ALBERTA ALONE

Cora Sandel

ALBERTA ALONE

Translated from the Norwegian *Alberte Og Jakob,*
Alberte Og Frieten, and *Bare Alberte* by
ELIZABETH ROKKAN

ORION PRESS NEW YORK 1966

839.823
F126

ALBERTA AND JACOB

PART ONE

The church clock shone like a moon in the night sky.

It struck, and weak little lights took shape out in the darkness and burned dully, lost in its infinity, scattered and lonely.

The clock struck again, and the lights multiplied, grouped themselves, formed lines and squares. Life stirred between them, a sleigh-bell tinkled, what might have been an empty sled could be heard jolting from side to side behind a horse on the hard-packed surface of the road. Something fell with a splash into the sea, a chain rattled. The sound of oars and creaking rowlocks came up out of the darkness, a boat thudded against timber, heavy feet in sea-boots clattered along a quay, someone shouted.

Out on the western fjord a ship's siren hooted. Red and green lights slid slowly out of the dusk. People were running with hawsers on the New Quay; at the Old Quay the bell of the Southfjord steamer was ringing, impatient to be gone at six o'clock. The eight arc-lamps in Fjord Street shone weakly in line, except for the one outside Louisa-round-the-bend, which was always broken. And windows, lit up in a flash, bright, strongly shining rectangles, joined ranks and fell into fresh lines and squares.

The clock struck one heavy chime on the quarters, four on the hour, and then, very rapidly, the hour itself. And Kvandal the tailor, who played the trombone in the Temperance Orchestra, was practising before opening his shop. At long intervals he would produce a single, tremulous note. These were a part of the regular early morning sounds, and a favourable wind could carry them all the way to Upper Town.

If there had been a snowfall during the night, the plough would fuss from one end of the town to the other with a great

5

to-do, with six horses, shouts and a cracking of whips, and Ola Paradise in charge. The roads were then officially open to traffic, and you could throng wherever you wished.

Theodorsen the baker appeared at the top of his steps. You couldn't see it in the twilight, but you knew he had flour in his beard and floury trousers. He looked up at the weather. Inside the shop Mrs Theodorsen was taking the loaves passed in to her through the hatch from the bakery, and stacking them slantwise on the shelves. Baker Theodorsen shivered a little and said Brrrr! Then he buttoned up his cardigan, took the snow shovel from the corner by the door, and set to work clearing a path out to the street for his customers.

Tailor Kvandal's music died away. Shadows came gliding between the houses, and shop doorbells tinkled. Hands moved in the Misses Kremer's window arranging coloured ribbons, hats on stands, christening robes, bridal and funeral trimmings. And there was Miss Liberg taking a hurried morning airing, and old Stoppenbrink taking his time, and Bjerkem on his way to school with a pile of exercise books under his arm, and Nurse Jullum the midwife on her way home. A new day was beginning, and no mistake.

It might be dark, with northern lights and swarming stars, and so cold that the snow squeaked under your footsteps. There might be a south-westerly gale damp with rain, and overcast, black streets; then the weathercock creaked on top of the church tower and the gilt signs outside the two bakeries rattled alarmingly. There might be moonlight too.

But mostly there would be thick snow, rounding off, smothering, muffling everything: shapes, colours and sounds.

When Alberta woke up in the morning she was always warm. It was the only time of day when she was not cold. Her limbs were snug and relaxed, physically at peace. Nothing could be better.

She would lie full length, her legs straight out.

The whole bed was warm, and her body felt as if it had uncurled, as if a shell surrounding it had been broken.

She stretched herself, feeling agile and supple, able to treat her warmth lightly. Sometimes in her arrogance she would stick one foot out into the cold simply in order to feel it warming up again as soon as she drew it back.

At night she would lie huddled and trembling beneath the blanket for hours, chilled to the marrow. She made herself as small as she could, drawing her legs up under her and hugging herself. The cold would sit between her shoulder-blades gnawing like pain. She carried it in her body all day, and it accompanied her to bed. Her feet, like blocks of ice, seemed not to belong to her, and she became cramped and sore from her huddled position.

After a while she would fall into a kind of waking doze. Her body slept, ice-cold, but numb and unfeeling. Up in her head her brain sat spinning, engrossed in its own affairs.

Time passed, hours went by. Through a thin web of half-waking dreams she would hear the church clock.

Then suddenly the warmth would come. It came like fever. She stretched her legs, and it was release from an instrument of torture; she relaxed her muscles as if after vigorous effort. She lay intoxicated and drifted into sleep.

When she woke she listened. Something ought to happen, the church clock strike, Tailor Kvandal begin, the Southfjord steamer ring its bell. She had to find out where she was in time, and how long she could stay comfortably in bed. But the Southfjord steamer rang three times, the church clock had the annoying habit of striking only once whether it was the first, second or third quarter, and Tailor Kvandal was subject to his human nature – he was not absolutely punctual. There were even mornings when he failed her altogether.

Eventually something happened on which she could rely. The stairs creaked beneath Jensine, who was going down them. Then she heard the door to the office, and a distant rumbling of coal. Jensine was lighting the stoves, first in there and then in the dining-room.

Alberta thought about all the stoves that were lighted every morning. The red glow from a stove door, the crackle of fire, were they not symbols of life's happiness? Warmth was life, cold was death. Alberta was a fire-worshipper in the full, primitive sense of the word.

Warmth made anything possible.

Warmth, and the cold gnawing in her back surrendered. Hands and feet came alive. She became more cheerful, more lively. Her limbs freed themselves from her body in unrestricted, beautiful movements; it was like putting on a well-fitting dress. She had a desire to talk and laugh, and a desire to sit still, busy with something.

Her face was no longer blue. She was a new person.

The stairs creaked again. It was Mrs Selmer.

She paused once or twice to do up the remaining buttons on her dressing-gown. The door downstairs opened and shut. And Alberta had stayed in bed too long again, and there was only one thing to do : get up with the greatest possible speed and the least possible loss of warmth, dressing herself more or less inside her nightdress, only slipping it over her head when all her underclothes were on.

As for the rest of her toilet, she hated the ice-cold water as much as the sight of her thin arms and sharp collar-bones. But neither were to be avoided. The mirror hung over the washstand, and Mrs Selmer was Argus-eyed. Not the slightest shadow on Alberta's neck had ever remained unnoticed the whole day through. While she washed she scrutinised her appearance with pessimism.

Oh to be different, in colouring and shape and dress, different in every way. That face in the mirror, was it really hers, the one she was to have all her life? Its features were so vague, she never really got to grips with it. Her hair hung smooth and unattractive round it, revealing far too much of her forehead; her complexion was blue and muddy.

And her eyes – yes, her eyes had a cast in them. Mrs Selmer sometimes called it a squint.

Alberta put up her hair in a curious manner, in a way that, without being either what Mrs Selmer liked and Alberta disliked, was nevertheless a compromise and a step towards reconciliation. Then she put on her dress. There were always a few eyes missing, and she hooked it shamelessly into the lining. This took some time. A disagreeable day of reckoning, when the holes and the crooked hooks would be exposed, was inevitable. But it was no use thinking about it.

Before she went into the dining-room she paused outside the door, just for a moment, a few seconds. She conquered something, and braced herself.

Then she went in to Mrs Selmer and the new day.

Inside the room the stove was crackling and the opening was bright. The fire could be heard and seen and would have given warmth had not the door to the sitting-rooms been open. It was supposed to warm up in there as well. But the sitting-rooms resembled the lean kine of Egypt, devouring all the warmth and becoming no warmer.

Mrs Selmer was sitting at table. Over her dressing-gown she wore her large check shawl. A novel from the lending library lay open beside her plate.

'Good morning, Mama,' said Alberta.

'Good morning, Alberta,' replied Mrs Selmer wearily and curtly, without looking up. Alberta sat down. The joyless still life of the breakfast table was immutable. The goat's cheese, the sour-milk cheese under one dome and the clove cheese under another, the bread basket. Two butter dishes, with dairy butter for the older generation and margarine for the younger, cream, sugar. But by Mrs Selmer's place was the coffee pot under its cosy. When the cosy was removed the coffee pot stood there like a revelation, its brass well polished, warm, steaming, aromatic, giving life and hope, a sun among dead worlds.

Alberta helped herself to bread and margarine with as little noise as possible. Cheese she took if the atmosphere seemed favourable. She cautiously handed over her cup, and Mrs Selmer filled it without looking at her. Not until the cosy was back in place over the pot once more did they glance up at each other, Mrs Selmer with a resigned look that crushed Alberta completely. She blushed and stiffened, her hands shook. Disarmed in the first round, she dared not ask for more coffee. If only Jacob would come.

Jacob had to be at school at half past eight. At twenty past he clattered downstairs, arriving out of breath with a 'Good morning, Mama. Good morning, Alberta.'

He tossed his books, strapped together, on to a chair, dragged his sleeves, which were far too short and which immediately crept up again, over his blue wrists, and looked from Mrs Selmer to Alberta and from Alberta to Mrs Selmer. He was sounding the terrain. Everyone did so in Jacob's and Alberta's home; it had become a well-developed instinct, an extra faculty.

'Jacob, Jacob, you'll be late,' said Mrs Selmer, putting aside her book. And Jacob assured her afresh each morning : 'No, I won't, Mama, I'll manage all right. I've got ten minutes.'

She cut thick slices of cheese and piled them on to his plate : 'Here you are, hurry up and get something inside you. You never eat properly – you get *up* too late, Jacob, my dear.'

Alberta left the table quietly, thankful for anything that drew attention away from herself. She sat by the dresser where the sewing basket stood – where the sewing basket always stood – took out a stocking and began to darn it. Sometimes this was not the right tactic, and she should have started on something else. But the basket was there, providing a kind of haven and a chance of salvation.

Frozen to the marrow, she twined her legs round each other. Her fingers were white and numb. If only Papa had eaten, if only Mama had gone upstairs, so that she could get hold of the coffee pot !

Jacob clattered out with a final : 'It's all right, Mama, I'll be there in time,' and disappeared.

Mrs Selmer sighed. And if it was one of the days when Alberta appeared in a slightly better light than usual, one of those unreal days of clemency which at any rate began well, she would be allowed to share in her concern for Jacob and his schooling. He was not likely to move up into the second year at *gymnasium*.

But if it was the kind of day – and this was most frequent – when Alberta was a cross and a burden from early morning onwards, Mrs Selmer would sigh without addressing her. She would sigh many times and not only on account of Jacob, not by any means only on account of Jacob. Alberta would cringe. She longed for Papa's arrival and feared it.

The stairs creaked heavily. Magistrate Selmer was on his way. He was large, and heavily built, the door seemed too small for his tall, broad figure, powerful in all its dimensions. His small grey eyes were tired and strained in his red face; the veins in them were like delicate tracks of blood. He carried the newspapers under his arm.

Now one of two things would happen. Either he said good morning, sounded the terrain, concluded with a 'Well, well—' and sat down; and then said something in a tone of voice implying that he wanted – wanted most decidedly – to be good-natured and frank, a tone of voice that was doing its best. Then peace or strife would depend on Mrs Selmer.

Or he did not say good morning, he said nothing at all. He sat down, was given his coffee, helped himself to bread and butter, unfolded his newspaper and still said nothing. But an inner struggle was taking place in his huge body. Something or other gave warning of it : a growl under his breath, a bitter mumble. Even the way he helped himself, even the set of his shoulders, seen by Alberta from behind, were full of ill omen.

Mrs Selmer trembled, looking at him sideways. Alberta trembled even more.

Then it came. He threw down his napkin, he threw down the paper. He pushed his plate away from him and moved something angrily, putting it down again with a clatter. And the storm broke. Strongly and with conviction and by no means under his breath he invoked the Prince of Darkness in several variants.

Nothing had happened necessarily. It need not have been a bill that had arrived by way of the office, nor did it have to be Jacob.

Magistrate Selmer's wrath piled up inside him for obscure and unknown reasons, and when the pressure became too strong there was, in accordance with the laws of nature, an explosion.

Mrs Selmer cried. She cried childishly and helplessly over her coffee cup, looking small and shrunken in her faded dressing-gown.

Alberta was also permitted to cry. Her tears, which unhappily welled up with ease, normally gave rise to vexation. On either side of the table she and Mama dabbed at their eyes with wringing wet handkerchiefs. The Magistrate had gone into the office.

Mrs Selmer pulled herself together and said jerkily: 'It helps me so much, Alberta my dear, that at any rate *you* understand – it's a great comfort to me'.

Alberta tried to say something, but had to give up. Racking sobs overcame her afresh.

Mrs Selmer rose, went round the table, patted her on the back and said soothingly: 'There, there, my child. We must remember that Papa is kind after all. He has many worries and difficulties, we mustn't forget that. But I do hope he'll control himself a little in there, so that the Chief Clerk won't hear anything – or Leonardsen. It's a perpetual anxiety to me, Alberta'.

But Alberta was already breathing more easily. Deep in her heart, beneath a chaos of evil and warring emotions, she had great sympathy for Papa, a great weakness for him. She knew that where the Clerk and Leonardsen were concerned there also existed a Magistrate-in-office, buttoned up, correct, his features tightly controlled. In fact, his mouth was slightly twisted. He could expunge the raging Papa of everyday life and put himself in his place, just as when one picture follows another in a magic lantern. She had an unreasoning faith that the Magistrate-in-office would always know when to appear at the call of respectability, cost what it might.

Mrs Selmer went to fetch a pail of hot water from the kitchen, and wandered upstairs to dress, red-eyed and resigned.

And the moment came for which Alberta had been watching and waiting. She forced herself to calm the last waves of tears, fanning herself with a rolled-up napkin until the worst traces had disappeared. Then she seized the coffee pot, carried it out to the cooking stove and put it on to heat. She kept her hands round it to warm them and to test the temperature. A blissful, torturing glow travelled through them up to her armpits and into her shoulders. When she could stand it no longer, when the palms of her hands began to burn so that she almost cried out, she fetched a slop-basin from the pantry, poured coffee into it and gulped it down through a lump of sugar held in her mouth.

I shan't have a tooth left in my head by the time I'm thirty, she thought, imagining she could hear them crack, while the scalding-hot waves of coffee washed through her, making her back ache. She drank it almost boiling, three or four cupfuls one after the other.

Jensine, who would have to cook more coffee for herself with the grounds and polish the pot into the bargain, muttered sourly : 'I'll tell the Madam, Alberta, and that's a certainty. I'll be glad when she comes in one of these days and catches you.'

Alberta turned, still drinking, and looked at Jensine with distended eyes over the rim of the bowl : 'I must have it, Jensine,' she managed to get out between two gulps.

Jensine went on muttering, but she never gave her away.

And Alberta was warm for a while, warm right down to her finger tips. Her blood beat strong and fast, and her blue face turned bright red.

Alberta was dusting. Grey with cold she pottered about in an apron and an old pair of gloves, armed with a knitted rag. She wore gloves more for their warmth than to protect her sadly neglected hands.

The grey light seeped slowly in through the ice-covered panes. There were six sets of windows altogether in the two sitting-rooms, all of them iced over. The little warmth from the dining-room had no effect on them. When Alberta started dusting she could only just see well enough to walk round.

Objects came to light in the same order each day, this year as last year. First the table in the middle with its plush cloth and small piles of illustrated leather-bound books. *Buch der Lieder* on top of *The Princess's Bridal Procession, The English Pilot* on top of Doré's Bible, the Norse Sagas on top of *The Arabian Nights,* Asbjørnsen's *Folk Tales* on top of Holberg's plays. In the centre of the table stood epergnes with visiting cards in them, and framed photographs.

Along the walls between the windows, behind the groups of plants, behind the ivy on its trellis and behind the big arm-chairs, pools of night still lay. Around them objects rose to the surface like skerries in the ocean : the sofa with all its cushions, the bureau with the clock on it, occasional tables with knick-knacks and books, the bookcase with rich colours and gilt edgings behind the glass.

Footstools emerged, and the pattern on the carpet. More and still more objects were touched by the grudging light of the dark season. Knick-knacks everywhere, knick-knacks and photographs, on Mrs Selmer's writing table, on the piano, on étagères. Small tables set aslant, small cushions of every size and shape, small pieces of fur. And a multitude of plant pots. Pots with palms and aspidistras or simply a dry stick, pots with crinkled tissue paper round them, majolica pots, pots large and small. They stood on jardinières, on steps, on pillars and on window ledges. In severe cold they were moved into the centre of the room at night and back again in the morn-ing. Alberta hated them.

She also hated most of the countless little objects she had to lift and put back in place every day. It was a quiet hate, expressed in her intense loathing at having to see the things, touch them, have them in front of her like a thicket through which she had to pick her way each morning – and in her tendency to put them down roughly and angrily.

As long as she still went to school and had nothing to do with them they had seemed like a magic world. There they were, either pretty or curious, if not the one, then most cer-tainly the other. Ever since she was small she had wandered among them on silent voyages of exploration – loving some of them, and admiring the rest.

But during the years she had spent at home she had learned to recognise their true nature : they were merely a nuisance and an encumbrance. She had already made one rule of life : to have few possessions, as few as possible, to look after and care for.

There were only one or two things against which she had acquired no grudge. First, the two little Dresden china figures, a shepherd and shepherdess each under a rose bush. The bushes had red, yellow and blue roses. The shepherd played his flute to the shepherdess, a dog lay at his feet. The shepherdess held her hat by its knotted ribbons in one hand, laying the other on her curving china breast, which burgeoned out of her delicate, slender waist as if from a flower vase. A lamb lay at her feet.

There was something about the smooth, shining forms of the tiny figures, their dancing-school grace and the colours of their clothes, that ensnared Alberta afresh each day, so that she paused when she reached them, held them in her hand for a while and looked at them more attentively.

She would never really be fond of the rose bushes; they were knobbly and uncomfortable to the touch. But the shepherd and shepherdess were smooth and good to hold, and they had something indefinable about them that made her happy. They were beautiful.

Then there was the red lacquer box from China. A curious world was carved in the lacquer and peopled its sides : men, trees, houses with balconies, people on the balconies, clouds, animals, all swarming mysteriously together. Somewhere on it there was a magnificent and terrifying dragon.

If you opened the box it was gold inside, a dark, deep golden lustre, beautiful and sinister. The box was a fairy tale, an unfathomable realm of mystery. Alberta opened it every morning and stood looking into its golden interior, where her face could be glimpsed at the bottom, faint and veiled as if seen through fantastic, costly hangings.

The Chinese box, the shepherd, shepherdess and bureau had all come from Grandpapa's house. A vague memory of a large low-ceilinged room with mahogany furniture and old portraits, where the light was green and cool from the foliage in the garden outside, lay about them like a faded halo.

When she was quite small Alberta had visited Grandpapa in the little town in South Norway to which he had retired.

The Magistrate was in the office, Mrs Selmer was dressing, Jacob was at school. For the moment nobody was asking for Alberta.

She put on the altered jacket, inherited from Mama, placed an unbecoming hat on her unbecoming hair, looked at herself despondently for an instant in the mirror, and went out.

The arc lamps hung in the falling snow like pale moons. But a warm, red glow fell on the snow from windows and shops, making it bluer round the patches of light.

Alberta gathered up her skirt and followed in Jacob's tracks. Ewart, whose business it was to hold a passage open to the middle of the street, was probably still on the office side of the house. Ewart came late, later and later every day, whatever the reason might be.

Kvandal the tailor was standing in the doorway of his shop in a fur cap and thick woollen cardigan. He did an old-fashioned kind of scrape towards Alberta. He had the family's custom in so far as he altered Papa's old clothes for Jacob. Alberta greeted him, stiff and tongue-tied as always, and hurried past. If he had called at the kitchen door with a bill recently she would turn red and hot.

But it probably could not be seen in the twilight. She blushed easily, it was one of her misfortunes, and she was thankful each time it went unnoticed. Invariably she blushed because of people, merely because for some unaccountable reason she had done so once. If she had the chance she unhesitatingly took any roundabout way in order to avoid them.

Quickly and quietly she glided down the street, a shadow among other shadows. Alberta always made herself as small as she could, shrinking inside her clothes, as if that would help. She held her hands clenched inside her cuffs, out of the cold, and had turned her collar up round her ears. With her stiff little nod, looking straight in front of her, she greeted Schmitt the butcher; Vogel the café proprietor; and Beda Buck, who worked in the Recorder's office and who shook her fist through the window at Alberta, because she was wandering about in freedom, while Beda had to sit indoors. Alberta smiled a half-smile at this, but hurriedly resumed her normal expression.

She caught her breath. A little way down the street Bergan the lawyer had come into view. His large, thick-set, slightly swaying figure was easily recognisable. He was one of the people who made her blush most, who made her helpless, crimson and tense.

For what reason God and Mrs Selmer alone knew. For Alberta was not in the least in love with Bergan, indeed, she would have been more than horrified were he to present himself as a suitor. But the thought that people might perhaps suspect her of being in love with him, and that Mrs Selmer might perhaps get an encouraging look in her eye if she were so suspected, was enough, more than enough.

Now he was coming towards her, he was coming closer, she felt tense already. What was he doing out of doors at this time of day, why wasn't he in his office? Oh, why did this have to happen?

And then Bergan went into the pharmacy, into the 'Polar Bear'. He moved calmly up the steps, and disappeared. Alberta's blush, which had already flamed up, faded away, her heart was released and started beating normally again, she was saved. But when she turned into the Market Square the tenseness was still in her body and prevented her from moving her head for a while, even though there was no-one there.

Here there was no traffic. The square was deserted right up to Peter on the Hill's house. Not a soul was in sight besides Schmitt the butcher's shaggy dog, lifting its leg by the bandstand.

Alberta ran. Past the fire station, past Peter on the Hill, from Lower Town to Upper Town, upwards, upwards, until she reached the main road into the countryside above the last houses. She stopped and turned, panting.

Her face glowed and her heart beat like a hammer. She breathed as if she had cramp. But her blood thrust warmly through her body, she felt it tingling in the palms of her hands and in her finger tips. It was some time before she got her breath again.

She was away from home, she was warm, she was alone. Priceless blessings, that might lead to undreamt-of opportunities. Every day she rushed up the hill at the same furious speed in order to win them.

She stood for a while and looked about her. The snowfall was slung like grey draperies about the light-abandoned world. It hung over the mountains, partly obscuring them; it stood like a black wall above the fjord to the west, like a grey one to the south above inner Southfjord. It shut out the view in every direction, and the river, which flowed dark and rapid at the very bottom of it all, seemed to come from nowhere, to be going nowhere.

The town lay below on the slopes running down to the river. With so much fresh snow on the roofs it looked as if a white fur coverlet had been drawn over it, with the lights that shone down there all day blinking out of slits and holes like cunning, drowsy little eyes. There was a large rent here and there : a spire, and a gable or house-wall of importance, where the bank, the school and the Lutheran meeting-house stood out. The sharp needle of the church tower had bored right through, and stood triumphantly up in the sky with pieces of the pierced coverlet hanging down about the pinnacle and gables.

The church tower was strange. It was an ordinary, ugly, yellow church tower built of wood. Alberta could see perfectly well that it looked like two excessively long, narrow boxes piled up on end, the one above the other, with an ice-cream cone on top. Nevertheless there was something distinctive about it. It stood straight up and down to good effect against the many horizontal lines drawn by the river and the main streets of the town; it changed and was new with every season. In summer it shone brightly against the grass-covered mountains and the river, which was then green, deep and opaque. Now it was grey in all the rest of the greyness. Only a shadow of yellow remained, a faint wash of colour.

But to turn one's back on the town and the tower was like

bidding farewell to this world and its glories. Although Alberta had done so time and again, year out and year in, she was still seized by the same uneasiness.

No snow-plough had gone inland across the bog. Only a few sleds from the farms had driven here early this morning, painstakingly marking where the road went, the road through emptiness out to nowhere.

In clear weather rounded, solid mountains, blue and distant, formed a wall in the far north of the province. Now there was nothing there, less than nothing, a colourless infinity.

Scattered across the foreground, half buried in snow, lay tiny summer cottages, their shutters closed, witnessing that people had been there once upon a time. A suggestion, a shadow of low, snow-clad birch thicket hinted at a line of hills; a steaming patch of horse dung, that organic life was still to be found on earth. There was no other focus for the eye. And a great feeling of desolation, something of what the lone survivor of a catastrophe at sea might be imagined to feel, chilled Alberta, shrinking her heart into a hard little whimpering lump. But she braced herself and advanced purposefully into the deep snow, into the eeriness, her skirt held high, her face flushed and hot. She was fleeing from her permanent conviction that she was a malefactor, from the painful self-knowledge which never left her – and there was nowhere else she could flee.

Her heart hammered so that she could feel it in her neck, and when a crow suddenly fluttered up from the ground she started so that she lost her breath and had to stop. But after a while a giddy audacity rose in her, and she opened the door a little to her dream world. Only a little – not wide open, without anxiety, as when she wandered about in the summer. Here in all this eeriness it was important to keep her wits about her. Her own terror was lurking in the air, it might grip her at any moment. She had to be on her guard against it and not allow it to get the upper hand. And not run, above all not run. She set herself reprieves and goals. The next curve of the sled tracks, the next piece of horse dung – and she would stop and get her breath and start back, as calmly as if nothing were the matter. But she kept on walking. Of the joys that could not be taken from her, walking was one of the greatest. To feel her muscles working, feel the healthy, wholesome warmth spreading over her body, while awkwardness and tenseness slipped away like a sloughed skin, leaving her body free, supple and relaxed as if after a bout of gymnastics. It was a resource from which she could gain fresh courage, the only resource Alberta had at her disposal for the time being, besides the coffee pot.

She walked, sank down into the snow, struggled up again and almost forgot she was frightened.

Then a flock of crows came flying straight towards her out of the driving snow. They screeched, screeched, and a gust of eeriness accompanied them and settled on the earth.

And the terror gripped Alberta. She gave in to it, turned and, seized with panic, ran, tripped, fell flat on her face, struggled up and ran again. Only when she saw the lights of the town did she stop. Her heart beat as if it would knock her down, and her hands shook too much to open the neck of her jacket.

Where shall I go, she thought : there is nowhere to go any more. On the other roads there are people, and up here the eeriness. I am trapped – this year as last year.

* * *

The lamplight fell on the table from under a red shade. In its circle there stood generous plates of cake and two dishes of jam, the silver basket with the teaspoons in it, the blue cups. Beyond, in the shadow, the tea-urn shimmered on a little table by itself, together with the Japanese tea-caddy and the slop basin with the curious, old-fashioned tea strainer on top of it. The faces were also in shadow, but hands moved under the light.

It was warm from the glowing coke fire and three lamps. 'Much too warm,' said Mrs Buck, getting up and fanning herself with a folded newspaper. She opened a window, and a cool stream of air was let into the living-room.

Alberta wrapped herself in the heat as if it were material one could pick up and feel. It was never too warm for her. Her hands and body and face felt different, and she sewed Mama's table runner quickly, not quite sure whether she was enjoying it, or whether it was merely the warmth and the cosiness of the lamp-light that made her feel like this. She laughed unselfconsciously at something Beda was telling her, and Mrs Buck cried : 'Just look at Alberta, she's so attractive when she laughs. Why are you always so serious, Alberta? Laugh, my girl.'

Alberta blushed, but was comforted by the fact that the light was red too. She withdrew into herself again for a while. One of her sore spots had been touched. She often heard the same thing at home, although the choice of words was different.

Beda never sat still for long. She threw down her embroidery, stood up, and wandered about with a lighted cigarette in her hand. She paused in front of the table, standing crookedly and daringly with her hip jutting out and her arm akimbo, making provocative remarks and gesticulating with the cigarette. Then she tossed it out of the open window, sat down and made a few stitches in her embroidery, while Mrs Buck cried, horrified : 'Darling Beda, are you crazy – throwing cigarettes out of the window !'

And Beda replied : 'Darling Mrs Buck, why do you think we have such a lot of snow up here? We can throw cigarettes out of the window without any danger of fire, my poor dear'.

'Yes, but my sweet little Beda, it might fall on somebody's head.'

'I'd love it to fall on Mrs Governor Lossius's head, when she's wearing her tulle hat – or on Lotten Kremer, when she's out in her finery.'

'Darling Beda, how you do go on.'

Mrs Buck laughed, but looked anxiously in the direction of the Archdeacon's Christina and Harriet Pram, who were so correct. They smiled and exchanged glances. But Gudrun Pram leaned back in her chair and laughed riotously.

Alberta sat wondering what was really wrong with Beda.

Both she and her mother were the bugbear of Mama and all the other ladies. They agreed that if Beda were not an old school friend and if it were not so embarrassing to break off the connection, there would be no question of their daughters frequenting that house. Beda was held up as an example of how a young girl should never behave. Her language, her manners, her clothes, her walk, everything was wrong. And yet the men were attracted to her like moths to a flame. In adolescence it had been the boys, now it was chemists and editors, mining engineers from Southfjord, and the new dentist; in other words, all young, presentable males.

She was hung about with skirts that dipped at the back. Small, slanting eyes, that could turn into narrow slits, a large mobile mouth with white, even teeth in a broad, flattened little Mongol face. Encircling the face were clusters of natural dark curls, which would turn snow-white early like Mrs Buck's. She had inherited her mother's deep dimples in her chin.

Beda said crude and vulgar things and made faces like a girl from Rivermouth. She was not afraid of dreadful words, and her language was almost like that of the country folk.

'Beda, my child, do watch your language a little,' sighed Mrs Buck; it was one of her refrains. But Beda did not watch her language. She put on an act and said frightful things just for the sake of it.

She dared the incredible. When tea was over, for instance, she would say : 'Now Mrs Buck, you must be tactful and disappear, my poor dear. We're going to talk about things that aren't good for an elderly lady's ears', leading Mrs Buck to the door as if under arrest. Mrs Buck would laugh resignedly and say : 'What will become of the child?'

Beda followed people on the street, mimicking them in broad daylight. She followed Lotten Kremer one Sunday, waddling her behind and mincing along; she had even gone so far as to follow the Governor's wife all the way from the bathhouse to the brewery, holding up a furled umbrella like a lorgnette. She used to follow the Recorder too, singing 'Adam in Paradise'. That was before she went to work at his office.

It was Beda who once pinned old Mrs Klykken's and Nurse

Jullum's skirts together with a safety-pin in the crush when the congregation was coming out of church, so that old Mrs Klykken's trimming was torn off all the way round; Beda who set fire to the splendid midsummer bonfire that had ten tar barrels in it, on the Flemming's summer property, so that it burned up in the middle of the afternoon, long before the guests arrived; Beda who fastened the outside hook on the door when Bjerkem the school-teacher was out in the privy, so that he was stuck there for an hour in the middle of the winter and had had chronic catarrh ever since. Her skirts aswing round her long legs, she had been the ringleader in boats and on skis, climbing on board the Russian trading ships to beg for sweets, and going to old Kamke to beg for delicacies.

She knew amazing things and was familiar with all that was mysterious and hidden. Beda read whatever she liked, without hindrance.

Mrs Selmer said: 'That terrible Beda Buck'; the Magistrate: 'If only she'd walk more prettily and use a different kind of language'. Then they both would trace the misfortune back to Mrs Buck, saying: 'One couldn't expect anything else, poor child'.

But the Recorder said in his quiet way: 'The most efficient person in my office'.

Headmaster Bremer pursed his lips and declared: 'Without comparison the best brain I have ever had in my class'.

And Mrs Buck herself would ask at every opportunity: 'Can you tell me what I should do without Beda, desperately impractical as I am?'

Harriet Pram leaned forward, looked at the photograph on the piano for a long time, and asked politely: 'Which rôle was this one, Mrs Buck?'

Mrs Buck screwed up her eyes short-sightedly: 'Oh, my dearest Harriet, that was in the journey to China, it was taken at the time I met Mr Buck, my dear, in Malmø. He sat in the stalls one evening and his face was as brown as an Indian's. He had put in with the *Augusta Amalie*.'

And Mrs Buck drew up her chair and recounted yet again,

with alacrity, the story of how that brown man sat in the same seat in the stalls for a fortnight. Then she gave in, left the stage, and went off with him to sea. 'Everyone thought it was a pity, of course, but he was a dashing fellow at any rate. Can you remember Victor Buck, girls?'

She looked up at the enlargement hanging above the piano in an oval frame, and nodded to it. 'Dashing', she repeated lingeringly. And she threw back her shoulders, stuck out her bosom, and concluded: 'Dignified – and a real *man*, nothing of the sissy about him. Practically all the girls were after him'.

Scattered about under the light from the variegated lamp-shades there stood and hung pictures of Mrs Buck in different stage rôles, and of Mrs Buck as the captain's wife on the *Augusta Amalie* – with and without Beda in her arms. Beda was born in Hull.

A reek of adventure and experience filled the room and lay about Mrs Buck's corpulent, white-haired, but lively and youthful person – something not quite proper, but amusing and enticing. She had been on the stage, she spoke Swedish in spite of all the years she had spent up here in North Norway, and she had seen a good deal of the world before Buck gave up sailing the high seas and transferred to the coastal service at home. Odessa 12.5.86 was written on one photograph, New Orleans on another, Port Said on a third.

'Damn it,' Beda would say. 'Why did you have to go ashore up here, when I was only a year old? You must have been bewitched.'

Mrs Buck had the same slit eyes as Beda, and there was a hole in her chin as deep as a scar. No-one had ever seen a similar chin-hole. It was difficult to keep one's eyes off it when talking to her.

The people she mixed with kept themselves afloat a couple of fathoms below the surface of society. They were Mrs Dorum the jeweller's wife, Mrs Kilde the clock-mender's wife, Mrs Lebesby the dyer's wife, Mrs Julius Elmholz, novelties and hardware. Well-situated, genial women, who travelled to Kristiania once a year, and abroad now and again, who were more expensively and better dressed than the officials' wives, the Governor's lady excepted. And young Mrs Klykken of course, who trumped everyone where clothes were concerned.

Mrs Selmer and her circle greeted them, chatted with animation and familiarity across counters with them, manned bazaar stalls with them, but never invited them to tea in any circumstances, and talked about them in a particular tone of voice and with a particular expression. Especially where Mrs Buck was concerned, they would drop their voices a little and cough warningly to each other when the young people were present. It was rumoured that she had a relationship with the Russian consul in one of the towns to the east. There must have been something in it, for why should Mrs Buck, who was Swedish and had sisters still living, stay up here years after Captain Buck's death, and what business took her eastwards three years ago? 'Well, don't tell anyone I told you, but there are all sorts, and poor Beda, that's what I say . . .'

And the ladies would raise their voices and remark : 'She is supposed to have been quite mediocre as an actress.'

But old Consul Stoppenbrink, who saw her on the stage twenty-five years ago in Gothenburg, when she was still called Ulla Liljekvist, would assure them : 'She was a lovely girl – a lovely girl – such a tiny waist', and blow a kiss with two fingers.

Tea had been drunk, and Mrs Buck had sung various numbers from her repertoire : 'Nitouche' and 'The Grand Duke of Geroldstein'. She retired, pursued by Beda. 'Very well, very well Beda, my dear. I'm going like a good girl,' she laughed. 'But don't say anything too shocking.'

Beda drew the portière after her. 'There, now we can be as indecent as we like. Christina, you're worse than any of us, you can begin.'

Christina smiled virtuously and cryptically over her embroidery : 'My poor Beda, you had better begin yourself'.

'No, since you came home from Germany, Christina, you're definitely the worst of all of us.'

In fact Christina had come home from Germany primmer and more embroidered, richer in domestic virtue, more admirable than ever. She fidgeted on her chair and smiled with embarrassment and scorn : 'Oh, Beda,' she said.

But Beda was merciless. 'My poor Christina, I told Bergan yesterday that if he wanted you, he'd better grab you now, for you're getting more depraved each day. Christina is going terribly downhill, I said to Bergan, no-one knows how terrible Christina is.'

Christina took offence, pursed up her mouth and sewed for dear life. 'If you did say that, Beda, Lawyer Bergan is sure to understand where the depravity lies,' she said with dignity without looking up.

Beda stood beside and a little behind her, and from time to time nudged her teasingly : 'Listen Christina. Christina, don't you think he's a lovely man, Christina? They say he has two of everything already, beds and bedside tables and – well, I won't go into details – it's only the proposal that's lacking. If only he could get round to it'.

Christina was furious. She sat with her back to the company and sewed like one possessed. The general opinion was that she doted on Bergan. 'Oh!' she exclaimed once, crimson with vexation.

Harriet Pram sewed in silence. She was cold and clear-headed, calm and correct, a little older than the others. She had been to Kristiania to take a course in massage and was far too refined for the tone adopted by Beda. She demonstratively started a cultured conversation with Christina across the table : 'Have you read Blicher-Clausen's latest, *Violin?*'

Christina grasped at the straw thus offered. 'No, but it's supposed to be wonderful. It was out when I asked for it, unfortunately.'

But Beda was not dismayed. She struck her breast : 'My God, how cultured they are! But Harriet, it's time you took pity on that assistant of yours, Dr Mo, for he's going with Palmine Flor. Someone saw them coming out of the Flors' summer cottage at midnight, so there's not much time to lose. The two of you could get more pleasure out of that money after you're married, my poor Harriet. They say Palmine's none too cheap – she likes fox-fur boas and feather hats'.

Harriet was well-bred and self-controlled : 'I'm quite sure that if Dr Mo has been seen with Palmine he must have been sent for as a doctor to the Flors. Besides, if your friends Kirkeby and Lett saw them, they'd do better minding their own business.

' – Or perhaps that's the sort of thing you discuss at the Recorder's office when Mr Jaeger is out,' she added coldly, with polite scorn.

'Of course, and when he's in for that matter,' replied Beda defiantly. 'We don't inhabit the higher spheres in our office, let me tell you. We take life as it comes – and after all, it is a cesspool. Besides, nobody would be ill up at the Flors' cottage – they do that down in town at this time of year.'

'Stop laughing so improperly, Gudrun,' said Harriet in sharp reproof. Gudrun Pram was weak with laughter.

'Oh, kiss my bottom!' remarked Beda scornfully under her breath.

And Gudrun wailed : 'I can't – I shall die . . .'

The warmth and well-being enfolded Alberta like a narcotic, half stupefying her, lulling her into a vague, bright, undefined world of fantasy, where nothing but enjoyable sensations flowed one into the other as in a pleasant dream.

She let her sewing fall and sat looking at her hands. They were no longer hers. Hers were purple everyday hands, on which Mama cast resigned glances, asking her to keep them under the table. These were a pair of hands out of a novel, white and slender, a little large, a little scrubbed, but beautiful. She could not stop thinking that they were beautiful, lying there in her lap, the skin transparent, with blue veins and pale pink knuckles. They belonged to a friend whom only Alberta knew – a happy, beautiful, carefree girl, who walked invisibly beside her, whom no-one saw but herself, but who lived a more intense life than any visible creature. Who knew everything, dared everything, hoped for everything and feared no-one and nothing, not even Mama – and to whom everything was granted : freedom, happiness, beautiful clothes. On Alberta's lonely walks it sometimes happened that the carefree girl blotted her out, materialised in her stead, became Alberta, but it was a miracle that brooked no witnesses. As soon as anyone appeared the transformation was over. There was the old Alberta, just as if nothing had happened, shrinking inside her clothes to make herself as unnoticeable as possible.

The girl's hands were lying now in Alberta's lap, white and warm, looking as if they were never dead from cold; and life was straightforward with small cosy worries of the kind the others had – dresses that would never be ready in time for a party, embroidery that would never be finished in time for Christmas. For what troubles other than these did they have, Harriet, Christina and Gudrun? Beda – perhaps she had more important ones and more of them, perhaps not – but neither she nor the others had the cold, and a guilty conscience waiting for them outside the door. These waited only for Alberta, accompanying her home like two bodyguards, not leaving her until she slept, standing ready at her bedside when she opened her eyes again.

But now they were outside at least. They were never so completely outside as at the Bucks'. In the first place Mama did not frequent the house, and this gave an invaluable feeling of security. And then nowhere else was so warm, so snug and so generous in every way.

Beda and her mother suffered from a chronic lack of ready money. They would turn their purses inside out when bills arrived, to demonstrate that there was nothing there. But they always had full cake boxes, an unparalleled supper table, a glowing coke fire, flowers, sweets and new music, fashion magazines and theatre journals. And Mrs Buck's little copper kettle, Coffee-Peter by name, stood permanently on the stove. 'You drink your tea,' Mrs Buck would say. 'I much prefer my little cup of coffee.'

'My dear, this is nothing by comparison with what we'd call an ordinary *smörgasbord* in Sweden,' she was in the habit of saying with an apologetic gesture towards the numerous dishes on the supper table. And she sent her delicious little sauces and yellow omelettes round the table with a : 'Just something warm' – which caused Alberta to think bitterly of the gruel and milk and the fried egg for Papa served in her own home.

Going home with Beda for supper was an oasis in life's desert. To be sure it felt deceitful. Out in the desert sat those nearest her, consuming grey gruel frigidly and with ill-humour. It was her duty to share these things with them. Once she had been seized with such a strong feeling of anxiety for everyone at home that she suddenly found an excuse for leaving. Dreadful scenes presented themselves to her imagination: Papa in full outburst, Mama small and shrunken, the tears trickling down her cheeks, Jacob cold, defiant, with set mouth. She rushed home – to find everything comparatively peaceful and idyllic. Since then she had stayed, and let herself be lulled to rest by the warmth and the well-being, forgetting for a while her travelling companions in the vale of misery.

It was at the Bucks' that she would become bold and say: 'Do you know, I almost think I'd like another cup of coffee'. And Mrs Buck would pour it out at once: 'Now that's sensible of you, Alberta, I like that. We know what's good for us, you and I.'

But the others were talking about the south, about going south. That most burning of all questions. Alberta was jerked back to reality again. It seemed to help a little to talk about certain things, as if it brought them a little nearer.

'All I need are some fine relatives down south like the rest of you – and no Mrs Buck to look after.' Beda said it in that quiet, introspective tone of voice she very occasionally adopted, as if talking to herself.

'But my dear, you have relatives too – and in Sweden into the bargain.' Harriet looked so innocent as she said it, although everyone knew Beda's aunts were only so-so. One of them was married to a station-master on a small local line, and the other was said to support herself by dress-making.

'I said *fine* relatives, my poor Harriet. You heard, and you know what I meant. Don't try to seem more naïve than you are.' Beda's tone was no longer introspective.

But Harriet was correct and ladylike : 'I really don't know what you call fine and not fine'.

'You know all right. When I talk to you, for instance, I mean what you mean, I run with the hare . . . And as for what you mean, my poor Harriet, if we couldn't tell by your appearance, we only need hear you say, "My aunt, the General's wife".'

Harriet sighed resignedly and let it be known that she considered it beneath her dignity to reply. She adopted the same attitude as Christina and sewed in silence. They glanced up at each other and smiled in complete sympathy.

But Beda had started on Gudrun. 'I suppose you'll be going to stay with your aunt, the General's wife, too, Gudrun, unless you take Stensett the schoolmaster, of course. They say he dotes on you so that he daren't hear you in class any more, he blushes furiously if he so much as talks to you. You won't get your matric., my poor Gudrun, but you'll get Stensett.'

'I don't want Stensett,' groaned Gudrun, gesturing away from herself with her hands. 'He has egg in his beard every morning and a patch on the seat of his trousers.'

Harriet coughed disapprovingly, and Alberta was afraid her turn was coming. They teased her about her father's Chief Clerk now and again, and it offended her, because he was the sort of person nobody would fall in love with, awkward, with clammy hands. Besides, she reacted to certain kinds of jokes like an innocent person under attack, becoming tense, incapable of adopting the same tone. Her future would never be in question. But beneath the knowledge that she was ugly, boring, hopeless and impossible, something fluttered – a yearning unrest. She carried it, as one might carry a secret hurt, an invisible injury of which one is ashamed, not daring even to touch it.

Fortunately her schoolgirl crush on Peter, the chemist's son, seemed to have been forgotten. It had been an unfortunate youthful aberration, a time full of anxiety, of much blushing and walking in back streets, her heart in her mouth. Meeting her heart's desire on the public highway had been more than she could bear. Peter Bloch was apparently completely unaffected, however, and the whole thing came to an end abruptly when he began wearing a bowler. It was immediately obvious that he was not the right one after all.

'And what about you, Beda, who will you have?' she threw out deprecatingly. 'Lett or Kirkeby or Bengtson the engineer?'

'Me!' Beda threw herself full length on to the couch and folded her arms behind her head. 'Do you think anyone will marry Beda Buck? No, I'm the sort of poor wretch men confide in and kiss to console themselves – I'm not the sort they marry. I expect I shall go the same way as Caroline Kamke. She had a child by a Lapp, so they all found themselves put to the necessity of marrying her off to old Isaac Hwass out east in Berlevaag. For you needn't think I shall end up like Jeanette Evensen, who's half crazy, all because she's never had anything to do with men.

'But you—' continued Beda, sitting upright on the couch, drowning the indignation of the others and prophesying with outstretched index finger towards Harriet and Christina : 'I'm telling you now, consider getting yourselves a man before the grey hairs and wrinkles come, for if you don't marry you'll not get so much as a kiss all your lives. Your sort have to do their sinning inside marriage – there'll be nothing for you outside, believe you me and Beda Buck.'

An hour later Alberta sat struggling with the lukewarm, grey gruel that had been standing in the oven and was now covered with skin. She had been late for supper. She always was when she had been out to tea, but it was overlooked because Alberta did what was expected of her in other respects, and because there had to be moderation in all things.

'I have plenty to scold about as it is,' Mrs Selmer had said once. 'If I were to scold her about that as well, it would be too much for me.'

Jacob sat at the other side of the table with *The Prisoner of Zenda*. He would look up now and again and make a face, and when Alberta had swallowed a spoonful of gruel he would pretend to belch.

But Alberta swallowed manfully.

Mama was in the large sitting-room playing the piano. She stopped for a moment when Alberta arrived, called, 'Is that you, Alberta my dear?' – and went on playing.

And Alberta, who always felt when she had been at some-one else's home, and most of all at Beda's, as if her home-coming was a rude awakening to bleak reality, and whose conscience troubled her because of it, understood at once that this evening there was a truce, this evening there was a fine, calm spell on life's voyage. Papa had gone to play cards with the Chief of Police. So Mama would go on playing for a long time, and she would be gay and talkative when she had finished, and tease Alberta and Jacob. Their sins would be as if blotted out.

Maybe she would even fetch jam and cakes. Worse things had happened.

* * *

Dinner, and the hanging lamp was lit. Mrs Selmer was at table. She did everything first : got up first in the morning, sat down first at table, finished her meals first and went first to bed.

Now she sat in her check shawl getting more and more tense round the mouth.

The Magistrate, on the other hand, was always late. He got up last and went last to bed, was always the last to be ready on every occasion and added greatly to Mrs Selmer's burdens, which were heavy and numerous enough as it was.

Jacob was like him. As a rule they both arrived long after they had been summoned, their eyebrows raised as if in apology. But Alberta, who had troubles enough in other respects, had adopted punctuality at mealtimes as a pro-pitiatory act. Now she was standing behind her chair, happy as long as Mrs Selmer's glance rested on the steaming beef collops and not in her direction.

The door opened, Papa arrived.

If he had exploded recently, this was now a thing of the past. He wished in fact to make up for his behaviour, and would therefore begin by apologizing for his tardiness.

But to Mama it was by no means a thing of the past. Besides, he had kept her waiting yet again. What with the one thing and the other there was no reason why she should be pleasant.

Alberta sent silent cries to heaven to make Mama pleasant all the same, but Mama was not. She replied curtly and coldly with pursed lips, and Papa said, 'Oh, so that's how it is, is it?' and went red in the face. He, too, pursed his lips. He looked at the beef with disfavour, turning over the slices contemptuously with his fork, while Alberta had palpitations and her hands turned clammy.

Papa chewed his meat demonstratively in order to make it clear to everyone how tough it was, and pessimistically contemplated his portion several times from various angles. Now and again he looked darkly at Jacob's empty chair.

Jacob arrived. He pulled down his inadequate sleeves and gave some explanation about a message concerning homework that for some obscure reason he had had to get from another boy, and the boy was not at home and Jacob had had to wait. This was believed by nobody and nobody replied.

'Sit down and eat,' said Papa roughly.

Jacob stopped mumbling and sat down. An oppressive silence fell.

Then Mama began. She began in the tone of voice that always spoiled everything – a cold, injured tone : 'Mightn't it quite possibly have happened as Jacob says?'

Papa flared up : 'I don't care a brass farthing for what Jacob says. It's his business to be home at a certain time, regardless of this, that and the other. I demand – do you hear – I *demand* that the boy keep up to the mark'.

Papa thumped hard on the table with his fist and went very red. Mama went white, her mouth a thin line. Alberta felt herself beginning to tremble, and Jacob put on his bad face, the cold obstinate face that always frightened Alberta.

For a while only the forks could be heard. Alberta looked sideways at her father's hands; they were shaking. He mumbled with twisted mouth. All of a sudden he put down his knife, pointed at the door and said roughly to Jacob : 'Go upstairs, get out of my sight'.

'Very well,' said Jacob, and got up.

But Jacob should not have said that. Papa struck the table and thundered : 'There's no need to answer me, boy, when I speak to you, all you have to do is obey and look sharp about it. Or I'll – now – out you go'.

He pointed again. And Jacob disappeared.

Mrs Selmer collapsed, a crushed, tiny figure, the tears trickling down her cheeks. Her entire appearance implied that both she and Jacob were being trampled under foot, the maltreated wife and child of a coarse brute. Unable to defend themselves against superior force, all they could do was submit.

The coarse brute was already fighting his anger. He looked crossly and questioningly over at Mrs Selmer, who did not return his glance, but looked straight in front of her in utter despair. The tears rolled down her cheeks, one after the other.

So he muttered a lot of bad words about environment, that caused him to lose control again, and yet again. Then he rose abruptly, pushing his chair noisily away from him, and left – closing the door behind him in such a way that everything in the room trembled and clinked.

Mrs Selmer sobbed for a while with her handkerchief pressed against her mouth, and Alberta wept silently on her side of the table. She wept for everything, for life in general.

Mrs Selmer wiped her eyes, arranged her shawl and ordered Alberta to open the window, ring for Jensine and explain that no-one wanted dessert so there was no need to bring it in. She went upstairs.

After a little while Alberta went upstairs as well. On the way she paused for a moment outside the closed office door. She could hear Papa behind it, and seized with sudden rage she shook her fists at the door and whispered devout administrations at it, of the kind she had heard issuing from his own mouth : 'God damn you to hell,' she whispered. 'Curse you.'

She repeated them several times and it made her feel better.

And she went on up to her room, sobbed violently for a

time, her fists clenched against her face, became calmer, wrapped herself in the travelling-rug Aunt Marianne had given her for her confirmation, and sat listening, waiting for Mrs Selmer to go downstairs again.

When the coast was clear, Alberta went in to Jacob.

He was sitting at the table leaning his head on one blue-grazed fist, playing with a penknife. His school books lay beside him, still strapped together.

The light from the lamp fell sharply on his face. He sat looking at the knife, and his mouth wore the expression Alberta feared most of all. Behind it lay all the dangerous thoughts that could lead Jacob astray, in wild directions that she was only vaguely able to imagine.

It was ice-cold in the room as it was everywhere else in the house. She could see her own breath, and Jacob's.

At first she found nothing to say, and remained standing in front of the table. Jacob looked up and asked with hostility : 'What do you want?'

Alberta did not reply immediately. There was no point in being too quick. She had to find a point of departure without worsening the situation. She sat down on Jacob's bed, hid her frozen hands in the blanket, and said nothing.

'What do you want?' repeated Jacob crossly.

Bitterness towards Jacob flared up in Alberta, and she replied, 'Nothing.'

'Huh – What do you want to come in for, then? Besides, Mama was here just now.'

'I know she was.'

'All right, so you don't have to come too. You're both after the same thing.'

Alberta was silent again. She got up and screwed the lamp to stop it smoking.

'Don't you want me to help you with your homework?' she said after a while.

Jacob made no reply. Then he flicked his knife; it stood upright, quivering in the table. 'I'll sign up for the Arctic,' he said roughly.

'No Jacob, you won't,' said Alberta vehemently. Something snapped inside her, and she began to sob. Jacob looked up, went across to her and patted her clumsily on the shoulder with a large, blue hand. His voice had altered : 'Come on, don't cry Alberta – do you hear me Alberta, you mustn't cry.

'Proper old leaking tap, that's what you are,' he added with an indulgent little laugh, his voice strangled.

But Alberta clutched his hand, for now he was close to her in every way. 'Jacob, can't you be a bit more punctual, for Mama's sake?'

'Punctual !' Jacob tried to free his hand. 'Huh – if only Mama hadn't started up in that tone of voice, Papa would never have got so furious, you know that. It's only because they quarrel so.'

'Yes Jacob, but at any rate we can try not to give them the chance,' answered Alberta philosophically. 'And you *must* see to it that you matriculate, Jacob,' she hastened to add, making the most of her chance, for it was not always so easy to get hold of Jacob's hand. She could see that he was trying to free it in earnest now.

'Come on Jacob, let's begin.'

For the moment Alberta felt strongly the drive that Jacob lacked. Jacob *must* matriculate, he *must* become an educated person – not a mere sailor and a dissipated character.

But the result of Jacob's examination on leaving secondary school had been worse than wretched and had cost much private tuition. Her own education had been sacrificed to it, for she had been taken out of *gymnasium* the previous year. His weekly reports left more and more to be desired, and the Magistrate prophesied the worst every Saturday : 'You'll grow up into an uneducated ruffian, my boy, mark my words. No-one will be able to tell that you come of a decent family'.

Now Alberta had yet another of her attacks of desperate optimism. They came upon her from time to time. It would be all right, it must be all right, in spite of everything, in spite of Jacob's own embittered aversion to school and everything that had to do with it.

'Wouldn't it be nice if you got a good report on Saturday, Jacob,' she said, in a different tone of voice. 'Hurry up and find me the books.'

'Ugh!' said Jacob, finally twisting his hand out of hers. He sat down on the edge of the bed with a morose expression. But Alberta was on her feet unstrapping the books on the table.

She read the time-table above the chest of drawers: 'German, History, Maths, Norwegian – you must have homework, Jacob, come along.'

Jacob rose unwillingly to his feet and brought pen and ink. He grumbled: 'If you think I'll get better marks because my homework's right, you're mistaken. Huh, I get delta however well I've learned it. The Head—'

Alberta was already struggling with x and y. She knew what Jacob would say about the Head and the masters, things it was best to ignore. For although they might be a little unfair and spoken at random, they were not entirely so, and it would be dangerous to embark on a debate.

Jacob had been completely at odds with society and the powers-that-be for a long time. Rebellion smouldered within him. Alberta still had an inherited respect for the mysterious and immense machinery in which Papa, the Head, the teachers and other officials were the cogs. It worried her that Jacob should have lost respect for it. It was these thoughts that would lead both of them astray, perhaps into real wrongdoing. It almost seemed as if Jacob was a somewhat wayward character already. Nothing ought to be neglected that might get him back on an even keel, and she energetically attempted to rouse his interest in an equation which she herself found thoroughly confusing.

After a while the equations lay there looking fairly plausible. It was better than a blank sheet of paper, at any rate. The German grammar was placed open in front of Jacob: 'I'll hear you after supper, and in Old Norse as well,' announced Alberta, standing with her hand on the door knob.

She opened the door. And she hesitated again for a moment, before saying rapidly and a little uncertainly: 'Don't be too late for supper, Jacob'.

And Jacob replied in the voice that made Alberta happy, and secure, and full of hope : 'I'll be on time, Alberta'.

In the kitchen with Jensine it was cosy and warm and smelling of coffee. Alberta hurried to fetch a cup from the pantry and served herself from the boiling kettle so that the grounds poured thickly out into the cup.

'It's not ready yet,' called Jensine, who was cleaning knives at the kitchen bench. 'Will you please leave the kettle alone Alberta, or I'll tell the Madam.'

Alberta drank it all. She was so cold after sitting still in Jacob's room that she could not feel her fingers. They were white and numb, and the cup she held seemed extraneous to them. Now the waves of coffee washed through her, scalding hot, paining her body and rousing it to life again. She picked coffee grounds out of her mouth, turned over the lump of sugar on her tongue and replied : 'If you knew how cold I am, Jensine.'

Jensine muttered over her knives. Not everything could be heard clearly, but cream, sugar and the Madam were repeated over and over again like a refrain.

'I take such a little, Jensine,' Alberta assured her, drinking quickly. And when Jensine turned her back for a moment and made a noise with the tap, Alberta poured herself yet another cupful and filled up the kettle from the water kettle beside it. She was in the pantry helping herself to cream when Jensine saw what was going on and rushed over. 'No, poor dear, now that's going too far. The Madam will think it's me – and if you've filled up the kettle with water again Alberta—'

'Only a little, only a little, just a tiny drop. Just let it boil a little longer, Jensine.'

She pushed Jensine in front of her out of the pantry. It was not wise to linger in there longer than necessary. Sometimes Mrs Selmer would get up in the middle of her after-dinner nap, driven by foreboding, and descend on the kitchen like Nemesis.

'All right Alberta, poor dear, I'll leave in the summer, and that's for sure and certain,' Jensine assured her, really angry now. 'If it were not for embarrassing the Madam, I'd leave this very minute.'

Alberta slunk away. Jensine made her feel a little ashamed and scared, but she was also thawed-out and warm. She stretched herself secretly. Jensine had threatened to leave for many years.

At the wood-box Alberta bent down as if by chance and collected sticks and bark into her skirt. Jensine said nothing to this, merely looking at her sideways and coughing significantly. She coughed again when Alberta moved off with her booty.

An undertaking full of danger, even for one expert at passing doors noiselessly. It was dark, and an accident might easily happen. Once a piece of firewood had fallen on the way through the dining-room, with highly unpleasant consequences. But nothing venture, nothing win.

Up in her room she lighted the stove. And when the birch bark began to crackle and curl the world was transformed. One after the other Alberta added the pieces of firewood, feeling a wild, intense joy at the sight of the flames leaping up round them. Then she crept on tiptoe down to Papa's office to steal coal.

Once there she moved like a mouse, feeling her way to the coal scuttle, fumbling and groping with her hands to find it. One might think Jensine had put it purposely outside the pool of light falling from the stove.

With every pore Alberta breathed in the stifling warmth, the permanent, pervasive smell of Papa's tobacco, that belonged to the inner office, while she picked up the coal piece by piece and put it in the shovel, making sure that nothing would spill and give her away afterwards, nothing fall and make a clatter. Papa was asleep on the other side of the wall, and in the outer office sat the Chief Clerk and Leonardsen, she could tell by the strip of light under the door.

In a little while she sat wrapped in the travelling-rug in front of her stove. She put her feet up on top, the fire roared, light flickered through the ventilating hole and fell on the floor. And a sheltered enclave, a place where it was good to be, slowly but surely came into being, spread, took over the whole room. A happy indolence pervaded her body and soon deadened the uneasy gnawing of her conscience.

She was acting meanly and she knew it. When the wood and coal in the cellar came to an end, it would provide an occasion for tragic scenes.

In the afternoon Mrs Selmer went out. She went out to tea or to one of her charities or to the lending library. It was important to manoeuvre so that she left the house without discovering Alberta's criminal intentions.

First of all Alberta must be in the dining-room when the after-dinner nap was over and coffee was served. She must look innocent, the soul of honour. After that the programme could be varied a little. She might sit with a stocking from the mending basket, imbued with domestic zeal, or she might take out the red and white table cloth. She might also be deep in something or other for Jacob, an essay, some arithmetic. In any case her alibi was in order, and Mrs Selmer would not feel impelled to reconnoitre upstairs, even though from principle she would contemplate Alberta's hang-dog appearance with suspicion and sarcasm.

The moment when the front door slammed behind her finally arrived. Alberta packed up again in order to return to her ill-gotten warmth. Then someone came through the office door, the flooring in the passage creaked beneath heavy footsteps, the dining-room door opened. It was the Magistrate.

'Hullo, are you here?' he said, obviously surprised to find Alberta.

She explained why she was there. And she wished, she wished to heaven Papa would not go over to the sideboard, but he did go. He bent down and took out the whisky decanter, poured himself a wine-glass full – so full that he had difficulty guiding it to his mouth – and emptied it in one draught. 'Ah,' he said. And he turned to Alberta and patted her on the head good-naturedly. 'Well, what are you going to do with yourself now, my lass?'

'I don't know,' replied Alberta. She drew slightly away from him but Papa did not seem to notice. 'All right, my darling,' he said, and left again.

Sick at heart Alberta wandered upstairs. She lighted the lamp and took out various things. A book she had borrowed, perhaps, or one of the poetry books from the sitting-room. Or maybe a little notebook, that led a secret existence beneath the woollen vests to the left in the chest of drawers. Sometimes she would not light the lamp, but would curl up on a chair in the comfortable darkness and sit looking out at the lights scattered along the river.

But if she knew for certain that Mrs Selmer would be away until supper-time, she might go down into the corner parlour, lighting her way with a match, and look for one of the forbidden books in the bookcase: *La Dame aux Camélias, Bel-ami, A Mother's First Duties*—

—And creep upstairs with it hidden in her skirt.

* * *

From time to time Olefine the dressmaker would come and install herself for two or three days upstairs in Jacob's room. She sewed blouses for Mrs Selmer and altered her old dresses for Alberta.

Olefine the dressmaker was pale, small and black-haired, and had a child by Isaksen the editor. Everybody knew about it.

When she had a fitting Alberta was always dismayed by the touch of Olefine's ice-cold, anaemic hands, which made her start and shrink away. But she liked to be in there with Olefine. It was warm, and coffee was served twice a day, coffee in a pot. When Olefine had drunk her two cups and pushed the tray away, Alberta would say: 'If you don't want any more, Olefine, I think I'll have a drop'. And she would pour it into Jacob's tooth mug and lose no time rinsing it clean again.

She was supposed to be helping. When Mrs Selmer came up now and again she would look sceptically at whatever Alberta had in her hands: 'Is Alberta of any use to you, Olefine?'

41

And Olefine would reply with her pale, tight little smile : 'Oh yes, to be sure she is'. And not a word more. Neither Mama nor Alberta were ever sure what Olefine really thought about it.

But when Mama had gone again, Alberta would lean over the table, rest her chin in her hand and watch Olefine's operations. Or she would stand at the window and look down into the street, tentatively leading the conversation on to various topics.

Olefine was not talkative. She answered with a brief : 'No, poor dear – thank you I'm sure – yes indeed, that's so'.

But Alberta, who was affected by the cosiness of the room as if by a stimulating drink, became good-humoured, chatty and bold, and attempted to broaden her knowledge of the mysteries of the town and of life in general.

Look, there were the two prostitutes going by. They were sisters, a little plump and getting on in years, and they wrapped up their heads and shoulders in large, brown shawls, which made them look as if they were wearing some kind of penitential costume. They would look out shyly or invitingly from behind their shawls, whichever happened to be appropriate, and they would often draw down one corner of their mouths at the same time. They lived on the west bank of the river near the distillery in a tumbledown little house, and had no permanent, official competitors, for Palmine Flor and Lilly Vogel did not consider themselves to be in the same class at all.

Another girl came to town occasionally, however. She was called Fanny and followed the fishing. When there was fishing to the south in Lofoten, she was there, and when the boats went eastwards to Finnmark, Fanny went with them.

She was tall, loose-limbed and blonde, and wore a large, furry, black hat on the back of her head. A dishevelled ostrich feather trailed from it. She was always laughing and had a vague look about her eyes; to tell the truth she usually looked a little drunk. And she was not afraid to appear in Fjord Street, surrounded by a positive thunder of sea-boots, arm in arm with her favourite. That was typical of Fanny. She didn't go round in penitential dress.

Fanny and the two sisters occupied Alberta's imagination now and again, just as they occupied the imaginations of Beda, and the Archdeacon's Christina, and Mama, and all the other women, although none of them would admit it. Mrs Selmer said of them : 'Poor miserable creatures,' as if she were referring to the lowest form of animal life.

The Archdeacon's Christina said : 'I can't see why you bother your heads about those disgusting individuals.'

Beda whistled significantly and pretended to know a lot about them.

Olefine lived on the way to Rivermouth and, it stood to reason, must have possessed a good deal of information. If only one could get it out of her.

'There are those awful girls.'

Olefine stopped the sewing machine and broke off the thread. She rose halfway out of her chair and looked down into the street. 'Yes, poor dear, I see,' she said. She smiled a little half smile and added : 'They have the day to themselves for walking'.

'They say it's dreadful in Rivermouth in the evenings.'

'Yes, so I've heard them say,' answered Olefine slowly, as if considering something privately. Then suddenly she declared curtly : 'But I'm not their keeper.'

The sewing machine droned on, and the subject of the two sisters was exhausted for the time being.

Alberta remembered that perhaps Olefine thought it embarrassing to talk about them, because she had a child herself. Once, a couple of years ago, Alberta had drawn her attention to Isaksen, who was passing by. After all, one wasn't bound to know that Olefine had a child by him, and it would be fun to see how she took it. She had replied in almost the same way : 'Yes, poor dear, I see.'

'Do you know anything about a girl called Fanny, Olefine?'

'Fanny – yes, I know there is a girl they call Fanny.'

'She's supposed to be a dreadful girl.'

'She's the same sort as those two.'

'Yes, but Olefine—'

'Oh – I know nothing about it.' Olefine bent over the sewing machine, pale and stubborn.

But Jensine, who had arrived with the coffee tray and had stood for a while listening, joined in the conversation : 'It's not always them you'd expect it of as is the worst. It may be the very ones you'd least expect it of'.

Jensine did not say it with indignation, rather with a kind of inner satisfaction. She chuckled a little inside, nodding prophetically at her own words.

'But nobody could be worse than Fanny, surely?' Alberta was full of expectancy, this was obviously a thread. She must grasp it tightly and draw it out in its entirety. 'Well, Dirty Katrine maybe, but she's so old.'

'I don't mean that sort, for that's the sort they be, and one can't expect more of them,' declared Jensine. 'I mean them as one can expect more of.'

Olefine nodded and helped herself to cream. 'Oh yes, it certainly takes all kinds, that's for sure.' She looked initiated, but she did not appear scandalised either. With her raised eyebrows and pensive eyes she almost seemed to adopt a waiting attitude, and it was impossible to tell whether she would smile or grimace.

'You mean Palmine Flor and Lilly Vogel.'

'Oh yes, them too. Of course I'm not saying they're among God's chosen children, but then they're not our betters' children neither.'

There was triumph in Jensine's voice. Olefine nodded, her mouth full of coffee, and made a small throaty noise in affirmation.

'Who do you mean?' Alberta had waited before firing her question. Her diplomacy seemed to be getting her nowhere, so she moved to the attack.

But Jensine and Olefine were prudent, and distressingly prone to talking in riddles.

Jensine put her hand over her mouth, tittered and said : 'Silence is golden'.

And Olefine looked vaguely over the machine into thin air

and had obviously been thinking about something else for a long time. 'How's it going with Marie at the Flemmings,' she said. 'I heard them say she wants to go south. That young Mrs Klykken has a situation for her in Trondheim.'

Alberta pressed her nose resignedly against the pane. It was not easy to unravel mysteries. No-one spoke straight out, neither books nor people. All those who were in the know were like members of a secret society, a freemasonry, in agreement that their shared knowledge should be kept to themselves. They tittered, they joked, they knew so much and took pleasure in knowing it. All about her the town was full of secrets. Behind all that she saw with her own eyes there lay a reality about which no-one would speak out loud. It lured and frightened, attracted and disgusted her simultaneously. In it unheard of, unthought of, and dreadful things were done, but people had a smile in their eyes and a chuckle in their laughter when they thought of them and hinted at them.

* * *

Between seven and eight o'clock the traffic in Fjord Street was considerable, particularly on the stretch between Theodorsen the baker and Louisa-round-the-bend. Beyond these two poles went only the energetic, the lonely, and those in love, people who deviated from the normal in one way or another. They walked to the east end of the wharf or out along Rivermouth, where the last of the street lights ended and the blackness of the winter night began.

Life collected in Fjord Street as in a canal, indeed it was channelled down the very middle of the street, for the pavements were full of snow. For this reason, and because the same people walked back and forth many times, the movement of the crowd was especially lively, almost intense – an incessant black stream under the eight arc-lamps.

The Magistrate and his daughter Alberta did not walk along Fjord Street as far as Louisa-round-the-bend like other folk. They had their own route and went along River Street, which was very dark and deserted in the evenings.

Young Klykken's living-room windows shone red, and a yellow border round a blind showed where the Catholic priest had his office in the Badendück building. But the other old houses with their wharves lay quite black, their dimensions unnaturally large in the darkness. You could see they were haunted.

Down on the Old Quay there was a circle of light under the lamp. There Papa and Alberta stood still, looking out at the dark river, where the current eddied cold and comfortless in the reflections from land. They discussed what kind of craft were lying out there, and contemplated the government dredging apparatus that could only be glimpsed in dark silhouette, freshly fallen snow along all its contours. Papa pointed outwards with his stick: 'They haul pretty large amounts up from the bottom here, by Jove. You get some idea of how much when you see the tip growing. It's a big undertaking. But we pay for it, it's the taxpayers who pay for it. All they have to do is squeeze.'

'I suppose it's necessary,' said Alberta. She said the same thing every time.

'Necessary, necessary, should damn well think not. I'd willingly go on taking a boat to board the steamer, as I have done all these years, to avoid giving them all that money.

'Now then, you know I don't mean it literally, Alberta, but God knows there's no sense in it, the sort of taxes we have now – they fleece folk, they fleece folk, the country's in a sad state of affairs.'

Alberta stifled a sigh. She had heard about taxes and the country's state of affairs as long as she could remember, had heard about it in the family circle and elsewhere, until it had seemed to turn into an unspeakably disconsolate little melody, endlessly repeated. It *was* so. In some place known only to God, far south in Kristiania, there sat an assemblage of inhuman, merciless people – peasant Members of the Storting, Radicals, heartless, uneducated persons – plotting the incredible in order to plunder and impoverish Papa, Uncle the Colonel, Aunt Marianne in Grimstad, and all their relations, friends and acquaintances. 'They' had their hand-picked men planted all over the place, in local government and town councils; gruesome, blood-smeared individuals like Ryan the butcher, who was terribly radical, and sinister, cunning people like Hannestad the schoolmaster, who was quiet, hollow-eyed and hollow-chested, and so radical that he even had a wife who was too.

But if it was no use talking about it? As long as Alberta could remember it had never been any use. Besides, it was an obscure and far from attractive subject.

'Imagine being the captain of a dredging barge,' she said apropos of nothing, in order to get away from it.

'Yes, by Jove, it's not a proud vessel exactly, and they send old-fashioned ones up north, but they do good service. We must be glad as long as no-one decides we're to have our own dredging apparatus here in town – God knows they're capable of it. One fine day someone who wants to call attention to himself will discover we need something more modern, and the ball will start rolling. Just squeeze the taxpayers a little, it's so simple.'

Alberta stifled another sigh. But now they were turning up into River Street again. And Papa halted and planted his stick deep in the ground. He did it exactly where he always did it, and he said exactly what he always said: 'You know, Alberta, I'd like to go round by the New Quay to see how things are getting on there. I enjoy looking at the new buildings.'

So, at their accustomed pace they went their accustomed way round the big Stoppenbrink wharves, the Magistrate large and heavy on his feet, slow of movement, Alberta thin as a shadow, her chin jutting out and her hands drawn up inside her sleeves. Still they met nobody. Who would go down to the quay on a snow-dark winter evening, when no steamer was expected? No-one but Papa and Alberta.

The desolation on the New Quay was oppressive and complete. In the light from the arc-lamp down below the snowed-in heaps of barrels and crates looked like the last surviving witness of a dead world. In spite of the cold a rank smell of cod-liver-oil and fish came from them and mingled with the smell of the filth left by the ebb tide. Like a pale arm the new stone quay could be glimpsed seawards in the darkness. Along its landward side lay small coastal trading vessels and heavy ten-oared rowing boats, their outlines drawn up in wool out of the new-fallen snow. There were river boats too, that had brought wood and kindling from the east. Furthest out, the harbour light glowed like a red full-stop.

A little path had been trampled in the snow by people going to and from the various craft, and Papa's and Alberta's programme included going as far out as the light reached from land. Wherever there was a mooring the snow had been swept into the sea, and the stone body of the quay showed through, smooth, iced over, treacherous to walk on.

Papa went first, feeling his way with his stick. Now and again he would halt and prod at a stone : 'Good work this,' he said. And he turned and pointed, today as on other days, out towards the harbour light and in towards the unfinished office buildings which rose blackly on land : 'That'll be a big installation when it's finished, by Jove'.

He pounded his stick against several stones : 'There are some fine pieces for you'.

Alberta mechanically placed her feet precisely where she always placed them. She knew every block and every juncture. If she departed from the ritual she did so with mature deliberation. The lights up on the river bend were not visible in the snow haze, and she drew Papa's attention to it. He agreed that she was right, it must be snowing over there : 'It never stops, by Jove'. – 'No,' said Alberta.

She fought against the exhausting, dizzy feeling she always got when one of her wanderings with Papa was drawing to a close, and they had to go back amongst people again – a painful, almost physical sensation of time creeping by.

Every time they turned the corner into River Street, and it became dark and silent round them, a feeling of expectation came over her. Something must happen; some decisive words, bringing clarity and giving hope, must fall. It must happen some time, perhaps today, why not? Papa must have some confidence to make to her, everything couldn't possibly be meant to continue for ever in the same way.

She remembered an occasion a couple of years ago. Papa had pounded once more with his stick, and said : 'Back we go, Alberta. We must keep at it – no use being down-hearted, by Jove.' It had been full of significance, rich in inner meaning and unspoken promises for the future. It was at the very least an admission that all was not as one might wish. Much could be deduced from it, and Alberta had done so and lived on it for a good while. But the need for something fresh had become pressing and acute a long time ago.

She longed, too, for him to talk to her as he did when she was small. He had talked about the stars and pointed them out to her, spoken of the bottomless depth of the universe and a god, more strange and fascinating than the God of school or of church, a god who was one with creation, a hidden flame that burned in everything : 'Well, well, Alberta, that's how we can imagine it to be, but none of us holds a patent in knowledge, by Jove, and I'm blowed if a priest in a pulpit understands any more than the rest of us'.

It became so easy to breathe – heaven and earth seemed aired when Papa talked like that. The old, strict, pernickety and punishing God, who kept such a sharp eye on people and boasted unceasingly of retribution, dwindled and disappeared. The smell of corpses, the horrible odour of churchyards and rotting bones, that hung round death, were no longer anything to worry about. She had never really been able to accept that the soul floated off somewhere else, how could anyone know? Suppose it did lie in the earth with all the others, writhing for air and waiting for Judgement Day? Her face turned hot and dry at the thought, as if the coffin lid were already pressing down on it; her hair rose up in dread. When Papa talked it was as if a fresh wind from heaven blew the horror away. One became nothing, a mere breath – but a breath that had nothing to fear.

But all that had been long ago. Nothing happened any more. She and Papa repeated the same words that they had repeated countless times before. They would turn back and go home, nothing had changed, everything was just as hopeless and just as oppressive.

'We ought to go home now, Papa.'

'How right you are, by Jove, we ought.' He pounded with his stick, and they went.

In silent agreement they always chose the streets where there were fewest people. They could go back the same way, they could also make a detour through shabby old Strand Street. But unless they were to appear downright laughable by wandering right round Upper Town, they would end up in Fjord Street just the same. This crowded thoroughfare could not be avoided in the long run.

Before they turned into it the Magistrate drew himself up slightly, threw back his shoulders, stuck out his chest, and brushed down his coat with his hand. Then he saluted those they met courteously and with extreme cordiality.

'You must tell me if there's anyone we know, Alberta.'

Alberta greeted them formally and diffidently. Her teeth chattered slightly, as always when she did not walk fast enough; her fingers and toes smarted with cold. But she was not afraid of blushing in this light, and there was a certain agreeable excitement in walking along, meeting all these people and feeling safe. It did not matter so much if the worst happened, and they were spoken to and stopped, when Papa was there.

The shops were still open. They shone in competition with the arc-lamps. Where there were large plate-glass windows all of a piece, as at Holst's and the Gentlemen's Outfitters, there was a city atmosphere, an atmosphere of the south, thought Alberta. You had to try to plan your way through the throng, to walk into it and out again as in great, milling capitals. You could pretend you were walking in one.

There was Beda with the chemists from the 'Polar Bear' pharmacy, and the new dentist. She laughed loudly and unselfconsciously, and sauntered carelessly along, swinging her muff. She put herself completely beyond the unwritten law that demanded of young girls in this town that they must walk stiff and straight as soldiers, their elbows at their sides, eyes front, with every sign of tremendous haste; and that they must greet others looking into space, almost without

moving their heads – certainly not in the way Beda did it. She
nodded so that her fur cap hopped forward on to her nose and
had to be pushed back into position again.

'Our worthy Beda has no *tenue*,' remarked the Magistrate.
'It is quite distressing to see. She walks so appallingly—'

'Harriet Pram, Papa.'

Harriet had a new winter coat. It had come from the
south and was trimmed with fur. You could see at once that
it had not been bought at F. O. Lenning's. She walked like a
soldier, but smiled when she greeted people and said good
evening in passing. She had learned that in the south.

'Remarkably pretty girl,' commented Papa. 'You should
apply yourself to becoming more like her, Alberta.'

'Mrs Lossius,' warned Alberta, glad to get away from the
subject, and Papa prepared himself for a fresh greeting.

The Governor's lady had a lorgnette, the only one in town,
which dangled outside all her furs at the end of a long gold
chain. It was, so to speak, a sign of her rank. Indignation
would have been roused far and wide if anyone else had
taken the liberty of wearing one. When you were not the
Governor's wife elementary tact required you to wear ordinary pince-nez – at least in town. As she passed she swivelled
it towards Papa and Alberta and called : 'Greetings from my
little girls,' smiling with a narrow, tight little mouth.

'Thank you very much,' replied Alberta with an evil pang.

'The Archdeacon's wife – the Weyers—'

Mrs and Miss Weyer approached slowly, arm in arm. Mrs
Weyer was gradually getting deafer and more difficult, and
Otilie's beautiful, kind, faded face gradually more patient.
It was generally accepted in the town that she had been the
loveliest woman anyone had ever seen. It was incomprehensible that she should still be unmarried, such a fine, sweet girl,
a pearl of great price. She was in her thirties now, terribly
old, and everyone had given up, except Mrs Weyer, who was
often deceived by renewed hope. They were with the Archdeacon's wife, who was small and transparent and had such
crystal-clear eyes that you could look right through them to
the bottom of her pure soul.

The Magistrate saluted the three ladies genially.

'Miss Liberg!'

'Oh, confound it!'

Miss Liberg bustled officiously past, righting her pince-nez to satisfy herself as to who was saluting her, and called out exuberantly: 'Good evening, Mr Magistrate, good evening'. One more glance and she would have stopped, but Papa resolutely quickened his pace, unrelenting as stone.

She was one of the energetic walkers and a teacher at the girls' school, feared for her talkativeness and for her declamation of 'The Ode to the Polish Republic'. On festive occasions both were seldom to be avoided.

'The Pastor and Mrs Pio.'

'Poor souls,' muttered Papa sorrowfully. 'It can't be so confoundedly easy.'

Mr Pio, Perpetual Curate, and his wife passed them slowly. They adopted the same speed as at a respectable funeral. Pastor Pio had thick lips in a small, bristling beard, and heavy eyes under heavy lids. Everyone knew that he had moved up to the attic last spring, and that it had not helped. Mrs Pio was having yet another baby and she looked tired and despairing, dragging a little on her husband's arm. Six children in eight years was a lot. The town conceded it and disapproved of Pio.

'Mr Bergan.'

In the lamplight and among so many people this was not such a great catastrophe. Alberta noted with pride that she only trembled a little when he went past. But when she discovered that Mama and a number of other ladies were standing below the steps of the 'Polar Bear' looking after him, the blood flooded into her face.

Mr Bergan the lawyer had bought a piano recently, and his home was said to be complete in every way. Surely he would have to make up his mind soon, but on whom would the choice fall? Since the arrival of the piano it had been a burning question.

He had light blue, slightly indolent eyes and increasing corpulence, topped with colourless hair which stood up straight like a brush. He greeted no one person more vivaciously than another, so it was difficult to make any prediction. If only he would decide on Christina it would be a great relief, thought Alberta.

Now she and Papa were passing the ladies outside the 'Polar Bear'. Papa saluted them with a broad sweep of his hat, turning deferentially towards the group; while Mama radiantly returned his greeting in a manner that differed from the others. It was clear that they had both lived in other, more gracious circumstances.

Immediately afterwards Alberta caught sight of Jacob a short distance ahead. He popped up, was lost in the crowd, and popped up again. Now he was saying goodbye to another boy, who turned and came back.

And Alberta saw with dismay that it was Cedolf Kjeldsen. He raised his cloth cap as he went by. It seemed to her that a smile passed over his strikingly handsome, aggressive face.

'Who was that, Alberta?'

'I can't imagine – someone who has been to the office probably.'

Thank heaven Papa was trusting and unsuspicious, shortsighted and easy to deceive – much easier than Mama.

Jacob could still be seen further down the street. Now he was turning in to the front door, and taking the steps in one bound, as he always did. He would be at home when they arrived, sitting in the dining-room with *The Prisoner of Zenda*. Papa's face would brighten and he would be kind to Jacob, and relapse into the hope that it might still be possible to make a man of him.

But Jacob would have that set of the mouth against which she was helpless. He would not see Alberta when she begged him with her eyes. He would not bother about his homework, but ask permission to go out after supper, explaining it away with a lie. Papa, thanks to his relapse and possibly for other reasons too, would give him permission.

Then Jacob would go to mysterious, hidden places – in the alleys and at Rivermouth – with Cedolf, who had come home from sea. And early tomorrow morning there would perhaps be a smell of drink, she knew where.

Alberta's thoughts distracted her, and something unheard-of occurred. She forgot to stamp the snow from her feet.

'Your feet,' called Papa in despair and resignation. 'Your feet, Alberta. When will you learn—?'

Alberta turned obediently and, with preoccupied expression, executed a step on the door mat.

Immediately afterwards they heard Mama. She was bidding exhilarated farewells to several ladies outside the front door. They could hear her witty and amusing remarks from well inside the hall. She was standing talking through the half-open door.

'Humph!' said Papa quietly, hanging up his coat and hat. 'Humph!' he said once more, and kicked off his galoshes.

Mrs Selmer arrived.

The cold made her look healthy and young, but her mouth, which had just been talking and laughing, had a sad, tired droop. She wandered round taking off her outdoor things without seeming to see Alberta and Papa. Then she stood in front of the mirror, arranging her hair and sighing deeply.

'Well?' said Papa tentatively. 'You all seemed to be in good humour. What was so amusing?'

'Amusing? I don't know that anything was amusing,' replied Mama wearily and coldly, as if from a long way off – still seeing nobody. 'I talked to the others a little, I'm sure I don't know what for—'

'What on earth are you standing about here for?' she exclaimed with sudden sharpness, inspecting Alberta and Papa as if she had just caught sight of them.

Alberta's heart sank. She made a cowardly movement towards the door, but happened to look at the Magistrate at the same time. His mouth twisted a little, very very slightly. Then he opened the door, clicked his heels, bowed lightly towards Mama, and said in a voice that in a curious way warmed Alberta: 'We're waiting for you, my dear'. And he stood holding the door open for her, his whole attitude one of respectful chivalry.

Alberta's heart swelled painfully with affection.

* * *

Snow, storm, delayed packet boats. Day-long, tense listening for the ship's siren, watching for Larsen, the postman, through the icy panes that had first to be breathed on for a while. Snow and still more snow.

'Isn't Larsen coming yet, Alberta?' asked Mrs Selmer, who was eaten up with anxious waiting on post days. She paced the floor, stopped at the windows, breathed on the panes and looked out, and when two hours had passed since the arrival of the packet boat and still Larsen had not appeared, she sent Alberta out to catch him at Kilde's, before he turned into River Street. 'And then come back with the post this way,' she called after her down the steps.

And she would search feverishly through the bundle of official circulars and newspapers. Her letters were easily recognisable from the backs of the envelopes, even if only a fraction was showing. They were so different from the Magistrate's.

What was Mrs Selmer waiting for, and what was Alberta waiting for? Mama's anxiety and excitement pulsed in her blood too. It was through the post that something wonderful must come, something that would bring to an end everything as it was at present, turn life upside down, open wide the future – the letter from Uncle the Colonel, who would invite Alberta to come south; or the discreet hint from good friends that some splendid post, Aker and Follo for instance, was free, and that Papa had every expectation, if he would apply . . . Or the unexpected announcement of a large inheritance, why not? It must come some day, this whatever-it-was – and it could not come otherwise than by post.

The living rooms were like an icy sea and the world outside a swirl of white and grey. The snow stood up like smoke from the roofs and was whipped into high crests round the corners, torturing the face and blinding the sight. It settled, packed and hard, on projections and ledges, closed up afresh each day the windows laboriously kept free of frost, filled cracks and grooves, entered like a cloud whenever a door was opened. Snow in the entrance in the morning, snow piled up against the street door, snow down one's neck and up one's sleeves as soon as one stepped outside. When the gale quietened now and again the snow went on sifting down from the thick sky like feathers from an inexhaustible grey quilt.

The houses became tiny, dwindled, and disappeared. Only the top half of Kvandal the tailor's house was left. The Telegraph Station, so impressive in summer with its long flight of steps, could soon be entered straight from the street.

The butchers' windows were covered with snow flowers. Karla Schmitt and Signora Ryan, who served in their fathers' shops, both had chilblains as in previous years. And, as in previous years, they became clumsy, cut themselves and were bound up with rags here and there. Alberta, who had been sent to fetch sliced meat, could not stop herself thinking of the moment when the knife had slipped and cut into the swollen, mauve-coloured fingers. Pressed meat and smoked sausage lost their appeal for her.

There was not much to see in the street any more. The few pedestrians were grey, unrecognisable bundles, who crossed in the teeth of the wind and snow with their faces hidden. But there came Kwasnikow stamping, and livened it all up. He was not grey, he was red, and the colour was most obvious in winter. His worn top hat, the joy of the street urchins, was not lording it as usual on his head. Kwasnikow was wearing a sheepskin cap with red ribbons hanging down the back, and a sheepskin coat with red edging to it. The snow powdered his red hair and his red beard, making both burn a little less brightly than in summer, but to make up for it his face, with its round, blue eyes, was more highly coloured than ever. It was full of tiny, red veins, broken by the wind and the weather and brandy; on his nose and cheekbones they clustered into three flaming roses. And he sang to himself, as was his habit when walking; a melancholy, monotonous, never-ending

56

melody. Once, long ago, no-one quite knew when, Kwasnikow had come from Murmansk with a Russian ship and been left behind, lying ill at the hospital. So he had found work with old Kamke and stayed for good.

Some distance behind him came the prostitutes in their shawls, snow on their heads, shoulders and other horizontal planes, like wandering monuments.

Every day the stifling dark nibbled a little more ot the weak twilight.

The lights were on all day. It was almost Christmas. Mrs Selmer's breakfast novel had disappeared. Her almanac, a pencil and a notebook had taken its place. Mrs Selmer leafed through the almanac, wrote notes, and made marks with the pencil, muttering to herself and drumming on the table with her fingers: 'Madam Svendsen says we shall be having *vol-au-vent* at the Archdeaconry on the first day of Christmas, so we can't have it on the third, it's out of the question. Otherwise I had thought of having it this year before the roast – last year we had tongue and green peas, so that's no good either. Oh bother, whatever shall I choose?'

She read her notes to herself and Alberta: 'Washing sixteenth and seventeenth, flead cakes eighteenth, wafers and Berlin rings nineteenth, boil ham in the evening, clean house twentieth, polish silver twenty-first, hang up curtains in the evening. Gingernuts, raisin bread twenty-second – no, I see we shall have to do them early too, Alberta, otherwise we shan't get out the plants and the carpets – scrub kitchen twenty-third – you'll have to decorate the tree, Alberta—'

Mrs Selmer speculated, drummed, muttered and scribbled more notes. And Alberta made the most of it, helping herself to cheese with her bread, and more coffee, while she replied, 'Yes, of course – yes, I expect that would be best,' in the tone of voice that by experience had shown itself to be most expedient when domestic affairs were under discussion. An interested, calm, friendly tone, which tolerably hid the blackness of her soul.

She was colder than ever. The curtains were at the wash,

and the windows stared blackly at her from all directions like empty eye-sockets. On the outer sills the snow lay piled high against the panes, the darkness and cold grimaced in without mercy. The dining-room stove seemed to burn to even less purpose than usual; the warmth was no longer devoured by the living-rooms alone, it seemed to be swallowed up in the universe.

Mrs Selmer drew her shawl tightly about her: 'Last year the flead cakes came to so and so much, but this year butter and eggs are dearer – and I sent something to your Aunt the Colonel last week, I thought I should – I daren't tell Papa – I don't see how I shall make the money go round, Alberta.'

She wrote a number of quick, small figures on a clean page in the almanac, added, subtracted, and counted on her fingers.

Alberta added and subtracted as well. All the prosiness and tedium of life was piling up ahead like bad weather forecasts. Her lonely walks, those fixed points of her existence, her innumerable secret visits to the coffee pot, her vice and stimulant, disappeared from view as lights are extinguished for the seafarer. The daily storms might turn into hurricanes and the approaching festival into a catastrophe, it had happened before. The cold, the dark, and the shortage of money, these three, these invincible three, each of whom alone could kill all joy, now concluded a terrible pre-Christmas pact to ravage life and lay it waste. Scrubbing and polishing days were gloomy and full of traps and dangers; the day when the one thousand and three potted plants had to be carried out and in again, washed and sprinkled, even worse – but it's an ill wind . . . Alberta's unfortunate person was generally put in the shade by the flead cakes and wafers, by burning financial problems, by Madam Svendsen who helped with the baking, and old Oleanna who helped with the wash. Besides, a couple of days in the kitchen rolling out flead cakes or laying Berlin rings on the hot plate would not be too bad. It would be warm in the kitchen, so warm that she could wear an open-necked summer blouse with the sleeves rolled up. Her skin would turn smooth and white, her hands beautiful and plump. Once in a while she would be able to fill up on a left-over piece of dough or some burned or other-wise unsuccessful cake, and there was no lack of coffee. On the other hand Madam Svendsen had red, running eyes, the sight of which ruined the appetite. She groaned from time to time and had to sit down and explain over and over again that it was the sores on her legs. Alberta was filled with horror at the thought of these legs full of sores, they obsessed her. She imagined them to be pale and bloody, could not get them out of her mind for long periods, and dreaded them every time Madam Svendsen came. What with one thing and another, there was a good deal to be taken into consideration.

But Mama was more conciliatory towards Papa. Her voice no longer turned cold and bitter, but she would explain patiently and pleasantly why such and such were necessary and why they cost so and so much. She did not emerge, as she normally did from her skirmishes concerning money, small and crushed, fighting her tears, the notes crumpled convul-sively in her hand. And Papa did not hand them over in a fury, but merely sighed a little and said : 'Well, well, if it's necessary' – or, 'You understand these things better than I, my dear'.

They discussed the party for the third day of Christmas at the breakfast table. There were even mornings when Papa, in high spirits, threw bank notes across the table to Mama, say-ing : 'If we're to have Christmas, then let's have a proper one – *après nous le déluge*'.

And Alberta at her mending basket felt her spirits rise, and it seemed as if everything could be borne if only Mama and Papa would behave like this to each other. But then she re-membered that it had been like this last Christmas too. For some mysterious reason it was like this once in a while.

It never lasted long.

* * *

'Are you up, Alberta?'

'I'm getting dressed. What do you want, Jacob?'

'I must talk to you, Alberta – you must let me in.' Jacob's voice was low and urgent. He grasped the door handle.

'No Jacob, do wait a bit – you are mean!'

Jacob was already in the room. 'I'm sorry Alberta, don't be cross,' he said quickly, short of breath.

Alberta groped for something with which to cover herself. Since Jacob's confirmation, when he began to wear long trousers, she had been shy of him, and it embarrassed her to have to display her arms and collar bone. Perhaps it was also a little because of Cedolf Kjeldsen, Jacob's evil genius, who had been to sea and whom Alberta dimly suspected to be a man of experience, capable of opening Jacob's eyes to all manner of things.

But there was nothing within reach. Not for the world would she cross the floor, so she remained standing in front of him, a little hunched, knock-kneed, her elbows pressed in to her sides, her hands crossed over her breast and the compromising collar-bone – trembling with cold and modesty.

Jacob did not even see her. He spoke quickly in the same low, urgent voice, and Alberta realised that her sensitivity was for the moment of no importance whatever. This was of those situations in which the barriers of everyday life fall, when people act without regard for trivialities, when one only made oneself ridiculous and insignificant by insisting on formalities.

'I say Alberta,' said Jacob. 'You've got to help me.'

'What is it, Jacob, what is it?'

Jacob waited for a second. It is no joke dealing someone a blow, even if you are in a hurry and action must be taken.

'Can you lend me twenty *kroner?*' he said, looking fixedly at Alberta. There was no other way out and he was beyond all scruple.

'Are you out of your mind, Jacob?'

'I must have it, Alberta, I must have it this afternoon, or else—'

'Or else?'

'Or else they'll send a bill for forty *kroner* to Papa.'

'Jacob!'

'Yes, you see, Alberta, it was a marble table – we sat on it, you understand, another fellow and myself, one on each side, and it cracked right across – and Krane won't wait. You see,

Alberta, we each have to find twenty *kroner* by this afternoon. He'd wait until then, he said.'

'It was you and Cedolf.'

'I haven't time for so many explanations – Mama may come any minute and find me here. And you know how it'll be if she gets to know, she'll lie about on the sofa and all that. You see, I *must* have the money, you *must* help me – I have to dash now – good-bye.'

And Jacob was gone.

Alberta stood there alone and tried to plumb the depths of this catastrophe. Her head whirled with one-legged pale pink marble café tables. Cedolf Kjeldsen's cheeky, handsome face, and Krane the hotel keeper's sour, pursed-up little one span past against a background of the horribly vulgar drinking-parties that went on in the small back rooms at the Grand, behind the banqueting hall. She had had a glimpse of one once when she was up at the hotel on an errand and took the wrong turning. The memory had remained with her in a reek of squalor. A disgusting, airless stench of stale, cold tobacco and drunkenness, slops on the tables, boisterous laughter. A hoarse voice, incessantly repeating damn, damn, damn from the centre of a group, one of the chambermaids on the lap of a man in shirt-sleeves. A commercial traveller in a state of dissolution, collarless, his waistcoat unbuttoned, who, glass in hand, had come to the door and called to Alberta : 'Come on in Missy, we were waiting for you. No, no, come on in' – and had made after her down the stairs calling pssst! The chambermaid had twisted herself off the lap on which she was sitting, had come and taken the man by the arm and brought him to order, whispering : 'Be quiet, Pettersen, she's one of the Magistrate's family – so be quiet now, do you hear?' – And it had been only the middle of the afternoon. People said it got worse later in the evening. Then Krane was said to hang dark blankets over the windows, and Palmine Flor and Lilly Vogel were there.

But it must not happen, it must not happen. The thought of what might come about, of Papa's fury and Mama's lamentations, made her feel physically ill. Cedolf had always been Papa's red rag and one of Mama's countless crosses, Cedolf alone was more than enough. The Grand, Krane, and forty *kroner*'s extra expenditure in the middle of the Christmas preparations was too much by far, and would bring about something very similar to Domesday. Papa might throw Jacob out of the house, give him up completely, beat him to death, kill Mama.

Alberta already felt that terrible giddiness that comes of enduring something, dreading something. It was an old acquaintance. When she had told Mama lies, done school work badly, stolen cakes from the sideboard, it had been there – and when she had had to take an exam or have a tooth pulled out – and the time she and Jacob had been out rowing on the river, were carried away by the current and came home in the middle of the night. It was like a sickness breaking out, a malignant fever.

Now she could hear Mama going downstairs. She pulled herself together, finished dressing and went down after her. As she entered the dining-room the street door slammed behind Jacob. She wilted and shrank under Mrs Selmer's gaze which, sharp with suspicion, was directed at her across the almanac.

'Strange that Jacob should be out so early today,' commented Mama, as she handed Alberta her cup. 'He had disappeared by the time I came down, and it's not more than eight o'clock. I can't understand why he should leave so early.'

'No, I can't either,' answered Alberta, blushing to the roots of her hair.

'It is also strange that you should be blushing,' continued Mrs Selmer. Her eyes never left Alberta, her mouth was sarcastic. 'Are you hiding something from me?'

Mrs Selmer was by no means trusting or easy to lead by the nose, and Alberta did not possess the saving grace of audacity.

'Of course not, Mama,' she said, but her hand trembled so that she had to put down her cup, and her eyes were wooden as they avoided Mama's.

'Take care,' said Mama. And Alberta felt the same anxiety grip her as when Mama had said take care to her when she was small : 'Take care, if I find you've been making a fool of me – you'll pay dearly for it, Alberta, my dear'.

Mrs Selmer's voice was pregnant with misfortune. There was a cold composure in it that froze Alberta. She tottered over to the mending basket and concentrated on rummaging amongst the stockings without bringing herself to begin darning them.

'Don't sit there rummaging,' exclaimed Mama irritably. 'Get out the silver and take it into the kitchen. My adult daughter should know that we clean the silver today.'

Alberta got up again, weak at the knees, opened drawers and cupboards and began to wander in and out, butter-fingered and clumsy, relieved each time she slipped past without being assailed afresh. But no-one avoids his fate for long : 'When did Jacob come home last night?'

'I don't know,' replied Alberta, feeling as if she were plunging headlong into the abyss. With any luck she was the only one in the house who did know when Jacob had come home. At any rate she was the only one who knew what he did with himself. The alleys, Rivermouth, the Grand – all that lay outside Papa's and Mama's range of vision.

She had lain listening as he crept up the stairs. It had sounded as if he was steady on his feet.

Now she was piling lie upon lie. Where would it end? If she were found out retribution was certain. Everything gave warning of it, Mrs Selmer's eyes, her icy voice. Oh – if only something would happen, anything, a catastrophe if necessary, as long as it put an end to this situation. It took nerve to deny anything consistently to Mama. Alberta felt with dismay that she had none. And now she would have to sit face to face with her the whole morning and polish silver.

If she had had the saving grace of audacity she would have asked with innocent voice and expression if Jacob had not come home at eleven o'clock, as he had said he would – but she did not possess it and was incapable of touching on the subject. Inwardly, she felt something give way. The moment when the sinner breaks down, and can maintain his stubbornness no longer, but prostrates himself and confesses all, seemed not so very far away for Alberta.

Mrs Selmer was speaking again. With the confidence of one who knows his time will come, she said: 'I don't know when he came home either, I was asleep. I don't even know where he was. I have my doubts as to whether he was with the rest of his class, as he said he would be. But I shall see to it that I find out, and I shall also see to it that I find out whether you have told me the truth today, Alberta.'

Then the stairs creaked. Papa was on his way, and Alberta was given a breathing-space. It was in everyone's interest to keep him out of it as long as possible, at any rate until Mama had discovered what was really going on.

The morning was endless. Alberta sat as if on live coals, scarcely daring to move so as to avoid attracting any more attention to herself than was necessary. She breathed more easily every time Jensine's many duties brought her out to the kitchen. She prayed to heaven that Jensine might stay there, but Jensine did not stay; she merely emptied her bucket in the sink, filled it with clean water, exchanged a few words with Mama and disappeared again. And the atmosphere remained as oppressive as before.

Once Alberta took courage and tried to begin a conversation on a neutral subject: the silver they were polishing, the abundance of silver that derived from Papa's and Mama's palmy days, a fairy-tale time from before Alberta could remember.

It was a complete fiasco. Mrs Selmer answered yes and no, all the while looking at Alberta like a detective who knows he has caught the criminal, and that it is only a matter of time before all is confessed.

Alberta went under again and surfaced no more.

Twice she got up and pretended to go to a certain place, simply to get out of Mama's atmosphere and think a little. In the fateful silence that prevailed it was impossible to follow the slightest strand of thought. She stood outside on the steps for a suitable length of time, twisting and rubbing her ice-cold hands and trying to find a solution. Faces whirled in her brain, popped up and vanished.

Beda? Beda would probably bring out a couple of ten *kroner* notes if she had them, but she never had any money except at the beginning of the month. And she would despise Alberta and say: 'You're a proper fool, Alberta, poor dear, to waste your time helping Jacob with a thing like this – don't bother Alberta'. Beda did not understand how things were. She had a mother who would say: 'But my dearest, darling, sweet little Beda, how could you do such a thing?' when Beda had done something terrible. A mother who was not in the least like Nemesis, but who was only a little extraordinary, a little scandalous – and a father framed behind glass on the wall. It was easy for Beda to be fearless and happy-go-lucky.

Christina? Impossible. Gudrun? No, none of her friends. The Chief Clerk – reveal to the Clerk that his superior's children could not find twenty *kroner* on their own – no! Leonardsen? His worn, obliging, little person, always suffering from a cold, appeared before her against the background of two small crowded rooms, stuffy with wet napkins, coffee and paraffin vapour – no, not Leonardsen.

Nor Jensine.

But then there was nobody else – then there was only one way out, a highly embarrassing solution, one that opened new depths for Alberta. She had resorted to it once before when money had to be raised. Now it almost felt like a compulsion. She knew it existed and could be turned to account, and that she would be unable to avoid it.

After dinner she waylaid Jacob in the hall. They whispered out there together.

'Can't Cedolf lend it you – he has his wages, hasn't he?'

Jacob looked away. 'He was treating me,' he replied evasively.

'I suppose he always treats you,' said Alberta bitterly, with some scorn.

'Mm-yes – I never have any money, you know that.'

'Yes, but you don't have to go to the Grand.'

'Don't have to go to the Grand?' Jacob's expression was suddenly helpless. 'We don't usually go to the Grand, it was only yesterday evening – and besides, I must be allowed to go somewhere. It's always so loathsome here at home. Papa can scarcely bear the sight of me.'

'I know Alberta, but it's no good preaching morals at me now,' he added deprecatingly when Alberta opened her mouth. 'If you can't help, never mind. I'll be leaving home soon anyway. Now or later, it makes no difference. And whether I leave on my own or get sent away makes no difference either. If it weren't for Mama, Krane could bring his bill – she suspects something already, by the way.'

Jacob turned up his collar and prepared to leave the house.

'You shall have the money, Jacob – I think – in a little while. Go upstairs and read, I'll come up later.'

'But can you manage it, Alberta?'

'I don't know, I'm going to try. Go on up, Jacob!'

The street was deserted immediately after dinner. That was as it should be, otherwise the expedition would have been unthinkable. But it also increased her feeling of being out on an unlawful errand, of this being a special time for deeds of darkness.

It was clearing up. A whiff of colder weather was in the air, and the snowfall had lightened towards the north. A star was visible through it; it twinkled weakly. Alberta remembered distractedly that the moon would soon be full. Perhaps it would shine the bad weather away until Christmas.

She felt as if her body were unreal, non-existent. If Mama or Papa had any inkling of what she was doing now, the day of judgement would probably have the same dimensions as if Krane were to come with the bill. One misdeed leads to another. Alberta and Jacob were on the slippery slope, rolling downwards at top speed. The next link in the chain would be to begin telling lies with audacity and cold-bloodedness, those two good and necessary weapons in life's struggle. Those such as Alberta who did not possess them by nature were ill-equipped, but it served no purpose to think of that now. A dangerous course had presented itself and had to be followed to its conclusion without hesitation.

There was Kvandal the tailor standing at his door. Was he not wondering where Alberta was going in the middle of the after-dinner nap enjoyed by officialdom and the higher business echelons? Could he not see it written all over her – did he not scent scandal through that flattened little nose of his?

Kvandal the tailor was one of the people who, she was certain, knew something positive about Papa's money matters. There might be some point in taking in the Archdeaconry and the Governor's family, the Prams and the Pios. Perhaps they went home from Papa's and Mama's parties after fine wine and plenty of food, thinking : 'Perhaps they're not so badly off after all'.

But Kvandal the tailor – he would smile derisively if he saw the spread. And Lian the shoemaker and Schmitt the butcher.

You see your home from one side, the inside. But it has an outside facing the town as well, in fact it has two, a front side and a back side. You yourself swing with it in its course and never see either the front, that faces towards the gentry and has a door on to the street, or the back, that faces Kvandal the tailor, Lian the shoemaker and Schmitt the butcher, and has a kitchen entrance. You can only guess how it looks.

The people who come to the kitchen door *know* everything that, with much care and sacrifice, is concealed from the rest of the world. You carry your head high in front of them, as high as you can – but unfortunately Alberta could do no more than that. And now she was making an admission to them. It is difficult to conceal facts – if you succeed in one quarter they will leak out in another.

Dorum the goldsmith – he had looked at her so craftily last time. He would look even more crafty now, most likely. And yet Alberta would lie to him, lie although she would blush to the roots of her hair. It was natural to lie to Dorum – if only it were equally natural to lie to Mrs Selmer.

It could be seen from a distance that Dorum the goldsmith

kept warm and comfortable in his business. There was no ice on the large plate-glass window, and you could see into the shop from a long way down River Street. A couple of country folk were inside trying on rings. Behind them Dorum's bald head shone like a moon under the lamp.

Alberta walked quickly past, as if she were going somewhere quite different. She went round the block at a speed suggesting haste and purpose. The next time she passed, the country folk were still there. The third time they were gone, but Mrs Dorum was in the shop, helping her husband to tidy up after them.

Alberta went past once more. She met Kwasnikow. He was drunk. He stood in her way, took off his top hat, bowed deeply, and placed the hat in front of her in the snow.

Afraid, Alberta started to one side and hurried on. She heard Kwasnikow speaking Russian in a threatening tone and stumbling after her. Was Kwasnikow going to stop her now? When he was angry as well as drunk, there was no getting rid of him. If he were to see her going into Dorum's, he would be capable of gathering a crowd outside.

Perhaps it had been stupid of her not to go in the last time. Mrs Dorum would hear about it just the same. It would have been best to go in and behave as if it did not matter, to take it easily and without concern. But again, for that sort of thing audacity and cold-bloodedness were necessary, those two stout weapons that Alberta did not possess.

She came out into River Street for the fourth time. Now the coast was clear. Mrs Dorum had gone, Kwasnikow made harmless. He had fallen into the clutches of P.C. Olsen, who was going his rounds. They disappeared from sight under old Kamke's doorway.

Alberta braced herself. What must be, must be. People had even gone to the guillotine. She grasped the doorknob, feeling as giddy as if she were doing it in a dream. The little bell above rang out as if disturbed.

'It's terrifically kind of you, Alberta.'

Jacob's voice was deep and rough with emotion. He looked

alternately at Alberta and at the two ten *kroner* notes she had placed in front of him.

'Put them in your pocket, Jacob, hurry, Mama might come – and you'd better be quick and get it settled.'

Alberta was out of breath, and spoke in gasps. She sat down on Jacob's bed and watched her breath; it rose like white smoke each time she opened her mouth. She felt ill at ease, for the deed was only half finished. For several reasons she ought to have gone herself, but could not bring herself to do so.

Jacob stretched two blue, grazed fists out of his shrunken sleeves, picked up the notes and stowed them away. He said without looking at her : 'How did you manage, Alberta – you haven't sold something again, have you?'

'I sold the bracelet.'

'The chain?' His face was full of dismay.

'The chain.'

'Oh, but Alberta – now it's you who are out of your mind – the chain from Uncle the Colonel! What will you say when Mama . . .?'

'I suppose I'll have to say I've lost it.'

'But then she'll be terribly angry, Alberta – and what about Papa?'

. . . 'But Alberta, surely you could have taken some other trinket, a ring or a brooch, you got such a lot for your confirmation.'

'It wouldn't have brought in enough, Jacob. And then Mama might have recognised them if Dorum had put them in the window. There are a couple of chain bracelets there already.'

'But neither of them is as heavy as yours, Alberta. Anyway, you must have got a lot of money for it, my goodness, you must have got at least a hundred *kroner*.'

'I got twenty-five.'

'Then he's cheated you, the scoundrel, you should never have let it go for that. Was it Dorum himself?'

'You get so little for jewellery, Jacob,' answered Alberta in an experienced tone of voice. Deep down she was bitterly disappointed at the pecuniary result of her expedition. If one were going to turn criminal, the rewards ought in principle to be greater.

'You should have gone to Vik as well – he might have given you more,' said Jacob, talking nonsense just like a man. He did not really know what he was talking about.

But he must have had an inkling all the same, for he added : 'But of course it was bad enough having to go to that fellow Dorum'.

And suddenly he took a couple of large strides across the floor, threw his arms round Alberta and thumped her hard on the back several times with the palm of his hand, knocking her backwards and forwards. In a choked voice, his cheek against hers, he muttered : 'It was terribly nice of you, Alberta – you'll get it back – when I start to earn money you shall have a much heavier bracelet, you can count on that, Alberta.'

'Jacob,' began Alberta, groping for his head. Her heart was overflowing, there was such a tremendous amount she wanted to say—

But Jacob saved himself, retreating into the middle of the room. He picked up his cap and turned up his collar. 'Well, I'd better sprint over to Krane, he might easily take it into his head to come here.'

He was already at the door when Alberta stopped him. She was going to find out about one thing at any rate, and the moment might never come again. 'Jacob, tell me, were there girls there?'

'Girls? Where?' Jacob opened his eyes unnecessarily wide.

'You know what I mean. They say Palmine Flor and Lilly Vogel are there in the evenings.'

'Phooey—' Jacob's voice was not in the least tearful any more, but full of scorn. 'I didn't see any Palmine or any Lilly either. You'll believe anything. But I must hurry. Good-bye Alberta.'

And Jacob was gone. Alberta heard him go out through the office door.

She stood at the window in his cold room, breathed on the pane, and saw him come out into the falling snow under the arc lamp at the corner, lift his cap to Kvandal, and be swallowed up by the darkness.

She had not had time to think of it before, but it had been lurking in the shadows, and now it emerged. She had disposed of a piece of property of real value, of the kind that only falls to one's lot at life's turning-points, given her by Uncle the Colonel 'not without sacrifice' – disposed of it for twenty-five *kroner*. The little ring last spring had been nothing, a mere trifle. Besides, Mrs Selmer had decided that Alberta was not to wear rings: 'Hands like yours should not be emphasized; on the contrary, they should be hidden, my child'.

But the bracelet!

' . . . We wish to give Alberta a memento for life on this solemn occasion, we do so not without sacrifice,' the letter from Aunt the Colonel had said. Alberta felt dimly that she had sinned against the class instinct for collection and preservation. The kind of people who went out and sold their possessions had sunk very low. She was one of them. The ground opened up beneath her . . .

Downstairs in the living-rooms Mama and Papa were asleep, each on a sofa, suspecting nothing of life's bitter realities. Jacob was impossible at school and sought out acquaintances from lower down the social scale; Alberta was unfortunate in appearance, incompetent in the house and not very presentable; that was as far as their knowledge and their anxieties went. If they had only known a little more they would probably have given up Alberta and Jacob altogether.

She was seized by great weakness and exhaustion – an overwhelming desire to lie down, to put herself at the mercy of darkness, cold and fatigue, to surrender herself. Was life really so bad, were she, Jacob, Mama and Papa really unhappy, or was it only something she imagined, and were they really like other people? Did everyone live like this behind their closed doors – was it only Alberta who was unreasonable and dissatisfied and who strained after impossibilities? Would there never come a time when anxiety and vague longing were quietened, when lies and evasions and all kinds of small, hidden irons in the fire would no longer be necessary – when life was enjoyable and straightforward? Suppose it did not come, suppose this were all.

A short while ago she had been standing in Dorum's shop. It was not an unpleasant dream. He had leaned ten fat fingers on the counter, given her quick, sharp looks over his spectacles and asked again and again whether she really wanted to sell. It was more reasonable to exchange it for something, she would get more for it – he couldn't give much in cash, it would scarcely amount to the value of the gold. He had brought out boxes with brooches and rings and said jokingly that a young lady could never have too many of them.

He had said exactly the same thing last spring, when she had gone to him with the little ring. That time it had been gloves for Jacob, who had been invited to a dance. Papa had said Jacob could go with a pair of his. If they were too big, it ought to be possible to sew up the finger tips on the inside. It was pay day and payment was due on the bank loan. He had forbidden, absolutely forbidden, the purchase of new gloves for Jacob. Mama lay on the sofa in despair and said : 'I am powerless, children – you see I am powerless'.

But Jacob got his new gloves, handed to him outside Kilde the watchmaker's, on the way to the party.

Dorum had said today as he had said then : 'Have you thought it over, Miss?'

Disgust for the whole business, the desire to give it up, had crept over Alberta like an infirmity. Anxiety that someone might come in, dread at the thought of finding herself outside again without having concluded her business, had come and gone like waves of fever.

When finally the whole transaction was over, and she stood watching Dorum unlock the drawer with the banknotes and take out two tens and a five-*kroner* bill, she felt physically exhausted.

And Jacob – he was on his way to the Grand on an honest errand in a sense, to protect Mama and stave off catastrophe. He would meet Cedolf, and in the back room some of the travelling salesmen were probably sitting drinking, the kind who were willing to offer anybody a drink. Besides, Jacob was not anybody – he was the Magistrate's son and by no means unwelcome there or in the alleys.

If she were the least bit brave she would have gone herself. Straight from Dorum's at that. She would have settled the affair for Jacob and made it unnecessary for him to set foot in the dens of vice any more.

But Alberta was incapable of settling matters. She had an ingrained fear of the spoken word, an irreparable horror of argument and explanation. She blushed, was prostrated, lost the thread and might well say something quite different from what she had intended. The mere thought of explaining to Krane why she was there made her go hot and cold.

Life is immodest in its demands and makes no allowance for individuals' differing powers of expression. Alberta was insignificant, that had been decided long ago.

A bitter feeling of impotence and of general doom came over her. She leaned her head against the window frame and sobbed.

A door opened below and Mrs Selmer called loudly and sharply up the stairs : 'Alberta !'

Alberta started like a dozing horse at the word of command. She went towards the door, hastily assuming her defensive mask on the way – that innocent, unsuspecting face, which so easily dissolved and was reduced to impotence at the first attack.

When she appeared in the light from the little lamp in the passage outside Jacob's door, the enemy assailed her without hesitation from the foot of the stairs : 'Oh, so that's where you are, and here I sit toiling in the kitchen, polishing and polishing, without it ever occurring to my adult daughter to lend me a helping hand. Will it please you to put in an appearance in the kitchen immediately?'

* * *

The moon had shone the bad weather away. A miracle had taken place. The world was no longer a grey and white swirl, a confused and formless chaos. It had crystallized into an open, generous landscape, firm and still. It seemed endless. The moon shone upon it without setting, hanging low in the small hours, turning white and losing strength later in the morning. But it recovered and changed to yellow, wheeled up into the bowl of the sky and shone huge, recreating and expanding the kingdoms of the earth. Distant mountain ranges, swathed in mist by the sun and the daylight, were pointed up and exhibited by the moon. Everything caressed by the sun and the daylight was drowned by the moon in oceans of blue shadow.

Alberta woke earlier than usual and saw a shining stripe between the curtain and the window pane. She struggled with herself, then abandoned her warm bed, was up on her bare feet and let the blind shoot upwards.

The cross made by the window was thrown far into the room along the floor, and outside the world lay like a new sphere, untrodden, unspotted, shining clean, full of enormous, fantastic forms.

Everything was thick and soft and generous. The coverlet of snow had spread everywhere, above and below, and was only slightly lifted by the houses beneath it. It hung and poured from roofs and eaves and filled the courtyard like a swelling eiderdown.

Behind Flemming's warehouse, which looked as if it were built of blue shadow and secrets, ran the river like flowing, streaming light. Beyond, the mountains raised up on their shadowed frames wide, shining plateaux towards the moon.

Above them stood Orion alone in infinity.

Alberta curled up on the chair with her legs under her. New snow and moonlight – the loveliest and worst of all – an experience each time. The world became still and open, nothing was frightening any more. She journeyed in a landscape without anxiety, and the mild, intense light fell protectively round her, recreating her appearance as it recreated everything else. She moved in it boldly, and even her face was easier to bear.

But a wound opened inside. Delight and melancholy welled

up simultaneously from the depths of her mind. She could not understand why nor protect herself from them. They streamed over her together with the light, making her shrink with painful impatience. Tears came, God knows how. One moment she was crushed to the ground by life's misery, the next, new strength coursed exulting through her – it was like madness.

If she could go out on skis now – or stay sitting here long enough under the moon, quite still – the sounds would begin inside her. Small stanzas would come fluttering, small webs of words with rhythm to them, and join up with other small webs that had come fluttering before, when she was alone and quiet and everything was beautiful. Or they might not join up with anything – they might just conceal themselves in her mind. You never knew.

Did they come from within or from the wide, mysterious landscape outside? They were there all of a sudden, demanding to be written down in the secret book under the woollen vests in the chest of drawers. The book was full of small, fluttering stanzas scattered among its pages. Some belonged together naturally and had become verses, others stood apart, waiting. Some seemed to wait in vain, while others found company when she least expected it.

A large number of them were useless, she had to choose and sift. Often a word was wrong, and it might take months to listen her way to the right one. Generally it was less a matter of searching than of listening – listening inwards. Taking pains seldom got her anywhere, the word so easily became false and failed to fit in. The stanza must be stored in her brain and come to fruition on its own. When that happened, the same wonderful and troublesome state of mind followed, the same happy intoxication and bitter disgust. Nothing was more painful than to tumble from the fluttering stanzas' airy regions down into Mrs Selmer's storm-laden atmosphere, a predicament that often befell Alberta.

When Mrs Selmer wandered upstairs after breakfast with her jug of warm water, Alberta saw her opportunity and stole out of the front door, in spite of the gingernuts and Madam

Svendsen, whose eyes had been watering since eight o'clock over a large piece of dough, which she was belabouring in the wonderfully warm kitchen.

Already when Alberta was dusting she had seen through the ice-covered panes a new sky, a suspicion of fire and colour. Now she ran up the hillside without looking about her, careful not to catch a glimpse too early and shatter the experience into small pieces. She was even cunning enough to wait while she got her breath and calmed down before turning round to find it all before her eyes like a revelation.

The landscape shone of itself, with a blue, cold, dead and muted light, under a sky that was kindled. In the lowest quarter to the south it was a delicate, crisp shade of gold, and the fjord had captured it in layer upon layer of answering reflections.

Soon the sky would look like a glowing bell of light above the earth. It would glow with all the colours of the rainbow from flaming red to deep violet, and the river would flow through the cold kingdoms of snow like a precious band woven of purple and green, gold and rose.

But to the north the moon hung white in an opaque infinity. The thin, crooked birch trees tentatively planted along the roadside stood bent beneath their furs of snow, sober as in a wood-cut, against the dead background. A bird took wing from one of them, a fleeting ruffle of feathers and a slow scattering of snow broke the silence. The air had a cool, bitter taste, as fortifying and refreshing as a drink.

And look, now the earth was visible in all directions, as far as the eye could see : in the middle the river flowing out into the fjord, with Southfjord, looking like an estuary, straight to the south; on the one side of the river the town, wrapped up in cotton-wool, like a collection of dolls' houses ready for packing, the warehouses outermost like a bulwark; it looked as if they were holding on to the town to prevent it from sliding out into the water. On the other side the steep, barren range rose straight up from the shore; on the sandbank at Rivermouth the cod-liver-oil factory like a snuffed-out volcano under its snow hat. Far, far out in all directions the landscape held up the sky like a cupola upon a wreath of rounded mountains. To the south they raised themselves higher and became peaks. To the east was the range from which the river came, cold and impenetrable as a fortress jutting from the wreath.

Somewhere below the edge of the bell of light the sun was shining on other lands and other people. That was where one longed to go, that was where one travelled, that was where life was lived and events took place.

Alberta sighed. She was tempted to stay up on the plateau; to walk on in the deep snow and go far inland across the bog before the snow-plough and the energetic walkers made the roads unsafe; to see the miracle accomplished; to see the glow turn blood-red and then fade, the mountains darken against a green sky, the moon be lit.

A star would blaze up from the depths of space. Only Orion's belt would be visible. It would go eastwards above the bend in the river and move slowly south. The northern lights would look like airy, tangled veils, would be rolled up, coil together, frolic and disappear. A breath from the universe, from all that is great, elemental and limitless, would fill nature. The peace of infinity would pervade everything, restless human organisms as well.

Look, the mouth of the river was already stained with purple.

But down there under the big roof north of Flemming's warehouse, Mrs Selmer was going to and fro in Christmas busyness, certain to have been dressed and ready long ago. She could not be seen, but Alberta knew she was there, she felt it instinctively. A mysterious force, strange currents against which opposition was both useless and unthinkable, compelled her back at a respectable speed, to all that she longed to escape from with all her heart.

* * *

Christmas came and went. It was what it usually was, what it had been as long as Alberta and Jacob could remember : a shining hope – and a flat, embarrassed wonder that yet again they could have been so trusting and naïve.

Hope is a frugal plant, that puts out new shoots in obscurity every time it is plundered. To stamp out hope would be a long undertaking, perhaps an impossible one. It lives on nothing, like yellow lichen on a stone, it lives in spite of everything – even in spite of the Chief Clerk, who was to celebrate Christmas with his superior.

'Do you think the Chief Clerk will leave early this year too, Jacob?'

'I expect so. I wish he wouldn't come at all.'

'So do I, but I suppose we have to invite him – and I expect he feels he can't say no. That's how it is, you know.'

'Ugh!'

'I wish I knew why he leaves. After all it is warm here on Christmas Eve, so it can't be because he's cold. What do you think it is, Jacob?'

'I don't suppose he thinks it's much fun here. That's not surprising.'

'No – as long as he doesn't notice that Mama and Papa—'

'He would have to be a complete idiot not to notice.'

'Oh but this Christmas we'll have a nice time, you'll see, Jacob.'

'Do you think so, Alberta?'

'Yes, of course – we'll do our best at any rate.'

Naturally the Chief Clerk would notice. He had always noticed, whatever his name and whoever he might be. Alberta could remember it ever since the time when she had found no other expression for her own troubled uneasiness than 'it's all so boring'.

Kvam was the only one who had noticed nothing. He remained talkative, riding his hobby-horses undaunted and unaffected by the shifting pressures of atmosphere around him. But after Kvam had come Bolling. An uneasy expression came into his eyes and already at tea he began to be careful. And the present incumbent was quiet and shy, excessively polite and excessively attentive, but he left before supper. He was determined to go, and stood firm in the teeth of Mrs Selmer's entreaties and the Magistrate's regrets, embarrassed but resolute. Bergan the lawyer was having a few friends in for goose and a bachelor party, it had become quite a tradition. He had promised to be there a long time ago. He was sorry not to be able to come on New Year's Eve either.

His brief attendance tortured Alberta, who was on guard against every word that was spoken. She was incapable of taking part in the conversation, and would sit on the extreme edge of her chair, only half-sitting, as if that would help.

Every Christmas she hoped afresh that things would go well, that they might get through it unscathed.

Christmas Eve was approached as if it were the moment of a visitation, when miracles could be expected. Everything presaged them : the closed doors of the corner parlour, the scents of the tree – a pine from inner Southfjord – of baking, and clean curtains. The arrival of wine and food in the kitchen, of mail and parcels to be hidden away, and of the annual bowl of bulbs – tulips and hyacinths – for Mrs Selmer from the Chief Clerk. It had pink and white crêpe paper crinkled and crumpled round the pot, and was one of the masterpieces from the Sisters Kremer's hat shop. Every year Mrs Selmer would say : 'Oh, how delicious ! I heard Lotten Kremer say they were expecting a great deal by the packet boat – they really are good at getting hold of flowers'.

And the bowl would be placed on the coffee table, from where it sent out an intoxicating scent of luxury and festivity.

But when tea had been drunk and the parcels opened, when the candles on the tree began to threaten the pine needles, and Mama had sung her carols and wept in a corner over her letters; when Jensine had been in to see the tree and drink A Merry Christmas and for the last time the Chief Clerk had put down the Christmas magazines, in which he had repeatedly sought refuge, and taken his leave; then the artificial atmosphere, towards which everyone had attempted to contribute to the best of his ability, and which had been in greater danger than ever before, immediately deflated. Mama opened a window to let out the tobacco smoke and the tension seemed to relax. No-one exerted himself any longer except for Alberta, who was always ready to indulge in naïve and hopeless endeavour.

The Christmas candles were extinguished, and with them the Christmas hopes. Everything was back to where it was a couple of hours ago. Ordinary life was back, in Mama's aggrieved voice, in Papa's muttering over the ham which was too fat, and the roast pork which had other defects. Danger lurked once more, and all kinds of mischief might occur.

Alberta went out into the kitchen to Jensine. To see her sitting there celebrating Christmas all alone, at a table spread with cakes and nuts, with her Christmas magazine and her package containing the annual dress length, gave her the same feeling of embarrassment as the sight of the burnt-out candles with their smoking wicks – as the sight of the parcels, which had only contained useful things they had needed for a long time. That was all, for us as for Jensine, this year as last.

'So Christmas is over once more, Jensine.'

'Yes, Alberta poor dear, he comes and goes as fast as he can. I'll be happy when the party's over too.'

'So shall I, Jensine.'

Alberta pressed her nose flat against the window pane. The moonlit evening was clear without a breath of wind, lights shone peacefully from all the windows. Not a soul to be seen besides Nurse Jullum's black cat, cautiously testing the surface of the snow on the roof of the porch.

The houses looked as if they held entertaining secrets. Behind the red blinds over at Doctor Pram's shadows moved in similar, even rhythm. They were going round the tree once more before blowing out the candles.

And Alberta abandoned herself to her hunger. It came like a severe, long-drawn-out stitch and remained gnawing at her body and limbs. Hunger for peace, joy, warmth – for God knows what, for God knows what.

It was strange, but it seemed as if it could be satisfied out there in the broad landscape that lay shining and enticing under the moon. Something was to be found out there at any rate : freedom – the beginning of all things. And did not the roads out to life lie hidden under the snow like strands in a ball of yarn? If only she could find one of them and follow it.

But much had to happen first. Everything had to be changed, for Mama and Papa too. To know that they were at home, still living in exactly the same way as now – no, in that case it would be better—

And Alberta realised that she was almost wishing her own parents were dead. She stiffened with contrition and horror. She felt as if she had looked down into an abyss and almost lost her balance. What sort of a person can I be? she thought with distress.

'Do come back, Alberta,' whispered Jacob from behind her, tapping her on the shoulder. 'It's terrible in there again, they're not saying a word to each other now. It's a bit better when we're there.'

Alberta rose from the chair in which she had been crouching on her knees. In Jensine's presence no discussion was possible, there was nothing for it but to go. So she went in with Jacob to the burnt-out Christmas tree and the burnt-out stove.

* * *

'Well,' said Mrs Selmer, casually putting her napkin down on the table, 'I'm afraid I have nothing more to offer you.'

Every glass was raised towards her, everyone smiled and leaned forward to catch her eye. Several waited, glass in hand, until she had time to look in their direction : 'Thank you. An excellent dinner.'

The Magistrate's turn came, and then the scraping of chairs.

Alberta rose and took the Chief Clerk's arm with a serious nod. She looked straight in front of her, thankful for the hubbub made by the chairs. All speech became useless and unnecessary, she could safely limit herself to a nod.

They parted in the sitting-room once inside the door, the Clerk with an indistinct mumble and a bow, Alberta still silent. Thank heaven Mrs Selmer was busy shaking hands.

Alberta fetched the flower vases from the dining table and distributed them in the sitting-rooms. Then she sat down under the potted palm with her hands in her lap, looking straight in front of her.

That terrible neckband!

It was made of green tulle, caught up in loops of frilled ruching over a stiff base which cut into the hollow of her throat and under her ears. It was much too high, and Alberta discovered to her sorrow that the colour in her face, which normally rose and fell, had stayed up there for good, kept in place by this new instrument of torture.

It was her Christmas present from Aunt the Colonel. It had arrived yesterday, the second day of Christmas, by the packet boat. It was a characteristic of Aunt the Colonel's despatches that they were always a little late.

When it was unpacked, Mrs Selmer had said with a sombre look at Alberta's hair: 'Hm, if you were pretty and soignée like other young girls, it might have suited you – but still, it is fearfully chic and the latest fashion, according to your Aunt'.

And Alberta knew her fate was sealed.

She moved her head neither to right nor left. When anyone spoke to her she turned the whole of the upper half of her body, and her overheated face became even redder. When she had the opportunity Mrs Selmer found time to direct a look of aggrieved and complete despair in her direction, even closing her eyes as if to avoid the sight. Alberta was even more hopeless, even further beneath all criticism than ever.

She sat under the palm tree, apart and to one side, as usual.

Round the circular centre table the conversation went back and forth between the ladies. It was as if they were playing ball with words, but slackly and without animation. Now and again the ball dropped to the ground and stayed there until someone made an effort and sent it on its way again. They had been in each other's company yesterday and the day before, which did not make matters any easier.

From inside the corner parlour the men's voices could be heard. They were talking about the war in East Asia and Port Arthur's prospects. Magistrate Selmer had everyone against him, he was the only one supporting the Russians. Now he was speaking quite alone in that deep voice he assumed now and again, and which never failed to make an impression on Alberta. It gave matters more weight, more moment.

The ladies fell silent and listened to the conversation. One or other of them nodded appreciatively at what was being said. The gentlemen's words were full of superior insight – a little too superior after a time, to be honest. One enterprising soul introduced a new subject.

Mrs Selmer was an excellent hostess. No-one could catch the ball as she did, send it on its way, keep it moving. She was inexhaustible, and it was only when she was occupied elsewhere that it really fell to the ground.

She came and went, settled cushions behind the backs of her guests, had eyes in the back of her head, took out photographs, pointed, explained. She said a great many witty and amusing things that made the ladies laugh, and showed herself to be superior to them all in the ways of the world and in light conversation.

On the piano there stood a youthful portrait of her in party dress with bare arms and bare neck, a fan in her hands. Her arms were incomparably slender, supple and beautiful, the position of the hands holding the fan full of grace. The large eyes in the small, short face had a frank, pure, childlike expression that one never tired of looking at. The mouth was so soft and young with small, innocent corners that curved a little upwards. And it looked as if the same tender modelling-hand had pressed in the two small dimples in the cheeks and the little dimple in the chin. She held herself erect looking almost as if turned on a lathe; narrow-waisted, not beautiful, but unspeakably charming and captivating all the same. Alberta knew it, and she knew that she would never be anything like Mama. It was her biggest and most obvious failing.

Mrs Selmer had kept her figure from that day to this, a little plumper, a little heavier, but with more or less the same outline. Her corpulence was evenly distributed over her body and had not accumulated in one place, as was the case with many of the other ladies. Her stomach did not stick out uncontrolled, or her arms burst out of the silk. She moved differently from the others too, with great lightness and assurance, and her skin was fair and smooth, almost without wrinkles under the blonde, frizzed hair that hid her own greyness.

The young Mama of the photograph was recognisable in everything except the expression and lines of the mouth. That small, pinched mouth, that could turn into a furrow in her face, was it really the same as the one she had had then? And the eyes, those Argus eyes, had they once looked so unsuspicious? Was it from having to live up here, enduring the cold and longing to go back to the south, from having insufficient money and disappointing children, that Mama had acquired a different mouth and another pair of eyes, or were there other, more obscure reasons? Beside Mama's portrait stood Grandmama's. Her eye-sockets were so deep. It was difficult to make out her expression, it seemed to have sunk back into the thin face. Her mouth was a firm-willed line. And Alberta suddenly shivered in spite of the heat of the room, her heart became small and afraid. Was it so, that generation after generation coerced the next, desiring only to fashion and form their lives in accordance with their own? Involuntarily she looked away from Grandmama down at the little drawer in the bureau where Mrs Selmer hid old letters.

It was not the first time Alberta had sat here under the palm tree puzzling about these things. This had become her permanent seat, her fortress, as the result of years of experience. A little nearer, and she would be indiscreet and obtrusive, pushing and forward, and might very well find herself playing a rôle that did not suit her – a little further away and she would be trying to make herself appear interesting and odd, different from other people. No, the palm tree was the correct strategic position for one lacking social talent and all external advantages.

In the corner parlour with the gentlemen sat Jacob. His situation was less critical. For a while he kept resolutely to a corner without anyone finding anything to comment about; for a while, later on in the evening, Papa became good-humoured, forgetting old scores against him. He would nod to him with raised glass and call: 'Wake up, my boy—' or: 'Cheer up, Jacob, you look so serious'.

Jacob was wearing his best confirmation clothes, and they suited him. When he wore them it seemed as if Papa felt affection and a renewed interest towards him.

Was Jacob looking serious? He sat with his arms crossed over his chest, surveying the assembly in silence. But the expression on his face, was it irony or hostility? Alberta did not like it, it disturbed her. She could see him through the door every time she leaned forward.

The Archdeacon's wife got her butter from Southfjord. She assured everyone, her eyes crystal-clear, that of course it was so much cheaper than buying it from Holst. The Governor's lady swivelled her lorgnette towards her and could not quite understand that, for Holst's butter definitely went farther. It came from the dairy in Flatangen and naturally was handled better than the country butter, there was less water in it. Her experience had been that it paid to buy from Holst, even if it did cost a little more.

The Archdeacon's wife, who was without guile and not quite of this world, assured them open-heartedly, her eyes just as clear, that really the butter from her butter man was every bit as good as the dairy butter. Mrs Bakke, the lawyer's wife, young, recently arrived from the south, and in her seventh month, looked about her innocently and said: 'My dears, I *must* find out which is better and most practical'.

The Governor's lady fell silent and pursed her lips. She had many good qualities, the Governor's lady, but did not brook contradiction; she had that little weakness. Mrs Selmer scented danger and interjected gaily : 'To tell you the truth, *I* use margarine for everyday' – betraying herself and throwing herself into the breach. And Mrs Pio righted her prostrate and encumbered form, revealed her enormous set of false teeth in a smile and found the courage to declare : 'So do I – so do I'.

The Governor's lady let it be known that she considered the subject exhausted. Demonstratively she picked up a book from the table, leaned back in her chair and leafed through the book. But Mrs Selmer was at her post. 'Have you heard what Professor Werenskjold said about Rikke?' she threw out, and a wave of excited interest travelled through the group. 'No, what has Werenskjold said – is it possible, has Werenskjold said something?'

Mrs Selmer nodded knowingly. She had sat next to the Governor's lady at dinner at the Archdeaconry. Mrs Lossius put down the book and resolved to let bygones be bygones. She righted herself in her chair and reported what Werenskjold had said, but with reserve and not at all exuberantly, for the sting still rankled a little.

'Oh, how wonderful, how simply wonderful! So Rikke will become an artist, I suppose, Mrs Lossius?' The ladies all spoke at once. The Governor's lady shrugged her shoulders : 'It is a very serious matter, and we would really prefer Rikke to use the gifts she has in some other way. After all, there are so many different fields. Applied art, for example, is the coming thing these days. But of course – if she decides after trying it out that she must take that course, we shall have to defer to her wishes'. Mrs Lossius was self-sacrificing and motherly, resigned in advance. And now she had got over her little ill-humour : 'Rikke draws night and day, writes Gertrude. She goes round with a sketch book all the time, literally all the time. You see, it was her drawing Werenskjold commented on. "Draw, draw, my child," he said. "That's the best thing for you".'

The unpleasantness over the butter forgotten, the tone was gay and sociable. Mrs Selmer, who did not intend to let any shadow of disagreement creep back, asked after Gertrude.

'Very well, thank you. Gertrude is practising hard. Both of them seem to be enjoying themselves too. Aunt Honoria writes that it's nothing but balls and parties, so I'm afraid there is sometimes too much of both fun and work. But we're only young once, Mama, writes Rikke.'

Mrs Lossius quoted amusing passages from her letters, and then swivelled her lorgnette towards Alberta: 'I suppose you hear from them now and again too?'

'Now and again, yes.' Alberta went even redder than she was already. It was a misfortune to be the object of everybody's attention. She replied curtly and with embarrassment to a couple of questions, looking as if hypnotised at Mama, whose eyes rested on her with undisguised displeasure. The knowledge that she was not gifted, not pretty, not amusing and sweet, not in Kristiania, nothing, paralysed her. It seemed to be her own fault.

Besides, her conscience was far from clear. In the first place there was the chain. It usually went with her party regalia, and it was miraculous that heaven and earth had not been shaken some time ago. She was prepared to bear almost anything as long as Mrs Selmer did not discover that it was missing. At the dinner table she had been silent and impossible. The Clerk had looked helpless more than once and had finally given up. She did not smile, she was serious all the time, an unforgiveable thing in company. Her condition was aggravated by the neckband, which she knew was just as irrelevant on her person as Mama's toque from Kristiania would be on Jensine. And it had been no better yesterday at the Archdeaconry or the day before at the Prams', even though Harriet, Christina and Gudrun had all been away on a visit to Southfjord, and had not, as in other years, blackened Alberta even more with all their virtues.

Mrs Lossius turned towards her yet again and asked a terrible question: 'And what are you doing these days?' she said with especial kindness, surveying her through the lorgnette.

Mrs Lossius had touched on a sore point, and Alberta suspected that such was her intention.

'Nothing,' she replied curtly. It was true that she did

nothing. She simply existed, did nothing and became nothing, while life rolled past somewhere far away, to the south.

But that was the wrong answer. Mrs Selmer turned pale with anger and hastened to interrupt : 'Alberta helps me in the house, it's very necessary. I get tired sometimes, Mrs Lossius. And then she coaches Jacob in some of his subjects'.

Alberta hated them all. They were fond of their own children and satisfied with them, but where others' were concerned their tact was cunning, their silence deceitful and their speech an open trap. She looked at young Mrs Bakke, who sat there newly arrived, looking round her with happy eyes, and thought : 'You simpleton, you innocent. You'll get like all of them in time, fat and heavy, with a double chin and uncontrolled stomach, false in mouth and eyes – perhaps your face will collapse and get hollow-cheeked and almost vanish round a large set of false teeth, like Mrs Pio.'

To live here amongst them, sitting round the coffee table embroidering, while they nodded knowingly to right and left and sent quick little side glances to see if it was true that you were expecting; and asked about one thing, while spying out another; and confided in each other when you had gone : 'Oh yes, no doubt about it, my dear. It can't be so very long now, when was it they married?'

To grow like them – to grow finally like the old ladies who could remember nothing but confinements.

Or to go round half old like Otilie Weyer, the Sisters Kremer, Jeanette Evensen, like something life had rejected and had no use for; to have been here for ever and to continue to be here always, while the days passed by, each one like the next, and Mama like old Mrs Weyer perhaps.

No, neither course, better to die, better to—

Alberta contracted her thin, wiry body inside her clothes and felt with relish that she had control of her muscles, that she held them in her hand like well-disciplined troops. She clenched her strong, even teeth, the only things about her person that could not be faulted, in a resolve that never, never should any of this happen to her. The thought of belonging here for ever gave her the same constricted feeling in her breast as when she was sent as a little girl to old Miss Myre, who lived by taking in repairs. In the little room with its stuffy atmosphere, where one could scarcely move between the chest of drawers and the bed, and where Miss Myre pottered about, small and yellow, short-sighted and finicking, wrapped in knitted shawls and smelling nasty, Alberta would always imagine how it might be if, for some reason, she was left with nobody but Miss Myre, and had to live with her, just like her. It had made her sick to think of it, and the day Miss Myre died Alberta had felt a secret relief. Because whatever happened, Miss Myre, at any rate, would be out of the question.

But the others might be in question, unless a miracle happened. It *must* happen, it *must* happen.

The Magistrate's voice could be heard among the gentlemen : 'Now listen to me, my dear Mr Archdeacon—' He continued in a low voice, and laughter rang out. Glasses clinked, toasts were drunk, and Alberta saw Jacob was laughing. She wished she were sitting in there, but it was unthinkable.

In there the talk was more interesting. Distant countries, world affairs, politics. Even politics were interesting, although Alberta knew nothing about them. She would learn by sitting in there. Here she was only told things she knew, on which she had already formed an opinion. And besides, ladies were stupid. Heaven knows what they learned at school. It couldn't have been much, they said the silliest things.

Through the door she could see Governor Lossius. His small, twinkling eyes under the grey, bushy eyebrows looked good-natured. So did Papa's and the others', good-natured and guileless. Men's eyes had something innocent about them. Men did not go in for quick side-glances at each other, as women did, averting their eyes again, and pretending they had been thinking about something quite different. They let them wander openly and honestly about the room and rest in the eyes of those with whom they spoke.

But both Papa and the Governor were very red in the face, more so than usual. Was it simply because of the warmth and because they were big, heavy men, or—?

There was the Archdeacon leaning forward. He was big and heavy too, but he had kept his natural colouring; so had Mr Jaeger, the Recorder. The Chief of Police, on the other hand, who was small and thin, was redder than any of them.

Unpleasantly agitated, Alberta shifted her position, so that she could see no-one but the Recorder. He was clean-shaven, tall, a little angular, a little nonchalant, with searching eyes and a calm smile beneath greying hair, hair that tended to fall over his forehead whenever he leaned forward. To see him sitting there seemed to be some kind of guarantee that everything would proceed properly. There was something reassuring in seeing him sitting looking just as usual.

He enjoyed a certain reserved respect because he was a man with unusual interests. The Recorder put a lot of his money into books and was interested in art. He subscribed to a large and expensive series of reproductions, *Les Musées d'Europe,* and old masters covered the walls of his rooms.

The gentlemen said of the Recorder: 'Good heavens, an uncommonly well-educated and cultured man'. The ladies: 'Gracious me, he's a splendid fellow, of course; they say he's wonderful to Beda and her mother, for instance, but somehow you never know quite how to take him, do you?' – They did not much like this reticent man, who was unfortunately a radical and probably something of a freethinker, since he never darkened the church door. They also had a number of comments to make on his appearance. His trousers had baggy knees, and his tie was usually a little crooked, yes, even a button might be missing from his person here and there. They had given him up as a candidate for matrimony after ten years of alternating hope and disappointment. It was now accepted that the Recorder would never marry.

But Beda would not tolerate any criticism of her superior. 'Jaeger's a poppet. Since I started working for him I've bitterly regretted singing 'Adam in Paradise' after him.'

He lent Beda books, and she often displayed knowledge of surprising subjects. 'I got that from Jaeger,' she would say in explanation.

Alberta was becoming drowsy. The air was heavy from the numerous lamps, from Mrs Selmer's incense, and from the tobacco smoke that invaded the room from the corner parlour. Dully she followed the ladies' conversation. They were talking about Madam Svendsen's ability. Mrs Pram could not understand how everything was always excellent at Mrs Selmer's, for she herself was so often unfortunate with Svendsen. The goose last year, for instance, she simply burnt it, and once there was salt in the ice-cream instead of sugar. Very vexatious. 'But I really haven't the courage to give her notice – may I enquire whether anyone else has?'

They talked about the Archdeacon's Christmas sermon, about poor relief, about the weather, about the scandal of Mad Petra, who was expecting a baby, and of Beda Buck, who had gone visiting the mining engineers in Southfjord with a party of gentlemen. 'Yes, really, it's a fact. First the idea was that Lett the dentist's sister was to come by the packet boat, but she didn't arrive, so Beda left just the same. What is one to say about a mother like that? I'm really sorry for Beda.'

Mrs Pram spoke her mind : 'Yes, her language is said to be so incredibly vulgar. Harriet says it gets worse and worse. The last time the girls were at the Bucks' it was so bad they thought of leaving – Alberta was there too, of course.'

'Is it true, Alberta, that Beda is so vulgar?' It was Mrs Lossius speaking, and she was swivelling her lorgnette towards Alberta.

But Alberta, who felt something snap inside when Beda's name was brought into the discussion, turned giddy. Her blood streamed to her head and she could no longer see clearly. 'Beda is certainly not vulgar,' she answered curtly and furiously. The blood sank back again, and she saw with horror the extent to which she had forgotten herself.

Oh – Mrs Selmer's expression !

Nobody said a word. There was an awkward little pause, in which Alberta felt like an outcast, beyond the pale.

Then Mrs Lossius rose and went uninvited to the piano. She really was kind, Mrs Lossius, and generous beyond all doubt, prepared to help Mrs Selmer over this quickly. She played *Marche Hongroise* by Schubert and a Liszt rhapsody. Afterwards the Archdeacon's wife sang 'The Great White Flock' and 'Hymn to the Fatherland' and 'The Seter Girl's Sunday', and then Mrs Pio felt ill and had to leave. Pio accompanied her, a little embarrassed and guilty. The ladies shook their heads and confided to each other that they had noticed it a long time ago.

The conversation flagged and seemed to be past saving. Then Mrs Selmer ordered tea, and the talk flared up again. Depraved Alberta was forced to run the gauntlet with the cream and the sugar.

* * *

The New Year came and went.

On New Year's Eve tradition and a certain feeling for propriety decreed that everyone should sit up until twelve o'clock. In silence, Mrs Selmer had brought out wine, nuts, apples, cakes, the remains of Christmas joys. They were eaten without a word. One and all were reading something. Now and again the Magistrate took out his watch and looked at it. When the stroke of twelve approached, he kept it in his hand, stuffing it back in his pocket the moment the church clock began, and as the last stroke died away he raised his glass and said : 'Well, a Happy New Year, and thank you for the old one.' – He raised his glass especially towards Mrs Selmer and said : 'Henrietta !'

Mrs Selmer's eyes filled with tears, this year as last year – as every year. Alberta's did too, the solemnity of the hour affected her strongly.

Then Papa made a speech. 'You, Alberta, I would ask to try to behave a little more in accordance with your Mother's wishes in the new year. I expect you know what I am referring to. And to you, Jacob, I need scarcely say in what direction all our wishes go. A Happy New Year, Alberta – a Happy New Year, my boy !'

Papa looked across at Mama, to see if he had done right.

But whether he had or not, nobody ever discovered. Mrs Selmer put down her glass and said coldly : 'I for my part have no more wishes – I know it's no use'.

She sighed, picked up her book and her keys, said, 'Goodnight' – and disappeared.

The ritual was over and everything was as before.

* * *

'I am astonished to see that you have given up wearing your chain, Alberta.'

'I suppose this is another of your bright ideas? Yet another way of being peculiar. You have to be different from everyone else so you mustn't wear jewellery – in fact, you must care for your appearance as little as possible.'

'You needn't think I haven't noticed that you have been hiding a good deal from me recently. I am not nourishing the hope of being allowed to know why our young Miss is so sober in her dress – I don't enjoy my daughter's confidence, unfortunately.'

'But the day may come, my dear Alberta, when you will regret that you didn't do more to make yourself attractive and that you had no desire to please your Mother, believe me.'

Mrs Selmer's voice was lost in a whisper. She sobbed.

Alberta knew from bitter experience that this was the prelude. Sooner or later the matter would come to a head, and she would simply be ordered to go upstairs, put on the chain, and come down again.

She carried on imaginary conversations with Mrs Selmer, saying, for example : 'I can't tell you now, Mama, the reason why I am not wearing my chain. It is best for us all that it should remain hidden for the time being. In a few years, perhaps—'

And she immediately felt dizzy at the thought of the consequences should she really express herself in such a manner.

She could not bring herself to say she had lost the chain, as she had first thought of doing. Mrs Selmer paralysed her.

There it was in Dorum's window. Alberta, who had been scrupulously keeping watch, saw it at once. So did Jacob. Now all that remained was for Mrs Selmer to notice that there were three chains there and connect the fact with Alberta's sobriety. She was quite capable of it. Her powers of discernment in unmasking crime were unparalleled. She might almost have been Sherlock Holmes.

Every time Mrs Selmer came home from town Alberta went hot and cold.

A misdeed, once perpetrated, is like a sickness. At night, when you lie awake, it rages in you like fever. When you wake up in the morning, you only remember at first that something is wrong, that something prevents you from breathing freely. It takes a little time before you realise what it is. It has sunk to the bottom of your consciousness and lies there like a weight.

But it floats up again. You recognise it with dismay and it remains with you all day long. And then again the fever attacks.

Beneath all Alberta's anxiety lay the longing to throw her arms round Mama and tell her everything, to unburden all her distress; a longing that was like an inborn infirmity which she had never learned to bear.

Besides – a bracelet, a heavy chain, was a beautiful thing to own and to feel round one's wrist. When her friends had leaned forward and fingered it and said: 'Goodness, how lovely!' it had made her happy.

Now it was gone.

PART TWO

It was getting lighter. When Alberta dusted a strange, pale light lay across the room, arriving earlier as the days went by. The darkness that had flooded in until only a blur of twilight was left, ebbed back. The blur took hold and grew.

The glow in the southern sky became brighter; the clouds took on a golden tinge. One day a lone mountain peak in the far distance was rose red, and the next day another.

One day the upper part of the mountain above the town was alight, as if from the reflection of a fire. The day after Alberta went up to Jacob's room a little before twelve o'clock.

Immediately afterwards Mrs Selmer arrived, as if by accident. They stood silently looking at Lake Peak far to the south. A halo grew round it, and became blinding. A sickle of intense light slid into view at the side of the peak.

'There it is, Alberta,' said Mrs Selmer breathlessly. 'Hurry – fetch Papa, Jensine, the Chief Clerk – they must come at once. I'm sure they've all forgotten the time.'

Alberta ran, called down the stairs for Jensine, and, out of breath, knocked on Papa's office door.

When she came back she had to shut her eyes for a moment. A miracle, a revelation, something beyond anything she had remembered or could imagine was there in the cut between Lake Peak and Flatang Peak shining straight into Jacob's room. And the room was illuminated slantwise from below, with long shadows falling upwards on to the walls – as strange and as wonderful as the décor in a theatre. The world was no longer cold and solid, complete and finite. It had dissolved into gold and blue.

Behind her she heard Papa, the Clerk and Jensine streaming into the room. Last of all came Leonardsen.

'Come along, Leonardsen, come right in,' said the Magistrate. And Mrs Selmer chimed in : 'Yes indeed, my dear Leonardsen, do come in. Then you can say you've seen the sun. It will be some time before it will be visible from the ground floor, as you know.'

There was a pause. Nobody found anything to say. Everyone stared at the phenomenon. And whether because of the unfamiliar light or for some other reason, Mrs Selmer's eyes filled with tears, this year as last year, as every year.

The Chief Clerk closed his mouth abruptly over something he had decided to say. Alberta noticed it, saw Mama's tears, and was embarrassed too. The Magistrate stood, watch in hand, examining it and the sun in turn, oblivious of the others.

In a moment of self-forgetfulness Alberta suddenly lifted her hands to the light to test its warmth. The Clerk was happy to find something to say. He smiled and shook his head : 'Oh no, Miss Alberta, it's too early yet'. Alberta blushed as if she had done wrong.

Now the sun was disappearing behind Flatang Peak, which was dark blue. When its last crescent had vanished, Leonardsen remarked timidly but sincerely : 'That was a fine sight to be sure'. The ice was broken. Everyone smiled and said something. Mrs Selmer assured him : 'How very true, Leonardsen'.

The Magistrate put his watch into his waistcoat pocket and announced : 'Three minutes, three minutes precisely, just as I said. You insisted it was four last year, Mr Chief Clerk, but you see you were wrong.'

* * *

Nothing could be bluer than the sky to the east of the river bend, thought Alberta. Nothing could be bluer, southern skies, the Mediterranean, nothing. And yet it seemed to grow bluer every day. Blue and bottomless. To look into it for long was like sailing out and sinking into infinity. You lost the feeling of solid ground under your feet, turned giddy, had to sit down in the snow so as not to fall.

Against the sky stood the range of mountains from which
the river came, sparkling with light as long as the sun was
up, rose red when it had disappeared behind the peaks at the
end of Southfjord, ghostly dead, cold and white when it had
gone for good.

The brief day was ending. The blue thickened, seeming to
turn into solid material behind the light-abandoned mountains, until the light of the first stars penetrated it like a
trembling, hesitating message from somewhere forgotten.

Since the sun and the daylight had come back, life had
changed. The roads were not snowed under again as soon as
the snow plough had cleared them. They lay solid and
frozen and screeched under foot. Ski-tracks led inland across
the bog, numerous, hard and confused near the town, fewer
and easier to follow the further you went away from it;
solitary, buoyant, when you went any distance. Through the
clear, still air the clatter and gliding of skis could be heard
continually.

Alberta was trapped no longer. She followed the tracks,
conquered the landscape afresh, this year as last, made new
conquests daily, she and her companion, that other invisible,
bold girl. Out of consideration for Alberta's old ski clothes,
lengthened once by Olefine and patched under the arms, they
went along the back streets in order to slip out of town unseen.
Her companion was better equipped. She moved so lightly
and gracefully in her becoming modern ski suit that Alberta
actually felt it in her own body. And when they had crossed
the open space just outside town and come to Peter Aasen's
birch thicket, they glided together and became one person.
After that nothing was impossible.

After that, imperfections no longer existed. Jacob was a
model of righteousness, Papa and Mama had overcome all
their difficulties and lived for ever in peace and understanding. They treated each other as once one summer day a couple
of years ago, a day Alberta would never forget. The weather
had been warm and still, several windows were open. There
was red currant jam in a dish on the table, mirrored beautifully in the water carafe. And a calm, happy conversation, in

97

which she and Jacob joined, coursed back and forth and created an inimitable atmosphere of security that Alberta could recapture at will. In this she would install her family before turning her attention to herself.

Herself – oh, she was far away, heaven knows where, out in the wide world. The sun was shining – perhaps palm trees were swaying too. But one thing was certain, she was as free and as light as a bird. She was the bold girl who had no need to hide her face, her hands or her thoughts, who was not afraid of people and who did what she wanted. – But what did she want?

The Archdeacon's Christina wanted to learn lace-making, weaving, elaborate embroidery. Harriet Pram talked about the Central Institute in Stockholm as if it were a place of salvation. Gudrun wanted to be an actress, Rikke Lossius an artist. Gertrude played the piano. Beda explained that if she were to do something she really liked, she would be a sailor. Sometimes they might add : 'If I don't get married, of course'.

But Alberta?

The truth was Alberta only knew what she did not want. She had no idea what she did want. And not knowing brought unrest and a giddy sensation under her heart. She existed like a negative of herself, and this flaw was added to all the others.

To get away, out into the world! Beyond this all details were blurred. She imagined somewhere open, free, bathed in sunshine. And a throng of people, none of them her relatives, none of whom could criticize her appearance and character, and to whom she was not responsible for being other than herself.

On Sundays she went to the Gronli farms with Harriet, Christina and Gudrun, and was simply and squarely Alberta. They took with them Danish pastries and oranges, ground coffee and lumps of sugar. The bad-tempered woman at Gronli made their coffee, gave them cream, and lighted the stove in one of the large, deserted rooms full of stale air, all for fifty øre. They danced with each other to keep warm, humming *The Blue Danube* in unison until the fire began to take effect. And sometimes a desperate gaiety would take possession of Alberta. Something would be unleashed, a sudden laughter, and she laughed simply to release it. It lay in wait for everything and nothing and infected Gudrun. In the end they could not stop. Harriet and Christina became annoyed and called them idiots.

Other parties arrived and were shut into other rooms. It might be a gay, fur-clad group that had come in sleds : Mrs Buck, Mrs Elmholz, Mrs Lebesby and Mrs Kilde – Mrs Selmer and her circle never went to the Gronli farms. It might be Beda with the chemists, the dentist and Dr Mo, in which case they might join them and indulge in a kind of circumspect gaiety, with Beda the life and soul of the party. It might also be Bergan and the Chief Clerk, in which case there would only be distant exchanges of greetings in the passage, for neither of them displayed any initiative where women were concerned.

But sometimes Palmine Flor and Lilly Vogel came with their men friends. Then the echoing house was filled with scandal. Corks popped, shrieks and laughter followed each other in waves, cigarette-smoke lay thick and cold in the corridors, doors slammed interminably. Palmine and Lilly rushed in and out in Lapp costume, their eyes dulled, curls wet with snow hanging about their overheated faces. Yelling, they tumbled on top of each other in the snowdrifts outside with the men in pursuit.

If Alberta's luck was out, Jacob and Cedolf came. They mixed with nobody, sat by themselves listening to the din, smiled faintly, said nothing and looked furtive. But a secret exchange took place. Alberta felt it and would become ill at ease and restless. Nothing could be proved, but anything guessed at. The air was full of secrets.

Harriet and Christina became tense round the mouth, and wanted to pay and go, saying that this was dreadful, they refused to listen to it any longer. Gudrun suggested staying for a little to see whether Lilly and Palmine really were drunk. Alberta was so restless on account of Jacob that she forgot her interest in the mysteries of life. She had to leave with the others, while Jacob stayed, and she dragged herself home, paralysed by the warmth at Gronli, preoccupied and aloof out of anxiety as to what might happen. The others gave her to understand that, without any doubt, they considered the situation to be critical. The way home in the cold twilight seemed endless.

The fact that Alberta went skiing in the middle of the morning was to nobody's credit. Mrs Selmer was quite aware of it. But she seemed to have given way on certain points, as if she could not be bothered any more. She said as much, too : 'It is not within my power to make a useful person out of my daughter. I shall have to give up the attempt.' She contented herself with sighing resignedly when Alberta sneaked guiltily out of the house in ski clothes after finishing the dusting, making herself as small and invisible as possible, but stubbornly resolved to accept any indignity provided she might finally get away.

The fact of the matter was, of course, that Alberta had too much time on her hands. It was not really proper, and it was embarrassing and difficult to explain away. Gudrun went to school, Beda worked in an office, Harriet and Christina helped at home, ironing, using the sewing-machine, making clothes, embroidering, baking; both of them patterns of virtue, pearls of great price.

Alberta dusted, cleaned silver and mended stockings. None of these activities was worth mentioning as a domestic achievement. She did them without any enthusiasm whatsoever, and there was nothing of the pearl about her – on the contrary, she was an affliction and a disappointment. She read, but what did she read? If only it were languages, if only it were the cookery book. But no, in addition to Mama's novels, which she skimmed quickly when they were left lying about, and devoured when they were hidden from her, she read learned tomes, 'Alberta's tomes'; Mrs Selmer could find no other way of describing such abnormal reading-matter for a young girl. Her friends were astonished and a little scornful when Alberta came staggering out of the library with them. 'How *can* you be bothered?' they said.

There was Lübke's *History of Art,* an old yellowed edition with poor woodcuts. There were twenty- and thirty-year-old works on the Stone Age, the migrations, Indian cave temples. She went haphazardly through the catalogue. And bad-tempered old Miss Jensen, who looked after the lending library as well as her books and stationery, had to climb the step-ladder to find them, tripped over her skirts, got dust up her nose, sneezed, and explained in an injured tone that this kind of book was never out.

Once it was Professor Monrad on aesthetics, a work that nearly took away Alberta's taste for further research, and which she very soon gave up.

The result was a flimsy, patchy knowledge about all sorts of things that no-one else wanted to know. She could for instance unexpectedly explain what a swastika was. What was the point of knowing that sort of thing? It was almost unseemly, and gave the impression that she was correcting other people. The ladies looked at her coldly and with astonishment, and Mrs Selmer felt no pride at all, quite the reverse. She pointed out on every possible occasion that reading learned tomes was a pure waste of time and no better than wandering about the streets. A way of making oneself unusual and eccentric, that was all it was, like straight hair and stiff-necked silence.

But Papa might pat Alberta on the head when he found her deep in a tome and remark, 'You're an odd child, I must say'.

She followed a blue, lonely track. It led her away from everyday and reality. Unfortunately it also led her back again, but then she had at any rate been away. She skied until she was buoyant and warm, losing herself in dreams and in the satisfying give of her body when she coasted downhill.

The sunset moved further and further towards the west, glowing behind new peaks. They stood deep blue, boring into the flaming sky, which gradually turned golden and then green behind them. – Eastwards above the river bend the first star had already appeared in the solid expanse of blue, and there was a new sound under her skis, that came with the evening – the sound of thin crust breaking.

And the painful, wonderful moment arrived, when the longing for something to happen – something, anything – almost anything at all – turned into an ache that could no longer be borne.

But when Alberta came clattering on her skis down the hard, much-trafficked streets from Upper Town – when she swung round and stopped as had been her habit ever since childhood, at the very moment when it looked as if she would shoot out on to the market place and into the clutches of P.C. Olsen – her conscience gripped her again. It thrived in the cold down here in town, between the houses where the lamps were being lit.

And when, a little later, she sat on the bench in the kitchen over the dinner which had been waiting for her in the oven, it was all over. She was the old, constrained, guilt-ridden Alberta, and the good, tired feeling of relaxation in her body had given way to troubling anxiety.

She lost no time pouring herself some coffee and adding water to the pot, to get the scalding hot drink inside her before Mrs Selmer, her after-dinner nap over, entered the kitchen like Nemesis.

* * *

'Well, well,' said the Magistrate with resignation, putting his large pile of newspapers down on the dining-room table; 'Well, well, you can go this time then, but you know I am not normally in favour of any running about after supper. It will please you to come home at the proper time.'

He sat down and ordered his newspapers for reading. They arrived in bundles twice a week, and he never succeeded in keeping up to date. He looked tired.

In the perpetual warfare waged with alternating success, which was his and Mrs Selmer's married life, he would on occasion capitulate, surrendering positions about which no open fight had as yet taken place, withdrawing from them quietly. This happened particularly if he had recently crushed his opponent in one way or another by brute force, with his heavy artillery. For his opponent invariably recovered and erected against him an icy wall of revenge against which he had so far been defenceless; whereupon he fell into uncertainty and tried to repair his erroneous strategy with an ignominious retreat.

Now he looked searchingly across at Mrs Selmer, but not the slightest expression betrayed her thoughts. Only when Jacob got up to go did she raise her eyes from her book and say: 'If your father has given you permission, naturally I have nothing to say. Good evening, my child'.

Jacob looked perplexed, but started to make for the door nevertheless. He paused for a second before opening it, and it seemed as if everyone was waiting to see what he would do next. Then he left.

Papa glanced quickly at Mama over his pince-nez, pursed his mouth and muttered: 'Wrong manoeuvre, futile sacrifice. Womenfolk – devils, the lot of them'.

Alberta ducked. Now for the storm. But Papa said no more and buried himself in his newspaper.

A wave of sympathy so strong as to be painful went through Alberta. Papa might be heavily armed with a great broadsword, he might be able to crush all that stood in his way; but he lacked those poisoned arrows that came whistling treacherously from behind the icy wall and remained quivering in the wound long afterwards. He was defenceless against them. They wounded him, and his perplexity was worse than any amount of Mama's tears.

As a contribution towards preserving the peace Alberta decided to take out her embroidery. Mrs Selmer then rose and disappeared into the darkness of the sitting-rooms. Shortly afterwards they heard her light matches, open the piano and strike a few chords.

An astonished 'Whatever next!' came from the Magistrate. He raised his eyebrows high up his forehead in increasing incomprehension of the female psyche. And he definitely gave it up for the evening, sucked at his pipe, and again bent over his newspaper.

But Alberta hastily fetched her confirmation-rug and seated herself quietly in a corner of the cold, dark sitting-room.

Far away in the opposite corner, beyond the black silhouettes of the centre table, the armchairs, the phoenix palm and the ivy, Mama sat playing. Two candles on the piano were alight. She looked so small and so inexpressibly lonely out there in the darkness, her shawl over her shoulders, sitting between her two candles, that something in Alberta melted and she was overcome by great tenderness for Mama. She wrapped the rug round her tightly and listened with a sob in her throat.

Mrs Selmer played the repertoire she had had in the time of her youth, old, well-practised pieces that her fingers never forgot, even though she never practised any more. Picturesque, tender, tuneful little melodies that conjured up visions before Alberta's eyes: *Scenes from Childhood, Carnival*. And then something unnerving and disintegrating, stealing in like an insidious and dangerous potion, making her weak, impotent and anxious: Rubinstein's *Night*. When Mama had played it to the end she sat still for a while looking down into her lap. Then she raised her head with a sigh. She raised her hands as well, and Alberta hoped she was going to leaf through the music and play more. But she clasped them together, closed the piano and snuffed out the candles.

An unreasonable desire to approach Mama, to give her a caress, came over Alberta. If she had dared, she would have gone over in the darkness and put her arms round her. But that sort of thing was not done. Mrs Selmer wandered past as if enclosed in an impenetrable aura, lighting her way with a match and taking a book from the bookshelf.

She said good night at once, a distant, cold good night, that did not appear to be addressed to Alberta and Papa. Then she wandered upstairs. She always went to bed earlier than anyone else in the house.

It was when the Magistrate was on circuit that the piano really quickened to life. No sooner had his heavy footsteps in the tall, furry travelling boots died away, no sooner were his and the Chief Clerk's bulging brief-cases and despatch boxes and the important package with the supply of bottles, carried down by Leonardsen, out of the house, than the piano lid stood open as if of its own accord, and the music was propped up, open and ready : Heyse's songs and Grieg's.

Mrs Selmer's somewhat slight, neglected voice resounded perpetually through the sitting-rooms : 'The princess sat high in her virgin bower' – 'I scarcely dare speak'. – The voice would break a little at the verse : 'I think of days gone by—'.

She also sang Schubert and mischievous little modern songs. She could sit for hours at the piano, and when she got up she would go round humming for a long time afterwards, while she attended to her innumerable flower pots and remarked thoughtfully from time to time : 'I see I shall have to transplant this one'.

She would send Alberta for some extra little delicatessen for supper and ignore her frailties. Cedolf and Beda were mentioned without the epithet frightful. A spirit of forbearance hovered over the house.

It was when the Magistrate was away that Mrs Selmer would put down the leaf of the bureau and sit at it. She sat there with many letters and faded photographs in front of her. There were withered flowers too that had to be handled carefully. If someone came in she would hurriedly put it all into a little drawer and push the drawer back into place; she would brush her hand across her eyes, as if to bring her thoughts back to this world. She might sigh. And she would rise with a tired, pre-occupied expression. That was all.

A few faded pictures, a few letters, a few mummified flowers that crumbled into dust between the fingers, were nothing. But they were fraught with destiny, sinister, deceitful and treacherous. The feeling hung about oppressively in an atmosphere which was otherwise fresh and cloudless.

Alberta bore a grudge against the little drawer in the bureau.

* * *

The Civic Ball took place at the end of March.

'No, we are not thinking of going this time,' said Mrs Selmer when the subject was raised at tea parties and soirées. 'Neither Alberta nor I have anything to wear. We shall stay at home this year.'

A few days before the ball she had a discussion with Papa in the office. They came in to dinner together, and Mrs Selmer said with finality as she entered the dining-room : 'As I said, the Governor's family is going, and the Klykken Juniors and the Prams. Mainly for the sake of the young people. The gentlemen will probably arrive later'.

Papa looked resigned, his eyebrows raised high. He ate in silence. Mama was conciliatory, almost friendly, not even taking offence when he pessimistically turned his steak over several times and called it a piece of leather, admitting that Jensine was undeniably careless now and again, the beef really was tough.

Towards the end of the meal Papa said : 'Very well, if you think we ought to go, then in heaven's name I suppose we must. It's so desperately expensive, that's all. But if you will get hold of the tickets, then – you know I—'

He shrugged his shoulders helplessly to indicate that he was a man overburdened with business and duties, and went in to his sofa and his newspapers.

Mrs Selmer opened the window : 'Oh Alberta, just run over and say I'll take the tickets they promised to keep for me'.

Alberta ran. The bracelet, she thought desperately, the bracelet. But Mrs Selmer opened another window and called after her : 'And then go to Olefine's and say she *must* give us a couple of days as soon as she can, it's to do with the Ball. Whether she's free or not'.

Olefine came. She hadn't time really, but Mrs Selmer generally got what she wanted.

Olefine explained her position in whispers. She was really supposed to be going to Ryan the butcher's, she had promised. To make a new dress for Signora. But as long as it didn't get about that she was at the Selmers' she would have to make some excuse to Mrs Ryan. Olefine whispered and looked about her anxiously as if the walls had eyes and ears. She fluttered her hand to emphasize how quietly and carefully the matter should be discussed.

Alberta's ball dress from last year was to be let down; once again she had grown. In addition it was to have new sleeves out of the material that, thank heaven, had been left over — short little puff sleeves. The old ones had come to her elbow.

'Short sleeves are pretty and young,' said Mrs Selmer, turning up the old ones to see how Alberta would look. 'You're shockingly thin, my child,' she added doubtfully.

Then she made up her mind. 'We'll have them short just the same, Olefine, it makes a change.'

Alberta stood in front of the mirror trying on the altered dress. She dragged and pulled at it, folded it up and let it down again, searching breathlessly and vainly for something in it that suited her. If she managed to make it pass muster in one place, it failed all the more lamentably in another.

She turned this way and that, lowered and raised her face, wondered whether she really was so plain, and thought : suppose it were sorcery, like the fairy tale. One fine day the spell would be broken, and an Alberta no-one had ever dreamed could exist would stand there, as beautiful as the princess.

Every time she had something new she locked herself in alone, trembling with excitement. Was it not so that a garment could work miracles? It was cast over the changeling, and hey presto, the spell was broken. He stood there in his true shape, young, beautiful, powerful, and had merely to pluck the joys of life like golden apples from the trees.

But it was not easy to find the magic garment. It was doubtful whether Olefine was even capable of producing it. Certainly it was not this altered dress. Alberta gazed at herself dispiritedly, by no means looking forward to the festivities.

* * *

The cold, grey half-light of the March evening fell cross the ballroom of the Grand. Krane was economizing on the lighting now that winter was so far advanced.

Alberta sat in the row of ladies along the window wall. One of the tall windows was behind her. She could feel the draught from it. If she turned she could look straight across Market Square to Rivermouth, where the mountains were standing on their heads in the dead calm. The reflections of snow and scree reached the sea-bed through infinite depths in a fantastic grey-on-grey pattern, and on the surface the current flowed in light little rings, dimples and whorls that never altered. There was a curious feeling of unreality in the fact that everything was going on its way quite unchanged, while in here there was a ball.

Up on the platform on the short side of the hall Mrs Selmer and her circle sat enthroned. Harriet and Christina were sitting there too; they had as it were withdrawn from the public eye. The time was approaching when the company would become somewhat mixed, when elements debarred from arriving at six o'clock would put in an appearance and take over the floor, and officialdom would retreat to its established positions. If you stayed sitting down in the hall you simply risked being asked to dance by any Tom, Dick or Harry. You could leave, to be sure. But nobody did.

For the moment there were only three or four couples on the floor and the music lacked ardour. In one of the back rooms, reserved for the occasion, the gentlemen had gathered for brandy and soda.

Alberta knew that Mrs Selmer had signalled to her several times to come and sit among her equals. She stubbornly pretended not to see. To walk up the long, now almost empty floor, alone, to arrive up there a target for everyone's eyes and the lorgnette – no, decidedly no. She felt plucked and bare in the white dress, which was too small, Mama and Olefine could say what they liked. She felt as if her unfortunate person was bursting through its splitting sheath under the public eye. Nervously she pulled at her gloves. They inched down over her sharp elbows all the time.

Pure chance, a stumble on the part of the Chief Clerk, who was no dancer, had washed her up here under the windows beside Lotten Kremer. It had not been the first time the Clerk had stumbled and lost the rhythm, it was perhaps the tenth. It became clear to him and to Alberta that they might as well give up, and she found herself sitting there. Lotten, who had not yet had one dance, but kept herself going by talking and laughing and behaving as if she were having a marvellous time all the same, had willingly made room. It was uphill work preserving this mood of gaiety with her sister Maria, who never said a word on her own initiative; besides, she was so old, certainly more than thirty, that it was no wonder she didn't even pretend to be enjoying herself any more.

Lotten was in sky blue with swansdown and long, white gloves. In her hair was the big, pink artificial rose that had been on a stand in the window of her hat shop a long time before the ball. Look, *this* is how it's supposed to be, with the stalk up and the flower down. Lotten knew how a rose should be worn, and serve you all right, she thought, referring to the ladies of the town.

She chattered ceaselessly and laughed strenuously at everything Alberta said. Alberta too became chatty, feeling a sudden sympathy for Lotten, with whom she normally only talked across the counter. As long as they were engaged in this animated conversation, Alberta had an excuse for not noticing Mrs Selmer's small signals and curious behaviour. Besides, she imagined what Lotten's position was like. If Papa were not the Magistrate, holding office in the town, his daughter Alberta would probably have been a wall-flower too.

Now they had all done their duty, those who were invited home now and again, and those whose parents were. She had danced twice with the Chief Clerk, who made her feel even more hopeless than she was already. She had danced with Bergan, who seemed not to advance at all, but simply turned on his own axis, taking his partner with him at arm's length like a distant satellite; with Dr Mo, who was from the south and indulged in unknown tricks; with the Archdeacon's

Henrik, who was out of step from first to last; and with the
Pram twins, who danced like the social lions they were, and
imitated Dr Mo.

She had also danced with Jacob. He was the most fun to
dance with. But Alberta was a little shocked to see him on the
floor. For Jacob danced with a self-confidence and conviction
that would not be quite fitting in a drawing-room. He danced
like a sailor, although he had never been to sea. Indeed, when
Jacob took the floor in his confirmation clothes, he seemed like
a stranger to Alberta. He looked attractive in a way that
appalled her. It dawned on her that strange girls in strange
countries would like Jacob, if he were ever to find himself
among them. The girls here liked him. That was why she was
afraid of Palmine and Lilly.

Then she had danced opposite Papa in the quadrille. Papa
went through the figures and bowed to her, gallant and
chivalrous as only he could be. In the chain she saw Mama a
little way ahead of her weaving in and out among the gentlemen, light-footed, gay and radiant, carrying herself like no-one
else in her old, much altered lilac silk. Now she was sitting
up there on the platform, a bright, festive speck among the
black silk dresses. Even the Governor's lady, who was dressed
in the very latest fashion from Steen and Strom in Kristiania,
looked less festive than Mama, so brittle, blonde, elegant and
petite. There was something about her that had nothing to
do with clothes, something that gave her whole personality
brilliance. Young Mrs Klykken was really the only one who
could outdo her; she got all her clothes from abroad and
was in light green silk, dark and slender as a heroine in a
novel.

But young Mrs Klykken stayed outside with the gentlemen.
She did not sit putting anyone in the shade, but shone quite
alone among black tails, white dress shirts, and red, animated
faces. Alberta had seen her through a doorway. She was sitting
on the arm of her husband's chair, with a hand on his
shoulder. She had pushed her gloves back over her wrists so
that her diamond rings were flashing – they said young Mrs
Klykken got one for each child – and she tossed witticisms at

the red faces and laughed, tilting her head backwards to show her long, white throat.

And all the red faces had the same, almost idiotically bliss-ful expression when they turned towards her, even Papa's and the Governor's. Alberta felt rather sorry for them. It was em-barrassing to see, as if they were being made fools of by young Mrs Klykken.

In the other back rooms refreshments were being served. The Kranes themselves stood behind a trestle table handing out ginger ale and beer, wine, coffee and hot chocolate. The hotel waitresses swayed in and out with loaded trays. The engineers kept open table with Beda as the centre of attrac-tion and Mrs Buck and Mrs Elmholz as chaperones. Gudrun Pram had a tendency to disappear out there, and Harriet be-came anxious up on her platform, stretching out her neck and looking as if at any minute she might shoot up out of her chair.

There was a pause. The music stopped. The couples dis-appeared from the floor. There was nothing more to watch and discuss with Lotten, and the coast was alarmingly clear between Mrs Selmer and Alberta, who nevertheless stuck temporarily to her position with her eyes turned in another direction. Then Lotten said : 'What's going to become of Rikke Lossius? They say she's going to be a painter'.

Alberta spied land again. Lotten was clearly just as inter-ested as she was in keeping the conversation going. To this extent they were allies. Eagerly she squeezed out all she knew about Rikke and stubbornly kept her eyes away from Mrs Selmer.

It was getting crowded down at the door. Young Theodor-sen, who had recently opened his own barber's shop, arrived at the head of a whole party. There were Elmholz's shop assistants and Weydemann the telegraphist, Karla Schmitt and Signora Ryan, Palmine Flor and Lilly Vogel. A number of strange young men who looked like commercial travellers were with them.

Suddenly Lotten Kremer gripped Alberta's arm, then just

as suddenly let it go. 'No, it was nothing,' she said shame-facedly, when Alberta stared at her. Perhaps she had forgotten that all the ladies in the party were her customers. At any rate she remembered in time – she had said nothing.

The new arrivals seemed to breathe new life into the festivities. Young Theodorsen had gone up to talk quietly to the band. It struck up *The Blue Danube* with dash and vigour. He danced out with Signora, and now in a trice the floor was packed with dancers. Krane became even busier. He brought small tables to put along the window wall, now that it had become impossible for all those wanting refreshments to have them in the back rooms. A gust of something new swept through the hall, something frightening and tempting. Alberta could see Mrs Selmer no longer. New arrivals streamed in through the door incessantly and joined the mêlée. The air thickened with tobacco smoke. It was now so dusky that faces and dresses appeared to be pale smudges, except near the windows where details were still visible.

The dancers formed a compact mass composed of revolving particles. The mass surged over towards the window wall, and a table lurched so that the people sitting at it had to defend themselves against bottles and cake dishes. It surged over towards the inner wall, and Maria Kremer opened her mouth at last : 'Let's try to get out now, Lotten, while there's still room'.

Immediately the floor was packed in front of them again, and Lotten laughed : 'No, my poor dear, it's no use trying. Besides, the fun's beginning now, that's what I think anyway'. Alberta did not like the ring in Lotten's laughter. It sounded so strange, as if in league with the half-dusk and the bewilder-ing, underhand atmosphere. She felt uneasy and wished she were sitting up with Mama after all as she usually did at this time of the evening. It was impossible to get there now.

There was young Theodorsen with Palmine. There was Lilly with a commercial traveller. There was Beda spinning past with a mining engineer, and Gudrun with another. There was Jacob – my God ! Jacob was dancing with the fair little girl who served in Holst's. What would Papa and Mama say?

And there was Cedolf. Cedolf, brown as a gipsy, with blue eyes and black hair, impudent and strikingly handsome in his shore-leave clothes. He was dancing with the new shop-girl from Haabjorn's, the one who was supposed to be from Kristiania and looked like it too.

Were not the young men holding their partners closer than before – were not the girls putting their arms round the men's necks with more abandon? There was Palmine – simply hanging on young Theodorsen.

Smiles and short phrases were exchanged in passing. The two engineers from Southfjord changed partners in the middle of the dance; they exchanged Beda and Gudrun. All four laughed and were lost in the mêlée.

All of a sudden somebody was pushed almost into Alberta's lap, and in trying to recover his balance stepped forcefully on her toes.

'Pardon me, Miss, I couldn't help it,' said an embarrassed voice. Alberta looked up. It was Weydemann the telegraphist. He had blushed to the roots of his thin, fair hair, and his large hands in their white cotton gloves twitched nervously.

'Not at all,' replied Alberta with as good a grace as she could muster, and blushed too.

Telegraphist Weydemann looked at a loss. Then he bowed.

And perhaps he did so merely in order to retire gracefully. But Alberta was disconcerted and did not quite know how to interpret it. She stood up in front of him, felt Lotten nudge her and imagined she heard a suppressed titter. Weydemann appeared to be even more at a loss and bowed once more. Then they were dancing.

Alberta had always felt sorry for Weydemann, as one does feel sorry for people for whom nothing turns out as it should in this world. For he came of a good family really, his mother was a Jaeger. She hoped Mama and Papa would consider it from this aspect when they in all probability caught sight of her. But she was far from being at ease when she did in fact pass the Magistrate, who was standing watching from one of the doors. Did he not readjust his pince-nez to make certain his eyes were not deceiving him? And when she and

Weydemann were pressed forward below the platform and waltzed round a couple of times right in front of Mama and all the ladies, her reputation was not worth a sou. Beyond all doubt there was quite a stir up there. She caught a glimpse of Mrs Selmer, who rose to her feet just as Alberta and Weydemann were swallowed up again in the throng. She slumped down apprehensively beside Lotten, inclining her head dumbly in thanks for the dance. An expedition to fetch her was presumably on its way.

'Well, what sort of a dancer is that fellow Weydemann? That wasn't what he meant at all, poor thing,' tittered Lotten.

'Wasn't it?' said Alberta unhappily.

But Lotten nudged her again. For someone else was standing before her bowing, a tall, strong fellow. Alberta looked up. It was Cedolf.

It was Cedolf! Looking down at her and smiling and bowing once more, blue-eyed and brown and impudently handsome.

The blood rushed to Alberta's head. This was an insult. But she had danced with Weydemann. And a compelling power seemed to emanate from Cedolf – she felt as if he were coercing her with his smile. Here, beside Lotten, among all these people, she was defenceless. There was no chance of turning her back on him and running. Trembling she rose to her feet.

Dancing with him was not at all disagreeable, it had to be admitted. On the contrary – it was miraculous, a suspension of the law of gravity. A suspension of the will and of responsibility too; a feeling of being disembodied and at one with the rhythm. Whatever else might be said about him, he could dance.

Now they were turning in front of Papa. And Papa wrinkled his forehead. It occurred to Alberta that he was saying something. Now they were dancing in front of the platform, and she caught a glimpse of the Governor's lady raising her lorgnette, and of Mama, who had been standing ever since the last time she saw her, and who now sat down. Mrs

Pram leaned over towards Harriet. They spoke to each other. Then they were all gone, and Cedolf was guiding her down towards the dark corner of the hall again.

Couples must have had a tendency to stay down there. There was a perpetual crush. Now the music changed abruptly to a gallopade and a wildness entered into the dance. A great knot formed, of couples colliding into each other in the dimness. Before Alberta knew what was happening she and Cedolf were in the middle of the knot, stamping on one spot without moving, shut in by a living barricade. On the outside young Theodorsen, the commercial travellers and the engineers with their partners blocked the way. They were laughing and singing in time with the music.

Alberta felt Cedolf take firmer hold of her. The others pressed her close against him. His large brown fist with the anchors on was no longer in her right hand, but was holding her arm above the elbow. She heard him say in her ear: 'Don't you be afraid'. And there was something in his voice, a dark purring, that made her afraid in earnest. Mortified too. What right had Cedolf to talk to her in such a voice?

His neck was close to her face, and thick, short, curly hair suddenly tickled her nose. Did she not almost press her mouth into Cedolf's neck, in the middle of the curls? Heavens, she must be out of her mind!

They were almost knocked over in the crush, and Cedolf lifted her up, smiling down at her as he did so. And something new and strange flowed through Alberta's body. It was like a deep call, a sweet, strong sigh in the blood. It passed through her and died away, leaving her behind, amazed, as if newly awakened from a dream and still listening after it.

At the same moment she caught sight of Beda in the dimness, Beda and Lett the dentist. And Beda and Lett were dancing cheek to cheek, Beda smiled as Alberta had never seen her smile before, and shut her eyes – it lasted for only a second, then it was over, and Beda and Lett were like other people again. Alberta asked herself: 'Is it real, is all this reality?'

Suddenly she was on the brink of tears of shame and anger.

The tumult, Cedolf's body against hers, Beda's smile, the wantonness about her, were violence and shock, mortifying and degrading.

'I won't dance any more,' she cried. 'I want to get out, we must try to get out.' She attempted to free herself from Cedolf, and saw his mouth curl up.

Now he was thrusting people to one side as if they were pawns, pushing and shoving to clear a way : 'Out of the way, fellows, we're not staying here stamping any longer'. And he galloped off with Alberta so that she scarcely touched the floor.

'I think you really were frightened,' he smiled, when she had been brought back to her seat beside Lotten. 'They were only kicking up a row,' he said.

Alberta, who normally blushed on every occasion, was pale for once, so pale that she felt it herself. She was crushed. She was miserable and disgraced.

Above her she heard Cedolf explaining to Lotten : 'They're crazy. It's that fellow Theodorsen and the commercial travellers that's the worst. You don't feel ill, do you?' he asked Alberta. 'You look so seedy.'

'No,' answered Alberta briefly, and now she blushed.

'Well, thanks for the dance then.' Cedolf bowed urbanely. She could hear that he was smiling, that he was talking with his mouth curled up.

'Thank you,' she muttered without looking up. Lotten remarked : 'Somebody's popular, I must say. The one partner more dashing than the last'. She laughed ambiguously : 'That Cedolf Kjeldsen's a nice fellow too'.

'Ugh – he's horrid,' said Alberta.

And she jumped, for someone had touched her on the shoulder. It was Jacob. He was in his overcoat, cap in hand. 'You must come now, Alberta,' he said. 'We're going home, we're all waiting for you.'

They walked home through the quiet, empty streets in the half-light. The short, transparent March night was over, the day was approaching. But it was neither dark nor light, it was pearl grey. Everything was pearl grey, the snow, the air, the mountains. They were still standing on their heads in the calm water, and a fishing smack was inching its way out of Rivermouth on the tide, mirrored blackly and distinctly. A long, light stripe followed it in the water like a line drawn beneath it all. The landscape seemed to be in light, half-waking slumber, and the houses slumbered with it. The blinds looked like closed eyelids. The crisp, frozen snow crunched like granulated sugar, making a jarring, disproportionate noise beneath the feet of the returning ball guests.

Her luck was out, Papa's and Mama's faces bore set expressions when they looked at Alberta and Jacob. They even turned away again quickly, as if they might be harmed by catching sight of something they did not want to see. Once Mama muttered to Papa: 'There are various matters I have to discuss with Alberta,' and Alberta felt a stab. 'The chain!' said the little stab inside her. As long as she was with somebody else nothing would happen. Perhaps nothing would happen until they were home in the cold, empty living-rooms.

She imagined Mama's icy voice: 'I cannot tell you how astonished I am. Weydemann perhaps, after all he comes of a good family really and I'm sure he's a nice boy – but that fearful Cedolf–'. And Papa: 'You must remember that you are a young lady, my child'. And Jacob: 'I say, it really was nice of you to dance with Cedolf, Alberta. He's a good fellow, you know'.

Behind her Mrs Pram was talking about young Mrs Klykken: 'Sitting in there with the gentlemen all evening – for my husband's sake I'd never do such a thing. But you may be sure the gentlemen think their own thoughts, Mrs Lossius'.

The Governor's lady was airing much suppressed indignation: 'We should have left long ago. The tone always degenerates later in the evening, it's scarcely right to allow the young people to witness all that goes on. But it was impossible to get the gentlemen away'. Harriet had been sent in time and again to remind them, and even Mrs Lossius had gone in once, all to no avail. She herself, praise be, had neither of her daughters there, but she was thinking of the others. As for young Mrs

Klykken, she ought not to forget her origins so quickly. She might be married to one of the town's leading businessmen, but after all she was still simply Sigfrida Flemming. There could be no-one who didn't remember her serving in her father's shop, looking like a simple little country girl with a gold cross round her neck and her hair parted in the middle. But then she came home from Kristiania and had grown into such a beauty – gracious me, she *is* beautiful – and young Klykken was completely stunned by her. She supposed that sort of thing went to the head when you came from simpler circumstances. It looked very like it. It was sad for the old Klykkens. Mrs Lossius tightened her mouth so that it disappeared into her face completely.

Harriet Pram assured everyone that she for her part had attended the Civic Ball for the last time, but Gudrun was loud in protest : 'Gracious, it was so much fun—'

She was frozen into silence. The others laughed a little and talked about something else, but no-one was vexed. Gudrun was pretty, with dark eyes, radiantly pretty. Then it's not so dangerous to be a bit glib, thought Alberta bitterly, as she walked along, eaten up by her various anxieties.

Under cover of the leave-taking with the Prams and the Lossiuses, Jacob whispered to her : 'Now for it, Alberta. But I'll go to sea. I'll not stay here to be nursemaided like a girl'.

After which the Selmer family continued its progress across the market place in ominous silence. Were Papa and Mama both waiting for the other to begin? Papa gave a preliminary cough—

Then someone appeared in the deserted square, someone in a hurry. It was Nurse Jullum carrying her worn, black bag, the one for which Alberta felt a secret terror.

'Heavens !' exclaimed Mrs Selmer. 'Go on, the rest of you. I must hear whether anything has happened at the Pios' or the Bakkes'.'

She stopped and spoke quietly to Nurse Jullum, who, looking in need of sleep, put down her bag and wiped her forehead up under her hat with her handkerchief. Papa said nothing. He would probably wait until the family was to-gether again.

Mrs Selmer caught them up. She was both shocked and animated and had completely forgotten Alberta and Jacob. 'A big boy at the Pios',' she announced. 'Over eight pounds. But it was a hard struggle. Nurse has not been out of her clothes since yesterday evening. Now she's on her way to Mrs Bakke, who has been ill since yesterday and does nothing but cry for her mother. I'll go up there, I'll change and go straight up. Mr Bakke is quite beside himself, walking in and out of the house with his hat on in utter bewilderment, poor man.'

Mrs Selmer was so kind in that way, absolutely wonderful. In a crisis there was no limit to her friendliness. You could always rely on her.

'Hm—' said Papa. 'It's not so easy, by Jove.'

Alberta dawdled about in her room, taking off her finery, still weak with anxiety. Sometimes it did turn out like that. Mama had actually forgotten, for the time being at any rate. She had gone straight up to her bedroom, changed, and disappeared. And Papa? Was he not really quite pleased to have the opportunity to forget? Papa, who underneath had the same soft spot for Alberta as she for him, and who never willingly scolded her for anything. No doubt the matter would be brought up again, but in milder form.

The sun of a new day shone on the upper part of the mountain from quite the wrong direction, contributing to the general feeling of unreality.

A night outside existence, yet giving her a glimpse into it; an intense and confusing glimpse, as if seen in a flash of lightning. All this unreality, it was real. This astringent taste of antipathy and sweetness, of alarm and longing, of wanting and not wanting, was that of life itself, Alberta knew that already. Even Nurse Jullum had not been omitted from the fantastic events of the night, she who was always there in the background with her terrible bag and her quiescent, know-all smile. Tall, thin, dressed in black, she appeared and conjured up the gathering storm like a sinister, supernatural figure.

Alberta was free to give herself up to her conflicting feelings and to a new anxiety, a new fear, born in her that night.

* * *

One evening Jacob raised his head from his plate of gruel and remarked : 'Skipper Danielsen is leaving for the Arctic on the twentieth. He'll hire me, if I want.'

Alberta dropped her spoon. Her whole being stood still. She glanced over at Mrs. Selmer, who looked as if someone had given her such a cruel blow that she could not open her eyes after it. She dared not look at Papa. What was going to happen?

The Magistrate did not answer immediately. When he finally did so, he said something quite unexpected. He described a careful circle round his plate and announced : 'I'm expecting by every post an answer to a letter I have written to my old friend, Shipowner Bjorn, in Flekkefjord. In it I asked him to keep you in mind, should he need an apprentice seaman. I have no doubt that he will do what he can.'

'That would be long-distance shipping,' said Jacob.

'Good gracious, yes. They carry freight all over the world.'

But Mrs Selmer collapsed in a heap. With her hand to her breast as if to stop her heart beating – or to keep it going, it was difficult to say which – she said in a weak, dying voice : 'And what about me! Nobody thinks about me. Nobody thinks of my feelings'.

'My dear Henrietta, nobody sympathises with your feelings more than I,' began Papa, 'But the boy must go out into the world some time, after all, and since he—

'God knows I'd rather have sent him south to the University or to the Military Academy,' he added. 'Then he could have counted on living with my brother Thomas, and he would have had the chance to become an educated lad and make a career – but unfortunately, it is some time since I gave up that idea. I have talked to the Headmaster on several occasions

recently, and he has given me to understand that – well . . .
And since Jacob himself desires to make a new start, I think
we ought to consider—'

But Mrs Selmer had recovered from her relapse. She was
white with fury. 'And here you all go making decisions and
arrangements without so much as mentioning the matter to
me. I am *quantité negligeable* – of no account – the boy's
mother is of no account.'

'My dear Henrietta, we have decided nothing. I have con-
sulted my old friend Bjorn as to how the matter might be
arranged. I have, as I said, talked to Bremer, and he con-
siders—'

Mrs Selmer girded herself in her armour of mortification.
She stopped eating, leaned back and stared into thin air with
a fateful expression in her eyes and with pinched lips.

The Magistrate surveyed her angrily above his pince-nez.
He muttered : 'So that's how it is !' His mouth twisted, and
he kept the Headmaster's remarks to himself for the time
being.

Tears began to roll down Mrs Selmer's stricken face.

Alberta saw clearly that this was the end. Papa was letting
Jacob go, giving him up for ever. From now on Jacob would
be wandering alone, a poor sailor. He would travel to far-
away ports, terrible ports full of squalor and girls. When he
was not out on the savage sea his environment would permanently resemble the back room at the Grand. And suddenly Alberta quite distinctly saw a wave washing over Jacob.
He was shipwrecked, sitting on a piece of wreckage, cold and
frozen, clinging fast with his blue hands – and at home they
knew nothing about it, nobody knew about it. He was alone
and helpless out on the Atlantic, far from everyone, abandoned
by God and his fellow men. All he owned in the world was
a miserable sea-chest, which was also floating in the ocean.

Alberta hid her face in her hands just as she gave way to
tears. She felt Jacob's hand on her arm, heard him say : 'Oh
no, Alberta, don't cry – there's nothing to cry about'.

She heard Mama say bitterly : 'Alberta, my dear – of what
use are our tears, yours or mine?'

She heard Papa mutter something about preposterous, over-excited females, and fled out through the door and up the stairs.

'Don't take it like this, Alberta. It's nothing to cry so terribly about.'

'But other boys leave home. I can't stay here for ever, having money wasted on me.'

'I *must* get away, Alberta, I can't stand it any longer. I'll never be any good here – it's no use *my* going to school – I'm too stupid, you see. Oh no, don't cry like that, Alberta, it's so awful when you cry.'

'Besides, all the teachers hate me, they're as beastly to me as they can be. It doesn't matter how hard I try. You said yourself yesterday, I *knew* my German, but Stensett gave me gamma just the same – he can't stand me, you see—

'And it's so miserable here at home – and cold and everything.'

'Listen Alberta. After all, I'll come home again. I'll go ashore pretty soon, you see – Cedolf and I, we've thought of getting a piece of land in Canada, that's the sort of place for fellows like us. If only I can get started on something like that I'll come home prosperous – just you wait and see, Alberta.'

'Cedolf *is* a good fellow, take my word for it – but he says that when he's home he gets so that he has to drink – and besides he never gets drunk, if that's what you're thinking.

'When he's at sea he never touches a drop.'

'Don't you see, Alberta, everything will get much better if only I can get started on something and begin to earn money – I'll help Papa with the bank loan, I promise you. – And you'll get back your jewellery and a lot more besides – are you listening, Alberta? Oh no, do stop it! Can't you stop crying—'

'I'll go teetotal if you want me to. Stop crying and I promise I'll go teetotal. – If I stay here I'll never amount to anything. – And you really must try to cheer up Mama a little. Can't you try to be a bit like she wants, it would be much better for you too.'

'If I had to stay here I don't know what would become of me – I'd probably get like Kornelius Kamke in the end. Oh, Alberta – if I could only—'

Jacob struck the air with clenched fists, as if clearing away obstacles. He would have liked to say more, but got no further and finished somewhat self-consciously and in confusion : 'Oh, I don't know'.

'Oh Jacob!' Alberta sobbed in the darkness and called his name. She cowered in bed, rearranging the blanket again and again, unable to get warm. And she thought and thought about him, shaking with sobs.

It seemed as if Jacob had led a lop-sided existence, never really fitting into the circumstances in which he was born – never living up to Papa's expectations.

She remembered him as a little boy. He had been slender-limbed, with large grey eyes and fair curls that were a sorrow to him because they were girlish. And he had had a tender, courageous little heart, that went out warmly to people and animals and never kept account of its gifts.

He had gone for Ola Paradise with his fists because he whipped his horse – and cried himself to sleep at night in desperation for the poor horse, who was driven every day by that terrible Ola, and could not be saved from his clutches.

He had gone for big boys who were unkind to the little ones, and got a thrashing and forgot it and did the same again.

He had come home one day leading a shabby little snotty-nosed boy from the street. The boy was wearing Jacob's over-coat, and Jacob's intention had been to install him in the nursery and load him with things from the middle drawer in the chest, his own drawer. But as luck would have it they met Papa on the way.

Papa was not angry with the little boy. He explained to him kindly and quietly that he had to go away again. But afterwards Jacob was caned in the bedroom by Mama because he had taken his coat off and put it on a stranger – a boy who might have all kinds of diseases and about whom she knew nothing.

Did Papa begin even then to suspect that Jacob did not have the right instincts – or was it later? When he was very small Jacob had been the pride and joy of Papa and Mama and everyone.

It was really when he started secondary school that matters became tragic. He had managed somehow to get through elementary school. It was then that he began to grow so enormously fast, and everything went wrong : his Saturday reports, the boots he wore out, the boys he was seen with on the street, the clothes he continually outgrew. He became big and tall, with arms and legs that always stuck out too far, and eyes that gradually turned shy and hid themselves.

Everything Jacob wanted Papa did not want, and everything Papa wanted Jacob did not – or could not – want.

Jacob wanted to be a Boy Scout. Papa called it nonsense, and after brief consideration refused to give him any money for that sort of twaddle. In his childhood boys had played Indians without it costing anything.

Jacob and another boy wanted to build a hut beyond the river bend and spend Sundays there during the holidays. When Papa learned that the other boy was Julius, the son of Karen the fish shop, the whole scheme fell flat.

'If only it had been one of the nice boys in the class,' said Papa.

After all, there was the Archdeacon's Henrik, a bookworm, admirable in every respect. There were the Pram twins, a little less admirable, but proper social lions with beautiful manners. There were boys from good homes all over the province. And there were the Headmaster's boys, notoriously perfect specimens, though somewhat reserved and self-sufficient. Suitable friends were by no means lacking – but Jacob spent his time with Julius and with Cedolf, with Klaus Kilde and George Ryan. He did not go collecting specimens on the mountainside in summer like the Archdeacon's Henrik, but frequented the quarries to the east of town, the wharves, every kind of craft, and Badendück's quay, among the Lapps and Russians. He had an unfortunate tendency to make his acquaintances among the lower ranks of society; to come home in the evening tattered, dirty and guilty, his clothes reeking of fish and tar, too late to do his homework which was set for six o'clock – too late for supper, when it was arranged that he must work first and go out afterwards – always with some misdeed on his conscience. Papa thundered and prophesied the worst, could not fathom what would become of the boy, and again came to the conclusion that he would be an ill-mannered guttersnipe. Mama wept and wailed, lay on the sofa, had little talks with Jacob in private. Alberta energetically put all her diplomacy into the service of a good cause. Jacob remained Jacob.

Schoolmasters came home to interview Papa, Papa went to interview the Headmaster. When Jacob moved up into the fifth form by the skin of his teeth, Alberta was in her second year at *gymnasium*. At Christmas she was taken out of school. Jacob had to be coached in several subjects – by Bremer and Stensett and Alberta.

And everything became worse than ever.

'I want to go to sea, Alberta, I don't want to stay at home,' grumbled Jacob.

A year later, when he once more slipped – or rather, was squeezed – through the needle's eye, he snarled : 'I'm not going to be a sabre-rattler or a clerk'.

'A clerk?'

'Yes, what else is Papa? He sits wearing out the seat of his trousers on an office chair. But I can't stand that sort of life, I'd have you know. I don't care whether I'm a gentleman or not, don't you understand. If only I could get to America.'

Alberta did not understand. Naturally, to ride round throwing a lasso on the Pampas or in Texas, to wear high boots, a highwayman's hat and a multi-coloured scarf loosely knotted round your neck and look for gold in Alaska, would be a wonderful sort of life, frightfully dashing. That she understood. But Jacob must not become anything like that all the same.

And definitely not a sailor.

Now and again a distant relative of Papa's, a captain on one of the Hamburg boats, would come visiting. He was well, nay, warmly, received. He and Papa drank toddy and chatted until late at night, and Mrs Selmer would join them with her knitting.

There was no apparent difference between him and the Magistrate. Nevertheless since Alberta was small she had known that he was not nearly as much of a gentleman as Papa – knew it without being told.

Jacob was not going to struggle and toil, only to become like that in the end, less of a gentleman and of a slightly lower class.

But Jacob became more and more at cross purposes with it all.

'Bjerkem hates me,' said Jacob. 'If he can do me a bad turn, he's glad. If that fellow Stensett can find an opportunity to crack down on me, he will. However well I've prepared my lessons they take it for granted I don't know them, just because it's me. The Head takes real pleasure in giving me delta.'

There were also occasions when he announced rebelliously : 'I'll sign on for the Arctic – I'll fail on purpose, then they can all go to hell'. And others when he explained earnestly to Alberta : 'You see, Alberta, digging in the earth, working with your hands, that's the sort of thing I can do, and going to sea and things like that. If only I could do something like that I'd be all right. But you see, I hate school more than anything. It stinks'. And Jacob shook his clenched fists at the sky in helpless rage.

Those of Jacob's companions who had gone to sea after their school-leaving examination came home again. They walked the streets with clay pipes, the beginnings of sea legs, and cloth caps; had tanned faces, spat far and spoke English. An insolent strength radiated from them and was apparent in their walk and their looks.

'I feel like a girl,' said Jacob furiously. 'All I need is spectacles on my nose like the Archdeacon's Henrik. I'm ashamed of myself.'

He accompanied them on board, was with them in the evenings, heaven knows where, and came home late, his eyes shining and his cheeks flushed, carelessly loud-voiced and noisy. Sometimes Alberta, who lay awake listening, would creep down in her nightdress as soon as she heard the distant sound of the front door, to shush Jacob and make him go quietly.

She confiscated the pipes and the quids of tobacco, packs of cards and photographs of ladies in tights, that she found in his pockets, so that Mama should not find them. She lied and covered up for him as best she could, and scolded him.

And Jacob assured her : 'I don't get drunk, Alberta, but I can't refuse when I'm offered a glass. Besides, if there were something else to do here, none of us would drink a drop, the others say that too. In places where there are theatres and things like that, out in the world, they don't drink. And a grown fellow must learn to hold it a little, you know'.

And Julius went off to sea again, but George came home. And George travelled south to the Seamen's School, but Cedolf turned up instead. Cedolf had had particular influence on Jacob from schooldays on. He was a little older and had stayed down a couple of years. If the masters really had a down on Jacob, it was perhaps mainly on account of his friendship with Cedolf.

Bjorn, the shipowner, had use for Jacob. Quite by chance he needed an apprentice seaman immediately. His S/S *Aurora* would be docking at Liverpool during the second half of the month to take on freight for Pernambuco. Jacob must make up his mind at once and leave as soon as possible.

It was like a bad dream.

Papa and Jacob talked at table about registered tons and deplacement. Papa seemed to see Jacob in a better light now that he had given him up. He talked to him in friendly fashion about the little town in South Norway : 'That was where your grandfather lived during his last years. You wouldn't remember him, my boy, but your sister should. You were almost five, Alberta, when you were down there with me. And it was at your grandfather's house, my dear Jacob, that I used to meet the old man, the present shipowner Bjorn's father'.

And Papa continued to talk about people and conditions in the south. He revived old memories, became animated by them, and ended up genial and good-humoured : 'As you see, I've spent some time among seafaring folk too. I'm not completely ignorant of navigation, and can talk about leeward and windward with the best of them'.

Light was cast deep down into the darkness of Alberta's childhood. It fell strongly and suddenly on unexpected things : on a bush with small, round sulphur-yellow roses. They smelt nasty, but attracted her hands, which stretched out towards them.

Jacob laughed. He and Papa were good friends. It almost seemed as if it were not so terribly tragic any more that Jacob was becoming a sailor, instead of a government official or an army officer. If it had not been for Mama, she might perhaps have begun to see the bright side. But a glance at her was enough for the abyss to yawn once more. Her face was swollen with weeping and she said nothing, but looked straight in front of her with hopeless eyes. She sat shrunken into her shawl, the personification of misery. Nobody would have recognised the elegant, vivacious Mama of social life. Every time her eyes met Alberta's a lump rose in Alberta's throat.

'Pernambuco – where's that, Alberta?' asked Mrs Selmer in a weak, almost inaudible voice.

'Brazil,' answered Alberta, feeling as if she were pronouncing sentence of death.

'Brazil,' repeated Mrs Selmer in an even weaker voice, scarcely more than a breath. She leaned her head against the back of her chair and shut her eyes.

'Now look here,' said Papa, red in the face. 'You're behaving, so help me, as if the boy were being sent to the devil. Of course we had other plans for Jacob's future, for many reasons – but we shall have to bear the disappointment. Apart from that I can't see that Jacob is in a worse position than any other boy who chooses the sea. On the contrary – he's joining a good shipping company from the start, an excellent company known to us, where they will most certainly keep an eye on him. If he behaves himself and makes progress, there's every chance that he may be able to work his way up in the same company. I think that, considering the circumstances, we have every reason to be pleased, and the boy himself looks forward to it with hope and optimism—'

Papa came no further in his speech. Mama rose and tottered towards the door, clearly summoning her last remaining strength. A groan escaped her, and she disappeared.

Papa struck the table, making everything on it jump. His mouth twisted violently. He addressed himself to his plate and was silent for a while, but his clenched fist, which still lay on the table, continued to tremble.

Alberta's desire for Papa to be right warred with a painful suspicion that perhaps he would just as soon be rid of Jacob, since he despaired of him anyway, and would therefore let him sink with deliberate intent. Judging by Mama, Jacob must be on the way to the bottom.

A memory surfaced, filling her cup of pain and anxiety to the brim. When Cedolf came home from sea the last time – it must have been last summer – she had confiscated among much else in Jacob's pockets a mysterious little piece of pink card with a printed inscription. '*Kommen Sie doch die schönen Damen zu sehen*', it had said – and a street and house number below.

'It's something I got from Cedolf, something he got in Hamburg,' replied Jacob when questioned. He reddened, snatched the card, tore it up and said : 'Besides, you've no business looking in my pockets'.

'Well, if you prefer Mama to find everything you keep in them, I don't mind,' said Alberta crossly, not attaching any further significance to the matter. '*Schönen Damen*' had probably meant dancers or something like that. But Jacob had looked so odd that she went on thinking about it later. And the light suddenly dawned.

It was showing the way to girls, to wicked girls, who lived in wicked houses, that little pink card. So it was true. Such places did exist, and as soon as a seaman came ashore he was probably handed a little message. Cedolf had no doubt been to see the beautiful ladies – he was capable of it.

At that time she had made up her mind more strongly than ever to save Jacob for an orderly life.

And now it had all been in vain. Now he was going out on the savage sea just the same, and down into all kinds of human filth. He would go ashore in ports, and everything horrid and bad and dreadful would happen to him.

Oh God! Oh God!

In the middle of the floor in Jacob's room there stood an open sea-chest. Inside, it had curious little sections along one end, and it was broader at the base than at the top. It was clearly meant to stand as long as there could be any question of anything standing. And there were handles made of thick rope for lifting it.

For Alberta it was a symbol of the seaman's tragic life, the sailor's rootless wandering, his poverty, his toil and deprivation, his struggle against the raging sea, all of which she could picture only too clearly. Perhaps it represented much the same for Mrs Selmer who, pale, with set face, was packing Jacob's outfit into it.

It all seemed to take on an entirely different complexion where Jacob was concerned, however. Whistling, he lifted first the one handle, then the other, rearranged the things Mama had put into it, and stood looking at the chest, swaying from his knees with his hands in his trouser pockets. He walked round it, bent down and inspected it intently from every angle, experimented with the locks and hinges, and behaved almost as if it were a fellow-creature of whom he was fond, but whose reliability he nevertheless desired to test.

Jacob had changed. He no longer avoided people's gaze, but looked straight at them. And Jacob's eyes were dark grey under the fair hair that curled thickly over his forehead. He smiled with a broad, frank smile that Alberta seemed never to have seen before.

He tried on the new, thick monkey-jacket he would wear in future instead of a waistcoat and shirt. It had a high neck and long sleeves – and the frozen schoolboy with the large blue fists sticking out of his short sleeves disappeared as if by magic. A broad-shouldered sailor with a smile in his eyes stood there instead, looking at Alberta from under his fair hair. 'Look Alberta, now the slavery is over,' he said.

To Mama Jacob talked in that voice of his that gave confidence. He sat with her a great deal. Often, if Alberta came in, she would find him leaning over Mama hurriedly withdrawing his hand, as if he had just patted her on the back.

His attitude towards Papa was that of one grown man to another. They looked at each other directly when they spoke; Papa even drew himself erect, smote Jacob on the shoulder and said : 'By Jove, you're not a child any longer, my boy'. Or he would talk half jokingly to Jacob, using sailors' expressions: 'It's up to you to do the navigating, Jacob, and keep a steady course'.

And Jacob answered in the same tone : 'Aye, aye, sir !'

But with Alberta he bubbled over with all kinds of things. 'I've finished with hanging about and being no use to anybody, don't you see, Alberta? Now I'll try to get Cedolf into the same company, and when we've saved as much as we need we'll go ashore. In Canada, you know, that's where there's money for hard-working fellows to earn. It won't be long before I can help with the bank loan and everything. On the other hand, if I had *studied*—' Jacob's voice was full of scorn, he pronounced the word with boundless disdain '—I'd have stayed here simply eating up money. Besides, I'd never have matriculated, however much you all coached me. No Alberta – I'm too stupid, you see, it would be no use for someone like me. But I'll do well all the same, you'll see – oh no, don't cry again, for heaven's sake. I'll go teetotal. I've told you, I'll go teetotal.'

And Jacob put his arms round her and shook her, but in a different way now, as if less embarrassed at giving way to such weakness. 'I'm not the kind of fellow you think I am,' he said.

'And then you must be kind to Mama, Alberta – can't you be kind to her? She has such a bad time, don't you see, she's not happy, and when a little thing like you frizzing your hair could please her—'

A little devil was roused in Alberta and she turned Jacob's weapon back against him : 'It's no use, Jacob, I'm too plain. It would be no use for someone like me. I'd only look silly, like those small dogs with thin, fair, crinkly hair. Don't you remember the one old Mrs Klykken had?'

Jacob stared at her uncomprehendingly. 'Good Lord, surely it doesn't matter as much as all that? The other girls all curl their hair after all,' he said, talking nonsense, just like a man. 'And you mustn't be upset, Alberta,' he continued, coming closer. 'Listen! You shall go to Kristiania. Just wait until I've saved a little. Now I can start earning my own living I feel as if there's hope about all sorts of things. Simply getting away from that feeling of being a criminal all the time—'

He stopped. Perhaps he realised he was harping on a sore point. 'And I'm jolly glad I don't have to go by way of Kristiania,' he said, changing the subject. 'Uncle the Colonel wouldn't want to meet a black sheep like me, Aunt even less.'

Alberta altered her route. She no longer walked uphill, where the roads were infested with people on foot as long as the sun was up, nor did she ski. The latter would have seemed like unforgiveable indifference at this time, when Jacob's departure was imminent, and would have taken her far from the focus of events.

She walked along River Street, along the quays, and in poky Strand Street, where small green hovels, their windows full of fuchsias and geraniums, stood crookedly supporting each other, and where nobody else walked.

She lived in an unreal world of fantasies about Jacob, and the good or evil that might befall him. Visions of colourful life in foreign ports flickered before her eyes : the tropics, Negroes, piles of pineapples and oranges. Then suddenly there was a storm at sea, the waves washed over Jacob, who was the last one left on the upturned hull, blue with cold and alone and struggling vainly for his life – sobs choked her. She also saw him coming out of taverns, a little unsteady on his feet, in the company of girls like Fanny, and she felt as if the ground were sinking beneath her. Under it all she nursed a hope; now and again it floated to the surface and pushed Jacob aside. A hope that now, somehow or other, it must surely be her turn. For the time being, Jacob was provided for, at any rate until he entered the school of navigation.

In glimpses she saw herself, free and unselfconscious, released from all that was unpleasant, out in the world. At the very least in Kristiania, perhaps in other places, preferably as far away as possible. She was cheerful and active, like the people who came home in the summer.

But then the realization of what it would be like to know that Papa and Mama were left here at home with all their problems, crept across the vision like a mist. She felt again that dizzying feeling of treachery, which gnawed at her night and day every time she was away from home, even during the week she used to spend in Inner Southfjord in the summer as a child.

One day Alberta was passing the spot where you could see right up Fjord Street and into Dorum's jewellery shop. Her heart missed a beat and her legs turned weak. For up in Fjord Street Dorum's door had opened, and out of the door had come Mrs Selmer.

She looked about her for a moment, up and down the street. Without noticing Alberta she gathered up her skirt and went down the steps, holding her muff out a little with one hand, as was her habit. Inside the window, between silver-plated jugs and trays, Dorum's bald head appeared. He craned his neck – indeed, he was quite clearly standing on tip-toe – to watch her go.

Alberta went home in a fever of anxiety, with pulsing blood and dizzy head. Now the hour of reckoning was near. How readily she would have directed her steps in a different direction! But the mysterious currents that emanated from Mama were as potent as ever. Alberta went straight home, certain of being unmasked as one who lent a helping hand to criminals, compromised her family, and squandered its possessions.

She presented herself in the dining-room more dead than alive. Mrs Selmer was sitting at the mending basket, without her shawl, still warm from her excursion in the fresh air.

'Oh, Alberta my dear, do help me to mark these socks for Jacob,' she said in a friendly, straightforward tone.

Alberta sat on the edge of a chair and prepared to mark the socks with trembling fingers. This must be a trap, and there was nothing for it but to walk into it with her eyes open.

But Mrs Selmer talked about Jacob's socks and his other things as if there was nothing the matter. Then she talked about Jacob himself and all the dangers he was likely to meet with. 'But I believe God will hear my prayers and hold His hand over him,' she said.

There was an air of mild resignation about her, a quiet, slightly hollow-eyed pallor as if after illness. Mama behaved like one who has concentrated his whole being on a decision – to bear her cross. Alberta, with her misdeeds and her bracelet, did not seem to exist.

Alberta's reason stood still.

The evening before Jacob's departure she and Jacob said good night to each other across the open sea-chest. They stood exchanging a few words, and Jacob leaned over from acquired habit and arranged the things in the chest, loosening one, packing another in more tightly. He had been living in it for some time. It contained everything in the world that was his, and it could not be tidied too often. Suddenly he raised his eyebrows: 'What on earth?' he said, and he hauled up from the depths an unknown object, a splendid new leather wallet. 'What on earth?' he said again, turning it over and over, his eyes large with amazement. Then he opened it.

Inside the wallet was a dizzy, unheard-of sum of money. Five ten-*kroner* notes, fifty *kroner*. And a small white card, on which it said: 'To turn to in a tight corner. From Mother, who loves you and will always be thinking of you.'

'Damn!' said Jacob.

'Damn!' he said again, and his eyes filled with tears. He had to turn away and dry them with the back of his hand.

'Where on earth could she have got it from?' he asked after a while. 'It's so unnecessary too, I'll get travel money from Papa. But I can't understand where it's come from. Fifty *kroner* – have you ever seen anything to equal it?'

Alberta shook her head. She had no words for what she felt – a great, painful tenderness for Mama.

The moment of departure had arrived.

Jacob's chest had been taken down. Ewart was already driving away with it on a sled. Mrs Selmer and the Magistrate in their outdoor clothes were waiting for Alberta, who was up in her room, making a last attempt to master her tears. They had been bubbling in her throat all through dinner. Now they threatened to overcome her.

There was Jacob behind her in the doorway. He threw his arms round her, thumped her on the back harder than ever and said in a husky voice : 'Good-bye, Alberta, good-bye. I shan't forget what you've done for me – don't worry about me, Alberta, I'll turn out all right, you'll see. And look, take it – you should have had it before now, but . . .'

Jacob pushed something into Alberta's hand, at the same time kissing her roughly, first on one cheek and then on the other.

Bewildered, she looked down at what was in her hand. It felt so familiar. Through the thin tissue paper covering it she saw the bracelet, the very same bracelet from Uncle the Colonel.

'But Jacob !'

'It's all right, Alberta, I only exchanged my gold watch-chain for it. Now I'm wearing this—' Jacob pulled at his sea-man's vest '—nobody can see that I haven't got a watch chain. I'll buy a new one when I get my wages if I can get ashore somewhere. I couldn't do anything about it earlier, because Papa would have found out, you see, and you know what would have happened then.

'And you must forget about the whole thing now. I've told Mama all about it, so you won't be bothered with it. Well, good-bye, we'll have to go now – promise me you won't cry on the quay. And Alberta – Papa and Mama – they have such a rotten time.'

Alberta had been speechless for some time from suppressed tears. She gave Jacob her hand and he squeezed it so that her fingers cracked.

Jensine was standing at the front door. She dried her hands on her apron, extended one of them and said : 'Here's wishing you well, Jacob'.

And so they went.

Jacob was to travel second class. This alone was inexpressibly tragic. It so clearly marked the step he was taking out of his own environment. With his matriculation in his pocket he would without any doubt have travelled first class south to the University or the Military College, and been a gentleman. Now he was travelling second and was only an ordinary fellow. It was beyond measure distressing and pathetic. Neither Mrs Selmer nor Alberta went down below with the luggage. Papa and Jacob dived down unaccompanied, like the courageous men they were, into the murky regions of the second class. When they came up again the Magistrate declared : 'By Jove, it wasn't so bad. On the contrary, it looked quite decent down there.'

But Mrs Selmer peered anxiously after someone who straddled a coil of rope and disappeared in the same direction. He had a celluloid collar and a carpet bag made out of a blanket and was decidedly suspicious in appearance. 'God knows what sort of company you'll be thrown into, my boy,' she sighed.

'Hm,' said Jacob. 'You don't think I could have made a fool of myself and travelled first, do you? The others who go to sea often sleep on deck. I'd have preferred to do that really.'

Every now and again somebody would come on board, shake Jacob's hand, exchange a few words with him, and leave again. Some of them were old class-mates, and some of them were people with whom Alberta had no idea he was on friendly terms : young Theodorsen, Signora Ryan, Karla Schmitt. Jacob seemed to have enjoyed wide popularity. And there was Cedolf ! He stayed waiting for the boat to leave. He and Jacob exchanged a few words over the rails now and again. Mama, Papa and Alberta replied to his greeting very curtly, and then looked as far as possible in another direction.

There was Beda pushing her way over : 'Can't you get me signed on too, Jacob?' she called gaily. 'Here am I longing to get out into the world. Tell them that if they need a first class apprentice, all they have to do is send for Beda Buck. It's no joke, I mean every word of it.'

Jacob answered her in the same tone, assuring her that he would get her hired. 'Many thanks and good luck to you,' said Beda, shaking his hand like a man.

There was the little fair girl who served in Holst's. She was coming up the gangplank, probably going to say good-bye to someone. And there she suddenly was, standing in front of Jacob, very red in the face : 'I just wanted to say good-bye and wish you a good journey'. Jacob was also remarkably flushed. He bowed repeatedly : 'Thank you, that was really too kind'. The little girl from Holst's handed him a paper bag : 'Just something for the journey'. She went redder still. So did Jacob, who bowed several times more and replied : 'Thank you very much indeed, you really shouldn't have bothered'. Then the fair girl left and Jacob's colour gradually faded away.

Alberta was on tenterhooks. Whatever were Mama and Papa thinking, what would they say? But they did not refer to the occurrence – perhaps they thought it didn't matter, now that Jacob was going away. They prepared to go ashore. The terrible moment had come when Mama hugged him for the last time, released him, turned away and left, her handkerchief pressed hard to her mouth, her eyes almost closed, all her strength concentrated on holding back an eruption of pain and anguish. As if in a dream Alberta heard Papa, who seldom mentioned the name of God except to curse, say quietly and seriously to Jacob : 'God be with you, my son'. Then she felt Jacob's hands, hard and warm in hers, and she was down on the quay again. The ship put out from land.

Blind with tears she glimpsed him aft. The propeller whipped up a whirlpool of froth and bubbling water between him and the quay. It grew, became broader, was impassable. She saw him wave. She heard Papa say: 'I must go home with your mother, Alberta, she's very upset. You stay as long as you can see each other'.

Now the ship was out in the middle of the river, now it set its course westwards. Jacob was only a small, black figure waving something white.

Alberta stood until it was just a dark speck with a streamer of smoke, far out on the fjord. She turned to go home. There was no-one left on the quay besides Cedolf, sitting on a barrel, swinging his legs. When Alberta went past he lifted his cap and said: 'We'll miss Jacob. Too bad he had to leave so soon'.

Alberta did not reply.

Up on the hill the fair girl from Holst's stood staring out to sea. She suddenly started, turned and disappeared down River Street.

At home it was dismally empty. No-one in the dining-room, no-one in the sitting-rooms. In the kitchen Jensine was polishing copper, looking as if she for her part was prepared for the worst, but did not wish to express an opinion. Alberta wandered upstairs. The Magistrate's voice could be heard through a closed door, matter-of-factly explaining something. Someone was in the office. Life went on, in spite of tragedy.

She knocked hesitantly on the door of the bedroom. Nobody answered. So she went into Jacob's room.

Mama was standing at the window, her complexion blotched, swollen, unrecognisable. And at this moment Alberta longed so much for tenderness and warmth, perhaps simply for Mama, that in a kind of delirium she went across and put her arms round her, and there they stood. Mrs Selmer leaned her head against Alberta and whispered: 'We must think of him, we must be with him in our thoughts, wherever he goes. I have had to admit today that it's best for him to go away'.

She sobbed, still leaning her head against Alberta; she was clearly not herself.

But she became so, bracing herself. Everyday life took hold

again, it had to be so. She dabbed at her eyes : 'We shall have to sort the washing this afternoon. Oleanna is coming to-morrow'.

She dabbed at her eyes once more and went towards the door. Then she remembered something : 'I take it that you will do your mother the pleasure of wearing your bracelet again, my dear Alberta, now that you have it back'. Her tone was not entirely free of sarcasm : 'You are clever at hiding things from your mother. My compliments,' she said.

Alberta was crimson and tense. Her heart sank to her boots, as usual.

'I must say I am overwhelmed,' continued Mrs Selmer. 'Really, the most incredible things have been going on behind my back.' She meditated a moment, as if not entirely sure of herself. But she soon recovered. 'I must be quite a monster, if my children cannot come to me with such a matter,' she said coldly. 'And heaven knows what Dorum thinks of us,' she concluded, as she left the room.

* * *

Sunshine every day. Vigorous trickles of melted snow under the hard crust – a strong, pungent smell of wet earth and mould. The slopes and mountainsides looked like speckled cows, white and yellow-grey – and in the yellow-grey there had sprung up small living, glistening shoots, thick, and red as meat, and already bursting here and there into luminous green.

Children were carrying pussy willow and golden dandelions, playing hopscotch and pitch-and-toss round the church, where the snow always melted first. But the snow still slid off the roofs, and water trickled and flowed from Upper Town down to Lower Town, where the slush in some places reached over the tops of one's fur boots. In the Market Square last year's horse dung was revealed.

At Gronli farms the cattle lowed restlessly in their stalls, the sheep were bleating. The chickens had been let out on to the sunny slope, and all kinds of strange bird songs had woken to life. After sunset the pungent odour of the earth rose up more strongly, and at night, which was almost as light as day, the speckled mountains stood unmoving, upside-down on the fjord and the river. Above them to the west hung a delicate shimmer of light.

People became restless and swarmed out of doors, later and later in the evening. They could be seen as black silhouettes against the green evening sky, bright with spring; the hard surface of the snow crunched beneath their feet. They walked two by two, looking for solitude. Even Bergan the lawyer and the Archdeacon's Christina would meet as if quite by chance and wander out along Rivermouth, for this was the way to go in the early spring, straight into the sunset. If they met anyone, Christina would shrink and almost disappear from coquettish modesty, but Bergan would look just the same. They were being talked about – to be sure people were talking.

Harriet met Dr Mo at Louisa-round-the-bend, and Dr Mo turned and walked out of town again with Harriet. She did not shrink in the least, but said good-day loudly and with a smile, as usual, and if anyone looked as if caught red-handed it was Dr Mo.

Gudrun accompanied her brothers, the Archdeacon's Henrik, and the chemists from the 'Polar Bear'. She admitted openly that she hooked on to anybody to avoid the company of Stensett the schoolmaster. She would stop people and ask them : 'Have you noticed whether Stensett has been this way, for if so I'll turn back at once'.

Beda walked with each and everyone. And she still skied to Gronli farms on the snow-crust that formed in the evenings, although the stone walls had reappeared a long time ago and on all the southern slopes you had to take off your skis and carry them. One evening when Alberta was wandering across the bog she saw Lett the dentist lifting Beda over a fence. He held her up against him for a moment before putting her down again. They disappeared into Peter's wood.

Alberta walked with no-one. This was in the nature of things, and Alberta's fate. With whom should she walk? Now and again she would meet the Chief Clerk, who also walked by himself, and this seemed equally natural whatever the reason. They would greet each other guiltily and continue their separate ways. Alberta blushed as usual when she was confronted in broad daylight, and wished that the Clerk would choose another way.

There was one person she would not meet under any circumstances, someone she took devious routes to avoid; whom she hid from, turned her back on and ran away from if there was no other way out : Cedolf.

If only he would go away. What was he doing at home all the time? Wasn't he going to sign on again, go away to the navigation school, to Canada, to Timbuktu?

She would not think about Cedolf. She loathed him. He was horrid. But she could not rid herself of the memory of his arm round her, of the new, strange feeling it had given her. If she had to pass him she trembled and turned crimson, and she saw Cedolf's mouth curl up as he greeted her.

She walked along the ice-crusted roads composing verses. It was a stupid weakness of hers, and it got worse at this time of year. The poems were about the mountains, the spring and yearning, the scent of the earth and the new moon, and came to her idly and easily out of the yellow-green air. So idly and easily that Alberta looked on them with suspicion and did not always grant them admission to the book under the woollen vests.

She found the first small leaf of lady's mantle with a dew-drop in it, heard a new bird song, and was intoxicated by such obvious trifles. But she took care not to mention them to anybody. The sunset, yes – but a leaf of lady's mantle ! It would show lack of judgment and a rather simple turn of mind, another defect to add to all the others. Mrs Selmer would call it affectation.

Uneasily Alberta noted how little she thought about Jacob. She had imagined she would be tormented with loss night and day, that she would never have a moment's peace. But now it all sank back into her consciousness, disappearing for long stretches of time, and then reappearing in the guise of a guilty conscience.

At home Mama stood in front of the window looking at the pale sky behind the dark roofs, and said : 'Heavens, summer is on its way again'. She sighed and drew her shawl round her : 'I'm so tired of being cold, Alberta, and of being lonely. But that's my lot in life I suppose'.

Alberta did not know what to say. She wondered whether she should embrace Mama, but was afraid that perhaps it would be the wrong thing to do. For the sake of propriety she stayed in the room for a while, and then went upstairs and sat looking at the river and the mountains. And she declaimed to herself verses by the Norwegian poets, taken from the selection in the bookcases downstairs, until she was warm and had a different face, one that she discovered with astonishment in the mirror. A face she did not recognise, a face that was more than plain.

*   *   *

It was summer in the south, said the newspaper. Mrs Selmer read out loud the number of degrees they had in the shade. She went across to the window, driving with wet and spattered with sleet, and dabbed at her eyes. The Magistrate remained seated, muttering irritably that well, in heaven's name, we must make some allowance for the latitude. 'Things are comparatively early this year,' he continued. 'I heard the Headmaster say that the Archdeacon's Henrik is supposed to have found a saxifrage. If we get a little sun things will come along quickly.'

Mrs Selmer shrugged her shoulders without replying.

Outside the turf roof on Flemming's barn was greening, and so was Peter on the Hill's slice of ground that was visible between the houses. In the Sisters Kremer's window the first straw hats were displayed on stands, and the Lapps had arrived at Badendück's quay. They lived down there under the piles of planks and strolled in the streets, hugging themselves in their reindeer skin jackets, their hands stuck into the arms as if into a muff. The street music had arrived too, five Germans blue with cold, wearing woollen scarves round their necks. They stood on the pavement surrounded by a faithful public of boys and Lapps, an infallible sign of summer.

But on the north side of the houses there still lay hard, grey patches of snow. And the south-wester hurled itself violently between the wharves, carrying the Germans' brassy notes in disconnected blasts across the town.

Alberta froze in body and soul. She struggled desperately with her umbrella when she was out on expeditions to the post office, but to no avail; the Magistrate's official documents got damp and sticky. Each time he objected afresh that there was absolutely nothing to be gained by fetching the post. It was much better to let Larsen bring it, as he should, then it would arrive dry and in proper condition. He would thank her not to do it any more, he had said so many times, but by God, you could evidently talk yourself blue in the face where some things were concerned. Could not Alberta, grown girl as she was, understand this clearly once and for all?

Alberta promised that of course she could, and next time the weather was bad the same thing happened, although she hid the big envelopes under her jacket. There was always a corner that stuck out and got wet. It was not easy to please everyone. Alberta was grateful to Papa for not flying into a rage about it. He had some patience, in spite of his hot temper.

Jacob's letters had arrived as they should, one from Bergen, one from Flekkefjord, one from Liverpool. They did not contain much except that Jacob was quite well. 'There's so much on my mind that I would like to have known about,' complained Mrs Selmer as she folded them up again.

'The important thing is that the boy is well and happy,' said the Magistrate. – Now it was the bad period when nothing would be heard of Jacob for a long, long time – when anything could be expected, anything imagined. Mrs Selmer sighed frequently and heavily, and Alberta felt more guilty than ever because she was as she was, adding to Mama's burdens. One of the greatest burdens was that Alberta never willingly accompanied her to church.

Mrs Selmer went every Sunday now. Previously she had

gone every other Sunday. It was no small sorrow to her that the Magistrate never set foot in the place, and that it was so difficult to get Alberta to go. Alberta employed the utmost cunning to avoid it: she was not ready dressed, had a pain in her stomach, a headache, had lost a button at the last minute. Mrs Selmer had to give up and leave, with pinched mouth and tragic eyes.

For Alberta could not stand going to church. She did not like it when Beda mocked the sacrament, sharing out cake at tea-time and saying, 'Take, eat, this is my body'. It offended something traditional in her and seemed to her unnecessary and vulgar. But she froze at the thought of going to church, being unmoved by it and thoroughly bored.

Before her confirmation she had honestly tried to get to grips with it and understand it all. Two afternoons a week throughout the winter her eyes had hung on Pastor Pio's thick lips, and she had listened intently to his slow, monotonous, slightly bleating voice, talking about sin and grace, perdition and rebirth in Christ. The class was held in the old girls' school, in a low-ceilinged room, where the air became thick and heavy from the smoking lamps and the breath of many people. After a while the voice seemed to be issuing from a cloud. However tensely Alberta listened, to her they were merely words, empty meaningless words. She would lose the thread for long periods at a time, and find her attention caught by something worldly: the velvet ribbon, for instance, that Signora Ryan never managed to tie tightly enough in her shock of hair, and with which she incessantly fiddled.

She received the sacrament and experienced nothing. Over at the other side of the curved altar rail she had caught sight of that nice girl, Ellen Ovre, who was now training to be a deaconess, her face tilted upwards, a remote expression in her eyes, completely ecstatic. Alberta had felt a prick of envy and inferiority. But just before the chalice came to her, Fina Zakariassen, who had a cold, snuffled lengthily and emphatically over it. Although Pastor Pio turned it a little and dried the rim with a napkin, Alberta was unable to think about

anything in the great moment besides putting her lips elsewhere than Fina's.

Then confirmation class was over and it all slid backwards
in her consciousness, to become something over which she
had exerted herself to no purpose.

Alberta found moral support in Papa. He might lapse and
say : 'If it means so much to your mother, surely you might – ',
but that was as far as it went. And after all, he never went to
church himself. He had never been. There had been times in
Alberta's life when she was ashamed that Papa was not to be
found in the front row in the chancel on Sundays, beside Dr
Pram, the Governor, the Chief of Police, and all the other
regular churchgoers. She had prayed for him at night, that
he might be converted and become like them. But it was no
use, and she gradually forgot about it.

An occasional Sunday would come along, however, when
it was impossible to get out of it. Pressure of opinion, unfortunate circumstances, made it unavoidable. Then Alberta
would sit as if on tenterhooks on the little bench facing the
congregation where Mrs Selmer had selected for herself a
permanent seat. The voice of the preacher above their heads
rose and fell. Each time it fell Alberta hoped it would be for
good. But no, it rose again in new, monotonous, incomprehensible turns of phrase, speaking of sin and guilt, grace and
hard-won redemption, words that gave her the same feeling
of pressure on her breast as Miss Myre had given her, as Nurse
Jullum and all the married ladies gave her. In church Alberta
longed more than ever for Papa's god, who only filled up empty
space and was content with mere existence; who left people
alone and pursued no-one, either with punishment or love.

If it was the Archdeacon, she would listen to him for a
while. He had such a kind face and talked in his natural
speaking voice. There was something simple and trustworthy
about him that made her think he wouldn't bother with it if it
were nonsense. Her old wish to understand was aroused. But
she discovered that ultimately it concerned all the same incomprehensible things; her mind became dulled, she lost the

thread and failed to find it again. Or she got a frog in her throat so that she had to swallow repeatedly; or her leg went to sleep, or she fidgeted, and Mrs Selmer would whisper despairingly: 'Sit still!'

When finally the sigh of relief that meant it was over went through the church, and the congregation rose for the blessing, Alberta was numb in body and soul, unable to feel her legs beneath her or to register any more impressions.

Sometimes the hymn could have a strangely liberating effect. One was borne aloft on the crest of a wave and glided out into quiet depths of peace and harmony: 'Praise to the Lord, the Almighty . . .'. But the long hymns with countless verses, harsh melodies and old-fashioned turns of phrase, with their talk of the pains of hell, the slough of evil, slaughter, blood and wounds, resembled a heavy, suffocating morass that had to be crossed. Pastor Pio had a deplorable weakness for them.

On the way home from church Alberta was still numb. She would hear the ladies discussing the sermon, hear Harriet and Christina take part in the conversation, expressing their opinions, praising, criticising.

She felt depraved, an outcast, because she had no opinion, except that it was all vastly boring.

One day the post really did bring something. A letter, surprisingly hard and thick, from Aunt the Colonel. Mrs Selmer seized it with anxious hands. The thick hard object was a photograph of cousin Lydia, in ball dress, with a fan, and flowers on her shoulder and in her hair. And her hair was above reproach, waved, and as well fashioned as if it were moulded round her face. An unspoken reprimand.

It was a three-quarter-length picture. Lydia was standing in half profile holding the fan in front of her, with a little world-weary, disappointed smile at the corners of her mouth, which looked as old and experienced as those of the wives, thought Alberta.

But Mrs Selmer declared that Lydia had really turned out very pretty, and that she looked so ladylike. Mrs Selmer sighed and concentrated upon the letter. After a moment she put it down again. She had to collect herself. Cousin Lydia was engaged.

. . . Quite splendidly engaged to an unusually promising young man of particularly good family. He was at the Legation in London, his connections and fortune provided him with the best of prospects. Neither Aunt nor Uncle could have desired a more attractive son-in-law. They had to face the fact that they would have to part with Lydia sooner or later. Now they thanked God for putting so noble and sympathetic a young man in her path. It was sad that she would have to go so far away, but she herself was radiantly happy.

Mrs Selmer again put the letter down. When she picked it up again and read on, her tone changed. It said that Uncle would like Lydia to see something of her own country before leaving it for what might be a number of years. So she and Aunt would probably be coming north this summer. They intended going as far as the North Cape, and it seemed to be a good opportunity for visiting their relatives for a few days. However thin blood might be, it was always thicker than water, wrote Aunt jokingly. Which gave Mrs Selmer occasion to remark that it was not as thin as all that, since Papa and Uncle the Colonel were brothers. 'But Aunt has the habit of saying things that are not very amusing,' she added, sitting with the letter in her hand, musing. 'That was a great deal all at once,' she remarked, giving Alberta to understand that she was not altogether delighted, that she was, in fact, not really delighted at all.

The first cruise ship of the year was anchored at Rivermouth. Small groups of foreign-looking people speaking English were in the streets dressed for rain and carrying umbrellas, looking cold and at a loss. Boys from the alleys gathered and followed at their heels. Forward souls accosted them and offered to show them the way to Badendück's quay, where the Lapps were. But P.C. Olsen was on his rounds and, when the occasion demanded, ordering : 'Get along home with you, lads – break it up'.

All along the street the small signs with 'English spoken', *'Man spricht Deutsch'*, had been hung out, along with the reindeer, seal and polar-bear skins. And even the Sisters Kremer had Lapp dolls, horn spoons and reindeer slippers thrust among the hats and the bridal and funeral trimmings.

* * *

It was summer, brand new, brought to maturity in a couple of short days. The greenness was immoderately green. It climbed upwards between the mountains' violet screes, was mirrored in the river, making it deep and unfathomable, covered all the slopes up to where the uncultivated land took over with heather and dwarf birch, providing a new, festive backdrop to life. The mountain range to the east hovered blue above all the green, eternal snow in its lap.

A hubbub of cheerful sounds rose up under the tall sky. They were hammering in the shipyard so that the world rang with the sound; they were hammering on board the ships, and singing, slapping their paint brushes, swinging their buckets. An exhilarating smell of tar and paint rose up from the harbour, awakening a desire to travel and thoughts of long journeys.

The planks of the wharves lay bare in the sun, steaming warm, wonderfully easy to walk on. But the last invincible grey snow patches hid away, dirty and sad, in the shade to the north.

The wind was in the east, bringing with it the rushing of the cataracts, a deep, churning hum that made one weak with longing and giddy with unrest. But if it shifted the slightest degree to the west, the smoke from young Klykken's cod-liver-oil factory hung greasy and oppressive above the town. The ladies held their handkerchiefs to their noses, and all flights of fancy were extinguished.

The rowan in shoemaker Schoning's yard, the only rowan in the district that had managed to grow to any height, tossed like a rich green plume above the shoemaker's roof and brought all kinds of colour to life round it. The houses were no longer grey, but red and yellow. The church tower was hung with ochre.

Along the brooks and rills there suddenly appeared luxuriant tussocks of kingcups, their stalks bursting with sap, golden yellow and shining against the black-brown peat. The cowparsnip had come up, heaven knows when; it was already tropical, heavy and swaying. The ditches were shaggy with lady's mantle and wild chervil. The Archdeacon's Henrik came home with the first *viola biflora* and laid it to rest in his herbarium.

People were moving up to their summer cottages. Harriet and Christina painstakingly carried glassware and other frail objects up the hillside. Palmine Flor and Lilly Vogel did likewise, not to be outdone by their betters. Young Mrs Klykken worked in gloves, setting shells in place, planting and sowing, while the silver ball in the centre bed mirrored it all.

Windows stood open everywhere. Curtains were carried inwards by the breeze, the hammer blows from the shipyard were echoed in the rooms. When they ceased, the cataracts roared evenly, now closer, now further away. The scents of tar, cod-liver-oil and sea shifted with the wind.

The supper table underwent a metamorphosis. Smoked salmon and gulls' eggs appeared and detracted from the clove cheese. Mrs Selmer's voice echoed with renewed energy through the sitting-rooms : 'Then I took up the paladin's cap all trimmed with gold and brocade . . . The knight he followed after me with a falcon on his arm'.

Alberta wore cotton dresses, and had new hands and a new face. She went along the back streets, to be sure, but it was summer in the back streets too, with grass in the gutters, warm sun on the grey walls, open windows, light-coloured blouses, the buzz of flies.

And she not only went along the back streets. She went across the bog, past Gronli farms, inland to where the mountains began. Bog-cotton and cloudberry blossom swayed in the wind amongst the heather and dwarf birch. The pale scrubberry flowers formed a thick carpet, alternating with delicate bracken and white lichen. Strange bird cries could be heard above the small lakes and deep bog pools that reflected rich, dark peat and sailing clouds.

Alberta lay down in the heather and plunged into dreams and unreality, while she half-mechanically arranged a posy of bell-heather and small, smooth birch twigs. She got up feeling giddy, as if she had been away for a long time. One day she saw blue smoke coiling above the slopes to the west. The Lapps had come to their camp at Big Gap.

In the evening she would lean out of her window, listening to the dip of oars and the music of accordions, her eyes following the eddies of the river until late into the night. For the days were succeeded by unreal, shining nights, when everything was dissolved into golden light and long, violet shadows, when the fjord lay like a bright, straining silken sail and the current moved like dimples in the deep green surface at Rivermouth. And a light-hearted summer night's mood full of music and laughter lay over the landscape – a mood that lived and died with the airborne blue smoke from many picnic fires along the shore and up the mountainsides. It was young Theodorsen and his crowd, Beda with her beaux, Mrs Buck and her circle. Cedolf too, who rowed past in his freshly-painted boat, probably going to fetch someone. He stopped rowing with one hand and raised it to his cap. Alberta pretended not to notice.

Sometimes she was still there at the window when the boats came home in the early hours of the morning with gold in their wake and accordions in the prow. She heard the steps of people returning home echoing clearly through the streets. Did she wish she were with them? Yes and no. Perhaps if everything, if she herself, were different.

The air was so warm and mild. Night and morning she would undress completely and see her body once again in the looking-glass. For in the small pieces of mirror at the bathhouse you could see nothing. And something happened from year to year. A little embarrassed and alarmed, a little ashamed and proud, Alberta stood and took in the fact that in spite of her lean, lithe figure she was a child no longer.

Every boat from the south brought new people. They strolled in the streets and walked differently from the people at home, looking secure and self-assured.

There was Augusta Bremer, who was studying medicine, was fabulously clever, and got distinction in all her examinations.

There was Peter Bloch, with whom Alberta had once been in love. Every year she wondered a little whether she would fall in love with him again. But Peter's face was just as odd this year as it had been last, in a straw hat as in a bowler, the features seemingly much too large. There could be no question of falling in love with him any more, and a good thing too.

There was the dentist's son Rasmus, and Peter on the Hill's daughter Matilda, who was something mysterious in Hamburg and who came home every year and horrified the town with her painted face, incredible waist and incredible bosom.

There was the Russian consul from the east, a short, lively, dark gentleman with olive skin. He spoke in broken Norwegian, paid formal visits on officialdom during the day, and at night went out to enjoy himself with Mrs Buck and her circle.

There were the new organist and important folk from the cathedral city, the Bishop and the Diocesan Governor. One party to entertain the gentlemen succeeded another. Madam Svendsen soon could not stand on her legs. Certain faces were redder than usual from too much festivity. And soon the most singular, the most exciting of all were expected: Rikke and Gertrude Lossius, with a cousin from Kristiania who was to spend the summer at the Governor's residence, and whom the Governor's lady referred to as Frederick.

Mrs Selmer stood at the window at midday, lifted the curtain and said: 'I thought I might catch sight of Gertrude and Rikke – they're bound to be out at this time'.

And she was quite right, there they were coming down

the street, even more marvellous than when they came home last year, in clothes beyond one's wildest dreams – the kind of clothes in which you could become a different person, thought Alberta. That was probably why they walked with more self-assurance than anyone else. Between them was their cousin, a tall, fair person with pince-nez, swinging a cane. He looked up and down the walls of the houses, adjusted his pince-nez, and wore a satirical expression. Alberta saw immediately that he was a person to be afraid of, and that he would make the streets terribly unsafe.

'Put on your jacket and run down to talk to them, Alberta,' said Mrs Selmer.

But Alberta had already disappeared in the greatest haste, and had locked herself in a certain place. She had suspected Mama would suggest something of the sort. But to go to meet them, to go entirely on her own initiative and address the person in pince-nez – most decidedly no! It was bad enough having to put up with so much else that was unavoidable, without rushing into misfortune.

Rikke Lossius pottered about in a painter's smock, humming. She had acquired a new way of looking at people – with her head on one side and her eyes narrowed. She was also very much changed in appearance, even more so than last year. Painted canvases lay scattered about her room on chairs and tables. The sofa was covered with them. They had a tendency to roll themselves up again, and they depicted women so naked that Alberta had never imagined anyone could look as intensely naked as they did. There was a man in bathing-trunks too.

Alberta sat on a chair in the midst of it all and looked about her with consternation. The same sight met her eyes wherever she looked: distressing apparitions in a kind of inert, resigned at-ease position, with their breasts in, their stomachs out, shoulders drooping, and equipped with such strongly emphasized details that she could scarcely believe her own eyes. Instead of feet and hands they had things resembling mittens and bathing shoes. The faces were mere blots.

So this is art, she thought in confusion, knowing only that she would defend it, if only in silence, on the principle that whatever scandalized the ladies must surely be of some value. She was sincerely grateful for the man's bathing-trunks. She had not dabbled about in boats all her childhood, not played about on the wharves and in the warehouses, without acquiring ugly memories that had stuck to her mind like revolting slime, memories that perhaps she would never shake off. Thank God for the bathing-trunks.

Rikke gestured with her cigarette towards her *oeuvre:* 'I've captured something of the movement in that one,' she said. 'There's something about the colour that's not at all bad. And this arm – when Ola Moklebust saw it, he said anyone could see that I *had* to paint, that I simply couldn't *help* it.'

'Who is Ola Moklebust?'

'My dear, don't you know? He's one of our very best young artists and an absolute pet. We've been spending quite a lot of time together.

'But you see, it's so hopeless up here,' she continued. 'People don't understand a thing. They're just shocked, as if it were pornography, which it certainly isn't, for heaven's sake. But I suppose this summer will pass too. Then I must see if I can get to Paris in the autumn – you know, Mama and Papa find it rather difficult to understand why *that* should be necessary. All the art school gang are going, and lot of other amusing people besides.'

'And Moklebust?'

'Oh yes, and Ola Moklebust. Yes, I *am* in love with him, there's nothing to be done about *that*. He *is* so delicious, and if I can't go I don't know what I shall do. I'll be absolutely furious with Mama and Papa.

'Yes, I suppose this summer will pass too,' repeated Rikke, as if implying that she had been through so much already, a little more or less would make no difference. She went backwards and forwards, moving canvases to give them a better light, and humming the stanza that she had been humming ever since she came home : 'Never look ba-a-ack to the time that is gone and the summer's withered flowers, but hope that the re-e-eddest roses may bloom once again in next midsummer's bowers. *I* hope they'll bloom in the winter, I'm so insane,' she declared, lighting another cigarette and extinguishing the match with an accustomed little flick of her hand.

From up in Gertrude's room came the sound of practising, scales up and scales down, resolute blows on the piano and valiant little trills. She had the piano up in her room out of consideration for the office. Now and again the practising would glide over into a quiet melody, and then Rikke would sometimes put her head on one side and say : 'Gertrude does play that beautifully, I must say. I heard Careno play it this spring – he wasn't at all impressive.'

The piano fell silent and Gertrude came into the room, good-looking, elegant and superior. She might stop and point at a study : 'That's delicious, Rikke'. Or she might stand at the window, look down into the street, and say : 'Who's that going by, isn't it little Harriet? What if I stole that Dr Mo of hers, and made a bit of mischief in this town? For we really must find something to do . . .'

One day when she was standing at the window she put her arm akimbo, drew herself up and asked : 'Now who's that handsome lad?'

'He's a sailor – I think he's called Kjeldsen,' answered Alberta, feeling false and villainous.

'My word, he's handsome.' Gertrude yawned. 'If I lived at home I think I'd make a set at *him*.' She yawned once more, and went.

'That's all right, as long as she doesn't make a set at Moklebust,' sighed Rikke. 'When Gertrude makes up her mind she's going to make someone fall in love with her, she can be so terribly attractive that I might as well pack up and go. And I'd even be happy if something could make her forget that man of hers. Oh yes, there's a man who wants to divorce his wife because of her, he has children too. It would be a catastrophe for Mama and Papa of course. I'm scared to death in case they see the letters. As if things weren't complicated enough as they are.'

AND JACOB

And she confided to Alberta that Gertrude was having a
difficult time because of her opinions : 'Of course Papa and
Mama are old-fashioned, you know, and Gertrude is terribly
modern and so frantically impulsive, she's incapable of compromising and being a little cautious. We're on tenterhooks,
Frederick and I. But just imagine, Gertrude has rejected seven
proposals already – seven! And I've had none. I think it's
about time someone made me a proposal too.'

Gertrude and Rikke were so secure, taking everything for
granted, moving through life like fish in their element, certain of being the first, the prettiest, the cleverest. They would
not tolerate contradiction – like Mrs Lossius their voices
quickly became ·a little curt and peremptory; but they were
kind and good-natured, generous with gifts and in giving
whatever help they could. Perhaps they appreciated Alberta
because she was so silent. Like a sieve, she drank it all in and
was never satiated.

Sometimes Frederick would come striding across the threshold with his pipe. Most of the time he sat writing. He was a
kind of author, this terrible Frederick with the pince-nez.

'Talented stuff, you know,' said Rikke. 'Quite remarkable
things. They'll cause an enormous sensation when they come
out.'

He would bow to Alberta and, fortunately, pay her no
further attention. She was afraid of him, in fact she was a
little afraid of all three of them. They lived on a higher plane,
they were so superior, knew so much about the outside world,
knew it in a different way than Christina and Gudrun, for
instance, who had not been born up here either. They were
purposeful and knew what they wanted. They subscribed to
the luxury of suffering for their opinions.

Frederick and the Governor's daughters confused her,
filling her with a new unrest and a longing for knowledge.
She had been looking for different books in the bookcase since
they arrived.

* * *

The cataracts churned evenly in the golden nights. Blue smoke spiralled lightly up above the dwarf birch trees from the many hearths and bonfires on mountainside and shingle, a pleasant smell of burnt twigs floated on the breeze. Boats with gold in their wake and accordions in the prow, oars at rest, rocked with the current all night long; the sound of voices and creaking rowlocks was carried right across from the other side of the fjord in the stillness.

The whole world was obsessed by the incessant light. Even the powers-that-be and the Church were to be found in the small hours, lying propped up on their elbows somewhere in the heather beside a dying fire, their eyes turned towards the unswerving sun.

No-one could equal Mrs Pram in her ability to take charge of a picnic. She was the one to decide who should be invited, who remembered that Miss Liberg and the Weyers were to bring the coffee kettle and a tablecloth. And she brought the most delicious sandwiches and even waffles as well. She was famous for her powers of organization. But when her health was drunk, she would point proudly at her daughters: 'I have such splendid helpers'. And Gudrun would raise her glass to thank everyone: 'The ones with egg and anchovy are my handiwork'.

Nevertheless the atmosphere among the ladies was not quite as it should be this year, and the reason was the Governor's family. Take Rikke, for instance. She went round with a sketch book all the time, except when she had her painting equipment with her. She would sit to one side on a stone, narrowing her eyes and holding her pencil out in front of her at arm's length, and would be occupied thus for hours. Between themselves the ladies considered that there was too much of it, and that it was poor manners. 'My dear, she surely has time to talk to the rest of us a *little*,' they would murmur, and agree that such behaviour went too far. They discussed her art in whispers: 'Have you seen it? Yes, isn't it fearful? Quite indecent if you ask me. – But it's supposed to be Art,' they concluded, as if repudiating all responsibility.

Then there was that fellow Frederick. He was polite and

handsome enough, in all conscience, but he was not a congenial young man. The ladies agreed that he looked critical, and that it would be just as pleasant if he were not included. He had the embarrassing habit of not laughing at young Klykken's stories. Young Klykken was really quite amusing, after all. If Frederick laughed, he did so some time afterwards, seemingly on his own account. But then he was probably so much more amusing himself.

Mrs Lossius was fractious, and as usual took it out a little on the others. Her voice would turn cold and discouraging, so that whoever she was talking to felt almost incriminated. Their agreement was tinged with self-defence. It was an honour, but not an entirely agreeable one, to be numbered amongst her intimates, as she sat in the heather, tapping her lorgnette nervously against her left hand, repeatedly returning to the same subject: 'You see, last year Rikke drew from plaster-casts. That was interesting. They were really beautiful things, it was a pleasure to frame them and hang them on the wall; figures from the Parthenon frieze for instance. But these *frightful* nudes'. Mrs Lossius had to be honest, she did not *understand* why it should be necessary to create ugliness when one's aim was beauty. She herself used to draw and paint in her young days, so she ought to understand a *little,* but she supposed it was true that she understood nothing. She pursed her lips together tightly.

Where Gertrude was concerned, she was such a good pianist, so thoroughly musical, that it was a pleasure to listen to her. But in other respects she had by no means profited by the winter. Mrs Lossius had observed many sorts of influence. It was not altogether easy when one's daughters were *too* gifted, it really wasn't. Mrs Lossius nodded in the direction of Harriet, who, well brought up and virtuous, was busy with the coffee kettle. 'You can be glad, Mrs Pram, that your daughters are not gifted in any particular direction.'

Harriet was appreciated as never before, by her mother and by everyone else. A sweet girl, they would echo after her, wherever she passed. Now and again a discreet conjecture was aired: 'I suppose we shall be hearing some news soon?'

For Dr Mo was equally helpful on every occasion with branches for the fire. He assured everybody who would lend him an ear, that he thought a fire out of doors was so exceptionally pleasant.

Alberta would lie on her elbow in the heather, listening now to one group, now to another. She selected her place round the cloth with care, preferably a little behind Mrs Selmer so as not to offend her gaze unnecessarily, taking care to turn to the assembled company the profile in which her squint was least noticeable. Gertrude and Rikke would sometimes pay attention to her and make her sit with them. Then she would listen to their easy, self-assured chatter about art, music, people and conditions in Kristiania with an agonizing mixture of bitterness, excited interest, and anxiety in case they addressed her directly. Frederick also played. Gertrude and he would hum together and nod in rhythm. They used expressions seldom heard in conversation in the town; quoted authors who appeared to be turning the rest of the world upside down, while everybody went about their business up here quite unsuspecting; reminded each other of discussions in the Students' Union; broached subjects that were only mentioned in a whisper with embarrassed sidelong glances here at home. Gertrude talked about everything in the same easy, rounded tone of voice that seemed to touch on the subject from above; her eyes would look far beyond the present topic of discussion. But she was often curt and spoke a little too loudly; her voice would become high-pitched and she would stir her cup of coffee nervously. Sometimes she did not even reply, but would suddenly hum loudly and fall into a state of anxiety. Then Frederick would look at her craftily with a sidelong glance and call her his dearest coz, as he lay tapping his cane against his leg. Rikke would become uneasy and murmur, 'Frederick!' When it was over all three made fun of everything in complete understanding and in an especially knowing way; when, for example, the Archdeacon's wife, full of goodwill, her eyes crystal-clear, went round pouring out rhubarb wine, and Frederick murmured behind her back: 'And behold, she is without sin'.

At times something would erupt in Alberta, an unaccustomed feeling of solidarity with the town's permanent inhabitants. Here one lived outside the world and acted accordingly. What business was it of these travellers from Kristiania? Just because some people had crawled up to a position where they could get a better view, they didn't have to . . . Then the hunger gripped her again, hunger to reach the view-point and see for herself.

One morning she was going home from a picnic with Mama through the silent, sunlit streets of Upper Town, where smoke was already coiling upwards from a few chimneys. They were without masculine protection. Papa and the Chief Clerk were on circuit again.

They met Kjeldsen the smith's cow on its way to pasture. It had a reputation for butting and wore protectors on its horns. Mrs Selmer retreated hastily into a doorway, while Alberta, as a representative of the younger generation, better equipped for struggle, nervously attempted to change the animal's course. Meanwhile Cedolf appeared. He arrived on the scene looking rested and brown, puffing at his pipe and whistling. 'Don't you be afraid,' he called obligingly. 'I'll hold her, please to come by. Is that your Mama over there?'

Cedolf seized the cow by the horns, leaping and tumbling with it, as resilient as a toreador, and lost his cap. Perhaps he leaped and turned a little more than was strictly necessary, perhaps he panted a little too hard, when they escaped past and he still stood holding the dangerous creature. But he was their rescuer and had the right to be treated accordingly.

'Thank you,' said Mrs Selmer coldly, 'Thank you, Kjeldsen,' walking on fast. Alberta accompanied her, her face crimson.

'How annoying to have to thank that fellow Cedolf for anything,' commented Mrs Selmer. 'But goodness knows what would have happened if he hadn't turned up. Cows are such fearful creatures.'

Alberta thought more than she wished about Cedolf's smiling, warm face beneath the untidy dark lock of hair. It remained in her brain as if photographed there. More than usual she felt as if it had been imposed upon her, a violation and an outrage.

It was the day of the picnic to Big Gap, the event of the summer. The elderly took carrioles or traps as far as was possible, and the provisions were transported on horseback over the last part of the way, across the plateau.

They had pitched camp in the middle of the Gap on the slope towards the sea. Everything was bathed in golden light and violet shadow. A reddish, fairy-tale sun hung low over the horizon, and the sea resembled an immense, brimming bowl of molten metal with a glowing sword plunged into it. A row of porpoises moved along the shoreline, leaving the sea swirling in their wake. Coalfish leapt, gulls circled, birds twittered in the heather, there was a pleasant smell of smoke from the dying fire. Like an enormous respiration the breakers rolled in towards the stones along the shore.

Alberta supported herself on her elbow a little behind Mrs Selmer and Mrs Pram, who were discussing the Bucks. The blue smoke rising from behind some large boulders further down was said to belong to Mrs Buck and the Russian consul. He was on his way through town again. Some other ladies were supposed to be with them. On the other hand Beda was here. What might that mean?

A little further off Harriet was taking advantage of the chance absence of Dr Mo to explain to Christina how the rumours of his affair with Palmine Flor had come about last winter. Disgraceful slander. Palmine had asked him to accompany her past some drunk Russians who were hanging about in the bend below the Flors' summer cottage, and he had done so, gentleman as he was. 'But you see how people are, vulgar and cheap.'

'Yes, indeed they are,' agreed Christina.

A little puff of wind went through the grass blades among which Alberta was lying. It seemed to waken something in her, to bring the loathing and longing with it. She suddenly got up and walked a little, pretending to pick heather. Then she sat down again a short distance behind Gertrude and Frederick, who were lying a little to one side with their backs to the company, looking out at the sea and talking in subdued voices. Rikke sat near them, sketching. Perhaps they would notice Alberta and ask her over. At intervals, when they raised their voices, she could hear their conversation.

They were again talking about things that were never discussed in the town, except perhaps occasionally by the gentlemen. 'I don't believe in *re*volution, I believe in *e*volution,' said Gertrude, stirring her coffee violently.

'Surely we all believe in *e*volution,' smiled Frederick. 'Each one of us believes we shall evolve splendidly according to his own recipe. I except those thrifty souls who believe in keeping themselves and theirs safe behind the assurance that there is no progress, that humanity is and always will be the same – but the others! Ask Pastor Pio over there, he'll tell you.'

But Gertrude took after Mrs Lossius, she disliked being contradicted. And she especially disliked her opinions to be the property of everyman, shared by clergymen. She became anxious and hummed.

'Oh, that's enough,' called Rikke, slamming her sketch book shut. '*E*volution and *re*volution. Look round you instead. When something as lovely as colour exists—'

'And Ola Moklebust,' said Frederick.

'Heavens, yes,' cried Rikke. 'I *am* in love with silly old Moklebust, but now I'm forgetting him a bit for the sake of all this.' She flung her arms wide. 'It's exquisite. A little too much Thorolf Holmboe perhaps, but lovely all the same.'

'Wonderful. And you know, Rikke, when the ladies put their heads askew and ask me if it isn't magnificent here, I always reply that it's unique. But I often think how it must look when the storms and the winter darkness set in, and they no longer have this blessed midnight sun as decoration. I'll wager it looks like what it is then – a place of exile.'

'The point is not to be here then.'

'I grant you that. But still I'm sorry for these people. There's something tragic about many of them, something has-been and coagulated. Take their hysterical emphasis of the bright side, there's something embarrassing about it, as if they were trying to hypnotize themselves. These old gentlemen, for instance – it's obvious that the majority of them live on memories and card-playing and alcohol, a little too much alcohol, and it's only human. What have they got besides their toddy? Politics, a little moaning about the lopsided way of the world – oh yes, the Chief Constable is a philatelist, I've heard—

'But any one of us may end up the same way, we who live down south thinking we're going to conquer the world. We may find ourselves sitting up here instead, thickening inside and out. Just imagine, some of them can't afford to apply for positions in the south again on account of the move. Like this Selmer, the Magistrate. I was talking to him the other day and he told me straight out, I can't afford to apply for anything in the south. He hasn't been down there for thirteen years. And then he was in Flekkefjord. Incidentally, he was a fellow student of Uncle Hans in Kristiania. You'd never think so, he looks at least ten years older. He's supposed to have been a very promising jurist once, and what is he now – fat, old before his time, and slightly alcoholic, as far as I can see – it's distressing.'

Alberta's heart had stopped, she was completely tense. Now she could hear every word they said, either because her hearing had become more acute or the breeze carried more to her. She tried to get up and go, but could not even move her head in another direction in order to look interested in something else. She sat there paralysed, like a chicken behind a chalk mark.

'Good Lord, they don't think it's too bad,' said Rikke. 'Many of them have no sooner left than they're homesick.'

'Yes, I suppose they get a sort of exile's mentality in the end, feel like strangers when they return to the world, and that they fit in best in their place of exile. That's what I call coagulation. No, to survive a number of years up here one would have to be either a very simple soul or richly endowed. The average person must find it soul-destroying. The Recorder seems to have his wits about him, by the way, he appreciates art among other things. But possibly he's one of the richly endowed, for all I know. In any case, he was born here in Finnmark.'

'He doesn't understand a thing about modern art, let me tell you. But I think they're rather touching, these old people. They *are* old, after all, and can't help but stay up here.'

'Touching, yes indeed. Good Lord, when they say to me with such happiness in their eyes : We've been brought so close to the world since we got the packet boat, you know, only two and a half days to Trondhjem – I'm touched every time. "Fear God and be content . . ." There's something so incredibly childish and undeveloped about some of them that they give the impression of being crippled and stunted. It can't be natural for young girls to be so desperately awkward and embarrassed as some of these are. This Christina – the Archdeacon's Christina – she squirms like a snake if she has to say yes or no, and Alberta Selmer breaks all records, she doesn't even say as much as that.'

'Yes, they are awkward and strange,' replied Rikke.

Alberta had felt her features harden, felt them knot themselves together into a painful, convulsive quivering. Rough fingers on open wounds . . .

Then it occurred to her that she must not be discovered there. She managed to overcome her paralysis, get to her feet and approach the noisy, laughing group round young Klykken. She went on picking heather, staring down looking for it as if it were of particular importance. Then she sat down a little way behind Mrs Selmer and pretended to arrange her flowers.

When she looked up again the men were flocking round the flat stone where the bottles were standing. Alberta suddenly crouched as if it might help. It did not. The Magistrate refilled his glass with much whisky and little seltzer – she had seen it happen before, there would be increasingly more whisky and less seltzer in Papa's glass – and skaaled with the Chief Constable, of whom she knew it was said that –

They were both very red in the face and deeply serious.

And the anxiety welled up in Alberta, gripping her coldly

and painfully round the heart, making her hands shake. Everything was rolling towards destruction, herself too, and nothing could be done about it. What she herself saw might perhaps not exist, it might only be imagination, an optical illusion. What others saw was given substance, reality – it *was*.

Oh but she had to, she would help, save, guard against it. Notice when Papa was on his way to the sideboard, get him to think about something else, apply herself to it seriously. Pity went through her in a warm wave. Can't afford to move south? Then they must be able to afford it, cut down, save, deny themselves everything, and get away from here, where Papa and all the others were on their way to perdition. She would spread the butter more thinly on her bread, wear Lapp boots in winter to save shoe leather, be the leader and set a good example – encourage and lead.

Then impotence crept over her again. She went on arranging her heather with numb, quivering hands.

Young Klykken was a wit. He always sat with the ladies, entertaining them, and was considered to be indispensable on a picnic. He had just been telling them about the last time he ate nuts, so that you could have died laughing. 'I spent the next few days getting all my teeth filled,' said young Klykken, with a killingly comical expression. My goodness, he can carry it off in style.

But they had finished with the nuts, and the mood was exhausted. Young Klykken had spoiled his audience. He had to be perpetually amusing, it was expected of him, and when he was not in good form the atmosphere round him tended to become a little flat. His wife sometimes came to the rescue and reminded him of one thing or another. Now she leaned forward smiling up in his face with sparkling eyes and flawless teeth : 'Imitate Gronneberg the Chief Clerk, you do that so well,' she said fondly.

A little way off the Clerk had landed himself between Otilie Weyer and Miss Liberg. Otilie was smiling, quiet and embarrassed, faded and lovely, as usual. Miss Liberg was in perpetual motion, continually straightening her pince-nez that had difficulty remaining perched on her agitated face, and leaning forward to look fixedly into the Clerk's eyes, her mouth churning like a mill.

Young Klykken allowed himself to be persuaded. In an undertone he mimicked the Clerk's cautious and elaborate diction, his somewhat over-careful pronunciation and small, self-conscious cough, his habit of pushing back his shirt-sleeves, as if to give his hands something to do. The ladies were helpless with laughter, with the exception of Mrs Lossius, who was always reserved towards young Klykken, and who merely smiled. Mrs Selmer also recovered herself quickly, to protest: 'I assure you, he is an exceptionally fine, good-natured young man. We appreciate him highly, and my husband would be lost without him'.

Old Mrs Weyer, who was vainly trying to follow the conversation, her hand cupped to her ear, persistently nodded encouragement to Otilie across the space between them. Otilie reddened. Mrs Weyer was equally hopeful every time a man came near her daughter. She seemed to be saying: 'Don't let Miss Liberg put you in the shade, go on, you must talk as well'. But Otilie remained silent. Otilie had withdrawn from the fray once and for all.

Alberta thought a little dully, half mechanically, that from now on she would try to be more friendly towards the Clerk, would try not to look obstinately in another direction to avoid shaking hands with him, try to say a little more than yes and no when he took her in to dinner.

There was Beda throwing herself down in the heather. She seemed restless, preoccupied and fretful. She was not listening to Lett, who followed her and squatted beside her, but looked down all the time to where the blue smoke, now thinner than before and fading, still rose behind the boulders. She nibbled at a stalk of grass.

'Oh, of course you will,' said Lett persuasively, continuing a previous conversation.

'Do be quiet, I've told you, no.' Beda did not seem to be thinking about Lett at all. It looked as if she wanted to shake him off, as if his presence disturbed her. Lett looked insulted, and nibbled a stalk too. Immediately afterwards Beda got to her feet and went over to another group. Lett retired in the opposite direction.

'Tangle in the thread,' remarked Frederick, who had moved nearer, together with Gertrude and Rikke. Rikke turned to Alberta and remarked : 'She is sweet of course, and terribly picturesque – but so hopelessly uncivilized'.

'Beda is certainly not uncivilized,' replied Alberta curtly. She was suddenly filled with enraged bitterness. She had a desire to be rude, to pull a face at Frederick.

She glanced over at him. He was lying looking at Beda, striking at the heather with a twig. His face had the same expression she had often noticed in men's faces when they looked at Beda. They fell silent – and stared – their mouths curled up a little, their nostrils widened, a foot or a hand became restless, and they made a few strokes with a twig or whatever else they might happen to have in their hands. And God knows whether their manner of looking at Beda was complimentary or disparaging.

Then Frederick turned and his eyes met Alberta's. He adjusted his pince-nez as he did so.

Quivering, her expression tense and glazed as if caught doing wrong, Alberta met his gaze for a moment. Her blush engulfed her mercilessly.

On the way home she was walking by herself, looking down into the bog, still collecting heather and unripe cloudberries, when Frederick suddenly appeared at her side. 'Never have I seen anyone so serious,' he said smiling, 'Or so silent. Do you really never say anything at all, Miss Selmer?'

Alberta made no reply. She stood still, as if waiting for some of the others, and turned away, tense and crimson.

'Come and walk with us,' said Frederick. 'Don't keep to yourself. It's not good for you,' he added. He had taken off his pince-nez, and was breathing on the lens and rubbing them. Now he put them on again as if to see her better.

Alberta was silent, bent her head, and contemplated her shoes from every angle. 'Look here,' said Frederick. 'What's the matter? Are you hurt about something?'

Alberta looked up, past him. Her eyes were full of tears and her face was hard and small.

'Very well,' she heard him say, in resignation. He raised his hat and left her. Some time later, when Alberta was pretending to be looking in quite a different direction, he was walking between Gudrun and Mrs Klykken. They were talking and laughing.

Alberta felt a stab. Oh God, to be pretty, to be spontaneous and self-possessed – and wise !

* * *

'Good heavens, are they those fearfully superior people from Park Street?' said Rikke, when she heard that Aunt the Colonel and Lydia were about to arrive. 'I know of them from the Association and the Promenade, they're incredibly stiff and starchy.'

And Gertrude exclaimed in her impulsive way : 'Heavens yes, those people who seem so shabby-genteel? Oh, forgive me, Alberta, they may not be in the very least'.

Alberta did not forgive her. She hid the words in her heart and brooded over them.

Aunt the Colonel and cousin Lydia *were* superior.

Even in their best, Mrs Selmer and Alberta were put wretchedly in the shade beside Aunt's and Lydia's imperturbable correctitude. Alberta miserably smoothed her bristling hair back behind her ears, but it continually came forward again. Her eyes never left Mrs Selmer's in a frantic attempt to keep up to the mark. Because of Aunt she was wearing the neckband and her chain and felt like a prisoner in irons.

At a little distance Lydia sat with her embroidery, which she would bring out, with a couple of words of excuse, as soon as she sat down. Not a hair was out of place. In fact her hair looked exactly like that of the ladies in the fashion magazines, and a little smile, the same as in the photograph, and which struck Alberta as being strangely wise beyond her years, never left her face. Now and again she would look up and smile more at what was being said, and it seemed as if some mechanism functioned inside her head, so unchanged was her expression in every other respect. She was pale with a completely straight nose and a narrow, oval face, and was considered to be outstandingly beautiful.

Aunt sat upright in the armchair and looked about her with shining eyes: 'I cannot tell you how happy it makes me to see that your home is so attractive and comfortable,' she repeated again and again; and Mrs Selmer, who had already replied vivaciously and cheerfully a couple of times, laughed somewhat nervously: 'Did you think we lived in a turf hut like Lapps?'

'No, goodness gracious me,' protested Aunt. 'But it is very far north, you know, and it's rather difficult for us who live in the south to imagine that you could live so admirably up here.'

The sun, pouring in through the open windows, was broken by prisms, and winked in the glass of the hundreds of photographs. Large vases full of bracken and buttercups, picked by Alberta for the occasion, stood on the piano and the occasional tables, giving an effect of luxuriance and richness. Mrs Selmer's La France had three large roses on it and stood turned inwards towards the room. The cataracts churned. The day was warm.

But Mrs Selmer must nevertheless have felt that Aunt had emphasized the admirable a little too strongly, for she interrupted her: 'Oh, heavens yes, it might be worse, but it might be better – the winter is long'. Her voice trembled a little as she added: 'We don't live here for pleasure'.

She rose and cleared away the books to make room for the tray Jensine had brought.

The Magistrate, sunburned and animated after his last circuit, asked after his brother Thomas, and Aunt assured him that he would more than anything have liked to have accompanied them, but his duties – and then the expense, of course, the confounded expense.

She splayed her hands on the arms of her chair and declared: 'We really couldn't afford this trip. Thomas often has no idea where the money is to come from, but for Lydia's sake we felt—'

She looked helplessly about her, although nobody had demanded any reckoning.

Alberta liked neither of them. She became anxious in their presence, her hands turned clammy. She noticed that they looked sideways at her when talking of other things, and once when the Chief Clerk was present, Aunt asked Mrs Selmer by means of her eyes and a little toss of the head whether he would not suit Alberta, whether it might not be conceivable—?

Mrs Selmer had shaken her head with a brief, sad little smile. Alberta felt their commiseration like a shirt of nettles about her body.

When she and Lydia were alone, Lydia would let her everlasting embroidery fall into her lap and talk about herself and the irreproachable young man whose photograph, in cabinet-size, lorded it on her bedside table at Mrs Korneliussen's private hotel. It had been clear to everyone that the Grand was unthinkable. Alberta could not understand how Lydia could allow the things she said to pass her lips : 'It's difficult being apart you know – almost as difficult as being together and just looking at each other and behaving ourselves. Heaven knows whether we'd have managed it either, if it hadn't been for this trip'.

She sighed, looked at Alberta almost despairingly and allowed her clockwork smile to function. Then she sewed again and said : 'I must finish my trousseau in time, soon I'll have other things to think about'. She leaned forward, touched Alberta's bracelet and assured her : 'I haven't anything as nice as that'. She looked at the red and white table-cloth and said nothing. And she smiled once more and again talked about her fiancé.

Alberta had the feeling that Lydia was thinking : 'You must keep up your spirits, my dear, even though you can never hope to experience anything similar'. She was glad they were not staying longer than between two packet boats, and that they did not intend to come ashore on the return journey south.

In the evenings, when they had been escorted back to their hotel, Mrs Selmer would lie on the sofa in despair over her daughter. She had kept up her spirits all day, and now her strength failed her. 'It was my hope that Alberta might make a good impression on her Aunt,' she wailed. 'I struggle and strive to do the best for my children, but it is all in vain, in vain, in vain.'

Her voice was lost in a whisper, she sighed : 'Other young girls are happy and gay, they talk and laugh, they don't behave like dumb fish'.

She exploded : 'Look at her, look at her appearance,' drawing the Magistrate's attention to Alberta, pillorying her. He considered her over his spectacles and remarked : 'Unfortunately I have to agree with your mother, Alberta. You do not take sufficient trouble over your appearance'.

Alberta stood in front of them, obstinate and mute as an animal. Only later did she cry in her room.

When Lydia arrived in the morning she had already written to her fiancé and was flourishing a large letter. She had also read some English, and was carrying her embroidery in her hand. She was perfect and a joy to all.

Alberta accompanied her to the Post Office with the letter. Afterwards they strolled in Fjord Street and along the quay. They met various people, and Lydia greeted these unknown persons politely, lady as she was. They met Beda out on an errand for the office, and Beda pulled a face at Alberta and nodded so violently that her hat lurched. Lydia asked : 'Who was that vulgar apparition?'

But later on, when Alberta was waiting for Lydia, who had wanted to go up to her hotel for a moment, Beda passed again. She arrived just as Lydia, trim and *comme-il-faut* with veil, gloves and parasol, was walking across the street. And Beda looked after her with narrowed eyes and said : 'Apple pie'.

What was shabby-genteel? Where did the gentility end and the shabbiness begin, or vice-versa? Were Aunt's words to

Lydia, when they were going out walking, shabby-genteel? 'Button up every button on your gloves, Lydia my dear. It makes such a bad impression to do it in the street.'—Was their discussion about how much they ought to give in tips shabby-genteel? Was Lydia shabby-genteel, when she walked the few steps to her hotel and said : 'I feel quite uncomfortable in the street without a veil'. Was Aunt shabby-genteel when she said : 'That's not *comme-il-faut*'. Or when she referred to the family name and smilingly, half jokingly added : '*Noblesse oblige*'?

Are we not all a little shabby-genteel, we who hesitate over a two-*kroner* tip and live in a house we are unable to heat? The thought struck home in Alberta painfully, and she was a qualm the richer.

On the last afternoon but one, she found herself alone with Aunt for a while. And almost at once Aunt broached the subject of Papa. She did so without transition or introduction, as if she had waited for this very moment and was now hastening to avail herself of it. 'Your father had every expectation of making a career for himself, my child,' she said. 'With his origins, his connections, his natural good qualities. But there is one thing he has never understood, Alberta my dear, and that's *money*.' Aunt laid her own particular emphasis on this most important of all words. She added : 'And we've all had to suffer on account of it'.

'Yes,' she said in explanation, when Alberta flushed. 'I think I ought to be able to talk to you about it now that you're grown up. Your Uncle Thomas has had to take the risk more than once. It's not more than a couple of years since he had to stand surety again, he and a couple of your father's old friends – and God knows how things are going with that loan, my child, whether it's being paid off properly – for Thomas is so generous that he would never mention such a thing, not even to me. If he has taken responsibility for something, he does so, without a murmur.'

'It's being paid off,' replied Alberta furiously. She saw Papa's face on pay-days, a certain expression he had, almost childishly tired and resigned; she saw his broad back in the shiny old coat that he wore when he came in from the office; the twelve cigars she had to run and buy when anyone was coming, because Papa never felt he could afford a whole box. – She felt a little faint.

'You mustn't get excited about it, child,' said Aunt. 'There's no reason for that. I'm talking to you as the grown-up, sensible daughter of the house. You are of an age when you can do a great deal, my dear Alberta, to see that your home gets on its feet again economically. The time has come when, with tact and circumspection, you can put in a word about thrift when necessary.'

'We are thrifty,' answered Alberta curtly.

Aunt ignored the interruption. 'We were all so glad,' she continued, 'not least for the sake of you children, when we persuaded your father to apply for a post up north. Your parents cut quite a dash, you see. Your mother was sweet and charming – a little insignificant, but sweet – it was only natural for your father to be proud of her and to want her to look beautiful. They sent to Paris for one thing after the other – and when one has no independent means . . . Then your father started to speculate, my dear, but he's no businessman, and that turned out as one might have expected.' Aunt suddenly struck the table. 'It was like a sieve in the end, my child, a whole lot of holes for the money to run through. Your father has never bothered to learn from life – your mother—'

Alberta's brain reeled. Mama's face over the account book, her miserable little figure in the shawl; the smoked salmon which, after long discussion, it was decided should be bought so that there should be a little in the house when Aunt and Lydia arrived; it all whirled in her head. In imagination she saw the persons who had once opposed Papa, secure, admirable persons with their own affairs in order, condemning him to apply for a post up here, beyond the world, beyond everything. As if in the foreground she saw Aunt's dress with its thousands of stitches.

And the blood streamed to her brain as it had at Christmas time. She was beside herself, wanting to say something, but only able to find one word. It stood out in her consciousness in letters of flame, blotting out everything else : shabby-genteel. She heard her voice hurling it three times at Aunt : 'Shabby-genteel, shabby-genteel, shabby-genteel !'

She covered her face with her hands and left the room sobbing. Behind her she heard Aunt's exclamation : 'Great God and Father of us all !'

On the last afternoon the Magistrate sent for Ola Paradise and the pony carriage to drive the ladies inland across the bog. In the hall, while everyone was preparing for the drive, Aunt seized the opportunity to make her comment : 'Can my brother-in-law really afford this? It's so pleasant here at home – this is quite unnecessary, you know'.

During the drive she several times suggested turning back. 'We've had such a lovely drive now, we ought to be satisfied, it seems to me.'

It was obvious to them all that Aunt wanted to bring the price down. But Ola Paradise had orders to drive past the Gronli farms. He drove and drove, his broad back adamant up on the driver's seat. He did not even look round to reply, merely spitting a notable distance as he spoke : 'Don't you fuss, I'll turn when it's time to turn, I have my orders'. To the general consternation he even drove a little further than had been agreed, and who could tell what he might mean by that? Aunt sat with one foot on the carriage step, ready to throw herself out if things should go too far. She remarked repeatedly : 'This is pure lunacy. Heaven only knows how much my brother-in-law will have to fork out for this little amusement'.

On the back seat beside Lydia sat Alberta, full of contrition. Every time Aunt opened her mouth she was afraid she would refer to yesterday's episode. But Aunt did not mention it and clearly had not mentioned it either, except possibly to Lydia. Did it not seem as if the two of them were sharing something special? As long as they told no tales to Mrs Selmer, it did not matter.

From time to time Alberta met Mama's tense look and

noticed the slight quivering and twitching round her tightly-pinched mouth. Each time it seemed as if yesterday's outburst was not so dangerous after all, but that it had been, on the contrary, justified and necessary, and that it was a good thing she had said it.

On the way home Alberta sat facing Big Gap. There she saw the mist. It lay like a thick, solid coil at the bottom of the gap. A few isolated, airy tufts, amounting to scarcely anything, had come loose and were drifting alongside the mountain. The mist from the sea.

Tonight the coil would swell. In the morning it would be everywhere. Then it would not be so admirable here any more. But by that time Aunt and Lydia would be rocking on the swell off the North Cape.

When the packet boat's pennant of smoke had disappeared westwards out on the fjord that evening, Mrs Selmer said, still standing looking after it: 'We couldn't have been more fortunate with the weather, but isn't the air a little strange this evening? Do you think there'll be a change?'

'It's the sea-mist,' answered Alberta. Aunt's hurried words, spoken in the moment when they were alone together in the hall, lay like a hard knot in her consciousness. 'I thought you had grown up, my dear Alberta. I see to my great disappointment that such is not the case.'

Fateful words, that were what they seemed – a death warrant.

* * *

Raw cold and sleet blew in from the northwest for the third week in succession. The landscape looked soured by too much moisture. The horsetail had ousted everything else in the meadows, the hay hung brown and depressing on the drying fences. The mist enclosed everything like grey felt. People in the know talked about drift-ice in the sea.

At the Governor's they had lighted the stoves, so effeminate and sensual were they. They were lighted elsewhere too, perhaps, but it was at Rikke's that Alberta shared such excessive luxury.

At home Mrs Selmer went from window to window, moving flower pots and sighing. She sighed over Jacob and over life in general, but over Alberta in particular. At suitable intervals she would glance resignedly at this perverse child, whose face was again blue, muddy and insecure. It came with the cold and could not be concealed. Even her squint seemed to worsen.

To be invited to Rikke's for tea was, in spite of Frederick, in spite of many things, a relief. Of two evils . . .

In Rikke's room the tea table stood in front of the open door of the stove, a tea table with silver, porcelain, golden marmalade. The glow of the fire reached far out over the floor, playing on everything and finding an answering reflection in Rikke's red silk dress, which was lying slung across an armchair. A slight scent of her eau de verveine and of good cigarettes hung in the air. From Frederick's room could be heard the notes of a violin, a couple of bars over and over again.

A weakness crept over Alberta, a drowsiness that permeated her whole body. She felt paralysed by the warmth, by everything.

She did not become outspoken here as she did at the Bucks'. Nowhere as here did she have such a discouraging sensation of being poor. Not only did Rikke and Gertrude inhabit regions which she had no hope of attaining, regions containing the tree of knowledge and much else besides; they moved therein with such obvious nonchalance, with such inevitability and superiority, that it almost seemed as if she had been invited over to see how clever and practised they were. It had been the same when she was invited, as a child, to play with Rikke's doll's house. Mrs Lossius helped Rikke a great deal with the doll's house; it gradually became a miracle of studied perfection. Rikke handled the things as if she had known them all her life. Alberta never learned to pick them up, but mostly stood watching, numb, an outsider.

She sat, awkward in speech and gesture, warming her ice-cold hands, while Rikke came and went, seeing to the tea and chattering : 'Heavens, what weather! There's no colour any more, and if you stand outside you freeze to death. I shall have to give up the picture of the Kamke quay. Once the Arctic mist comes in it puts paid to everything. Moklebust and all the others are painting with all their might and main down in the Setesdal valley, having a wonderful time, and of course they'll have heaps of things ready for the Autumn Exhibition, while I—' Rikke gestured with her hands to imply that she was destitute. 'And yesterday that Signora Ryan came to ask whether I taught painting on velvet! What do you think of that? On velvet! They ought to have heard that at the art school. Well, well, it'll be nice to have a cup of tea at any rate.'

She disappeared. Alberta thawed out, settled herself more comfortably in her chair, and attempted to enjoy the interlude as much as she could. Warmth was warmth. And as long as Frederick kept on playing—

At once the violin ceased with a discordant stroke across the strings. She could hear his footsteps crossing the floor, and there stood Frederick in the doorway. Alberta's heart jumped.

But Frederick was so wrapped up in the music that he continued humming from where the violin had left off, smilingly beating time with an outstretched index finger, and peering at her over his pince-nez. Then he sat down, his legs straddled and his elbows on his knees, rubbed his hands together and remarked : 'It's cold, but playing the violin warms you up, it's the only thing that warms you properly. If only it were not so confoundedly difficult'.

He snapped his fingers and bent them backwards and forwards. Alberta sat on the extreme edge of her chair, as if it might help. 'Is that so?' she answered stupidly.

Frederick considered her meditatively above his spectacles. Since the picnic at Big Gap she had noticed him taking a curious interest in her. She had felt his eyes on her, always with the same searching look as if he were trying to find the answer to something. Tense and ill-at-ease, half insulted, she had studiously avoided him, acted deaf and blind when he looked as if he might approach her, found one excuse after another to get away. They had conversed very little.

Now it looked as if Frederick was prepared to ignore all this and pretend he had not noticed it. Alberta's obstinacy rose.

'Listen,' he said. 'I've asked you this before – do you really never say anything of your own accord?'

'Oh, now and again,' replied Alberta evasively and even more stupidly, feeling quite idiotic. One stupidity presumably gave rise to another.

'Well, that can't be often, so help me.' Frederick laughed and Alberta could not help laughing too, although she hastened to control herself. Frederick took off his pince-nez, breathed on the lenses and polished them, while continuing to regard her with his short-sighted, persistent stare.

'You laughed at any rate,' he said. 'It suited you.'

Alberta flushed crimson.

'Tell me, what do you do in the winter?'

'Oh—'

'In the summer you all seem to exist for the scenery. If one gets into trouble for saying this place is far north, the midnight sun is unanimously invoked. But when that's gone—'

'The light can be beautiful in winter too.'

'Well, all right, that may be possible.' Frederick's voice was impatient, he looked somewhat astounded. 'But you're not going to tell me you can live solely on the light and the memory of a few sun-filled nights and – let us say – tea and a little local gossip and a little handiwork?'

'That's not my impression,' he said, more to himself, looking into the fire.

Alberta did not reply. This Frederick had a supreme ability for putting his finger where it hurt most. What right had he to sit here prodding her nerves to the quick? In distress she reacted as those in distress will – with irritation.

Frederick was still looking into the fire. 'All due respect to those who set the tone up here,' he said, 'But what have you got besides the most banal social life?'

The blood mounted to Alberta's head again, and as usual

she said the wrong thing and said it coldly and provocatively, with a provocative toss of the head : 'We have cards and toddy'.

'I beg your pardon?'

'Oh, nothing.'

Frederick suddenly slammed shut the book he was holding, threw it on to the table, got up and paced the floor, his fingers in the armholes of his waistcoat. He stopped once and smoothed back his hair.

But Alberta sat there wretchedly. God knows who put the words into her mouth. They were not her own. They were foreign to her, stupid words behind which she hid herself. Her own never saw the light of day, they died unborn or withered on her tongue and were born distorted. She was disabled, she was without the use of speech, she would die of muteness.

Frederick halted in front of her : 'You're not happy,' he said quietly, as if concluding a train of thought.

Alberta's face was suddenly wet with tears. She turned away from the fire to hide them. But Frederick took one of her hands, held it in his and patted it : 'What a great ass I am,' he said in altered voice. Then he released her hand and paced the floor again. The door opened. Rikke and Gertrude arrived in procession bearing tea and toast. A cheerful conversation about the latest news from Kristiania flowed over Alberta's head.

The cold and rain continued. Rikke was forced to move her easel indoors for good and bring home her half finished work from the Kamke quay. It hung slackly, billowing on its frame. She took up Alberta seriously, fetching her daily and in person : 'You *must* come. You're the only person one can talk to here, you and Beda Buck, but you know *she's* too much for Mama. We scarcely see anything of Frederick; he sits up in the attic writing, when he's not playing or out walking with those teachers of his. My goodness yes, he's taken up with them now. They trudge for miles across the bog in the wet, he and these dried-up schoolmasters. Gertrude practises and writes to that man of hers. I'm left to pine on my own – thank goodness I've got you'.

She made Alberta sit in a comfortable chair, and nestled into another with her legs under her and a pile of reproductions in her lap, holding them out at arm's length, explaining and discoursing about them, knocking the ash from her cigarette and narrowing her eyes.

And Alberta curled up, tried to give herself over to the warmth and the well-being, thawed out a little, feared and hoped that Frederick would appear. She seemed almost to be getting accustomed to being there.

The art she had read about in old, yellowed books, of the period of the worst wood-cuts, was given substance; pictures that had been only printed titles, a few letters, suddenly became a small world of reality. She had seen some of them at the Recorder's house the few times she had been there, but had never dared to go close to them, inspect them and ask questions. Now their secrets were revealed, and at times she forgot herself and her anxieties.

Rembrandt's Polish rider, for instance, what was he riding from, what was he riding to? The four edges of the picture seemed to enclose the wide world itself. He rode through it, released from all that had been, moving untrammelled towards all that might be. An aura of freedom and loneliness surrounded him, making one hot and cold, making the heart beat faster. Alberta put the picture down and then took it up again. 'It's incredibly beautiful,' she said. 'You can have it if you like,' answered Rikke generously.

She brought out Dutch interiors, and Alberta was encompassed by their neat, cosy comfort as by pleasant warmth. Stillness, a glint of sunlight, practically no people, the perfect place to be—

But Rikke was expatiating about composition, values and perspective, and the pictures fell apart. It was the same when the Archdeacon's Henrik pulled a flower to pieces and added up stamens, germen, petals and calyx – a scented whole disintegrated into nothing. Confused, Alberta looked from what she had in her lap to Rikke's studies on the walls, meditated on the fact that both were supposed to be art, and became even more confused. She listened absent-mindedly to Rikke who, heaven knows how, had started to talk about Moklebust : *'He's* talented, you see, and sweet and naïve. *He's* impulsive. When he meets a pretty girl in the street, he kisses her. He *has* to, he says'.

Rikke raised her eyebrows and stared in front of her with large, dreamy eyes, as if she sank and disappeared in such mysterious depths. But she hauled herself up again and declared encouragingly : 'Well, well, Alberta, your turn will come'.

She narrowed her eyes at Alberta and exclaimed : 'Of *course* you're picturesque. If only you had a little colour. But what Frederick says is true, it comes from inside and only momentarily. He says that when you learn to use that cast in your eye, and make yourself a bit more approachable – you *are* stiff, Alberta. Good Lord, is that something to blush for so dreadfully? I think he's right and you're nervous'.

Frederick's footsteps could be heard in the attic. He was pacing the floor up there. Alberta sat on the edge of her chair, prepared for flight. If he were to come in and sit down she would move even further forward, as she listened anxiously to his and Rikke's chat. Sometimes the atmosphere in the Governor's house was charged on account of Gertrude's opinions. She and Mrs Lossius each sat behind closed doors, each with her tightly pinched mouth and her irreconcilable opinion of, say, marriage and divorce. Then Frederick would come into Rikke on tip-toe, stretch himself and say : 'Ugh, one daren't breathe here'. And turn to Alberta : 'I must find comfort in your fount of oratory, Miss Selmer'.

He remained sitting with his elbows on his knees, rubbing his pince-nez : 'There really are some lively people in this town, you know Rikke. I've managed to discover them. Living, uncoagulated tissue in various layers, small colonies of cells – one at the top round Headmaster Bremer, one further down round Hannestad the schoolmaster. People who are not living on what they brought here with them, or on inherited notions, but on new ideas, with their eyes turned outwards towards the present. They keep up with the times, they keep up to an amazing extent. And then there's the Recorder, Jaeger. He's a unicellular organism, he lives alone. – That's significant, by the way – the people up here who subscribe to anything beyond the Family Magazine shut themselves in with it'.

'Ugh,' said Rikke. 'These schoolmasters, is there really anything more to them besides worn clothes and shortage of money, hurry and scurry and spectacles?'

'Their clothes may be worn and they are short of money, but they don't wear lorgnettes, Rikke.'

'Now that's naughty, you should be ashamed of yourself!'

'Good Lord, but we both agree that it's an apparatus for the hindrance of the sight, more or less.'

'My goodness, yes,' laughed Rikke, without prejudice.

Frederick turned to Alberta again. 'If you persist in this flow of chatter something will happen to your tongue.'

Alberta laughed self-consciously. Her feelings were strangely erratic. This critic from Kristiania, at one moment she felt hostility and bitterness towards him, the next, unexpected confidence.

'Seriously, you must overcome this. You must learn to talk, to express your opinions.'

'I have none, I'm stupid.'

'Then say stupid things,' exclaimed Frederick. 'Say them, for heaven's sake, or your words of wisdom will never get a chance to see the light of day, supposing there are any coming to maturity deep down inside you. It's dangerous to keep silent like this.' He leaned forward and looked into her eyes.

At home that evening Alberta put the looking-glass on the window-sill to get a better light. She looked for what was supposed to come from inside her. But she only discovered a small, indistinct face with a squint.

The face became bluer the longer she sat.

* * *

The mist lifted as if a curtain were drawn back. But behind the curtain autumn had been waiting. Now it was present in everything. In the air that was far too clear, the mountains that were far too blue, in the permanent, flat patches of mist that encircled them. It sat red in the rowan tree above the shoemaker's roof, and yellow, brittle and frozen in the dwarf birches on the hill; in the darkening evening and the flaming early evening clouds, in the moon that had reappeared and was turning more and more yellow.

It was also autumn in that everyone was leaving. That stage had arrived, this year as last year. They all left at once, by the same boat. One was forced to accompany them on board, to be left standing on the quay, to see lights and lanterns disappear – to go home again.

It was a quiet, light evening. The moon had made its first serious appearance. It hung warm, round and unnaturally large above the mountains, reminiscent of decorations and autumn festivals. Like an enormous gold ducat its reflection floated and bobbed in the waves at Rivermouth.

The packet boat had all its lights on and looked more European and magnificent than on any other night of the year. On board all was bustle and animation. People bumped into one another in the corridors, no-one could find his cabin. The boat was full of people from further east, and reservations had been made in advance from places further south. Mrs Lossius was nervous : 'I told you so, children. If Papa had listened to me and spoken to the Captain when he was on his way east, you would have had a cabin to yourselves amidships. Now you'll have to put up with the ladies' saloon at the very best, and I think it's appalling that you should have to sleep in there with the rag tag and bob-tail. But nobody listens to me'.

She urged them to wait until the next boat, called after Frederick and the Governor, who ran from the Captain to the Mate and from the Mate to the Captain : 'It's no use my dears. I've spoken to the stewardess, she says it's hopeless'.

'If only someone could make Mama keep quiet,' sighed Rikke. 'I'm *not* going ashore, now this everlasting summer is finally over. Have you ever seen anything so irrelevantly lovely as that moon?'

But in spite of everything Gertrude and Rikke were given a cabin, the Captain's own. Mrs Lossius thanked him personally, and Frederick mopped perspiration from his brow: 'Heaven help us, what a fuss. Yes, I've found room in the chart-house. Yes thank you, Aunt, it'll be very comfortable'.

The Archdeacon's Henrik and the Pram twins were going south for the first time. The Archdeacon's wife and Mrs Pram tripped round in a tremendous state. There was nothing to sending one's daughters away; it was much worse with boys, they felt.

And there was young Theodorsen, who was also leaving. He was with a large crowd: Signora Ryan, Karla Schmitt, the fair girl from Holst's, Cedolf, and others. Augusta Bremer was there looking neat and tidy, with everything in order.

Harriet Pram stood with her family group, smiling happily, giving the twins little sisterly pats on the back, and sighing: 'Dear me, you are lucky to be going away'. It was clear to everyone that she really thought she was better off where she was.

The ship's bell rang for the second time, there was sudden crowding and confusion. Hands were shaken, quick kisses exchanged, many small cries crossed in the air. Alberta, following in Mrs Selmer's wake, fought against a painful feeling of unreality. It was all so bitter that it surely could not be true. It must be a lie, a stupid mistake, that nothing should have happened, that this year as last year, as in all the years past and to come, as far as the human eye could see, she was to be amongst those not going away. An insane notion that something beyond the bounds of reason and possibility might still happen, stirred in her. She smiled mechanically, shook hands, mumbled short phrases of farewell and was shoved hither and thither.

Now everyone was crowding towards the gangway. Gertrude kissed her on the cheek once more, Rikke twice. And there was Frederick. There he stood in front of her, a summer's bête noire, someone who put his finger roughly on sore places, someone whom she had gone by back streets to avoid. Now it seemed as if he, more than anyone else, was leaving her behind alone.

She must hide it, she must hide it at all costs.

'Thank you for a pleasant summer,' said Frederick. 'Goodbye. Until we meet again,' he added, and smiled.

But Alberta looked up with the hard, locked little face she could sometimes present, and answered stiffly and coldly: 'Thank you. Pleasant journey'.

Frederick looked somewhat dismayed. He stood for a moment as if expecting her to say something more. Then he released her hand and took that of the Archdeacon's wife, which was held at the ready, extended into the air.

Alberta's heart sank as if with irretrievable loss.

At the last moment Bergan the lawyer arrived, with the intention of going on board to take his leave when all the others had finished. He swayed heavily on the gangway. The ladies on the quay became nervous and slightly irritated, but a fantastic possibility occurred to Alberta: the ship would not leave with Bergan on board. But there he was on land again. And there went the gangway. The ship glided away from the quay, the propeller churned, the water foamed and swirled about the stern. The packet boat was off.

Now it was rocking out at Rivermouth, festive and magical with all its lights shining, a dark silhouette islanded in moonlight, a pleasure boat on Lake Maggiore. It seemed to hesitate a moment, lying quite still before setting course westwards for good. People were waving. Three cheers came concisely and vigorously across the water and were answered by a group of which Cedolf seemed to be the leader. 'Youth,' smiled the Archdeacon's wife. 'Youth.' She looked out across Rivermouth with her crystal-clear eyes full of moonlight. And she put her hand into the Archdeacon's and declared cheerfully: 'Our boys are in the Lord's keeping'. But Mrs Pram had to be supported by Harriet.

For a moment they all stood silent. The departure of this autumn ship gave rise to many different thoughts. Something came out of hiding in the most hardened.

The Magistrate broke the ice. He pounded with his stick : 'Well, off they go once more. The summer's over. We must hole ourselves up for the winter again – and try to make the best of it,' he added in English, which he sometimes spoke in moments of stress. He looked enquiringly across at Mrs Selmer, who of course took it tragically, with distant expression and bitter mouth. The moonlight inconsiderately revealed two big tears on her cheeks.

'Hm,' muttered the Magistrate, looking away again. But now the steamer was only a dark patch far out. People were beginning to go home. He pounded again authoritatively and encouragingly, and officialdom marched off in small, conversing groups, with the exception of the Bremer family, who took their leave pleasantly and went their own way. Mrs Selmer watched them go : 'Just fancy, Mrs Bremer is supposed to be fearfully clever. She's interested in the rights of women and all sorts of things. With only one maid and all those children I think it's marvellous'.

'Some people are so indescribably capable,' replied Mrs Lossius icily. She was not in favour of extremes in any direction, and the Bremer family were slightly *too* capable, slightly too good for this world. It sounded like a reprimand : 'I must say I think it's difficult enough to cultivate one's interests with *two* maids. Oh dear, I do hope my little girls will keep warm on deck'.

Dr Pram reminded them that it was less than two and a half months until the dark period began, and less than four until Christmas. The Archdeacon replied : 'Yes, indeed. Time passes'. Mrs Pram remarked : 'Soon we shall have to take our winter clothes out again, and we put them away only yesterday'.

Antipathy towards them all erupted in Alberta. She felt utterly paralysed by numbing, inner cold. And suddenly she saw the supper table, illuminated by the hanging lamp, far off in a great darkness; supper tables in an endless row, with their atmosphere of depression, and grey gruel. She shuddered with horror, simulated a headache, and obtained permission from Mrs Selmer to go for a walk in the moonlight.

In spite of its chill the evening had something of southern luxuriance about it. It must have been due to the large, warm moon. It was troubling, unseemly, ironic.

Already Rivermouth was a little sinister. Boats were arriving daily with their catch from the Arctic, and the men roared out of them after long hardship and asceticism, to rollick in and out of the taverns, stand loitering on corners with dreadful girls, and shout after the passers-by. Another evening Alberta would scarcely have dared come here. But now she was in flight and noticed nothing. And she was possessed by a fixed, idiotic idea : to go the same way as the steamer.

She had come to Louisa-round-the-bend. The street lay long and gloomy before her, completely deserted. A single soul was visible, a person in skirts, far off. She looked like a working-class woman, an unknown person of no consequence, who in any case was going in the same direction as Alberta, with her back to her.

So she let the tears come, abandoning herself to her anguish and distress. She seemed to see herself from the outside this evening, a failure, ugly, ignorant, full of aversion for everything life had earmarked for her, full of impossible, hopeless, vague longings. They stifled her, they were more than she could bear. She did not go so far as to scream out loud, but she pressed her clenched fist against her mouth to avoid doing so.

Finally she sat on a boulder on the shingle and sobbed openly without hiding her face. It did her good. The tumult within her seemed to melt down and subside. Inertness followed in its place, a great, thoughtless exhaustion. She sat looking out over the water without thinking.

The water rose and flowed round the boulders. When she kept quite still she could hear a swarming in it, a tiny teeming sound of activity and labour. It was full of secrecy, of a mysterious, hidden will to conquer by stealth. The moon had rolled up high in the sky and become small and yellow.

And her mind was rocked into complete peace and became like the sea, without a ripple. All that was painful and troublesome sank down, and something scattered collected itself and floated to the surface instead. Small stanzas followed one after the other in disorder, without beginning or end.

Then they stopped. No more came. Alberta sat for a while fumbling and found nothing. But they would come. She would listen her way to them, find a beginning and an end The poem would be about what it was like to long in desperation and in vain.

Hope was born in her anew. Perhaps something wonderful and impossible might happen one day after all. It was not quite so unthinkable as it had been a short while ago. She made a resolve. She would go back to school, persuade Papa, become knowledgeable and free in spite of everything, become something.

Suddenly someone was standing behind her. She looked round terrified. The woman on the road had been Jeanette Evensen. And although Jeanette had never done harm to a cat, Alberta froze with fear. She had been taken by surprise, and Jeanette's grey, expressionless face with the untidy hair looked so strangely petrified under the moon.

She was queer. Some said a little crazy. Everyone knew it was because she was not married. She always looked unkempt and dishevelled, and dressed below her station in life in old, ugly clothes. But sometimes she would wear a rose in her hat or pinned to her breast.

She was in the habit of lying in bed and getting up late in the afternoon. She did nothing and was no mean burden for old Mrs Evensen, who was a widow and had a small shop selling sewing things, knitting wool and other oddments. Mrs Evensen's windows never looked like other people's in the summer; scarcely had a La France blossomed before Jeanette had taken it. She even took the buds.

She could sometimes be seen from the shop, sitting erect on a chair with her hands in her lap in the inner room. Mrs Evensen would open her heart to the customers, sighing deeply.

Now Jeanette was standing there on the shingle, just as if she wanted to remind Alberta of her existence and of how things could turn out, for she said nothing, only stared tensely out across the water. A fresh stab of fear passed through

Alberta. She got to her feet and edged away. They said people like that were worse at full moon.

But Jeanette said peaceably: 'I thought I'd go out on the rocks to look for shells, but the tide's coming in'.

'Yes.'

'I needed those shells so badly.'

'Oh yes?'

Alberta remembered now that Jeanette was in the habit of embarking on sudden, useless enterprises that she never carried out. She obviously had some plan.

'I didn't even bother to get dressed before I left. I thought I'd come out as quickly as I could.' She smoothed down her skirt and her hair with her hand and smiled dazedly.

'Oh, never mind.'

Alberta was no longer afraid, but ill-at-ease and uncertain. She had never spoken much to Jeanette and all she wanted to do was to get away. But Jeanette said: 'I'd really appreciate your company. I was quite relieved when I saw you sitting there on that stone, so many bad folk as there are in Rivermouth'.

So they began to walk the long way back to town. Jeanette chatted incessantly, mostly about how she never achieved anything: 'I never sleep, let me tell you, and then you never get anything done, you can't even get up. Just imagine, Mama *chivvies* me out of bed. Would you believe a mother could be so hard-hearted?' She halted and looked anxiously at Alberta.

Alberta answered yes and no more or less as she should. She soon discovered that it was as well to take care to reply correctly, for when Jeanette was displeased with her answer she would stop once more and go into the matter in detail. Exhaustion crept over Alberta. The courage and faith she had found a little while ago seemed to have been blown away. The lines of verse were probably of no value, a poor mimicry of something or other, a bit of jingle she had learned by repetitive reading. It was probably only a delusion that she had been liberated by them. And now they were gliding away from her. She seemed unable to remember them.

Everything was dead, joyless, sickening, without hope.

PART THREE

No-one saw anything of Beda Buck any more. It was odd.
Alberta had been up to ask after her twice, but the doorbell
must have been out of order, for she could not hear it, and
nobody answered. In Fjord Street, which was re-established as
the main traffic artery in the evenings, now that autumn was
approaching, Lett, the editors and the chemists promenaded
without Beda. It was being talked about.

She did not go home at her usual time any more either. You
could still catch sight of a dark knot of hair and a few un-
governable curls now and again above the Civil Service
Calendar that lay on the window-sill of the Recorder's office,
but not all the time as before. And Beda never looked out of
the window, caught sight of you and grimaced or shook her
fist. Alberta missed her. There was something worrying about
it.

One day, when Alberta was wandering across the bog, she
met Beda and the Recorder. They were walking slowly, and
stopped from time to time. The Recorder was speaking
quietly and urgently, and looked serious. Beda looked down
as she walked, with a strangely stony expression. When she
raised her head and greeted Alberta her expression was foreign
to her, miserable, with something diminished and completely
preoccupied about it. Alberta had never seen her so careless
in her appearance before; her skirt was shorter than ever in
front.

'Goodness,' thought Alberta. 'Beda is being reprimanded
by the Recorder.' The thought had something oppressive and
heart-sickening about it, as if some evil and inexorable fate
was suddenly threatening everything and everyone, not just
Beda.

That afternoon Alberta rang the Bucks' doorbell again. Still it did not ring, and she tried the handle. The door opened. She heard voices and went into the hall. The door into the living-room was ajar. Inside voices were raised in sudden, violent exchange.

'You are so utterly unreasonable, Beda. You really are impossible.'

'I'm not asking you for anything. Just let me paddle my own canoe. I shan't be the first.'

That was Beda's voice. New and strange, and yet Beda's. So full of bitter, cutting defiance.

'Dear child, you must let us use our heads a *little*.' Mrs Buck's voice was no longer shrill and upbraiding. It was deep, and trembled with the suppressed tenderness that rounded and filled it, in contrast to her dry, sensible words.

A third person spoke in support of Mrs Buck : 'Yes, indeed'. The person sighed.

Alberta was about to leave when Beda appeared in the doorway. 'Oh, it's you, Alberta. I thought I heard someone. No, don't go my poor dear, I'm glad you came.'

'Oh dear, I forgot to lock the front door after me,' said the third person in an undertone from inside the room.

Beda took Alberta and led her into the living-room, where she made her sit down on the couch. 'My poor Alberta, I ought to have been as good at Norwegian composition as you were, then I could have gone abroad and become a writer. Or I ought to have been a boy, then I could have gone to sea. I wouldn't have stayed a day longer in this filthy town.'

Beda's face was flaming with irritation. She kicked at a small footstool so furiously that it shot across the floor.

Mrs Buck was sitting by the window. Her eyes were red and she looked dishevelled. Mrs Lebesby, Dyers and Cleaners, sat up high on the piano stool, her travelling coat buttoned, her hat on her head, and a very solemn expression on her face.

Alberta did not know what to make of it. They were all behaving so strangely. There must be something the matter with Beda's job at the Recorder's. It couldn't be anything else.

'If only I had seventy-five *kroner* to get myself to Kristiania.'

'Dearest Beda.'

'If only I had them. You wouldn't need to bother about me any more.'

'Seventy-five *kroner* – oh Beda, you wouldn't get far on seventy-five *kroner*.'

'I'd get far enough,' answered Beda bitterly. She moved towards the door.

'Where are you going, child?'

'To put the kettle on. I suppose we may as well offer them something, since they've come to see us. Since when have we been so mean in this house that we don't offer so much as a cup of tea? Please take off your hat.'

Beda disappeared.

'Good Lord, how could she say I was mean,' sighed Mrs Buck. She raised her hands from her lap in a helpless gesture and let them fall again, as if to say : 'Am I to sit here and be blamed for that too?'

And she took out a damp, tight little ball of a handkerchief and pressed it to her eyes. A sob escaped her. Mrs Lebesby's face assumed the fervent expression of sympathy that the situation demanded. 'There, there, Ulla,' she said soothingly.

But Mrs Buck continued to dab at her eyes with the wet little ball, remarking jerkily : 'Oh Alberta, my dear – life is nothing but sorrow and deception – the world is vile, thoroughly vile—

'And what a fool I am,' she exclaimed suddenly. 'So innocent and so foolish – oh Alberta—'

Alberta prepared to ask a circumspect question. But Mrs Buck was talking again. 'My little girl, my poor little girl,' she sighed, and suddenly her voice became stronger. 'I'm telling you, Alberta, never trust a man, for they're the vilest of them all – except Victor Buck of course. Oh, if only my darling husband were alive—'

She sat looking at the enlargement above the piano with wet, exhausted eyes.

So Alberta knew that it also had to do with a betrayal on the part of Lett, the dentist. For it must be Lett. She tried to imagine what the situation might be, but asked no questions. Those who truly sympathised were evidently supposed to understand such things automatically.

Besides, Mrs Buck went on to say : 'You'll hear all about it in time, Alberta, my dear, you'll hear all about it in time'. She sighed, or rather groaned, and disappeared into the kitchen too.

Alberta's eyes met those of Mrs Lebesby. But Mrs Lebesby closed hers and shook her head resignedly. Her mouth was tragic and fateful. Clearly words were inadequate.

As Alberta passed through the kitchen on arriving home, Jensine, who was standing stirring the porridge for supper, remarked : 'Things are only so-so at the Buck's, I understand.'

'What do you mean, so-so? Besides, I haven't been there.'

'Oh, my poor Alberta, you needn't bother. I was at Theodorsen's getting the bread, and I saw you on the Buck's steps as clearly as I see you now.'

Alberta was caught out. She did not want to discuss Beda with Jensine, but it had been stupid to lie. Jensine was triumphant. 'Oh yes,' she said with a little laugh, stirring resolutely, 'Soon it won't be any use denying either the one thing or the other. They say that fellow Lett denies everything.'

'How do you mean, everything? That he's going to marry Beda?'

'That too. Oh no, fine folk aren't any better than other people, I've learnt that much in this town,' declared Jensine, who came from the outer islands.

'If what they're saying is true,' she added, 'I'm sorry for Beda. But then she's a flighty one, they all say as much.'

Alberta left the room. She was reluctant to talk about Beda with Jensine, who was partial to riddles besides. There was something disquieting about the whole matter. Alberta dared not admit it, but she began to have her suspicions. She forced them back.

It must not be true!

* * *

'What is it, my child,' asked Papa, looking up from his work with tired, red-rimmed eyes. 'I'm particularly busy today. What is it?'

'I can wait until later.' At the moment Alberta had no objection to a postponement.

'No, no. Out with it.' The Magistrate let it be known that he was listening, although his pen continued to wander across the paper.

Alberta swallowed. She had sought this interview herself, muddled herself into it entirely of her own accord. For a moment she thought how easy it would be to muddle out of it again, to ask for a couple of *kroner* for something and allow heaven and earth to remain undisturbed. Then she blurted it out: 'May I go back to school again Papa? Will you allow me to enter *gymnasium?*'

Papa dipped his pen in the ink without looking up. His tone implied honest regret that the suggestion had been made when he said: 'Go back to school again! What sort of an idea is that?'

'I'd like to learn more.'

'Hm. Yes, that's very laudable of course. But after all, you do read, my child, you do have the opportunity to read. And I see with satisfaction that you often choose books from which you can learn something, you don't just read all these preposterous trashy novels that are being written nowadays. I appreciate that. I may not have remarked on it, but it has pleased me. If there is anything you are especially interested in, I could perhaps provide you with more recent books, through the Recorder, for instance. He has an amazingly wide selection, by Jove. Unfortunately I'm quite unable to afford such things myself, much as I would like to.'

'But Papa—'

'All the same, you are not to study, my child, As you know, I have always thought it a lot of nonsense, this matriculation business. After all, there are so many other things for a young lady to do – domestic accomplishments—'

Oh those words! Alberta had heard them before. They had condemned her to dusting and idleness three years ago. If Mrs Selmer had been present, Papa would most likely have turned to her, as he did then, and said : 'Find Alberta some employment in the house'.

Her completely innocent and unsuspecting Papa had handed her over, lock, stock and barrel, to Mama. Alberta had been disarmed and silenced by a helpless : 'I simply can't manage it,' that had seemed to escape him involuntarily after what had gone before. So she had begun to stay at home.

Now her eyes hung on Papa's lips. Would he say the same thing again today? For then the matter would be closed. But he did say it, tired and worried : 'I simply can't manage it, my child. It would be too much for me. I have a number of obligations to meet, as you know'.

Alberta knew. It was the bank loan.

The battle was lost for the time being. What argument could be used in the face of Papa's 'I simply can't manage it'? To claim one's rights, to demand anything from such an utterly exhausted and harassed Papa, who could do that? Not Alberta.

But she had not mobilized all her courage, not summoned up her strength over the past two weeks, for nothing. Those who are not bold by nature can be rash, once they have unleashed themselves. Alberta had something in reserve. It would be an exaggeration to say that she directly attempted to exert pressure, but at any rate she came out with it. As considerately as possible she announced : 'In that case, I'll look for a post, Papa'.

'I beg your pardon?' said the Magistrate.

'I'll try to get a post as a governess. I must tell you Papa, I can't bear simply hanging about here at home.'

Albert was in deep waters. She had said what for years she

had dared only to think. She had to shut her eyes for a moment.

But the Magistrate had put down his pen. 'I've never heard anything to equal it,' he said, in his consternation moving the paper-weight and everything underneath it from one side of his desk to the other. 'You can't bear hanging about in your own home, my child?'

He rose, went to the window, and stood for a moment looking out. His hand jingled in perplexity with the bunch of keys in his trouser pocket.

'Good heavens, is it so difficult for you youngsters,' he said in a different tone of voice. 'You, who have life in front of you,' he added more quietly.

Alberta winced. Out of pity for Papa. Out of irritation. It struck her that the words he had spoken on the Old Quay many years ago, that little encouraging 'back we go', of which she had annexed her share and on which she had based her hopes, had been spoken solely to himself, not to her at all.

'When you're not pretty, you have to try to be something else – a bit clever—'

Now the water was over her head, rushing in her ears. It was not she who had said those last words in a bitter voice, it was someone else.

But Papa had espied land again. He turned, sat down, and crossed one leg hopefully over the other : 'Pretty? Good Lord, my child, if only you'd take a little trouble over your appearance, you'd look really attractive. I must admit your mother is right when she says—'

'I want to travel, Papa, and besides, it would be a good thing if I could earn something on my own. After all, it's almost a necessity.'

'A necessity! Necessity!' The Magistrate tasted the word, and repeated it once more. 'It depends what you mean by necessity. I consider I do what I can to provide you with everything you need, Alberta. I do as much as I possibly can.'

But the last argument had had some sort of effect at any rate, for he changed his mind and declared : 'Well, well, if you really want to I shan't oppose it. I am not in favour of young ladies taking paid positions. It wasn't done in my day, but nowadays everything has been turned upside down. As I said, if you needs must, and if you can find something decent—

'Though I doubt whether that will be so easy,' he added in a brighter tone of voice.

'The trader on Røst* has advertised for a governess.'

'On Røst! But – I've never heard of such a thing! You have no idea what it would be like, child. Røst!'

Alberta nearly let slip something reckless to the effect that nothing could be worse than here. But she stopped herself in time.

'It's further south,' she said.

'Yes, yes, I suppose so, but—

'Now then, that's enough. By Jove, I have work to do, my child.' Papa made a gesture towards the desk, obviously considering the subject closed, as long as it concerned the island of Røst.

'I'll apply for the post then, Papa.'

Magistrate Selmer looked at his daughter despairingly. Then he said : 'Speak to your mother, then we'll see'.

And he bent over his papers.

Alberta paused in front of the sitting-room door until her heart began to beat more slowly, and her breathing became normal.

Had she hoped for support from Papa, for direct co-operation on his part? Had she simply hoped that, with the island of Røst in prospect, he would have admitted the necessity of sending her back to school again?

In any case she had not envisaged having to confront her mother immediately. Now she stood there, collared by circumstance, trying to screw up her courage. She opened the door, crossed the floor—

'Mama,' she began.

Mrs Selmer looked up surprised from the stitches she was

*Røst : the most remote of the South-West Lofoten Islands, north of the Arctic Circle.

counting. A direct approach from Alberta was not part of the normal routine.

'Yes, what is it?'

'There's a post I'd like to apply for, Mama.'

The needle with the stitches on it sank down into Mrs Selmer's lap with the rest of her knitting. 'What did you say?'

'If I can't go to school any more, then I'd prefer to try to find myself a post.'

'I'd prefer to try to find myself a post!' Mrs Selmer repeated such unprecedented words with incredulity. 'What sort of an idea is this, may I ask?' she said icily.

'I want something to do, I want to earn my own living, not just hang about here.'

'I cannot tell you how astonished I am, my dear Alberta, at the tone you adopt. Just hang about here! As if I did not do my utmost to find you employment. As if it were not your primary duty to help your mother. But of course, it's more amusing to sit hunched up over those useless books of yours.'

Mrs Selmer was fully armed by now. Surprise had momentarily paralysed her, but that had passed. 'God knows how ashamed I often am when I hear how domestic and practical the other young girls are. They apply themselves, they help, they relieve their mothers of their burdens, while our young miss—'

'Mama—'

'Yes, I'm taking full advantage of the opportunity to broach the subject. You are a great grief to your mother, Alberta. Not satisfied with applying yourself to looking like a common girl – I said a common girl, there is no other expression for it – but you—'

'Mama—'

'May I ask whether you have spoken to your father about this?'

'I said I wanted to apply for a post.'

'Did you? And what did he say to that?'

'He said I should speak to you. He said he had no objection.'

'Did he? In other words you went there to get his approval first.'

'Mama—'

'May I ask what sort of a post you have in mind? Perhaps the whole thing is cut and dried, without my knowing anything about it. It wouldn't surprise me.'

'I haven't applied for it yet, but the trader on Røst has advertised for a governess.'

'On Røst!' Mrs Selmer looked dazedly at Alberta. Then she leaned her head against the back of her chair and shut her eyes. 'Røst!' she breathed. Her strength had clearly abandoned her.

It was incredible, but Alberta really had sent off her application. After innumerable drafts the document was ready. Now it was on its way to those wild, strange people, the household of the trader on Røst, who required a young lady, with school-leaving certificate, willing to help with a little office work, music not necessary.

She went round in a fever. What had she embarked upon? If she had not had time to think the matter over properly beforehand, she did so all the more thoroughly now. It oppressed her like a nightmare day and night.

She saw herself sitting at a school table with children round her, children who had to be taught something, and kept respectful. She saw her squint, saw the children making faces at each other, saw bills that did not add up, office books in confusion, ink blots, erasures. The sickening giddiness that followed her misdeeds gripped her.

The situation at home was unbearable. Alberta sought refuge in the bog, which lay bright and luxuriant with colour in the thin, clear autumn air. She ran between the tussocks for a while, lay down in the heather, absent-mindedly ate the overripe crowberries, and collected heather and birch twigs into a bouquet. And her anxiety subsided. A hot wave of boldness came over her. Why not, why not she just as much as anyone else?

Pictures of life on this island in the middle of the sea pre-

sented themselves to her imagination. Naked cliffs, screaming, circling sea birds, long rollers, were what she glimpsed.
And a house. Not sheltered by trees, not enclosed by a
garden. A house all by itself. A few waving grasses in a
crevice in the rock. People – of few words and reserved, as she
had seen them at the trading posts deep in the fjords, with
kind, slightly wondering faces.

Then suddenly she saw shoemaker Schoning's rowan tree
swaying, green and luxuriant, with thick blue shadows beneath it, like a plume above the shoemaker's roof – the fullness
of summer; the lush flora of the roadsides, reeking of warmth;
round, yellow, nodding buttercups. The magnificence of the
bog's autumnal carpet, spread out at this moment before her
eyes, impressed her as never before. Her heart dwindled with
loss. But it expanded again. The infinity above and around
her out there on the island in the ocean beat against her, a
breath from space, from simplicity and boundlessness. Immediately she longed to be there, to have the untrammelled,
open horizon round her, to be a speck at the centre of its
immense circle, to be receptive and to listen. New verses, new
dreams awaited her there.

She would send money home every month—

Then Jacob's face appeared. She heard him say : 'Mama
and Papa – they have such a rotten time . . .'

She rose abruptly to her feet and hurried back. The currents from home had reached her.

Mrs Selmer lay on the sofa. She lay there as never before,
crushed, all her strength gone. She dragged herself in to
meals, her look was distant, her mouth bitter. Now and again
a solitary tear would trickle down her cheek.

The Magistrate periodically muttered to himself, his eyes
testing the terrain. Then he would turn to Alberta and embark on a conversation of no consequence in an unnaturally
lively tone of voice. The island of Røst was not mentioned.
The atmosphere was deathly oppressive.

This went on for a week. By that time Alberta was almost
ready for anything, capitulation, an oath devoting herself to

the domestic virtues. Then the Magistrate unexpectedly came
out of his office with the reply in his hand. Somehow Larsen
had stolen a march on her. 'I took the liberty of opening it,'
said Papa. 'Here you are, my child, read it yourself.'

Quivering, Alberta ran through the short missive and
handed it in silence to Mrs Selmer. Mrs Selmer read it. Then
she sat upright on the sofa. 'Heaven has heard my prayers,'
she murmured.

Papa patted Alberta on the head : 'I'm sure it was for the
best, my child, for you and for all of us. Your chance will
come in one way or another, you can be sure of that'.

The position on Røst was already filled.

Was Alberta disappointed or relieved?

She was empty. After a week brimful of hope and fear, she
had nothing to hope or to fear for. She went about feeling
embarrassed, less certain than ever of how she should occupy
herself.

Beda was still not to be seen. And now everyone was silent
about her. A mysterious, ominous silence one did not dare to
break or to puncture with questions. Alberta often went past
the Recorder's office, but nothing happened, and she wandered aimlessly.

In shabby Strand Street the sun still shone between the
grey walls. It seemed as if all the old, unpainted wood down
there had stored the warmth and was giving it back, now that
the air had turned cold and autumnal. Here grass grew in
the gutters. Framed by all the grey it looked greener than
ordinary grass. Behind the small window panes fuchsia and
calceolaria glowed. A lapful of summer had hidden away
down here and been left behind.

No-one walked there. And the Kjeldsens, who once lived
there, had moved to Upper Town long ago. When Alberta
was small, they had lived in the little corner house, that was
so old that the inside walls were of timber. She had gone
inside once, and still remembered the timbered walls that were
painted blue and on which nothing hung straight. The
pictures and the clock hung stiffly outwards at an angle from

the nails on which they were suspended. She remembered a chest of drawers with two china dogs on it, a sofa covered with imitation leather, a shut-in smell. And Kjeldsen the smith, who sat drinking coffee out of a saucer, with a completely black face.

The sight of this innocent house was suddenly disagreeable to her. Was it not in some strange manner in league with everything that was trying to hold her back, with everything that was treacherous and oppressive – Nurse Jullum and other dark powers? She imagined how it would feel to be tied, to live for ever between a chest of drawers and an imitation leather sofa with two china dogs and the old Kjeldsens. A stupid thought, which nevertheless caused Alberta to quicken her pace, as if fleeing from it.

She turned down on to the old Stoppenbrink quay that once, long ago, before Consul Stoppenbrink built the two big new wharves, had been busy and full of traffic. Alberta used to play here sometimes as a child. Here she and Beda had once stolen a big piece of candied sugar from an open sack, kept it for two contrite days, and then crept down again and left it on an empty barrel, for in the meantime the sack had disappeared. The Archdeaconry boat used to be tied up here, and there had been much coming and going of wharf hands and country folk.

Now the quay was abandoned and desolate, all its doors shut. Alberta's footsteps rang empty and hollow as she went through the dim, roofed-in passageway. The sun was hot on the little bench right at the end by the landing stairs. It was warm and quiet. She could look right across Rivermouth, where there were no autumn colours, only boats and water and sun-warmed wood. Not a soul was in sight besides an an old man in a boat a little way out. He stood scratching the back of his neck. Alberta sat down and sank into vacancy. Beneath her the sea busied itself, lapping round the posts with gentle little gurgles. The tide was coming in.

She started. There were footsteps on the quay. Someone was coming, a black shadow in the darkness under the wharf. Alberta looked involuntarily for the old man who had been scratching his neck, but he had disappeared. Oh well, it was probably someone coming to hail the boat. But something about the footsteps made her unseasy.

The figure came out into the sunshine. It was Cedolf.

She was petrified. She had no desire to meet Cedolf down here alone. He would talk to her—

She looked about her, down into the water, out after the boat, trembling and paralysed. Then she arrived at a desperate decision, broke the spell and began to hurry up the quay, towards Cedolf and past him, crimson, staring straight in front of her, as if he did not exist. He stopped, lifted his cap, she sensed that he was saying : 'Excuse me—'

She hurried on as if blind and deaf. Her heart pounded. It pounded wildly. For Cedolf was coming after her, coming with long strides. She began to run, knowing as she did so that this was one of the most stupid things she had ever done.

The old Stoppenbrink quay was long. Today it was endless. If only she were out of the shadow and in the steep little square between crooked houses that led up to the street.

Suddenly she stopped. For flight was useless. Cedolf towered in front of her in the dimness, unnaturally tall. She looked in all directions to avoid meeting his eyes. Eventually she could do so no longer. They both stood for a little, looking at each other, still out of breath from running. And now Alberta's fright melted away. Outraged dignity had the upper hand. Even the anxiety in Cedolf's hands, which alternately clenched and unclenched themselves, left her unaffected. Just let him try—

'Will you be so kind as to let me pass,' she said from the superiority of her position as Alberta Selmer.

Cedolf did not reply. He stood his ground. 'What did you want to run away for?' he asked, his voice quivering and outraged.

Alberta was silent. She walked round him, saying nothing. But there was Cedolf in front of her again, and this time he openly barred her way. He was highly insulted and held her to blame : 'What did you want to run for, I'm only asking.

What have I done to you? When you set eyes on me, you might be seeing the devil himself,' he said, emphasizing 'devil', as if to make sure of conjuring up that unsympathetic character.

Was Alberta afraid again? She replied curtly, but more meekly : 'I didn't see who it was'.

'Oh, so that's it, you didn't see who it was?' Cedolf's voice was full of scorn. 'No, you never see. All you see is that it's not one of your grand folk, so he must be a dangerous scoundrel.'

'I told you, I didn't see who it was, Kjeldsen.'

'Grand folks' little girls,' said Cedolf ambiguously and without answering, apparently to himself. 'What do you think we want of you?' he said, suddenly including vague masses of humanity in the question. 'What do you ruddy well think we want? Do you think we'd bother to run after you only to—'

Alberta interrupted him. Outraged dignity was again uppermost : 'You seem to be running after me'.

'Yes! I found myself put to that necessity,' said Cedolf with emphasis. He stood swaying from the knees, very much in the right. 'I have something to give you from Jacob. He wrote particularly that it was to be delivered to you personally, and that no-one should see. But that was the worst part. I've gone round with it on me for more than a fortnight, but no sooner had I caught sight of you than you disappeared again. I'm leaving soon too. Today I was sitting up with Klem the carpenter's family, and saw you going down here, but if I'd known I was going to frighten you out of your wits I'd have stayed where I was, and sent it back to Jacob – well, here you are, take it, now it's off my hands.'

Cedolf had taken a blue envelope with Jacob's handwriting on it out of his inside pocket and handed it to Alberta. He took a deep breath, as if relieved of a heavy load.

Alberta might well feel a fool. 'Thank you,' she said meekly. 'Thank you very much, Kjeldsen.' – She felt she ought to say a bit more and fastened on Jacob : 'You've just had a letter then?'

The situation was thoroughly embarrassing and beyond

saving. And Cedolf was not quite himself any more, not just cheeky and self-assured. He had become more human, a big, injured boy. She wished she could put things right again.

'I told you, it was a fortnight ago,' answered Cedolf, a little absent-mindedly. 'Jacob's all right, they were lying in Bahia for coal. He's pleased with life. He's been lucky, has Jacob,' he continued conversationally, and suddenly seemed to have decided to take up the subject in all its ramifications.

But Alberta, who felt that this was bringing them closer together than she wished, asked no more. Besides, Cedolf was Jacob's evil genius. She prepared to take her leave coldly and politely.

As if Cedolf saw what she was thinking, he said : 'But you think me capable of anything. You thought I led Jacob astray'.

'You got him to go to Rivermouth and the Grand,' answered Alberta curtly. The whole thing must be brought to an end. She had not the slightest desire to discuss these matters with Cedolf any further. But right was right.

'To Rivermouth! And the Grand!' The same helpless expression she had once seen on Jacob's face came to Cedolf's for an instant. 'But where can we go? Can you tell me where we can go in this town?

'Besides, it might have been Cedolf Kjeldsen who held him back, when others wanted to offer Jacob drinks. That can happen too. He was inexperienced, was Jacob.'

Alberta started a little. Could it have happened that way? What did it matter, it wasn't seemly, this conversation with Cedolf on a quay. She brought the subject back to the letter, waving it a little. 'Thank you very much then, Kjeldsen. It was kind of you to come after me with it. I'll write and tell Jacob I've had it.'

Right through it all she had felt Cedolf's compelling power. It was not simply that he was tall and handsome, he was almost *too* handsome, it was too much of a good thing. Rather it was something in the voice, a dark timbre it took on now and again. Or – God knows what it was. Perhaps it was only Alberta's own miserable nature.

A little reluctantly she extended her hand. She could hardly avoid it. She would go now, irrevocably : 'I wish you a good journey—'

But Cedolf held on to her hand : 'Yes, I'll soon be tossing on the briny again'.

'Yes, you will. Pleasant trip. And many thanks.' Alberta withdrew her hand.

'I expect I'll be leaving on the next boat for Hamburg.' Cedolf seemed to have something on his mind. He was uneasy, uneasy in his arms and his hands.

'I want you to believe that I've never wished you any harm,' he said suddenly.

'Of course I've never believed you have,' answered Alberta, her voice at once failing her. It was the dark timbre in Cedolf's—

'Jacob's told me what a fine girl you are. There aren't many like you.'

'Good-bye then, Kjeldsen, pleasant journey—'

'But it doesn't matter to Miss Selmer what Cedolf Kjeldsen says, I suppose.'

'I must go now, good-bye.'

And Alberta really did. If only she were out of the dimness here under the wharf, out in the light on the slope up to Strand Street. If only she were well away from here.

But Cedolf still had something on his mind : 'Fare you well'

Alberta stopped. God knows why. She was somehow unable to go on. She was seized by inertness.

Then it happened.

As if guided by fate, by something inevitable, Cedolf moved nearer. And she was paralysed by it. All she saw were the beautiful, deep-set eyes, that came closer and closer, with something stiff and tense about them. Her hand was not free any more.

Then Cedolf's face was there, his mouth was on hers. 'I don't wish you any harm,' she heard him murmur, and in his voice was the same warm magic as in the spring, when he had said : 'Don't you be afraid'.

She sank back helplessly against the wall, and let Cedolf kiss her.

But when he tried to put his arm between her and the wall and draw her to him, she came to her senses, slipped out of his grasp, tore her hand out of his, and ran.

'Whatever is it?' exclaimed Jensine, as Alberta rushed through the kitchen.

'Nothing!'

Up in her room she tore off her hat, stood for a moment looking into her eyes in the mirror, blushed crimson, hid her face, and went and washed it and her hands.

She sat at the window. Her heart would not stop beating. It pounded as it did when she had run up the hills without stopping, as if it would knock her down. She sat staring out at nothing, feeling her eyes unnaturally large in her face. She went over to look at herself in the mirror again. A stranger was there. A new and unknown Alberta.

There was so much grown-ups and old people neither knew nor suspected. They went about so innocently, busy with this and that, thinking that was all there was to it. They knew nothing of what was insidious and dangerous, of what was coiling and twisting beyond all reason in hidden places.

Beyond all reason. For she would not, could not, live with imitation leather sofas and china dogs. She would die of it.

She hid her face again, aware of her own degradation.

'If only I'd gone to Røst,' she whispered, and repeated it mechanically several times with her thoughts elsewhere. 'Beda,' she whispered.

Then she remembered the letter, lying crumpled on the wash-stand. She had gone through town, through the kitchen, with it in her hand, quite openly, this secret document, a confidential missive from Jacob. Heaven knew what it might contain.

She tore open the envelope with trembling hands. In it lay two ten *kroner* notes and a little piece of paper: 'Dear Alberta, buy yourself something nice with this. Something you want and like. More later. I'm fine. Yours, Jacob'.

Alberta sat twisting and turning the little piece of paper. Then something was released in her heart, and she wept copiously over everything at once : the island of Røst, Beda, herself, our complex and erratic nature, and Jacob. Over life in general.

Alberta did not go out for two days. She found all kinds of excuses to keep to her room, and displayed an unusual amount of interest in the red and white tablecloth besides. Sometimes in this life one needs a refuge, a fortification to which to retire. Then one turns to whatever is available.

Now and again she glanced surreptitiously, searchingly and enquiringly at Mama. But when she surprised Mama looking back at her, surreptitiously, searchingly and enquiringly, Alberta disappeared from the sitting-room for good. Upstairs she sat for hours at a time inspecting herself in the mirror.

On the third day Jensine, who had come from the baker's, remarked : 'I heard Mrs Kjeldsen saying to Mrs Theodorsen that that fellow Cedolf went south today on the Hamburg boat'.

That afternoon Alberta hurried out along Rivermouth, restless from sitting indoors and from a suppressed need to be alone with life's problems under the open sky.

At Louisa-round-the-bend she almost ran full tilt into Mrs Selmer and the Magistrate, walking peacefully down one of the cross-streets from Upper Town.

'Heaven preserve us, child, how you run. What's the matter?'

'Nothing,' answered Alberta, her heart sinking. In that respect she was unchanged.

'Well, I must go home, but you young things ought to take a walk in this fine weather,' said Mrs Selmer, throwing them together. She looked preoccupied as she did so, as if thinking about something completely different, but she had a glint in her eye as if she was secretly a little amused, and Alberta noticed it.

'I'm going home too,' she said sulkily. Then she caught the Magistrate's eyes, full of unhappy astonishment. She remembered her intention to be kind. Besides, she already felt a little faint on account of her bad conscience.

'Well – yes, all right – I'd like to.'

And they wandered out of town along Rivermouth together.

* * *

Sounds travelled so strangely at Rivermouth and on the river during the autumn evenings. It was as if the thick darkness, black as velvet, carried them. Voices, the stroke of an oar and the creaking of rowlocks came clear and distinct across the water, as at no other time.

Gudrun, Christina and Alberta lowered their voices involuntarily and spoke softly, as they sat one evening at about ten o'clock in the Archdeacon's skiff, scarcely able to distinguish one another. Alberta and Gudrun were each carefully resting an oar; Christina was on her knees in the prow, on the look-out for posts and moorings lurking in the darkness. They were between the wharves in the old harbour and had happily avoided bumping into rowing boats and sailboats and the Russian ship, which was taking on fish from Badendück. Now they had to find their way to the Archdeacon's mooring innermost on the Kamke quay, which was an awkward manoeuvre, and walk along the pitch dark wharf among barrels and crates, the worst part of all. If only Beda had been with them. She was so brave.

Crash! They bumped into something big and black, that towered above them. Alberta fell backwards across the thwart and got her behind wet : 'You might have gone back for the scoop, Christina,' she whispered in annoyance. 'It was mean of you. What did we bump into?'

'It must be Badendück's steps, you're rowing too fast.'

'Nonsense, it's you who's not looking out.'

'Oh yes I am,' answered Christina angrily. 'I wish I'd left you behind on the other side – I wish I'd never taken you with me at all.'

'You needn't bother to take us with you another time, then you can sit all by yourself on the other side, poor thing. Who got the boat free again, you I suppose?'

They quarrelled volubly under their breath, and it did them

good. The eeriness seemed kept at a distance. It lurked ready to pounce in here between the great wharves, about which so many tales were told.

For a couple of hours they had fought against the current swirling out of Rivermouth on the ebb tide. The cold fright that had crept over them when, laden with frozen cranberries, they had come down to the shore below the mountain and discovered the boat lying far up the shelving beach among the boulders, was still with them. The lengthy business of getting it down again, the tension as they rowed and rowed while nothing changed its position on land, while darkness fell and the lights were lit over in the town, still quivered in their remarks.

The Kamke quay was particularly sinister. Old Kamke's father was supposed to haunt it. None of them would admit they were thinking about him, but all three were doing so.

'As long as you know about it, Christina, we can leave the oars and everything in the boat until tomorrow. It'll make such a din if we take them all up, we might wake someone. Who knows what sort of people may be hanging about behind all the barrels further down the quay.'

'We *must* take them with us. I *daren't* go home without them,' whimpered Christina. 'And you'll be good enough to wait and help me,' she bullied. She was sitting for'ard, was responsible for everything, it made her fractious. It was well known that the Archdeaconry family was unreasonably per-nickety about the boat. They would even unhook the rudder and take it home.

'I hope we don't meet Kwasnikow,' said Alberta in order to blunt her own fear. 'I'm thinking mostly of him.'

In her imagination she saw Mama waiting to write *finis* to the escapade, sitting upright with blank expression on a chair in the dining-room, the attitude Mrs Selmer always adopted on occasions such as this. Nevertheless she was longing for the moment when the porch door would close behind her, and she was safe at home again.

There, they bumped into something else! 'What a fool you are, Christina, can't you look out?'

'*Look?* Did you say *look?*' Christina was about to say more. She began : 'If you think I'm—' then suddenly stopped, and all three sat quiet as mice, paralysed with fear. They had all heard it simultaneously, someone walking slowly along. One minute it sounded as if it were coming down the quay, the next as if it were going away.

'Oh God!' whispered Gudrun. 'Shhh!' pounced the others.

They scarcely dared breathe, and a wave of relief went through them when the footsteps seemed to fall away from each other and lose their rhythm. There were at least two of them. And they were people. Drunk and dangerous perhaps, but still people.

'My God, I thought it was Kamke,' exclaimed Gudrun.

'How stupid you are,' sneered the others. 'Imagine, Gudrun believes in old Kamke! Oh Gudrun, you are a joke.'

Now they could hear voices, the voices of two men, of a sudden violently raised and mingling in angry exchange.

'Oh, I hope they're not from the Russian ship,' whispered Christina, and a bitter feeling of helplessness crept into the other two.

Then the footsteps stopped. Quite clearly, spoken normally and very calmly, a sentence came through the darkness : 'Sir, you are a blackguard'.

'I beg your pardon?' came the answer, sharp and furious, considerably less calm.

'Irrevocably a blackguard,' repeated the first voice. 'It gives me great satisfaction to tell you so, and I will gladly repeat it in the presence of witnesses.'

The voices flowed together, the sharp, furious one in a confused torrent of words, the calm one in short, cutting phrases : 'Precisely – exactly – I agree with you entirely—'

'Damn you,' shouted the sharp voice, 'I repeat, I don't even know if I'm responsible. I have considerable doubts, and with good reason—'

'The only responsibility you have now is to make yourself scarce,' answered the calm voice coldly. 'Now we've got you covered it's all we demand of you. You're finished in this town, Sir.'

'May I ask,' shouted the furious one, intending to continue with a long dissertation about having to answer for this and it would cost him dear. But he was hushed up : 'For goodness sake hush, man, don't scream like that – you'll make a scandal—'

The voices were lost in mumbling, the speakers moved away. And now it was clear that they were not on the Kamke quay at all, but on one further away.

The three in the boat sat in dead silence. Nobody wanted to be the first to speak. '*Haben Sie gehört,*' whispered Christina finally, as if it was necessary to fool listening ears.

Alberta and Gudrun attacked her together. 'You're not to go telling anyone about this, Christina, we're telling you now. So just you keep your mouth shut.'

'And why should *I* be the one to say anything?' asked Christina, insulted, and she may very well have been right. Perhaps she was no more of a tattler than most; but she was mistrusted on account of her notorious reputation for being a pattern of virtue, who liked to sit with her elders round the tea table and chat precociously. Over the years she had been suspected of various treacheries, without anyone being able to accuse her directly.

They brought the boat in and moored it, handed up the oars and rudder and left everything tidy. None of them was frightened any more. Each was wrapped in her own thoughts. Christina was speechless with affront, Gudrun and Alberta only exchanged words when necessary. All were bursting to discuss the incident, to find out what the others thought about it, but they felt embarrassed and no-one would begin. Besides, Christina had her insults to nurse. When she disappeared through the back gate of the Archdeaconry, laden with equipment from the boat and still speechless, the others relaxed. 'What do you think will happen, Alberta? You heard who they were?'

'Yes.'

'But he told him he ought to go away. He'd better make himself scarce, he said. Can you understand that?'

'No, it's frightfully odd.'

'Do you think it's true what they're saying, Alberta, that Beda's going to have a baby?'

'Don't be so silly! Who says that?'

'Oh, a lot of people. The maids at home. Olefine the dress-maker. They say so at school too.'

And it was not that Alberta had not heard it. But she had rejected it, denied it consistently, as if things could be undone by keeping silent about them. 'That's just nonsense, surely?'

'But supposing it's true?'

'It can't be true.'

A window opened above them. Mrs Selmer's voice came through the darkness: 'Is that you, Alberta? Heavens, my child, we're sick with anxiety. Where *have* you been? Hurry home, Gudrun, your mother's quite desperate'.

And Alberta and Gudrun went their several ways, heavy with the knowledge that Jaeger, the Recorder, had called Lett the dentist a blackguard on a deserted quay in River Street, where he had thought himself to be without witnesses.

* * *

See, how crisp and light the shadow of shoemaker Schoning's rowan had become. It was a round, gently swaying mass of shadow no longer, but a lattice-work of thin, blue branches, restlessly flickering over the pavement. Soon not a red leaf would be left on the tree. The clusters of berries swayed on the bare twigs, and the sky behind them was ice blue.

One morning there was newly fallen snow in the mountains. It lay halfway down them, and a raw cold, naked and biting, set in from above. It arrived in the night and dug its claws into Alberta, gripping her from behind between her shoulder blades and buckling her tightly into the old enforced position with her legs drawn up and her arms crossed over her breast, keeping her awake for hours. Now she wrapped herself in a nightgown again, shivering and quaking, with the prospect of her own greyish-violet winter face in the mirror.

Mrs Selmer sat at the breakfast table with a shawl over her dressing-gown. She looked at Alberta resignedly as she handed her a cup of coffee, and according to established tradition Alberta sank conscientiously into the depths, flushed and quivering. Automatically she continued Mrs Selmer's train of thought : 'I have so few pleasures in life. I don't think I should be deprived of seeing my only daughter looking a little attractive. But even that is denied me'.

Alberta sat at the little table where the mending basket stood – where the mending basket always stood – took a stocking and began to darn it. Frozen, she twined her legs round each other. Her fingers were dead and numb. If only the Magistrate had eaten, if only Mrs Selmer had gone upstairs, so that she could get hold of the coffee pot.

And she ran up the hillsides. This year as last year.

On her birthday at the end of the month Alberta as usual received a potted plant from the Chief Clerk. There was nothing surprising about it. The Clerk had always been attentive in this way, both to Mrs Selmer and Alberta. It was taken for what it was – a courtesy.

For two years it had been a pot of Michaelmas daisies. This year it was neither more nor less than the big blue hydrangea that had stood resplendent in the Sisters Kremer's window for several days, attracting attention and admiration. Mrs Selmer had even asked about it the other day just to find out what it cost, and, believe it or not, it was ten *kroner*. For this reason she exclaimed from a full heart : 'Mr Gronneberg must be mad, to go to such expense. It would have been quite sufficient to give less.'

Alberta was hostile towards the hydrangea from the very beginning. In any case she felt not the slightest sense of ownership towards these annual offerings. It was Mrs Selmer who received them and put them in an advantageous position in the sitting-room, Mrs Selmer who drew the attention of visitors to them and said : 'Isn't it lovely?' Alberta's was the blame when they lacked water and hers the unpleasant duty of thanking the Clerk, a duty she carried out as quickly and in as low a voice as possible, being supported by Mama, who always emphasized the excessive amiability of the enterprise.

This year the plant's dimensions, together with something indefinable that hung in the air, oppressed Alberta. Since it came into the house she had continually felt her heart thumping. It was as if it were held in a vice and were beating to free itself. She tried vainly to shake off this uneasiness. It occurred to her that Mama was emphasizing more strongly than usual that the plant was Alberta's. '*Your* hydrangea,' she would say, and she never tired of pointing out that a hydrangea at this time of year was something quite out of the ordinary, a work of art.

Alberta demonstratively held her tongue when its merits were under discussion, defending herself with her sole weapon – silence.

*　*　*

Mr Selmer, Magistrate, and Mrs Selmer.

It was written on a small, hard, unsealed envelope with a local postmark. Alberta peeped into it on her way home with the post.

She remained standing as if rooted to the spot, looking alternately down at the two cards it contained, and then straight in front of her. 'Oh!' she said. 'No!' she said. And the painful pressure in her breast suddenly increased, her heart pounded as if to free itself. She had a desire to hide the cards, to throw them away, but realised that it would be of little use. So she took them home.

On the one there stood : Beda Birgitte Buck. On the other : Adam Jaeger, Recorder.

'Nothing less than a blow in the face to all respectable people,' asserted the Governor's lady. 'We can assume that the child is that fellow Lett's, I suppose. And now we shall have the pleasure of seeing the worthy Beda amongst us as the Recorder's wife, we shall even be compelled to receive her in our homes. Just imagine it, picture the situation to yourselves. It will be far from pleasant, let me tell you. It's true they say the Recorder is thinking of applying for a transfer south, but that won't happen immediately. What? Could the child be his? Well, in that case all I have to say is what kind of morality is it that allows such a relationship with one man while spending day and night with the other. After all, they've been seen at nightfall all over the place, Beda and her dentist. I'm so glad now that we never set foot in his office, but kept to old Oyen, even if he is old-fashioned and it hurts. Yes, he *is* ham-fisted, but he's thorough, and you can't complain about his reputation.'

The Archdeacon's wife objected with crystal-clear eyes that after all, for the Recorder's sake, one must – one could not very well do nothing. 'And besides, now Beda is marrying such a splendid man, perhaps – It's amazing what a difference a change of circumstances can make, Mrs Lossius.'

'Naturally, one must do something. That's precisely what is so disagreeable. If I didn't have to, I shouldn't give it a thought.' The Governor's lady was irritated over the matter, taking it as something of a personal affront, and bore contradiction with less patience than ever. As far as a change of circumstances went, she doubted whether anything would affect Beda. 'I am deeply distressed on the Recorder's account,' she announced in conclusion.

Mrs Pram honestly thought that if Mr Jaeger wanted to go off and get married in his old age, he could surely have found himself something better. 'We had given him up,' said Mrs Pram. 'He had been ranked with the confirmed bachelors long ago. But just think, if only he had chosen Otilie Weyer for instance, what a joy for us all. They say she doted on him the first few years after he came here.'

Papa said: 'Ha-ha – the Recorder – ha-ha'. He laughed inwardly a little and looked at Mrs Lossius, who also laughed inwardly, lifted her glass and said: 'Skaal, Mr Magistrate!'

But Mrs Selmer surprised them all. 'I can't be anything but sorry for Beda,' she said. 'The difference in their ages is great. I don't suppose it will be so easy for her.'

'Easy!' Mrs Lossius had to repeat it, so indignant was she. 'So easy! May I ask why it should be easy? If it should turn out to be difficult, it's really only what Beda thoroughly deserves. For the Recorder's sake we must hope for the best, but otherwise—'. Her lorgnette struck her left hand in a series of nervous little taps.

The general consensus of opinion amongst the ladies was that the Recorder was doing it out of chivalry, because he was so fearfully chivalrous. Mrs Selmer was quite alone in declaring, mischievously and cryptically : 'What have I always said, you never know where you are with that man. He's an old slyboots, let me tell you'.

To be honest the town did not know what to make of it. Was the child Lett's or Jaeger's? Was the Recorder taking Beda out of compassion or love? Was Beda taking the Recorder to save her skin, or was she in love with him? Did she start a relationship with him as soon as she had finished with Lett last summer, or had it begun before, or had there never been any such thing?

Lett the dentist had left, rumour had it, following a violent encounter with the Recorder on one of the quays, during which the two gentlemen were said to have exchanged insults and been finally reduced to fisticuffs, hitting each other with their sticks. When Alberta and Gudrun tackled Christina about these rumours, she said that by God she hadn't breathed a word. And perhaps it was so. Who could guarantee that nobody else had heard the two vociferous gentlemen that evening?

Olefine the dressmaker was significantly silent over her sewing machine, but Jensine seized every occasion to point out that many people had prophesied that Beda Buck would come to a bad end. 'And what can you expect of simple folk, when grand folk are no better than they should be? Anyway, we only have to wait and see whether it's a little Lett or a little Jaeger,' chuckled Jensine.

Mrs Buck's closest acquaintance, the ladies Dorum, Kilde, Lebesby and Elmholz, insisted to all who would lend them an ear, that the Recorder had really loved Beda for two or three years, but had held back on account of the difference in their ages. But then this summer . . . Then when he came and asked to have the wedding immediately, Mrs Buck had said : 'But my dear Mr Recorder, Beda has nothing. She scarcely owns anything but the clothes on her back'. To which the Recorder had replied that that was not what he was asking for.

At home Mrs Selmer sat speculating over the affair with her knitting and her book. When for strategic reasons Alberta sat down beside her with her everlasting tablecloth, Mrs Selmer would speculate aloud, holding her knitting up in front of her to cast off : 'This affair of Beda's is really a terrible business. I shan't tell you what is being said about her, Alberta, I only hope none of its gets to the ears of you young girls. She must know herself how matters stand. But if she was really fond of that fellow Lett, I cannot do otherwise than feel bitterly sorry for her, poor child, for in that case she has many a sad day in front of her. For my part I shall be as friendly as I can towards Beda – she may find she is in need of a little friendliness. You must sew her some little thing, Alberta'.

'Go up and congratulate her yourself, Alberta, she'll be so pleased, she's all alone at home,' was Mrs Buck's reply to Alberta's careful : 'Congratulate Beda for me,' when they met a couple of days later outside Kilde's shop. And Alberta, who had thought of nothing but Beda since the cards arrived, went with beating heart.

Beda was sitting sewing on the couch. 'Is that you, Alberta? How nice of you to look in.' She put down her sewing, but did not get up. Her face when she lifted it was sunken round the eyes, patchy and brown, so changed that Alberta's heart sank.

'Congratulations, Beda,' she said, troubled, and extended her hand. 'It was quite a surprise.' She could hear how strange her voice sounded.

'Yes.' Beda smiled a little crookedly. 'I'm a little surprised myself. You never can tell, as they say. I expect it was the last thing you all expected in this town, that the Recorder would marry Beda Buck.'

Her tone was facetious. Nevertheless it dismayed Alberta. The whole thing dismayed her. She did not know whether Beda was happy or miserable, and it did not seem to matter.

Reckless Beda, reckless with money, clothes and everything else, reckless with herself, the bold representative of defiance, now sat quiet and changed with her sewing, Nurse Jullum's certain prey. And she was to marry an old man, a man of over forty, a man like Papa, thought Alberta, although she knew the Recorder was considerably younger. In a short time, only a few months, it would be Beda the ladies would be discussing : 'How are things at the Recorder's? She should be near her time now'.

It was too outrageous, it was unbelievable, it must be possible to prevent it. Alberta wanted to take hold of Beda, to persuade her to back out in time, to make her see that it was insane. But something restrained her.

'I must be glad to be getting such a good husband,' said Beda quietly. She had taken up her sewing again.

'Is that for your trousseau?' asked Alberta for something to say.

'Yes, that's what it's supposed to be.'

There was a pause.

'He's so kind, Jaeger, I don't know how I shall ever be able to make it up to him—' Beda took up the conversation again. 'He wants to apply for a transfer south as soon as possible.' It was almost as if Beda was apologizing for herself.

'So I've heard.'

'Yes. He doesn't want me to stay here for the rest of my days. It's very kind of him. We're going abroad too, later on.'

'How marvellous !'

Was Beda really looking forward to the future with optimism, or was she simply bracing herself to meet it? It sounded to Alberta as if she were mechanically repeating something learned by heart.

'You're going to get married soon, I understand?'

'As soon as the banns have been called. That's why I'm so busy, as you see.' Beda held up her sewing in front of Alberta, and the same crooked little smile again came over her face. A completely strange, new smile, so unlike the old Beda. The wide mouth over the even teeth was no longer animated. It was closed and there was something secretive about it.

'What are they saying in town?' she asked. 'How about Mrs Lossius, what does she have to say for herself?'

'They're surprised, of course.'

'Oh indeed? Well – they'd better prepare themselves for a few more surprises,' answered Beda curtly, and made no further comment on the subject. On the other hand she invited Alberta to visit her when they were married: 'We're not having a big wedding. It will be very quiet, but afterwards you must be one of the first to come and see us, and you will be very welcome'. She smiled again and extended her hand. Alberta could stand it no longer. Her mouth trembled and she failed to utter a sound.

'But Alberta, what's the matter, how silly you are—' Beda's own voice was trembling, nevertheless. Alberta, who turned away to dry her eyes, did not know whether it was laughter or tears. 'It's just that it's so strange that you're getting married,' she managed to say.

'You're right, it is strange. But I'm going to have such a kind husband. I couldn't have found one kinder.'

'No.'

And they had nothing more to say to each other. They stood shaking hands for a while, considerably embarrassed.

'Well, I just wanted to congratulate you.'

'Thank you for coming.'

Alberta left her. She saw Beda in the old days, following the Recorder through Upper Town, where he had then lived, tilting her shoulders a little, as he did, and singing 'Adam in Paradise'.

She saw Beda's pale, closed, distant face up on the bog some time ago, heard the Recorder's calm, cold words through the darkness that memorable evening: 'Sir, you are a blackguard' – and Lett's furious: 'Damn you, I don't even know if I'm responsible'.

She heard Mrs Buck: 'You must let us use our heads a little'.

Then all else was pushed aside by Beda's face as it had looked that spring, in the short moment at the dance when she had laid her cheek against Lett's: the sweet, tender smile, the closed eyes, both as if spun together and entangled with the deep call, the strong, demanding sigh in Alberta's blood, her paralysis under Cedolf's kiss.

Life was a trap. Even Beda, frank, courageous Beda, was she not sitting there like a fly on flypaper, having, as far as one could see, kicked out and then given in?

* * *

That letter from Uncle the Colonel – had Mama left it lying on the sewing table, open, out of its envelope, on purpose?

There it was, anyhow, and Alberta found herself alone with it. It was folded over in the middle. On the part facing upwards she caught sight of her own name at the first glance.

She hesitated no longer, but leaned over and read :

'. . . and I understand to the full, my dear sister-in-law, your anxieties on Alberta's account. Lacking the opportunity, as you do, of giving her a more extensive education, it is reasonable that your mother's heart should turn in its anxiety to a good and suitable marriage as a solution – all the more reasonable when we consider that woman's natural place is and always will remain the home, whatever people may say. Within the four walls of a home your daughter will find the surest happiness. Now it is my impression that our dear Alberta is a thoroughly good, well brought-up young girl, with an excellent brain, but of a . . . to be sure, loving and winning – but nevertheless modest appearance, together with a quiet and somewhat timid personality. In these circumstances I believe very little would be gained either for her or yourself by allowing her to spend a winter down here. Among the young ladies of this town, some of whom, I must admit, old man as I am, are unusually vivacious and beautiful, she would find it difficult to make any impression. You would also be compelled to put yourselves to quite disproportionate expense, in order that she might merely be enabled to present a tolerable appearance, as her birth demands and

warrants. The expense of the carriage for our Lydia
alone has been particularly heavy on my budget during
the current winter; but since, by reason of various circumstances, and in spite of the fact that we ourselves
have never been in a position to reciprocate adequately,
she has been accepted in those circles which entertain a
great deal down here, I decided I ought to sustain such
expense. This has shown itself to have been entirely
justified, since it was precisely in these circles that she
met and became more closely acquainted with the exceedingly pleasant and sympathetic young man who is to
become our son-in-law.

'The position is quite different for your Alberta, who,
as you know, has grown up quite outside these circles. It
would of course not be particularly easy for her to gain
access to them. The fact that you yourself have celebrated triumphs both in the Association and in private
salons would scarcely be sufficient in this case, nor would
the fact that she was living with us. Your time down
here was too brief, and it was too long ago. I am afraid
that our dear Alberta, even if she paid the obligatory
visits, would find herself leading a somewhat unheeded
existence. Such is the world and the people in it. In
addition, when present at such events to which she
might have some expectation of being invited, she would
in all probability, mainly on account of her lack of
acquaintances, come to play the less amusing rôle of a
wallflower, a humiliation to which she should not be unnecessarily exposed. You know from your own experience, I am sure, my dear sister-in-law, what importance
society attaches to external appearance. With an appearance and conduct such as yours, one could make an
impression almost anywhere. All doors are open to the
lady who is both beautiful and distinguished; she is welcome everywhere. Those less richly endowed on the other
hand should rather seek happiness in quieter and more
modest circumstances, and heaven forbid that it should
be suggested that they hereby choose the worse part.

But to be brief: you should look for a husband for our dear Alberta in the circumstances she knows and to which she is accustomed. There she will have every prospect of winning the respect and the love of a worthy and honourable young man. I understand that at the great trading posts up there in your Arctic regions there resides a veritable trading aristocracy (the so-called "lords of the headlands"), many of whom, it is said, keep quite impressive households under the circumstances, and whose sons are on no account to be despised as mates. Would it not be a task for your anxious mother's heart to bring it about that Alberta might one day sit secure and happy in the position of rightful lady of the manor on one of these aforementioned headlands? This is only a suggestion *en passant;* there are of course other prospects of meeting "the right person" up there. Many young men of excellent family apply to go north when they begin their careers, in fact, I hear that you already have an efficient and sympathetic young man in your employ. I assure you, a wise and tactful mother can do much in a matter such as this, I would even go so far as to say that it is a most important part of her duty.

'This is, my dear sister-in-law, the humble and well-meaning advice of an old man experienced in the ways of the world, in a matter that is of particular weight and import as much for you and my brother, as for your daughter.

Your ever devoted T.B.S.

P.S. The date of our Lydia's wedding has been somewhat advanced. It will now take place next month. My wife will write to you about this in more detail. She and Lydia send you most affectionate greetings.

Alberta put back the letter as it was, went upstairs and sat by the window. For once she did not cry.

She sat, her blood running cold, imagining the small moves being made backwards and forwards concerning her inconvenient self, with whom none of them really knew what to do. She sat for a long time, dazedly feeling something stiffen and remain in her face, feeling pain from the clenched hands in her lap. She hated them all.

'I'm glad I kissed Cedolf,' she said eventually through clenched teeth, 'Very glad, very glad. Come back Cedolf, and I'll kiss you again. As much as you like, as much as you like.'

* * *

The Clerk's hydrangea seemed as if it would never fade. The weeks went by, and all that happened was that its flowers assumed a semi-artificial, slightly dessicated appearance. 'By Jove,' said the Magistrate. 'Never seen a plant last so long.'

Alberta watered it reluctantly and insufficiently. She had an antipathy towards it. When, one day, she came too close to it, the smell of it, chilly and sickening, made her recoil. And it occurred to her that the hydrangea smelt of corpses. It smelt like old Mrs Veum when she lay dead. The three clusters of flowers were three well-preserved relics. After that she avoided it when dusting and passed it by purposely with the watering can.

But Mrs Selmer drew everyone's attention daily to the fact that it was wonderful how the hydrangea was lasting so long. She would notice that it lacked water, and advance with can upraised : 'Alberta, you've forgotten this poor plant of yours again, and here it is flowering for us so nicely. It's sad to see, my dear, that you have no feeling for this sort of thing'. Mrs Selmer watered it thoroughly. 'But things will surely be different when you have your own home one of these days, if not before,' she said, sighing.

Then she would invite the Clerk to supper again, although he had been quite recently. It seems to me that he is getting more attached to us,' she would explain. 'I do think that's nice.'

Perhaps he was. He came when invited, at any rate, was more talkative, more outspoken, stayed late.

Alberta froze up, remained on her guard, and ignored all her former intentions to be kind. She perched on the edge of her chair more awkwardly than ever. If she met the Clerk's eye, she immediately looked away again. Under their shyness was there not something she had not seen before : tenacious, obtrusive determination, a kind of triumph? They defiled her. 'Leeches,' she thought. 'Leeches.'

The sum of her conversation was yes and no. She contributed absolutely nothing to these social occasions. Nevertheless, Mama had recently seemed to be eyeing her more hopefully and indulgently, even to the extent of treating her with a certain amount of deference. It increased her repugnance and uneasiness.

One day she met old Mrs Weyer, leaning on Otilie's arm. Old Mrs Weyer stopped and shouted : 'And what about the Recorder, eh ! What about the Recorder !'

'Yes—'

'Well now, I hope we shall be hearing some more pleasant news soon. It won't be long now, I hear.'

And old Mrs Weyer slapped Alberta hard on the shoulder several times : 'Yes-yes, yes-yes, a good husband, a good husband. Just wait, my child, you'll feel like a new woman after the first confinement. Confinements cleanse the body, let me tell you,' she shouted into Alberta's ear. Alberta shrank back, horrified.

'But Mama,' sighed Otilie unhappily. She whispered to Alberta : 'Poor Mama, she gets more forgetful every day. You mustn't mind what – she's getting you mixed up with someone else,' she said, attempting to gloss it over.

But Alberta rushed away as if pursued. It was no figment of her imagination. A horrible notion, a breath of nightmare, glimpsed far out on the edge of evil, uneasy dreams had suddenly taken shape and become real. Now it was going about freely, haunting the streets and the market place.

Was it not grinning at her from all the eyes she met?

She rushed home, and upstairs, to bury her head in the pillow. Something seemed to rise higher and higher about her, a revolting slime. She could no longer breathe—

That night she did not close her eyes. Her thoughts circled endlessly round one idea : to get away, free from it all.

There was an English ship anchored at the Klykken quay . . .

In her search for a hold, for a thread through the passing days, something from the time when she worked regularly, when she went to school, Alberta had joined the gymnastic society. Her old gym costume still fitted her, the fee was a bagatelle. Mrs Selmer, whose ways were past finding out, produced her objections in a tone of capitulation : the company was mixed, it would be most unpleasant to have to come home so late in the dark, she would have been pleased if Alberta indulged herself in the same sort of pleasures as Harriet, Christina and Gudrun, but good heavens . . .

Alberta had gone to Mr Kirkeby the editor, who was the demonstrator, and joined the group. Now she went twice a week, enjoying the opportunity to move about freely and get warm.

She was in fact more at peace in certain respects. Mrs Selmer did not sigh over her so much, and looked at her searchingly rather than with resignation. Alberta interpreted this in her own way and made use of it cautiously, with all her wits about her. But sometimes she would turn bold and abuse her position, as is only human. Did she not simply get to her feet one evening when the Clerk was there and announce that she was going to the gym? One chooses the lesser of two evils : to be an object of ill-concealed curiosity and banter was bad enough – to sit here with her parents and the Clerk was worse.

But it was a case of the biter bit. Just as Mrs Selmer, her eyebrows raised, was about to express herself, the Clerk remarked obligingly that in that case it would be a pleasure to fetch Miss Selmer after the session.

'It's not necessary, thank you,' snapped Alberta.

But Mama cut the discussion short : 'Yes indeed, it's necessary, my dear. I am *so* grateful to Mr Gronneberg. I always worry about your coming home. Thank you very much, Mr Chief Clerk.'

Alberta left in a fury.

At ease in the stale, heavy air that remained thick in the gymnasium after the men's group, she wondered how she could get through this situation. To be met outside by the Chief Clerk, to be simply fetched, to be accompanied home in the sight of all, would be unbearable. She would run the risk of being congratulated in the street tomorrow by all and sundry.

She would have to go home early, find an excuse, steal a march on him. Sneak out during the next march, perhaps, as she went past the door.

At the bar Palmine Flor was just stepping out of the ranks and preparing to turn a somersault. She put her heels together at attention, threw back her shoulders, stuck out her breast, smiling and twinkling at Kirkeby from under her golden curls while she waited for the word of command. He was finding it difficult to keep a straight face and not smile back.

One—two—

Alberta suddenly put a hand to her heart and stood staring, holding her breath, her eyes distended. Something terrible was about to happen, something contrary to nature, to all instinct. And nobody seemed to notice. They were all standing at ease, chatting quietly. Nobody rushed up and tried to prevent—

She felt sick and closed her eyes. And it was done. Palmine went over the bar on her stomach. And Palmine was pregnant. It was when she had stood to attention that Alberta had realised it.

It was done. It was as if something soft and small and defenceless had been crushed and trampled on, just as when Ola Paradise in his drunkenness had dashed a blind, new-born kitten against the wall of Ovre the baker's shed. Everything stopped, you dared not breathe, not look, something moaned and whimpered deep inside you.

Involuntarily Alberta looked round her. First Beda, now Palmine. Were there more? It was an epidemic, it seemed unavoidable. That Palmine could do such a thing, that she could do such a thing.

Palmine could. She did not use gym shoes like the rest, but wore high-heeled, pointed dancing shoes. She swung herself through the apparatus, a little heavily, but with precision; made a tiger-leap over the horse, lay horizontally in the air with upswinging legs and thick stomach, and sailed smiling down towards Kirkeby, who caught her in his outstretched arms and held her for a moment before putting her down. Kirkeby was the kind whose hands seemed to stick, reluctant to let go. They often wandered about a bit when they got the chance. He had a reputation for it.

'What's the matter?' asked Karla Schmitt suddenly, pushing past the others towards Alberta. 'Do you feel ill? You look as if you'd escaped from the graveyard.'

And Alberta gratefully put her hand in Karla's and allowed her to lead her out. For everything was floating round her, and she was sweating as if she were seasick. Crushed, she sank down on to the bench in the cloakroom, and Karla quickly moved away clothes to let her lie down, rolling up a coat to put under her head.

'Here you are,' said Karla, bringing water. 'You mustn't faint.'

Alberta swallowed a little water, squeezed Karla's hand, closed her eyes, and surrendered herself to her indisposition. When it was over and she could sit up again all the others were streaming out of the gym. She was doomed.

Outside stood the Clerk, polite, smiling, punctual, right under the lamp. He attracted attention, as she had expected. The small groups that passed turned to look at him and Alberta, buzzed, whispered, smiled.

Of a sudden all that Alberta had repressed during the previous months exploded. She did not attempt to hide her ill-temper, answering curtly and angrily, without looking in the Clerk's direction, walking ahead as if she were about to run away from him. In reply to one of his cautious remarks she stopped suddenly and stamped on the ground. The next moment she burst into dry, tearless sobs.

She heard him beside her, unhappy, obliging : 'Dear Miss Selmer, is it in any way my fault? Have I been so unfortunate as to hurt you? If so, it was entirely unintentional – I deeply deplore—'

'Yes, go on, deplore, deplore, deplore,' shouted Alberta scornfully. 'Go on, deplore.'

Then she controlled herself and managed to say : 'Forgive me – please forgive me – but everything is so loathsome—'

There was a pause.

'But it seemed to me that recently – Have I really not insulted you?' said the Clerk at length, hesitantly but with insistence.

'No, no. Only – don't send such large flowers – don't come and fetch me – don't come at all—'

There was another pause. The ground sunk beneath Alberta's feet. What had she said? Wasn't it too much, hadn't she gone too far? It had slipped out in a sudden flame of fresh irritation. Thoroughly unhappy she walked on, waiting for him to digest it.

'No, no,' he said quietly.

They had arrived at the Selmers' doorstep. Alberta extended her hand. She felt a certain warmth towards him : 'Thank you very much for seeing me home'.

'It has never been my intention to pester you, Miss Selmer.'

She met his eyes uncertainly in the lamplight. Was not that little look of triumph more cunning than ever? Was he not standing there safe and sound, while she—

But she was suddenly relieved that what had been said could not be taken back in any case.

'Good night, then.'

'Good night, good night.' He bowed, stood and waited while she went up the steps. As she closed the door behind her he turned and went. Alberta watched his back as it was swallowed up in the darkness and was seized with pity for it. It looked lonely. Poor fellow, if he really had believed that she, ugly and impossible as she was, could be had for the asking, there was nothing strange in that – on the contrary, he might well—

Alberta smiled to herself.

Mrs Selmer was sitting in the dining-room with her keys and her book, ready to go upstairs. She had waited for Alberta, had sat up later than the Magistrate, contrary to her custom. A little tray with cakes and jam stood on the table.

She pushed it across to Alberta and remained seated, talking in random.

Mama's mischievous searching expression was so distasteful to Alberta that she abandoned the idea of telling her she had felt ill. She tried to get down a little of the food and behave as if nothing was the matter. But she could not manage it, and put down her knife, just as the flush reached her face. There she sat, crimson and trembling.

'And did Mr Gronneberg come to fetch you?' asked Mrs Selmer.

'Yes – he came.'

'It was nice of him, don't you think?'

'Yes.'

'It seems to me he has become remarkably attentive this autumn.' Alberta looked up, on her guard, and trembled even more.

Mama smiled. 'Would you accept him?' she said.

Alberta felt herself turning white.

She rose and looked Mama straight in the eye. 'I would *not* accept him,' she said, her lips tight, yet with surprising clarity. And she walked past her out of the room.

* * *

Between seven and eight o'clock the traffic in Fjord Street was considerable. It was frosty and the autumn evening was dark. Under the eight arc-lamps the stream of humanity flowed quickly and smoothly, egged on by its awareness of the snow and the winter perhaps already lying in wait up in the mountains, perhaps ready to descend on the town that very night. People walked fast, talked loudly, inaugurated their new winter clothes upon the bare paving stones of summer, knowing that the snowstorm would soon tear and pull at their finery, making it dishevelled. Now was the time for display and gratification, for taking a few quick turns between Theodorsen the baker and Louisa-round-the-bend.

Harriet Pram and Dr Mo had announced their engagement. They were walking arm-in-arm for the first time. Harriet was wearing a new boa, earrings, a veil and white gloves. Palmine and Lilly stopped and stared after her, scarcely able to believe their own eyes.

She was openly radiant. Her good evening was louder and more cheerful than ever, and her thanks when someone stopped to congratulate them were pearls of laughter ready waiting. Dr Mo lifted his hat, embarrassed but smiling. He had a new stick with a silver handle.

A little way behind them came Gudrun arm-in-arm with Christina, who shrank and crumpled up and was no longer walking with Bergan. It had not come to anything between them, whatever the reason. Each was walking by himself again. Bergan was quite unchanged, but Christina was if possible even more modest than before.

Gudrun would stop people and say: 'Honestly, I'm going to accept the first person who proposes, with the exception of that fellow Stensett. If you only knew what fun it is to be engaged.'

Christina might make herself small, but was brave enough to joke about it. Perhaps she wanted it to be known that if she was walking alone, she was doing so of her own free will. Giggling, she asked whether Gudrun had forgotten the song: 'No, better say no, and show them the way to go; And then you'll avoid the infant's cry and a hullaba-loo-ba-lo'.

Gudrun assured her at the top of her voice that there might easily be an infant's cry just the same and a great deal more hullabaloo, and Christina said: 'Hush, don't be so silly'.

Papa and Alberta did not walk along Fjord Street as far as Louisa-round-the-bend and turn there like other people. They had their own route and turned down into River Street, which was very dark and deserted in the evenings.

Young Klykken's living-room windows shone red, and an edge of light round a blind showed where the Catholic priest had his office in the Badendück building. But the other old houses lay quite black, their dimensions unnaturally large. They were said to be haunted.

Papa and Alberta walked down to the Old Quay, stood still in the circle of light under the lamp, and looked out at the river, where the eddies moved cold and comfortless in the reflections from land. A fishing boat with red and green lights was drifting out on the current, and Papa conjectured that it was a Russian boat. 'Bound to be the one that's been tied up at the Kamke quay, loading dried fish.'

'Perhaps so,' answered Alberta.

They went down on to the New Quay, wandered out as far as the red light at the end of the breakwater, and Papa remarked: 'By Jove, I wonder how many more times we'll be able to walk out here this autumn. The snow may come before we can say Jack Robinson'.

'Yes,' answered Alberta.

'You're very quiet, my child. Is anything the matter?'

'No—'

'Cheer up, Alberta! No use being down-hearted. You're young,' added Papa, as if he meant: 'It's no problem for you'.

'It's awful to be young,' said Alberta, and held her breath for an instant. Was she on the verge of talking to Papa?

He came to a halt, shocked: 'Awful to be young? Stuff and nonsense, child, that's just a phrase you've picked up somewhere. You young things don't know how fortunate you are. To be young is *everything*, child. Wait until you're old'.

'Life's horrible,' said Alberta in repressed rebellion.

'Now listen to me, a young girl has no right to say life is horrible. Mercy on us! But it's these novels again, these damned problem novels. A lot of these muddled scribblers ought to be hanged, indeed they ought.'

They were silent for a while.

'I suppose we ought to go home,' said Alberta inertly.

'How right you are, by Jove, we must.' Papa pounded with his stick, and they went.

In Fjord Street they met Harriet Pram and Dr Mo, who were still out.

'Extraordinarily pretty girl,' remarked Papa, 'And Doctor Mo is said to be a promising young doctor. Well, well, it must be gratifying for the Prams.'

A subdued light shone from the Recorder's living-room windows, probably from a table lamp. He and Beda had just returned from a short journey to the city where they had had a civil wedding. It had taken everyone by surprise. Neither of them had yet been seen in public.

Outside Kilde the watchmaker's there was a mob of street boys, country folk, youths from Rivermouth. Above them all could be seen Kwasnikow's fiery red hair and beard and Crazy-Philomena's flowery hat with the veil. The hat bobbed back and forth throughout the violent altercation that was taking place between herself and Kwasnikow.

He was drunk, and had the appearance of an ancient child, blue-eyed and lisping. His nose and cheekbones looked like three roses painted on his face. In Russian, Swedish and Norwegian he defended himself against Philomena who, tiny and furious, hissed in his teeth.

Alberta suddenly caught sight of the Clerk among the spectators. He stood watching for a moment, then disappeared.

'Lousy Russian,' spat Philomena.

Kwasnikow took her by the shoulder, shook her backwards and forwards, and shouted threateningly : 'I give you payment for this, Philomena, I give you payment'.

The crowd yelled with glee. Someone shouted : 'Here's your topper, Kwasnikow!' The weather-beaten top hat, Kwasnikow's summer wear, inherited from Kamke, was planted on his head from behind. It was grey with dust and had a dent in the middle.

'What's going on?' asked Papa sharply.

'Kwasnikow wants to murder Philomena,' explained a boy, forgetting, as Kwasnikow seized Philomena again, all respect for the Magistrate, and shouting in ecstasy : 'That's the boy, chew her up, chew her up!'

'You rascal, I'll ask the police to take care of you. Where are they, in any case? It's too bad they're never on the spot when they're needed. Ah, there's Olsen. Let's get along then, Alberta. Excuse me, be so good as to let us pass—'

A way was made for Alberta and Papa. P.C. Olsen arrived

AND JACOB

at full speed with a stern face, shouting : 'Move along there !'
to the crowd, which retreated, but immediately gathered
again.

'That poor fellow Kwasnikow,' said Papa, completely forgetting the boy the police were to take care of. 'He hangs
about here – but Alberta, wasn't that Gronneberg standing
over in the corner by Kilde's?'

'Yes, I think so.'

'He disappeared so suddenly. How odd of him to leave like
that, without speaking to us.'

'I don't suppose he saw us.'

'No, no, it's possible. But he seems somewhat changed these
days. I'll wager there's something the matter. I should be sorry
if—

'He's no Adonis,' said Papa, quite irrelevantly. 'But he's
clever, and very useful to me. I should be sorry to lose him,
by Jove.'

Mysterious words, that could be interpreted in more ways
than one. Alberta glanced at Papa searchingly, but looked
quickly away again. Papa was looking straight in front of him
like the Sphinx.

Mrs Selmer was sitting at the supper table gazing across it
blankly. Her reply to their greeting could scarcely be heard,
she hardly seemed to see them. They were late too, in addition
to everything else.

The Magistrate tentatively began to converse about Jacob.
Mrs Selmer replied in the tone of voice that always spoiled
everything. He muttered : 'Oh, so that's how it is, is it?' His
hand shook.

Mrs Selmer turned to Alberta. 'Did you see anything of the
engaged couple?'

'Yes.'

'The Prams must be very gratified.'

'Yes.'

'A few people do have something to be pleased about. I met
Mrs Bremer today. She was so sanguine – the Headmaster has
decided to apply for Kragero.'

'Really?' The Magistrate looked up with interest. 'Kragero! I'd have thought the position here was better.'

'Mr Bremer says the children are stagnating here.'

'Stagnating!' Papa chewed over the word, and Alberta's heart shrank. 'Stagnating,' he repeated. 'That's a strong word, by Jove.

'Nonsense,' he suddenly decided, resolutely describing a circle in his porridge bowl with his spoon. 'Nonsense.' He muttered under his breath, and his hand shook. Jensine, who had just arrived with his fried egg, eyed him askance.

Mrs Selmer stared resignedly into thin air, in silence, letting it be known by her expression that she would not deign to argue with unreason itself.

'How does Jensine put up with a family like ours?' thought Alberta. 'How can she stay here of her own accord, when she could be in all sorts of other places? She isn't a sister or a daughter of the house.'

Mrs Selmer disappeared immediately after supper, retiring without a word. The Magistrate looked askance at the closed door over his pince-nez, remained seated until her footsteps reached the top of the stairs, rose, and went across to the sideboard. Alberta half rose in her chair, almost stood up, but it was no use. He filled his glass to the brim. 'Must have something to sleep on,' he explained.

When, a little later, Alberta put her arms round his neck to say good night, her face was suddenly wet with tears. Papa had never plagued her, he had always left her alone. He never sighed, but a certain tired expression in his eyes when he removed his pince-nez stabbed her like a painful stitch. Papa was one who had found more than his match in life, and never complained. She could rage at his closed door, clench her fist, call down God's curse on him, but an irreparable weakness and anxiety for him was there, always ready to flame up, beneath everything else in her heart. He was as men are, his worst enemy, and needed her there.

Alberta did something unusual. She kissed Papa twice. He looked up, surprised, saw her tears, and exclaimed: 'Good gracious, Alberta, a big girl like you? Whatever next, you cry-baby!'

But he held her closely and kissed her emphatically back again. Altogether it was quite a little scene, without either of them knowing how it had really come about.

'Off to bed with you, child.' Papa pointed to his eternal pile of newspapers : 'I have a little reading to do'.

Alberta wandered upstairs and sobbed into her shawl until she was calm again. She remained sitting in the dark without attempting to light the lamp and go to bed. Her thoughts floated up from obscurity, the one evolving out of the other, falling away and making room for others, as thoughts do, while the restless little lump that was her heart moved painfully and irregularly; thoughts that had acquired something mechanical about them, a tendency to rise and spin in the same ambit as soon as she was alone, sending waves of blood up to her face, giving her a feeling of suffocation.

Now and again she mumbled words into the darkness : 'To be offered frugality in love, no insult is greater – none——

'—but the colliers will come and go, and I'll never have enough courage – Beda, yes, she could have done it. Now she sits sewing under the Recorder's lamp instead, knowing that the faces are pressed up against her window, tight as a shoal of fish— — — —

'—and this is only the beginning.'

Alberta felt her face grow old and shrivelled at her own words. She was a shadow already, half old, distressing, comic. Something happened from year to year, suspicion became knowledge, bad dreams reality.

A weariness crept over her, more intense and pervasive than any she had known before. It sat in her back, sapping her strength. She sank down into it as if it were an abyss, sank inwards into gaping emptiness. It was as if she were sinking back into—

Did she not glimpse an endless, grey ocean, as light and colourless as a misty autumn day? Was it not in and behind

235

all things – was it not that which one slipped into, became united with when death came?

Death?

Perhaps something scattered and finely dispersed is always lying in the mind, waiting for a long, quiet moment in which to flow together and condense. Something indefinable.

Alberta rose, drawing her shawl about her. One more nightmare had taken shape, one she had glimpsed farthest out on the edge of evil dreams. For days and nights she had suspected that it was moving towards her, and had wept with horror under the bedclothes. Now it was upon her, and she could not avoid it. To live with this deep weariness, this disgust for all existing possibilities, this endless oppressive grey-ness of everyday existence behind her and before, this fear of life – she could not bear it. But then she must do it – *must* – the sooner the better.

It was late. The final creak of the floor boards under Papa's heavy tread had died away long ago; it was a while since the church clock had struck its four slow quarter-strokes followed by eleven very fast strokes on the hour.

When she was out of the back door and the autumn dark-ness enclosed her, malevolent anxiety settled like a mask over her face, stiff and cold, yet burning and pounding painfully out through her ear lobes. Something knotted itself in the pit of her stomach as when, as a child, someone had done her an injustice. But just as she had occasionally, in spite of her fear, crossed Dorum's threshold, and Papa's, and contradicted Mama, so she took one step forward, then another. She walked across the yard and down to Flemming's quay as she used to walk through dark rooms when she was small; not too fast, struggling to keep calm as if to deceive watching eyes – half senseless with fright.

Now she could distinguish dark from dark. The piles of barrels and crates rose up threateningly on either side. The knot tightened in her stomach. Her body seemed to be dwindling and shrinking with agonizing fear.

At the same time everything was strangely unreal, as if she

were already outside life, out in a world of shadows, where
what she was doing was fated to take place in accordance with
inexorable, cast-iron rules – one action inextricably linked to
the next, dragging it after. First this, then this, and no way
back.

She felt as if she were re-enacting something she had done
once before in some obscure past, as if she were once again
carrying out something difficult, sinister and inescapable.

She did not think, but she wept calmly, making no sound.

She was at the steps. It was low water and far down, a
black, repellent abyss. As if remotely, from far away, she sensed
that here it was shallow, with large boulders, she must go out
in one of the boats; remotely too, she sensed her own horror.
She found the boat chain, climbed down backwards, holding
on to it—

Then she slipped on the smooth steps, hung by her arms on
to the chain, clawed the air with her legs and found no foothold, while her blood ran cold from top to toe, and she wailed
aloud in fear. Her skirts and legs were in the water. Her
clothes absorbed it and she was dragged down by an icy and
terrible gravity.

Shortly afterwards Alberta lay full length face downwards
on the quay, clawing at the planks beneath her, breathless and
whimpering with exertion and fright; no longer daring to
move, or to believe that she was on dry land.

One thing was hers. Her bare life. It was hers still, hers – it
throbbed and hammered through pulse and heart, quivering
in every muscle. They had not succeeded in driving her into
the sea, and never would. Something had been roused in her
down there in the icy cold as it crept up round her body. It
had been terror, violent beyond control, but it had also been
something bright and hard, a raging refusal. It had been like
touching bottom and being carried upwards again.

Below her the water slapped lightly against the stones.
There it was again, that little swarming sound of activity and
labour. The tide was coming in. In a kind of demented rapture she lay listening to the incoming tide and to her own
throbbing blood.

Once Alberta was inside the back porch, enfolded in the little warmth that seemed to reside in the staircase when one came in from outside, she collapsed. Her legs gave way, gusts of heat and cold passed through her. A feverish shivering rose from her wet skirts. And the terror, which had lain in wait and seized her as she groped her way back up Flemming's quay, making her stumble and run in panic, still moved like puffs of wind over her body.

Voices had whispered behind her, hands had clutched her. – Miserable and idiotic, here she sat on the stairs. Only one thing was lacking – that she should meet Mama. Then her expedition would be described as it deserved, as foolery and showing off. And she would be utterly prostrated, for the laws of nature cannot be changed.

No matter. She had brought one thing back to the surface with her, life. Life, that at any time, even at its most wretched, bears every opportunity within it as does the dry, inconspicuous seed. No-one sees them. But they are there.

Alberta opened the kitchen door cautiously. Her wet skirts slapped heavily about her legs. Then a chill went through her once more and her heart stopped. For through the kitchen window and a window lying at an angle to it she saw a light. The person carrying it was shielding it with the other hand, and Alberta first saw only the light-encircled black hand, as it passed the opening between the curtains. Then the candle must have been put on a table, for the glow from it fell steadily and clearly on something white, moving between the table and the sideboard. And the whiteness was no ghost. It was Mrs Selmer, Mama herself. Alberta felt rather than saw her.

She held her breath, and squeezed herself into the darkness between the kitchen cupboard and the wall, prepared for the worst.

But the candle remained in there, stationary. Alberta peered out. She saw Mama hold something up to the flame and inspect it, touching it with a finger as if making marks. It sparkled for a moment, opaque, golden, like a large, round topaz. It was the whisky decanter.

Mama put it down again. She remained standing above the table, leaning on her hands. Her face sagged as if her legs were failing her. The candlelight fell on it strongly, and Alberta could see her expression, an expression so empty, so tired, so bereft, that she herself seemed to shrivel too.

Mama stood thus for a second, perhaps two, perhaps longer. Time stood still while it lasted. Essential facts were revealed, a whole sequence of cause and effect was exposed. Mama's true face, moulded by life and the years, was in there by itself in the dark, as if the strife and turmoil of everyday had parted to let it be seen. Simultaneously, memories floated up from the deepest layers of Alberta's mind: memories of Mama's hands, cool and firm, good and safe about her head, of warm kisses from Mama's mouth, of tender smiles; memories of times long ago when everything had been different. And something that had frozen and died one evening in the dining-room put out fresh shoots in her mind.

Now the candle was being lifted, now it disappeared. Alberta heard a door, and the night settled down on everything.

When the church clock began its twelve strokes she found herself in Jacob's room, heaven knows why. From some sort of need to be with him for a while as best she could, from old habit. For leaning her forehead against Jacob's window frame she had ridden out many an inner storm, found calm after many tears of distress.

His books still stood on the shelf. There were invincible ink blots left on the unpainted wooden table – they could be glimpsed even in the dark. And that indefinable smell of the wharves that Jacob had had in his everyday clothes and which had transferred itself to the rest of his belongings, to Mama's despair – did not a little of it still hang in the air?

When she had crept past the bedroom door a stripe below it and the rustle of a book had betrayed the fact that Mama was not asleep. Papa was snoring with a loud droning sound.

Alberta was back again. Back to it all, to all that was warped and desultory, to the lies and evasions and small, hidden irons in the fire, to humiliation and hopeless longing, to the grey road of uniform days.

To live in spite of it, to live on as best she could, with her two warring natures : one that willed, no-one knew how far – one that could let itself be bound any time and anywhere. To live and lie and listen her way forward, to seek haphazardly in her tomes, to wait and see—

Everything was unchanged and the same. But Alberta had been in touch with what lay beneath and behind ordinary existence.

Behind Mama's bitter little everyday face, behind her almost convulsive party face, a face which was the real one, and which was deathly tired and corroded by lonely anxiety—

Behind Papa's little catchword, 'Cheer up, back we go,' the set features of one without hope—

Beneath her own weariness and despondency a stubborn will to continue, a hungering uneasiness, that could only be quieted by life itself; that could intoxicate itself with small, fluttering verses on a clear evening in spring or a moonlit night in August, yet hankered restlessly and desperately for something else, something undreamt of, far distant and obscure.

Over it all flowed everyday existence, turbid and shallow, with many small backwaters and eddies—

People swarm about together. The one knows so little about the other.

It occurred to Alberta that ultimately Jacob was the only one who turned his true face out to the world, a face full of undaunted confidence in his own two strong arms.

The street lights had been extinguished a long time ago. The church clock shone alone, like a moon in the night sky. Alberta was still standing with her nose against the pane. Then she picked up her wet skirts, shuddered with cold, and went to her room.

Soon it would be another day.

ALBERTA
AND
FREEDOM

PART ONE

When one's clothes drop off and one stands without a stitch on in front of a stranger, one's predominant sensation is not that of modesty, but rather of being unprotected, of disquiet in case someone should come too close and do harm, an anxiety of the flesh, so to speak. There is the sensation of solitude too, similar to finding oneself alone in a deserted part of the country. One never gets used to it, it is the same each time.

Alberta took off her clothes as if she were jumping into the sea, a little giddily, feeling that it was a matter of now or never. She undid one button here, another there, and her clothes slid down round her all at once. Before they reached the floor she seized them, stepped out of them and put them in a heap on a chair. Then she stepped on to the model's stand and faced reality boldly. She did not slouch ashamed with her hips or her head, but clenched her hands slightly and looked Mr. Digby straight in the eye, while she gradually took up her position. Then she ' stood '.

Mr. Digby gauged the distance, righted his spectacles, put his head askew. With rounded gestures he implied directions, giving orders in his incorrigible English accent: ' Comme ça... comme ça.' Finally he announced curtly but pleasantly that that was good, c'est bien.

And time began to creep painfully forward in the way Alberta remembered from her childhood; the way it could creep in church, for instance, or when she went out with Papa and they walked and walked and never got on speaking terms with each other. She could sense physically how it crowded slowly past her, tenacious, absorptive, exhausting, how it could be heard and felt. To stand there doing nothing else but stand, came to feel like being stretched on the rack. Her limbs ached and turned numb. But that was not the worst. The gnawing in her mind was worse, a steady murmur as if from an exposed nerve.

There was something she ought to have been doing, something besides standing there. It was only that Alberta could never find out what. She earned one franc twenty-five an hour, and managed to exist as long as it lasted, without being a burden to anyone. She should therefore have had a clear conscience.

She could see her body in the long mirror, thin and lithe, clad in spare, lean muscles which arched and curved a little here and there, not much, not more than was fitting. A controlled nakedness, without exaggeration, without any gross stamp of sex. If she had to be a woman she could not very well demand to be encumbered with less.

Out of doors it was an early, tempestuous spring; indoors the house was cold. Mr. Digby's studio, which was first-class and faced north, without disturbing reflections, was full of a stale winter clamminess. Alberta quickly turned blue and muddy, especially on the lower half of her legs. And it was not only warmth that escaped from her pores; it was life itself slowly filtering away. An insidious wastage of energy was taking place.

Mr. Digby was no slave-driver. At brief intervals he would ask pleasantly whether Alberta was tired, whether she was cold, while he strode forwards and backwards on his short legs between the canvas and what seemed to be a permanent observation point in the middle of the floor. For her part, Alberta stood for her three quarters of an hour without sagging at the knees, however much she might tremble and sway. She had some kind of foolish and unreasonable notion that the more doggedly she stood, the more would she placate certain mysterious powers which habitually force us into circumstances and situations we hate and abhor.

Round, honest, completely innocuous, Mr. Digby's eyes viewed her through the spectacles, relinquishing her not a moment too soon. Precise to the minute, by which time Alberta was empty-headed and paralysed, beyond hope or expectation, simply a stupefied body, he said: ' Rest yourself, Mademoiselle '. He continued to come and go, to narrow his eyes, gauge the distance and add small dabs of colour, look satisfied and hum. He had the fearful diligence of the dilettante in his blood.

Alberta wrapped herself in her coat and huddled over *Le Journal*. She finished reading the short story for the day which she had begun in the Métro, gobbled down theatre, art and literature, murders and sensations, but consistently skipped all politics. Finally she looked through the advertisement colums, noted that ' Wonderful Remedy for Wrinkles ', Pink Pills and Rubber Stockings, Crème Simon and ' Abbé Soury's Rejuvenating Elixir ' were there as usual, and that the background to existence was to this extent unchanged and completely normal. Sometimes she took advantage of her breathing-spell to complete a recently scamped meal, and chewed a little bread, fruit or chocolate.

The worst thing about it was the passing of time, the next worse the people who dropped in and stood watching, ' admirers of Mr. Digby's art '. Every time the door opened to let one of them in Alberta was on tenterhooks, wishing she could vanish into thin air. Yet again she had a secret iron in the fire, and was travelling along one of life's small murky back streets, as she had done since childhood. These intruders to whom she owed nothing at all caught her red-handed. Well-dressed, exceedingly respectable, often somewhat elderly, they belonged to a category of persons from which she hid and whom she deceived without exception.

They were dangerous. It was true that Mr. Digby lived in Passy, in a quiet, prodigiously correct *quartier,* apparently as distant as it possibly could be from the milieu which Alberta normally frequented. Nevertheless her luck could fail her at any time. The very thing one wishes to hide has a curious tendency to sift up into the daylight. Both Mr. Digby's and Alberta's associates moved about freely, could meet, become acquainted, and could in no way be prevented from doing so. The possibility of catastrophe was always there. On the other hand, one does what has to be done. She had to take the risk that went with it.

Tensely, a little convulsively, she would stand enduring the strangers' gaze, racked by defiance and antipathy. She understood the model who once, at Colarossi's, suddenly pulled a face at someone who had come in and just stood and stared. She understood the prostitute who hurls a contemptuous term of abuse in the face of the woman walking by. She felt an obscure solidarity with them.

'Eh bien,' said Mr. Digby. 'I thank you.' He put down his palette and rubbed his hands.

When Mr. Digby said as much as that, it meant he would not be needing her any more. There would be no more five-franc pieces to earn for the time being – solid, weighty coins that made her feel solvent; or pieces of gold, ten francs, twenty francs, that gave her the over-confidence of the rich, making her step light, her face new, her mood extravagant and reckless. It meant that she would be free and unemployed again and would have her alibi in order. It meant that she would be able to expand a little. Once again Alberta had scraped a means of existence. As far as the human eye could see, it had been brought to a conclusion without catastrophe.

'I thank you,' repeated Mr. Digby. 'I am very pleased with you. I shall be travelling in the South, in England, in Brittany. I shall be coming back to Paris in October. I may then need a model who is a little more comme ça.' His hands indicated generous curves and his eyes widened enormously behind his spectacles. 'I don't know in advance, I never know in advance. I am a very capricious man, very capricious. But if . . . .' And he nodded encouragingly at Alberta.

246

Mr. Digby had said almost the same thing this time last year. He skimmed the surface of this foreign language in short sentences which often petered out. It never occurred to him to speak to Alberta in English, nor was it necessary; he managed to say what was important and to imply the rest.

With short, hurried steps he went into the apartment next door, and spoke quietly to someone inside. There was a rattle of coins. Alberta thought urgently: Will it be seven or eight or nine times? Will he deduct for the time we had to stop because he was taken ill? Or the time someone arrived unexpectedly from England? Then it will only be just enough for the rent. If he does deduct it I ought to say something, but I'm stupid about things like that. I ought to say, for instance –.

Mr. Digby returned with Mrs. Digby. Jokingly he referred to her as ' my jury ', putting two new twenty-franc pieces and five francs in small change on the table. He had not deducted anything. Alberta, whose whole body was relishing the feeling of clothes about it again, appropriated the money carelessly, a little offhandedly, as if she collected such sums daily. ' Thank you,' she said.

With admiring cries Mrs. Digby inspected the picture. As always when a work was finished she appealed to Alberta: ' It's very beautiful, isn't it? Such delicate colours? Mr. Digby's a real artist, yes indeed, a real artist. I do hope you're not too tired? It must be very, very tiring. But I expect it becomes a habit, doesn't it?' She went up close, small, friendly and short-sighted, and raised and lowered her lorgnette all over the picture, inspecting it with the air of a connoisseur. It was sleek and sugary like the lid of a chocolate box, similar to the rest of Mr. Digby's production, a collection of rose-pink ladies, all more or less ' comme ça ', against the same background of faded lilac and iron grey. They embellished the walls from floor to ceiling.

Politely Alberta expressed agreement. She put on her hat and powdered her nose.

' And if,' said Mr. Digby, ' When I come back?'

' Just get in touch with Alphonsine. She always has my address.'

' Very well. Still Madame Alphonsine. Very good ... I thank you.'

Alberta's hand was shaken first by Mrs. and then by Mr. Digby. And she hurried across the neat courtyard. White shingle, newly spread, difficult to walk on, forcefully accentuated its length and breadth. Budding box bushes, clipped low, framed a centre bed. Small-leaved ivy, trimmed and refined, covered the walls with an even, monotonous green, and, clipped as if with a ruler, framed handsome doors with shining brass plates and large studio windows with raw-silk curtains inside. A concierge, looking like the housekeeper of an elegant residence, appeared watchfully at her window. She nodded to Alberta, because although Alberta obviously had to be considered a questionable character, she was not the worst kind, but on the contrary looked comparatively respectable.

The wind blew in gusts. It was one of those March days when sharp, warm sunshine alternates with cold wintry blasts. Along the road, which was bordered by low walls with gardens behind them, naked branches tossed in confusion against racing clouds and sudden depths of ultramarine sky; at the edge of the pavement on a corner was a handcart full of violets and mimosa, like a festive cockade on the ragged clothing of the day.

Alberta turned another corner and found herself beneath the tall iron skeleton of the Métro, between barrack-like blocks of flats that cast clammy shadows. A train passed noisily above her head. Soon afterwards she was sitting in one herself, travelling high in the air between earth and sky over Passy bridge, across the Seine.

There was a rustle along the benches as newspapers were lowered and people looked out. Far below lay Paris, bright in sudden sunshine beneath a tremendous sky full of moving banks of cloud. People, cars, *fiacres* bustled about like toys. To the north-east above Menilmontant was a coal-black shower of rain; directly beneath, the Seine like flowing metal. A tug with a string of barges behind it, working its way upstream, hooted piercingly and belched out thick black smoke, making the sharp light even sharper.

A wave of expansiveness passed through Alberta, washing away fatigue and stale cold. She felt her face changing to an expression that men found disquieting. God knows how it came about. It was suddenly there, making them turn their heads towards her, jerkily, hurriedly, as if in surprise. It was no special distinction, for it can happen to almost any woman. But at least it was a kind of guarantee that she was reasonably like other people, not remarkably ugly, not directly repulsive. And if the person in question was not himself an affront, it sometimes helped her to expand a little more.

The train rattled through the Grenelle district, alongside broad avenues with tree-lined walks down the middle. Some of the buildings were old-fashioned and squat, a bit decayed, a bit rotten with damp, some were brand new in *Jugend* style, shining like butter in the sun. Suddenly it was all gone. White tiled walls and arched roofs, variegated posters darkly illuminated, slid past. An intrusive reek of cellars and disinfectant filled the carriage. And Alberta again felt the fatigue in her limbs. Underground she flickered out.

She alighted at Montparnasse, coming up into the daylight again behind the railway station, in the shadow of the high wall and of the bridge that carried the trains out of the city on a level with the second floors of the houses. Here the pleasant parts of town ended, here the large, depressing working-class districts on the other side of the Avenue du Maine began. One was always met by a gust of greyness and narrow circumstances. Here Alberta could not help thinking of death sentences and executions. Perhaps it was because of the wall.

She paused and looked up at one of the houses in the

Rue de l'Arrivée. ' Hôtel des Indes ' was written in huge gold letters on a balcony railing right across the façade.

From a railing several storeys higher something white fluttered for a moment, a cloth, a handkerchief, fastened up there. It was carried outwards by the wind and then slackened again. Alberta made certain it was there, then hurried away underneath the bridge where there was a blaze of fruit, flowers and vegetables on handcarts in the semi-darkness. She bought violets and a spray of mimosa, made a couple of other purchases, went into a dairy.

Then she disappeared inside the Hôtel des Indes.

* * *

To come up from the hard street. To kick off one's shoes and stretch out one's whole length on something, a bed, a divan. To relax in every limb, while the little spirit stove hums gently. To have a cup of tea, or perhaps two, some biscuits, marmalade, a couple of cigarettes – and the numbness arrives: that blessed state of indifference out of which the will towards life is born anew.

Hungry? Yes . . .

But not as when she used to come home from skiing as a child and grabbed something or other on the way through the kitchen, because she could not wait until her ski clothes were off and she was seated at table. Not that healthy, demanding voraciousness that made all food taste good and satisfying. No – now there was the eternal dissatisfaction of the body, which remained after she had eaten, which could not be quieted, only deadened and diverted. With tea, for instance, and cigarettes.

Alberta lay on her elbow on Liesel's bed, listening to the singing of the spirit stove and smoking a Maryland. Liesel came and went, fetching cups and spoons from the wardrobe, wiping them and arranging them in the sunlight on a chair with a towel over it. Her black dress, poorly cut in one piece, tended to hang askew. She pulled at it repeatedly and stuck her nose into Alberta's flowers now and again as she passed them. They stood resplendent on the mantelpiece and were multiplied by the mirror behind them. ' *Reizend,*' said Liesel. ' *Wunderbar. Wie freundlich Albertchen.*'

The balcony doors were ajar. The narrow, oblong room, which obtained all its light through them, was filled with muffled noises from the street, smoke from nearby chimneys and the steadfast old bedroom smell that goes with cheap hotels. It is no use trying to air it out, it seeps back in again from the staircase.

Only now did Alberta realise how tired she was, a tiredness like disintegration. It would take at least two hot cups of strong tea to pull her together again. She exhaled small puffs of smoke and exchanged everyday remarks with Liesel. Brief as a code they dropped from them both: ' Well? ... Oh, all right .... No news .... *Gar nichts.*'

On the washstand lay a quarter of a pound of butter wrapped in paper, because, as Liesel said in her housewifely manner, it keeps better on marble. There were also mandarin oranges and two small cream cheeses, which were Alberta's contribution. Liesel's wash-bowl bristled with paintbrushes put to soak.

Alberta looked round for the study of the Pont Neuf. It was on the floor, leaning against two chair-legs and facing the wall, a bad sign. Traces of yellow ochre along the edge of the canvas frame and on the skirt of Liesel's dress emphasized the connection between them.

Now she was warming the teapot. Tilting it with both hands she made a small amount of boiling water flow here and there inside it, while she watched it thoughtfully: ' Fräulein Stoltz makes tea with the egg water. I think that's too economical. There we are Albertchen, the butter was fresh today.'

She straightened her dress and sat down. It was one of her absent-minded days, when she would be a little round-shouldered, a little despairing and lost in her own thoughts. Today it would be no use asking how the Pont Neuf was going, someone had probably stopped to watch Liesel and disturbed her. One of the barges in the foreground had perhaps disappeared when she got there, or something unexpected had displayed itself in the motif: a fresh pile of sand, an unsuspecting fisherman on his camp stool. She had no doubt ruined her picture again and was dejected and untalented. It happened sometimes.

'Thank you.' Alberta took the cup Liesel handed her and gulped it down eagerly like a drunkard at last getting a drink. Without a word, as if following a ritual, Liesel filled it again, and Alberta emptied it a second time. Then she sat up, put her feet into her shoes, and moved nearer. The strong, hot liquid was taking effect.

'Finished with Papa Digby for the time being,' she said, buttering a biscuit. 'That's the rent, ten francs extra, five for the garçon. I'll buy those unbleached chemises from the pawnbroker's, Liesel, cut them up at the bottom and make them into combinations. That'll be seventy-five apiece. I won't get any at Bon Marché under five francs.'

Liesel's eyes focused again, returning from a great distance. She doubted whether the project could be carried out. Alberta would have to insert gores, it wasn't as simple as she thought, and it would take a long time to sew the seams by hand. But Alberta had her plans and her faith in them would not be shaken. 'Gores? Of course not. When you're as thin as I am!' As far as the seams were concerned, you could always make large stitches. She knew a concierge who took in machine sewing, five centimes the metre, but she'd rather save the money. 'And I must wear something underneath,' she said. 'Soon I shan't have a rag left to send to the laundry.'

'Nor I,' sighed Liesel, who needed a petticoat, stockings, shoes. It was fatal when it got to the point where those kinds of things had to be replaced. You *had* to have them. And the possibility of getting a new hat or a new dress vanished for uncertain period of time. If only the five-francs man would turn up!

'Oh, it's no problem for you painters!' Alberta thought enviously of the five-francs man, who went round buying studies lock, stock and barrel, large ones and small ones all for the same unchanging average price. Last year he had bought everything Liesel had for a hundred and thirty-five francs. A painter could suddenly conjure up unprecedented sums of money. But the five-francs man was something of a mystery; he arrived unexpectedly or he did not come at all. It was useless to try to find him, write to him, ask people to send him along. He was as capricious and erratic as the weather. You might hear that he had called on such and such a one, and then perhaps hear nothing for a long time.

To have in one's possession a production that might be the object of enquiries from the five-francs man was in any case a basis to life. A quick glance round Liesel's room, where canvases were stacked one behind the other all along the walls facing inwards, ascertained that Liesel could do business in the grand manner again whenever she wished, if her luck was in. And if in addition you got a regular allowance from home, you were by no means so badly off.

' Painting's expensive,' protested Liesel. ' *Es kostet furchtbar viel, Albertchen.* Chinese white costs a fortune, let alone colours like cadmium and carmine lake.' Alberta was lucky, she needed no working capital. Liesel could not understand why she took jobs as a model, how could she, *aber gar nicht.*

' I can't do anything else,' said Alberta.

' You can. French. Writing.'

Alberta looked impatiently at Liesel over her cup. ' Can I live off the two pupils I taught last year and teach no longer? Can I, Liesel? Or can I hope to get more in this country? They all go to the French, you know that as well as I do. And write! I can't write. I'd rather be a model.' She took a large gulp and put her cup down roughly. Liesel made mountains out of mole-hills. She had not lived in Paris long enough.

Besides, Liesel herself posed. Alberta pointed this out, knowing full well that it was a lame argument. Liesel posed for Eliel. She made coffee for him and sewed on his buttons.

If only she could persuade him to adopt a collar and tie and stop looking like a shoemender.

' I pose for the head,' said Liesel. ' For the head Albertchen.'

' I know – and for a hand, and for a shoulder. If it goes on like this ... '

Liesel did not laugh.

Usually she shared the joke, laughing at the shoemender, admitting for goodness knows which time that, yes, she had turned down her dress one day when Eliel's model had been unable to come. She had thought she could do it for Eliel, who was so hard-working, so talented and so splendid – and she would laugh again.

It was tempting to tease her about it. Eliel had been endlessly busy with that portrait of her. Alphonsine hinted that he burst his buttons on purpose when Liesel was coming, so that she could put them on again for him, and sit there looking domestic and charming while she did it. And Liesel would laugh.

Now she supposed curtly and coldly that she had finished sitting for Eliel. As Alberta knew, some visitors were coming from Sweden, a Swedish girl to whom Eliel would be showing the sights. He wanted to have the plaster bust ready by that time, so that he would be quite free – it was understandable.

' Yes,' said Alberta. ' I suppose so.'

Suddenly Liesel smiled. There seemed to be a hint of defiance in her smile, and she looked directly at Alberta. ' Ness looks like a shoemender too, without his collar and tie.'

' Yes,' said Alberta, amazed. ' Of course he does.'

The years went by, the seasons changed. Through it all Alberta and Liesel found themselves in the same situation, monetarily and otherwise. They made no careers for themselves. Even Liesel, who had talent, was endlessly marking time. She paid her subscription to the Indépendants, but never got as far as sending in anything. She went summer after summer to Brittany with the fixed purpose of submitting a painting to the Autumn Exhibition. She came home again, still without anything she thought would be suitable, still, without managing to produce anything.

Alberta considered this. She sat looking at Liesel, who was wandering restlessly about the room, a biscuit dripping with marmalade in her hand, picking up everything leaning against the wall and turning it to face the light.

Most of them were life studies, and looked as life studies usually do: one straight leg, one limp; sagging shoulders, arms and hips; stomachs like balloons; chests that cried out for orthopaedic treatment. A few were promising, most of them had been retouched too often. Except when providentially stopped, there nearly always came a moment when Liesel lost her head and changed a fresh, pure colour combination, a design that was good already, into something hard, dry and dull. Her work sometimes looked as if it had been spoilt purposely and in anger. Sudden thick, meaningless brush strokes would be drawn in, or irrelevant, alien planes of colour inserted, that did not fit in and killed everything else round them. Afterwards she would get nowhere with it.

She came from some small town in one of the Baltic provinces, Alberta had long ago given up remembering which. The Baltic provinces are confusing, rather like the Balkans. On the mantelpiece in cabinet size sat Liesel's mother, a small, round, German-born *hausfrau* with white bands round her neck and wrists, surrounded by her four daughters, Liesel among them as a little girl, sitting on a stool in front of the others. Above the bed hung a faded picture of a young, thin man with a long black beard and deep-set eyes: her Russian father, who had died a couple of years ago. He had been the one to sympathize with Liesel and take her part when she had wanted to paint. She had spoken two languages as a child, German and Russian, and often mixed her clipped, inadequate French with them both. She was still wearing out her mourning clothes.

When Liesel nodded in the direction of the mantelpiece and said: '*Sie sind alle furchtbar gut, aber* . . .', Alberta understood to the full what she meant. Liesel seldom said anything else about them.

She was a little round-shouldered, a little slow in speech and manner, with skirts that dipped at the back. But she had large grey eyes in a pale, oblong face, skin smooth as cream and a little nebula of freckles across her nose. She had a red mouth, and a mass of smooth black hair twisted round her head in solid, shining plaits. All in all Liesel was handsome and the object of a good deal of attention. Doubtful individuals at the studios would kiss her, hotel residents tried to get into her room at night. She was less inured than Alberta to such phenomena and unable to appear icy and unmoved; her cheeks flamed and a frightened expression came into her eyes. And she was sought after more unscrupulously than ever.

Now and again, when Liesel completely lost courage, decided she was utterly lacking in talent, and made up her mind to give up painting, a rich merchant who lived in her home town and wanted to marry her, and who was favoured by her relatives, would figure in her conversation. Alberta had no patience with him. There was an air of bad novels about him and he was quite uninteresting, even perhaps an hallucination. She wished Liesel would stop bringing him into it.

Liesel continued rearranging her canvases, fetching them out from the corners and from behind the wardrobe. Soon they were all over the place, leaning against chairs and table-legs, on the mantelpiece and along the bed. She folded up her family and put them on the table to make room, and finally turned round the study of the Pont Neuf, placing it in front of all the rest. It showed a section of the quay, a couple of tall, leafless trees, some barges, and in the background the arch of the bridge, all of it basically good, with a certain heavy richness of colouring. But there were angry-looking ultramarine lines drawn criss-cross over the barges. They did not appear to belong any more, being quite out of keeping with the rest of the picture.

Alberta said nothing and watched. She was used to these sudden displays. Other painters did the same thing. In the middle of a mouthful they would be impelled to turn round everything leaning against the wall. They would be made cheerful and hum, or become absent-minded, irritable and inconsolable.

' I shall end up like Potter, Albertchen, like Potter and Stoltz.' Liesel sat down and contemplated her display despondently. ' That's all for this year. I don't suppose even the five-francs man would take it.'

' Nonsense, Liesel. You have talent. Marushka says so, Eliel and Ness and everybody say so. If only you could stop spoiling them all the time. Potter and Stoltz . . . '. Alberta shrugged her shoulders pityingly.

But she did not like her tone of habitual encouragement. And as she spoke she saw a whole series of elderly women perpetually trudging round Montparnasse. They were beyond any reasonable age, forty, fifty, even older; they had wrinkles and untidy grey hair, and they dragged themselves round with large bags full of brushes over one arm, their camp stool and easel under it, a wet canvas in each hand and their skirts trailing behind them. They sat at street corners and in parks and on the banks of the Seine and painted; fussing and wearisome, they filled the academies and life-classes, disappearing during the summer perhaps, but reappearing in the autumn, as inevitable as the season itself; they lived on nothing, making tea with the egg water, like Fräulein Stoltz. She was one of them, Potter another. Originally they came from different countries and had their own peculiarities. Now they were here, and behaved and painted more or less the same, all of them. It was they who filled the walls of the outer rooms at the Indépendants, the rooms one always hurried through to reach the new, the shocking, or simply the proficient. The thought that it was possible to go on living here like that, and to be nothing more than an elderly, ugly, poverty-stricken dilettante, bred disquiet.

'You *mustn't* spoil everything, Liesel. You must put a stop to it and begin exhibiting your work. If only you could leave them alone while they're still good.'

'I *feel* colour,' said Liesel, pressing her clasped hands to her breast and staring wide-eyed in front of her. 'I feel it physically, Albertchen, it hurts me inside sometimes, but ...' She closed her eyes, her head sank forwards on her graceful neck '... It's the *drawing*. I suddenly see how wrong it is. I want to put it right, I *have* to put it right, and then it all goes wrong. I don't know how it happens, something compels me. I haven't any real talent – I only have a little, and that's worse than none at all.'

Here comes the merchant, thought Alberta. She believed in Liesel's talent, as one believes in the earth beneath one's feet; she took it for granted and saw nothing tragic in her distress. But Liesel suddenly walked past her out on to the balcony, leaving the door open behind her, and stood out there, leaning on the balustrade with both hands. After a while she turned her back to it, supporting herself against it with her elbows. She leant her head back, and looked down into the Rue de l'Arrivée.

Like a light picture in a dark frame she was enclosed by the doorway and the open doors with their filthy curtains sticking to the panes, all of them that solid grey of the streets through which railways pass. A ray of the setting sun fell upon her in a beautiful alternation of light and shade, modelling a section of the plaiting encircling her head, the tense sinews of the neck, the breast forced upwards by her stance, the drooping wrists. A breath of wind carried her skirt a little outwards and sideways, almost wrapping it round her leg. The loose-limbed figure in the worn black dress was given a plastic gravity it normally lacked, the hair acquired an alien sheen of metal. Liesel was suddenly statuesque out there between earth and sky. She addressed the Rue de l'Arrivée quietly in her clipped French: ' My life is not interesting.'

Surprised by the brief, gently-spoken phrase, Alberta went on listening. Whether or not it was because Liesel was standing out there looking statuesque, the words grew in the silence they left behind them, turning into an oracular pronouncement, casting a sharp, unexpected light over the past and the future. One of those appalling seconds when one sees one's existence and is made giddy by it, had suddenly occurred. Deep down Alberta was gripped by the thought: Nor mine, nor mine. It goes on and on and is not interesting, as Liesel says. I don't even know what I want to do with it. I am like someone who has set out from land and is letting himself drift.

An uncomfortable chill crept over her, her heart became small and hard, hammering as it used to at home when she had done something wrong or something unpleasant was about to happen. She heard her voice dwindle and freeze as she said: ' It *will* be interesting, Liesel, of course it will. Wait till you start exhibiting and get properly under way. Thank you for my tea.'

She laced up her shoes and put on her coat, bracing herself as she got ready to leave, trying to find that feeling of freedom which, like an intoxication, can sometimes turn walking into a dance, reminding herself that now and again one lands on small islands of joy. Of course they would get somewhere, not just Liesel, but herself too. It was already something of a feat not to be lying becalmed in quite the wrong place – and after all, this was life, life itself, irreplaceable.

' Are you going to the evening class, Liesel?' Alberta half hoped that Liesel would consider further effort useless this evening. They could then go out together, laugh about things together, and finally laugh at themselves. Once you get as far as that, things begin to look brighter.

But Liesel was going to the course. She had paid for it, so she had better . . .

' What a reason!' she said. She suddenly slumped down on the bed and laughed despairingly. ' *Wie alles tragikomisch ist, Albertchen.*'

'It is indeed.' Alberta laughed with her, liberated, and at once felt immensely grateful at the thought of how much they had laughed off together, she and Liesel, through the years.

* * *

The Hôtel de l'Amirauté in the Place de Rennes looked respectable and inspired confidence: the name in enormous gold lettering across the façade, the laurel trees in green tubs at the entrance, the open vestibule with its red carpet, comfortable basket chairs, green plants. In the doorway Monsieur, as well-dressed as a dummy in a tailor's window, with waved hair and a ready smile, always and instantly at your service. Inside the office Madame, young, beautiful, irreproachable, in her white silk blouse and with her long shining nails. Into this correct establishment walked Alberta. This was where she lived.

Monsieur's greeting was unexceptionable. It was not the same as his greeting to the naval officers from Lorient and Brest, his smile was not in evidence, but Alberta had not expected it to be. Madame, on the other hand, greeted her strikingly coldly, looked her up and down and then stared at the bag she was carrying. Alberta stopped, and opened it in her direction: 'Only some fruit Madame – fruit, newspapers . . .'.

'*Ça va, ça va.*' Madame gazed absent-mindedly at the bag. Clearly she had been thinking about something else for some time. She leaned forward over her little counter, her hands clasped, and pronounced: 'You know, Mademoiselle, when one leaves bits of bread lying about on the floor . . .'.

'I do not leave bits of bread lying about on the floor.'

Madame looked at her even more coldly. 'The *garçon* reported that there were mice in your room. I went up there today to see for myself. There was bread on the floor.'

Alberta reddened. ' I did put some bread on the floor yesterday evening.'

' When food is left lying about in corners, you get mice. That is obvious,' stated Madame. ' The scraps attract the mice, you see.'

' I put bread on the floor so that the mice would leave me alone and stop attacking me in bed. There have always been mice there, yesterday was the first time I ...'. Alberta's voice trembled and so did her legs, which did not seem quite real beneath her.

' Don't leave scraps about in the corners and you will get no mice, *voilà*.' Madame handed Alberta her key and turned smiling to a new guest, who was being led in by Monsieur with demonstrations of respect. The conversation was closed. Alberta, her face darkly flushed and her heart hammering, wandered past the open door that led into Monsieur's and Madame's private dining-room, a small room that obtained its meagre light from the courtyard. A rich reek of good food wafted out. A thin old lady in a light grey shawl was setting the table, picking up a table-napkin which was already in place and putting it down a little differently, judging the effect and righting it again. Her yellow hand trembled unceasingly, her head twisted incessantly on her neck. When Alberta went past she looked up with the short-sightedness of an old woman.

' It's me, Madame Firmin, the Norwegian.'

' Ah, is it you, is it you? Good evening, *ma petite*.'

And Alberta began the ascent.

The red matting continued between the flights of stairs, one floor, two floors. At the third Alberta quickened her pace, swinging round extra fast at the landing and looking stiffly in front of her. At once a door opened ajar:
' Mademoiselle Selmer!'

' Mademoiselle.'

' Always in a hurry, always busy! And I who am so much alone!'

' But Mademoiselle.'

' Come in a moment, have a cigarette with me. We could

go out and dine together. I should be so pleased if you . . . '

The pale, fair, somewhat rigid figure in the doorway was correctly tailored, tall and slender, dressed to go out. She stared with piercingly blue eyes at Alberta and stepped aside to allow her to pass.

Alberta gripped the banisters and made no move. She could see into one of the hotel's best rooms giving on to the street, one of the newly decorated ones for which the young Madame was responsible. Inside, the airy curtains were half drawn; they moved slightly in the draught from the door and filled the room with a subdued, rose-coloured light. Nickel taps and other modern fixtures shone. It was the kind of room one dreamed about in winter, when a small box of coal cost one franc fifty and the icy north wind chased the dust clouds down the street. Fruit, that had not been bought from a barrow, was in a bowl on the table, golden pears, blue grapes. A hat was lying there, a pair of gloves, a blue fox fur. A cubist study was on the floor, leaning against the legs of a chair.

' Come in and look at my latest work. Let me have your opinion. What do you think of it?'

' It's beautiful, very beautiful Mademoiselle . . . Mademoiselle . . . .'

' Wolochinska, Wolochinska! Is my name so difficult to remember? *Mon Dieu, mon Dieu!*'

' It is very beautiful, Mademoiselle Wolochinska,' repeated Alberta, looking at a confused puzzle of deep, somewhat turbid colours, with which Wolochinska was wandering about in order to place it in a better position. She drew back the curtains. The daylight fell palely on the thick layers of colour and on her own angular features under the smooth, close-cropped, very fair hair.

' Come in, don't stand out there. You actually look as if you're frightened of me.' Wolochinska laughed uneasily.

Alberta laughed even more uneasily. ' I'm busy – there's something I must do this evening, some correspondence – I'm sorry, I hope you will excuse me . . . . Your picture is very beautiful, very . . . good evening, Mademoiselle.'

Alberta was already on her way up. Wolochinska called out after her: ' You are unkind! Unkind! Don't you know what loneliness is?'

' Oh yes,' called Alberta. ' Yes, Mademoiselle.' And she fled, two steps at a time.

The red matting gave way to coco-nut. Soon this gave out too. The doors were different, the windows low and small. Finally Alberta groped her way forward in the darkness under the roof to a door that was hers, opened it, divested herself of her outdoor clothes and carefully removed two eggs and other provisions from inside her blouse. Then she sat down on the bed with her hands pressed against her heart as if to control it.

It was a small, stuffy attic room, smelling of mice. It had a sloping roof with a square skylight which was left open day and night, but it made no difference. An unchanging quantity of stale air, that seemed heavy with the dust and reek of generations remained immovable in the room, fed by suspicious-looking old armchairs, the proximity of chimneys and the collective bedroom smells of the whole hotel, stored in the upper part of the staircase.

Dusk was already falling. The lower half of the furniture disappeared in shadow, the fragment of sky had a thin sheen of gold. When Alberta had sat for a while, she heard a faint, gurgling sound from the wash-bowl. She went over and looked down into it.

In the grey soapsuds a mouse was swimming round and round; at intervals it would try to climb up on to the rim, but plopped back again. Alberta watched it without surprise. She went out on to the staircase and peered down into its murky depths.

When she had waited for a while, a white apron and a swinging feather duster came into view between two doors and disappeared again. The muffled tones of a song, uneven and melancholy, rose momentarily upwards: ' *Et le pauv' gas, quand vient le trépas . . . serrant la médaille qu'il baise, glisse dans l'océan sans fond . . .* '

' Jean,' called Alberta.

A hand placed a full toilet bucket and a mop out on the landing and was gone again.

' Jean!'

' Mademoiselle.'

' Would you please come up?'

Jean popped up out of the darkness, red-faced, red-haired, illuminated by the fast disappearing daylight from the sky-light. He was in shirt-sleeves, a bibbed apron, and armed with a feather duster.

' At your service, Mademoiselle.'

Jean was not in the least alarming. Alberta therefore informed him boldly that there was yet another mouse in her wash-bowl.

' Another? It's because they're thirsty. They suffer from thirst just as we do. Besides, the weather is sultry, it wouldn't surprise me if we had a storm.'

' Sultry?' Alberta remembered the restless, windy spring outside.

' Yes, sultry. I'll take it away.'

Jean commandeered the bowl and disappeared. He was back instantly.

' What have you done with it?' asked Alberta, stricken with guilt.

' I killed it,' Jean told her without visible emotion and without going further into the matter. ' Mice are vermin, as you know. I told them downstairs that they were bother-ing you, and Madame came up, but...' Jean gestured apologetically with the feather duster '... *vous savez*, Madame! And there was bread in the corner over there. I hadn't noticed it. Madame did. It was unfortunate.'

' Yes,' admitted Alberta and sat down, suddenly tired of it all. She could not be bothered to defend her little vagary any further; it was doubtless stupid, as was so much else that she did.

Out of habit Jean made several passes with the duster over the furniture within reach: ' The old lady would have sent up a mousetrap and perhaps the cat as well. This one

264

grimaces and says it's no use letting out rooms to artists and foreigners, they're *malpropre.*'

'*Pardon?*'

'Oh,' said Jean quickly. 'I, who look after the rooms up here, know better than anyone that it is not true where you're concerned. You are not an artist, you are very clean. You know how to behave. There are foreigners and foreigners. The Hungarian musician further down the passage, on the other hand, and his madame – they stopped up the water-closet again only yesterday. Madame had dropped a whole bunch of radishes down it, it ought to be obvious that you can't do things like that. She showed me that they were worm-eaten, as if that were any reason. She washes her paintbrushes under the tap out here. Your hands get covered with paint, just look at my apron. And this porridge that foreigners eat, she makes it in her room, in spite of the rule against cooking. It boils over. It's disgusting. If I've been up once I've been up ten times with a bucket and cloth. It's a waste of breath explaining anything to them, they don't understand a word. I shall have to report them to Madame.'

Alberta, who had once been green and inexperienced too, felt sympathy for the ethereal, pre-Raphaelite lady she met on the staircase now and again. It was she who, with a strong Danish accent and extremely limited vocabulary, initiated the couple's transactions with the outside world. 'Key, if you please; water, if you please; letter, if you please?' She had long, narrow, impractical hands, large vacant eyes, a personality full of anxious reserve. It was rumoured that she was in hiding with her musician. She would probably be scared to death if Alberta were to try to help her by addressing her in Norwegian and interpreting for her. Both of them had a way of going in and out, of opening their door just wide enough for their thin figures to pass through, of turning the key in the lock, that cut them off from all advances. Nothing could be done for this couple, whose existence was only noticed on account of the accidents they caused, and the occasional long-drawn

265

out, smooth tone of a violin that reached Alberta across the roof through her skylight.

On the other hand it was not so amusing for Jean and his countrymen to have all these helpless people from various parts of the earth in Paris, trying to make a fresh start in a life they had never attempted before.

" I know it's a nuisance,' admitted Alberta. 'But don't say anything to Madame. They'll be leaving soon, they're not the kind who stay long.'

Jean shrugged his shoulders : ' The old lady was patient, she went up to the rooms, talked to people and explained. The young one . . .

' The old lady's a good woman,' he asserted. ' But now she's finished and so are we all. The young one's turning everything upside down. Even up here under the roof she's going to have new wallpaper, and heating and electric light. Yes, Mademoiselle, and hot and cold water like the first and second floor rooms. It'll mean the end of living here for thirty-five francs a month, the end of artists and people like that. They want it to be a big hotel, as it used to be in Monsieur Grandpère's time, they want to modernize and compete with the Hôtel Lutétia. You'll see.'

I'd better give notice before I'm thrown out, thought Alberta wearily. She said : ' It'll mean richer guests and bigger tips.'

' It'll mean the end of me,' replied Jean. ' Of a country boy like me. It'll mean chamber-maids in black with white caps on their heads. Madame will throw both of us out, Mademoiselle, you as well as me. She gave Aristide the sack so that she could take on someone who had worked at the Hôtel Wagram. Yes, he's worked at the Wagram, that new fellow. As if he's any more clever than the rest of us. He looks like an advertisement for brilliantine, that's the only difference. In my opinion the old lady would do better to clear out.'

' Perhaps so.'

' The young one has taken over the till, that's only right and proper, she is the daughter-in-law, Monsieur's wife.

But she pretends not to hear when the old lady tries to put in a word, is that any way to behave? And Monsieur!' Jean gestured away from himself with his hands, hunching his shoulders: 'Poor fellow – he'll be a cuckold before the year's out. She makes up to the hotel guests behind his back, she's that sort. If she were my wife...' Jean suddenly fell silent.

A memory came back to Alberta. A clear, mild autumn day, an attractively-lighted, peaceful interior that had been like a revelation after the darkness of the stairs, an artist's attic perhaps, almost a studio, with sunshine falling from above in a flaming parallelogram on the red-tiled floor; a kind old lady in a light blue shawl, who mischievously put her hand in front of her mouth and whispered: 'No bedbugs – believe me – you can sleep here in peace.' The sensation of happiness, peace, security, given by it all, of having finished with dark, oblong hotel rooms, as narrow as corridors and lying opposite the staircase, filtering machines for noise, draughts and stale air, cheap, the cheapest there were . . . .

'I must go,' announced Jean. 'I can't stand here chatting. Some of the guests never leave their rooms, so you can't get in until late in the afternoon. What a filthy *métier* this is! *Oh là, là* – I had enough of it, more than enough, a long time ago. By the way, one of those gentlemen was here, the short one – I said Mademoiselle was not at home. If I may give Mademoiselle some advice, it would be best not to leave water in the bowl when Mademoiselle goes out.'

'No,' said Alberta submissively. 'I shan't do it again.'

Jean displayed his goodwill by cursorily waving his duster a couple of times over the bedhead, and retired.

Alberta was alone. She remained standing for a while, her arms hanging at her sides, as if crestfallen. The sounds from the street and from the interior of the house reached her like the last sounds from the outer world to one immured.

In the mirror above the grate, weakly illuminated by the fading twilight, she could see the contours of the unknown girl whom she met in the mirrors wherever she set up house, a figure she would never be rid of and never understand, never quite succeed in getting to accord with her inner self. In this light the cast in her eye could not be seen and shadow mercifully covered much else. Only a slender apparition with her hair down around her ears stood there.

During the years down here in Paris she had learned to accept the figure in the mirror for what it was. She no longer attempted to adapt her awkward person to custom and fashion, but adapted her few cheap articles of clothing as far as possible to herself. Was she ugly? Probably. But here in Montparnasse people wandered about with snub noses and many kinds of facial faults and were quite acceptable. They thought up an outfit that suited them, procured themselves style, *genre,* a cheerful disposition, and did not look too bad. The aching wounds of Alberta's childhood, the smarting feeling that she annoyed people merely because of her appearance, had almost healed. Only when she met visitors from home was she reminded of it.

She wandered about the room, climbed up on to a chair and looked out of the skylight, arranged the flowers on the mantelpiece and gave them water, lighted the spirit stove. Soon she would only see the surfaces of things. The darkness flowed higher about them, seeping up from the corners, like the sea at home gaining slowly on the seals and the rocks. Only the front legs of one of the two ancient, suspicious-looking armchairs would remain standing for long out under the skylight, while the black marble profile of the mantelpiece became sharper.

It was time to light the lamp, to take out pen and ink, grammar and dictionaries, to fill her evening with studies or writing. There was no-one to hinder Alberta. She had studied French thoroughly, taken coaching, attended lectures, learned many long poems by heart and practised her ' r ', filled countless thick exercise books with inflections, had, most decidedly, continued to live in Paris ' for the sake of the language '. She was an advanced student; the literature was open to her.

She did not really do her reading here. She did it at the booksellers' counters under the arcades of the Odéon Theatre, at the *bouquinistes'* along the Seine, at the Ste. Geneviève Library. She seldom managed to buy a book, and those she owned she knew by heart. Her studies had not proceeded without cost, they had swallowed up whatever money there was to be swallowed, and more. She had been given help towards them, and as a result they had become a hobby-horse for those who wanted her to return to an orderly existence, a trump card in the letters from home, something she should come home and ' put to good use '.

As for writing, according to Liesel, she knew how to do that too. Moreover it kept her busy, according to what she herself had so brusquely said to Wolochinska.

Now and again, assailed by desperate shortage of money and reckless enterprise, she had recourse to it: when there was no other way of conjuring up the rent, when her shoes had become impossible or the need for new clothes glaring, when she dared not ask for further credit at the shops, and Mr. Digby was away or had no need of her. It was an alibi, when such was needed, but otherwise it was merely one of her chance expedients, something she could do because she had learned it at school, as the result of training, aptitude, and because it was expected of her. Articles about this and that, the Flea Market and the Fourteenth of July, a fête in the Tuileries Gardens, the Seine flooding its banks; things of which she needed to know nothing beyond the evidence of her own eyes, topics behind which to hide herself and her lack of knowledge and experience, a collection of words to throw in the face of the equally stupid, ignorant reader, confusing and startling him. She found a topic, stowed away impressions into a suitable number of lines and signed it A.S., doing so with reluctance and shame, feeling that she was doing violence to something in herself, and that what she had described was untrue, because it was shallow and merely superficial.

Sometimes she did write differently. But it was not the sort of thing that could be used by the newspapers. It could not be used for anything at all, was most unlikely to bring in a sou, would not even be accepted for printing. In other words, a form of idling. Alberta had always had many forms of idling. She frittered away her time with virtuosity.

Other people had a purpose in life and struggled towards it, or at least they had some kind of work. Their lives did not resemble an obscure path which wound round and beyond them in the darkness and which they could not reach.

Apart from the first couple of effervescent years, when everything, the language, the city, the museums, the past and the present, had surrendered of their own accord when she attacked them like a famished soul who at last sits down at a table set with food, Alberta did not yet know what she really wanted. She still had only negative instincts, just as when she was at home. They told her clearly what she did not want to do. Her whole being cringed when faced with certain situations and certain people, certain activities and certain surroundings, so that she felt it physically in the form of fever and pressure on the heart. Afterwards she was left free to reject what she did not want and without the slightest idea of what she should do with herself.

She had made one or two attempts to overcome this. A helpful Swedish lady had found her a post in the Scandinavian *pension* where she lived. Alberta would thereby avoid something she knew with certainty she did not want, and which yet again threatened on the horizon: going home. Because of her knowledge of French she was to be at the service of the guests, accompanying them to town, helping the ladies to change their purchases in the department stores, clearing up their misunderstandings with the servants; in emergencies to be prepared to wash a blouse, iron a creased dress, see people off at the station.

It had meant a heated room, three square meals a day, the chance of getting presents and tips, in fact, clover for someone like herself. On the seventh day Alberta had quietly sneaked out after having shown herself to be quite impossible, burnt holes in a silk blouse, and lost her temper with an old lady who wanted to go into Lafayette and change two small embroidered table-napkins after they had begun to roll down the iron blinds in front of the windows.

It was winter and raining in torrents. Just before dinner, when the guests were in their rooms and no-one was asking for her, Alberta had stolen downstairs in a daze, betaken herself to a sinister, but cheap hotel in the Rue St. Jacques, and gone to bed there, ill at ease and miserable.

The feeling of being abandoned and lost, that she was left alone with in that small, gloomy room, that smelt mildewed and uninhabited, the damp sheets, the candle-end that smoked and burned out, the cold dawn that eventually came, were impressions that still remained with her and always would. The next day she had written an embarrassing letter in a café, apologizing and asking for her trunk to be given to the messenger. Afterwards she had tried to avoid Scandinavians.

She had fallen back on casual and ephemeral pupils, newspaper articles, wandering about, reading. It was then that she had confided in Alphonsine who, after a certain amount of hesitation, had put her in touch with Mr. Digby. And she went and took off her clothes in front of this strange man. It was disagreeable, it was mortifying, but it was life's bitter law and no worse than much else. It was nothing to make a hue and cry about, as they would have done at home.

A violent fever of activity would occasionally possess her, a restless urge to use her energy, to use it for almost anything: to run down street after street to find places where such and such took place during the Revolution, to get up in the middle of the night and write long, effusive letters to Jacob, to begin studying something, to patch up her ignorance.

She had thrown herself blindly into one thing after another, had trudged systematically round museums for weeks, sat in libraries poring over works on this and that, including anatomy, made notes and traced charts of the human body and at times derived a secret gratification from what bored her. Perhaps precisely this was necessary if one wanted to learn to work at something. Until one day she finished just as abruptly as she had begun.

She was shallow, soaking up knowledge and quickly satisfied even if the subject really interested her. The thought would occur to her that perhaps it was resistance that was lacking, friction against the disapproval of others. And she would feel more negative than ever.

For long periods she would be numb and indifferent. She only had energy enough for everyday matters. The world about her seemed like a film, comic and gripping by turns. And she was away from home, she had achieved that at least. This was the plank on which she floated, which she was must not abandon, whatever happened.

And the days would pass. Until life suddenly seized her by the scruff of the neck and gave her a good shaking. There she would be without a sou – or she would get a letter urging her to come home – or someone employed by her relatives' secret police would turn up – or somebody would say something, as Liesel had done today : ' My life is not interesting.' Such things roused her, waking her to bitter reflection. But they did not reform her.

Alberta got to her feet, put her eggs on to boil, looked at the station clock to see what time it was and curled up in bed to wait. The bells of the trams sounded shrilly above the traffic, a train whistled. She watched a little pool of water that Jean had spilled when he took the bowl away. Firmly circumscribed, it stood in low relief on the red floor, reflecting the delicate golden light from the ventilator.

After a while something happened near the pool. A nimble little silhouette scurried out from the darkness under the sloping roof, paused and sniffed the air, sitting for an instant on its haunches with its tiny forepaws lifted – Alberta could see its little nose moving – scurried forward again towards the bright water, and drank. Like an ornament its tail lay curving behind it.

She watched it with composure. It was a fact. In a little while another one came, a new fact. Alberta's room was overrun with mice, but rooms can be overrun by worse creatures. Mice do not bite. They smell, but they are not alone in that. She was acquainted with animals that smelt as well as bit.

And she let them run about. It was only when she came across them in the wash-bowl that she failed to cope with the situation.

Later in the evening Alberta went out and wandered about the streets.

This was the refuge of many at this time of day: the homeless, the lonely, the disgraced, the puzzled, who do not know what to do with themselves. No-one is so impossible that he cannot feel he belongs here.

She walked down the Rue de Rennes, the greyest, hardest, bleakest of streets. There one met no acquaintances, there one was an anonymous person going by, a working girl on the way home, a prostitute on the way out, a straw in the current . . . .

Down, up, down again, first along one pavement, then along the other. The traffic was thinning out. After a while the street began to resemble an empty stage, where a rowdy drama had been played. Pieces of paper, banana-skins and cigarette stubs had been left behind in the gutters, and took on the appearance of uninviting props as the evening progressed. All the shutters high up on the houses were closed.

From the bars light shone cold and white. Silhouettes glided out and in, the clamour of gramophones came unevenly through doors that swung open and shut, snatches of music were thrown out from small orchestras. The passers-by began to look as if they were out on suspicious errands, Alberta too. Words were thrown at her from time to time, occasionally amusing, in some cases complimentary, never crude and vulgar as at home. The worst was the brief, low '*Tu viens*?', naked as an order to a slave. But if one walked quickly and pretended not to notice, the matter would lapse quite naturally. Sometimes it would be made good again with an apology: '*Pardon Madame*'. Alberta was never afraid in the street here, as she had been at Rivermouth and in the alleys at home in the small Arctic town.

It was lonely, and the loneliness rose from it all like bitter cold. No-one would hear if something happened on a deserted stretch of street, no-one would open the shutters to see who it was that screamed.

But nothing happened. And even the bleakness had something of adventure about it. Walking in the street can be like following a river. There may be plenty of traffic on it, or else it flows dark and forsaken, with scattered lights along the shore. It leads people towards each other, away from each other, there is no knowing where it can finally lead, or to whom.

The city streets, where you run to get warm in winter. Alberta had an extravagant weakness for them.

* * *

' How about going to Versailles, Liesel?'

Alberta leaned across the waxed cloth on the pavement table outside The Coachmen's Rest, a modest restaurant which she had frequented during her early, hesitant days in Paris, and where she and Liesel sometimes went in silent agreement. She watched Liesel expectantly. Absent-mindedly, in a slightly hunched position, Liesel was struggling with a tough chicken wing, muttering from time to time something about '*Uralter Hahn*'.

' We could get the two o'clock from Montparnasse.'

' No,' said Liesel. ' I have a life-class.'

' Today? But Liesel, if you haven't started by this time . . .'

The spring sky was tall and pastel blue above the city.

The waves of sound had a new tone, a light humming, peculiar to the season. The fresh colour of the new leaves was just as astonishing in the street scene this year as last year, as every year. The air and the light raised everything to a higher pitch, to the border of unreality. A hint of water and meadows was adrift in the atmosphere. Spring with all its happiness and sorrow had conquered the city, giving one the desire to do ridiculous things: to hire a cab by the hour and damn the expense, buy masses of flowers and beautiful things, eat outside at Leduc's every day, dine at D'Harcourt's at dusk with a lighted lamp on the table. One's old hat was an offence against the scheme of things.

At least one could go to Versailles. It cost thirty-five centimes, but lay within the bounds of possibility. Alberta already felt the warm sunny air that hung, heavy with the scent of box, above the flower beds there; already lay on her stomach in the grass, watching clouds and insects on their capricious ways, while Liesel sat on a camp stool, sighting with a brush, narrowing her eyes and painting. Blue shadows moved slowly round a piece of sculpture, across a lawn, up the gigantic pale green wall of an avenue. Patches of sunshine played over the elm trunks, the clock in the Palace chapel marked the hours, paying them out in ringing coin and with royal generosity. One had passed over into timelessness and abundance.

But Liesel wanted to go to her class. 'It's still full there,' she explained. 'And there's a new model who's supposed to be exceptional. The evening class is not enough. Besides, only dilettantes and old ladies go, not real artists. It lacks atmosphere. I must go to life-class today,' said Liesel. She looked nervous and distressed as she struggled with the chicken.

'Are you feeling well, Liesel?' The fact was that Liesel looked quite tousled although she had lowered the neckline of her dress even more this year, put the roses on her hat in a different position so that the faded parts were almost hidden, and sat equipped for the season, her Botticelli shoulders rather too bare, but with veiling over them.

'Well? Oh yes, thank you.' Liesel had not slept. But apart from that ...

Why had Liesel not slept? 'Is it those people next door again? You must ask for another room, Liesel.'

'*Ach,* you only move next to others who are just the same. You know how it is, Alberta.' And Liesel didn't care, *aber gar nicht.* She pretended not to hear. She spoke the last sentence vehemently, and flushed.

'No, no.'

Suddenly Alberta noticed a tear rolling slowly down Liesel's face. Liesel wiped it away, quickly, roughly as if to punish it. Another one followed.

'It's my nerves,' she mumbled in apology. 'It's because I'm tired.' She dried her tears more thoroughly and openly, looked up and attempted an embarrassed little smile. 'What will you think of me, Albertchen?'

'Why nothing.' Involuntarily Alberta put her hand on Liesel's, a rare and little used expression of sympathy, that made both of them look embarrassed. She withdrew her hand at once, regretting the gesture. Now Liesel was really crying; she sniffed and had to blow her nose. Alberta's gesture had evidently only made matters worse; she was silly about things like that.

There was nothing she could do but wait until it passed. Liesel dried her eyes, her face blotched and miserable, and tried to hide herself from the world under her big hat. When she had recovered a little she said, as if concluding a train of thought: 'Don't ever let anyone kiss you, Albertchen. I mean unless he's terribly fond of you.'

'No,' said Alberta hesitatingly.

'Once they kiss us the game's up.' Liesel sniffed and searched for a dry corner on her handkerchief. She did not look up.

Dread crept over Alberta. Had Liesel gone and got herself involved in something? It subsided at once when she heard that it had to do with Eliel. 'Of course you understand it's Eliel?' Liesel dabbed at herself with the handkerchief.

276

But Alberta, who for a moment had thought of hotel guests and other doubtful individuals, breathed again, relieved and a little embarrassed. 'Eliel! But he's certainly fond of you, Liesel.'

'Oh, not a bit of it.' Liesel gestured away from herself. 'The Swedish girl, Albertchen, the Swedish girl. It's now three weeks since she arrived. Potter has seen her with Eliel, they were sitting in chairs under the trees in the Luxembourg Gardens looking as if they were enjoying themselves.' And not a word had Liesel heard from Eliel during that time. If that wasn't a bad sign, Liesel didn't know what was. But she supposed men were like that.

It's mean of Eliel, thought Alberta. Cunning or mean or both. She set about comforting Liesel, pointing out that now and again the sort of people one had to look after from morning to night did come to Paris and one never had a moment's peace. It probably wasn't much fun for Eliel. Liesel would see.

Liesel wanted nothing more than to be comforted. She looked at Alberta with shining eyes, saying at intervals, 'Do you think so, Albertchen?' In between she returned to her original argument that if only she hadn't let herself be kissed she would never have got into this state. She quoted an observation made by Potter who, when asked what she thought about the situation, had said bluntly, 'Well, if he's hard up for a girl . . .'.

'Don't take any notice of Potter. She's old, I'm sure she's never . . .'. Alberta broke off. It was the same as with so many of Potter's bald, bitter utterances: they tore away the ground from under one's feet, making life uncertain and rough, ugly and unkind; one suddenly found one was freezing, standing unprotected in a desert of ice.

'Yes, there you are,' said Liesel. 'That's how you get if you're like Potter. One must have someone to love, Albertchen. Those who say so are right, Marushka is right.'

Alberta shrugged her shoulders, without going into the question. But she found something really consoling to say:

' I expect Eliel's trying to make you jealous, Liesel. I shouldn't be surprised.'

Wide-eyed, Liesel whispered fervently: ' Albertchen – sometimes I've almost thought so myself. And if only he comes back . . . .' She smiled. At the same time there was something defensive in her expression, she seemed ready to make an argument.

Alberta attacked neither attitude, advised neither for nor against and made no more bantering allusions to Eliel. He was no longer merely the big, good-natured blunderbuss about whom one made little jokes, at whom one laughed a little, behind his back and to his face. He had conquered Liesel. It gave him an unexpected halo.

Alberta had known him when he was making heavy weather as a newcomer who could not go to the post office alone nor come to an understanding with his concierge without help. It had fallen to her lot to help him over the worst, find him a cheap iron bedstead at the junk shop, arrange for his milk delivery, and so on. His expression, as happens when men are helped with things they are quite incapable of arranging on their own, had become dreamy and strange when he looked at her, *distrait* when they were alone together. But Alberta was on her guard. All her life the only men who had ever been in question had been those she could not tolerate, and she had finally acquired a certain dexterity in putting matters in their place with small means: a tone of voice, facial expressions, sudden formality. She carried out her mission without anything transpiring, and the constraint that she had felt fell away and was gone. What remained was a somewhat passive friendship, which found expression in occasional loans of money.

And here sat Liesel, altered by anxiety and longing because of Eliel. Alberta felt the same slightly embarrassed wonder she had felt in her childhood, when she had been unable to find amusement in the others' play, and she realised that it was due to lack of ability. Eliel – it was possible to fall in love with Eliel. Here sat Liesel who had done so. It was possible for him to be a dream hero, an obsession, a song in the blood.

He was plagued by catarrh in winter, and was in the habit of sniffing. In fact, his nose twisted round in his face. Presumably, that kind of thing had to be ignored.

Quietly, with shining eyes and a little smile that tried to hide itself, but constantly reappeared, Liesel talked about Eliel: of his talent, his industry, what he said on this occasion and what he did on that, how she had to laugh at him sometimes and how touched she was sometimes and how stupid she had been and if only she had not ruined everything. But he *was* intelligent. And he was *fundamentally* handsome. Alberta had said herself once that he looked handsome when he was at work.

'Of course, Liesel.' Alberta saw Eliel's tall, slightly stooping figure, surrounded by numerous large sculptures, which in some curious way seemed to be related to him, dragging limbs which they could not quite control, looking as if halted in the middle of a hesitating, half implied, fumbling and helpless gesture. She remembered an inner clarity, which would suddenly seem to shatter his heavy expression while he worked, the strangely intuitive life in his hands when he kneaded the clay and forced form out of it; the calm, legitimate triumph with which he would slowly turn the modelling-stand and show the world a new creation, the toss of his head as he did so, as if he had emerged victorious from a long, hard struggle : the essence of the man. And here sat Liesel, ignoring all that was unimportant and looking victorious too. Besides, she was starting to talk about her work. Nothing seemed lacking to her.

'What are you thinking about, Albertchen?'

'No – it was nothing. Go on Liesel.'

Liesel was only going to say that she seemed to have definitely ruined the Pont Neuf picture; she had gone down to improve it, and the trees had become light green in the meantime, and then she got the disastrous idea of – well, there it was. But she was going to take her drawing seriously and not think about colour any more: life-class from this afternoon on, and not just because Eliel might be there. She pressed her bosom and her clasped hands against the edge of the table and looked at Alberta solemnly.

Alberta was thinking that this afternoon there was only one thing to be done, she must get intoxicated in her own private way, and forget Eliel and Liesel and everyone who had everything she herself did not have and never would.

La Villette St. Sulpice.

Past St. Germain-des-Prés, across the Place St. Michel, over the Seine; La Cité, past Porte St. Martin, Gare-de-l'Est; through broad and straight, narrow and crooked streets. Streets smelling of petrol, perfume, powder, and streets smelling of oil, chipped potatoes, pancakes. Regular, correct streets, where the houses stood looking just what they were; and others where signs, awnings, posters and advertisements of all kinds crowded each other, dissolving and displacing contours, charming away all underlying planes in a confusion of intricate pieces. Streets that buzzed with cheerful human life, while two rows of light-coloured treetops united in the far distant haze; and gloomy streets, full of clammy shadow, clammy fate, something oppressive and uneasy that kept the sun away. Small parks, paradises gay with flowers and playing children; and the obscene horror of the slaughterhouse.

To plunge into it. To drift, wander about, watch, absorb it all, with no other purpose. To take one of the old-fashioned horse-buses, which still swayed along here and there – not the bright red motor-bus, which bustled about in certain streets. To dismount and take other buses, penetrate unknown territory, buy fruit from carts and eat it sitting on benches, hear the clock strike in different ways in different church towers and know that it didn't matter, no-one knew where she was, no-one knew where she belonged. At the bar where she drank coffee and cracked a hard-boiled egg against the counter, she was someone who came and went and no-one could give any information about her. It made Alberta feel something approaching *schadenfreude*.

There was an outside seat on the horse-bus, nearest the coachman and just above the horses' broad, pitching haunches. There you pitched high above everything too, you had a clear view.

Childhood tendencies are not easily escaped. They lead one further, lead one far. Alberta had had this inclination to drift since she was small. It could be roused by many things: tedium, weariness, physical unrest, a blue sky or a grey one, joy, an inexplicable impulse. It had acquired the addition of curiosity which did not make it any more permissible.

She could follow people unknown to her up and down streets, getting on and off the same means of transport with them to see where they finally went; listen intently to conversations between total strangers as if her whole existence depended on it; seek out places where she had no business to be, because some small feature gave her the feeling that something was happening there. Certain streets and houses had an inexplicable fascination for her; she drifted back to them time after time in order to stand there for a while, to watch people going out and in. Blindly, unable to give herself any valid reason for it, she absorbed impressions as a sponge absorbs moisture.

She would return home from her expeditions tired, hungry, knowing that she had yet again used money, time and shoe leather to no purpose, and yet strangely satisfied, as if deep and mysterious demands in her had been pacified for a while. Her brain teemed with fragments of the conversations of strangers. Disconnected pictures of the teeming life of the streets succeeded each other, shutting out regret and uncomfortable thoughts.

If only that were all. But one night a little while later she would perhaps be sitting up with smarting eyes and feverish pulse, scribbling illegibly on paper torn with abandon out of the nearest exercise book, which would then be ruined.

Something she had witnessed had clothed itself in words in the secret recesses of her mind. Or remarks she had heard blazed up out of her memory, appearing to her like mysterious knots into which many threads of human life converged, entwined themselves and retreated into the obscurity from which they came. She wrote them down – and before she was aware of it, was engaged in a struggle with the language as if with a plastic material, trying to force life out of it as Eliel did with his clay. Reality lies hidden in outward occurrences, the words one hears are for the most part masked thoughts. But there are glimpses which enlighten, remarks which reveal. Alberta sometimes thought she had grasped something of it. And she fought with the recalcitrant words, they were like a mutinous flock tripping each other up. When they were eventually written down, conquered and in order, a lull fell in her mind after such unprofitable midnight turmoil.

In the morning something was there. It looked strange and unrecognizable, and belonged to some sequence, heaven alone knew what. It was blocked on all sides, there was no way out in any direction. To find it she had to know more about life, much about life, everything possible about life and more than can be observed from the roof of a horse-bus. As the waterfall sucks and pulls, so can the teeming streets suck and pull. A yearning would seize her to swirl with it, if only to see what would happen, and a yearning to track down its myriads of secrets.

This business with little scraps of paper in the night-watches was another sore spot on Alberta's conscience. The following day she would be dazed and incapacitated. And the pile of loose sheets in her trunk had been lying there for a long time, filling it up and making it untidy. They fluttered about in it indiscriminately. One day she would have to come to some decision about them. She could not be for ever opening it, slipping more into it, and shutting it again. But she had an unhappy weakness for this muddle of scribbled pages.

Buried in her memory there lay a fragmentary landscape. A shadow moved in it, appearing now here, now there, a naïve figure making up poetry. The background shifted. It might be as unreal as a theatrical décor, a blue and gold mountain range, illuminated from below by an unnaturally low sun; it might be eddies in the current, a river eternally flowing, deep with grey upon grey or green upon green; a bank of snow in thaw beneath a light that was neither day nor night, neither winter nor summer. And it might be almost nothing, a dull speck in infinity, shut in by mist, rain, snowstorms, as by enormous draperies. The shadow was always the same, in an altered jacket of regrettable cut and with her hands tucked up inside her cuffs.

Like a piece of reality crystallized out of it all there once had existed a battered exercise book, filled with bad echoes of mediocre poets. It had come to light in the trunk one cold, raw winter afternoon in the Rue Delambre and turned out to be something to laugh and cry over, certainly not something to be found by anyone after one's death; on the contrary. It became a hastily flaming, bright warmth, towards which Alberta held her ice-cold hands for a while, and to this extent it actually proved useful for an instant. Alberta did not like thinking about it.

One day the scraps in the trunk would have to go the same way.

*　*　*

` *Mon enfant* – beware of yourself – don't be too kind, too docile . . . . '

Alphonsine spoke slowly, with long pauses between her words. She had pushed the glasses and plates aside and spread out the cards, in apparent disorder, over the table. With her chin on one hand and the other planted with straddling fingers over a group of three or four, she gazed at them meditatively. She was reading Liesel's horoscope.

283

Liesel was sitting beside her on Marushka's divan, rather low down, on account of a broken spring. She stretched out her neck to listen, pouting with half-parted lips, while blushes and involuntary little smiles came and went in her face. Now and again, with an ironic *ach* or *doch,* she let it be known that she was by no means taking it seriously.

Beside Liesel was Alberta, uncomfortably squashed. Then the Russian, one of Marushka's numerous acquaintances who unexpectedly appeared and disappeared again. He had addressed Alberta in Russian and Italian with the same meagre result; she did not understand a word of either. Now he was being brutally and baldly offensive, pinching her arm, treading on her toes, leaning forward to stare into her face as if she were passive out of slow-wittedness.

But nothing is less dangerous than rough handling; it can quite safely be permitted. And demonstrations were out of the question as far as Alberta was concerned. If she could not escape quietly she would rely on her old weapon of silence, sitting stiff as a post, acting deaf, blind and numb, a strategy which in the long run is enough to render anyone harmless.

On the other side was Marushka, who had kicked off her sandals and drawn up her naked feet under her skirt. Her short little toes, of which she was so proud because they were not marked by shoes in the slightest degree, flexed and moved. She leaned forward with her elbows on the table and a cigarette in the corner of her mouth, watching the horoscope.

Across a muddled still life of bottles, glasses, fruit peelings and ash-trays Alberta defended herself through the tobacco smoke against several pairs of eyes. Openly amused or tensely enquiring they moved between her and the cards : Potter's eyes, screwed up into slits in her tired, ageing face; those of the Finn, Kalén, small, slanting, dimmed with wine; those of the little Swedish woman – the one who had run away from home and begun to paint, and whom Kalén was currently escorting everywhere.

calling her his ' little angel ' – stiff, light blue, round with tension; Sivert Ness's eyes, strikingly clear and sober in his crooked Norwegian face; and high above them all, Eliel's. He had materialized again, in new corduroy trousers, the kind worn by workers in the street, wide in the legs and narrow at the bottom, and he seemed animated. A little way back from the table, mounted on Marushka's tall painting stool, he was enjoying the situation unreservedly, safeguarding himself by muttering: ' Huh – what a lout – an utter lout – I'd like to beat him up . . . '.

A Dane, a bespectacled, silent and random person, not an artist and quite uninteresting, was sitting low down and somewhat outside the group on an overturned chair. Eliel had fished him up in a café somewhere or other, dragged him along with him and introduced him to the company with the whispered explanation: ' Bet you anything the fellow has money, lives at Neuilly, I know that. We'll let him buy a sketch at least. One must fool the peasants when one can.' The "fellow" had been sitting looking about him with disoriented spectacles. Now he had suddenly heard something he understood and said with conviction: ' Beat him up – yes, that's what we should do.' But Eliel bent down and spoke to him quietly, and the question of beating up the Russian was dropped.

The hot weather had arrived, it was summer. The only movable pane in the big side window was thrown wide open. Pallid light fell through it from a threatening and stormy sky. They were in one of the numerous tiny studios in number nine, Rue Campagne Première.

' Here is happiness for you,' said Alphonsine. She looked at Liesel seriously, leaning her index finger on one of the cards. ' Happiness. Assuming that you don't let your heart run away with you. Beware of your heart.'

During the short pause, while Alphonsine pondered again, Potter leaned across the table and remarked quietly in English to Alberta: ' Men are like hungry dogs. Haven't I always said so?' And she switched over to her slow, tedious, incorrigible American-French and commented out loud, to the whole company: 'It is woman's misfortune to think with her heart. Man thinks with something a little lower down.'

That awful Potter! A small storm blew up round the table. Alphonsine said, 'But you are shocking, Madame.' A quiet, reproachful 'Potter!' came from Liesel. Marushka called out seriously, with raised eyebrows, 'We too, we too, often, but yes.' Above it all could be heard Eliel's 'For shame – a female like that.'

'What? What did she say?' The little Swedish woman was roused from the confusing conversation she was having with Kalén, who was quite drunk, and looked round innocently. Kalén put his hand on hers: 'Never mind, never mind, my angel. It was nothing for little angels. But the old woman, so help me, ought to . . .'.

The Dane had understood nothing. He enquired politely what it was all about. And Eliel, who probably felt he had a kind of responsibility for the man, explained perfunctorily: 'Ugh, the old woman is talking through her hat, she's a man-hater. But Marushka really is damned outspoken.' Eliel appraised Marushka thoughtfully, and Liesel became restless and her gaze wandered.

Sivert Ness said nothing. He never did say much, this quiet, indefatigable boy from Eastern Norway who was incredibly industrious and incredibly poor in a tumbledown studio in the Rue Vercingétorix. He sat rolling a cigarette. When he raised his head, it was to look at Alberta, who out of habit immediately jerked her eyes away. She did not like Sivert Ness. He was a silent, self-assertive fellow in ugly thick country clothes, an admirable person of course, and a fellow-countryman. But she had no interest in exchanging glances with him.

At the same moment the Russian pinched her arm again, his foot caressed hers under the table, his knee pressed upwards. And Marushka, stretched full length on the divan behind them, whispered happily and vivaciously into her ear: 'It's obvious who he likes best, who he wants. It's you. He's an opera singer . . .'.

Alberta turned scarlet, spiteful, hard, merciless. She felt shame and anger written on her face. Opera singer! She was not sure why, but the fact only made matters worse, unendurable. In stinging clarity a sudden explanation presented itself to her. He and Marushka were old acquaintances from far back, something between them was perhaps over now. Liesel's relationship with Eliel encircled her like a protective aura; men have a nose for that sort of thing, they prefer not to get in each other's way. Potter was Potter and incredibly old, over forty, it was maliciously whispered. Alphonsine . . .

Alberta ought to suit this opera singer on his way through. She was disengaged, suitably young, healthy, clean, undemanding, harmless, cheap in more ways than one, as good as free. She squinted in one eye, but that was of no importance in this context.

That was what the people who spoke to her in the street thought too, the ones who said ' *Tu viens*?' into her ear. And those who were shy and circumspect, with a cunning will deep in their eyes. The sort of girl you can take liberties with.

' I'm going, Marushka. I'm going home.' Alberta rose to her feet and struggled to get out. But Marushka held on to her from behind and whispered in her ear: ' Now don't be foolish. You have the summer in front of you to sit alone in that attic of yours. We're eating at Leduc's. I'll pay for you.'

Above the murmur of all the voices persuading her to stay, to take no notice, and so on, Alberta suddenly heard the spectacled Dane say, earnestly and confidentially: ' Listen, if you really would rather go, will you permit me to see you home?'

She sat down at once, replying no, thank you very much, boldly and defensively. This stranger, who had the same feeling for where the line should be drawn as herself, was definitely not going to assume the role of some kind of rescue operation, sent out by the forces of respectability. She was where she wanted to be, all things considered, coarse-grained overtures included. Besides, Marushka's words had sent a gust of the bleak attic through her, a premonition of the sickening feeling of desolation that summer evenings in the city gave her. Soon enough she would be able to sit at home evening after evening and boil her lonely egg. She laughed nervously and said to Marushka: 'Well – if you'll lend it me, then.'

'C'est ça.' Relieved that all ill-humour was over, Marushka kissed her quickly on the cheek and spoke to the Russian in his own language. He looked astonished and deprecating, shook his head and laughed. Immediately afterwards he was there again, quieter than before, more secretive, more insistent.

Between the clipped trees in their green tubs outside Leduc's it was crowded. The Americans predominated, taking up as many as two of the long tables, young men with studio shoulders and bare heads, women of all ages with veiling on their hats and round their necks, hung about with long necklaces of amber, amethyst, greenstone. They sat with their elbows on the table and smoked with a remote expression, greeting Potter nonchalantly and absent-mindedly, and Marushka, who was going from table to table shaking hands, warmly.

A short, sharp shower had fallen. There was a scent of earth and wet leaves, the air was heavy with spicy perfume from the Japanese rowan trees on the Boulevard Edgar Quinet. The evening sky hung sick and thundery between the rooftops.

Pock-marked Germaine waited on them. She was friends with everyone, moving people together to make room, laughing and throwing out swift repartee to right and left. Potter took Alberta under her wing: 'Poor little thing, come over here.'

Alberta was overcome by the weariness that was always a consequence of her incursions into social life. She sat withdrawn into herself. Mechanically she expressed agreement with the little Swedish woman, who was exclaiming over and over again: 'So charming to be out all together like this – just like this – how charming Paris always is in any case – how charming everybody is. I think everyone is so terribly kind . . . .'

'Yes,' said Alberta. 'Terribly kind.'

The Russian had transferred his attentions to Germaine. He seized her round the waist when she passed, followed her indoors to the bar, disappeared with her into a corner. Alphonsine looked after them and shrugged her shoulders: 'She's not as stupid as all that.'

Alphonsine had ordered a solid and sensible meal. *Entrecôte* with potatoes and salad, cold rice pudding with *compôte*, and that was that. No coffee. She ate calmly, with reflection, tearing pieces off her bread and chewing at it, talking no more than was necessary. Then she calculated what she would have to pay, put the money on the table, lit a cigarette and leaned back in her chair. *Voilà*, I've finished. If anyone wishes to hear my opinion on the Government or Monsieur Fallières, this is the moment. All you need do is present yourself.

Alphonsine did everything calmly and thoroughly. She was no longer young, but she was a sought-after model, because she was perceptive, punctual and without caprice. She had eaten, and now she was resting. She had taken off her hat and hung it on one of the ornamental trees. Above her short, broad face, in which the skin and muscles were stretched spare and taut across the cheek-bones, red hair jutted out in a thick wave and was gathered up diagonally on top of her head in an oblong roll. A painted mouth and two large irises, green as a cat's, stood out in violent contrast to her powder-white skin. Beneath her eyes it looked as if brownish blue shadow was eating in deep. It gave her a ravaged, battered, almost defaced look. She smiled with large, strong teeth.

Alphonsine was a friend. You could confide in her and meet with understanding. She read horoscopes and always found something to say that was encouraging, cautionary, or in some way to one's advantage. Always ready to do a favour, she had found Alberta the job with the harmless Mr. Digby over on the other side of Paris and kept quiet about it. Alphonsine made one feel safe.

Now she stubbed out her cigarette and announced that she was leaving. If the others intended to finish up at Montmartre or Bullier's, they must not count on her. She had been on her feet for eight hours, she had to be at work at eight o'clock the next morning with her bed made and the bedclothes properly aired. She could not stand coming home to an untidy room. Goodnight everybody . . . .

As always when someone leaves, the conversation flagged a little. An American woman expatiating on cubism at the next table could be heard so clearly for a moment that everyone smiled. Then Marushka said, ' Lilac – isn't it?'

The light from the arc-lamps among the leaves still had the same magical effect on Alberta as when she had first experienced it. Fantastic, theatrical moons suddenly light up, and a mysterious world of green leafy cascades and black shadows, of moving circles of light and dark silhouettes, is created. People glide in and out of it as if on a stage, one feels as protected and secure as in moonlight; secure from the day with its many evil hours, from the endless summer night outside.

The American's words about cubism had taken effect, Marushka was in full feud with Kalén, who was making fun of the new theories. In his calm manner, which was further emphasized by his slow, hesitant French, Sivert Ness joined in the conversation. Usually he sat listening most of the time. Now he confessed that he was not a cubist, that he had bought Gleize and Metzinger's book. Yes, indeed, he really had. If only it weren't so damnably difficult. In the first place he didn't know the language well enough. If only he knew more French – he muttered the last sentence in Norwegian and looked at Alberta.

Kalén exulted. He was now really drunk and slapped Sivert on the thigh. ' Ha, ha, my friend, French won't help you there. Drivel, drivel, the lot of it. " Obscurely said is obscurely reasoned," has my friend ever heard that saying? A great poet said it, a very great poet, whom my friend does not know – yes – and that book is obscurely reasoned. Everything they say is obscurely reasoned, except for the place where they say that some of them are making a miserable *pretence* of being strong and deep, while others, *whom the authors do not think fit to mention* – mark that my friend – *move freely on the highest level*. What they mean by this pronouncement is quite clear – quite clear, yes – besides, if my friend is short of money, he could make better use of it. Does my friend even know what a theorem is? I can see that he does not. But these cubists demand of their readers that they meditate over certain of Rieman's theorems – it's ridiculous of my friend to embark on such a thing.'

Sivert did not say much in reply. He treated the drunkard reasonably, admitting that – yes, oh yes, of course. Kalén, who had talked himself into an angry, threatening mood, slouched over his glass again, pacified.

Marushka and Potter had become heated on the subject. And Sivert, never one to miss anything, turned his attention to them. In her circumstantial manner Potter contributed the usual argument about stove-pipes. The cubists painted stove-pipes, grey and brown ones, why? Or they took apart a coffee-grinder and placed its various sections around each other, on top of each other, inside each other on the canvas. Why? If you asked them they said that was not what they were doing at all, even though it was obvious to everyone. They entrenched themselves behind formulas and set phrases that no-one understood, themselves least of all; they were really quite at sea. ' *Yes,*' said Potter. She would not allow Marushka to get a word in edgeways, but shouted her down and insisted that she knew cubists who sat for long periods at a time holding their heads in desperation when they were painting, simply because they didn't know *how* they should do it. ' *Fumisterie* ', said Potter, blowing smoke down her nostrils. ' Hot air. Humbug.'

Marushka had fallen silent. She looked as she sometimes did when she spoke Russian with Russians about Russia. Her dark eyes, which normally danced in her face with vivacity, seemed to look inwards, lost in contemplation. In a low, deep voice she said, ' They are creators, seekers – they are pioneering a road . . . '.

' . . . that leads nowhere.'

' Yes.'

' No.'

That was how it always ended, in airy protestations. The antagonists leaned back in their chairs and did not address each other for a while, each convinced of the other's lack of judgment. But Liesel eventually contrived to put in her little confession of faith. ' I'm *not* a cubist. Even the cubists themselves say one is born to it or not. I'm not. You must be yourself.'

' Quite right,' cried Eliel emphatically. And Liesel blushed happily and looked about her to hide it. ' Mutermilka ', she said, and went on to talk about the Polish artist who was her ideal.

At a couple of tables put together a little further away, Norwegian voices exploded. Alberta had gradually come to hear Norwegian from the outside, as a foreigner might be supposed to hear it. It can sound musical, being securely embedded in a light, strong, slightly differentiated register and having its own clear, staccato melody. It is without evasion, going directly to the point, an honest, forthright language.

But when many people converse together, the brief sentences, the disconnected, self-sufficient words dart at each other like angry barks: ' *Nei. Jo. Javel. Ikke tale om. Tøv. Paa ingen maate. Tvert imot.'* They strike hard against the eardrum and the voices swing upwards on the final syllable as if in defiance. When women speak, it sometimes seems as if they intend to talk their opponent down, talk him to exhaustion, so that he is incapable of more. They lean forward, transfixing him with their eyes, and talk loudly, categorically, unanswerably, until suddenly a feminine voice, low, clear and flexible, darts light as a bird up and down its small, pure scale, so that one listens to it as one listens to music. And that too is Norwegian, and resembles no other voice in any other language.

The little Swedish woman had fastened on to Alberta. A stranger to the circle, really only acquainted with Kalén, who was also an outsider, she probably felt impelled to associate with the women. She had her worries, and sighed : ' If only he could leave the liquor alone! He's such a wonderful person in every other way, fundamentally so distinguished and kind. But unhappy, you see – he's tried to kill himself, oh yes, not once but many times. You think you've gone through a lot yourself, and even then it's nothing when you compare .... If only one could help a person like that, do something for him .... '

Alberta had heard the same story before. Kalén hung about, always drunk, occupied year out and year in with a drama that would never be finished, sometimes fighting and causing scandal, frequently disagreeable and quarrelsome. He always had some sighing female newcomer in tow, while his Swedish wife, who was a masseuse and led a neglected existence in the Rue d'Assas, paid his café debts and got up to make gruel for him when he came home in the small hours. One's sympathy for Kalén became a little blunted over the years, giving it expression easily became a matter of habit. ' Yes, poor fellow,' said Alberta, thinking about something else.

She was half watching the Dane, prepared to be on the defensive with him. People passing through, needing someone to pilot them round, fell all too easily to her lot. She thought she felt the spectacles directed towards her now and again.

He did not say much, perhaps because the confusion of tongues put obstacles in the way. He had a thin, irregular face which the spectacles made even more irregular; they continually caught reflections from various angles and hid his eyes. When he moved, the padding in the shoulders of his jacket was pushed upwards. His voice reminded her of

293

Rasmussen. Every time it reached Alberta, memories floated up piecemeal. She could hear Rasmussen saying, as they walked past the Galeries Lafayette, for instance, where cheap remnants were lying in heaps outside, ' That's your colour – you ought to buy that piece – then you should make it up thus and so.'

She never bought it. However cheap it was, it was still too expensive, because it had to be made up. But she learned a lot about herself from Rasmussen, as they drifted all over Paris together, on foot and by horse-bus. One day he had had to give up painting and go home, for mysterious, rather vague reasons. Alberta had the impression that he was going to work in an office, and that it was to be some kind of transition to something else. She missed him very much. He had stopped writing a long time ago.

' *Skaal,* Albertchen – where were you then?' Liesel, a little distance away, lifted her glass towards her, smiling. Liesel was no longer disintegrating and depressed, as she had been a short while ago. She radiated a kind of quiet, concerted glow, which she seemed to force back, but which kept on breaking through. As the evening wore on her eyes seemed to darken and become veiled, because of what she was drinking or perhaps for some other reason. Presumably everything was settled between her and Eliel. That very day Liesel had said: ' We are happy, Albertchen – *aber so.*'

Something had come over Eliel too. Not only had he acquired new trousers; he had an artist's cloak, which he slung round him with a single gesture, and a new, broad-brimmed hat. When one examined Eliel more closely, he was new from top to toe. Besides, he was beginning to get a tan. The summer was Eliel's best time. Then he acquired an even, warm patina, which contrasted well with his teeth and his eyes and made him look younger and as handsome as a peasant. Alberta had occasionally felt a pang when Eliel made his annual appearance in this condition. But she remembered the catarrh in winter and various other things, and then it was over.

Now, however, Eliel was really good-looking. New clothes certainly made a difference. A new love affair too, no doubt.

The Russian wanted to go to Montmartre. The little angel's eyes brightened, she clapped her hands and cried: 'Oh yes, do let's. I've not seen belly-dancing yet. I'd so love to see belly-dancing. Just to see it, that's all.' But the proposal came to nothing for lack of support. During the discussion Liesel and Eliel miraculously disappeared. Potter left too, lonely and dragging a little as she went along the pavement. Kalén was heavy-eyed and quarrelsome. He announced that the devil could take him if the angel was going to any Montmartre this evening, no. She fell quiet and did not insist, her face turning small and distressed. Shortly afterwards they too were gone.

Marushka commandeered a cab and packed those who remained into it. They drove round the Luxembourg Gardens. It had again rained a little. The wooden cobbles in the Rue d'Assas shone like varnish in the wet, reflecting street-lamps and occasional pedestrians. There was a strong scent from invisible trees in blossom.

Alberta had the Russian's knee against hers, he was treading insistently on her toes. An understanding had to be reached before it was too late. It couldn't be so utterly hopeless, surely. She sat knowing that she found herself in the cab for one reason only, fear of coming home and being alone.

She was finally accompanied by the Dane and Ness. They talked to each other about the country. The Dane was going to the country, to a married sister of his. He turned to Alberta and explained that he lived in Neuilly with the same sister. 'Really,' said Alberta, tired and empty-headed.

Outside the hotel entrance this person, so completely ignorant of the circumstances, who had nothing whatever to do with her, suddenly decided that she was still his responsibility. 'Now are you sure you'll get in all right?

We'll wait until we see you safely inside. Good evening, it has been most pleasant, *au revoir*. We'll wait here, Ness and I.'

It took some time for the door to open. Alberta explained: 'Jean is asleep. One always has to ring several times. Do go, please.'

Ness was standing in the middle of the pavement. He intended to get up early next morning, as usual, and showed his impatience. 'Miss Selmer will get in all right. Besides, there's traffic on the street.'

But the Dane would not budge: 'We'll wait here, Ness and I.'

Sure enough, Jean was on duty. In the circle of light from the little pocket torch which he directed towards her as if she were a burglar, she glimpsed his face, heavy with sleep and warmth. He was lying fully clothed in his stockinged feet on a camp-bed in the little room beside the office, and muttered incoherently when she gave him her name. And he pointed the torch at the shelves on the wall so that she could find her key and her candlestick.

* * *

The furnishings were the depressing kind in brown-painted wood that seem inevitable in all administration. The light was poor and grey. There was a smell of poverty.

From old habit, perhaps from atavism, Alberta looked furtively about her on the way in and squeezed herself quickly through the door. Taking everything into consideration from childhood onwards, she was once more embarked on one of the small back ways of life. Once right in, such notions fell away as if she were throwing off a burdensome old garment. She was quite simply herself, and felt relieved. A failure, a little on the side-lines of life – yes. But so were the other people who came here. Nobody expected her to be any different, nobody was any more successful than herself. On the contrary, a quiet acknowledgement of life's difficulties, of the fact that it consists of alternatives, was in the air. The low-voiced people who gathered here recognized in each other reliable individuals, who gave guarantees, and they exchanged glances full of understanding and little smiles. No-one needed to brace himself to persuade the others of facts.

The bench under the window was Alberta's habitual seat. She was away from the light, could see all who came in, and right into the little window where a bald head with grey bristling moustaches and spectacles appeared from time to time. The head directed its spectacles towards one or another of those waiting, mentioned a sum with a not unfriendly ' *Ça va?*' to follow. The person concerned would get up and go forward.

Taking everything into consideration, it was an obliging head. It looked at one seriously, but without disapproval. It was the same to everyone, to the lady who nervously and surreptitiously took a ring out of her handbag, to the woman fumbling with trifles in a knot of cloth. It listened to what people had to say and went to the trouble of giving explanations. Not all heads in windows did that.

She could trust it. When, for instance, it said ' *Quarante francs, ça va?*', Alberta made no objection. She took its infallibility for granted in such matters, considering besides that if she did not get an enormous sum, no enormous sum would be demanded of her when it was time to come back again. And all the little things she had been given at her confirmation or which had been Mama's, the brooches, the rings, the necklace, the watch, had disappeared into the unknown – the enormous, grey complex of buildings that surrounded her and filled the *quartier*.

What is property? In the final instance a piece of paper, which renews your admittance to life for a while, a ticket to it, so to speak. If your luck is in you celebrate it with a brief reunion with something you thought you owned once. Round the corner, in the Rue de Regard, there was a door, a mysterious place, where a sparse gathering, silent as a congregation awaiting the miracle, sat on benches in rows. It was there. There you bought dearly the illusion of owning your property for a while. Putting it in was almost a more cheerful business than taking it out, for you could never really afford the latter.

Money in your pocket makes your step light. It is a sort of credential, giving one again the right to exist and look people in the eyes, to do things that increase one's well-being and self-respect: to ask about prices, choose food-stuffs, take them home and eat them, pay debts, smarten oneself up. On the way across the courtyard Alberta reacted as she usually did when she saw the word '*Matelas*' above a door: Thank God I've not sunk as low as the mattress yet. I haven't one, but even so.... She also noted with satisfaction that she had no intention of turning the corner into the Rue St. Placide and borrowing more money on the basis of her receipt. She was not as depraved as all that.

The municipal guard in the gateway twirled his moustache and smiled at Alberta as she passed. He did so out of good nature. Alberta did not misinterpret it either, but smiled back at him.

It was an evening in July following a completely still day. The heat outside beat down on her sickeningly and suffocatingly. The sun had gone from the street, but the asphalt gave off heavy, accumulated warmth. Thick with the reek of fatigue, dust, petrol and food, the air hung immovable between the walls.

Under the café awnings people were crowded round the small round marble tables. Blue syphons, golden, red or emerald liquids shone dully, sugar dripped glutinously into turbid absinthe, glasses and coolers were hazed over by quickly melting ice. The sight of a lump of ice sliding cool and smooth down into a vermouth reminded Alberta of a seal she had once seen at a circus. It had had a little rubber bath-tub to flop in and out of. It was immediately succeeded by another image, which floated up from hidden depths and remained for a second behind her eyes: a few small houses, half buried in snow under a grey sky, uninhabited, ice-cold.

Alongside the pavement the last fruit and vegetable barrows were moving slowly along under the impatient ' *Avançons messieursdames, avançons,*' of a policeman. A reek of decay, of things stored too long and slightly fermented, followed in their wake.

It was summer again, exhausted and cheapened, unaired and a little dirty, as it so quickly becomes in the paved streets. It breathes freely in parks and quiet residential districts; there, full of dark, melancholy sweetness it lets itself be surprised, but it yawns on the asphalt, trampled and soiled. Trees appear as if dying, animals and people half die. Alberta knew all about it, she had experienced it many times. For the first time she felt her courage flag on seeing it.

Slowly she wandered upwards, looked critically at the fruit barrows, studied the menu outside Léon's Restaurant, but left again. It was not the moment for extravagance, even though she had the rent, that nightmare of all the impecunious, in her pocket.

' Liesel!'

With her back towards Alberta, loaded with paper bags and parcels, Liesel was standing beside a late barrow, choosing from amongst the day's last squashed peaches. She started and looked up, her eyes wide in surprise, and collected the things she was carrying into one hand in order to give her hat a shove. It appeared to be losing its balance on top of her coiled-up hair. ' Albertchen! *Wie geht's*? It's close this evening, *aber so, nicht wahr*? That one and that one and that one, *ach nein,* not that one, it's rotten, but that one and that one.' Liesel picked and chose outspokenly from among the peaches. The fruitseller, a coarsely built woman with honest eyes and skin like copper, muttered something to the effect that if the customers were to take matters into their own hands trade would soon take a turn for the worse, then suddenly changed her mind and laughed: ' *Enfin,* it's the end of the day, and Madame is charming. Here you are, over a pound, *ma petite.*' She handed Liesel the bag and winked at Alberta: ' Her husband's fortunate, he has a thrifty housekeeper and a charming *amie,* he'll have a good dessert this evening. And you, *ma petite dame?* A pound for you too, *n'est-ce-pas?*'

She filled another bag quickly. ' There, thirty centimes. They were fifty. I'm honest, I admit you couldn't offer them to the President of the Republic, but they are good, they are juicy, believe you me. You'll be satisfied.' Holding the coin Alberta handed her tightly between her teeth, she fumbled in her bag for change, and then wandered on with her barrow. ' Good evening *mesdames, bonne chance.*'

Liesel blushed her pale blush. ' Did you hear what she said, Albertchen? It's just as if they can tell.'

' They say that sort of thing to anyone who's pretty, Liesel.'

' They can tell,' insisted Liesel. ' But they like it. Here it's the way it ought to be, not wrong as it is elsewhere. She saw very well that I had no ring. Look, not a single rotten one. I always got rotten ones before. *Am* I pretty, Albertchen?'

Timidly, with a shy little smile, Liesel produced this decisive question. At the same time she stopped, loaded Alberta with her bags, drew out her hatpins and stuck them in again differently, brushed dust off her dress. And Alberta, who knew what it was all about, and honestly thought Liesel was pretty besides, nodded in confirmation: ' Yes, of course you are.'

There was no doubt as to where Liesel was going. The days were past when she was on her way to Alberta's, or on her way home to light the spirit stove. Feeling a little flat, a little left behind and out of things, Alberta thought: Liesel might ask how I am. But Liesel said: ' I was looking at the hats in the window on the other side of the street. You know, the place where they're all the same price, four-ninety-five. But they're so boring, Albertchen, *so bürgerlich.* The ones we put together ourselves look better, more artistic, *nicht wahr?* There's one in Bon Marché – Marushka said she'd help me with it. It only needs a flower or two, *fertig.* But fourteen francs just for the form, *unmöglich*. Especially now. I've done something very reckless, Albertchen.'

'You're always doing something reckless.' The words came out of Alberta's mouth unintentionally, from fatigue, half-teasingly. She regretted them instantly. Liesel's face seemed to fall for a second. At any rate she said in a thin little voice: ' It's true, I *am* reckless. Not a month goes by but I'm in torture – but in *torture*. And yet it's been no more than two so far.'

Faces she had watched turn miserable here on Montparnasse, disappear and turn up again even more miserable – or simply disappear, paraded before Alberta. Indifferent, casual words from street corners and cafés rang in her ears: ' Mm – yes – things went badly for her, you understand – she got pregnant.'

Cold alarm for Liesel gripped her. Then she thought: After all, it's Eliel, Eliel's decent and kind. And simultaneously Liesel said firmly and with intensity: ' I've only done what I had to do. It's as natural as being alive. I'm in *love* with him, Albertchen, I'm in *love* with Eliel. You see how mad I am to say it out loud in the street.'

Liesel's little confession was completely drowned by the traffic, a lorry thundering past making it as inaudible as a sigh in an avalanche. Nobody had heard it besides Alberta. Nevertheless Liesel looked about her fearfully and ascertained with relief: ' No-one we know, *Gott sei Dank*.'

It was a fact that the most incredible things, truth and untruth in confusion, leaked out from Montparnasse to the rest of the world, finding and causing alarm to unsuspecting relatives, even as far away as America, giving rise to turmoil and catastrophe. It probably would not take long for a rumour to reach Liesel's cabinet-sized family. They were quite obviously unsuited to receive news of this kind.

' They think you ought to be married *und so weiter*,' said Liesel, as if Alberta had spoken aloud. ' They might decide to come, and disturb Eliel.'

And Eliel must not be disturbed. He was so gifted.

Someone was supposed to have used the word genius once at the Versailles. Besides, he was ill-suited to dramatic conflict, it was quite unthinkable that he should be involved in any such thing. Liesel emphasized still further the gravity of the case; 'No-one knows besides yourself, Albertchen, no-one, and you will be careful, won't you?'

' Of course I shall, Liesel.' Alberta was not the kind of person to give anyone away. Keeping silent was one of the things she really knew how to do. It offended her a little to have it enjoined on her. Coldly she asked, ' Where have you been?'

Liesel smiled her new, disingenuous smile: ' I told you I'd done something reckless – yet again.'

Alberta looked her up and down. She was wearing her eternal black. The dust showed up terribly on it in summer. Altogether it was ill-suited to the time of year, and Liesel was perspiring, pale with the heat. Alberta noticed that it had been cut down still more, the sleeves only reached to the elbow. Her hat was the faded violet one from last year, enormous, as fashion had then demanded, with small red roses round it. Liesel's bags clearly contained food from the barrows. But from her little finger there dangled a light little package.

' You're looking at my dress, Albertchen. Should I have left the sleeves alone?'

' No, no. What's *that*, Liesel?'

' You'll never guess.'

' Something from Bon Marché?'

' *Gar nicht, gar nicht.*'

' Then I don't know.' Alberta was suddenly tired of the joke. The money she had in her pocket no longer had any effect on her; she felt superfluous and futile. But beside her Liesel was saying: ' I *want* to be beautiful, Albertchen, I want to be beautiful now. I want to be ... ' She looked round enquiringly and found a word that expressed her thought: ' *Troublante. Troublante*, like the Parisian women. You can laugh, *aber* ... '

'*Troublante* is the right word. That's what we want to be. It's just that we're not properly equipped.'

'There, you see. Albertchen!' Liesel's voice assumed a confidential tone. 'I've just come from "*Cent Mille Chemises*" – *Hunderttausend chemisen*. I've bought a frilly nightie, *ganz allerliebstes,* nineteen francs ninety-five.'

Liesel nodded in the direction of the little package. But Alberta, who knew no better than that Liesel's wardrobe cried out for other replacements, and who was in addition short-sighted and stupid, exclaimed from an honest heart: 'Have you become a millionaire or completely mad?'

'Mad, Albertchen, mad, not a millionaire. I haven't the rent for the fifteenth, but still ...' A shadow passed over Liesel's face, then she suddenly exclaimed: 'It can't be helped, Albertchen!'

Her voice became still more confidential, filled with fervent, repressed emotion: 'I'm going to stay with him all night, for the first time. I'm not going to get dressed and go home again. We shall sleep together and wake together. It'll be more proper, more natural, won't it? I've wanted it all the time. One *wants* it, Albertchen.'

The tram to Fontenay aux Roses came into view at the bottom of the street, and Liesel set off for the tram stop at top speed. 'I *must* catch it. He *never* eats a proper *déjeuner,* only sardines *und so was.* I *must* get hold of a chop before they close out there. I've got the mayonnaise and ham and Brie and fruit here. You'll come out soon, won't you, Albertchen? Just imagine, he hopes to sell the group – the small, patinated one. Then we'll go away to St. Jean du Doigt – as long as Potter or Marushka don't decide on the same place. He wants to make sketches of me in plastolin, he says I resemble a Cranach, that I've given him an idea! For a large figure, Albertchen!' In all her busyness Liesel found time to look up at Alberta significantly. Her life was no longer uninteresting, she was everything, she was a Muse. She had the right to ask for a little assistance with nondescript everyday matters. 'Oh, would you mind taking a coupon for me, please?'

Alberta took the coupon, and Liesel mounted the congested tram-car, hot and flustered, her hat awry. Struggling to protect herself and her packages she stood in the crush on the platform, jostled back and forth, out of breath and radiant. Her breast rose and fell, her lips glowed as if painted. A couple of youths with cigarettes stuck in the corners of their mouths nodded at each other, and exchanged complimentary remarks: ' She's charming, *la petite,* very charming – if only it was worth the trouble of paying court to her.'

It was clear to everyone that it was not worth the trouble. A motherly old soul made room for her: ' Here you are, *ma petite dame,* you can stand more easily here with everything you've got to carry. I know what it's like to take the tram-car at this time of day, when one has done one's shopping.'

Liesel became even more radiant, in happy connivance with the whole world. She looked down with emotion at Alberta, left alone and probably looking a little pathetic. Just as the tram-car started to move, Liesel had an impulse. She leaned out and whispered at the last minute: ' You should find someone, Albertchen – Marushka is right – you should . . . '

Her final words were swallowed up by the noise. Liesel was gone.

Up in her room Alberta gasped in the enclosed atmosphere that met her. Quickly and roughly as if in desperation she tore off her clothes, threw them on to the bed and rubbed herself down with a sponge. Then she lighted the spirit stove, sat down naked among her clothes and sucked peach after peach.

At first she thought about nothing at all, keeping hateful thoughts successfully at a distance. They can resemble greedy birds round carrion. They circle round you in narrower and narrower rings. You throw them off, they return once more. Finally they alight on you, flapping their dark wings and hooting in your ears. They tear at your heart with their sharp beaks, and your heart writhes in pain, and sometimes stops.

For the time being Alberta had sufficient food. After the peaches came the eternal eggs. She stuffed bread into her mouth while she waited for them to boil, then ate and cleared away, threw a kimono round herself and opened the door out on to the stairs, leaving it wide open.

The staircase windows were open on to the minute courtyard, deep as a well. It was dinner-time and the house was quiet. The sound of forks could be heard from downstairs in Monsieur's and Madame's apartment and the clink of dishes from the kitchen. Looking over the banisters she could see Jean and the new *garçon* going downstairs for their meal. They buttoned up their waistcoats on the way and smoothed down their hair with their fingers.

She sniffed towards the draught which she hoped would come. But the heavy, dead air did not move. Nothing moved, nothing could be heard, but the light scattered sounds of cutlery and the muffled noise of the street. Nevertheless Alberta paced between the window and the door as if on guard, listening, prepared to turn the key in the lock instantly.

She was used to the summer emptiness of the upper storeys and knew its dangers and advantages. These depended to a certain extent on the menservants, whose rooms were also up in the roof. But here there was only respectable Jean trudging round. She had nothing to fear from that quarter, nor from the couple further down the corridor.

But the unexpected can happen.

She remembered an evening last year, heavy, suffocating, with peals of thunder far away. The demands of the body for fresh air, dammed up in her summer after summer, had all of a sudden become unbearable. Carelessly she had thrown the door wide open and stood on a chair, naked under the kimono, with her head out of the skylight, inhaling through every pore the small puffs of wind that moved now and again across the rooftops. The countless rows of yellow chimneys were pallid beneath the gathering storm. To the south, above Vanves and Malakoff, the metallic sky exploded in flash after flash of lightning, and an occasional violent gust of wind promised release. She seemed to feel how her blood drank the air in her lungs and flowed on, giving life to the dry network of veins. The draught played with the light material of the kimono, fluttering it momentarily. She was bathed in air, inside and out, and mind and body expanded to receive it. On a corner of the boulevard she could see the dry curled-up leaves, which the exhausted city trees strew about themselves at the height of summer, swarming along the pavement, all in the same direction, like scattered Lilliputian armies in flight. The whine of the trains at Montparnasse cut through the air.

Then her heart gave a jump as she realised that she was not alone. She looked down, and there the man stood, fat, bearded, in shirt and trousers, his chest bare, and dark with animal hair. In the sick, thundery twilight he looked unreal, especially as he did not speak, only stared at her. Alberta did not speak either. Dumb and tense she climbed down off her chair, and drove him out backwards in mutual silence, while her brain hammered with the realization: We're alone up here – it's a long way down – he'll get to the door first – if he shuts it, no-one will hear us.

He did not shut it. As silently as he had come, he disappeared again, in slippers or his stockinged feet. A lock that turned quietly out in the darkness was the only indication that he had actually been there.

He had been neither a vision nor a rapist. Alberta saw him again the next day on the stairs, a commonplace traveller in a top hat and waterproof. An ordinary man, who lived cheaply on top floors and sought cheap pleasures, led astray by the open door and the woman in scanty attire inside. It might have been worse.

Other memories from the top floors of other hotels lay stored up in her memory, uglier, more dangerous. She did not like meddling with them. And this last incident had been almost the most vexatious. The fact that she could not leave her door open on a suffocating evening unpunished, because she was everyman's booty, a woman, had left her bitter.

She walked a little way down the stairs and looked out of the low window. Now they had finished eating down there, only the clinking from the kitchen could be heard. At the bottom of the courtyard's depressing shaft someone was squatting, playing with the hotel cat. It was lying on its side, half on its back, striking out lazily with its paws. It was Jean sitting there. He had just hosed down the yard. A ring of small black puddles had been left round him in the depressions in the asphalt.

Someone was coming up the stairs, and Alberta drifted in again, shutting the door. She could go out walking, as was her custom, or she could go down and sit on the boulevard. She was free to do so, it was a harmless, cheap evening's entertainment, shared by thousands, by large sections of the population. The melancholy summer evening in the city, she had admittance to that: to its dying, sickly green light lingering in the window-panes high up, the suffocating atmosphere with its sudden puffs of fresher air which slap feebly at the café awnings, chase the dust upwards and die away again; to its gasp for tranquillity, which is drowned in the clamour of gramophones and the clanging of tram-cars. Tired, low-voiced or silent people sit on the benches. If they tilt their heads backwards they can see the sky, thin, clear as glass, far too light, pitched to hang whole and free above a scented landscape, drawn taut in bits and pieces above desert formations of stone and cement. Even the trees along the pavement look foreign and irrelevant, as if picked up from a Noah's Ark and set out in rows, artificial, unnaturally dark.

Alberta had experienced it summer after summer. It is then that the lonely cannot withstand their loneliness any longer, but come out from their hiding-places, and walk quietly down the street as if they had a route and a purpose. It is then that poor, elderly women get something impracticable and out-of-date from their drawers, something that suited them once, put it on and go out in it, guilty and uneasy, a little wry in the face.

There were evenings when a compulsion, an inner necessity, made Alberta seek out precisely this; when, with a kind of appetite, she inhaled the heaviness of the atmosphere, all it carried with it besides the reek of the day: human frugality, fatigue, resignation, unsatisfied longing. Something in her was nourished by it, and began to put out painful shoots. But it had to happen in freedom and according to her own choice, not as the only way out. It easily acquired a tinge of necessity and of touching bottom against which she had to be on her guard. This evening it was not worth going down to sit on a bench. It could be worse alone with herself down there than anywhere else.

Should she go to see Liesel? Look out for her when she came from her evening class? Ignore her slightly tired surprise and force an entrance to her sooty, narrow balcony, barely separated from the neighbours by a low trellis? Comfort herself with the thought that even if Liesel might perhaps have preferred to go to bed, she was at any rate sitting on her balcony enjoying this asset, a thing she seldom dared do when she was alone, because she would be accosted and pursued across the trellis.

No. That had come to an end. Liesel was with Eliel. She was no longer the rather lonely girl, who trailed her painting things and her long, black dress around between Colarossi's, the banks of the Seine and the Luxembourg Gardens, returning home untidy, dusty, dirty with paint and ravenously hungry, and who would explain despondently: 'There were four of them watching today. I can't do anything if someone's watching. Everything was different when I got there – now I've spoiled it again. I'll never be any good – my life is not interesting.'

Ever since a day last winter, when Eliel had taken her hand in his, lifted it towards the light, inspected it from every angle and asked if he might model it – 'It's so unusually beautiful and full of character ' – Liesel had gone through the usual stages in the correct order, sitting for a hand, for the head, for a shoulder, for everything, sewing on buttons and making coffee, collapsing like an empty rind, and blossoming like a rose; and had now invested half her rent money in a frilly nightdress. And all of it without Alberta really being aware of what was going on. Now Alberta was left by the wayside, while the others drove on with everything settled and a final ' You should find someone too '.

Find someone! Alberta stood up and walked restlessly about the room. Women repeated it in every tone of voice, wherever she happened to be. From old Mrs. Weyer in the little town at home, who had patted her on the shoulder and repeated ' A good husband, a good husband . . . ', to Marushka, who smiled introspectively at her memories and said: ' Why live as you do, *mes enfants*? To what purpose? Love gives happiness – what would life be without love – I'd wither up and die, I admit it frankly', and to Alphonsine, whose green eyes studied her through and through, and who stated quietly ' *Il vous manque une affection, Mademoiselle.*'

But Alberta remembered Liesel on one occasion last winter, when Marushka had yet again been giving her variation on the theme. It had suddenly struck Liesel. She had heard it many times before, but now it struck her. Her eyes had become big and shining, like those of a child who has been given the answer to decisive questions. Something had happened to Liesel at that moment. Perhaps it was then that she had changed course and gradually steered towards Eliel, who had been tacking round her for a long time, allowing him to approach, as if testing him.

Then the Swedish girl had come – the one thing after the other.

' A good friend – two arms round you at the end of the day – that is what I wish for you, Mademoiselle.'

Alphonsine again. Her reflective and divergent answer to some comment Alberta had made about unsuccessful attempts to work, the incompetence from which she suffered. No-one could, like her, strike down into one's daydreams and light on to what they were really about, whether one admitted it to oneself or not. She did not carry on insidious propaganda like the married women at home, who knew no rest until the whole world was caught in the trap in which they found themselves: food and servant worries, gynaecological troubles, Nurse Jullum the midwife like an official executioner in the background. She did not share Marushka's attitude either; Marushka, who glided from one affair to another incredibly easily and insouciantly, banishing all scruples by the device of trusting in her lucky star.

Alphonsine brought out one's weaknesses, holding them up to the light for an instant. She would shake her head seriously in denial, if one day Alberta were to broach the question, expose her wretchedness, and say: 'Who, Alphonsine? Who? The man in the street, who says *tu viens*? The hotel guest who tries to get into one's room? The fairly good-looking fellow who wanders about the studios looking for love, gratis, and whom almost anybody can have once or twice? Or the kind of person from whom mind and body shrink, one with catarrh, one with an obstinate will deep down in those cautious eyes?' She would say: 'But there are others, Mademoiselle.'

'Not for me,' said Alberta bitterly, out loud. She continued her train of thought: 'Tenderness? What about tenderness, Alphonsine? When you have lived next door to all kinds of people, and the walls are thin, you begin to find it a little difficult to believe in that. At first you are frightened, thinking of madness or confined animals, finally you understand. Groans, struggle, a smothered bellow in the darkness, a heavy silence as if death had supervened, the snoring. The snoring! Or women's tears, streams of bitter, upbraiding words. What happened to tenderness? It must have been lost on the way?'

Alphonsine would probably smile a melancholy smile and know better. And rightly so.

Alberta was sitting on her bed in the dark, her arms round her knees and her chin resting on them. Suddenly she got down, found a light, and dressed herself feverishly. Now the evil had reached her heart, anxiety gripped it. That vague anxiety for life as it reveals itself step by step; anxiety that in spite of everything it might slip through her fingers unused.

She ran downstairs, bought the evening papers, *Le Rire*, more cigarettes, even an expensive literary monthly, drank a vermouth at the zinc counter in the building next door, wasted a lot of money in great haste.

* * *

Gare Montparnasse. The train to Brittany, at the front near the engine, in the sun, far beyond the station building. Alberta's friends travelled third class. Anyone travelling second was likely to be someone from home and therefore more or less under suspicion, people who came to Paris to rush through the Louvre, spend their days in the big stores and their nights at the Place Pigalle, stick their noses into Alberta's affairs and say stupid things about the French and about Paris.

Her friends had uncomfortable and inelegant luggage, packets of sandwiches and bottles of wine in the compartment with them, as did Liesel and Eliel now. Liesel's rug strap bristled with dangerous easel-legs, her canvases were everywhere in the way. And when Eliel put her travelling bag down on the step of the carriage the sound of glass that came from it made her open the bag quickly and with trepidation. Its contents were swimming in red wine.

With a sigh Liesel applied herself to picking out toilet articles, paintbrushes, rolls and ham in paper, all of it saturated and dripping with wine, while the stream of travellers parted on either side of her as if round a carrier of disease. Eliel assisted her, a little stiff and piqued.

Now they were inside the compartment, quarrelling loudly as to the practicality of having bottles in hand luggage. Alberta could see them in there as flushed, bewildered shadows behind other passengers. Liesel span round and round in confusion, pointing up at the luggage racks, parleying about her canvases. It was not an easy matter to dispose of them. Eliel wiped his forehead, rearranged things, and stowed them away. He repeated at frequent intervals, and his French was even more clumsy than hers, 'One does not pack glass comme ça'. Liesel: 'It was for your sake. I was thinking of you. But never again . . .'

Alberta knew what would happen. Soon, within ten minutes at the most, Liesel would beg Eliel's pardon for being stupid and for losing her temper besides. And Eliel would say graciously 'Never mind', and lose his tense expression. But only if Liesel begged his pardon.

There she was in the window. 'My poor Alberta. The rest of us are leaving. You – you stay behind.'

Alberta shrugged her shoulders: 'It can't be helped.'

'But I'm glad you're moving into Eliel's studio. It's almost the country, Albertchen. You'll have six weeks completely to yourself out there. And there are *no* bugs.'

Other passengers jostled Liesel aside. Eliel pushed his way forward instead, calling through the hubbub: 'My clay, my dear Alberta, you will remember my clay – to dampen it I mean – the syringe . . .'

Liesel: 'The flowers, Albertchen – the cat, poor thing – the key is with Madame Lefranc . . .'

Eliel: 'The syringe is on the stand – the clay in the box must be dampened too – the water bucket . . .'

Alberta pulled herself up on to the step to hear better, but the train started to move, and she was lifted resolutely down again by a passing guard. Eliel reappeared for the last time: 'The water bucket is standing in the broom cupboard – Liesel asks you to remember the flowers.' He wiped his forehead. Behind him Liesel was smiling, exhausted and happy. Alberta nodded her understanding. They were gone.

Half stunned by heat, light and noise she watched the

long train glide past her. It was overflowing with passengers: middle-class families with children; people with painting equipment; peasants; here and there a priest or a nun who, undisturbed by their surroundings, fingered their rosaries and twitched an accompaniment; English, German, American tourists. It was going to the sea, to fresh air, clean water, an open sky, quietness; it left at midday, every day. When the summer in Paris reached the point when it was reminiscent of an unaired room, Alberta accompanied one group of friends after another to this train, this year as last year, as every year.

From the tracks, which are carried into the city between two streets on a level with the second floors of the houses, she could see in through the windows in the Rue de l'Arrivée. Everything there was grey with smoke from the station. On Liesel's balcony in the Hôtel des Indes a man was standing in his shirt-sleeves, brushing his trousers. Liesel's room had been rented out again already. A vision of blue sea and white sand, of lady's slipper, white clover and ragged grass waving in the wind, that rose in Alberta's mind every year at this precise spot, was projected for a second against the background of grey houses, then dissolved and disappeared. Her legs felt suddenly heavy, the walk into the shadow of the station too long. Her steps seemed to make no progress.

In the depressing flight of steps leading from the station down to the street, there was something that almost resembled a draught, in spite of the dead, stagnant heat. It rose up from below, sickening and impure, full of vapours, but crept upwards nevertheless bringing relief to her body, then over her face and neck, making the flounces round her low-cut dress flutter, lifting her skirts a little. People walked slowly here, taking their time. Alberta paused for a moment.

A stranger's breath on her neck, a bated ' *Tu viens?*' close to her ear, made her turn round. A fat man, glistening with the heat and carrying a suitcase in each hand, was regarding her genially and with expectancy. She hurried down the steps.

The square outside lay like a desert landscape in the sun, barren, trackless, full of dangers. Across broken-up tram-lines, between heaps of sand and stones, Alberta gained the pavement on the other side, went into her hotel, began the ascent.

On the landings used sheets lay in heaps. Inside a door Jean could be seen manoeuvring his brush over the mantelpiece. He was humming his everlasting ' *Et le pauv' gas, quand vient le trépas* . . . '.

On the second floor Wolochinska's door was standing ajar. Alberta was about to swing past, but the opening widened suddenly, and Wolochinska stood there, tall and slender, in a kimono. Behind her on the table were travelling bags and toilet articles, on the floor a large trunk with painting equipment round it. It was clear that she was leaving.

' Mademoiselle Selmer – you can do nothing in this heat, in any case. Come in and have a cool drink with me. I was just thinking of ringing for one. Make yourself comfortable in here for a while. Look at me . . . '

Wolochinska smoothed a large, beautiful hand over her body. Her flat figure was clearly modelled under the thin material; large, embroidered storks clung about her. Alberta halted. She had a slight pang of conscience, because she had not been more friendly towards Wolochinska. One should be sorry for lonely people. At the same time she felt an instinctive uneasiness in the presence of this Polish woman, who showed her a persistent goodwill she neither understood nor returned. ' Are you leaving?' she asked and feigned astonishment.

' Yes, you know that. Come in for a moment.'

Alberta entered, ill at ease.

Wolochinska pushed a cigarette box towards her across the table. ' Sit down. Take a cigarette. What will you have, a vermouth, a grenadine? Thick with ice? What do you say to that?'

'Thank you,' attempted Alberta deprecatingly. 'I – I must go soon. There's something I have to do.'

'Always you have to go. Always. One would think it was a disease, a nervous disease.' Wolochinska laughed her forced laughter.

But Alberta found a little formula, which she thought quite felicitous. It was also true to a certain extent. ' I have to live,' she said.

Wolochinska's face altered. She looked at Alberta with a new expression in her eyes. 'Yes, yes of course. I am stupid and insensitive? Forgive me, my dear.' The large beautiful hand sought Alberta's across the table, she was forced to take it for an instant, felt that it wished to hold on to hers, withdrew her own and smoothed it over with a smile. ' It was nothing. I hope you have a pleasant summer – that it will be pleasant where you are going. It's Normandy, isn't it?'

' Seine – Inférieure. Near Fécamp.' Wolochinska's face had stiffened again, with that tense expression that Alberta did not know how to interpret. She felt she had seen it before in a completely different place, but could not remember whose it was or where. Wolochinska was staring above Alberta's head, and said as if lost in thought : ' So you will be staying here?'

' Yes.'

' Why?'

Alberta shrugged her shoulders. ' I always spend the summer in Paris, I . . . . ' She stopped. She did not wish to explain how impossible it was to strike out into the unknown when one's livelihood depended upon the pawn-broker. ' I love Paris,' she explained.

' In August too?'

' In August too.'

Wolochinska got to her feet, strode about the room, stopped, stubbed out her cigarette against the mantelpiece, and said without looking up : ' Come with me.'

She turned and looked intently at Alberta.

Alberta was also on her feet. ' It's impossible.'

' It is possible. It's entirely up to you. I invite you.'
Wolochinska continued to look at Alberta, who was feeling
thoroughly uncomfortable. This was so strange. Perhaps it
was Polish.

' You are very kind,' she began. ' But there can be no
question . . . '

' Listen to me,' said Wolochinska. ' I feel affection for
you, great affection. I am alone here, without friends. We
shall be completely independent out there. I hate *pensions*,
I have rented a little house and shall have someone to
look after me – after us. You will be able to bathe, rest,
do just as you please, and I – I am a lonely person,
Mademoiselle Selmer.'

' Yes, I know,' said Alberta, confused by the perspective
thus unrolled before her eyes, at once frightened and
tempted as if in front of a trap with a titbit. Again she saw
Lady's slipper, the wide sky, white sand, everything she had
in the course of time come to connect with holidays away
from town. And the expression on Wolochinska's face was
suddenly helpless, almost forlorn, her mouth drooped and
looked destitute. ' Yes, I know,' said Alberta again to gain
time.

Then Wolochinska came straight towards her. Alberta
extended her hand, prepared for an understanding squeeze.
But Wolochinska did not take it. She gripped Alberta by
the shoulders, looking into her eyes with her hard, blue
gaze. There was just time for Alberta's discomfort to
change to anxiety – and then she was given a passionate,
imperative kiss full on the mouth. As if stung by a wasp
she drew her head away.

' Come with me, Mademoiselle!' Wolochinska tried to
seize her hands.

' I cannot, Mademoiselle. You are very kind, but – I
wish you a pleasant summer, I wish . . . ' Alberta was
already in the doorway, something seemed to be suffocating
her. At the same time she thought feverishly: That wasn't
what she meant . . . it is I who . . .

Behind her she heard Wolochinska: ' Little ninny. Cold

little ninny from the North. What did you think? You have a nervous disease, Mademoiselle Selmer.'

Alberta reached her own door and shut it behind her. Her heart was pounding. She rubbed her lips with her handkerchief, remembering simultaneously who it was Wolochinska had resembled for an instant. A sailor on a quay once upon a time. Like a sudden glimpse from a great hidden common life the same feeling had lit up two quite different faces in quite different circumstances. ' But on that occasion I really wanted it too,' murmured Alberta to herself and became a little calmer. Fair's fair. ' And I can't stand anything like this,' she said aloud.

Although it was nearly three o'clock the bed was unmade, the slop-bucket full, the heavy air tinged with tobacco smoke. She felt sudden violent disgust for the life she led. It smells of old bachelors, she thought, and snuffed the air in her own room with repugnance.

' Jean!'

No answer.

' Jean!'

Jean appeared from the obscurity of the staircase.

' It's nearly three,' began Alberta, still out of breath after the episode downstairs. It relieved her to have something urgent to do.

Jean admitted that he knew it was. But he had unexpected guests on the first and second floors. He had hoped Mademoiselle would be out this evening, as Mademoiselle often was. He also pointed out that the heat was trying up here in the middle of the day. If Mademoiselle went out earlier. Mademoiselle got up late.

Alberta could not deny this. She stood on the landing in the half-light outside her door and acknowledged that it was all her own fault, while Jean plodded in and out with slop-bucket and water-can, shook the sheets through the staircase window, went over the floor with his swab, and the mantelshelf, table and chairs with his feather duster. She did get up late, it was one of the things on her conscience.

'Leave the flowers, Jean, if you please.'

'But they are wilting, Mademoiselle.'

'It doesn't matter.'

Jean shrugged his shoulders as if repudiating all responsibility, made a sweep round the peonies on the mantelpiece and had a final look round the room. 'I cannot see anything more that I can do for Mademoiselle for the time being.'

Then Alberta said, and the words seemed to come out of her mouth of their own accord: 'I shall be moving out tomorrow or the day after.'

Jean's eyes became round as saucers in his freckled face. He flushed slowly, until his whole face was red. Then he said severely: 'You can't do that, you have to give a month's notice.'

'I shall have to pay for the rest of the month.' Alberta felt her astonishment increase. 'Nobody can stop me from moving. I'm going to live at a friend's house to look after it while they're away ... I ...'

Here she was justifying herself to Jean. That was rather unreasonable. It became even more unreasonable. Jean said, his face dark and his voice upbraiding: 'And you never said a word.'

'I didn't know before. It happened suddenly – my friends decided at the last minute. And since I shan't be able to stay on here in any case – it's going to be altered, you told me so yourself.'

Jean lowered his eyes. He stood stroking the end of the bed with his duster, watching its movements. 'I know of an hotel on the Avenue du Maine,' he said, still not looking up. 'A pleasant little place, simple, without restrictions. The old lady will recommend me to the owner, she knows him. It's an establishment where you can make yourself comfortable, come and go and make your arrangements as you please. Not like this place. I thought perhaps it might suit you too.'

Jean looked up and stared straight in front of him. He had an expression that Alberta had seen before on other boys, on Jacob. That was how they looked when something had gone wrong, at once offended and distressed. '*Enfin* – with things as they are . . . '

Alberta's thoughts jumped to the Avenue du Maine. She would have to live somewhere when Eliel came back. But she did not like the hotels there, they looked mouldy and airless, and the avenue was not at all pleasant in the evenings. She said: ' You could give me the address. It's kind of you to bother about me.'

Jean fished a printed card out of a battered wallet and handed it to her: *Maison meublée Chauchard, electricité, télephone etc*. Alberta took it. ' Thank you.'

But Jean stayed where he was, stroking the end of the bed with his duster, and said reflectively: ' One could see you were a *demoiselle* . . . an . . . an educated person, more educated than oneself – one can see it from your books. But . . . ' Jean made a gesture with his duster, his speech became more resolute and seemed more outspoken. ' On the other hand, Mademoiselle lives like this, all alone. To speak frankly, you seem to me to be a young lady who has met with misfortune.'

' But other women have lived here alone,' answered Alberta, a little confused. ' The Americans, for instance, and Mademoiselle Wolochinska. I'm not the only one. We have not met with misfortune, we . . . ' She had the word ' work ' on her tongue, but changed her mind: ' We study.'

' The American ladies were two,' explained Jean. ' They were painters and getting on in years. Mademoiselle Wolochinska is also a painter, she is not young either. You are young, and you do nothing.'

Alberta flushed deeply. His last words cut her like whip-lashes. As if from a great height she seemed to glimpse how utterly inexplicable and unjustifiable a phenomenon she was.

' I am here to study French,' she said curtly.

' You know French. You speak it very well for a foreigner. You speak almost like one of us. Why should you want to learn more?'

' But . . . to teach.'

' In your own country, then?'

' Yes – in my own country,' answered Alberta in a low voice.

Jean was looking past her, up at the blue of the skylight. It seemed as if he was seeing it all out there, when he replied: ' At home we live in a village, Mademoiselle. We have a cow and a pig, we have earth, potatoes, cabbages, the sardine fishing. When it is warm and still, as it is today, I wish I were there. Today the sea is as white as milk in the sun – it's market day in Pont-Croix.'

' You are homesick?' asked Alberta.

' Homesick? No. But I want to go home again, certainly.' Jean's gaze returned from the blue of the skylight. He looked at the wall behind her and swayed from the knees as he lectured her about himself: ' When I had done my military service, I thought I ought to see Paris. Later I thought I ought to stay until I had saved up enough for a boat. In the old lady's time it was all right, she is a good woman, but the house has changed. It's no use any more for a country boy like me. Besides I've had enough of it. It's a filthy *métier* running up and down stairs like this emptying slops, I'm going to leave it to the Parisians. If I get that job on the Avenue du Maine I shall take it. But in a year I shall have enough for a share in a boat, that's always something.'

' Yes, of course,' said Alberta encouragingly, vaguely relieved at the turning the conversation had taken.

' After forty years as a fisherman you get a pension,' said Jean. ' From the state.'

' Oh, really?'

Jean nodded, staring across the floor. There was something he wanted to say, and he suddenly took the plunge: ' Well it's like this – sometimes I've thought, this young lady, she is always alone, it doesn't look as if it has come to anything with the other gentlemen – perhaps she would be happy with us in the country. She must have a little – she does nothing to earn her daily bread, at least not as far as I know. She is modest, content with little, clean. Cleanliness is something I appreciate. I have always thought that if I married, it would be to a clean person. Well – perhaps I have been mistaken.' Jean looked straight at the wall again, suddenly piqued, although Alberta had not said a word.

She stood confused, embarrassed, touched, angry, thinking: He can't mean it seriously, and at the same time she had an obscure feeling of reparation and rehabilitation, a feeling that one misunderstanding in some way cancels out another. A sensation similar to the one she had had in her childhood when they said to her: ' Think how thankful many people would be to have a dish of bread and milk ', passed through her mind. The vision of a white beach and tossing Lady's slipper in ragged grass, that had haunted her today, was there again, urgent and insistent.

But she saw imitation-leather sofas and china dogs too, although perhaps they possessed neither of them where Jean came from. She felt the atmosphere of disapproval that she, incompetent that she was, always created round herself. And straight in front of her were Jean's round eyes, his freckles and sandy hair, the eternally unbuttoned waistcoat.

' You'll soon get married to a girl from your own village.' Alberta attempted a little conviviality as best she could.

' Perhaps,' said Jean. ' One must have somebody.' He looked dissatisfied, at the last moment caught sight of a little island of dust lying on the mantelshelf, wandered over to it and wielded his duster. And he withdrew with a ceremonious ' Mademoiselle '.

Alberta was left standing. Today she could have gone to the country. She could not complain that opportunity had been lacking.

Pigs and cows, cabbages and potatoes, something secure to live on, a place to belong to that was not in Norway, that was, on the contrary, so incredibly distant from all that had gone before that perhaps nobody would ever hear of her again – it was ridiculous, but part of her reached out after it. In her position she ought perhaps to reconsider it before definitely breaking off negotiations.

If only Jean had looked like some of the men she had met at Marushka's. Or at Colarossi's, when she went to fetch Liesel. Proud conquerors in Spanish cloaks, buoyant Americans, who frequented the studios. Or the sailor on the quay, Cedolf, whom she had known many years ago.

Then there had never been any talk of pigs or cows or any other kind of settled existence. Cedolf, for instance, had taken advantage of a moment of weakness and kissed her without ceremony. He had kissed someone else at the next port of call. Cedolf was like that, all those who resembled him were like that.

But Jean was Jean. And she was too shabby-genteel. At home they called it ' fine '. Too restless as well, too afraid of plain sailing, monotony, any situation that lacked possibilities. And too incompetent. She would hang about, clumsy and in the way.

Suddenly a cluster of petals loosened and fell from the pink peonies on the mantelshelf, lying on top of each other like small turned-up childish hands. Mechanically Alberta began taking the pictures off the walls. She was going to move, she had better take steps to do so.

And once again she took apart the interior she had put together up here, building it up from the possibilities at hand. The death-mask of the young girl said to have drowned herself in the Seine, the photograph of Jacob in working clothes on deck taken by an itinerant photographer somewhere in South America, the Manet and Gauguin, Rembrandt and Van Gogh reproductions, all jumbled together just as they made an impression on her and were daringly acquired, the drawings by Eliel and Marushka, Liesel's colour sketch, the books in yellow jackets. Everything had had its carefully planned place, some of them had fulfilled double roles, having pleased the eye and hidden ugly patches of wallpaper, everything had appeared to advantage in the tranquil light from above. Even the strong lustre that the earthenware jug on the mantelpiece acquired in the middle of its belly at this time of day had played its part in the whole. That corner of the room became dead when Alberta now emptied it of wilting peonies and dried it.

It had been made for flowers, and flowers had filled it, from the first moist violets in February to the cheap glory of phlox, dahlias and sunflowers in late summer. Some of them she knew from her childhood. They had come into the house in connection with some festivity, or at Christmas time. Or they had flaunted themselves, few in number and prohibitive in cost, in the window of the Sisters Kremer's shop. In certain cases, such as the roses, they had been coaxed out with endless care indoors, the object of rivalry, envy, secretiveness. Mimosa one only read about in bad novels; it was as unreal as counts and countesses, as Monte Carlo and Lago Maggiore. One scarcely believed in their existence.

Here one bought them all in heaps from the barrows, getting an armful for fifty centimes. They had glowed as never before under the skylight, kindling a festive bonfire in the room. They did not last long up here under the roof; they faded quickly and the petals dropped for lack of air, from too much stagnant heat. But there was richness and extravagance too in the quiet decline of the flower petals, in their piling up on the glossy black marble shelf. Alberta never took them away until they had all fallen.

She sat down and looked round her at the moment of departure. Here an oil stove had stood. Madame Firmin had lent it to her the first winter. It had shone red and warm, awakening a desire to sit busy with something or other, and had driven old chills out of Alberta that she had carried in her body from the sunless rooms in the Rue Delambre and thereabouts, where the autumn damp stole into one like an incessant fever and remained until the spring was far advanced.

Once she had lain ill up here. Jean had come up from below with camomile tea and hot soup. Via Liesel the rumour spread of the comfort in which Alberta lived. The ancient bourgeois hotel was infiltrated by an inflammable and incorrect public, individuals with a fantastic cut to their cheap clothes, bearing milk bottles and damp packages, and keeping blackened spirit stoves on the washstand. But Liesel had not come. She already lived five francs cheaper.

The young Madame had come one day, and she could freeze out anybody she chose with her two cold, clear eyes, her unhurried inspection of one's person, her silent nod in the direction of the regulations on the walls. She had frozen her mother-in-law out to the small rooms facing the yard and her husband out to the doorstep, where he stood like a figure in an advertisement.

Later that afternoon, when her packing was almost done, somebody knocked at the door. It was Jean. He had the clean towels for the day over his arm and therefore had sufficient excuse. With his back to her he busied himself hanging them up, draping them meticulously on the rail. His back looked piqued. Alberta felt strongly the necessity for saying a few words, something friendly and cheerful. She tried in vain to find them.

Then Jean spoke, looking past her : ' *Enfin* – with things as they are, I went down to the old lady and said, " Mademoiselle has always been *comme il faut*, always paid on the nail, she is a lodger of long standing, it would not be more than reasonable were she to be excused paying for half the month ". It's abominable, let me tell you,' he suddenly flared up, looking directly at Alberta. ' In this house they are rich, *oh là, là*. And for Mademoiselle it means throwing money out of the window. It's not right.'

' But Jean . . . ' Alberta shrugged her shoulders, a habit she had acquired down here when something was inevitable and had to be endured.

' It wasn't worth the trouble. The poor old lady said : " In my time no-one would have made difficulties. I was reasonable, I got on well with people and took pleasure in it, even when they lived up in the attic, but now it is over, my poor Jean ". That was what she said, Mademoiselle, " Now it is over, my poor Jean ". It is sad.' Jean looked accusingly at the wall.

' Thank you all the same. It was kind of you.'

' At your service, Mademoiselle.' Jean again looked piqued. He turned hither and thither a couple of times, as if searching for something. He lacked the feather duster with which to wave himself out. Out he came, however. His slippers could be heard for an instant going down the stairs.

At once Alberta felt terribly lonely. Her thoughts jumped experimentally over to the hotels on the Avenue du Maine.

PART TWO

Alberta woke with a start, and sat up.

The first grey light was barely visible through the curtains drawn across the large windows. The trill of a bird could be heard outside. In one of her collar-bones there was a stabbing pain which throbbed in competition with her heart.

She lighted a candle and moved it searchingly above the sheets and blankets, lifted her pillow quickly, with an accustomed, competent movement. Then she moistened her finger and brought it down with an exultant cry on a flat, dark little disk the size of a lentil, took it to the wash-bowl and dropped it in. A couple more were already lying there kicking.

And she took a bottle from the chair beside the bed, poured some of its contents out into her hand and splashed it over her smarting collar-bone. The stinging liquid ran down over her breast and was sprinkled round her. A light, round fleck appeared on the blanket – and another.

The sprinkling of ammonia rose suffocatingly in the clammy air that filled Eliel's studio. Shapeless masses of clay, wrapped in wet cloths, made it heavy with raw vapour. Only one of the many window-panes could be opened.

Alberta lay down again, tried to forget and doze off, but failed. She lay looking out at the grey dawn that slowly filled the room. Her blood beat painfully and uneasily. The bird's trill outside had become a chorus, drowning preludes.

Eliel's mattress smelt musty. It was the one she had

326

helped him to find last winter, when he had just finished a large work, and that atmosphere of enthusiasm, emotion and fussy solicitude that an impecunious and awkward talent periodically rouses suddenly came into being round him. After two years in Paris Eliel owned nothing, apart from his modelling-stands and his clay, besides a basket chair with a hole in the seat, an iron bedstead with uneven legs, a bare divan, a table, a stool and a couple of cups. This state of affairs had given his circle of acquaintances a bad conscience.

In the corridor at Colarossi's, among the many notices about this and that pinned up by the artists, one had caught Alberta's eye about a used, but good mattress offered for sale cheaply in the house next door. She had had one of her sporadic attacks of pluck and initiative. It was as if she wanted to rehabilitate herself now and again in her own eyes, to accomplish something. Up breakneck steps, built on the outside wall of the house, she had betaken herself to the place in question and concluded the bargain in a sickening atmosphere of uncertainty and poorly concealed male banter. The owner had turned out to be owners, a band of Swedes and Norwegians living together. All of them were at home, sitting or lying, each in his lair, on a confusion of ramshackle beds and suspicious-looking divans, all of them with faces she recognized as having seen on Montparnasse. One of them removed the pipe from his mouth and got up from the object of the sale.

The journey out to Eliel's studio with a messenger and the mattress had been long and slow. A flush played over Liesel's pale face when the door opened. She had just begun sitting for Eliel. With her finger on the lid of the coffee-pot she stood leaning over his cup.

Then she clapped her hands and called out ' *Wunderbar*!' and explained that the thing would have to be beaten.

Under protest Eliel had beaten the mattress until sunset. The cloud of dust rose from it just as thick and unaltered. Over and over again he gave it as his opinion that it *was* clean, that Liesel and Alberta were crazy about dust. When darkness fell, and the dust could no longer be seen, merely sensed as a discomfort in the air about them, Liesel resigned herself. The mattress must have been stuffed with dust, they would have to put it in place. When Alberta saw it again it was covered with an ' Assyrian ' drapery that had cost eleven ninety-five in Lafayette's bargain department.

There were bugs in it. Liesel could say what she liked. But Alberta was lying on it for nothing. In this circumstance there was a certain balance that accorded with the laws of life and prevented her from complaining. At the Hôtel de l'Amirauté there had been mice, a species to be preferred. But it had cost her thirty-five francs a month to live there.

The dawn floated slowly down from above, releasing Eliel's sculptures from the darkness, making them stand out in relief. They stood there, a strangely troubled world of plaster beings, vainly trying to lift their heavy limbs towards each other. Among them were the bust of Liesel, slightly built with sloping shoulders, pouting mouth and stylized plaits, and the block of marble that had been so expensive and was to be Eliel's first sculpture in genuine material. A brass instrument of torture was stuck into it; it had bored a sharp hook right into one nipple, which was almost loosened from the block, and another hook into the navel. These two small forms had something spontaneous and alive about them, which differed from the rest of Eliel's work. Alberta could not help thinking about Liesel, and felt tortured every time she caught sight of the hooks in the marble.

The casts on the walls showed up in relief, all the attempts at human anatomy, arms and legs, hands and feet – the inevitable young girl from the Seine, the wounded Assyrian lion dragging its hind leg.

On the clay crate stood Eliel's primus, which he had brought with him from Sweden and of which he was proud. There had been a time when the vicinity of the primus had consisted of empty sardine tins and Eliel's coffee-cup, which he had taken out and rinsed under the tap in the yard every time he used it. In the quick course of time Liesel had succeeded in leaving her mark on her surroundings. On the wall there now hung three small saucepans neatly in a row. There was a kitchen cloth on a nail and a small shelf with cups and dishes. A couple of chequered cushions were placed on the divan. Eliel's books were arranged neatly at one end of the table between two round stones – all Liesel's work.

The birdsong outside was drowned by the other sounds of day. There was the rattle of the first tram-car; there was the whistle of a train above the Parc de Montsouris; there was the yawn of the man next door. Someone was drawing water at the tap outside.

A beautiful, calm light filled the studio from above. Eliel's cat, a young black and white tom, arched its back and stretched itself, climbed with dignity out of its box, went to the door, mewed . . . .

And Alberta had to get up.

Above the door the ivy hung in cascades; on it stood ELIEL in large, black, uneven lettering. Rumour had it that Eliel was also called Svensson, a name he must have left behind him somewhere *en route*. Now he was called Eliel; on letters, on leases, on pieces of sculpture, on Montparnasse. Eliel, the sculptor.

In small flower beds beneath the ivy Liesel had, as one might except, planted flowers: nightshade and snapdragon and the delicate white flower called ' The Painter's Despair '. Against the wall grew clusters of bittersweet with their small dark violet and flaming yellow corollas. It looked pretty, brightening the grey, rather gloomy walled passage that led to the studio and only caught the sun for a short period each day. Many of the people who came to draw water or visit the privy, which was situated at an angle to Eliel's door, paused to look at the display. They were men in shirt-sleeves, with bare legs and slippers on their feet, artists from the adjacent studios, and now and again a model with her coat slung loosely round her nakedness. A few of them expressed surprise that anything could grow in there in the shade. The studio lay behind a large block of flats and the remains of an old garden. There was a scent of box in the evenings. With a favourable current of air, drifts of scent came from the park as well. It was almost the country.

There was a painful time of day – the hour when it arches over and goes downwards again. It does not correspond to high noon, but occurs a couple of hours later. The sun left the passage, the ivy turned blue. That was the time. In the hotel room it had been when the lustre died on the belly of the earthenware jug. The room had at once become strangely threatening and desolate.

Yet again she had not come to terms with herself today; she had not come a step nearer those admirable, industrious souls who accomplish something. She had promised herself yesterday that something would happen. She had been going to scrape together some material and write an article, if nothing else, earn fifty kroner. Now the day was waning and she sat there, silent and obstinate inside, with five or six lines on the paper.

Alberta got up, lit a Maryland, stroked the cat, sat down again. Nothing was improved by these measures, nor by her taking out Jacob's photograph and looking at it for a while – the one taken on the deck of a ship.

He was thin, with one of those faces so spare that the small knots of muscle on each side of the mouth are exposed and become visible. There was something brave about them, something of the indefatigable, hardy wanderer through life. For the ninth year Jacob was living on the other side of the globe, in South America, Africa, Australia, a casual and hard-working life; at sea, down the mines, on farms, now and again in factories – and then at sea once more. There were times when he did not write for long periods, and others when he reported: I have a good job now and am saving money. I think I'll stay abroad for another year.

There was never very much more in the letters from Jacob. For years he had written: I think I'll stay for another year. Behind those words lay Jacob's dream: to save enough to buy land somewhere, preferably in Norway. It seemed to have petrified into a couple of sentences, which were no longer even correct Norwegian. Heaven knew how much of the dream remained?

But Jacob remained true to himself, taking no short cuts or avoiding ordinary honest labour. One day, in spite of everything, he would perhaps succeed in the task he had set himself, quite quietly, simply and straightforwardly. It would only have taken more time than he had expected.

However it was, Jacob was not rootless and restless, without purpose, without duties, living short-sightedly for the moment, keeping himself alive from one day to the next and doing nothing else besides; someone superfluous, who might as well disappear, and perhaps it would be quite a good thing if she did.

As if looking towards the end of a dark tunnel, Alberta could glimpse a final perspective. Someone with outstretched hand stood at a corner – a bundle of rags was lying on a bench somewhere, under one of the arches of the Louvre, where there were always people sleeping at night. The bundle was herself, had been someone like herself, paralysed and confused by her own life.

She fled. She could go out and sit on the fortifications in the worn, trampled grey grass, looking out over the infinity of small allotments outside them. The sky was wide in this part of the city, with clouds drifting across it like heaps of enormous eiderdowns. Children played, mothers sat on the grass with their sewing, simple housewives from the back streets. As the evening wore on couples arrived and lay down in the grass close together, speaking in low voices, biting straws. Flocks of sheep tripped past. In the still afternoon light, with a shepherd boy following them, and a dog, with the ringing of bells

for vespers from churches in the distance vibrating in the
air, and smoke from bonfires drifting in from the gardens
outside, they seemed merely an innocent idyll; until
suddenly one or more of them fell, stretched their legs in
the air and their tongues in the dust, turned up their silly
eyes and were roughly shifted out of the way and left
lying. The slaughterhouse would have them. Dead or alive,
they could be fetched later. Old, rebellious agonies of
childhood rose impotently in Alberta, an anger as if she
herself were suffering torture. There was nothing to do but
go.

She wandered inwards towards the city, drawn along in
the dusk by the crowd of people as though by a stream.
The thudding sound of countless footsteps on the asphalt
beat soothingly round her, life unfolded about her like a
teeming, many-scented twilight flower, smelling of sweat
and labour, exhaustion, frivolity, all desire. But something
quietly shining also emerged: the feeling of human freedom, that grows out of an honest day's work. It appears
in voices, in footsteps, in numerous small gestures, is
inherent in the way a napkin is tucked underneath someone's chin, wine is poured into a glass, a newspaper is
spread out. It excited Alberta, making her walk faster,
as if that might help her.

Up from the Métro exit pressed the mass of humanity,
compact as a crawling animal, and was divided, groaning,
into sub-species. There was one especially for whom
Alberta had a fellow-feeling, perhaps on account of her
sessions with Mr. Digby – the one who had struggled
through the day standing behind a counter. They seemed
to have a weakness about the knees. It made her think of
the cab-horses which with pendulous lips were driven
round, seemingly supported by their harness and their
speed. The inexorable demands of the day must similarly
have kept this species on its feet.

Silently and speedily a mysterious element glided
through the swarm; they came from backyards, suburbs,
goodness knows where. The stocky fellow with pomaded

hair and his cap down over his eyes, the hatless girl with the hard face who came after him; the one with a hair style that would stand up to anything and stay neat through scuffles and love-making. They came with the darkness like the cats, and shared the stealthy silence of dangerous and nocturnal animals. Alphonsine called them suspicious types, and she did not exaggerate.

Now the flood was in full spate, carrying Alberta along with it. Almost before she realised it she was down at Montparnasse, in her old haunts, was washed up at the Cabmen's Rest, and found calm over a plate of onion soup.

Occasionally Alphonsine came.

She made herself comfortable on Eliel's divan, blew smoke-rings at Alberta, and studied her with her green eyes while the water boiled for tea.

The door out to the passage was open. The sharp, brief afternoon sun lay like a flaming puddle in Liesel's little flower bed, shining through the broad leaves of the night-shade, igniting the snapdragon like an intense flame against the brick wall behind them, making the grass border round them bright as an emerald. Alberta loved this short moment of the day; it made up for a good deal. And today, with tea and fruit on the table, with the blue smoke from their cigarettes drifting in beautiful whorls and with Alphonsine, in white with green earrings that matched the colour of her eyes, on the divan, it gave Alberta an intense sensation of lazy, sun-filled summer days. If it were not for the gusts that wafted from a certain place from time to time! They undeniably spoiled the atmosphere.

Alphonsine talked about her ' little artists ', about every-thing she was doing now in their absence. She was making herself dresses, was going to re-cover her divan, would spend a fortnight in the country with her friend.

' I'm not one of your little artists,' said Alberta. ' It was kind of you to come, Alphonsine.'

' I have a kind heart,' said Alphonsine simply. ' I

happened to think about you the other day, the little Norwegian girl. I said to my friend, she is alone this *demoiselle,* I shall go and see how she is.'

She stubbed out a cigarette against the table and said in a different tone of voice: ' I am fond of my little artists and their friends, I wish them all well, I would like everyone to be happy.' She smiled her conspiratorial smile and studied Alberta, who bent her head and stroked the cat in her lap.

' Are you happy, Alphonsine?' Alberta's question made her tremble a little. It had come out so brusquely.

Alphonsine meditated for an instant. ' I am not unhappy,' she said reflectively. ' And I was happy when I was young. What do you expect? One must not be ungrateful.' And she summed up her assets: ' I have my work, my friend who is kind to me, good health – that is much. I have had my sorrows like everyone else. My poor husband died, my child too. I was young, I had to live, I became a model, what else could I do? But *le bon Dieu* let me meet good people, I have never had reason to complain. My little artists have been charming, yes, all of them. And if I was bereaved sometimes, I also found comfort. One must be reasonable and not want the moon.'

Alberta said nothing. She felt a pang of bitterness: I don't want the moon.

' But still,' said Alphonsine. ' When I think that I too could have had a little child to go and look after in the country as so many others do – he was so sweet, my little baby, he was three weeks old, he was smiling already ...'

She flicked ash off her cigarette and sighed. Alberta looked up sympathetically, but found nothing to say. Her understanding of the loss of a child was limited. There was something distant and foreign about the whole thing.

Alphonsine did not go into it either, but changed the subject. ' It is a beautiful thing to live only for one's work, one's ideals, but a woman is a woman. And as long as she meets the right man. Mademoiselle Liesel ...'

Alberta pricked up her ears, but Alphonsine again

changed the subject: 'Men are big children, Mademoiselle. They are easily spoilt. And when they are spoilt they are insufferable – but there...'

There was a sudden crunching of footsteps in the passage. Alberta nodded towards the door of the privy. 'It's only someone going there. It's a nuisance having it here when so many people use it.'

But the steps went past the place in question and stopped outside. Someone knocked cautiously on the doorpost, a voice asked in Norwegian: 'Are you there, Frøken Selmer?'

'*Værsaagod,*' answered Alberta without enthusiasm. 'Come in, Ness.'

Sivert Ness reddened slightly when he caught sight of Alphonsine. Then he greeted her with country familiarity: 'Good day, Madame.'

'Monsieur.' Alphonsine's tone was dry. She flicked ash off her cigarette again, a gesture she sometimes employed as if to dissociate herself, to repudiate responsibility. She edged further along the divan and smoked with a distant expression, definitely apart.

Sivert Ness took a Maryland from the yellow packet Alberta pushed across the table, lit it, put it in the corner of his mouth, and asked whether she had heard from Eliel.

She had his blue, momentarily much too glittering eyes directed straight at her. She sensed a loneliness as great as her own behind his visit, the hunger for human society that can be damned up inside one in Paris in the summer, when one cannot speak the language and all one's acquaintances are away – a hunger perhaps for female company too. She was used to Ness's occasional appearances, to his sitting there, as if defying everything, a little short, but square and thickset, a black lock of hair falling over his forehead, and eyes that did not seem to suit the rest of him – they were too pale and looked up with a sudden darting movement. There was something familiar in his little gleam of sly triumph which could suddenly wedge itself up from beneath much honest, simple uncertainty. Strength, and an obstinate will lived behind much else in them and dared to believe in itself now and then. Perhaps she imagined it all. He was the only other Norwegian she ever saw.

To atone for her curtness she asked about his work, what he was doing, if he was not going to the country this year either.

' The country! I'm thankful I'm here at all. Besides, one can get out of the city now and again. To St. Cloud, Meudon, down the Seine.' His eyes held Alberta's for a second. ' It's refreshing to take a boat trip in the heat.'

What the tenacious eyes had meant and wanted on previous occasions had been uncertain. These at any rate wanted company on possible excursions. Perhaps also help in buying shirts at the Bon Marché, in abusing his concierge, in getting something translated, in obtaining French lessons. Here she was again, sitting with someone whose eyes forced themselves on her. But she would not be looked at in this way, with a glance that in its uncertainty yet had certainty behind it. She was not the kind they could get to do this, that and the other, those who did not dare set their sights higher; she was not the unassuming, suitable girl they had had the good fortune to run into, those who did not dare to dream audaciously. It was her fate to be encumbered with them.

This one was not really shy, on the contrary, he was only unfamiliar with things, a little unpolished, a little afraid of rowing out farther than the boat would carry him. He had more of the persevering leech about him than Grønneberg at home, more masculinity too.

On closer scrutiny there was a fearful strength in his hands. They were tranquil, staying in one place, never moving without a purpose. Sivert Ness did not pick at his sleeves, he had no nervous gestures. It was said on Montparnasse that he had talent. Provisionally he was accorded sympathy for his industry, his poverty, his home-made clothes, his ignorance of so much. But he was not like Eliel, who submerged himself in his wretchedness until somebody did something about it. Sivert managed somehow, in fact he was very capable of doing so when it was necessary. Self-denial came to him naturally and as a matter of course.

One must never feel that a man is touching. Alberta knew this from many years' experience. They interpret it in one way only. Then you are left, either ridiculous or encumbered.

'Another cup of tea?' she said, acting the hostess. She wanted to get away from the Seine and St. Cloud, having no desire to go to these places with him.

'Thank you very much.' Ness had really only intended to look in and get Eliel's address – he took out a notebook and a pencil – 'But if Frøken Selmer has another cup, then . . .'

He drank with his elbows resting on his knees. It looked as if he was sitting on a wooden crate in the kitchen, thought Alberta, and was in spite of herself a little touched at the simplicity of this. Finally he revolved the cup to get at the rest of the sugar, and her feelings became even more disturbed, as feelings can be in dreams, where they stream in and out uncontrolled. There had been something in Sivert's manner just then of the poor boy who must manage as best he can, of the toiler who sits down for a moment to rest – of Jacob. Yes, perhaps Jacob too sat like this, worker that he was, far away in strange countries.

But Sivert put the cup down, wiped his mouth, looked up, straightened himself, and the disturbance in Alberta subsided at once. She decidedly did not like his eyes.

Unasked, Sivert announced that he had finished the picture of the Rue Vercingétorix, the one with the four catalpa trees round a – well, a little house with posters on it, which was perhaps not worth mentioning. Would Alberta like to come in and look at it one day? He intended to try to get it into the State Exhibition at home this autumn, it would have to be sent soon.

'Thank you very much.' Alberta ignored the question. She hastened to suggest that it must be terribly distracting to stand like that painting in the middle of the street?

' Distracting? Yes, I suppose so, of course.' It seemed as
if Sivert had not given a moment's thought to this aspect
of it and now brought it up out of his mind for consideration. He smiled, sat leaning forward again with his
elbows on his knees and looked away across the floor:
' The children at home were worse.' He remembered a time
when they had hidden behind a stone wall, ten or twelve
of them, and thrown burrs at himself and the picture. Well –
it didn't happen again – for once he smacked his tranquil
hands together, linking the fingers hard. And again Alberta
had a vague impression of strength keeping silent and
waiting, achieving its aim simply by being there, even
though Sivert most certainly had not kept silent and waited
on the occasion in question. A chill crept over her at the
sight, she actually felt a little afraid of those hands. *Huff,*
she thought.

Then she shook it off; after all, they were nothing
whatever to do with her. She mentioned Liesel, from whom
she had heard, all the time side-stepping a question that
Sivert had asked as if by chance – ' Are they staying at the
same place, Eliel and Frøken Liesel?' – talking about things
Liesel was busy with there, a market scene with peasants.

Sivert smiled again. ' Women,' he said.

Alberta made no reply.

' But isn't it just like a woman to want to do something
like that?' persisted Sivert, his eyes glittering.

' What do you know about it?' And yet again Sivert did
not row out farther than the boat would carry him. ' No,
no, that may be so,' he smirked.

A little later he asked, and now he seemed to have come
to the point: ' Don't you find it lonely out here?'

But Alberta had changed since that first summer, when
the loneliness had almost taken her breath away and she
had allowed people to approach her, merely because they
were people, and had had cause to regret it. With assurance,
a tone too high, she replied that it was wonderful to be
alone, she loved it.

There was a glitter again in Sivert's eyes as if of disbelief.

as if he had caught her out lying. He was insufferable. Immediately afterwards he took his leave and went.

Alberta politely accompanied him to the door, and closed it. The sun had gone, someone was going to the privy, there was no reason to keep it open any longer. She turned and met Alphonsine's green eyes. Alphonsine shook her head energetically: 'Not that one, Mademoiselle.'

'But Alphonsine!'

'A specimen like that. They do not have two sous, but to Paris they must come. They must have models, and love, free models and free love. But both cost money here on Montparnasse. Only the foreign *demoiselles* are naïve enough . . .'

'Alphonsine.'

'A fellow like that needs you, I can see that. But when you are worn out with standing for him and sitting for him, going hungry and cold with him and perhaps submitting yourself to all sorts of things for his and his art's sake, he will become successful one day, and then you can pack your bags. I've seen it happen, I've seen it happen many times. I am old, as you know.' Alphonsine smiled, tired and omniscient.

'But Alphonsine, I shouldn't dream of having him. Besides, there's no question of – he's a fellow-countryman, after all! We are Norwegians and acquainted, that's all there is to it.'

'He wants you,' answered Alphonsine drily. 'And that is dangerous enough, *ma petite. Attention* – it is Alphonsine who tells you so.'

Alberta suddenly laughed out loud: 'What nonsense! There's no danger of that, I assure you.'

'Very well, all the better.' Alphonsine flicked ash off her cigarette. 'It looks to me as if he has something up his sleeve, that fellow.'

* * *

A hundred in the shade.

The asphalt was like over-heated metal, the air out in

the sun a burning helmet. The trees died, curling up their leaves in a last painful spasm, and letting them fall. Alberta felt she knew how the roots in the tiny round patch of soil allocated to each of them sought vainly in all directions after escape and salvation.

Horses collapsed, humans too. Every day the newspapers reported many cases of prostration. The half-naked labourers engaged in the inevitable summer road repairs were reminiscent of penal colonies in the tropics, of atrocities and merciless torture. Their eyes looked dead under their straw hats, the sweat streamed off them. But their brown torsos were bronze against the dark corduroy trousers and the flaming-red scarves that held them in place. The invincible Sivert was sure to be out painting them.

In the Seine the fish floated belly upwards, dying in their thousands in the thick, slimy water, which stank of rottenness and chlorine. When Alberta crossed the bridges in the evenings on her horse-bus ride, her body pressed up against the weak, scarcely noticeable draught made by their speed, she saw them and listened to the other passengers discussing them and the possibility of epidemics. They could be brought about by less.

In front of the small shops and the house doors chairs were dragged out, forming a continuous chain through the city. Low-voiced, almost silent people sat out there, thousands upon thousands of people of small means, their faces pallid from the heat and the still air. On the benches under the singed trees there was not an empty seat. Working folk ate their supper there, tearing at their long loaves with their teeth and drinking their wine straight from the bottle.

Alberta was seized by uncomfortable longing. She was suddenly reminded of the slap of water against the piles of a jetty, long, shining breakers, the smell of salt water and the newly-ebbed tide; of sitting in the prow of a boat on a night of sunshine, turned away from the others, one hand in the water, watching the smooth, cool shape of the displaced water round the boat, the shoal of coalfish leaping like silver-fish in the sun, boats further off, the oars at rest, with gold in their wake and accordions in the prow.

Or she remembered how the air had tasted sometimes when one went out of doors. Mild air with the thaw in it; air in transition, just as the cold was about to set in. It lay sparkling on the tongue, fresh and mild as water.

She pitched home again, the streets were quieter. Small stumps of conversation reached her from the pavement, settling in her mind like a sediment composed of other lives. A mother's: ' If only you had finished your soup – people who don't finish their soup . . . '. An elderly man's: ' It's the fault of the Government. France is governed by idiots. If only we had another Government . . . '. A young woman's angry ' Nothing doing tonight, *mon ami*. I shall turn my back on you, and serve you right.'

At intervals a flutter of relief seemed to go through the atmosphere, like the last gasps of a sea animal on land. From the Pont Neuf she could see the moon rising in the south-west over Charenton, a red, drunken, crazy August moon.

When she finally alighted from the tram-car at Porte d'Orléans and walked home along the fortifications it was sailing high above the roofs and the silent treetops, shining, yellow, in the company of a small star.

It was a fortnight since Alberta had spoken to a soul besides the *épicier* and the concierge. With them she discussed the temperature, agricultural prospects, their children's and grandchildren's conditions, endeavours and expectations, the occasional newspaper scandal, the behaviour of the cat, the dog and the canary since yesterday, and the blunders of the Government, which Alberta did not understand and on which she commented in the dark. Whereupon it was over for the day. The studios round her were deserted. No-one came any longer to the water-tap and remarked on the flowers.

With the window and door open, naked, her kimono slung across a chair-back within reach, she sat in Eliel's broken basket chair with one of his books and a Maryland, got up now and then, poured water over herself and sat down again. The air in the room was stationary, an evil-smelling mass. The large clay sculpture in its cloths was stinking. It caught at the throat as one came in.

The cat, too, rose occasionally from its favourite position on one of the stands, stretched itself, walked round itself a couple of times and lay down again. Or it went to its saucer on the floor, where the milk quickly turned sour.

It was an effort to go out when evening came. A kind of fear of doing so began to creep over her. But she knew it of old, knew it must not get the upper hand. And she went; a little dizzy and uncertain to begin with, a little wry in the face. She sat on a bench in the Parc de Montsouris.

This was where the summer found sanctuary. Heavy and dark with maturity the trees and bushes trailed their foliage on the ground. The twilight was scented, people sat silent on the benches. A late bird flew home, the first bat flitted soundlessly past. Arc-lamps were lighted here and there, hidden behind the enormous crowns of the chestnut trees, casting large circles of greenish light over the lawns. Someone ought to have danced in that light, fauns and nymphs, the Russian ballet.

Occasionally someone would whisper, ' Are you alone, Mademoiselle?' She would reply politely and evasively, and betake herself in a little while to another part of the park.

Alberta's limbs became as cool as marble in the heat; if she put her hand into the neck of her low-cut dress her shoulder was as cold and smooth as polished stone. But it opened up sores in her mind. She came home to the stinking studio, and suddenly tears misted her eyes and she hid her face in her hands.

And the night took its course: a torturing confusion of waking dreams; a series of painful, insecure sojourns in mysterious border regions with an occasional violent, brutal jerk back to reality, splashing ammonia on stinging collar-bones, feverishly writing on scraps of paper that were thrown unread into the trunk; a painful awakening as if from the dead when the cat mewed to be let out.

There was something she should have experienced, something besides this. There was a path somewhere that she could not find. It was and it was not her own fault.

'The ignorant man watches every night, anxious about many things. He is exhausted when morning breaks, but his sorrow is the same as before.'

His sorrow is the same as before. It was written in the *Edda*, in Eliel's copy between the stones on the table. An old truth, therefore.

On a day of the same stagnant heat Alberta opened, from a sense of duty, Eliel's large, zinc-lined clay crate. Averting her face to avoid the sight of the wood-lice scurrying in all directions inside it, she manoeuvred the unwieldy syringe and rearranged the clammy cloths that were lying over the clay. Then steps approached along the gravel path and went past the privy. Ness, thought Alberta. Thank heaven the door's shut and I've got some clothes on. It might have been worse.

Someone knocked. She answered: 'Who's there?' At once the door opened, and Alberta jumped up, dropping the cloth and drawing her flimsy garment closer about her, uselessly folding her arms, and stood as if paralysed with her legs pressed together while her flush engulfed her mercilessly. She felt utterly at a loss just as in the old days at home, while the thought pounded inside her: How shall I move? I can't move.

'Er-huh, what are you doing? What's that dreadful stuff in the crate?'

It was the Dane with spectacles standing in the doorway, not Ness. To Ness she could have said a few curt phrases: Wait outside – come again later – it's not convenient just now. What was she to say to this one? Tall enough to block the sun out, he stood there with his hat in his hand, mopping his forehead with his handkerchief. His shoulder-padding was awry, his spectacles caught a green reflection from the big window at the far end of the studio. If he was a vision, an optical illusion, he was at any rate fully equipped. In great confusion she heard herself explain : ' It's clay.'

' Is it? It looks unappetizing, I must say. But I know nothing about that sort of thing. Listen, have I come at a fearfully inconvenient time?'

Now something seemed to have got locked in him as well. He said, stammering. ' You must tell me if you would prefer me to go – I . . . I . . . ' Then he interrupted himself : ' But it would not be very kind of you to let me go immediately in this heat. I'm almost dead.'

Alberta looked up, met a smile under the spectacles and found unexpected composure : ' I was about to change my dress – would you mind waiting outside –and taking a chair with you?'

' Will you come with me out of town somewhere or other afterwards? On a boat down the Seine or something like that?'

Alberta considered for a fraction of a second. Then she said : ' Yes, I'd like to.' Great relief welled up in her at once, as if she were about to be liberated from prison.

She stood immovably, while he tactfully possessed himself of the nearest stool and disappeared with it. Behind the closed door Alberta rummaged nervously amongst her two dresses, although in view of the temperature only one of them was remotely suitable – the sleeveless one.

* * *

' Have you considered staying here for good?'

The question, apparently casual, fell a little to one side of the conversation, and Alberta felt her old defensive mechanisms at the ready. Consider? She had considered nothing. Does one consider that kind of thing? One crawls up on to dry land somewhere and awaits the next possibility. She had had to escape, and she escaped here. She answered with her usual curt ' I don't know '.

' You've spent a good many summers here?'

' Seven, including this one.'

' And you've never been away?'

' No, never.'

' But why not? There's so much that's beautiful to be seen elsewhere in this wonderful country. Is it your work that prevents you?'

' I don't work,' answered Alberta with embarrassment. This was an awkward moment of half-truths and empty replies behind which to conceal herself. One leads whatever existence one can; hers was not worth displaying. As a rule she did not invite anyone to examine it either. It passed on Montparnasse, but it was not suitable for well-brought up people from orderly circumstances. Nevertheles, here sat one of them tampering with it. It was her own fault. She should never have come.

' Oh, don't you? I understood Eliel to say you wrote for the newspapers?'

' No, far from it.'

' I must have misunderstood him then. Never mind – but surely one can do nothing in the country as well?'

Nothing . . . . For an instant Alberta was about to answer irritably. Someone or other was always cropping up, finding her sore points and prodding them. She controlled herself, thinking: If the worst comes to the worst I shall have to give Ness a few lessons. Casually she answered : ' I have a couple of pupils.'

' Oh, have you? In French? Well, that's work. And teaching, I certainly know about that. And these pupils, don't they go away either?'

' No,' answered Alberta.

' Listen, you mustn't be annoyed. You are quite right, I ought to mind my own business. It's just that I think you're looking pale. And then this fearful heat, and the air in the city. It can't be good for you to stay here summer after summer.'

' But if I prefer to stay,' said Alberta, mollified but

depressed by this complete stranger's thoughtfulness for her person.

The stranger looked at her speculatively through his spectacles. He was sitting with his back to the light, his elbows on the table and one muscular, sunburnt hand resting on it. When they were not concealed by reflections his eyes were grey, observant, now and again a little distant as if in meditation. His face was decidedly irregular. It was difficult to deduce anything from it besides the fact that it was clean-shaven, tanned and bony, with a broken nose. His name was Veigaard, an ordinary name, that seemed to go in at one ear and out of the other. Combined with what he gradually revealed about himself, the total impression was one of somebody keeping in step, somebody from the ranks of the admirable, the irreproachable. She might wish she resembled them, but she was not on good terms with them.

Behind him, dark leaves and branches formed a rich pattern against the grey-green water of the Seine; in front of him on the cloth were two half-emptied wine glasses, coffee-cups. Capricious blue coils of smoke from a pipe and a cigarette rose up; he waved them away from time to time as if in impatience. They were at Bas Meudon, at a small restaurant on the very edge of the river, one of those that base their trade on fried river-fish.

Alberta, however, sat illuminated by the evening sun which shone in on her through the branches. It was one of her misfortunes that she always found herself in a bright light when others were protected by shadow. Since childhood she had had a compulsion, never entirely overcome, to hide her face and her person, and this cropped up periodically from its repressed condition. Involuntarily she held her head askew, so that the profile in which her squint could least be seen caught most of the light. She was a past master in being sensible of its play over her features.

' You're a strangely stubborn little girl, I must say. So you're here all by yourself? All your friends are away, are they not? Fru Marushka and Frøken Liesel and the

American lady, what was her name? Potter. And the Norwegian painter?'

'Ness? He's not in the country.'

'Indeed, so he's here? Hm – and of course there's the Russian opera singer.'

Alberta's colour rose with sudden fierceness, throbbing in her ear-lobes. 'I don't know him – he was only passing through.'

'Come, I didn't mean it seriously. And you must not think I was not concerned for you that evening at Fru Marushka's. The man ought to have been kicked out. But Eliel asked me not to interfere. I couldn't help being a little amused, though; he certainly didn't get anywhere, it looked so funny. Now don't get annoyed with me again. A lout like that. Has Fru Marushka many friends of that calibre?'

'One or two,' said Alberta and bravely met the spectacles for an instant. She saw a hint of amusement in them and was a little confused by it.

It was the kind of conversation that is kept going with some trouble, thanks to one of the parties. It drags itself heavily along the ground, refusing to take off and gather speed, so that the words may lure each other along. Altogether Alberta regretted the whole enterprise, although she was sitting carefree at table and had chosen the restaurant herself. An old awkwardness crept over her, an invincible inner stubbornness.

She had not brought out anything more about herself. But a couple of remarks had been unavoidable. Then the speculative eyes had looked even more speculative. Alberta had occasionally done a right-about turn as if in front of a dangerous fence which she had decided at the last moment not to take, hastily entrenching herself behind the language, her alibi in situations such as this. She could not help thinking how much more pleasant it would have been to sit here with Rasmussen. But of course that would have been out of the question; they had bought waffles at St. Cloud, their debaucheries had never amounted to more.

Occasionally the conversation fell to the ground completely. The pipe puffed on the other side of the table, it was poked and picked at, tapped out and filled afresh, the eyes above it becoming distant as if occupied with something else. But they returned. And the voice resumed with new courage, broaching quite different topics: It was warm in the country, but it was nothing by comparison with Paris. Of course everyone had warned him against coming back again at this time of year, but it had been impossible to work out there; the house was full of guests from morning to night. Then there had been this room, which a French student had put at his disposal for a fortnight. It was in such a pleasant spot, next to the Luxembourg Gardens and near the museum. He could look down into the Gardens – but there... 'And you never feel homesick?' attempted the voice again.

'Never,' Alberta assured him callously. Again she met his eyes for an instant. It seemed unavoidable, even necessary in order to vindicate her words. The pipe puffed several times.

The Seine below them became more lively towards dusk. Crowded steamers called at the quay, there was a hum of voices, singing and laughter. Rowing-boats slid past beneath the branches hanging out over the water, and an occasional canoe, manoeuvred by half-naked rowers. The little garden of the café filled up. With every boat more guests arrived and were packed together like sardines, while pleasantries were exchanged between the tables. Bombarded with good advice on all sides as to how it should be done, the proprietor climbed on and off chairs, lighting the paper lanterns festooned between the trees. They made a fantastic glow against the light evening sky, the treetops darkened to silhouettes, laughter rang out, it was no longer possible to be sure from which direction it came, the air was warm, pure, full of scents. 'Let's have some more wine,' suggested Veigaard.

The frankness and compulsion to examine oneself and one's life in detail which steals over people sooner or later when they sit on a bench in a French open air restaurant, had suddenly come upon him. They find everything falling into perspective, they check their accounts and sum them up. He leaned forward across the table, puffing at his pipe, and explained that Paris was *the* city to work in, there was no doubt about it. He must spend a year or two down here, finish writing his thesis, learn the language, get on intimate terms with the French mentality which was and always would be the salt of the earth. But he had to pay back his study loan and had other obligations as well. He had thought it over and decided he'd have to hold out a little longer at home, drudge along with the boys – yes, he taught at a school in Horsens, and gave private tuition in mathematics besides. It was by no means dull, boys were never dull, whatever else they might be, it was just that he would like a little time for himself. But there – he would probably get it one day.

Alberta listened to it all with polite attention, putting in a yes or a no now and again. Academic degrees were referred to in the course of the conversation, he also mentioned his subject in passing, the structure of pure thought. Alberta saw lines and squares in the air for a moment, and failed to connect anything with it.

He began to talk about his sister, who was married to a businessman down here, a Swede dealing in timber and pulp. They were doing well, had a large apartment on the Avenue du Roule, a country place in Calvados, an automobile, two lovely children. ' But there – of course she is well off in many respects . . . ' Veigaard paused and rummaged in his pipe with his penknife.

Alberta registered that there was something the matter with his sister. She looked as interested as she could and said: ' Really?'

A melody suddenly awoke out in the dusk, played on a single violin, a waltz of the kind that break out all over Paris, are on everyone's lips for a while, and die away again, displaced by a new one. ' My word, he plays well,' said Veigaard. ' He has a good instrument too.' Alberta wisely kept silent. She did not know how to talk about music. As a rule it was in some way fateful for her, passing into her blood like an animating or dissolving stream, making her sad or almost uncontrollably merry so that she had to resort to silence so as not to misbehave, causing her to see visions. Another waltz came out of the darkness. The little garden roared with applause.

A young man came into the uncertain light from the lanterns, and went from table to table, hat in hand. Veigaard put a two-franc piece in the hat, and thanked him for the music, expressing his appreciation in his awkward French and extending his hand to take the violin, holding it with care, giving it back again with a smile and a nod. The musician smiled too, introspectively and with melancholy. He remained standing at Veigaard's and Alberta's table, and played, as if directed at them, one of Chopin's nocturnes. In the brief silence that followed he wrapped his violin in a kerchief and disappeared, silent as a shadow, thin and pale, gaunt inside his clothes, while the applause roared up behind him, apparently too late and to no purpose.

To Alberta it seemed as if the undertow of the great world outside was seizing her. Hunger submerged her, flooding mysteriously and confusingly like an intoxication through her veins. With boundless emotion, a warmth that could carry her with it into any situation, she heard herself speaking hurriedly for a moment without knowing what she was saying. And when Veigaard looked after the violinist and said: 'But all the same, how sad it is!' new warmth flamed up in her at these ordinary words, something resembling tremendous gratitude.

From now on a conversation was brought into being across the table. Alberta felt her listening to be different, her brief, half-finished comments to be alive, woven into coherence. She told him something about herself too, something highly irrelevant besides. It was not quite clear how she embarked on it. It was about sensations she had had when she left home, the naïve feeling of having at last thrown herself out into the effervescence of life, that had gripped her already on board the boat. It was comic to think of it now.

' Come – I don't think so,' said the understanding man on the other side of the table.

She had arrived in Trondheim in the evening. It was already dark, and raining, the cobblestones glittered wet in the lamplight along the quay. The cabs had their hoods up.

There had been something in the sound of the horses' hooves against the cobbles, in the clatter of the wheels up along the riverside that, more than the large houses and the many lights, had struck Alberta as continental, a part of the teeming world. They had no cobblestones anywhere in her small home town. It had been fearfully naïve.

' Yes, but quite natural. That was the way you should have felt. And then ... you came down here?'

' I spent a winter in Kristiania.'

' Eliel said both your parents had died. And almost simultaneously.'

' It was an accident,' answered Alberta. She side-stepped it and said something quickly about the necessity of going abroad, one could not stay at home for ever. But she had liked the tone of Veigaard's question. There had been no hint of intrusive sympathy, no attempt to probe; it had been refreshingly matter of fact.

On the other hand she now sat listening to her own voice, as if it were acting on its own account. It was talking somewhere up in the air in front of her, like someone else's. I must be a little drunk, she thought, appalled. What am I saying? Thank heaven this is a fleeting acquaintance, someone who will perhaps be mentioned somewhere or other several years from now, and of whom one says: Good Lord, I'm sure I met him once, now I come to think of it.

Herr Veigaard's face had become quite indistinct. Only a pale orange-coloured light fell on it from a dying lantern directly above his head. But his pipe glowed now and again. After a while the inadequately lighted face said: ' Why are you so quiet?'

351

' Am I quiet?'

' Yes. But now you're beginning to feel thoroughly tired.'

' Perhaps so,' said Alberta. And at once she felt all the fresh air she had breathed and the wine she had drunk like a compelling weight in her body and her limbs. She could have put her head down on the table and fallen asleep.

' We'd better see about getting home again. *Skaal,* and thank you for coming. It was sweet of you. But it was a good idea of Eliel's too, to write and tell me you were living out there. Otherwise I shouldn't have known a soul — it would have been no fun at all.'

He accompanied her as far as Montparnasse, where Alberta took the tram-car. Veigaard repeated how pleased he was to be living on this side of the Seine. It wasn't at all comfortable to live as he had done the last time.

' It was too genteel,' said Alberta sleepily and know-ledgeably. ' Precisely,' answered the Danish voice, as delighted as if she had found the solution to vital problems. A little astonished she looked up into the two spectacle lenses, which reflected the lamplight and hid his expression. ' Thank you! Thank you for coming!' said the voice again, rising from the first thank you up to the second. ' And *au revoir,*' it said, and went down again.

Even more astonished, Alberta pressed the hand held out to her, thanking him in turn. Once inside the tram-car she sank down inert. In bed at last, she fell asleep, for once, immediately.

* * *

The days undeniably held something new. Alberta admitted it to herself, if not earlier, then certainly on the morning she lied in Ness's teeth in order to keep the afternoon free for her new acquaintance. Before she would simply have said no, she did not wish to. Now she piled up untruths and covered up her tracks after her.

Ness had cropped up again tanned and looking as if burnt solid and indestructible by the heat and his work out of doors in the sun. He was handsome in his peasant way, and would have looked almost like a gipsy if it had not been for his eyes which were too pale, too china-blue. Blue eyes can be beautiful with black hair, but in Ness they were all wrong.

He wanted to go out of town to paint, but he was not very familiar with the surroundings. Could not Frøken Selmer show him some good motifs? They could take their food with them and have a picnic. In the woods somewhere?

Alberta assured him that she was engaged. Visitors from home. She recommended to him Charenton, Vincennes, knowing that wherever else she might be going, it would not at any rate be in that direction. Had he never been out that way? It was exceedingly picturesque.

When he left she felt a little sorry for his back, and could afford to be. It looked lonely.

And she rummaged amongst her dresses, again decided on the sleeveless one, and went out, perspiring with heat, to the Luxembourg or the Parc de Montsouris. Or she prepared the tea-table with the door open to the passage. Fifty kroner for an article, which she had long ago ceased to expect, had fallen like manna from heaven. She could entertain in style with good tea, good cigarettes, flowers on the table. It was a quiet period where the door of the privy was concerned, which also made for a certain festivity, a circumstance of which Herr Veigaard was, however, completely unaware.

Besides, he never sat down for long. He emptied his teacup quickly and was ready to go, out of the city or over to one of the parks; was, in fact, far from having a due sense of appreciation of the occasion. Alberta sometimes felt a little put out by this, a shadow of resentment on behalf of all good-for-nothings. She had put a cushion in the broken chair, nobody could see that there was a hole in it, nor feel it if they sat down. All in all, she had done her best. But in such matters one noticed clearly where the frontier went.

In fact, shadows would pass through her memory. She remembered a ball to which she had gone that winter in Kristiania, at the home of one of cousin Lydia's friends who, to the general rapture, had invited Alberta, even though Lydia was married and had left home. A most unusual kindness therefore.

It had been held in large, high-ceilinged, rather empty rooms somewhere to the west of town. Alberta had sat out a great deal. She knew no-one and was a complete outsider. But occasionally someone would come and present himself.

Then she asked herself, as she circled with them, silent and stiff: Why did he do this? Was it out of pity or because he could find nothing better to do for the moment? The thought was not new, she had brought it with her from the Civic Balls at home. There in Kristiania it was presented in its extreme form, there no-one had any obligation towards her.

It was still with her. It reared up like a dragon when Veigaard remarked casually one day: ' We're like two people washed up on a desert island, aren't we?'

They can do nothing else but cling together – the thought was painfully insistent. Alberta did not show it, merely nodded and laughed a little. In the last resort of course that was what it was; all this bespectacled person from another world wanted of her was company on the island. As far as she could see he managed very well in other respects, wandering round churches and museums in the early morning ' before the asphalt begins to fry the soles of your feet ', then sitting over his studies at home, over in the Luxembourg Gardens, or in libraries, finding his own way everywhere with his halting French. He had told her that he was not going to set foot in the big stores; he had been there with his sister, it was dreadful.

The position was not without its difficulties. It was no longer a secret that Alberta did not have a single pupil. ' Well now, and what about these pupils of yours?'

Veigaard had said the second day they were out together.
'When do you have them? In the mornings perhaps?' He
looked at her with amusement, puffing at his pipe. And
Alberta, completely taken by surprise, blushed flaming red.
She, a past master in defensive measures, had forgotten to
include her pupils in her time-table. This fact, not the lie
itself, embarrassed her. There was nothing for it but to
laugh and give in, saying airily that oh, it didn't matter
about them just at the moment.

Veigaard laughed too. 'Oh, indeed!' he said. A little
later it came, however: 'But that you should simply hang
about here like this – I don't understand it.'

Even the temperature led to the discussion of personal
matters. Alberta and Veigaard sat a great deal, on chairs,
on benches, in small cafés, all over the place. And they
could not sit as dumb as fish. Neither could they talk
endlessly about what they saw, had seen, intended to see.
And Alberta could not say much about her experiences
before Veigaard had found a thread to pull. And pull he
did, speculating, puffing at his pipe, amused, then quickly
turning serious again. 'Indeed, so you have . . . so you
are . . . so you are used to . . .' he insisted. He wound up
the threads too, he remembered things, and, mathematician
that he was, he put two and two together and made four
out of them without difficulty. Since the matter of the
pupils Alberta's standing had become quite insecure. Again
and again she had had to abandon her position and search
for entrenchments further back in time. A not inconsider-
able portion of her casual and good-for-nothing existence
in hotel after hotel, without aim or purpose, had already
been wound up. Sometimes she said: 'I'm afraid it will
get back home.' 'No, no, no – you know I'm not that sort
of person,' said Veigaard.

He was not entirely irreproachable himself. He had a
divorced wife at home in Horsens. He spoke of her as if
he had a guilty conscience. 'Such a shame – a sweet, good
little girl really – but it was a childhood engagement, and
they don't turn out well as a rule, one grows up so very

different. I take much of the blame for it, I should have known better. But there – she's young, she could be happy in quite different circumstances, if only the old people at home would stop trying to patch it all up again, but that sort of thing is the breath of life to them. Sometimes you just feel like running away from it all.'

Oh do you? thought Alberta, feeling almost rehabilitated at the thought that people with orderly lives could have those kinds of feelings. She surprised herself wondering what this man looked like when he was not sunburnt. A wan teacher, probably. There was no risk of her falling in love with him at any rate, not with a teacher in spectacles, living in a Scandinavian country. All her instinct for self-preservation rose against it, and present circumstances seemed to preclude such an eventuality absolutely.

One afternoon Alberta went over to Neuilly with him, to his sister's home. He had left some books there when he was last in town. Now it appeared that he needed them. No-one was home, but the concierge had the key.

It was in a large, silent house with red carpets on white marble staircases and a concierge in black, similar to Mr. Digby's. She inspected Alberta from top to toe and informed them in a tone implying that she washed her hands of them, that a couple of the servants happened to be in town: Joseph and the cook. All Monsieur had to do was ring.

Alberta thought better of it and hesitated. If there were people in the apartment it was a different matter, she would not fit in there. But Veigaard persuaded her: 'Of course you must come in. They are a charming couple, married; they've been with my brother-in-law for years, and I think they'd go through fire and water for him. They're the type of old French servant you don't find anywhere else. And you'll see how my sister lives.'

This decided Alberta. This sister, married to a kind and distinguished man who was far too old for her, who was loaded with comforts, but was not allowed to move so much as a flowerpot in the well-arranged bachelor home into which she had moved, was not without interest. Once Veigaard had let slip a nasty expression: Old man's love. He had tried to cover it up again, but what's said is said. Alberta felt she had peeped inside the troll's mountain.

Joseph opened the door. He had a round, placid face, covered with tiny, superficial wrinkles, which contracted jovially at the sight of Veigaard, but smoothed out into worried, slightly dismayed gravity, when it appeared that Alberta was a member of the expedition. It looked as if some friendly remark he was about to make suddenly withered and died on his lips. He went before them, however, showing the way into a large, dim room, where subdued light fell in stripes, threw back the shutters and opened the windows. When he left, Alberta sensed that he did not quite shut the door behind him.

Veigaard had already disappeared into his room. Alberta sat in a heavy Louis-Quatorze armchair, feeling utterly out of place. In her faded, sleeveless, rather too low-cut dress, her home-made hat and her sandals, she contrasted strongly with the furniture in royal styles, the battle scenes in heavy frames on the walls, the collection of old china in show-cases, and much else. Above all, with Joseph. Through the open windows she could see an iron railing. Beyond it the leaves of a plane tree moved lazily in an almost impercep-tible breeze, which died again immediately. The smell of good food mingled with the room's atmosphere of stale air and polish; it had followed Joseph. She felt that she was under surveillance, and jumped when a large golden-bronze time-piece suddenly began to strike six clear, vibrating strokes, as if to emphasize that this was going too far. Her instinct for flight was aroused.

But there was Veigaard with the books under his arm, suspecting nothing, naturally, just like a man. And just like a man, he had an absolutely desperate idea: ' What a good smell. Oh – she makes wonderful food. We'll get her to serve us a splendid little dinner. There may not be very much of it, but what there is will at any rate be excellent, I can guarantee you that.'

'No, thank you very much,' cried Alberta deprecatingly. But Veigaard was already at the door: 'Joseph!'

Past him Alberta could see a dining-room which, with its dimensions, its dimness, its weighty baroque, strengthened even further her resolve to get away.

They negotiated in low voices through the door. Veigaard racked his brains arduously in French. Joseph replied with terrible correctitude and a shade of chill regret: 'We were not prepared for guests, Monsieur – Monsieur can surely understand . . . .'

'But you can find something surely,' insisted Veigaard. 'We don't mind waiting. Marie-Catherine prepares such wonderful food – *très bon* . . . .'

'Impossible, Monsieur.' The undertone of distress in Joseph's voice at what had taken place was the last straw for Alberta. 'I don't want anything, I want to go,' she said curtly and loudly.

The tall figure at the door turned, hitching up his trousers, which he wore belted in summer: 'I'm awfully sorry, but he won't do it. I don't understand what's the matter with them today. They are usually so ready to please, nothing is ever good enough. I went out to the kitchen to say good-bye to Marie-Catherine – she too was not her usual self.'

'Come along, let's go.'

'If only I could explain myself properly. The whole thing must be a pure misunderstanding.'

'Is this the way?' asked Alberta, wishing to initiate the retreat.

'Yes. No! We'll go another way, so that he won't have to see us out. I'm so annoyed, I'd prefer not to see him again. Come this way.'

They wandered through rooms in which all the shutters were closed. Weak light fell in horizontal stripes. Alberta saw dimly collections of furniture under dust-sheets, glimpses of gilding, chandeliers in tarlatan bags, mountains of bric-à-brac. Somewhere the light caught a prism, was broken, shimmered softly and trembled, rainbow coloured, surrounded by the dimness. The floor was soft and deep underfoot.

Old repressed antipathy stirred in her. She had a rooted fear of rooms full of objects. They weighed one down and held one there, exerting force and discipline. Anyone married to all this was truly to be pitied.

She stumbled against a table and hurt herself. Something on the table tottered, but was saved at the last moment by Veigaard: 'Careful! Did you hurt yourself? It's a bit too full in here – like a bric-à-brac and antique shop. But there are beautiful old things amongst them. It's a pity everything is covered, it might have amused you to see . . .'

'Oh no, thank you.'

'There we are, here's the hall. Now let's go quite quietly and we shall have given him the slip. But there – he doesn't mean any harm . . . .'

They were almost out of the door and were about to draw it to after them, when Joseph suddenly appeared. Consternation and sorrow were written in his obliging face, as he uttered in a low voice, as if confidentially and exclusively to Veigaard, his own and Marie-Catherine's regrets. They regretted, they regretted eternally. Would that Monsieur would understand! Their only desire was to be of service. But if Monsieur wished to receive guests up here, would Monsieur then be so kind as to announce it earlier, and – Joseph's tone became almost pleading – to the master himself? If, on the other hand, Monsieur wished to live here for a few days, there was nothing to prevent him doing so; he and Marie-Catherine would be here until Wednesday, they desired nothing more than to oblige Monsieur . . . .

'What is he talking about?' asked Veigaard. 'I don't understand the half of it.'

Alberta prevailed upon herself to act as go-between and explain. 'Oh, what a lot of nonsense,' said Veigaard angrily.

359

' Such hair-splitting. Tell him to go to the devil. And he'll be hearing from my sister and brother-in-law.'

Alberta reported the final sentence to Joseph. He listened without looking at her: ' *Bien, Mademoiselle.*'

She ran down the marble stairs with the red carpet, heard Veigaard explaining behind her that by Jove he couldn't make out what was the matter with the fellow, felt the enquiring eyes of the concierge at her back, and at last found herself in the street again.

The evening sun was low in the west. The plane trees drooped with every leaf and every flap of bark. The shade, which a short while ago had lain in deep pools beneath them on the pavement, crept tall and thin up the walls of the houses. Farther in above Paris hung the compact sky that a scorching day leaves behind it. The air seemed filled with golden dust.

Alberta walked quickly, irritated by the whole situation, trying to walk it off. She should have known better than to get mixed up in this, the whole thing was all her own fault.

Veigaard, however, had not finished with it: ' How extremely annoying. What on earth was the matter with them?'

' You can't improvise a dinner at short notice,' suggested Alberta.

' Food? Fiddlesticks! Of course they had a house full of food, they have plenty of everything. If I know them, they had at least a whole chicken out there in the pot.'

Alberta gave up replying and simply concentrated on walking. At Porte Maillot Veigaard insisted on having something to drink. ' I am both thirsty and furious,' he explained. And they sat down somewhere in the dust and the noise, in the used breath of the city, as it is spewed out in the evening along the big highways as if through ventilators, thick with petrol and vapour.

Still Veigaard had not finished. Somewhat mollified he said: ' It must be a misunderstanding. They are excellent people really.'

Alberta was tired of the whole question. She shrugged her shoulders: ' Yes, that's precisely why. They were right. They were defending the house they serve. They thought I came from the street.'

The words had fallen out of her mouth, a little indifferently and flippantly, a little too nakedly. One does not say things like that to respectable people from Scandinavia. Now the expression hung in the air, out of place and oppressive. She thought: When I occasionally do speak the truth, I always say the wrong thing. I ought to hold my tongue.

' You're joking, aren't you?' The spectacles were turned towards her enquiringly for a moment, giving her the impression that they did not find the joke appropriate. She tried to gloss it over: ' I mean that we from Montparnasse – we foreigners – here in these *quartiers* where they are not used to us . . . '

Silence. Several puffs from the pipe. It was knocked out hard against a chair-leg, scraped inside, harshly and punitively handled, as if it belonged to the guilty party. Then he said angrily: ' I can't stand hearing you say such brutal things. It – it doesn't suit you at all. Oh – but God knows there are a great many things I can't stand, Alberta. Yes, I'm sorry, but sometimes I want to scold you like . . . '

' Like the boys at home,' came provocatively from Alberta. She looked straight into the spectacles.

' Yes, like the boys. Oh – I know perfectly well you don't do anything really wrong. But you hang about here scamping life. Yes, *scamping* it. What sort of an existence is it? You don't paint, you don't write, you don't do an earthly thing. If things haven't gone wrong yet, they may do so. There are some people who hang about here just drifting, do you want to become one of them?'

Alberta winced, she saw clearly for an instant the bundles of rags lying on benches. Then she said, and she felt her forehead flushing with defiance: ' That's not what we were talking about.'

' That may be so, we are talking about it now.'

'What is "wrong"? Where does right end and wrong begin? Hasn't everyone the right to do what he pleases with himself? Is it wrong that I work as a model? That I earn my daily bread as best I can?'

At once she wanted to bite off her tongue. Why should she have said that? *Epater les bourgeois,* was that what she wanted to do? If so, she had failed. Veigaard did not look at all shocked. He said more calmly than before, lighting his pipe: 'That too? I'm not surprised. Not in the slightest. It fits in excellently with the rest of it.'

Alberta sat silent for a while. Astonished she surveyed this stranger, with whom she was suddenly on such good terms that they were quarrelling about her most sensitive points, and by whom she was in fact being scolded. Here she sat without defending herself.

A moment later she noticed something new in Veigaard's manner of looking at her, with quick little side-glances down over her dress and up at her hat, speculatively puffing at his pipe.

A strange and unaccustomed little sensation as if of power stirred deep in her mind.

* * *

'So Kristiania didn't turn out to be quite as you had expected?'

'Expected?' Alberta smiled a little wryly. How could she explain how it had been to a person like Veigaard? A stinging gust of narrow circumstances, of endless struggle to overcome fresh obstacles, arose from what he occasionally said about himself. He had given coaching, and yet more coaching, from before he matriculated and right through examination after examination, and still had some way to go in the same fashion. He and Alberta might be compared to a skilful, persevering swimmer and a hen fallen in the water. Things that for her were insurmountable obstacles, air in which she could not breathe, would seem silly trifles, childish excuses for idleness, to someone like him.

They were sitting in the grass in the Allé des Marmousets at Versailles. Between them on a cloth were the remains of a meal. If Alberta craned her neck she could see the top of the enormous living green wall behind her disappearing into the slope up by the Palace. It was still warm in the sunlight. But from down below the shadow, blue and indolent, crept upwards at an angle, giving everything dimension, a liberating breadth.

The park satisfied a yearning derived from her childhood for masses of foliage and summer richness, abundance of sun and shade, warmth, scents and fruition. With the same avidity as on the first day she absorbed the spicy perfume of box and roses, the taste of hay and running water, that flowed in from the spacious countryside roundabout, the sheltered tranquillity of it all.

Now Veigaard's question awakened old, tarnished memories. She saw the grey-brown, sooty, trampled snow lying used and shallow along the pavement, shabby tumbledown façades, low decayed fences, the whole scene inexpressibly dirty and mean; remembered a strange light-shunning Sunday stillness, closed milk shops with three lonely bottles of Bavarian beer on display in the window, and one in particular that used to be open. Her mind hard and shrivelled, she stood defiantly outside and became absorbed in its poverty. Besides the three beer bottles it displayed a dish of palely baked cakes, a cardboard box with liquorice pipes in it, another with small champagne bottles made of pink sugar. The bell above the door rang from time to time, a customer slipped in or out, guiltily carrying a cream jug.

There had been something sly and suspicious about everything and everyone in these parts of town on a Sunday. The few people who went in and out of the filthy doorways gave the impression that they never emerged except when the city was desolate and abandoned. They hurried in and out, rounding the corners quickly as if afraid of being seen. Even the solitary dogs, who bustled, sniffing, in and out of the doorways, lifting their hind legs, did not do so in the same confident and officious manner as elsewhere.

The junction of Munkedam's Way and Engen Street. the small streets leading up from the West Station; all the young people were streaming up to the woods. Alberta had neither ski equipment nor friends. At home in Park Street sat Uncle and Aunt expecting visitors. In order to avoid them and to get some exercise, she had gone out. A desire to dive as deep down into ugliness as possible, since she had nothing else to dive into, had driven her down here.

The height – or the depth – was reached by going down the revolting steps between what was known as 'the bazaars', up to or down from Victoria Terrace. There was a stink of urine on the landings, great gobbets of spittle lay on the steps. Here there was no white, untouched snow or crystal-clear winter air, only filth and degradation.

Only one thing was more degrading, more tormenting: to *walk* up into the woods with Uncle and Aunt, slowly in galoshes like an old person, while youngsters on skis and toboggans swarmed everywhere; to be amongst those who halted circumspectly at the side of the road to stand and watch if someone came whizzing past. Her whole being, body and soul, felt mortified. A feeling of ignominy overcame her, undeserved and more bitter than she could bear. Better Engen Street instead.

One day when she was walking up the hill with them. attired in galoshes, a skier coming at full speed down the track leading from the Corkscrew slope suddenly swung round and stopped, came back, bounding on his skis and calling out to Frøken Selmer, and introduced himself to Uncle and Aunt. It was Frederick Lossius, an acquaintance she had made a couple of years ago in North Norway. He had heard that Alberta was down here, was happy to run into her, and so forth. Would she come out tobogganing with him one evening? Or skiing in the woods one Sunday?

Alberta said no thank you, she had no equipment. It was true. She had given away her old, worn skis with the bamboo bindings to one of the poor boys from Rivermouth when she left home. She could not have appeared on them in the south, nor in her ski suit. She had supposed in her recklessness that life was going to be different.

Oh, but she would have to get equipment in any case, insisted Lossius. 'You can't live *here* without sports equipment, it's quite unthinkable.'

Aunt had interrupted: Alberta's plans were uncertain for the moment, nothing quite settled, best to wait for a little before making any purchases. Thank you very much, Mr. Lossius.

He took his leave and continued down to town. He had only meant to be kind. If he was unsuccessful, then it didn't matter, and good-bye. But for Aunt it was yet another occasion for emphasizing that Alberta would have need of every *øre*, whatever she decided to do: commercial college, cookery school or arts and crafts. There were so many things one would like to have, but .... that young Lossius was said to be a fearful radical. You could see that. Distressing for his parents – nice people.

'Where were you then? You haven't answered my question. Never mind – I can guess.'

It was Veigaard. He was lying on his stomach in the grass, leaning on his elbows, without hat or spectacles. The flesh round his eyes twitched nervously now and again, as it does in people who strain their sight. Then there would be a sudden gleam in them and his look would sharpen; it could be directed at Alberta almost piercingly at times. And again the strange little sensation of power would stir. deep inside her. She was actually something of a problem to this man. It was not entirely unpleasing suddenly to say things which made him puff at his pipe, to say, for instance. as if *en passant*: 'That was the hotel where I found an aesthete standing in the middle of the room one dark night.'

'An aesthete?' he puffed the pipe, at once disorientated.

'Yes, one of those fellows from all over the globe who hang about here. If you ask them whether they write, paint or sculpt they answer, a little evasively, that they are aesthetes. Just like that. This one was Hungarian. I had forgotten to lock my door.'

' Hm.'

Usually that would be all. Alberta had only been scolded on that one occasion at the Porte Maillot. There was a little excitement in it just the same, rather like daring to go out on thin ice. It might break.

But fearful notions could occur to her. Just as now when Veigaard was lying there passing his slender, muscular hand through his hair, which was a little long and tended to fall over his forehead, a gesture he often employed, and a highly unmotivated desire came over Alberta to take his head in her hands and lay it in her lap. She was flooded with quite unwarranted pity for it. It was as if there were a double substratum to her personality, or perhaps several. Full of contradictions, she wanted and did not want. It was as well that irreproachable persons, with their emotions in order, could not see inside her.

It was late in the afternoon. People were leaving the park. Mothers with handwork folded up their small camp-stools, called playing children to them and trooped off, patiently carrying dolls and small buckets, spades and skipping-ropes and teddy bears. From the Hôtel des Reservoirs came the clink of crockery and slamming of cutlery, from the villas beyond the strumming of pianos and laughter of children, fragments of conversation, the thump of croquet mallets, all the pleasant small sounds of summer.

' How did you find out you were interested in French?' The grey eyes looked searchingly at Alberta, and she reflected, attempting to grope her way back to the vague ideas that had become decisive for her at that time. It had not just been Paris with all the promise contained in that short, bright name, it had been something else as well: roots that sought new and completely foreign soil, the hints, the anticipation, the scintillation that arose out of the little she knew of the country, and out of every word in the useless sentences she had learned at school: 'The cherry trees of my uncle are more numerous than the apple trees of my aunt'. 'The house of my cousin is larger than that of my brother'.

'This is where one wants to come,' she said. And Veigaard was satisfied with this profundity: 'Yes, of course it is.'

But Alberta suddenly felt communicative: at the end of that winter Aunt Marianne had invited her to Grimstad.

She came to a steep, stony little town composed of small white houses with red roofs, to the last remnant of the South Norwegian winter, to a hint of spring; evenings with a green sky behind the dark silhouettes of houses and trees, the beginnings of birdsong in the woods. The roofs did not drip, nowhere did the water go above one's galoshes, there had after all been very little snow. The landscape lay, not white, but brown, yellow and grey under the glass-clear spring sky in which a marvellously large star would blaze out and the moon hung like a sickle with a dark circle inside. An altogether new and foreign spring. And suddenly one evening something wonderful, something she had never experienced before: the flight of grey geese.

Aunt Marianne was small and thin, almost transparent, not at all as Alberta had imagined her. She had looked perplexed and anxious when Alberta decided on Paris, chafed her two thin little hands together and said: 'But alone, my child? Alone? In my time it would have been absolutely unthinkable.'

Then she must have asked Doctor Kvam for advice. He was a white-haired old gentleman who was a frequent visitor, a friend and contemporary from her youth. At any rate it was from him that salvation came, suddenly and unexpectedly. He thumped on the floor one day with his stick: 'If you're to go abroad, you must go when you're young. Let the little girl leave. The sooner the better. Times have changed, Marianne.' And he and Aunt conspired together, wrote to Uncle in Kristiania, moved heaven and earth.

Alberta was given presents, kind people subscribed, old friends of Mama and Papa, suddenly emergent distant relations, mobilized by Doctor Kvam. She left with a respectable sum of money sufficient for a year's stay. It had been kind, terribly kind, nobody was obliged to do it. Alberta was filled with the uneasy joy that results from that kind of thing. When she thanked Doctor Kvam he had slapped her on the back: 'God be with you, my child. Greet the Pont Neuf from an old Parisian.' Now he and Aunt Marianne were both dead.

Alberta fell silent. Again she felt the acrid after-taste left by gifts of money. Such gifts resemble stringent medicine; you are forced to accept them if you are to get on your feet. But they leave a paralysed spot, a dead place in the mind where nothing will grow.

Veigaard got to his feet. As if concluding his train of thought he said: 'You had to go abroad. You had to come here. But you must see about getting more out of it than you are doing. Now let's go and have coffee at that little place you told me about, down by the canal.'

They watched the sun set from the terrace of the Palace, sitting between scattered, silent or quiet-voiced people, while the Palace stood on its head in the fountains, golden-green from the vanishing day. Above the elaborately clipped trees in the beds below them the shadow crept victoriously forward. The angelus bell rang from the chapel, the scent of box was interlaced with stock and heliotrope and the breath of the meadows outside. Far off in the deep perspective above the canal hung a rusty sky, tarnished with soot and piled-up heat, splintered by an occasional distant flash of lightning.

There would be no storm. It would come perhaps tomorrow, perhaps another day. The metallic clouds thickened, gathering into layers; above them rose enormous eiderdowns, tinted with the distant, vanished flush of sunset.

'How pleasant and fresh it is now,' said Veigaard. 'Shall

we go for a short walk along the canal before they close? And round by the circular fountain? You remember, the one where the water is coloured by the patina of the central figure. We'd have time for that, don't you think?'

Yes, Alberta thought so.

The park was teeming with night-life. Crickets sang round them, the grass and foliage rustled quietly, small dreaming birds gave an occasional pipe, and the scents were strong in the twilight. A young frog jumped out of Alberta's way, she jumped herself, both of them stopped to look at each other. A small, velvet-brown body, that stretches itself to leap and collects itself together again to sit; black eyes like pearls, intelligent, intently observant; a slightly deformed, minute person, a mysterious little fellow-wanderer on the turning earth, belonging to the evening and the forest.

Veigaard suddenly started to talk about his childhood. He recognized the sound of gravel underfoot in darkness under trees, remembered how, as a small child, he had driven home with his parents from a party on just such a warm, dusky night in August. He was sleepy, nodding on his mother's knee. But when the carriage entered an avenue, he awoke. The gravel had sounded different beneath the wheels under the trees, different from the day-time, deeper, more secretive. He must have been quite small, he remembered no more than that.

'That's how one does remember,' said Alberta. In her, too, pictures streamed up from the depths of her mind, memories of a large garden, of flowers. She saw small, round, sulphur-yellow roses, a tall tree with a broad crown in the middle of a courtyard. A walnut tree. It must have been in Flekkefjord, which she had visited once when she was quite small.

'I say, where are we exactly? And what was that we heard a while ago? That rolling of drums in the distance? Surely it wasn't . . . ?'

'Oh, heavens,' exclaimed Alberta. 'The park's closed.'

Her heart turned over. She was the guide, she was responsible. She stood and looked about her, but saw only the darkness of the forest rising upwards, mysterious walls of trees stretching to the sky; a hint of light up there, an even weaker one on the path beneath their feet.

' By Jove, we must hurry,' said Veigaard vehemently. ' Are you sure of the way?'

Sure? The earth sank beneath her, she attempted to consider the possibilities. There was no way out through the Palace any more. They had walked along the canal, round the arm of the enormous cross of water it forms at the Grand Trianon, continued along it, turned into a side-path at an angle, come out into a large avenue and left it again. They had walked quickly, stimulated by the evening air, seized by the thwarted need for exercise that piles up during heat-waves. She had been listening to what Veigaard was saying, and had not paid very much attention to . . .

Everything was so terribly big too, the distances so enormous. Now in the darkness it engulfed them as sea and darkness had done at home sometimes, an enormity reducing one to nothing.

We must try to get out through one of the side entrances. The Palace is closed. God, let it be this way!

Beside her she heard Veigaard: ' Come, at least let me take your arm. It's as black as pitch. Then we must put our best foot forward. Whatever next!' He was not in a good temper. His voice seemed to be keeping his feelings under control.

The darkness thickened round them. Alberta assured him that of course it must be this way. She purposely ignored his question as to whether she had been in this part of the park before, repeating that, as far as she could tell, they would come out at the Trianon. If she remembered rightly, there were watchmen's houses there; they would have to knock.

And indeed, it was getting lighter in front of them. They suddenly found themselves out in a large, circular clearing.

From it avenues, black with night, led in all directions back into the darkness. Veigaard counted them. ' Seven,' he said. ' I make it seven. Can you decide which is the right one?' Alberta looked around her desperately. All seven of them seemed to be constructed out of obscurity.

She stood hesitating. Then the truth had to come out. ' I don't know where we are,' she admitted.

' This is a nice kettle of fish. But there – I had my suspicions. When does the moon rise?'

' Late tonight. Towards morning sometime.'

Alberta really did feel like the boys he scolded, and like the eternally ill-fated person she was. ' I'm exceedingly sorry – it's all my fault, I... we must try, it's not fenced in everywhere.'

' Oh, we're equally to blame,' said Veigaard curtly.

Inertia crept over her. If they had come out on the Trianon side they would not have been far from town. Now it was impossible to tell where they were. They might walk and walk for a long time without finding a house. Even if they got out of the park, it would be like trotting haphazardly round France. She felt dead tired at the very thought; like a criminal awaiting judgment too. If only Veigaard would say something. There he stood, coal-black and silent.

' Does nobody live inside the park?'

' There's a house somewhere near the canal. I don't know whether anyone lives there. If only I knew which direction it was.'

Fresh silence, then curt, cold words out of the darkness. ' There's only one thing to be done, wait until dawn. I can smell hay somewhere close by. We shall have to pack you down in that. The night is warm, so you shouldn't take harm, it could have been worse. Now just wait a little.'

She heard him pushing through branches, then a thud, as if he had jumped over a ditch, and grumbling. And she allowed herself to be taken by the arm and led away, acquiescent as if under arrest. ' I am more upset on your account,' she managed to say.

' Oh, I expect I shall survive. Just as I thought, here are some big haystacks. Be careful, there's a ditch here. Let me help you.'

' But I don't want to sleep,' attempted Alberta.

' The dew is falling heavily already. Down in the hay it's dry. Now then, down you go. We're not having any colds and that sort of thing.'

Oh – woman is in truth man's burden. Alberta felt it clearly at this moment. Had Veigaard not had her to drag along with him, he would have walked until he came to a house, and slept there, satisfied. Now he was burdened with a being who could not be expected to hold out for any length of time, who might catch cold, and so on; who, besides, was the cause of these developments, and whom his sense of honour forbade him simply to leave. Miserably she waited, while he pulled and rummaged in the hay, making a kind of nest for her. If only he would speak, but no. ' Thank you very much,' she muttered, when he laid a great armful of hay over her and roughly packed it together. ' Now try to get a bit of sleep; you must be up at first light,' came curtly out of the darkness.

There she lay looking up at the sky. Little black clouds were drifting about between the stars. The treetops stood mysterious and enormous against it, swaying gently now and then. Warm streams of air lapped her face, full of the scents of all kinds of flowers, sweet and bitter mingled. The crickets chirped as if for dear life. It sounded as if someone was incessantly shaking a large box of needles.

Sleep? She wasn't going to sleep. If she had dared, she would have talked to drown all her embarrassment in chatter. She heard a match being torn off, heard the small puffs of the pipe being lit. ' How are you over there? Are you at all comfortable? I can't tell you how sorry I am about this,' she attempted apologetically.

' Will you try to get to sleep,' came the severe reply. And Alberta fell silent, not daring to say more. Suddenly she yawned. A drowsiness that she remembered from her childhood and never experienced in her adult life came over her, comfortable and overwhelming.

She woke suddenly. High above the treetops sailed the moon in infinity, the moon of her childhood, shining and yellow.

Small, thick clouds drifted past, quenching the yellow of its light before reaching it, green as tarnished silver when they were right in front. When her eyes followed them she seemed to be sailing herself in a soft, scented cloud. It smelt of hay.

There was Charles's Wain, unnaturally large, apparently alone in the sky. It had been overturned, and was lying with the chariot-spokes sticking upwards, like a toy left by a child. There stood the enormous formations of the trees, coal-black against a colourless sky, against the grey, silent depths of space. Now the treetops caught a metallic half-light, midway between silver and gold – now they were melted, dissolved and made unreal by the moonlight. Now and again a murmur went through the wood, was drawn along close to the ground, then rose upwards and was released in quiet rocking. The night was like a dark material wrapped about her, saturated with extract of all that grows. Somewhere close by, a cricket was almost shrieking.

A sudden notion that perhaps she was dead and beyond the grave occurred to Alberta. No – she was on earth, more on earth than ever before, deeply and wonderfully united with all its life.

Something moved close to her, hay was drawn over her and tucked in. A hand, quickly withdrawn, moved over her cheek. A sweet sigh of recognition went through her, she was taken back to a time long, long ago when someone else had tucked her in. She had been woken by it, had felt safe and happy, and had fallen asleep again.

She was cold. The dampness was creeping up her, involuntarily she made a movement so as to get further under the hay. Then the attentive hand was there again, tucking it up under her chin and round her shoulders. She looked up for his face, it was already gone. The sky above her was greying with something which was neither light nor darkness. A deep cooing came from somewhere in the wood. A voice said: ' You ought to get up now and move about properly.'

Not yet. Alberta stretched herself lazily down in the hay. Not just yet. She wanted to return to this dreamless sleep, the best she had ever tasted, wanted to go down again into the sheltered chasm of forgetfulness. She seemed to have been sleeping away years of restlessness and fatigue down there. And she dozed off.

' I'm not going to let you lie there one minute longer.'

Alberta looked up. The sky had a dull flush, but down on the earth the pale, greyish light which was neither day nor night, only a waiting, still lay. She was cold and a little stiff. Nevertheless these brief hours of sleep in the fresh air had renewed her, as a bath may do. She rubbed her eyes, plucked from her hair the straws that were hanging in her face and said: ' I've never slept so well in my whole life.'

' Will you please get up, and at once.'

Alberta sat up. There was Veigaard, his face grey and tired, his collar turned up and shoulders shivering. He was stamping his feet and had a homeless look about him, like a poor fellow who has nowhere to go for the night. His pipe was sticking up pathetically out of his pocket. But he was no longer angry, on the contrary he said in a surprisingly hilarious tone of voice: ' It's plain to see you've been having adventures. Straw in your hair, dew in your hair. You should always have it down on your shoulders, it suits you.' And he busied himself plucking straws off her, long ones that would not brush off.

Alberta knew very well that her hair, which did not look especially attractive put up, fell beautifully and coherently when she took out her hair-comb and let the coil glide down until it lay half undone on the nape of her neck.

Without answering she lifted an arm, which she also knew to be beautiful, and as if in a dream plucked out straw from his hair and his upturned collar. The grey, tired face in front of her altered at once to an expression that was familiar and intimate, that had something in it of the courageous wanderer through life, of a man's strict frugality, of Jacob, of Papa. Old and new feelings flooded into her in a confusing blend. She heard herself laugh an entirely new little laugh, sensed something she had never sensed before in gesture and movement. It streamed from within her, forcing its way out, whether she wished it or not.

– Something soft and gentle. And it was not humiliating or mortifying. It was submission for the first time to a law of life, an unfurling of herself like a leaf in the sun. Perhaps it made her, the ugly duckling, beautiful. At any rate it made her different, giving her something of the inevitability of a bird or an animal, the innocence of a life lived in the present.

She looked up, into a face so deathly serious and tense that the small muscles on either side of the mouth came into prominence. She felt a little giddy. She laughed again to cover herself.

They ran through the grass which was grey with dew. It was a struggle for Alberta, she felt stiff and distant. The hems of her skirts were wet and slapped heavily about her legs. But Veigaard was merciless, run she must.

They crept through a hedge and negotiated a ditch out on to a country road, an endless avenue. A peasant on a load of vegetables told them the way to Versailles, round the park. And they ran again, until Alberta could run no longer and declared that she was warm.

It was day. The air was already quivering with the coming heat. Along the roadside grew the plump, shaggy childhood flora of Lady's mantle and wild parsley. There is something erect, something wild and warm and invincible about them. Equipped with such strong roots that not even the thickest layer of dust from the country roads ever chokes them, they grow along the roads of half the world, and stand each day dew-fresh in the morning light. It is like a greeting to walk along the road and see them coming continually towards you on either hand.

Versailles was still asleep, with hushed, empty gardens and closed shutters, when Alberta and Veigaard entered it, hand in hand like two schoolchildren. 'Now we must see if we can find something to eat,' said Veigaard. 'For we're both decidedly hungry.'

Outside the café just across from the station a yawning *garçon* was sweeping between the tables. Very tactfully he interrupted this task to go in and provide the matinal couple, irrelevantly gay and dishevelled in appearance, with something to eat. 'Hot coffee, plenty of coffee, coffee at once,' ordered Veigaard. He sat down with his elbows on the table and struck his fist into the palm of his hand, like someone who has made up his mind on a grave matter.

Tame sparrows approached them, sweeping the air with their wings, settled on the backs of the chairs around them and chirped urgently. Still cool and new, the day lay beneath the great elms on the Avenue de Sceaux.

* * *

'Things can't go on like this, Alberta. Not a month, not even a week longer. Some arrangement must be made for you.'

Alberta shifted restlessly. 'Making arrangements' could only mean wresting from her the only thing she had succeeded in conquering in her whole life. She was about to say something. Then Veigaard said: 'If you refuse to come home with me now, then you must move in with a family. I won't have you living here like this.'

But Alberta would not go home. She wanted something quite different. She kept silent, searching quietly for arguments.

'Yes, I know what you're going to say. You're going to talk about freedom again. Freedom? What sort of freedom do you have? It's a miserable life, that's what it is, and you are far too good for it. You're not free, you're an outlaw.'

There Alberta sat. She shook her head now and again, said yes, of course, yes, yes. And she shut herself in again behind her obstinacy, her brief, sulky, ' If you knew how everything really was, Nils '.

But Nils had again concluded a train of thought: ' That obstinate mind of yours is worth a better cause, dash it. If only you could use it to work your way through...'

' Through what?'

' Good Lord, Alberta, through anything. We can all of us do something. And you – sometimes I get the feeling that something is on fire inside you. But you're certainly not going to find out what it is in this way. Here you are, here you've been for seven years. You know the language, and in spite of your ignorance you are informed about a great many things. If only I could fathom what it really is I like about you. When I examine you closely, I must say I don't understand it at all.'

He drew Alberta's face towards his, pressing his nose against hers repeatedly: ' Stubborn, stupid, ignorant.'

' Ugly,' completed Alberta.

' Ugly? Yes, hideous as the devil. A little heathen, an anti-social individual, a hopeless character. But there – on Wednesday I shall go home and marry someone else, a respectable, sensible little girl, who knows what she wants. And the little memory of Paris will become just one of those little memories one has...'

Alberta turned her face away, pulling away from him. What he was saying hurt her deeply. ' I know what I want,' she muttered.

' No, indeed you don't. You live in perpetual opposition and believe it to be freedom, independence. You are more stupid than I thought, Alberta.'

' Oh?'

' *Still* more stupid than I thought, and that's saying a good deal. But I'll tell you what you are doing...',

Veigaard took her by the shoulders and turned her face towards him again : ' You are stunting yourself and freezing here too, you never do anything else, dash it, only in a different way from up there at home. You are stagnating, that's what you're doing, destroying yourself for lack of all sort of things, from food and air and proper clothes to . . . to affection and care. You must get out of this, out of this sordid existence in seventh-rate hotels.'

Yes, said a little voice inside Alberta. Yes, yes, yes, it's true, all of it. She found escape in the new element within her, what in her innermost mind she called being ' different towards Nils '. It consisted of an indeterminable number of small cadences, gestures, expressions, a way of snuggling into her clothes and laughing, a low, clear sparkling laugh – a laugh that she herself listened to with amazement and which made her think of the chuckling of the decanters at home, when good wine was poured from them, a festive and superfluous little sound. ' You'll come down here again soon, Nils. You'll apply for the grant and get it. Then we'll rent a room in the house where you're living now, one of those with a view of the Gardens. There are no bugs there. And you have no idea how cheaply one can live down here. Or how practical I am. We could be so happy. Like many other people here. And no-one would need to know, no-one.'

Each day was a fight about the same thing. Veigaard would arrive brandishing his pipe and armed with new arguments. He would brush Alberta aside and begin at once : ' You're longing to go home, Alberta.'

' Am I?'

' Your face went so small that evening we were sitting at Lavenue's and the violinist played " I Gaze on the Sun ". I saw it clearly. And you're not just longing to go home, you're longing *for* a home, like – like all homeless people. For a place to belong to.'

But Alberta shook her head and denied it. ' I shall never be of any use doing that,' she said quietly.

The pipe puffed: ' I wish I knew what you think it would be like. I have a sofa and a few chairs left me by my mother, an old-fashioned Pembroke table, books; a couple of rooms all told. I kept no more than was strictly necessary after the divorce. And I don't intend you to stand over a cooking-stove. We could be together, each doing his own work, quite simply. I haven't the slightest interest in all this business of running about with newly baked cakes on a dish and pulling down curtains and hanging them up again. If I did, the old marriage would have sufficed. It was perfect from that point of view, I suppose.'

But Alberta knew better. She pictured to herself washing day and the Christmas house-cleaning, felt all the critical small-town eyes pressed up close against the window-panes, saw herself, the good-for-nothing, going from defeat to defeat. And she attacked him in turn: ' *You* long to get away. You long to come here.'

' I shall come here. It's just that I can't run away from everything there at home on the spur of the moment.'

' Don't *run* away from it. Go home and make your arrangements and come back again.'

' My arrangements might take a year, perhaps two. Even if I get this grant, which you think is hanging on a tree all ready for me, I shan't be able to leave immediately. But let's leave the matter there. You'll have to stay here, and we'll just have to find something for you.'

Alberta sighed. She too had her life, that she could not run away from on the spur of the moment; it was just that it was so difficult to sum it up in words or discuss it matter-of-factly: immense, chaotic possessions for which she had fought and held out, the streets, the throngs of people, the flowers, being outside it all; the vague certainty that it was here, in spite of everything, she should seek and find the way she should go. Her way.

Mists of doubt clouded her mind. This chance traveller passing through, what had she to do with him? The lone-liness had played her a trick. Was she not behaving as if ready to cling to anybody? Once he had left, would she forget him in, let's see, how long?

Nothing is incurable, everything passes. From the first stab that gives warning of danger, right through the fever of restless dreams, one most certainly reaches freedom again. One day the whole thing has dropped out of one's thoughts, and is left behind, forgotten.

His eagerness to take her with him made her feel at times like a pawn, to be played against another pawn. She remembered things he had said: ' We had been married a year, then I simply couldn't go on. When a man can't, then it's no use. There's nothing he can do about it. Well, then it all became tragic, and so it still is in a way.'

His observations on these matters were few and brief. But Alberta glimpsed a face, a contour, blonde and passionate, continually blotched with tears and continually telephoning. She thought: I won't get mixed up in all that, I won't.

Marriage – the very word dragged, it sounded compelling and burdensome. She remembered her friends who had married in the small town at home. The church would be packed, the town dressmaker almost dead with exhaustion. The next day the new bride would be standing in Schmitt the butcher's or at Ryan's, feeling the meat with her finger to see if it was tender; then she would call at Holst's to ask them to send home such and such, taking with her a good piece of cheese for supper, while people asked each other all down the street whether they had seen her, and went a different way in order to get an opportunity of doing so.

No, none of that. There were four days until Wednesday. Then the worst would be over.

But she longed for him every minute he was away from her. He lived in her, possessed her. The French call it having someone in the blood. Nothing is closer to the truth. And when he unwillingly muttered one day, under his breath: ' If only I had you, I'd know how to hold you, that's all there is to it,' anxiety and sweetness quivered confusingly through her. She felt a slow cajoling call in her body to submit and give herself, to be humble and serve.

Then she would go to meet him as light-footed as if she were flying. She laughed her new laughter. In her were gestures she had not known about, as natural as the swaying of branches in the wind, cadences she listened to with astonishment. There it all was one day and nothing could be done about it. For long periods at a time all their difficulties seemed to be forgotten. Alberta felt the new element in her being play like a spring of water that has finally found its way out into the sun, bringing liberation and deliverance. She would search his face with her index finger, looking for the two small knots of muscle on either side of his mouth: ' You haven't put them on today. That's not fair, you're cheating. You will please put them on every day.' A calm certainty grew in her: It will work out all right, it will work out in some way or other. Until suddenly Veigaard would be cold and distant, although not a single word of disagreement had been spoken. He would shift his position, lead the conversation on to quite irrelevant matters, raise a wall of correct, ordinary words about him.

And the daylight would lose its brightness. Alberta would sit numbed, searching for what she had done wrong, finding nothing. And would herself shortly become a little cold and stiff, paralysed by what was unexplained, and by an old, painful thought: Perhaps there was something repulsive about her after all.

* * *

The days passed. The enormous gladioli of late summer were already in flower round the circular fountain in the Rue Soufflot. The beds in the Luxembourg Gardens were full of dahlias. The mornings were a little misty, as if carrying the autumn in wraps.

A chill would go through Alberta at the thought of being alone again. Then she would suddenly feel relief at the idea of putting the whole thing in perspective. It had come so close that it was tomorrow morning.

She was sitting in the red armchair by the window. Veigaard was packing. He had acquired new books and a new trunk, had bought some knick-knacks for his relatives at home and a ring for Alberta in an antique shop in the Rue des Saints-Pères: an old ring, a dark amethyst with tiny pearls round it. He had found it and bought it on his own. Alberta got a lump in her throat and felt heart-sick when she looked down at it.

Neither of them said very much. Veigaard's face had that tense expression that made Alberta think of life's hard journey. She felt strongly the necessity to steel herself now towards the end. Nevertheless there were words that seemed to be lying on her tongue, ready to pop out now and then. She would not say them. She might regret it terribly, and fail to keep them in the long run. Now it must be left to fate.

Veigaard suddenly turned round, putting down a pile of books that he was taking to the trunk. He half sat on the edge of the table and slapped his knee with a paper-knife: ' For the last time – are you coming with me?'

' Give me a little time at least,' said Alberta yieldingly, feeling a hypocrite. She would never want this. She got up and sat close to him on the table and stroked his hand, outlining yet again a provisional plan that she had conceived: first, he would be coming back for Christmas, for the whole month. She would book a room here in good time, arrange everything so nicely. He should sit undisturbed the whole day, make enormous strides with his dissertation, no telephone would ring, here no-one ever used the telephone, the table would stand exactly like this one so that he could look out over the Gardens. But at dusk they would fan the coke fire in the grate so that it glowed and cast its light over the whole room, they would have chestnuts with freshly churned butter. On Christmas Eve, midnight mass at St. Sulpice – turkey at D'Harcourt's afterwards. It was always full of students there, gay and lively.

'Yes,' said Veigaard wearily. 'I'm sure it would be nice. And then?'

'Then?' Alberta faltered a little. 'Well – then you'll stay perhaps?'

Veigaard looked even more weary. 'And supposing I can't? Supposing I have to leave again, leave the . . . the coke fire and all the rest of it?' He suddenly had the ravaged expression that she remembered from the morning at Versailles, that look of the toiler who must keep going and has no other pleasures in life. And he looked at her strangely wide-eyed. Alberta was reminded of a poor man watching sumptuously dressed rich folk. She was greatly moved.

But Veigaard said, and his mouth curled up bitterly as he did so: 'So we must arrange something for you, Alberta. I suppose it is too much to expect you to come with me on the spur of the moment. I need someone there at home, I expect it's that that makes me unreasonable. It's not good for a man to be alone, and in my situation it's terrible.

'Well – then I saw you sitting there at Fru Marushka's that evening. You sat as if alone amongst the others and you were – different. I had a strange feeling that I had always known you. And that morning at Versailles I had the . . . the impression that you felt the same. But you do not, and I cannot expect you to so soon. I thought it would be so natural for you to come home with me, because of the way you live down here, with your roots groping about haphazardly in the air, so to speak. I thought we might be able to help each other as best we could. I meant well in my fashion. But there – now we must find some arrangement, you must get something out of the winter, and then . . .'

Alberta was on her feet. Waves of emotion went through her, appearing as flecks before her eyes. She could hear her heart beating loudly as if measuring a moment of destiny, felt her eyes widen in her face, heard herself say in a deep, slow voice: ' I mean well too. I want you to be free and ... happy and ... have everything you wish. There's nothing I couldn't do for you. I'll tell you everything I've not told you before, not even mentioned – do whatever you want .... '

She saw his eyes, wide and dark like her own. When she put her arms round his neck he drew his face back a little, but continued to look at her, as if trying to see into the depths of her mind. She thought: If I must I shall even conquer the innermost, shining white fear of anyone coming near me, I shall do it now. And suddenly these dark eyes which continued to look at her sent the blood flooding through her veins. She felt her own expression altered by it, as if it were sinking back, turning inwards. She heard Veigaard say, his voice trembling, ' Alberta '. He seized her wrists. But she forced herself up against him, tensing her body like a spring – and suddenly had his arms tightly about her.

* * *

It had rained for the first time for weeks and a smell of fresh leaves came from all the trees. The air was spicy and as buoyant as in spring when Alberta and Veigaard jogged up towards the Gare du Nord in a cab.

Alberta was wearing an old, white embroidered petticoat under her dress. She caught herself sitting thinking about this ridiculous circumstance. Nobody wore such petticoats nowadays, they were antiquated and a little comic, and it had worried her yesterday and this morning. Now it would show when she climbed out of the cab. It looked terrible with her dress, giving the effect of a country woman dressed up in her Sunday best. But sometimes you have to wear whatever you possess.

Veigaard was holding her hand in his, thumping it up and down as he recapitulated: ' Now – a week today my sister comes back to town. I shall write to her as soon as I get to Copenhagen or on the ferry. Then she will help you, Alberta. – Yes! To find some respectable lodgings and whatever clothes you need. I will not have you going round looking like this. I may like you as you are, but no-one could call you well-dressed exactly. Something radical must be done. And those old sandals of yours, I don't ever want to see them again.'

Alberta flushed, again remembering her petticoat and the episode with Joseph. Here she sat, tamed, with her wings clipped for all time, strangely bound to Veigaard and dependent on him. She did not know whether this was a good thing or not, but was simply compliant to the extent of apathy. For an instant she saw clothes, beautiful clothes such as she had passionately wanted to own, clothes that suited her. But deep down in her mind lay something resembling a little ball of mist, an immovable nothing. It was by no means certain that it would not start to swell and hide what was uppermost in her now.

'You must discuss your journey home with her as well, Alberta. And then come when you wish. When you are quite certain you want to. Not before.'

Alberta pressed his hand in reply. It was gradually borne in on her: Now you are sure of me, quite sure.

They were halted by the traffic. Veigaard looked at his watch and his small gesture made Alberta think of executions, the moments just before. They were probably like this. Perhaps they contained the same microscopic amount of curiosity as to how it would feel when it was all over. She sat drinking in all her impressions of the life about her in quite a new way: the air, the sounds, the light murmur of the city on a clear, beautiful morning. There it was still, she had not left it, nor let it slip out of her hands. In a short while she would be alone with it again.

Then warmth and tenderness filled her mind. She pressed his hand hard, spoke about freedom, the grant, the peace he would at last have down here when they finally got as far as that, the libraries, the freedom from everything that was tying him down.

Veigaard suddenly sighed. 'I've been thinking,' he said,

' that perhaps I ought to apply to get into a school in Copenhagen. It wouldn't stop us going abroad when we had the opportunity.'

But Alberta started as if stung. Uncle and Aunt went there every year. Cousin Lydia came through on her journeys to and from England. There the whole thing would be displayed to the public gaze in the most fearful way. She heard her own voice, shocked and mortified: ' Copenhagen! That would be ten times as bad, Nils,' and regretted it at once. He had been sitting thinking this out. She pressed his hand with all her might: ' Of course you'll get your grant. Why should we want to go to Copenhagen?'

But Veigaard's voice sounded tired and a little cold when he replied: ' Well, well, I expect I shall apply.'

The painful astonishment that follows the breaking of something precious by mistake, came over Alberta. He was out of humour, it was dreadful. There was no opportunity here in the street to use the kind of argument which had proved to be more successful than talk and reasoning. Anxiously she looked up at him, watching his face for signs that it would clear. And thank God, now he was squeezing her hand again! Yes, she was indeed a different person today, overflowing with gratitude for a mere smile.

He took out his notebook: ' Have I got it correctly? *Poste restante* Alésia? Since it is so important to keep Eliel out of it. Though I must say I'm glad he'll be back in a couple of days. It's always somebody, and you can't really have anything to do with Ness. You shall hear from me from Cologne. And you are to be a good little girl, no more sessions out there with that revolting old Englishman, no more aesthetes in your room at night.'

He suddenly threw his arm round her and held her tight: ' I have a strange feeling that I ought to take you with me now, this very minute, just as you are and whether you want to or not. I don't like leaving you behind alone at all. But you will stay at a decent hotel for these few days until my sister comes, won't you?'

' Yes, of course,' Alberta assured him. She knew of one

up on the Boul' Mich' which was excellent. She would stay there. She kissed him quickly and passionately on the cheek. His jaw was crooked with emotion.

At once the traffic began to move, the cabman whipped up the horses, and they rolled on at a gallop. There was no time to spare.

Afterwards everything happened in fast tempo; it was impossible to collect herself or to think about anything. There was the trunk that had to be weighed, the difficulty of finding a porter, the crush at the entrance to the platform. When they finally reached the train Veigaard scarcely had time to kiss her once and squeeze her hands in his. A conductor, who was slamming the doors, parted them: 'If you wish to leave, Monsieur, into the carriage with you.'

Alberta stood on the station platform. The train was already moving. Then suddenly something seemed to give way, something forced itself up, she had not said – she wanted to say that –

But she was already drowned by the noise. She saw a last smile, a wave of his hat from the rear platform. And Veigaard was gone. She was blinded by her tears.

Two days later Alberta was sitting in the Parc de Montsouris. There had been nothing in the post yesterday, nothing by the first post this morning. But it would come by a later post, the more certainly so, the longer she had to wait. Much could happen to hinder one on journeys. She felt a secure anticipation, a calm joy, which included the next moment, and the next, and the next.

A child threw its ball to her. A little surprised at herself, she caught it and threw it back.

Then they were in full swing. Alberta had never really played in her life. She had been awkward and ignored. Now she played and laughed aloud with the child. A little way off, its mother looked up from her sewing, let it fall in her lap, and watched them with smiling eyes.

PART THREE

Her hand trembling, Alberta put the book down and did not pick it up again. Some words in it had hurt her, stinging like salt in a wound. Hard, merciless, true, they had reached their target unswervingly. The words of a man, thought by a man, written by a man. They sank into her mind with painful gravity. Her heart stopped for an instant, as with all of life's shocks.

She took out other books, changed her place among the readers, turned over the pages for a while, read a few lines. They danced up and down, she did not take in their content. It was no use pretending it didn't matter. The dreadful words already lay like stones in her soul.

She started to shiver, raw cold attacked her through her coat between her shoulder-blades, a gust of the falling darkness and the lonely evening. It was closing time. A desolating stir was produced by the banging of cupboard doors, the rattling of bunches of keys, hurrying steps on the stone floor. Along the counters all the many-coloured volumes were piled up in heaps and disappeared as if by magic. The librarians' long grey coats fluttered behind them in the draught of their haste.

In a trice it was all empty, grey, deserted. Once again life had taken her by the scruff of the neck and she found herself defenceless against it. With her freezing hands clenched inside her cuffs Alberta hurried out of the Odéon arcades towards the railings of the Luxembourg Gardens and continued alongside them. The pavement glistened damply; it felt cold and glutinous through the soles of her shoes.

A bluish mist filled the Gardens. Behind the strong silhouette of the railings the tree-trunks appeared one behind the other as in a dissolving water-colour. A last remnant of yellow was left in the treetops, a hint of vanishing sunset-red hung in the air above them, light fell from a row of windows at the Senate. Untouched by trends, sentimental and traditional, the day died its quiet, natural death above the lawns. Out in the streets it was killed by the newly lighted lamps.

There was a smell of roast chestnuts and rotten leaves, petrol, perfume and damp soil. The last gladioli shone hectically under the arc-lamps round the fountain at the Rue Soufflot. Red in leaf and stem, a dark, muddy colour that contrasted violently with the clear flame of the flower, they looked as if they blossomed in fury and defiance.

People had the haste of autumn in their step, hurrying from something, to something. They seemed relieved and expectant, renewed and rejuvenated. Or they ran because they were cold, like Alberta.

Only the blind newspaper-seller fumbled slowly along the railings as usual, his back against them, holding on with one hand and stretching out the other. Quietly he mentioned from time to time the few papers he offered for sale, this year as last year, as every year. He held his head a little askew, his extinguished eyes mirrored the lamplight. No season would alter him now.

Alberta halted, looking for a tram-car. Then somebody stopped short in front of her, a small, buoyant person, who rose up on her toes as she did so: Marushka. She was dressed for autumn in new clothes. A long-stemmed rose was pinned to the white fox fur round her neck, her fur hat was set at an angle on her boyish head: ' Mademoiselle Alberta! Where have you been? What are you doing, where do you live? At Montrouge? A side-street off the Rue d'Alésia? *Mon Dieu,* what an idea! With whom are you hiding all that way out there? But you don't look well.

You're pale, you've become thinner. You're not ill, are you?
You're blushing? Why are you blushing? You don't look
happy. Surely there's nothing the matter? Seriously?'

' No, of course not,' said Alberta.

And Marushka went on to talk about something else, but
Alberta still felt her eyes on her face like two small
sympathetic searchlights. ' And Liesel? *La petite* Liesel?
No-one sees anything of her any more either. But there,
she's lost her heart to Monsieur Eliel, oh but of course,
everybody knows that.' But Marushka had heard that she
was going to Colarossi's again, and it was madness, sheer
madness, after that picture of hers at the Autumn Exhibition. It was just what Marushka had always said, Liesel
had been wading about in old impressionism until she did
not know what she was doing. Now she had managed to
shake that off this summer, and had achieved comprehen-
sion, simplification, expression : three preliminary sketches,
three colours more or less, brown, green, black, the whole
well concentrated, a little thin perhaps. Marushka had
taken several of her friends over to see Liesel's work,
people with a critical sense who understood these things,
there had been no disagreement, she has a fine talent, *la
petite*. Just the fact that she got in without any support
whatsover, just that! And then she goes back to Colarossi's
again, to that fearful dilettante milieu, among a lot of old
maids. Marushka herself had joined up with Russians,
Frenchmen, Americans, Scandinavians around a studio
down on the Boulevard des Invalides, in an old monastery
there. She would willingly try to get Liesel in there, although
it was crowded. There was comradeship there, a really
artistic atmosphere, earnestness. Everyone would certainly
do their utmost to find room for Liesel. If Alberta would
tell her so? Marushka had gone out to Eliel's place one
day, but nobody was at home, nobody had opened the
door at any rate. Liesel's picture had been hung well,
didn't Alberta think so?

But Alberta had not yet been to the Autumn Exhibition.

' Not yet? But it closes tomorrow, the fifteenth. So you

haven't seen my work either, a still life, a landscape, both of them marvellous? *Mon Dieu*, what will become of you?' Marushka shook Alberta's arm, looked at her even more searchingly, stood on tiptoe, high on her elastic insteps, strong as a dancer's: ' Listen to me! My little finger tells me there's something wrong. Don't go fretting and getting thin blood. Come up one day and we'll have a talk. It's not nice of you never to come. I'm engaged this evening, but one day soon, you will, won't you? *Au revoir, courage!*'

And Marushka was gone. Together with an athletic American-looking man she disappeared quickly down the Boul' Mich'. She turned once and waved to Alberta.

Somewhat stunned, Alberta mounted a Montrouge-Gare de l'Est. The poverty-stricken feeling she already had increased to the point of hollowness. She shrank into the woollen human warmth of the tram-car as into a shelter, and sat for a while thinking about Liesel, as one thinks about somone half forgotten. She saw her seldom, only knowing that she lived with Eliel and that it was ' *reizend* ' but difficult because it had to be kept secret. It had come about quite by itself. On their return from Brittany late one evening Liesel had driven home with Eliel to stay the night, and had been there ever since. She had spoken of the sun and the sand in Brittany, of swimming in the clear, salt water – green and translucent so that every stone could be seen on the bottom – of her picture, which had suddenly come to her, she was not quite sure how, of Eliel's sketches and of the acquaintances they had made out there, with the same over-excited brightness in her eyes, the same nervous haste. Her face had gone thinner under its freckles. They had spread from her nose in all directions this year, as last year, as every year. They disappeared in the winter. Her busy, slightly encumbered figure, weighed down with food parcels and bags of paintbrushes, stood for an instant, wide-eyed and sloping-shouldered, almost frightened-looking, before Alberta's inner eye. How was Liesel really? Then she thought: Liesel has Eliel. As long as she has Eliel . . . . And the malicious man's words that she had read at the Odéon were there again, gnawing into her further.

But when Alberta left the tram-car at Montrouge Church, there was Liesel, carrying out some kind of transaction across a cart with fish, snails, sea-urchins and crab, slow, creeping animals fighting against death. She was as usual laden with purchases and in addition was eating something which on closer inspection turned out to be a slice of Swiss cheese. Absently she looked up: ' Oh, it's you, Albertchen. I haven't seen you for ages.'

It was a crab that the fishwife was weighing in her hand. She was holding it out towards Liesel, praising its qualities. Lying on its back, its claws crumpled together over its deathly-pale stomach, it immovably awaited its fate, as the fishwife swung it up and down, assuring her: ' Heavy, full, all alive. Look!' She prodded it with spirit, making its claws stretch and crumple, stuffed it into a bag and handed it to Liesel. Then she turned to Alberta: ' And you, Madame?' A fresh crab was being weighed in her hand.

' No thank you,' said Alberta deprecatingly. ' Not if you gave it me,' she exclaimed.

' You are mistaken, quite mistaken, Madame. Crab is excellent food, nourishing food, healthy food.' The fishwife turned to another customer.

' But Liesel! What are you going to do with a crab?'

' Cook it, Albertchen. Cook it.' Liesel pushed her hat straight and took a bite of cheese.

' But we don't cook *crabs*,' said Alberta in sudden revolt. There was something unprecedented, almost degrading about this crab, there ought to be a limit to one's submission to the laws of nature.

' *Ach*,' said Liesel, ' We cook anything, Albertchen. Just you wait until your turn comes. Eliel loves crab. I bought a cooked one *chez* Hazard the other day, but it gave him stomach-ache. This time I thought . . . '

' Is that cheese you're eating, Liesel?'

Liesel stuffed the rest of the cheese quickly into her

mouth and laughed a little self-consciously. Yes, just imagine, she got an absolutely irresistible urge to eat some *Gruyère*, couldn't help buying it and eating it at once. It was a good thing it was dark and that this was Paris. All in all she had been very well in the country and now had such an appetite that it was quite embarrassing. Eliel thought it was still the effect of the sea air. But there was always something to bother one. Now Liesel had toothache, such a nuisance. She hadn't slept all night. The Austrian medical student they met at St. Jean du Doigt had written a prescription for something to hold on the tooth, but it had not helped. Perhaps Liesel would have to go to the dentist, and it was so expensive here. Could Alberta see, she was swollen on the one side?

'Be sure to go in time, Liesel,' advised Alberta somewhat mechanically. She had caught sight of a large piece of octopus amongst everything else on the handcart. The thought struck her: Yes, yes, I would have cooked crab; I would have cooked octopus if I'd had to. She felt bitterly alone beside Liesel, who was on her way home to cook crab for Eliel. She was listening through everything Liesel said for something Liesel did not say; she had been doing so throughout the autumn each time she had met her. And she listened for the same thing when Eliel spoke, and complete strangers. No-one mentioned what she was thinking of, no-one ever said they had heard anything. Once, immediately after Eliel had come home, he had asked whether that Dane had called on her, whether he had been friendly? And Alberta had answered as calmly as she could that, yes, they had gone out together a couple of times, he wasn't at all bad. Since then there had been nothing but silence. Sometimes Alberta felt as if there were a conspiracy against her, as if the whole world were in agreement not to say a word. A foolish desire to shake people – But speak out, can't you – would come over her. If she did not do so, it was because we really can remain on the verge of action for a long time without doing anything.

She remembered her conversation with Marushka and reported it. But Liesel rejected the idea. What was Alberta thinking of? Scandinavians and Russians? And Liesel, who was by no means good at hiding things, blushed and was overcome with embarrassment, giving herself away completely. Incalculable catastrophes might occur in Sweden and in Russia if rumours began to circulate. Eliel could not marry, however much he wished to. There were big Swedish grants for which married men could not apply, and naturally his art had to come first. Of course it was dilettantish and boring at Colarossi's, especially now when she really had got to grips with something, but there was no choice for the time being. It was no good working at home in the studio. Eliel never stopped turning the stand, he walked about the whole time. However Liesel placed herself, he intruded into the motif. Besides, they were in debt for yet another piece of marble, so there could be no question of renting anything. But worst of all were the days when she had to lie up in the loft.

And Liesel explained. It was if anyone came so early that she had not had time to get dressed. Eliel had many acquaintances now. Some Swedes had come to Paris this autumn, who were interested in him and thought he might get a grant. And Liesel was so tired in the morning, even though she had felt so well in the country. She could not understand why. Perhaps she had over-exerted herself with too much posing out there, at any rate it was difficult for her to get out of bed, sometimes she wished she could lie there all day, just for once. But the food had to be cooked. Some cleaning had to be done. Eliel didn't think it mattered, but Liesel could not bear it to be so dirty. The floor seeemed to dissolve into dust, breed dust. Well – so there would be a knock on the door before Liesel was up, and then she would have to *stay* there. But it was such a strain. She had to be as quiet as a mouse. She was afraid, afraid of sneezing, for instance. Sometimes they would stay for hours. Once a whole crowd came, decided they would fetch a model, and sketched from nine to twelve. That was one of the days when Liesel had had toothache. She couldn't say anything, it wasn't Eliel's fault, after all. Besides, he would only suggest that she move back to the hotel again, that it would be best for them both. But Alberta would understand that she didn't want to do that. She looked up eagerly: 'It seems more devoted when we *live* together, more natural, don't you think?'

'Yes,' said Alberta.

In spite of Liesel's tribulations she felt infintely poor by comparison. When Liesel, with a final, somewhat uncertain, 'You'll come and see us soon, won't you, Albertchen?' collected her paper bags more firmly about her and went, the street at once took on a hostile and evil appearance, and all the passers-by seemed rootless and homeless.

Alberta's street looked sinister after dark. There was only just sufficient lighting; but it was not dangerous. The people who lived here were not bad people. It was simply that none of them had been successful.

Madame Caux looked searchingly out of her window. She had enteritis and the swollen stomach that accompanies it. There was always a half-empty milk bottle in her vicinity, and her eyes were gentle and long-suffering. She had had a kind of liking for Alberta from the very first, treating her obligingly and with kindness, in spite of the fact that she demanded of her a certain amount of equanimity where the unavoidable dispensations of providence were concerned, bugs and draughts, for instance. Madame Caux had a couple of standard answers for those who complained: 'Well, even if there are a couple of creatures here, we can't very well tear the house down. You must be more careful about shutting the window, *ma petite.*'

On every landing there burned a naked gas jet. It flickered forlornly, spreading a light as wretched as charity. It did not conceal that the jute on the walls was torn and flapped in the draught, but seemed placed precisely in order

395

to illuminate the gravest damage. At every turn of the stairs one was met by it as by a symbol of grudgingly shared out goods.

The air thickened on the top floors. It was stored up here as in all houses and had received an additional contribution of the stronger exhalations of working people. As soon as Alberta came up she had to open the window. In a favourable wind the autumn fog streamed damply up towards her from the fortifications and the country beyond. If it was less favourable, the smoke from adjoining chimneys was blown in, thick and visible as at a railway station.

She reached her small, ugly room.

The tablecloth was green, a piece of thick woollen material Alberta had bought cheaply at the Bon Marché together with the table, the chair, the mattress on legs. To avoid the junk shop she had foregone all hint of elegance. The objects stood reduced, so to speak, to their original idea of simplicity. But in the evening the green tablecloth acquired an unexpected significance one would not have believed possible. When the candle was lighted in its candlestick, its scanty gleam included scarcely anything besides this; it seemed unable to reach any farther. And the objects on the table which could not be put anywhere else, the inkwell, the blotter, the box with writing paper in it, acquired an uncomfortably predominant aspect.

She would find herself sitting looking at them. There was nothing else at which to look. The window-panes were full of darkness. The walls enclosed her at a pace's distance, dark brown, heavy in colour, as if they were trying to force the eye back to the table. The framed reproductions that Alberta had hung up only reflected the candle-flame. Nothing singled itself out, everything was too close. The pottery jug stood empty and desolate in a corner on the floor for lack of space.

So it usually ended in Alberta sitting at this green table, as if taken by the scruff of the neck and placed there. She assembled lines, crossed them out and tore them up. Letters she would not think of sending materialized under her hands, a confused collection of words, which tumbled over one another on their way up from hidden places in her mind. And brief, bitterly polite notes, a mere couple of sentences, an address, a greeting, an initial below.

She never sent them. She had sent two. First, a letter, then a brief note. She had felt faint when she posted them. It had seemed to her that she was writing to a complete stranger, or to a figment of her imagination, or that she was perhaps a little mad. No reply had come to either of them. Nothing ever came. She could equally well stand up and call out of the window, out into the night. It would be just as effective, and less bitterly humiliating.

Every day the time came when she had to go home to all this. The Odéon, the museums and the libraries closed. She could not continually sit in churches. The street became damp and raw. And even if she still considered all possible eventualities, sickness, catastrophes, lost letters, and did foolish things as if under hypnosis, running to the *poste-restante* window time after time, even though the woman behind it had long ago started to look at her sympathetically as at someone deranged, taking the Métro over to the Avenue du Roule, sitting on a bench there staring up at a row of windows, the evening set a limit even to this. She sat there feeling a stab each time she caught sight of a sign of life up there. A hand would draw the curtains across, the electric light would be switched on here, switched off there, someone's shadow glide behind the panes. Or a lady would come out of the street door. She might be anyone from the large building. She might also be . . .

Alberta struggled with a desperate and stupid desire to run after her, speak to her, *take hold of her*. A fearful and mysterious attraction seemed to emanate from her. And yet she did not even look the same all the time, being sometimes fair, sometimes dark, sometimes young, sometimes old, now and again elegant, now and again simply dressed like a servant. One day she was holding a child by the hand, another, two small dogs on a leash. Once Alberta was compelled to hurry past her and run back again in order to see her face, but she was wearing a veil, and it was already dusk. One day two ladies came out of the door together, and Alberta felt the same about them both, searching hungrily for something in the walk, in the stature of both of them.

Whatever the appearance of this lady, when she vanished from sight, took a cab, mounted a tram-car, went into a shop or down the Métro, she took Alberta's vitality with her. She felt she could not be bothered to drag herself home again. For her too, she had words on her lips, which died unborn, lay in her mind and turned to poison.

Sometimes Alberta would feel that the concentrated agony she continually carried within her must be able to work miracles. The thought that now, in a second, something would happen, that the whole thing was really only a delusion and a nighmare, obsessed her. In a waiting attitude she would raise her head, hold her breath, stare as if magnetized towards the door. But the door did not move. Nothing came fluttering in underneath it, no gliding square of paper, rustling a little as it did so.

And the pain would be there again, like a sword along the spine. Mortification and anxiety and regret crept interlaced through her mind like cold snakes. She wept painful, tearless sobs, wretched and smarting, a grimace merely; a caricature of the liberating stream that cleanses the mind and from which one rises assuaged, even perhaps born anew.

In all her veins there beat an urgent, all-embracing hunger for warmth. The words forced themselves up towards her lips and insisted on being spoken, she whispered them, dry as if from thirst. Memories lay in her, a kind of futuristic picture. She saw a chin, a slightly crooked mouth, two eyes, a hand, a hat. A hat! She saw it out in the darkness and was not always quite certain how far the limits of reality went.

Occasionally footsteps would approach down the passage outside, and stop outside her door. They were no miracle.

They belonged to Sivert Ness. He was the only person who had come to see her since she moved there.

He would sit on the divan, broad-shouldered and squat, looking across the floor as he spoke, with one composed, loosely-clenched hand lying on his knee. His thick country clothes smelled of homespun cloth in the autumn rain. Now and then he would look up, and the gleam would come into his eyes, a gleam Alberta scarcely noticed any more. He sat there, at any rate, and helped her through an hour of miserable loneliness; and she had to give him his due and listen to him abstractedly.

Sivert was always tackling something or other. With a small phrase-book sticking up out of his pocket he used all the free time he allowed himself for seeing the sights. He did not wander round in a desultory fashion, like Alberta, but went nosing after all kinds of museums and collections, including those that artists seldom visit, coming from the Hôtel des Monnaies, the Musée de la Marine, or the motor and machinery collections. The latter had been an accidental discovery. ' I couldn't believe my eyes,' said Sivert. ' I suddenly found myself in the middle of a lot of boats. Splendid things. Models of everything you could think of, from three-masters under full sail to ironclads, old and new all mixed up together. I must admit I didn't know such things existed in the Louvre. I'm going there again. If there's anything I enjoy looking at, it's ships.' Pleased with himself, he struck his fist into the palm of his strong hand.

Sivert's other news was that he had sold pictures at the State Exhibition at home that autumn. It had made him even more composed, and a little more prosperous-looking, but not much. He still wore his home-made clothes and affected no Spanish cloak. But he admitted that he was thinking about a winter coat. And he had bought himself a stove, had got it cheaply from the junk shop down the street. It had been there all last winter too, but then he had not been able to consider it. Now he was busy walling it in. It would be a nice bit of work when it was finished, it would be pleasant to get up in the morning even when it was cold outside. Otherwise it was awful in winter in these studios built directly on to the earth, he had thought he would rot last year, it had rained so much.

It began to dawn on Alberta that Sivert was really a sailor. She could clearly imagine him in blue shore-leave clothes and a cloth cap, imagine him jumping from thwart to thwart in a boat, casting off, applying himself to a pair of oars so that the water boiled round them. It seemed all wrong that he should be here in Paris, wearing a hat and occupied with painting. However, it was easy to imagine him sitting in his leisure hours like sailors on ocean journeys, patient, infinitely strong in his patience, making elaborate sailing ships inside bottles, or embroidering blankets and cushions with two crossed flags and flowers. Everything about him that was practical and self-supporting, the underwear and socks that he told her he mended and washed himself, his thickset, four-square shoulders, the short, strong legs, all were those of a sailor.

His clothes were confusing, wrongly giving the impression that he was a countryman. But these too were explained. One evening Sivert took out a little photograph to show Alberta. She saw an ordinary white country house with attics and a veranda. It had been taken a little crookedly. An elderly man was standing at the bottom of the steps, on which two women were sitting. Sivert pointed : ' That's Father, there's Mother, there's Otilie.'

Alberta politely attempted to distinguish the faces, but gave up. The picture was so small. She could see that his father had a long beard and both women smooth, parted hair, the older with a kerchief tied under her chin. The farm was called Granli, explained Sivert : ' Quite an ordinary name. But there are in fact some fir trees about that didn't get into the picture. Father was a sailor before he started farming. Mother comes from farther up country, from Land.'

The homespun clothes, thought Alberta.

' They're a bit pious at home,' said Sivert apologetically, putting the picture back in his wallet.

' Oh?' said Alberta.

They talked besides of Liesel and of how she had got into the exhibition. Sivert could not believe this was anything more than an accident. Yes, the picture was good, he would never have believed Liesel could have produced it, but now we'll see, he said, ' Ladies ... '. Besides, Sivert had to admit that he thought it must be a bit strange for Eliel. Liesel's picture had been very well hung, but Eliel's sculpture was hidden away in a corner.

Alberta suggested somewhat indifferently that Eliel might be sufficiently gallant to be pleased about it. ' He ought to be,' she said.

' Yes, I suppose so. Of course. But all the same ... ' Sivert stared thoughtfully across the floor as if trying to put himself in Eliel's place.

He left early. He had to go and wall up the stove. As soon as it was ready he would begin working with a model. ' It's hellishly expensive, but there's no help for it.' And he was gone. And there was nothing for it but to go to bed.

But when the noise of the street died away, a new world seemed to come alive around her. From every joint in the large house came noises she had not heard before, which awoke with the darkness. Through the thin walls, beneath the badly-fitting doors, they filtered out unhindered, collecting in the stairwell as in a canal and vibrating further in one's every nerve. Scolding, and the cries of small children, sudden flickers of conversation, the anguished moaning of women caressed by men and sometimes struck by them, the creaking of beds. An occasional loud comment, meant to be heard : ' And in the presence of children! People ought to be ashamed!'

Alberta attempted to hold on to the flickering patterns that form behind the eyeballs when one shuts one's eyes hard. The patterns shift, growing out of each other, colour within colour, whorl within whorl, figure within figure. She glimpsed landscapes, animals. Strange, unearthly flowers

exploded in the darkness, the one out of the other, snakes
writhed about each other. It was beautiful or frightening,
according to how it turned out, a fantastic primeval world,
hidden within reality, visible when one looks inwards.

Until all of a sudden she sat upright on the divan, her
heart hammering, staring hungrily at the door.

* * *

' I don't know what else to do, Alphonsine.'

Alphonsine removed her pince-nez, rubbed the lenses,
and sat holding them between two fingers, with one elbow
leaning on her knee, staring in front of her.

Pince-nez did not suit Alphonsine, they seemed irrelevant
to her person. Alberta was never convinced that Alphonsine's were anything more than a toy made of ordinary
glass, an amusing little object she happened to possess.
They were, however, real. She also had a case, in which she
placed them with care. Now she tapped with it thoughtfully: ' To be frank, it's no life for you, *ma petite.*'

' But Alphonsine, I must live.'

' Of course you must live. That's exactly what you ought
to do, *live.*' And Alphonsine got up, suddenly put her hand
under Alberta's chin and turned her face up towards her:
' Do you know that you are of an age when one is supposed
to be happy, *ma petite*? All this is stupidity. You live in a
hole.'

' I beg your pardon, Alphonsine?'

' A hole. I don't at all like the way you live. Why have
you left Montparnasse and your friends? Only yesterday
Madame Marushka asked: " Have you seen anything of
the little Norwegian girl?" She had met you at the Luxembourg Gardens, and you had promised to go and see her.
But you don't go. She asked after Mademoiselle Liesel too.
I said nothing. I never say anything. But Marcelle, you
know, my friend Marcelle, was out at Monsieur Eliel's one
day to find out if he needed her. She posed for him last
year. Well, she knocked, she heard someone run up the

steps to the loft just as the door was opened. She came in, Monsieur Eliel was alone. But that brooch was lying on a chair – you know, the one Mademoiselle Liesel always wears, a cameo – and on the steps up to the loft there was a garter! And in the middle of the floor a clay figure, an enormous contraption, the kind Monsieur Eliel always does, female, with shoulders *comme ça*, like a Botticelli. And Marcelle, she is a tease, Marcelle, she can never leave anyone alone, she said: '*Eh bien* Monsieur Eliel, you are managing without a female model at present. You are satisfied with small details that remind you of women, small hints, so to say. That's clever.' She pointed at the brooch and the garter. And Monsieur Eliel, who is not very quick-witted, went as red as a turkey-cock. It was a little unfair of Marcelle, but Madame Marushka laughed heartily when she heard about it. But there, we all hope she is happy, *la petite* Liesel, since she loves Monsieur Eliel. But you! You wouldn't hear a whisper from me if you were living with a man. But to go and install yourself like that among working folk – oh, I know they're good people – but all the same, a milieu that is not yours. Why on earth do you want to live out there?'

'But,' began Alberta. 'In the first place it's cheap. Twelve francs a month, Alphonsine, twelve. Then it's not far from Eliel and Liesel. And I have nothing against seeing different aspects of life.'

'You don't need to look there for the aspects of life that should interest you first and foremost at your age. You have education and a good upbringing. Yes, yes, yes, anyone can see you come from a respectable home. I don't know much, but at least I understand that. And among those people out there ...'

'But I have nothing to do with them, Alphonsine. I only live there.'

'But you ought to have something to do with someone. I've been saying so for a long time. Another cup of tea?'

Alberta looked up from the Oriental pattern of one of the cushions on Alphonsine's divan. She was lying on her elbow tracing the same whorl with her finger, a whorl that again and again led her back to the beginning, continually growing out of and back on itself.

' Yes, please.'

Alphonsine poured it out of the big silver plated teapot, put three lumps of sugar in it, which she knew Alberta liked, and pushed the biscuits closer. ' Get some strength. You look as if you need it!'

Alberta already had the winter's lurking sensation of influenza in her body. It came with the autumn fogs. She was perpetually cold and could never swill down enough cups of tea, as hot as possible. She took several large gulps, then raised her eyes and met Alphonsine's above the cup. And suddenly the tears were flowing down her face, silently, without a sound or a sob, but impossible to hold back. Embarrassed she fumbled for her handkerchief.

' *Voyons!*' said Alphonsine. ' *Voyons!*'

But Alberta was at the point when the barricades fall. Smiling bitterly through her tears she quoted : ' *Les femmes s'attachent aux hommes par les faveurs qu'elles leur accordent. Les hommes – guérissent – par les mêmes faveurs.*'

Alphonsine had put her head on one side. Amazement was written in her face. Alberta's tears still flowed copiously.

' What's all this?' asked Alphonsine at last. ' A quotation?'

' It's from La Bruyère.'

' La Bruyère? Is it now? He is not so stupid, Monsieur La Bruyère.' Alphonsine strummed with her fingers on the table as if to gain time. Then she said : ' Has someone made you unhappy, *ma petite*?'

' He never writes, Alphonsine.' Alberta twisted her sopping wet handkerchief round her fingers, feeling as if she were tearing something to pieces, something secret, holy, flaying it and throwing it away in shreds. But she could not stop herself.

'And what about you? Do you write?' Alphonsine seemed to be searching. Her voice was cautious.

'No – I mean, I have written.'

'Hm. Perhaps you should do so again.'

'No, Alphonsine.'

'And there was no misunderstanding, no disagreement?'

That was the good thing about Alphonsine, she kept to the point and asked no more than was absolutely necessary. It was as if she knew all life's alternatives and only needed small clues to clarify them. She did not assume that one had no brains and did not give advice at random. Now she seemed to hesitate: 'Are you sure the fault does not lie in yourself? Men take offence easily, they have much self-esteem. If their masculine dignity is hurt ... '

'There was no misunderstanding at the end,' said Alberta. 'That was only at the beginning. He wanted to take me back to his own country ... '.

'And you did not want to go?'

'No, yes, of course, I mean ... we could have been so happy here, Alphonsine. But finally I nearly agreed to ... '.

'Was it America?' asked Alphonsine.

'No. Not as far away as that.'

'Well, well, console yourself, *ma petite*. If he is fond of you ... '

'He has been married before, Alphonsine. He was divorced.'

'Oh,' said Alphonsine, and became serious.

Then Alberta felt her face shrink. Something inside her was just as ready, in spite of everything, to crumple up and wither as to unfurl itself and blossom. It must have been hope, imperishable hope. Now it suddenly became microscopic, and Alberta shrank with it.

Alphonsine patted her on the cheek: '*Courage*! If there's anything to him, he'll turn up again. Besides, we don't know what's the matter, it might be any one of a number of things. And if he doesn't, then another will. That's life, *ma petite*, that's how it is.'

No-one will come, insisted a voice inside Alberta. Life

405

is over, death is all that's left. But Alphonsine continued:
'One does not die of an unhappy love affair. *Bon Dieu*, I
should have died many times! It is hard while it lasts,
but it passes. Well, well, so you are abandoned and
penniless. It is much all at once.'

'Yes,' said Alberta.

Alphonsine flicked the ash off her cigarette: 'Mr. Digby
is not in Paris. You don't want to go on the streets or
turn on the gas, and you are right. What about your
fellow-countrymen?'

'Ness is the only one I know.'

'You avoid them. There's a whole crowd of them on
Montparnasse. It is not wise of you to keep away like that.
Look at the Russians, they stick together, they help each
other. None of them go about lonely as you northerners do.
I know types ... '

'Yes, I know,' said Alberta, a little fatigued. 'It takes so
long to explain, Alphonsine, how small Norway is, how
careful you have to be to avoid rumours getting home, how
one loathes the way one lived there and would rather put
up with anything than be forced back into it again.'

'And you can't work? Put something together for the
newspapers?'

'Not now, Alphonsine. I can't think. It's as if I were
dead,' said Alberta with sudden candour.

'*Pauvre petite.* I shall have to find something for you,
since you insist. A respectable type, with whom you will
run no risks. To start with we shall have to cheer you up
a little. You are alone too much, go out too seldom.
Tomorrow evening you're coming with me and my friend
to the Gaité Montparnasse. It's not like the Folies Bergère,
but the artistes can be good. And my friend is a good fellow.
You will be doing us a pleasure if you come.'

Alphonsine always spent Saturday to Monday with her
friend. The rest of the week he worked in an automobile
factory at the other end of town. He was a mechanic. 'A
mechanic,' said Alphonsine. 'You know where you are with
him. The artists, they come and go, they love here and

love there, believe it is necessary for the sake of their art and call it temperament. They are nervous and difficult, they have even more self-esteem than the rest of them. I've finished with artists in that respect. There are good types amongst them, I don't deny it, *mais enfin . . .* '

Alberta hesitatingly expressed her fear of being a nuisance. She was given the same unaffected reply as always: ' *Que voulez-vous,* Mademoiselle? I have a kind heart.'

* * *

Alphonsine's friend smoked a pipe. This made Alberta a little miserable from the start. His nose looked as if it had been through some accident; it looked like a boxer's. But he was sedate, dependable and dressed in his Sunday best, with hair that lay in little curls on the nape of his neck.

Alphonsine introduced Alberta as ' one of my little artists who needs a bit of starch '.

Monsieur Louis took the pipe out of his mouth and laughed genially: ' One must not take life too seriously and let oneself get thin blood.' And he gave a little lecture on this calamity.

Alphonsine supported him. ' There, you see, Mademoiselle. Learn from the men, they know the art of taking life easily.'

The Rue de la Gaieté smelt of pancakes, potatoes in oil, chestnuts. Hissing fat spluttered, cinematograph bells chimed, gramophones buzzed. A continuous stream of faces came towards one along the pavement, looking hard under the sharp lights of the bars and the *variétés*: red, white, black, tired eyes, brazen eyes, against a restless background of variegated posters. A tram-car advanced slowly, ceaselessly ringing its bell, through the noisy, nervous Saturday evening crowds.

Alphonsine had booked seats in the pit. Cramped and confined between her and Monsieur Louis, who unceasingly

407

did his best, smiling at Alberta at every witticism, having evidently promised himself that she was not to be allowed to sink into melancholy for an instant, Alberta struggled against a boundless feeling of loneliness. Wherever she looked in the packed little theatre in which the air hung stiff with powder, dust and tobacco, and the smell peculiar to old theatres, people were sitting in pairs. When she caught sight of a woman who looked as if she were sitting by herself a few seats in front of her, all female loneliness seemed to engulf her. The reserved, slightly discouraging, unaccompanied lady, the one whom nobdy meets when she alights from a train or goes down a gangplank, who looks round her for a porter when others are surrounded by expectant friends – she who, in a railway carriage or a tram-car, cannot take her eyes off the babbling, laughing child on a strange mother's knee, who bends down to pat an animal on the road because her hands never receive caresses, and are restless from their vain search for something to enfold – oh, Alberta recognized her now, knew who she was, distinguished her without difficulty from the others. She had never seen her before.

Simultaneously the performance on the stage seemed to be ploughing deep furrows in her mind. The sentimental singer in evening dress, who sang of moonshine and couples walking two by two, the innocent young girl who attempted burlesque and was whistled off the stage because she irremediably descended into vulgarity, the man who imitated Polin and sang soldiers' songs, and the one who imitated Chevalier and sang topicalities: behind it all, the good as well as the bad, life's tragedy lay bleeding. Alberta would have preferred to weep when the laughter rang round her.

The star turn was the woman who sang about the apache in a deep, slightly rusty alto. She had a simple black dress, hair hanging about her ears, a large red mouth, slanting eyes. A sigh of expectation went through the audience.

The apache's tricks in deceiving the police, his slave-owner relationship with his sweetheart, his bloody deeds

in poorly lighted suburbs, his meeting with the guillotine
one morning in the dawn outside the La Santé jail. The
prostitute's contempt for the men who pay her, her hatred
of the lady who passes by, her savage tenderness for the
man who comes home with blood on his sleeve knowing
that all is up with him, her loneliness the morning his head
falls, and she sees nothing, only hears the roar of the crowd.
Brutal and naive romanticism, anything but original, the
period's species of cheap romance. But it expressed simply
and truthfully human defiance and human passion, tenderness and boldness, rawness, sentimentality and fierce,
primitive philosophy. When the singer, her hand on her hip,
finally slung out her last refrain, ' *Je m'en fous, de tout* ', it
came from the heart and went to the heart. The audience
stamped in ecstasy and the dust rose.

Monsieur Louis leaned over towards Alberta and Alphonsine : ' *Eh bien* – either you like this *genre* or you don't.
Some people lap it up.'

Alberta had lapped it up. Her mind was like a ploughed
field, utterly uncritical. Anything whatsover with a message
from life was accepted by it as by fertile soil, but now it
affected her differently from before, as new and fearful
tragedy.

On the way home Monsieur Louis offered them a drink at
the big café on the corner. The violent white light made
their faces hard and lined, as if harrowed. In the mirror-
lined walls around her Alberta could see various versions
of herself, full profile, semi-profile, full-face and from
behind. They all looked pathetic and windblown. She could
not let herself look like that, so cowed and miserable.
Involuntarily she straightened her back, talked, smiled and
drank a toast with Monsieur Louis.

' There, you feel better now, don't you? It gives you
something to think about to come out, even though it
isn't the opera?' Monsieur Louis left no stone unturned in
his attempts to cheer her up, telling her stories about his
military service and discoursing to her on the disadvantages

of living alone. It was not natural, as she perhaps knew and could easily imagine, not good for the health, not salutary: correct, simply stated facts with which Alberta had to agree. Alphonsine nodded approval. She sat with one elbow on the table, sipping the drink she was holding, looking round her with calm, green eyes that seemed to have seen through everything, understood everything and forgiven everything. She looked surprisingly bourgeois in a big skunk collar and she was not smoking.

Both of them accompanied Alberta to her door. It turned out that the staircase light had been extinguished long ago, and Alphonsine decreed that Louis should accompany Alberta with his torch. She would wait in the doorway. She kissed Alberta good-night on the cheek: 'Now you will sleep, won't you? Right through till morning? Like a good little girl.'

Making cheerful conversation, Monsieur Louis escorted Alberta upstairs, exclaiming *zut* and walking on tiptoe on the landings to emphasize his consideration for the sleeping inhabitants of the house, remaining with the light while Alberta searched for the keyhole.

He shook her hand heartily in farewell and assured her that it had been a great pleasure, then swung down the stairs in great leaps. Alberta heard the door open and shut behind him and Alphonsine. And nothing could alter the bitter fact that they were leaving together and were two, while Alberta was only one. Small and cold at heart she fumbled for the matches.

Everybody was two: Alphonsine and Louis, Liesel and Eliel, the apache and his girl, Marushka and – someone or other.

Alberta sat down on the divan. From old habit she tucked her hands up into her sleeves and remained sitting thus, hunched and drooping, lacking the energy to undress. Refrains flooded through her, entered her blood, danced witch dances in her brain, mingled with the noises of the house which were gradually reaching her, and resulted in a bitter brew of defiance, dejection and desperation.

Since La Bruyère's hurtful words had settled in her mind
she had not written a line, not even in order to tear them
up again. An empty paralysis could seize her for long
periods at a time, spreading into her arms and hands. Her
limbs would turn to lead, her brain to fog behind her
forehead. In a kind of dull amazement she remembered
times when adversity had cut into her as sharply as toothache, becoming an aching spot, localized and fierce, or a
throbbing fever throughout her body. She had had small
childish worries: something she had done wrong, the rent
that hung over her head, the *épicier* who had reminded her
of what she owed him, anxiety for the morrow. And further
back in time the worries of others, the sorrows of adults
that can devastate a child before the skin has formed on
its soul. It had all expressed itself as something frightful
and acute. But beneath the dreadful thought had existed
others, which sooner or later would push it aside and
come to the top. Hope, the untiring, again put out surface
roots into nowhere, in spite of everything. The pain could
not go on for ever, nor did it.

This evening she seemed to recognize that everything
comes to an end, even pain. It burns itself out finally. One
dies of it, or it passes out of one's system like an ache that
is over. All that is left is a calcification in the mind, a hard
scar, that cannot be affected again.

For the first time for a long period Alberta supposed she
had better see about doing something, pulling herself
together, quite apart from what Alphonsine could find for
her.

Suddenly she stiffened. Someone was outside her door,
close up against it. She felt rather than heard the proximity
of a person who was standing, then noiselessly shifted his
position and went on standing. Clothes brushed almost
unnoticeably along the wall. Appalled, Alberta seized the
key, holding it tight with both hands. The large, hostile
house around her was at once frighteningly full of dangers
against which she felt herself to be powerless.

Then a furious whispering began outside, the voices

threatening time and again to break out into normal speech, and again dropping to a whisper. Then they exploded into a noisy exchange of violent abuse:

' Old criminal!'

' Old camel!'

' Pig!'

' Cow!'

A door was hurriedly closed, a key turned in the lock. A moment of deep silence followed this most wicked and extreme of all French terms of abuse. The person who had said it was already in safety. Now the other party called with all her strength on heaven and the inhabitants of the house to witness that the fearful word had been spoken.

Farther down the corridor doors opened and shut. Assurances that the old idiots would be thrown out, that the scandal had gone on long enough, that it was someone's intention to inform the watchman, the manager, the commissioner of police, rent the air. A woman's voice called out emphatically: ' Old shit. Garbage!' A man's exclaimed with dignity: ' Be so good as to be silent, Mesdames. It is almost midnight.'

Alberta opened her door a crack.

On the opposite side of the corridor stood a man in his nightshirt, trousers and slippers, shielding his candle to protect it from the draught. In the room behind him someone was coughing lengthily and tearingly. The commotion was subsiding with an after-swell of scandalized muttering behind the doors farther along.

The man gave Alberta a melancholy smile: ' It is your neighbours to the right and left, Mademoiselle, two poor old women who are a little ... ' and he pointed significantly at his forehead. ' They compete with each other in listening at your door and peeping through your keyhole, this evening it has been really shocking. It's nothing to be afraid of, but it's very annoying. They've woken my wife too, and I had just got her to sleep. She is not well, unfortunately.' The tearing cough came again from behind him.

Alberta murmured something sympathetic, expressing

the hope that Madame would be able to sleep again and that she would get well. The man gave her the same melancholy smile, and Alberta suddenly shivered as if chilled by frost.

But once behind her closed door she felt something brace itself in her mind, a furious reluctance to go under, to perish in filth, cold and loneliness. In our innermost being there is a tough sinew that binds us to life. In the last resort everything depends on that. It can fairly beckon to us, flash in the darkness. Alberta was sensible of it now. She *would* have warmth and joy and find them for herself, as best she could.

*   *   *

Alberta was woken by the water-tap farther along the passage. There was a shuffling of slippers along the tiled floor, the tap was turned on violently for a moment. There was a shuffling again. In a little while the tap started running once more.

Madame Bourdarias was fetching water in a bucket; the jet of water slammed against the bottom of it. The old women on either side of Alberta fetched theirs in a scoop or a jug, something that filled quickly and overflowed. The doors banged continually. There was a succession of hurried footsteps going to a certain place. The plug was pulled, but it never worked properly the first time. It was pulled with increasing irritation. Finally the water crashed down.

Through the mansard window Alberta could see the sky. ' There you are,' Madame Caux had said, when she threw open the door for the first time. ' Look at the view, breathe the fresh air. This is much better than the lower floors. I'd much rather live here than on the first or second floor, *si* Mademoiselle.' And Madame Caux threw out her breast and inhaled eagerly. ' Much better than downstairs. And nobody above your head, no clattering heels when you wish to sleep, no piano late at night. Only quiet people who have their work to do and go to bed early. Twelve francs a month, almost gratis.'

Under the window stood her trunk with her books on top of it, difficult to get into. A closed coffin.

The sloping roof was so low that she could only stand upright close to the one wall; but if she absolutely had to stand, she could do so. Tired of looking for the cheapest possible room, Alberta had taken it.

Outside it was pouring with rain. A raw wintry draught was blowing between the window and the crack under the door. Shivering, Alberta plucked up courage and splashed herself with water while the spirit stove whistled.

There were the concierge's footsteps along the passage. She paused. Yet again she looked through the pile of letters. There was a rustling down by the floor. Something was being put under one of the doors, a voice called, ' Thank you, Madame Caux '. The footsteps advanced, and again stopped. From unbroken habit Alberta held her breath, her coffee-cup trembling so much that she had to put it down. But the footsteps continued, heavy, slightly dragging.

So Alberta did what had to be done if she did not want to fall into utter decrepitude and become like the old character who had had the room before her, and of whom legends were told in the house. He never made his bed, the room was a nest of fleas. He was lonely and suspicious and allowed no-one in until one day Madame Caux reported him to the Poor Relief, and they came and took him away.

Alberta aired and tidied, fetched water to wash the tiny floor, pretending to herself that it was important.

The usual bloodstains led from Madame Bourdarias's door to the water-tap. It hurt Alberta to see them; she felt as if stabbed with an awl in her sensitive parts. A person could be as destroyed as Madame Bourdarias and still stay alive. The first time Alberta had noticed the red drops on the floor she had thought: Someone has cut his finger; the second time: it must be someone who suffers from nose-bleeds.

The third time she drew Madame Bourdarias's attention to the horrible stains; she was the only person she knew, and she had just arrived with her bucket. A quick flush had spread over the thin face with the kind, patient eyes, the voice begged indulgence: ' It is I, Mademoiselle, it is I. I assure you I do what I can, but as soon as I take hold of anything, lift something, it happens just the same. At the hospital they say I must stay in bed, they want to keep me there. But what would happen to my children, Mademoiselle?'

Alberta stood rooted to the spot, searching for something to say, finding nothing. Madame Bourdarias was back at once with a cloth to wipe the floor: ' The worst of it is the young people in the house. The thought of them troubles me. It doesn't help much to clean it up, see here. And one becomes modest as one gets older, Mademoiselle. Just as modest as when one was growing up.'

Alberta was alone again, shocked as if she had witnessed an act of cruelty. The next day she had made an awkward attempt to carry the bucket for Madame Bourdarias. A thin red hand, hard and rough, pushed her own away from the handle: ' I have four children of school age, Mademoiselle, and I help in three households. One bucket of water more or less ... '. And Alberta saw the naive, almost unnecessary intrusiveness of her action.

She had lived up here as one must with something that is more than one can bear, holding her breath and with her eyes shut. The red patches on the floor, the cough from the room across the passage, the man who lived there with his sad smile, always carrying something, milk bottles and dripping packages of food or long rolls of drawing paper, his skin yellow-white as silk above the black beard – these things had of course hurt her, as the whipped horse on the street did, or the ragged beggar with his outstretched hand. She remembered for a while, then thought about something else.

She had scarcely noticed the two elderly women who were her neighbours. With faded hair, clothes, eyes, on terms of enmity with each other and the whole house, strangely alike, they padded about like grey shadows, as frightening as everything life leaves behind unused. They reminded her of dusty old objects that nobody wants any more. It probably would not have surprised her if one day she had found them set aside in a corner out there.

Now it had all become horribly tangible. She looked round her room as if it were a chamber of horrors. And for the first time for a long period she again considered ways of escape.

There was really only one. She must see about writing something again. Even if Alphonsine found what she called a respectable type, it would be no use Alberta presenting herself just now. She looked like pictures she had seen of famine areas in India. Her ribs resembled a comb, her shoulder-blades protruded from her back like two abortive little wings. Her collar-bones, her childhood affliction, again stood out in relief. She was shockingly thin.

And now her body demanded food. Voracity suddenly possessed her. When she thought about it, it was quite a long time since she had eaten properly or even considered what she ate. What had she picked at recently? *Pommes frites,* boiled beans, chestnuts, spinach, bread. In her imagination she saw large plates of hot soup, steaming portions of meat. Her coat was thin, her shoes barely possible, her sandals out of the question in winter.

She owed money everywhere. In the dairy, at the *Epicerie* and the bakery. Soon it would be the rent. And panic seized her. Life had taken her by the scruff of the neck again, and was shaking her hard.

It was no use surveying her belongings. She owned nothing that would be accepted in pawn except the mattress on legs. Quite apart from other discomforts resulting from the transaction, her reputation in the house would sink to below zero if she allowed it to be carried away. It was unthinkable.

She would have to write again and borrow in the meantime, scrape material together as best she could, trim it and send it off. It had worked before, it ought to work now. Blue with cold, her fingers stiff, she set to, out of practice and reluctant, attempting to find the smallest thread that lay, thin and miserable, hidden somewhere in her mind. She ought to be able to tell the person from whom she was going to borrow that this was her article, here it was in her hand. In a few days the fee would arrive.

Instinctively she sought out the pleasant moments in the life about her, remembered the occasional glimpses she had had of Madame Bourdarias's room in the evening where four children, well cared-for and respectable, happily saved from all adversity, sat gathered round the steaming soup tureen on the red check tablecloth; while the enormous pitchpine bed, and the huge hanging lamp which all the poorer classes in Paris acquire as soon as they are able, seemed to fill the room. She included too the slender, clear-eyed young woman farther along the passage, the one from Auvergne, who always carried her baby in her arms and was always singing to it; monotonous, repetitious melodies, peasant airs to which one automatically beats time. That was the sort of thing people liked to read on Sunday afternoons after coffee, they liked above all idyllic scenes and the pleasant side of life. For a moment Alberta considered bringing in the bloodstains, but resolutely skirted them and contented herself with implying depravity in the character of the eldest Bourdarias, who was at the hobbledehoy stage and a worry to his mother. He always left a whiff of cigarette-smoke and an echo of ' *Quand l'Amour Meurt* ' in the composite atmosphere of the corridor.

The *épicier*? His colourful still-life on the pavement down in the depths brightened the grey street. It produced rather cheap effects, but was a relief for the eye. And it provided an opportunity for word-painting in a way that might give rise to an encouraging little remark in the editor's reply: ' Your last article was very entertaining. We look forward with pleasure to more from your pen.'

Cabbage, carrots, fresh wet lettuce, apples, oranges, eggs coloured with carmine, blue grapes, golden-yellow marrows; and as a realistic, but not too shocking addition, his trade in living and dead rabbits, small furry animals that he kept in crates under the tables outside. They nibbled lettuce, sitting on their haunches with one paw uplifted, snuffing the air with mobile, anxious noses. But fate plays with life and death, the *épicier* would come for them. He would look up and down the street, whistling and chatting with the passers-by while he squatted down and fumbled with his hand in the crate. And he hauled out a portion of life, a cowering bundle of terrified nerves suspended from two long ears, and disappeared with it into the darkness of the shop. Straightaway he was back again with a corpse, the thinnest, most pathetic of all small corpses, a flayed rabbit. He added it to his exhibition.

Here Alberta suddenly stopped. Paralysed by the superficiality, the one-sidedness and cheapness of her account, she sat, despondent to the core, hollow with cold and incompetence. She tore up what she had written and put on her coat. Liesel and Eliel were in for it. It was imperative that she have proper food. She went out into the drizzle.

From the outset it did not look promising. There seemed to be nobody at home. Alberta knocked several times and was about to go away again when the door opened suddenly. It was Eliel, looking unnecessarily surprised: ' Look who's here, Alberta! I thought I heard someone knocking.'

Alberta told him, somewhat astonished, that she had been knocking for a long time. ' Would you believe it?' cried Eliel. ' Here I am, sitting with Dr. Freytag. We were having quite an animated conversation, it's true, but still . . . ' And Eliel introduced Dr. Freytag, a tall, thin man with thick, tightly curled hair. He rose in the darkness of the studio and bowed coldly to Alberta, and, for no apparent reason, she felt an immediate antipathy towards him. He was the Austrian Liesel had mentioned occasionally, one of their acquaintances from St. Jean du Doigt.

Eliel did not invite Alberta in. He let her stand out in
the rain while he informed her that Liesel was not there.
He did not know where she was living. He turned to Dr.
Freytag and asked him if he remembered where Liesel had
said she was going? Was it not so, that someone had
arrived whom she had to look after, someone travelling
through? Freytag shrugged his shoulders and eyebrows
apologetically as one who knows nothing and cannot help
in the matter. The whole manoeuvre filled Alberta with a
kind of unease, not solely derived from the fact that she
was, to say the least, not wanted. Dr. Freytag's presence
also prevented her from asking Eliel for a casual loan,
which she otherwise could have done on the basis of much
mutual assistance over the years. Confused and blank, she
prepared to leave, full of inexplicable anxiety. It was not
lessened when Eliel suddenly, quite at random and as if
speaking over her head, made some bitterly humorous
remarks about the rain: 'It's terrible how it goes on
raining. It's shameful. Enough to make you pregnant.'

This old joke of Eliel's which Alberta had never found
amusing, appeared downright macabre at this juncture.
Was Eliel a little unbalanced? Was he a little drunk? It
had not rained for more than a day. An old Parisian like
Eliel should not get pregnant for so little. It could rain here
for weeks and months at a time. She asked him to give
Liesel her greetings and left. 'Yes, of course, indeed I will,'
he called after her in an extravagantly bright and cheerful
tone of voice. And Alberta was out in the street again. And
everything was worse than before. There was treachery in
the December day, pain rested crushingly upon the world.

Dusk was already falling. The winter darkness of the
city comes gradually, grey as death. Alberta wandered down
towards Montparnasse, uncertain as to what she should do,
uncertain as to what had really happened to Liesel. Had
she been up in the loft all the time, kept up there by Dr.
Freytag? Or had something happened to her and Eliel?
Had they fallen out? Had they been discovered and
exposed? Was there really nothing the matter, or was

something mysterious and inexplicable, distressing and inevitable, going on? Oh, it was probably only shortage of money and the weather that made Alberta see the black side of everything. Eliel had probably been the same as usual, a little thoughtless and scatter-brained, wrapped up in his own affairs.

Alberta wandered into Colarossi's. It was unlikely that Liesel would be there. But there was the warmth for the models. She could stand there pretending to look for her, waiting for her.

Correction was under way. A grizzled, friendly little gentleman in grizzled clothes with a red ribbon in his buttonhole went from place to place, began with an encouraging *pas mal, pas mal,* and continued in a lower, confidential tone, accompanying his words with rounded gestures across the paper, small curves of the hand, small shrugs of the shoulder. Finally he seized charcoal or brush, made merciless strokes right across the work, nodded benevolently and went on.

Alberta stood waiting as long as she decently could. The warmth streamed soothingly through her, while she made herself appear to be looking for someone across the thicket of easels, swinging palettes, skewed heads and brushes held convulsively at arm's length in a last hopeful assessment.

And she pushed her way out again, between ladies flocking eagerly round mediocre studies, past the fanatical German who interested himself solely in movement, and really had brought it to the point where his drawings resembled the jointed figures made of wood and wire one buys at the ironmonger's. Just then someone was accusing him of drawing sticks, not legs. He punched his painter's stool with clenched fist, declaring: '*Es giebt überhaupt keine Beine nicht. Es giebt nur Stöcke.*' And Alberta suddenly felt what an elevated form of existence it was to be able to stand in a well-lighted, well-warmed place maintaining opinions of this kind; opinions of any kind. And what a categorically low form it was to trudge along the muddy, rain-wet streets looking for her next meal.

In the Rue Delambre there was a little shop where for years she had indulged in culinary extravagances. It sold chocolates, sweets, coffee, spices. It was always a place where she could go and stand for a little in the light and warmth, looking at it all. A chocolate bar for three sous was sufficient excuse.

The air was always the same in here, heavy with vanilla and stored coffee. Behind the counter was one of the two deformed sisters who took it in turns to stand there. She interrogated Alberta with interest as to how she was, whether she still lived in the *quartier*? Oh dear, had she moved? But she remained faithful to her former purveyors. It was kind of her, very kind. Would she like Salavin's chocolate, or another brand? Her small purchase was by no means treated as of little account, on the contrary, it might have been a matter of importance. In the meantime sister number two, who was exactly like the first, their mother, also the same but older, and their father, white-haired, his pen behind his ear, were all called in. The father dealt with the paper work of the business and always carried a pen. They all gathered round Alberta, asking about the state of her health. Mademoiselle was still in Paris? Mademoiselle was happy in Paris? Mademoiselle had again spent the summer here? But there – one had Bellevue and Meudon, was it not so? One had the woods at Clamart. And near by were the Luxembourg Gardens, which were splendid.

The space was minimal, the view on to the grey street miserable and dull. A red cretonne curtain divided the shop from a dark little back room which served as sitting-room, dining-room, office. But each time the curtain was raised Alberta saw the hanging lamp illuminating a table set for a meal. A long shining loaf reflected the light, a soup tureen steamed on the check tablecloth, a bowl of salad looked newly tossed and inviting. And hunger for proper food again hollowed into her breast, while she kept her side of the conversation going as best she could. Had not the family been to the country this year either? Was it not so that they had relatives in Brittany?

Oh yes, yes indeed. But everyone could not travel, it was impossible because of the business. So no-one did. They had each other, they did not know for how long. They kept together. Besides, they went on trips on Sunday afternoons, attended the open air concerts at the Tuileries Gardens in the evenings. They would really be very ungrateful if they were not satisfied.

When Alberta left them, knowing that they were gathering round the steaming tureen again, she thought of how she could have been like them, placid, industrious, frugal, friendly, easy to meet, closely tied to her children. How would life have turned out then? That year in Kristiania, for instance? There had not only been Engen Street. There had been the museums, the Abel statue and the Viking ships, the Deichman Library, uncle's bookcase which had been quite comprehensive. There had been two or three plays at the National Theatre. Above all there had been the National Gallery which she had visited often. But all this had only increased her dissatisfaction, creating fresh disturbance in her mind. And since? Reasonable conditions had been offered her time and again. She could have gone home with her knowledge of languages, and lived on them simply and respectably. She could have –

Alberta suddenly started walking quickly uphill in the direction of the Rue Campagne Première. She would not give up. Not yet. And she regretted nothing. She could not have acted differently on any occasion. There was something she had to do, she was searching for it. It led her on to painful and desolate paths through cold and loneliness. She could only wish she were someone else, that she need not be the person she was.

Now she wanted food. It occurred to her that if only she could get a couple of proper meals inside herself, if she could avoid, if only once or twice, the warmed-up beans, the half-cold chestnuts in the sad glow of the candle, she would get back her equilibrium again, find the courage to get to grips with something, even with her writing. To someone who takes the short view a meal can seem like a stage on one's journey, a new chance. If I get that far, I shall also get a little further. But with the sum she had in her pocket it was useless presenting herself anywhere, even at the Coachmen's Rest. She hurried on.

On the gloomy staircase of number nine she was stopped for a moment by a scene on one of the landings. A model with a man's coat slung about her was engaged in a cheerful tussle with a painter in a smock. They were fighting over a pipe, disporting themselves and laughing, then they suddenly fell silent and struggled on, their faces tense and serious. Alberta continued with their faces imprinted on her mind, blinded by them for a second, as if she had seen fire break out; empty and poor after the incident, as if left sitting in the ashes.

On the next landing she met Potter.

Potter was carrying an empty milk bottle, and transporting lettuce leaves and gnawed chop-bones packed loosely in a sheet of newspaper. In the wretched light from the gas-flame she looked older than usual, harrowed and sad. It struck Alberta that plenty of women of Potter's age were doing just this when evening came, their hands clutching the rubbish from a small, lonely household. It gave her the feeling of being condemned to death, with the mode of death demonstrated to her: to wither, to wither. Like Otilie Weyer at home. Like Potter and Stoltz and the old fools in the corridor where she lived. She began to feel desperate.

But Potter's face brightened, as lonely faces do when they meet someone. Was Alberta coming to see her? If so Potter would turn round and go up again. She was on her way to the garbage can, from there she had thought of going out to eat and then on to the evening drawing class. It was a long time since she had seen Alberta. Where was Alberta living now? What was she doing? She had got thinner. There was nothing the matter, was there?

' No, of course not.' Alberta attempted to laugh it off.

' I miss you,' said Potter. ' I like you. And I wish you would work. Work now while there's time. When you get old it's too late for everything, for that too. Don't let the men hinder you, dear. They hinder us at our best time, then leave us behind. I could tell you things, plenty of things. Won't you come up with me?'

Potter looked at Alberta hungrily, as if out of a long grey day's loneliness. And the painful question one should really only put with forced assurance to those who are in the same situation as oneself, and whose opinion does not matter, popped out of Alberta's mouth. Slightly appalled she listened to her own words: Could Potter make her a small loan? She happened to be in difficulties. And she muttered something about a letter that had been delayed.

She regretted it at once. Potter's expression changed, as if she had heard something shocking or scandalous. She said pityingly, ' I'm afraid I can't, dear.'

Her voice a tone too high, Alberta hastened to assure her that she was expecting it every day, it would be all right, and Potter's expression returned to normal. Oh, she was glad to hear Alberta say so. Delays in the mail were disagreeable, very disagreeable. She hoped it would turn up soon. *Au revoir* dear. And she went on down with her chop-bones.

Outside Marushka's door Alberta paused, and took a deep breath. Marushka was not the kind of person from whom one could not ask a favour, but money was money. Alberta should have been hardened, but she was not. She knocked.

Under normal circumstances Marushka would now either not answer or utter the traditional ' Who's there?' from immediately behind the door. Neither of these things occurred. From far away, as if from the farthest corner of the studio, there came a loud, clear and unreserved ' Come in '.

Astonished, Alberta opened the unlocked door, and remained standing in the doorway, uncertain, a little numbed by the heavy, spicy warmth that met her, a blend of perfume and heat that was almost paralysing. The curtains were drawn across the windows, the grey evening was shut out. There was a red glow from a small paraffin stove down on the floor, and above the divan a single gas-jet was lighted, with a rose-coloured silk shade over it. Under it Marushka was enthroned with her legs drawn up beneath her, supported by brightly coloured cushions on all sides like the inhabitant of a harem.

She was wearing a black kimono with gold embroidery, one of the expensive items of clothing one sometimes picks up and admires, but never thinks of buying. Her slender, short feet stuck out naked and childish from under the hem. Her pink toes were stretching themselves, as if pleased with their freedom. Alberta could not help being reminded of children she had helped with their clothes. In her lap Marushka had *Omar Khayyám* – recognizable from its soft leather binding – in her hand a cigarette. From the low table beside her an airy blue arabesque from an incense lamp coiled upwards. Half-blown Riviera roses were standing about, the silver vase with the cigarettes in it was shining. Books lay carelessly in heaps. The whole picture contrasted so strongly with the meanness of the staircase, the rain and early darkness out in the street, that Alberta needed to collect her wits. She was used to coming across Marushka in all sorts of situations: in a painter's smock, smeared with colour, or sitting on the edge of a table eating one of her extraordinary meals, the ingredients arranged round her in their respective wrappings and a jar of jam from Felix Potin in the middle of it all. This was new.

Marushka remained seated without moving. And indeed the light had been so well calculated to fall on her that it would have been a pity. Between the kimono and her short hair her face, neck and breast had something satisfied and creamy-white about it, a strange, thick fullness, here and there toning into the rose-coloured light from the lampshade. It was suddenly clear to Alberta what Liesel and Sivert meant when, with their heads askew and their eyes narrowed they agreed that there were possibilities in Marushka, that she ought to be built up in thick colour with a palette-knife. She was by no means free of smallpox scars, but this seemed to contribute to the richness. Just as astonished as Alberta, she asked without preliminaries: ' What is it?'

' No, nothing.' Alberta was thrown off balance by the circumstances, and felt herself to be as much out of place as she possibly could be in Marushka's studio at that precise moment. It was not she who should have come in. She prepared to withdraw.

But now Marushka rose to her feet and came tripping on naked toes across the floor, small, rather broadly built, above all buoyant: ' There *is* something the matter. I can see there is. Come back tomorrow. I – I'm expecting some-one, to be frank.'

' Yes, I understand that.'

' Is it obvious? *Tant pis.*'

' I'll go, Marushka.'

' Listen . . . ' Marushka seized Alberta by the arm. ' Is it money? I can see it's money.'

The flush rose in Alberta's face. ' I'll manage somehow.'

Marushka was still holding Alberta's arm. She rattled on quickly, as if every second counted: ' I've paid the cleaning woman, and had a parcel from Bon Marché, I haven't a sou. But tomorrow I'm going to the Rue de l'Arbalète to meet some of my fellow-countrymen. This evening – I'm prevented . . . . '

Alberta felt her shoulders sag. Marushka's many puzzle pictures on the walls around her, their colours deep and beautiful as carpets, but their construction such that one always felt like tidying and rearranging them, danced in front of her eyes. For a moment she glimpsed Sivert and Alphonsine, but they disappeared again at once. Something inside her gave way.

' Must you have it today? Listen . . . . ' Marushka's face

glowed with a new idea: 'Hurry to the Mont de Piété with something or other. If you go now you'll get there before they close. It's not at all unpleasant, they treat you very politely. You can redeem it as soon as you have the money again.'

Alberta smiled bitterly: 'If only I had something to take there.'

'You must have something, a ring, a watch, a bagatelle. Preferably something on you. I don't think you'll have time to go home first.'

Then Alberta's weakness overcame her: 'All that I had, on me or at home, found its way there long ago.'

'*Comment*?' Marushka slapped Alberta on the back. 'Why didn't you say so at once? Look, take this!' And she fluttered on tiptoe across the floor, came fluttering back again, and hung her watch on its long chain round Alberta's neck. 'Here you are, *ma petite*. It's a good watch, twenty carats. You'll get at least a hundred francs for it.'

Blood-red, Alberta seized Marushka's hands, trying to prevent her, to take off the chain again. But Marushka held it in place with her strong little hands, stuffed the watch down the neck of Alberta's dress, and pushed her out of the door. 'Yes, yes, yes, why not? I don't need to look at the clock all the time. Alphonsine has a watch, and so have most of my friends. There are clocks in the street, at the station and the cafés, the world is full of clocks.'

'But Marushka, I don't know when I shall be able to redeem it again.'

'*Tant pis, tant pis*. While I remember, Liesel, go and see Liesel, I saw her the other day, she looked as if – there's someone on the stairs! Go now. Come again soon, *au revoir, courage*, off with you!'

Marushka gave Alberta a quick kiss on each cheek, span her round, shoved her out on to the landing, shut the door. Her tiptoe fluttering was audible for a moment, then there was silence. She was posing amongst her cushions again.

Far below the footsteps did not stop anywhere, but continued upwards. Simultaneously relieved and depressed,

Alberta went down to meet them. In a while she would eat warm food, soup, meat. She would be able to pay the rent punctually without having to take refuge in the little speech she had already begun to prepare and rehearse so as to be able to deliver it easily, in an off-hand manner: a misunderstanding, a delayed letter, pure mischance, a matter of a few days . . . .

She would be able to buy herself a lamp, something to read . . . .

The footsteps were just below her. Hastily she composed her face in case it was someone she knew and must greet. But it was one of the Americans, one of the many from Montparnasse. He looked searchingly at Alberta, as men do look at strange women, enquiringly, appraisingly. And she heard him knock at Marushka's door, heard a loud, clear 'Come in'.

A sensation resembling cramp seized Alberta's heart for a moment, a privation, raging as hunger. Then she went on her way with the watch, hurrying along the wet, glistening pavements, knowing she only had a few minutes left.

She arrived just in time to see the heavy doors swung to and bolted.

Back in her room she lighted her candle. The flame cast shadows up the walls and was reflected, thin and flickering, in the glass covering the reproductions.

She remained sitting with her coat on. This was one of the moments when she hated herself and everything about her, her wicker trunk and her worn soles, the whole of her shabby and purposeless existence. Reluctantly and with difficulty burning tears forced themselves out of the corners of her eyes. As if on its own account her mouth whispered defiantly: 'I *will* have a different, comfortable life, warmth, someone to be with, pretty clothes, fur round my neck, books that are mine and that I don't need to stand reading at the Odéon.'

An old and evil thought reared its head, watchful as a

poisonous reptile: I could go on the streets, earn ten francs, twenty francs, hide them in my stocking and earn more, I, just as well as others. I belong to myself, I can do what I please with my body. No-one can touch my soul. I could do it from cold, from the desire for human warmth. If I'm no good at anything else, I could always be of use on the streets.

Then her defiance melted. She sat there knowing that she would not do it, and that she wanted to even less now than before.

She must have a slight fever. Her ears were buzzing, she was cold inside and unreasonably warm outside. She had kicked off her shoes and her soaking wet stockings. With her hands tucked up inside her sleeves and her feet under her she remained sitting, while the packet of spinach she had brought home with her disintegrated from the damp and dripped greenly on to the chair beside her. And she dozed upright like the cab-horses.

When someone knocked she knew at once who it was. As if in a dream she opened the door, without changing her position and without saying anything, remaining sitting with her legs under her looking up at Sivert Ness, who stood there looking larger than usual in a new thick winter coat, his hat in his hand. She could not see his expression. The light did not fall that way. But she felt his eyes on her and met them haphazardly.

That was his hand, feeling her shoulder and her arm. She heard him say: 'But you're soaked, you're sitting here soaking wet. You mustn't do that you know. Nothing on your legs, and it's cold in here and everything – whatever next.' He leaned over, felt her saturated shoes, and shook his head: 'Everything wet through. This is sheer idiocy. It takes less than this to make you ill.'

That was his hand in her sleeve, drawing out hers, clasping it. It had hold of her, the strong hand she had gone half in fear of. She winced as if she had burned herself.

something inside her was shattered. Then it was over. She pressed the hand.

'Like a live coal,' commented Sivert. And he leaned over her and said in a tone of voice that she would not have believed him to be capable of: 'Well, there's only one thing to be done. For you have a fever. I can see it from your eyes.' He looked round for a moment, as if summing up the situation. 'You can't stay here, there's nowhere to set up a stove even.' And he leaned over her again. 'There's a red glow right across the floor in my room.' He began putting on her stockings and shoes as if she were a child, tying tight solid knots that could not come undone.

Alberta was filled with gratitude simply for his presence and for the warmth that flowed from him. Giddily she put her hand on his shoulder. Sivert looked up, held both her arms firmly for an instant, then released her. 'Now we must hurry,' he said.

PART FOUR

The north wind blew cold and hard, chasing clouds of dust down the streets. When Alberta went from barrow to barrow making purchases and saw the grey, frozen faces crowding round her, Sivert's stove seemed an unjust advantage with something of immodest upper-class luxury about it. She noticed how many in the crowd smelt unpleasant, unwashed and stuffy and thought: No wonder – you can't reproach poor people for being dirty. If you have few clothes, live in cramped conditions and are always cold, keeping clean becomes an insoluble problem. And she felt a sensation that was almost deceit towards all those around her who she knew would go home and continue to feel cold.

When Sivert had raked out the embers in the morning and riddled the ashes, the stove shone far out over the floor, creating a circle of warmth. Into it was brought Sivert's zinc bath-tub, heavy and unwieldy to normal folk, but a bagatelle to him. Then all she had to do was get into it, scrub herself red and warm with the heat from the stove-hole glowing straight on to her skin, and curl up on the divan in an aroma of coffee.

For the first few days Alberta had stayed in bed with fever. She just sensed that two large, tranquil hands shook up her pillow now and again and turned it, that she was supported in bed and given something to drink; and she dozed off again. Then came an evening when the fever had gone. In rare high spirits she sat on the divan, wrapped in Sivert's new winter coat for lack of a dressing-gown, ate greedily, talked and laughed, all the time with the feeling that it was really another person sitting there, quite a different person from the old Alberta. Or perhaps it was that one life lay behind her, a new one was beginning. For better, for worse, it was so.

The weather was just as unpleasant as when she had arrived, with rain streaming over the panes in the skylight and dripping in several places on to the floor. Sivert had put dishes and bowls underneath. He himself sat in his usual manner, as if on a crate in the kitchen, listening to Alberta and putting in a word here and there. The stove burned as it should, casting a long red glow.

It was then that an ache took hold of Alberta, sorrow, longing, sympathy, fate, bitter necessity, all mingling and streaming towards her heart. Human loneliness suddenly became so clear to her. Here they sat, she and Sivert, as if drifted together, shut in by the rain and the darkness. How good Sivert had been to her! And she did something she had to do, it seemed predetermined that she should do it; she put her hand on the nape of his neck.

He sat turned towards the fire, so she did not see his eyes this time either. When he stretched out an arm and calmly drew her to him she felt an instant of tremendous distress, but made no resistance. And all that was mute in Sivert engulfed her.

Afterwards she smiled as best she could, the tears streaming down her face, a circumstance that did not seem to astonish Sivert in the slightest or put him at a loss. All in all, Sivert was easy-going about things like that. He made no enquiries about the past or the future, but took everything as it came. And it was good. There was obliteration in it. Shoots, that had once put out tendrils to no purpose and been singed off, were kept in check.

He would walk humming between his easel and his observation point in the middle of the floor, painting artichokes and other vegetables, making the utmost use of the grudging daylight. When Alberta had the meal ready on the table, he would rub his hands together with satisfaction, find it excellent, and, far from leaving the most boring part of it to her, would help with the washing up and clearing away.

She had begun mending his socks and repairing various garments that were lying about. He never asked her to do so, he had managed it himself very well and could presumably manage it still. The tidiness of Sivert's wardrobe was amazing. But when she sat down to it a second time he made no objection.

He had had a model the first few days. Alberta, lying dozing in the loft, heard at intervals his broken French as he talked to the model below. He did not attempt to hide the fact that there was someone upstairs, but went imperturbably up and down to see how Alberta was. ' Is that your lady friend up there?' asked the model. ' Yes,' answered Sivert. ' Has she influenza?' ' Yes.' ' Yes, it's the time of year for it now.'

Sivert finished his studies of the model in a few days. Then he began on the artichokes. Sometimes he made a quick sketch of Alberta, as she sat sewing. In the afternoon he went to life-class.

Then Alberta was left alone for a while, and it was a painful time, full of uneasiness. She ought to work as well, sit down and write something, see about earning some money. She had warmth, peace, someone to be with. She postponed it from day to day.

Once she went back to her room. It was comfortless and unlived-in, dusty and cold. She sat on the edge of the open trunk, looking for clothes she wanted, coming across loose sheets covered with writing, and also a little ring with an amethyst which she had taken from her finger and dropped into the trunk one evening that autumn. Now it lay there casually among so much else, a little stray object of pity. It looked at her upbraidingly, and she wept over it for a while. A thought that had sometimes brushed her mind fleetingly, reappeared: Death?

It can come like an icy wind striking down people like pawns with a single breath and bringing desolation to numbers of homes at one fell swoop. Having experienced it once, it remained for ever a reality to be reckoned with. She had never thought about it before.

But many of the circumstances of life were equally possible. A man comes to feel sorry for the little wife, red-eyed with weeping, who wants him back on any terms; perhaps he becomes fond of her again. It probably happens often. And La Bruyère certainly knew what he was talking about. What with one thing and another, there was no need to go so far as to think of death. Alberta had in any case arrived at the stage when she could bear to look at the whole thing in perspective; she was no longer a bundle of aching nerves meeting an endless series of painful moments as one might a whipping. She lived on, and wished to do so; and took what life offered, whatever it might be. Still, she would frequently see fragments of a face. The memory of a hand, a touch, a tone of voice, would strike her unprepared, as if from behind. The sound of Sivert's shaving in the morning – like someone peeling a raw potato – would perhaps continue to scrape her nerves for a long time, painful and too familiar as it was. But everything passes. She would not suffer like that a second time. A hard spot forms inside, that cannot be attacked again.

She read the sheets of paper for a while, since she was up there. They surprised her, they resembled small fragments of life piled in confusion. She thought vaguely that perhaps they could be threaded together into some cohesion. What would that look like? Then she packed them in again.

In the corridor she met no-one. It was the lunch hour and quiet on the stairs. Madame Caux looked out of her window: So Mademoiselle had moved to friends during the cold period? She was wise. Whatever one might say about the attic rooms, they were not warm. No, there were no letters. If anyone came asking for Mademoiselle, what should Madame Caux say? That Mademoiselle was away for a short visit? Staying with a friend? Coming back soon. *Bien,* Mademoiselle.

And Alberta left with something of a guilty conscience. In a way she had abandoned her own existence, the cold, depressing house, the many people who were forced to go on living there.

Sivert's paintings consisted of landscapes, life studies, street scenes, still lifes. Their strength lay in their colour. Abundance as from a bouquet of flowers met the eye when Sivert propped his canvases along the wall, a collective sensation of flesh, clouds, green and stone grey all united, a sensation almost of scent. His technique was not new or unusual. He took an interest in the numerous contemporary experiments in that direction, but continued imperturbably to paint in his old manner, an uncomplicated simplification uninfluenced by any ' isms '.

' I must paint as I see it,' said Sivert. ' I can't do anything else.' In spite of this he often came home with books and brochures on new forms of expression, Cubism and Futurism, Orphism, Dadaism and Synchronism. He studied them seriously and reflectively, finding out what all these strange words really entailed. Where Eliel only sneered and poked fun, where Kalén became angry and aggrieved, Sivert sat and cogitated. ' I'll try to find out what those fellows mean, at any rate,' he would say, and stuff the pamphlets into his pocket until the next spare moment.

When he submitted a picture to Alberta's judgment, she stood a little embarrassed. It was the same with painting as with music: she was repelled or fascinated, strongly and decisively, but she found it difficult to say why. Besides much else she lacked critical ability. She wished she could find something to say besides ' It's beautiful, Sivert, it's excellent '. She was not good at that sort of thing.

On the other hand, she thought she did understand the total sum of strain and will-power that lay behind a complicated work. Now, when she watched Sivert painting every day, she could be stirred by his struggle with the motif, as

435

one always is stirred by masculine toil. He stood there, frugal, industrious, untiringly pursuing what he wished to reveal, sometimes from canvas to canvas. He had a peculiar way of suddenly painting with his thumb, of entering personally into the work, as if boxing with it. For him this was life's hard journey. And she was seized with a desire to be useful in her way, with carefully prepared meals, and so on.

One day when he was painting one of his still lifes, the eternal refuge of all impecunious painters, Alberta said almost at random – she was sitting thinking about one of Marcel Lenoir's pictures, a Golgotha scene with solidly composed, strictly simplified groups in a solidly composed, simplified landscape with shadows from great masses of cloud drifting over it: ' If I were a painter, I would paint life.'

She shut her eyes. There was a sudden flickering behind them. People were moving between groups of trees and high cliffs. Children played and ran, couples walked close together, or apart, as if they were strangers. Here was a woman sitting alone, weeping, here was another suckling her child, here was someone working, here sat a couple of old people . . .

' Life,' smiled Sivert. ' That's quite a tall order.'

Alberta opened her eyes. He was just going back from the picture, inspecting it, adding after mature consideration a new smudge of colour. ' Non-painters always want to do symbolic things,' he said. ' It's a certain sign of dilettantism.'

But Alberta, who still glimpsed a little of what she had seen, continued: ' Life. In the middle of it all I would put the tree of good and evil, full of apples.'

' Ouch,' said Sivert. ' Art is teeming with that kind of allegory. At home we have Vigeland, fortunately without any tree of good and evil, as far as I know.'

' That may be so,' persisted Alberta. ' I would put in people I knew, Alphonsine and Madame Bourdarias and you, Sivert, painting artichokes.'

It was good to sit and talk. It made the time pass.

'It would have to be kept strictly simple,' said Sivert after a while. ' Sculptural, almost.'

'Precisely. It would all have to be contained in the positions, the gestures.'

Sivert fell silent again, painted, moved forwards and backwards, went across to see to the stove. As he was squatting there, he said: ' Yes, the motif is really not so important. It depends on how it's done.'

The next day, when Alberta unloaded her purchases on to the table, he shoved a rough pencil sketch across to her. ' Look,' he said. ' Something like that?' And he explained the foreground figures to her: 'I haven't brought it off, but I thought this position should be thus and thus. And like this here. I've only drawn it straight out of my head.'

Then Alberta again did something she had to do. It hung in the air and seemed to be simply a continuation.

Quickly she took off her clothes, and posed in the warmth near the stove. ' Like this?' she said.

' Yes,' said Sivert eagerly. He had already taken out his sketch book and was drawing.

But when Sivert held her close to him and warm currents flowed through her from his hands, then they were two lonely, frozen people, who crept together beside the fire of life and warmed themselves as well as they could. It was neither wrong nor shocking, as some arrogantly insist. It was their simple right.

The spark kindled by two poverty-stricken souls somewhere in the darkness of infinity. Should they not be allowed to have it? A great affection for Sivert arose in her, a desire to give and give again. And a shadow of guilt towards him, as though there was much for which she had to compensate him. It was warm and safe in his arms, shut off from the world and the cold.

But then Sivert wanted to sleep. It was awful how quickly Sivert wanted to sleep. He yawned and gave the wrong answers, while Alberta still had a great deal on her mind, things which seemed to lie dammed up inside her and were waiting their turn to be said. She had them on the tip of her tongue . . . .

Suddenly Sivert gave a lengthy snore. He woke in the middle of it, sat up and said: 'What?'

'Good night, Sivert,' said Alberta, crestfallen.

But sometimes she would lie on her elbow watching him when he slept. He was handsome then, and looked like a child or a young boy. The thought that he would die one day occurred to her. She, too, would die. They would disappear from each other, sink down each to his own part of infinity, exist for each other no longer. The smell of his hair, the warmth of his arm, his even breathing, would all wither and be extinguished.

A boundless feeling of loneliness seized her. Her face was wet with tears. Sivert slept.

So she went from barrow to barrow in the mornings, multiplying and adding, had worldly cares and was not entirely useless. She was full of gratitude for it. When she came home she would sometimes feel she must go straight over to Sivert and say: 'How happy we are, Sivert.'

'I'm glad you think so,' Sivert would say, painting on imperturbably. Sometimes he would turn his head slightly and give her a quick kiss. And Alberta told herself that she had not expected him to put his palette aside, but he might have done so for a moment at any rate. She regretted having said anything, it would have been better not to.

They had come to each other each from his great loneliness. They had drifted together somewhere in time and space and accommodated themselves there as best they could. Sivert was no hero of romance, no conqueror in a Spanish cloak; but he was healthy and strong and capable. And she did not notice the glint in his eye, which she disliked, any more.

Without a collar and tie he looked like a shoemender. Alberta wished she did not have to see him dressed like that. On the other hand most men looked the same in that brief, ugly neckband with the nasty little round button. And Alberta was certainly no romantic heroine. The old, embroidered petticoat was far from being a thing of the past. It reappeared again and again, even at this time of year, and was by no means the only detail of her wardrobe that she wished was otherwise.

There was something mute about Sivert. Sometimes it would occur to Alberta that he had something of the enigma of an animal, a passivity of whose content she was ignorant and never became any wiser. And she realised that herein lay something of Sivert's fascination.

When they had been alone for some time, working together, chatting together, preparing meals together, everything felt extraordinarily inevitable and simple, as if it ought to be so. But when they met other people, or met each other again after being parted for a few hours, she would feel strangely disappointed and flat for a while. She might go over and straighten his hat or pull at his tie, as if she needed to correct her impression of him.

*   *   *

When Alberta knocked for the third time on Eliel's door and nobody answered, she remained standing for a while, perplexed. It was a long time since she had seen either Liesel or Eliel. They lived as if immured. Or they were living separately again. No-one knew anything about them any more. Alberta had been to Eliel's door in vain. Marushka's hastily interrupted words that evening in the Rue Campagne Première had sounded like a mysterious warning of danger. Even Sivert was strangely reserved about the matter. It almost sounded as if he could suspect anything when he said: ' They'll turn up again.'

One evening he was able to report that he had met Eliel at the Versailles. ' Well?' asked Alberta eagerly. ' Yes, well, Eliel could not understand why he was never at home when people came and knocked. It was a strange coincidence. Liesel was quite all right, she still had visitors in town.'

439

' Do you believe that, Sivert?' asked Alberta. 'Yes, why not?' said Sivert.

Now Alberta was standing there, no nearer her object. She fumbled in her handbag for pencil and paper, intending at any rate to write a note and stick it in the door. Quite by chance she looked up, straight at the high little window, the window of the loft. And she caught a glimpse of Liesel's face, pale, large-eyed, before it disappeared again, so quickly that Alberta asked herself for a moment whether it was her imagination, something she thought she had seen.

' Liesel, she called, full of uncontrollable anxiety.

No answer. But now Alberta called again as if constrained to shout something down. It had been Liesel. She knew it with fearful certainty. And she knew more. A series of small circumstances she had scarcely noticed suddenly formed a straightforward sequence. What happened to so many women, what happened to others Alberta had known, what could have happened and still might happen to herself, had happened to Liesel. Now she had shut herself up there, in hiding. Alberta called again with all the intensity one can put into a call: 'It's me, Liesel. It's Alberta.'

The window opened quietly. Hoarse and thin, terrified of being heard, came Liesel's voice: ' Don't shout, Albertchen, for God's sake.'

' But what's the matter, Liesel? Are you ill? What's going on? Can I help you?' Alberta scarcely knew what she was saying any more. Liesel's thin voice cut her to the quick.

' The key is on top of the door,' whispered Liesel. 'You can come up for a moment. You must go again at once.'

Alberta opened it. The heavy smell of the clay made breathing difficult. Eliel's latest enormous work stood wrapped in wet cloths from top to toe, reaching such a height that the room was darkened by it. The winter damp lay clammily over everything, the paper was loosening from the wall beside the door. And an untidiness, that was unlike Liesel, prevailed everywhere. Clothes belonging to

Eliel lay about as if he had changed in a hurry. The washing-up from several meals spread itself round the primus and overflowed on to the floor. No cushion covered the hole in the basket chair, it gaped emptily and frankly. The stove was burning, but in a heap of ashes. From up in the loft came Liesel's hoarse voice: 'Don't look at anything, Albertchen. I haven't been down for some days, I know it's terrible there.'

Alberta went up the steps to the loft. Liesel was lying on Eliel's iron bedstead with the crooked legs, and it seemed to Alberta as if there was nothing left of her but thick plaits and large eyes, she looked so bloodless. Her hair was dishevelled, and she hurriedly hid her plaits behind her back.

'But Liesel!' exclaimed Alberta.

Then the tears rolled quietly down Liesel's face, many of them. She said nothing for a while. Then she lifted her head anxiously, and looked at the watch lying on the chair beside the bed: 'Eliel has gone out to get plaster. He's going to cast his big figure soon. He's in a hurry. It's to be ready in stone for the Spring Exhibition. ... As soon as I'm on my feet again, he's thought of asking Ness for some help with the moulds.'

Alberta felt a pang at her mention of Ness. But she said nothing. Everything in there was so oppressive, from the atmosphere to Liesel's tears.

'He won't be back for a little while,' Liesel decided, and dried her tears. 'Would you give me a drink, Albertchen? It's over there. It's difficult to breathe in here, don't you think?'

'I expect it's the clay,' said Alberta, relieved at every word she could say that had nothing to do with the situation.

'It is the clay. When you stay indoors for a long time it seems to end up here.' Liesel put her hand on her breastbone. She drank thirstily, and then lay down again with a sigh: 'Perhaps I shouldn't have sat up to look out of the window, but I couldn't help it. The time drags so when Eliel is out, *aber so*. In the evenings, when he is at the Versailles, I sometimes feel I shall go mad. But of course he has to go.'

' I don't think he has to go at all. He could easily stay at home with you,' said Alberta, shocked. ' You have the worst of it, Liesel,' she blurted out, regretting it immediately, afraid of having gone too far and broached the subject too roughly.

But Liesel looked straight in front of her: ' It's important that he should put in an appearance and pretend there's nothing the matter. He *has* to go.'

' How long have you thought of staying up here, Liesel? I'm sure it's not good for you, you ought to . . . '

' Until Monday,' said Liesel. ' Not a day more. I long to get out into the fresh air. I was down the other day, but it made me ill, so I had to come up and lie down again.' She looked at Alberta for a while. Then she said, smiling almost pityingly: ' You don't understand anything, do you, Albertchen?'

Suddenly she held out her hand: ' I'm glad you came. It's a good thing somebody came.'

Alberta squeezed her hand. All kinds of misgivings confusedly occurred to her, misgivings that hurt her physically. She dared not ask any more.

' But the worst is over, after all. I'll soon be better again,' whispered Liesel. The tears began to roll down her cheeks once more. ' But I'll never be the same again, Albertchen, never. I feel as if I was destroyed, disfigured, mutilated.' Liesel's lips trembled suddenly as if she had cramp, she wrung Alberta's hand, her eyes widened as if she saw horrors: ' The " duck's beak ", Albertchen – that's the worst of it. They have something they call the " duck's beak ". They *force* their way in with it. I cried each time, I cried the whole night beforehand.

' In the end all I wanted to do was to give up, but once you've begun . . . It might have turned out a cripple, Albertchen!' Liesel hid her face in her hands and sobbed. ' It was so . . . so humiliating – so degrading . . . so . . . To lie there and let them do it to you!' she exclaimed with loathing.

'But Liesel!' said Alberta helplessly. She only partially understood, dimly sensing some ill-usage which appeared to her to lack all reasonable dimensions. Liesel explained a little more calmly: 'If only it helped at once. But I had to go time after time. I was almost in the fifth month. It was – it was a little child that came, a little body, naked, bloody, with arms and legs and everything.' And Liesel wrung and chafed Alberta's hand as if in delirium. 'I felt so sorry for it, so terribly sorry for it, when they went and threw it in – Albertchen! Don't *ever* do it, whatever happens!' Liesel sobbed desperately. 'I shall see it for the rest of my life, Albertchen.'

Her voice deepened with accumulated resentment and scorn: '*They* don't understand anything. They go round humming when it's over. A small operation, they call it. Imagine – on a healthy person. I have never been so healthy in my whole life. If only I hadn't been so desperate.'

Liesel clasped Alberta's hand with both her own, half raising herself in bed. 'But have you noticed what awful legs Eliel has, what large, tramping feet. And the way he sniffs!' A look almost of evil joy suddenly passed over Liesel's face. She fell back in bed. 'I was ill all night long, I thought I'd die of pain and fever.'

'Liesel!' Alberta, completely at a loss, patted her, gave her a drink, attempted to tidy up a little. She found no words. Liesel lay there, exhausted, her forehead beaded with sweat, breathing strenuously. After a while she said more calmly, in a different tone of voice: 'The worst of it is that I've become so spiteful. Yes, Albertchen, spiteful. Malicious. I wanted to do it, and yet I feel I can't stand Eliel any more. As if it were his fault. Yes, for you don't think Eliel wanted to do it, do you?' She raised her head and looked at Alberta intently.

'No –,' said Alberta uncertainly.

'*You mustn't think it was Eliel.*' A reflection of Liesel's former pale flush passed over her face, and she said as if in quick parenthesis: ' Naturally, he really would have liked nothing better than to have a little child. I ought to be ashamed of myself. It's been worse for Eliel than for me, worse for him, do you understand? And heaven knows what would have happened to us if we hadn't known Dr. Freytag. He helped us for nothing, although he was running a risk. Oh God, Albertchen – you won't say anything, will you? There's a grave penalty for it.' Liesel looked at Alberta terror-struck.

' No, Liesel.'

' I'm mad. I'm utterly unreasonable. Here I lie, getting wine and everything. Yesterday I had champagne. They are so kind to me. And it's not Eliel's fault he can't marry *und so weiter.*'

' You'll feel better when you're up and out of doors, Liesel,' said Alberta haphazardly. Tears were trickling down her cheeks as well. ' You'll get well again, of course you will.'

Liesel looked at her earnestly: ' Do you think so? Do you think I can become just as fond of Eliel again? When I get out and I'm not in here all the time? I do so want to. Can you forget the unkind things I said about him? He has suffered too. Over and over again we thought it was done. A long time goes by before you will admit that it is so, you try to believe all kinds of things instead. And Dr. Freytag was away for a while. And then – then it all became so terrible.'

Liesel glanced uneasily at the clock. ' You must go now. Eliel mustn't suspect that anyone has been here. To think that you never noticed, Albertchen.'

' I haven't seen you for a long time, Liesel.'

' No, and I am thin. I don't think anyone noticed. Are you still living in that horrid little room?'

' Yes,' answered Alberta a little hesitantly. ' But I'm thinking of moving,' she added, in order to come slightly nearer to the truth.

' I almost think you're lucky, not .... At least you don't have to be afraid of ... ' Liesel looked up at Alberta, who reddened at once. And Liesel's face reminded her for a moment of those of tired women, when they sit looking after young girls. ' Marushka,' she said. ' She's managing all right?'

' She's managing all right.'

' She's been married,' said Liesel. ' They always manage. Thank you for coming. Go now, hurry.'

And Alberta went. Out in the street she paused. Something told her to go back to her cold little room again, to her miserable, lonely existence there; a longing came over her to be the old, impossible and real Alberta, free in her fashion, free above all of the cold anxiety which she would not allow to come to the surface, but which was latent in her mind.

But she went down towards the Rue Vercingétorix as if drawn there.

When Sivert received a message from Eliel a few days later about the casting, Alberta decided to arrive as if quite by chance during the afternoon. ' Perhaps I shall meet Liesel,' she said. ' And they know nothing about us two.'

' Come, by all means,' said Sivert, imperturbable as always. ' I shan't give anything away.' With amazement Alberta felt a slight bitterness at Sivert's words. They were, after all, correct and appropriate, spoken with good intent, and yet wrong, wounding and spiteful. She thought what had occurred to her several times already : Sivert and I get on best when we have no contact with the outside world. As soon as we do, something goes wrong.

At the door of Eliel's studio she stopped short.

It resembled a place left in ruins after an earthquake. The plaster lay all over the floor, looking like collapsed houses, bulky and apparently immovable; heaps of large lumps and small lumps, heaps of rubbish and dust. A layer of white powder covered everything, lying on all the projections, hanging heavy in the damp atmosphere. clogging the throat and nose as soon as one entered.

Eliel and Sivert were moving busily about in it all.

445

Nothing appeared to be immovable as far as they were concerned; they were lifting and transporting great pieces, imprinted with gigantic fragments of the human form, which added to the impression of natural catastrophe, doom and destruction. Here giants had lived and moved.

In a tolerably clear spot stood Eliel's round bath-tub. To this the giant imprints were transported, and washed down with soapy water so that the cavities bubbled and shimmered with rainbow colours. Eliel and Sivert looked as if they had had a miraculous escape at a time when the destruction had long been under way. They were in overalls, covered with dry lumps of plaster, and had plaster lumps and dust in their hair. Sweating and hot, in full swing, they breathed deeply and rubbed their hands in satisfaction over a tremendous piece, wrested from chaos. Eliel splashed the sponge over it so that the soapy water shimmered like phosphorus. He called to Alberta: 'Look who's here! You've come just at the right time. Liesel is here, she's making coffee. Come in, if you dare, and join us.'

Sivert called: ' I've been given quite a job. I feel like a plasterer.'

Both of them gave the impression of being very much at their ease, lifting and carrying, washing and rinsing and tramping about ankle-deep in rubbish, with the same intense satisfaction as boys in a demolished building. They shared a wordless understanding, reaching agreement concerning their manoeuvres with the aid of glances and silent nods. Once Eliel said: ' This is awfully kind of you, Sivert Ness, let me tell you.'

In the corner by the door Liesel was keeping house. Dusty and wan, with her dress hitched up about her, she was setting the coffee-table. She sat down now and again rather suddenly and for no apparent reason. She seemed to slump down on the divan, while she continued to rub what she had in her hands, cups or spoons. It hurt Alberta to see her and she slumped down with her. She took the coffee-grinder, which Liesel handed over in an attack of weakness, and ground it unthinkingly, with short pauses and much wastage of coffee. The whole thing gave her the frightened feeling she used to get as a child, when a game that was being played around her suddenly, without anyone understanding why, became deceitful and dangerous, changing its character and going too far.

She felt a desire to seize the others by the arm and say: Let's stop now. The game's up.

Alberta had been in bed for a long time when Sivert came home that evening. He stretched himself as if after a good day's work, announcing with satisfaction that it was all finished. The figure stood there and only needed polishing. Then there was the cleaning of the studio. It was filthy. He supposed he'd have to give Eliel a hand with that as well.

' I think Liesel looks poorly,' said Alberta from up in the loft, not knowing why she said it. She had not mentioned Liesel to Sivert, she had not been able to bring herself to do so.

His reply made her suddenly pay attention.

' She'll get well again,' said Sivert. Alberta heard him walking about below, turning round pictures that were leaning against the wall, as he often did when he had been away from home for a while. He was greeting them on his return.

The words were not important. But his tone affected her strangely.

* * *

Alberta was sitting in the Café de Versailles, jammed in tightly, nervously turning the pages of the Norwegian newspapers. She had pulled herself together and written a couple of articles again. There had been nothing else for it. Without a word Sivert had so far borne their common expenses. In the long run this was impossible for many reasons, among others the fact that he was no Croesus.

Besides, Alberta had private obligations. She had kept on her room, needing it as a retreat and an alibi, and she had not pawned Marushka's watch, but had handed it in to her concierge a few days later.

She was tense and anxious. What she had patched together had been unlike her usual style, a little drastic, perhaps a little too realistic. Perhaps she had gone too far and it would not even be printed. Then she would be back where she started. She threw aside *Aftenposten,* there was nothing there, and looked round for *Morgenbladet.*

The café was packed. Tobacco and heat lay in the room like wool, hanging in layers beneath the ceiling. The contents of glasses glistened dully in the heavy air. The music, the voices, the tramp of dancing feet farther in seemed to come out of a mist. The whole atmosphere lay about one like a nauseating and used, but comfortable and protective old garment, good to turn to after draughty studios that lay on the bare earth or up under the sky, after rooms without stoves.

It was difficult to find the newspapers, difficult to read them. Norwegian voices exploded and Danish ones bleated penetratingly. An occasional Swede would also deliver an opinion after more mature consideration, and then shout down all those sitting round him. Kalén was wandering about, in the worst possible humour, provoked by *grippe* and spirits, causing a disturbance and giving offence wherever he went. At Alberta's side was the little Swedish woman, who had been keeping company with Kalén since the spring. Suddenly he began treating her worse than anybody else. She sat on the verge of tears, picking at her handkerchief, dabbing her face with it furtively and repeating: ' If only I could get him to go home. He's ill, his temperature was a hundred this morning. And now some- one has offered him absinthe. That's the worst thing that could happen. If he were not such a splendid person when he's sober . . . '. And she snuffled.

Kalén stopped in front of a young woman, a painter,

newly arrived from Kristiania, and asked her aggressively whether her name was not Frøken Olsson?

' No, far from it. Absolutely not.' The newcomer ignored the drunkard demonstratively.

' But Frøken Olsson has in any case come here to try to learn to paint? Is it not so?'

' My name is *not* Olsson,' came the reply in an offended Kristiania accent.

' It's of no consequence, no consequence at all, what Frøken is called,' persisted Kalén. He had taken up his position supporting himself with both hands spreadeagled on the table, and was not going to be budged. ' Frøken can be called Olsson or Svensson or Karlsson or what the devil she likes, that's not the point. Frøken must be called something in any case. The point is that Frøken should go home to Norway and have *children* instead of hanging about here throwing Papa's money away learning to paint. For Frøken will never succeed. She should go home tomorrow and get herself a *child*. Then Frøken will be as *useful* as she could possibly be – '

' Now then, now then,' intervened appeasing voices from several directions. Above them the Kristiania accent could be heard, high-pitched and cultivated: ' What *sort* of a frightful individual is *this*? He's not just drunk, he's *mad*. *Can't* someone get rid of him?'

The Swedish woman squeezed Alberta's hand: ' If only I could get him away from here. But I scarcely dare speak to him.'

Someone had persuaded Kalén to sit down. They were holding on to him, agreeing with every word he said: ' Yes, of course, quite right. So very right.' And he slumped down temporarily, dulled and pacified, as if the sting had gone out of him for the time being. Alberta searched anew through the pile of newspapers. She could still hear the voice of the Norwegian girl: ' *Huff* – is that *gruesome* man still here? I don't care in the *slightest* whether people are drunk, I assure you, as *long* as they don't get vulgar.' It reminded her so strangely of an unknown country a long way away, called Norway. That was how they talked there, underlining the words heavily, eager to air *their* opinions, *their* views, in some way different from *everyone* else's. Alberta glimpsed blue hills, air grey with snow, scattered habitation that seemed to force you to shout loudly. Otherwise perhaps nobody would hear you. People there did not live close to one another.

Alberta also listened involuntarily for the Danish voices. Their cadences touched her in far too intimate a way.

But the Swedish woman suddenly commented with a repressed sob: ' It's my wedding day today.'

Alberta put down the paper. It was the least she could do.

' The terrible thing about marriage is that you wait the whole time for the other person to say something quite different from what he does say, and to do something quite different from what he does do. ... I don't suppose you understand what I mean ... '

' Oh yes,' said Alberta.

' You see, my former husband was a scientist, a zoologist. He spent all his time at the museum with the stuffed animals. While I ... '. And the Swede assured Alberta that she still had the revolting smell of the chemicals in her nose, and could recall them whenever she wished. And then the boa constrictor too, so utterly revolting. She had had to go past it on her way to the offices in the museum. It stood in a corner, quite a dark corner. The terrible thing was that you did not see it until you were right on top of it, so that it made you jump. It gave her such a turn every time, she never got used to it. Alberta could imagine for herself how disgusting it was with its enormous, thick body, coiled round a tree-trunk. It made you feel throttled.

' But did you have to go there so often? Your husband came home at night, surely?' Alberta asked haphazardly, mainly for the sake of saying something.

' Of course he did, but very late. Always too late to go out and see or hear anything. He sat late over his books, he had so much to get through. I just went to bed, you see.'

'Oh,' said Alberta, embarrassed and helpless.

'So then I got the chance of coming down here and began to paint, which I had always had an inclination for. And I have made valuable acquaintances, I've come to know elegant people who have become of importance, real importance to me, people with tragic lives . . . .'

Kalén, thought Alberta mechanically.

'It doesn't stop one feeling a little sad on such a day. Memories come back. A fine man in any case, a truly fine man,' she snuffled.

'That's what you always say.' It was Kalén, who had freed himself again and now stood towering over the table.

'I beg your pardon? What do you mean?'

'Little angels always say, when they have left a man, that he was really so fine and sweet. Is it to improve your consciences or what? To be a bit noble afterwards? That's easily done.'

'Oh – !'

'What was your husband?' asked Alberta mistakenly. She had forgotten the chemicals and the boa constrictor, and merely wanted to show what interest she could, besides making it clear to Kalén that nobody was bothering about his tactlessness.

'A custodian,' came the quiet reply.

But Kalén exploded with the uncontrollable laughter of a drunkard: 'Custodian! Ha – ha – ha!'

'Is that so terribly amusing?'

'Rich. That's rich.' Kalén struck himself across the knees, seized a glass that was not his own, and swung it aloft: 'Skaal for the custodian! Health to him! I shall enjoy that for a long time . . . ha – ha – ha!' And he emptied the stranger's glass before its owner could stop him.

There was a stir. The owner of the glass, a quiet, bespectacled Swede, rose to his feet muttering something about educated people, ordinary manners. Well-meaning souls interposed themselves to explain. Meanwhile the little

Swedish woman got ready to go, pale and dignified: ' I
can't put up with that drunk fellow. I'm going now.'

Alberta said she would accompany her. There was an
atmosphere of catastrophe, of breakdown, in the fracas.
They helped each other with their coats. She nodded to
Sivert, who was sitting chatting to some Danes at the next
table.

Suddenly she heard a woman's voice in Danish: ' It was
a terrible accident. So frightful for his wife too. Yes, they
were divorced, but when she heard about it she went
straight down. But it was all over. He never regained
consciousness.'

Alberta stood as if petrified.

' A car accident, wasn't it?' That was Sivert, sympathetic
and careful as one is when asking about that sort of thing.

' A big lorry, one of those monsters that come at you
like a stone-crusher. Just as he was coming out of the
railway station in Cologne and was about to cross the
street. He was knocked down violently, fractured his skull
and suffered other injuries besides. I thought perhaps you
knew him. His name was Veigaard. He was an odd
person ... .'

Alberta supported herself against the table, a chance
table, with chance faces round it. They looked at her in
amazement. She looked back at them for a while.

Then something snapped. And she laughed out loud, a
hilarious, forced, unnatural laugh.

Everyone looked up, Sivert from the contemplation of
his two composed hands. He rose and came towards her,
speaking quietly and urgently, half jokingly: ' Listen
Alberta, have you had too much to drink? You can't stand
here laughing when the poor chap's dead. So help me, Kalén
doesn't seem to be the only one drunk here tonight.'

He took her arm, implying that he would accompany
her, that now they must concentrate on getting away. A
little farther off, between the tables, the Swedish woman
stood waiting for her, miserable and dispirited.

Then Alberta pushed Sivert away, went through the

swing-doors quickly, looked round for a moment. as if uncertain which way to go, caught sight of the tram-car that passed her street standing at the tram-stop, and ran to catch it. It moved off at once.

* * *

Each time Alberta woke in her comfortless little room with the comfortless sounds of poor people's grey lives seeping in through the gap under the door – the shuffle of slippers in the morning rush, the tap perpetually running, the slamming doors – she received a stinging, rough reminder that there is a worn, hard little path across the fog-bound marsh, where we can see no further than tomorrow. There is a ridge that one can grope for, hard to the feet, but safe: toil, honest toil, no matter what. Perhaps something will get frost-bitten on the way and shrivel up, but there is no need to lose one's foothold or one's way. And one's weakness will not become open to anybody who happens to be in possession of the small skeleton keys to it: tenderness in the voice, certain words that one craves to hear, that single one out from other people and run rippling through body and soul like a healing spring, kindness in a difficult moment.

She felt again, like the ache of an exposed nerve, the old longing to discover her own form of toil and to work at it. Hard, bitter, healthy toil, serving as a safeguard against all that was weak and hesitant in herself.

The rest was like playing blind-man's-buff; we rush about, our eyes blinded by our own longing. And death plays this game too, using his dagger quietly and from behind. Nothing seems to have happened. Or one has the impression that something quite different has happened. Until suddenly the cards are laid on the table in circumstances that make one laugh aloud as if in delirium. The game was up a long time ago.

Death can also amuse himself by reversing the fortunes

of the game in one throw. Alberta had seen that happen too.

A variegated web of violently contrasting light and shade was drawn unceasingly through her memory. A summer night in a haycock, the mingled scent of flowers over her face, dry, fleeting warmth from a hand touching her cheek, the secure feeling of being tucked in, just as when she was small.

A morning grey with dew and approaching daylight, a sudden play of new forces in her body, a face that looked at her, so tense with gravity that two small muscles appeared on either side of the mouth.

A misty morning outside open windows, the strange, new little sound of raw potatoes being scraped, the mixed scent of roses and freshly made coffee, the notes of *Santa Lucia* from a barrel organ near by.

The warmth of another person through a whole long night, the feeling of having reached one goal on a long, laborious journey, all that she had felt on waking, until the daylight and the street and a thousand glimpses of others' lives about her had succeeded in rousing old unrest to life again.

A moment at a railway station, when words she had not brought herself to say, decisive, strong words, forced themselves to her lips too late and to no purpose.

And a turbid dream that had taken hold, unreasonable, confused, until she was suddenly woken, roughly and mercilessly, by the cards being brutally turned up.

The rest she was only capable of seeing in relation to something old, something she normally kept locked well down inside her mind. Now it was unlocked for her, she lived through it all again. An icy wind seized her, whirling her with it through a piece of existence that seemed to be the hereafter, where day and night were one. Then she was dropped down into a churchyard in front of two large black holes in the snow. Stunned she stood watching coffins lowered into them and knew that now life would begin again, but otherwise, and beyond belief.

All thought of death, all conception of it, was indissolubly bound up with that first time, a winter evening at home in the small town, the wedding day of the new district physician from Flatangen. The arrangement had been that Alberta was to have tea ready when Mama and Papa came home. They would probably need something warm. Mama thought it would be cold down on the quay.

Alberta stood at the window in one of the dark sitting-rooms and watched them all go past, all the guests at Dr. Berven's wedding: Berven himself and his bride, who had come from Kristiania a couple of days previously and was so lovely, the Reverend Pio and his wife, the Governor and his wife, Mama and Papa, Beda and the Recorder, Dr. and Mrs. Pram, Dr. and Mrs. Mo, the Dean and his wife, almost twenty of them in all.

They came out of the darkness, walked quickly in procession through the circle of light made by the street lamps, and disappeared into the darkness again. The gentlemen walked with their coat collars turned up, Dr. Pram in a fur overcoat, his stick pointing straight up into the air out of his pocket as was his habit. The ladies fussed with their trains, pausing momentarily to get a better grip. The lace shawl, which the Governor's wife was wearing over her fur hat, slipped backwards. She stood still in the circle of light while Harriet Mo helped her. Mama looked up and gave Alberta a little wave.

Behind them came the street boys and youths, the maids who worked for various people, Lilly Vogel arm in arm with a girl from Namsos who had become her boon companion since Palmine Flor had married and become so respectable and superior.

Everything had been so ordinary. Alberta remembered clearly that Jensine had passed by the dining-room on her way up to bed. With her alarm-clock in her hand she had come into the dark sitting-room and stood for a moment in the window as well: 'Are they on their way down now? Look at the maids from the Prams' and the Recorder's. Beda's supposed to be not at all bad to work for. They want to go down and have a look as well when it's Doctor Berven who's leaving with a new bride and under his own steam. Well, nobody's going to get me down to the Stoppenbrink Quay at this time of night, thank you very much. I've lighted the spirit stove, the water's on.'

'Thank you, Jensine.'

Alberta was left to walk up and down in the cold, dark room. The light from the dining-room shone in across the floor. She walked across it from darkness into darkness, whimpering a little to herself, as she was used to doing when she was alone: 'I won't go on, I won't go on.' Her thoughts struggled with old, hopeless problems.

An evening like countless others when Papa and Mama were out without her. Only married couples had been invited.

She went out to see to the stove. It had been turned up too high. The kitchen was full of cold steam. On her way back into the hall something reached her, a hubbub from the street below, the hum of many voices, loud shouts that cut through them.

When she got to the window the street was black with people. They came running from all directions, from the alleys and down from Upper Town. Boys, old women who had scarcely given themselves time to throw on a shawl and were still fumbling with it as they ran, one or two men who cleared themselves a way by elbowing people aside, Mad Petra . . . . They converged in the middle of the street as if in a canal and streamed westwards.

Through the open window she heard Tailor Kvandal calling from his doorstep: 'Keep calm, dear people, keep calm!' Nobody listened to him.

A few short sentences freed themselves from the hum down below, a few impossible, brief phrases: 'Stoppenbrink's old quay – all the fine folk in the sea – they can't see to get them up again.'

The words affected Alberta like unexpected and unmerited blows, making her angry. That was her first reaction and the last she remembered clearly. Afterwards she

456

remembered in bits and pieces, as one remembers dreams.

She ran along the street with all the others, occasionally hearing shouts behind her: ' Alberta, poor thing ... Miss Selmer ... oh, don't let her pass, what if she ... can't someone ...'. A few tried to take her by the arm. She had to tear herself free.

Then there were all the lighted windows in Strand Street, normally so dark – it reminded her in an irritating fashion of Christmas Eve – and black groups of people who stood in the way everywhere so that she could not get through; from time to time a kind of procession, several men carrying heavy, mysterious burdens; shouts from down on the quay, lights moving down below, backwards and forwards.

Perplexed and seemingly quite outside it all Alberta drifted from group to group, shoved in the back by people trying to get through who did not see who she was. She remembered Jeanette Evensen's voice: ' Are they dead?' A man's voice answered curtly: ' They're dead.' Alberta's anger returned. The whole thing seemed to her like an idiotic, simple-minded joke, a tasteless performance, stupid beyond belief.

Somebody suddenly seized her by the arm and led her forward. A voice said with authority: ' Make way, this is one of the next of kin.' She went obediently and heard the voice say: ' You mustn't be upset. And you mustn't be frightened. It may not be so bad.' Alberta was given the feeling that now everything would be put to rights, soon the nonsense would come to an end.

They entered a passage. A small kitchen lamp hung on the wall. And suddenly it all became even more confusing. For the person holding her arm and talking to her so reassuringly was Ryan, butcher and radical, dripping with blood and a danger to society, one of the bogeymen of her childhood. The most fearful rumours concerning the slaughterhouse in his back yard were passed from child to child.

Afterwards she vaguely remembered untidy rooms, the small, simple, stuffy rooms of the poor, where people in

457

full evening dress and dripping with water were lying
anyhow, on sofas, beds, wooden benches, tables, the floor.
Some simply lay there, others were being attended to,
having their arms worked up and down above their heads.
She remembered Dr. Mo, so wet that he left great pools
behind him wherever he went, but fully active, giving orders
and feeling pulses, listening for heartbeats with his head on
someone's breast – remembered that she seemed to find
Papa lying quite still on a sofa, his face surprisingly young,
manly and resolute – remembered that someone took her
away, she did not know who.

· Lie down for a bit now, Alberta, poor thing, please do.'
The words were deeply imprinted in her memory, together
with a hand that was lying on her knee when she opened
her eyes. A working hand, red and rough, inured against
everything and by everything. Confused, she looked into
a heavy, masculine, leathery face, not familiar and yet not
quite unfamiliar. It was a while before she realised that
it belonged to Anna Sletnesset, a person seldom seen out
of doors. She sat with the sick and with women in childbed.
As if in a disordered dream this face from life's periphery
was suddenly in the very centre of existence.

She was sitting at the other side of a small table, leaning
over it to talk to Alberta. She seemed to have been talking
to her for a good while already: ' What's the use of sitting
here dozing off? It'll make you ill too, and what do you
gain by that? Put down that fellow Dante and go to bed.
I'm here, I'll tell you at once if there's any change.'

But Alberta would not go to bed. Giddy and sick she
sat trying to collect herself after her brief nap, to read the
book she had taken at random from the bookcase. It was
Dante's *Inferno*, the old Danish translation. The table from
in front of the window had been moved over here, one
of the lamps from the sitting-rooms was standing on it with
a handkerchief over one side of the globe. Everything was
wrong or upside-down in one way or another: in the
shadow, Mama's bedside table, full of medicine bottles

and glasses with spoons in them, on a pillow further away Mama's immovable face. The air was heavy with illness and medicaments, and with a thick, even warmth which Anna Sletnesset, this innocent person from the street, carefully kept at an even temperature and controlled with a thermometer. Without hesitating she ordered magical quantities of coal and wood to be sent up, and Jensine brought them without protest.

Something inconceivable was happening. The dream went on and on, timeless, bound by neither day nor night. Down in the sitting-room lay Papa, white and still, his face young and manly, but sharper over the bridge of the nose from day to day. Out in the town lay several others who were dead, many dangerously ill, some dying. A couple of doctors had come from elsewhere, Dr. Mo was no longer on his feet, Dr. Pram was dead. A strange doctor came and went and told Alberta that it was providential that she had Anna Sletnesset; many more like her were needed now.

She remembered that Mama woke from her fever once when the doctor was there, that she lay there with her eyes clear and calm and asked whether she was in danger, she wanted to know the truth. The doctor's reply had burned itself into Alberta: ' You are in danger, Madam, but we are hoping for the best.' And Mama's lingering reply, as if given after serious reflection: ' It doesn't matter. I have been dead for a long time already.' And she asked after Papa, whether he was still asleep, whether he was always asleep now? ' The Magistrate is still asleep, Madam.'

' He needs to rest,' said Mama, her eyes already retreating again, as if on their way inwards towards something mysterious. Immediately afterwards she lost consciousness and did not return.

Much of this came to Alberta as knowledge she had to acquire afresh each time she woke after brief and unwilling slumber. Together with Anna Sletnesset she watched constantly, and would not go to bed, but sank from time to time into a painful, restless sleep in a sitting position.

Was it the same night that she had stood at the window

459

looking at Orion? She remembered getting to her feet, stiff with fatigue. In spite of the warmth in the room she felt thoroughly chilled as soon as she moved, her whole body trembling as she stood with the blind drawn to one side. There was a hard frost, the dark sky glittered with stars, Orion among them, easily recognizable. The belt's three suns glowed more brightly than everything else out there. Far off the church clock shone like a moon in the night sky. Which night out of many? The clock said five minutes past two.

It was then that Alberta was overwhelmed with anxiety on account of what was stirring deep inside her. She knew the feeling of old. It was like standing on the edge of deep water and fainting. What did she want, what did she desire, when she gave herself time now and then to desire and want?

Then she was sitting beside Anna Sletnesset again, trying to keep her head from nodding, refusing to sleep. She heard Anna say: 'Now you *are* going to bed, Alberta, poor thing.'

She was lifted, carried, put down. Her shoes were taken off, a blanket laid over her.

It was good . . . good.

' Alberta, poor thing, you must get up now.'

It was Anna Sletnesset again, the doctor too. He was standing in the middle of the room looking sympathetic. Both of them took Alberta by the arm and helped her across the floor. Her legs felt as if cut from under her. She shook with helplessness.

' Have I been asleep?'

' Yes, poor thing.'

Anna's voice was different, so disquietingly mild.

' Is Mama dead?' Alberta heard herself say these strange words. She felt as if someone was standing beside her saying them.

' No, but the end has come.'

Then she was standing by Mama's bed. The face on the

pillow was still, white, tranquil, the eyes clear and shining. Mama said nothing, but she looked at Alberta with an open, pure expression, like a child's. And it seemed to Alberta that she had never seen Mama before; tenderness, regret, longing flooded into her as she knelt beside the bed.

An anxious, enquiring expression came into Mama's face, she moistened her lips with her tongue. Now she will ask for Papa, thought Alberta, agonized. What shall I say?

But Mama said slowly and indistinctly and as if with infinite longing: ' Jacob.'

Then it was terribly quiet. And her expression disappeared, withdrawing inwards and backwards. Two empty, staring eyes were left behind. Blinded with tears Alberta saw Anna Sletnesset's rough finger gently draw the eyelids down over them. ' A beautiful death, Alberta, a beautiful death to be sure,' Anna whispered, patting Alberta on the arm.

Alberta's tears suddenly stopped. She got to her feet, and accompanied the doctor downstairs. Politely and tactfully the stranger offered her his condolences and shook her hand.

She could still remember the sensation that had come over her when she had seen him out and gone in again through the cold rooms. It was like coming home from school and finding the curtains had been taken down: a sensation of something missing, of nakedness, of a cold wind that blew straight in unchecked.

Then she was in the kitchen. She could still see the lamp she put down on the kitchen bench, the cold meat she found, off which she suddenly began to carve slice after slice, her own blue hands doing it. A raging, ravenous, hunger had possessed her. She stuffed the slices into her mouth with her fingers, swallowing them without chewing properly.

And she went up to Anna Sletnesset and Jensine, who were busy seeing to things up there. They took her and put her to bed, undressing her like a child, and giving her

461

hot-water bottles. For she trembled and trembled and could not get warmth into her body.

It was only when it was all over that Alberta found out what had really happened. Rotten, its piles and planks riddled with worms, the old Stoppenbrink Quay had suddenly been unable to hold up any longer. It had broken down beneath all those tramping, gay people. The tide was up, it was freezing and dark. The sequel she knew already. Some drowned, nearly all the survivors fell dangerously ill with pneumonia and all kinds of complications after the shock they had suffered. Several died. There was a mass burial with the flags flying at half-mast all over the town.

Uncle Thomas himself travelled north. He helped Alberta to make arrangements and decisions. With her full approval everything was sent to be auctioned. It had brought in a sum of money for herself and Jacob. Her share had been used up long ago.

When Alberta now woke in the little room in Paris and lay thinking back over her life, she felt as if she had really only been dreaming now and again, or that she had come into it by mistake. But they were dreams that left reality behind them.

There was Sivert, for instance. He was as real as could be. And he put in an appearance daily. He did not ask directly for any explanation, but sat there as if on his wooden crate with his elbows on his knees and his hands clasped, looking thoughtful. Sometimes Alberta would catch a hesitant expression on his face. He was probably wondering whether she was quite in her right mind.

He did not say much. He went so far as to imply that the timing of the crisis could have been better chosen. He was already in full swing with his composition, had almost come so far as to hope that he might be able to try it out at the Spring Exhibition. Strange that this notion of living in her own room should have come just now.

He would sit for a while, ask as if *en passant* whether she would not come out with him to eat at any rate. Then

AND FREEDOM

he would give her some packages he had put down by the
door when he arrived. There would be bread, fruit, cooked
vegetables, sometimes a grilled chop. Alberta felt terribly
humiliated. On the other hand both her articles had been
sent back to her with a few apologetic words. Unfortunately,
the material was not quite suitable this time. However,
something in the style in which she had written formerly
would be welcome, and so on.

Mumbling with embarrassment she thanked Sivert for
what he had brought. She would pay him back when she
had the money. Sivert shrugged his shoulders: 'That
doesn't matter,' he said. 'And I can't sit watching you
starve to death up here.'

She went and posed for him now and again, in order to
do something in return. But it was far from being the same
as before or quite what Sivert wanted. If only she got up
early in the morning. But she was tardy, and did not turn
up until almost lunch-time. He had to hang about waiting
for her without being able to start on anything else instead.
Then they had to eat. Then perhaps the lunch did not suit
Alberta. Occasionally she had to go and lie down on the
divan for a while, seized by a strange and obscure indisposition. What with one thing and another Sivert sometimes
wandered about a little impatiently, rattling his canvases
and brushes. A sigh would escape him.

Nevertheless Alberta had put on weight since she had
been eating properly again. Her figure was rounder than
before. Every time she pulled herself together and posed
again, unwilling in body and limbs, she caught sight of
herself in Sivert's mirror. It was not as large as Mr. Digby's,
but you could see quite a lot in it all the same. Every time
she thought: I owe it to Sivert to pose; it's the least I can
do for him. And she posed from old habit, until she
trembled and swayed, feeling as if she were placating
mysterious powers whose habit it is to force us into
situations to which we are averse.

One day Alberta was sitting on the edge of her trunk,

463

rummaging amongst her scraps of paper. The window was open. The smoke of bonfires drifted in the air from the thousands of small allotments outside the fortifications. Warm sunshine alternated with cold wintry gusts, the clouds raced overhead with sudden depths of ultramarine sky between them. It was one of February's sporadic spring days.

She read them, put them down, read once more. Involuntarily she began to put some order into the muddle, sometimes finding several scraps about the same thing. In the course of time she had come upon new characteristics, had noted them and thrown them in. Laid out in small piles it almost looked like a collection of material. For some reason she knew more about people and their relationships than before, and could continue here and there. Where she had once broken off because she only glimpsed obscurity, full light now fell; where she had faced mute darkness, light began to dawn. She now suddenly saw through conversations, short exchanges she had written down hastily with the feeling that something lay behind them; she saw the people concerned coming and going before and after, moving in surroundings she had not known she could imagine.

Slightly astonished, half amused, she sat dabbling and reading, took a pencil and made a correction here and there, improved words and expressions, and then sat still, holding a little bundle of papers, her head resting on the window sill in a warm gleam of sunshine. Only then did she realise how tired she was. Tired of longing, making mistakes, being cold, pining, fussing about the wrong things. She closed her eyes, still seeing the sunshine as red light beneath her eyelids. It was good to sit like that, her body relaxed, to feel the sun and the air on her face, not to be cold.

And something dawned on her. All the pain, all the vain longing, all the disappointed hope, all the anxiety and privation, the sudden numbing blows that result in years going by before one understands what happened – all this was knowledge of life. Bitter and difficult, exhausting to live through, but the only way to knowledge of herself and others. Success breeds arrogance, adversity understanding. After all misfortune perhaps there always comes a day when one thinks: It was painful, but a kind of liberation all the same; a rent in my ignorance, a membrane split before my eyes. In a kind of mild ecstasy Alberta suddenly whispered up to the sun: 'Do what you will with me, life, but give me understanding, insight and perception.'

She went over and lay down on the divan, making herself comfortable. The sun reached right in and shone on her as long as it was there, the red light still flickered behind her eyelids. New possibilities dawned on her, something more than the old newspapers on the table at home: *Morgenbladet* and *Aftenposten*. Other forms of writing were possible besides putting together casual articles for these two. New, bold ideas stirred in Alberta. Supposing she were to try! To try to find form for a little reality, not just continue to write horrid, well-bred essays about purely external events, eye-catching and easy to read – she, as well as so many others. When she was less tired she would do something about it, try to put something from the trunk into shape . . . .

Someone knocked. From acquired habit Alberta stretched out her hand, turned the key and sat up on the divan: 'Come in Sivert.'

But it was not Sivert, it was Liesel. She stood in the doorway, astonished, and said apologetically: 'It's only me, Albertchen.' Alberta, too, was astonished, and lay down again. Liesel had become so infrequent a visitor since she had moved out to Eliel. With her wan, small face beneath her thick braids she was not quite the old Liesel any more. 'I only wanted to look in,' she explained.

'That was nice of you.'

'Are you resting? Are you posing for Mr. Digby again?'

No. Alberta was only a bit tired, slept badly at night, had bugs and noise to contend with. One thing after another.

'Really?' said Liesel, sitting down and looking at

Alberta. Suddenly something strangely experienced came
into her expression, and it struck Alberta as lightning
strikes. For an instant she was made so giddy that the divan
seemed to disappear from beneath her. Things that had
and had not happened recently lined themselves up for
inspection. Cold sweat broke out on her temples. She had
asked life to do with her what it would. That had not been
necessary. Life had begun exaggerating some time ago. This
was impossible. At the same time she knew that it was so.
Where had her thoughts been? Preoccupied with a series
of old and new events, whose horror had bewildered her,
which she could not keep apart from each other and still
had not fully grasped. In the meantime rough reality had
gone its way.

' Where can I find water?' asked Liesel.

' Out in the passage. Take a cup with you.'

Liesel came back with the cold water and Alberta drank
thirstily. The roof of her mouth was suddenly dry and she
felt as if her throat was parched.

' Is that better?'

' Yes, thank you.' Urgently impelled to chatter away the
whole impression, Alberta asked after Liesel. How was she?
How was her painting getting on? Was she going to exhibit
again at the Spring Exhibition? She must certainly do so.
Beneath her words the thought insisted: It can't be true,
it's impossible, impossible, it's death . . . .

Liesel told her she could no longer paint. If only she
could! She got so fearfully tired, did not seem to have the
energy. Besides, she could not work on anything but still
lifes, and even that was not feasible when Eliel had a
model. She could go to Colarossi's, but – . And she
confessed that she had become so incredibly lazy in the
mornings. She found it almost impossible to get up, and
then she would lie in the loft for the best part of the day
because people were always dropping in. Eliel declaimed
from the Edda : ' Things go from bad to worse if you sleep
late in the morning. He who acts quickly is half rich
already.' Could Alberta hear that she could speak Swedish?

Liesel smiled a little, and repeated the foreign tongue slowly, childishly stammering, marking the rhythm with her head. ' But it's no use, Albertchen. I'm quite impossible. And yet I must pull myself together. One day Eliel will go back to his own country, and I'll be left high and dry.'

' He'll take you with him, surely, Liesel?'

' *Ach*, he can't marry, Albertchen. Family life doesn't suit artists, especially sculptors. They must be bachelors, free of all ties.'

Alberta lay staring at Liesel. She had been through it all, the anxiety, the uncertainty, the continually teasing hope, the torture. Now she was pitiful and annihilated, an echo of Eliel. Suddenly Alberta hated Eliel.

At that moment there was another knock, and this time there was no doubt as to who it was. A faint hope of saving the situation flickered in Alberta for an instant against all reason; she put her finger to her lips, and Liesel sat tense and quiet as a mouse. But the knock came again, even the locked door was rattled: ' It's Sivert. Are you there, Alberta? Here I am with my hands full and I'm in a hurry.'

Crestfallen before the inevitable, Alberta opened the door. Sivert entered firmly, carrying dripping packages, a long loaf of bread sticking up out of one coat pocket and a bunch of celery out of the other. Liesel stared at him, clearly putting two and two together.

Sivert also looked overcome for a moment. Then he evidently thought he had mastered the situation splendidly: ' Look at that! I come up here once in a blue moon and kill two birds with one stone!'

Alberta's attention was caught by one of the packages. It contained boiled, white beans. She had disliked the look of it as soon as she saw it. Now it was lying on the edge of the table turning into a revolting blur of wet paper and thick, yellow pulp. She felt it slide into her, and began to sweat as if seasick. She clenched her teeth desperately, answering briefly with words of one syllable: ' Yes. No '. She would not look at the package of beans. But when she did not do so she saw them even more clearly in her imagination. They ought to have been wrapped up and not left lying about like that. But she could not go near them, and it did not seem to occur to either of the others. They were simply sitting, looking embarrassed.

Then she half rose: ' Go out, get out of here,' she shouted. And the worst happened. Sivert and Liesel instinctively shrank back as close to the narrow walls as they could. ' Oh,' groaned Alberta, and lay down. She turned her head a little: ' Please go, Sivert.'

And Sivert went. Liesel helped as well as she could, with towels she found hanging on the wall, cleaned up Alberta and gave her water, looked irresolutely at the result of the catastrophe. Alberta got up wretchedly, found the floor-cloth and tried to remedy the worst of it. Liesel took it away from her: ' Lie down again, Albertchen.'

In a short while she was back, sitting on the edge of the divan: ' Is it Ness?' she asked gently.

' Yes.'

' Perhaps I should not have come, Albertchen, but I didn't know anything about it. The whole thing is so unexpected. You didn't even like Ness.'

Alberta hesitated, searching for an answer. Then Liesel said: ' To be honest, perhaps it's a bit accidental who it is. But we want to love the person it happens to be, don't we?' She looked at Alberta almost entreatingly.

' Yes, Liesel, of course we do.'

But Liesel said eagerly: ' It mustn't turn out as it did for me, promise me that. You'll regret it your whole life, Albertchen.' She leaned over closer and looked into Alberta's eyes, her pupils dark as forest springs with repressed vehemence. ' You're never the same again, nothing is the same again. I want to love Eliel again just as much, but I can't. Now you mustn't be upset, you must talk to Ness about it.' She kissed Alberta on the forehead: ' Dear little Albertchen.' And Alberta suddenly felt that it was a great comfort and support that Liesel knew this.

' Only today I thought I could see some way in my

work,' she said, half to herself. 'I had such a desire to write, but in quite a different form from before.'

'Oh –.' Liesel gestured away from herself with her hand. 'That's precisely when it happens, when we think we're beginning to achieve something. Then it comes and interrupts it all. I was afraid of it the minute I came into the room, Albertchen. I could see there was something.'

Now life and death depended on Sivert. Now everything in her that was not him had to be hidden away, she had to cling to the person she loved. Liesel's words came back to her again and again: Perhaps it's a bit accidental who it is, but we want to love the person it happens to be. And she searched for every good feeling she had for him, trying to imagine that nothing had happened to make everything meaningless and impossible for her in one blow.

She went and posed for him as best she could, but she did not go as often as before. One day, standing at his easel, Sivert said: 'Why don't you come and stay here for a while again, Alberta?'

'Not yet, Sivert.' Alberta suddenly burst into violent weeping.

She heard him behind her: 'Tell me what it is, Alberta. For I can't make head or tail of it all.'

But Alberta could not get it out.'It's nothing, nothing,' she said. Sivert sighed.

With new eyes she watched the small white bundles the working-class mothers carried with them when they were out of doors. They had nobody to look after them, they were tied by them from morning to night, forced to forget everything else for the sake of the white bundle, sacrifice everything for it. And Alberta felt mutinous. She thought: I'm not ready with myself yet, I haven't achieved anything, must I start thinking only about someone else, unable even to look in any other direction? At the same time she surprised herself noticing how such bundles were carried and dressed, and attempted instinctively to catch glimpses of the tiny, well-wrapped faces. She vainly tried to imagine what her child would look like. It was all misty, she could see nothing.

But here again was one of the things she could not take in immediately.

Then she told him.

They were sitting on the fortifications in last year's grass, sitting there like other couples. Out above Fontenay the moon was rising. Smoke was drifting from the bonfires. It was a mild evening, far too early.

' We're going to have a child, Sivert.' It dropped from Alberta's lips like something ripe, something she had to say at that precise moment.

' What?' said Sivert. ' Are you sure?' he added.

' Yes.'

He sat tearing up the grass, looking down. Alberta's heart made a few painful, unaccustomed movements. She felt fate itself so close to her, so immediately above her, that for an instant she seemed to feel the thread being spun.

' We shall have to see about getting rid of it then, Alberta,' said Sivert quietly.

Alberta got up. She swayed slightly when she was on her feet. Sivert held her, intending to give her support. She drew herself away and began to walk.

He couldn't quite take it in, he said.

' It is so,' said Alberta roughly.

' Yes, yes, now don't get upset, Alberta, it's nothing to worry about. They say it's a trivial matter if you catch it in time. I know several people . . . '

Alberta felt her face turn white. Hurt and shame writhed painfully in her. If only Sivert had said something else she would really have loved him for it. She continued to walk, not bothering to answer. Now and then his hand touched hers. At a corner he took her arm, and she just missed being run over. She twisted away from him again, turning off near the Rue d'Alésia.

'Can't you come home with me this evening, at least? So that we can talk?'

'No,' said Alberta.

At the entrance to her street he attempted to kiss her and tried to hold on to her hands: 'Do you think I don't understand how upset you are? But surely we can talk about it. Perhaps it's a false alarm . . . .'

She pushed him aside, ran along the pavement, pulled the bell violently. Contrary to its custom, the door opened immediately. Without looking round at Sivert, whom she could hear coming after her, she slammed it behind her. She felt as if turned to stone in face and soul.

Sivert was there the next day. He sat on the divan in his usual position, his hands a little less tranquil than usual. One of them rubbed the other continually. And he admitted that, to be frank, he had wondered occasionally whether trouble was on the way, had been devilishly afraid of it, to be honest.

'Have you?' said Alberta.

Yes, after all, she had been rather strange lately, to put it mildly, as far back as the time when she became hysterical at the Versailles, and went off without saying a word.

'If you so much as mention it!' exclaimed Alberta.

'No, I needn't mention it,' said Sivert meekly, already complying with the situation to a certain extent.

He changed the subject to his future, his art. At home at Granli they could not help him much. They had no more than just enough. The farm was small, and there was still a debt on it. The money he had had from the sale of his pictures this spring was as good as finished. Now he was applying for a grant. But . . .

He felt damnably helpless. It was not a small thing for a man in his position to take on. Merely the responsibility! Had Alberta thought what a responsibility it would be? Obviously there was nothing a man wanted more, when he could manage it, than to . . .

He also referred to her future, her freedom and her work.

471

Had she realised what a tie it would be, considering how they were placed?

Alberta listened to him without altering her expression. Something inevitable had occurred to her. Its shadow lay cold across her life. Throw off the burden – yes, she would do it, if it were possible. But it was not possible. Sivert's solution was no solution.

He continued: If only circumstances were different! Alberta must not believe that he didn't . . . . Well, well, when she had thought things over a bit they would be able to live calmly and happily again.

Alberta got up, sat down, watched the movement of the clouds across the sky outside. She seemed to have difficulty talking. Her lips seemed to have stuck together and refused to co-operate. At last she said tonelessly: ' I'll take some hot baths, Sivert, very hot. It's supposed to help sometimes. As for the other – I won't do it.'

And she thought: If baths helped, the world would be a very different place.

Alberta had taken hot baths. In the Rue Delambre and the Rue d'Odessa and the Rue d'Alésia, so as not to attract attention by going time after time to the same place. She had almost scalded herself, had held out until her heart refused to do so any longer and everything whirled round her, had let the hot tap run so unreasonably long that she had been threatened with having to pay for two baths instead of one, next time. But the situation remained unaltered. Sivert said yes, but she must put herself in his position. Alberta continued to sit with her stony expression and said, ' Naturally '.

She had a few words ready to the effect that he should leave her alone, that she could manage by herself, that he need not come again. But they were never spoken, they died unborn like so many of Alberta's words. Saying them would have been equivalent to cutting an anchor-rope and drifting out to sea alone in an open boat.

And Sivert repeated that as long as one did not let too

much time pass, it was not the slightest bit dangerous. That doctor Eliel knew was supposed to have said it was nothing, a mere trifle. Afterwards one was as free as a bird again. Good heavens, if only Alberta realised! It was an everyday matter.

'And Liesel?' Alberta heard a threatening note in her voice.

'Well, what about Liesel? Is there anything the matter with Liesel?' Sivert had seen Liesel in the street quite recently.

'Oh!' exclaimed Alberta in agitation. Like a caged animal she paced the two steps between the window and the door.

Then Sivert said: 'Well ... what was Eliel to do, poor fellow? He was in no better position. Is a man really to let his whole future, all his opportunities, slip out of his grasp for the sake of someone unborn? Is that reasonable? I must say I more than understand him,' asserted Sivert. 'And he's had his share of trouble too, you can be sure of that.'

Alberta had halted. 'Eliel?' she said, holding her breath. 'But surely it was – ?'

Sivert looked at the floor uncomprehendingly for a long time. 'Yes of course it was this doctor who did it, naturally, that's obvious. It was certainly very fortunate for them that they knew him. He seems to be a nice fellow – human – '

'You must go now, Sivert,' said Alberta, her hands over her face. And Sivert, who occasionally behaved with surprising tact, got to his feet and took his hat and coat. He remained standing for a while, as if waiting for Alberta to uncover her face and at least look at him. But she did not do so. He sighed despairingly, and went his way for that day.

'But it means utter ruin, Alberta,' he said a few days later. And for the first time Alberta saw a pale, ravaged, almost contorted expression in his face. Then sympathy began to steal in on her, with a strange stubbornness and slowness. The hardness in her began to yield as if gliding away sluggishly, almost imperceptibly.

She said nothing. But she put her hand on Sivert's arm for a moment. To her, too, it seemed like utter ruin. But these forces catch up with you sooner or later. You may see an avalanche coming, or floods or other catastrophes, but nobody has ever suggested you can avoid them by so doing. One single, narrow, rough track was left to her and Sivert, difficult to follow, precarious and discouraging. She already felt her feet stumble many times, felt the weight of her burden. But the alternative was ruin too, and Sivert would not attempt it with her.

Suddenly his face was on her shoulder. He hid it there for a second or two. It was a boyish gesture – like that of a big boy who has done something wrong and does not know what the devil he can do about it, and has a moment of weakness with his sister or his mother. She bent her head and kissed the troubled boy's forehead for the first time for a long while.

As if by tacit agreement Alberta came again and posed for Sivert. Neither of them referred to it, they simply resumed the practice. It was the first time Sivert had worked on a large composition. He had come some way with it too, had made a number of sketches and begun to collect them on a large sheet of pasteboard. Sivert was not one to risk a canvas before he knew what he was doing, and that precisely. Alberta tired quickly and had to lie down on the divan, and this also took place tacitly, without discussion. One day it struck Alberta that perhaps she instinctively glimpsed salvation here – perhaps, deep down beneath everything else, she had begun to take thought for the morrow as well as she could, for someone besides herself. From now on she was more pleasant to Sivert, more talkative. The painful petrified feeling seemed definitely to have dissolved.

And then Sivert gradually arrived at a decision too,

without superfluous talk. Strictly speaking, he needed female models in this condition. They could carry themselves in proud triumph, or they could wander about, weighed down by anguish and distress. Life manifested itself in them in more than one way, and it was ' an ill wind ' ... The proverb showed itself to be true now, as so often before.

She had begun to adopt hole-and-corner methods of reaching her room, making herself small on the stairs and choosing dark times of day, taking to the habit of throwing her coat round her shoulders, in and out of season, letting it hang loose and open. Nothing was very noticeable yet, but her dresses had begun to feel tight. She avoided conversation with the inhabitants of the house as far as possible.

One day Liesel came up.

' Have you talked to Ness, Albertchen? What did he say?'

Alberta was seized with fellow-feeling for Sivert, perhaps too a touch of feminine reluctance to admit to herself or to anyone else that, however much may have taken place, men are apt to see beyond women, to pay attention to other things besides them alone.

' He said – well, yes, not much. We must keep it dark for the time being, of course. You understand ... .'

Did Liesel understand! With tears in her eyes she took Alberta's hand and held it to her cheek for a moment. ' Are you happy, Albertchen?'

' Happy? You know, Liesel, we have no idea how we shall manage.'

* * *

One hot August evening they were wandering down the Boul' Mich'. Alberta was now a little less cautious, and ventured more often down into town. At this time of year there were no dangerous acquaintances in Paris, and she had a nervous compulsion to move about.

The new St. Michel-Montmartre motor-bus was standing ready to leave. And Sivert was quite prepared to improve matters as well as he could. He did not flinch from promenading abroad with Alberta, by now considerably altered; he found things to do in so far as it was possible. He suggested a trip on the upper deck.

Sivert did not look at all happy. But he did look as if he had decided to struggle through. Alberta, on the other hand, had her petrified feeling, something frozen in the mind that only made itself felt at intervals. She seemed to congeal over and over again. Something was happening that was so overwhelming, she could not really take it in. It made her apathetic, almost indifferent. It would have to end as it might, preferably in death.

They bowled along through the oppressive streets. It was no longer the same as in the horse-buses that pitched along at a walking pace or a slow trot, according to contingencies, while snatches of conversation rose up from all the people sitting on chairs on the pavement. Now everything was drowned in the noise of the motor.

The air in the streets ascending towards the Place Clichy was worse than ever, a revolting brew of the stink of petrol and stagnant vapours. '*Huff*,' said Sivert. 'Why did we come here? It would have been far better to take a tram-car out of town. It'll be pleasant to get back home.'

But further along the Boulevard Clichy something was happening. People were crowding round large tents pitched lengthways under the scorched trees on the walk in the middle of the street. The roaring of lions came from one of them. In front of another a Negro armed with a shield, arrows and a lance, tattooed and wearing a metal pin through his nose, stood on a platform above the crowd. The muffled sound of war drums arose, as threatening as distant thunder about him. Farther off a steam roundabout span round to loud music, and announced its departure with a shrill whistle, very up-to-date of its kind. A switch-back was in full activity to the accompaniment of clattering and shrieks. Enormous posters announced that here man-eating tribes from Central Africa were on exhibition. The smell of fried apples, pancakes and wild animals cut through the heavy air.

' Come on, let's go in,' said Alberta suddenly. They were standing in front of the Negro's tent.

Sivert demurred for an instant: ' I'm not sure that it would be wise for you to go in,' he said. ' I've heard that . . . '. He would like to see the blacks himself. ' Even if it is only trickery, they can be very picturesque.'

' I *want* to go in,' said Alberta curtly. She felt the cold stubbornness that often had the upper hand in her now. If it was ill-advised, so much the worse.

Once inside the tent Sivert wanted to take her out again. ' The smell,' he said. ' It's enough to finish you.'

But Alberta could stand it. A deep sympathy, something compelling, had seized her as soon as she entered. These Negroes squatting round simulated camp-fires or wandering round on flattened, naked feet, grinning at each other and exchanging comments on the sightseers which were certainly not flattering, perhaps exceedingly coarse – she felt a warmth for them, a searing pity, similar to the pity one feels for inefficient jugglers and performing animals, for all poor things that have to put themselves on show.

They were all ages, old people, young ones and children, the majority men and young boys, but an old man and a couple of old women too, looking like the mummified heads one sees in museums. In one corner a war dance was taking place to the accompaniment of the drums, people were gathering there, standing on tiptoe to see over each other's heads. Sivert jammed himself in with the rest, sketchbook in hand, asking Alberta to wait for him and to go outside if the smell was too much for her.

She wandered round the big tent, watching the weaving and other handwork that was being shown in the corners, and then stopped in sudden surprise. In the far corner there was a separate section, a smaller tent raised inside the large one. Illuminated by a hanging lamp a young Negress was kneeling inside it. She was holding a child in her arms, and had pushed her sleeveless red dress down from her shoulder and taken out her breast to give to the baby. He was loosely wrapped in a brightly coloured cloth. Alberta could only see the back of his head and one strong little hand which struck again and again at his mother's flesh, gripping it with pleasure. Just as Alberta approached, he relinquished the breast. The mother put him down on a blanket on the floor while she put her dress straight. Then she bent down and loosened the cloth, and remained looking down at the child, who stretched himself, satisfied, while his eyes slowly blurred with sleep. He was a sturdy baby, probably a few months old, round and firm as a little baroque angel, in spite of the city air, the dust and all kinds of wrong conditions.

The mother wrapped the cloth round him again, picked up the child and rocked him gently, watching him intently. Behind her the walls of the tent gave continually under the pressure of the crowd outside. She seemed to be unaware of anything but the child she was holding.

Alberta had never seen such sweetness in a face, such placid, infinite tenderness, such tranquil, intense happiness.

The child was asleep. The mother looked up. Her eyes were as frank and soft as those of a gentle, beautiful, shy animal. They glittered moistly, blue as enamel round the large, brown pupils. The mouth beneath the small, flat nose was paler than the face, scarcely red, but generous with the same animal goodness, making Alberta think of the dumb devotion of dumb creatures, their instinctive and primeval expression of it. She was reminded of the doe that licks its calf, of horses nuzzling each other.

The Negress looked at Alberta. The large, moist eyes looked her up and down. Then the lips parted in a smile full of understanding, she nodded delightedly a couple of times from Alberta to the child and back again. And she slid carefully down into a sitting position on the floor of straw and branches with small woven mats scattered here and there over it, leaned once more over the child in her arms and remained sitting thus, as if lost in patient, joyful submission. She did not move again.

But something was released in Alberta's heart. For the first time she felt without defiance and coldness that she was to become a mother. The approaching enemy was a little naked child, infinitely defenceless, with only herself to turn to and trust. Boundless sympathy for it streamed towards her heart and eyes, and was released, warm and wet on her cheeks.

Sivert arrived. He was full of the war dance, which had certainly been genuine enough, by Jove. But it was high time they went, it was a wonder Alberta had not even felt sick. Was she crying? Well, what was the matter now?

'I'm only a little tired,' said Alberta.

People were filling the tent, hiding the young mother. There was nothing more to wait for. Sivert led her towards the exit: 'We'll find something to drink somewhere,' he said. 'Something cool and refreshing.'

That evening Alberta went home with Sivert. She accompanied him to the door and went in with him, without either of them referring to it.

But when they were inside the studio and he had lighted the lamp, he said half jokingly: 'Are you still there? Well, I think that's the best thing, don't you? It can't be very pleasant going up and down those stairs any longer, I imagine.'

He looked about him: 'We shall have to arrange things as best we can here.'

Then Alberta went over and took Sivert's hand. And she did as Liesel had done with hers, laid it against her cheek.

ALBERTA ALONE

PART ONE

The cart taking Liesel and Jeanne was at the top of the slope, standing still against the light wall of mist. They turned and waved, Liesel with quick graceful movements of her wrist, Jeanne with a broad swing of the arm and a high, piercing *'Au revoir'* which the wind blew down to them piecemeal. The children were lifted off, the baker swung himself up instead. A final gust of fresh bread on the breeze, the altered ring of the hooves striking the road as the horse began to trot. Liesel and Jeanne waved once more. Then they were gone.

'It's lifting. It's going to be fine. Just as I said.'

'It's going to be fine.'

'Soon it will be your turn. Sivert will be coming back a rich man, and you'll be off to meet him.' Pierre turned his head and looked at Alberta for a second.

Her heart gave a painful little jump. The words, 'Sivert, rich man', provoked her. What was disturbing about them? On the contrary she ought to—She laughed a little. 'Rich?'

'It's always a beginning,' Pierre said reprovingly. 'If he brings off this deal—and he will. You'll see how it goes afterwards. What a good thing the baker came this way, or we'd never have got Liesel to the train. Jeanne does enjoy going to town.'

There was an undertone to his voice, almost as if he were saying: 'At least I can do that for her'. He was standing a little in front of Alberta with his back to her, his right hand thrust deep into his pocket, as was his habit, so that his trousers were pulled askew; he was still looking upwards even though there was nothing to be seen any more.

Fond of Jeanne all the same, thought Alberta.

She felt chilled, and hid her hands in her sleeves. The early morning mist lay damply on everything, and the night had not yet released her: the long night hours when her heart punched out the seconds, passed, passed, passed, passed, and sleep descended only momentarily, loose and full of holes. What was the dream she had had? A bad one as usual? The times were gone when dreams had been a refuge, a land of promise. They had turned into a purgatory where she stood face to face with her own inadequacy, her disquiet and anxiety.

'Streets, shops, purchases, a meal at a restaurant—strange what a weakness women have for all that.' Pierre shrugged his shoulders, turned and looked in the direction of the sea, screwing up his eyes.

Strange? thought Alberta. No, it's not strange.

For an instant she visualised the narrow, crooked street of the town with its domed cobblestones, the low, dark little shops, the peasant women crowding everywhere with their baskets and their big skirts, the market place packed and noisy with men and animals, the heat of the midday sun beating down on it all. A longing to go from window to window, to stand rummaging amongst materials, perhaps to buy them, a truly feminine longing came over her; and a longing to sit under the trees outside the hotel, eating shrimps, released from the daily round.

She stood watching the children coming down the slope: the little girl leaping, arms and legs flying, the boy walking slowly with bent head, absorbed in stroking his finger along the stone wall. His tan was too thin, too transparent, reminding her of the coffee they used for the first wash of colour in the school drawing class at home. One longed for the next time, when it would be the real thing.

The dungarees she had made him were far from flattering, too long at the back, awkwardly cut. The woollen jersey he had on to protect him from the chill had felted into a comical shape from poor laundering. With torturing clarity she saw it all.

The little girl, on the other hand, came running boisterously, her tan healthy and complete, as if she had several summers' sunburn in her skin, the one on top of the other. Her bare arms and legs stuck out of faded, but normal, well-cut clothes. Jeanne was clever, her child strong and tough.

In a moment Marthe would reach her father, throw her arms round him—

Then Alberta noticed that Pierre was humming. Involuntarily she turned towards the sound, so unusual was it. He was still looking down to where the sea lay behind the mist, and he was humming; one of the tunes one has always known but not where it came from, something or other out of an old opera. It was unheard-of behaviour for Pierre. Alberta could not remember hearing him hum before. He hummed nicely.

Then everything was drowned in eager children's talk.

The little girl clung to her father's arm, jumping up and down. 'Why didn't you look at me? Why are you looking the other way? I ran all the way down from the top and you're looking the other way!'

'Hm,' said Pierre, taken by surprise, and smiled his crooked smile, which consisted in drawing his mouth to one side. He made a movement as if to lift the child. Nothing came of it. His hands, which had been halfway out of his pockets, returned to the bottom of them. 'Another time,' he said.

'I may not run another time. But today Tante Alberta is going to look after us all day. And if there's not enough of the cold pancakes for lunch she's to give us soft-boiled eggs, and if the butcher doesn't come before dinner she's to give us yesterday's soup and something made with eggs, and fried potatoes. But if Jean-Marie brings any fish, she's to boil them fresh and ask Jean-Marie to clean them. He might as well considering the price he asks for it. But Papa is to have the cold chop as well, because he needs more. And at five o'clock we're to fetch the milk and the fresh butter, and afterwards we must be quiet and not disturb Papa, for we are to play up here round the house while Tante Alberta cooks dinner. And Papa is to send off he knows what by the postman, and afterwards he is to write his book. But we are to bathe at two o'clock, for then it will be high tide. And for our snack we shall have—'

485

Pierre put his hand over his left ear.

'Marthe, Marthe, Marthe, have you finished?'

'Now I've finished,' explained the child in all seriousness. 'Except that *Tante* Alberta must fasten the shutters in our room, because *Maman* forgot. And Papa is to be sure to take his medicine.'

'He's to be sure to, is he?' Pierre stood with an ambiguous expression on his damaged face. His scar was two white lips that would not tan, pressed tightly together in the black beard. His mouth—was it sad or defiant, contemptuous or patient, or a little of all these things? Pierre lived behind a mask, brown above his pallor, and angular, with deep saucers of shadow beneath the cheekbones and temples, the lower jaw crooked and wrongly-shaped from the sword-thrust.

For the time being he would go upstairs. He would say, 'Well, you must excuse me,' and go upstairs. And his typewriter would clatter until lunch. And until it was time to bathe. And until dinner time. Or he would disappear outside amongst the grassy slopes, his old beret askew on his head, taking pencil and paper with him. Both kinds of behaviour were in order. He was a man, a breadwinner, a writer of repute into the bargain. It was Alberta whom Marthe would nag all day long and talk to a standstill with Jeanne's decrees; Alberta's child whom she would tyrannize with her excess energy until there was trouble, and the day became dark with scolding and tears. Alberta would not scold. She was a woman and no more.

Tired out already by the coming day she faced it as best she could. A fear that had haunted her in recent years, of not appearing sufficiently motherly and domesticated, often drove her to simulate cheerful enterprise.

'I expect we'll manage, Marthe. Don't look sarcastic, Pierre.'

'Sarcastic?'

Pierre looked at her for an instant. His expression was blank. It was impossible to know what he felt and did not feel. He looked away again, and the slight irritation, which Alberta had unexpectedly felt, subsided.

A rent had appeared in the mist. Behind it the day lay

ready, clear and warm; a tarnished silver shilling of a sun, a scrap of very blue sky. The spider's web on the nettles glistened with dew like fine pearl embroidery. The slopes that ran down towards the sea became more distinct, then the white strip of sand and the long sandbank beyond, dark, hostile, exposed as far as the edge of the gunmetal sea that suddenly caught lustre from above and lay there like newly-polished pewter. A boat with slack sail resembled a shadow.

It would not be one of the days smelling of seaweed and salt, but of flowers and hay from far inland. The wind came caressingly in light, warm puffs, turning aside into one's ear, playing round it and moving on. The simple flora of the meadow curtseyed before it, a wasp was buzzing about already. After a few minutes only a little coil of mist was left up in the air above the surface of the sea. It floated away like smoke as it disintegrated. A mild warmth, full of promise, reached them.

The boy had paused a short distance away; he was standing with his back to them, picking lichen off the wall. The nape of his thin neck was exposed to the light. He looked round, with a strange little face that cut Alberta to the heart. She remembered what she had dreamed.

The boy had bought a large silver dish with a lid, a frightful object in Jugend style. It stood there, polished and shining, its contents steaming. Music was coming from somewhere, a thin, tinkling sound like a musical box.

It was the dish playing. A musical dish that played as long as there was anything inside it. An expensive and useless item, vulgar and ostentatious, that played weakly and tirelessly. Tot had bought it, he was proud of it—

No!

She could not help going over to him, tilting his face upwards from behind and examining it. The eyes that were much too blue met hers for an instant, then looked away to watch the dissolving mist. She flinched from uneasiness and longing, old hurts that were tender to the touch. Then the boy twisted away, and she was left empty-handed.

'Alberta!'

'Yes?' said Alberta. An expectation passed through her mind, fleetingly and gropingly; nothing that could be put into words, not even into thought. As if Pierre could help!

But Marthe, who had been watching all three of them, as only Marthe could watch, with bent head and eyes that jerked sideways and up and down, tugged at her father: 'Go in and write, go in and write. So that you can come with us when we bathe. Go in and write, go in and write.' She went to the other side of him and pushed.

For once Pierre was angry. The colour rose violently in his badly repaired face. He picked up the child with both arms and put her down again hard, as if he had a nervous compulsion to move something about. And he quickly hid his injured hand in his pocket, while his colour rose even higher.

Then he was just as suddenly himself, with his pale sunburn and calm voice, his expression blank and closed. It allowed none of his thoughts to escape, and shut off access to him: 'Mind your own business. Run along and play.'

So that's what his anger is like, thought Alberta; a flame that blazes up and which he masters. Fortunate for Jeanne. Very fortunate.

'What were you going to say, Pierre?'

'Oh, nothing—'

Marthe was standing where he had put her down, within hearing distance, still squinting up at them. Her lower lip pouted. Jeanne in miniature, although Jeanne never stood like that. She must have done so once upon a time.

'The sugar bowl is full of flies.'

Without having been indoors, Marthe announced this unpleasant fact, which no one dared challenge. The sugar bowl had not been put away; it was still standing on the breakfast table, which everyone had hastily abandoned when the baker's horse, neighing and irritable from having been pulled up so abruptly, stuck all four legs into the crest of the slope, spattering the pebbles downwards. There was every reason to believe that the flies had come in long ago. They came from the bricklayer's cowshed, and were a scandal and a public nuisance that Jeanne, armed with a rolled-up newspaper, fought with great energy and vigorous commands to her troops: 'There, Pierre! Hit it, Alberta! Take proper aim, Liesel. *Mon Dieu*, how clumsy you all are!'

If Jeanne had been at home—

'The bread basket is full of flies.'

Marthe stood, pouting and squinting up at them. 'The butter is full of flies.'

'Go in and put them away then. Don't just stand there talking about it.' Pierre took a couple of steps towards his daughter.

'I am to be out in the sun,' explained Marthe. '*Maman* said so. The spring was so poor, we must make the most of it now.'

They might have been listening to Jeanne, a Jeanne transposed back to childhood. Pierre's eyes wavered, met Alberta's, slid further on at once. 'Go in and put them away,' he said curtly.

He gave a swing of the shoulders, as if pushing away an incumbrance, and another of the head, as if coming up from a dive. He laughed his curt little laugh, that had nothing to do with merriment. 'Have you ever heard anything like it! Seven years old, and we might as well have the police in the house. We're under surveillance, Alberta.'

Over by the wall the boy turned his head now and again. It was impossible to tell how much or how little he understood behind that alien little face. It usually turned out sooner or later that he had understood an astonishing amount. He looked lonely. Alberta resisted her desire to go over to him again. She would be repulsed, she knew.

The sea on this side of the dark sandbank had become shining blue from the reflection of the cleanswept sky and the fine offshore breeze. Two deep chords filled the air, advancing and receding, rising and falling, growing evenly in volume. The tide was coming in. It was the same enormous breathing Alberta had heard once a year at Big Gap, when the brief summer was at its height. Here it was never silent; it merely alternated in strength according to the ebb and flow of the tide. Eternally restful, it supplied a framework and a rhythm to everyday life.

The larks were already hanging, invisible and untiring, somewhere up in space. The gulls planed on their wings, almost grazing the slope and then screaming. And Alberta's dejection gave way. The day and the song of the sea had had their effect. Sun on the boy's neck, she thought. I ought to be happy. Perhaps the children will behave themselves.

For mist and driving drizzle had hung over the world for days on end, hemming them in. She looked about her. Today it was all spacious and open just as on the day of their arrival, when, although tired and numbed by the journey, it had struck her with such force that she had had to shut herself away from it and pretend indifference, until she had rested and collected herself. Here was everything she had sighed for vainly for years. Slopes, exactly as she had imagined them, with ragged grass and white clover, a scattering of lady's slipper and cinquefoil, an occasional long, flat rock sticking up, yellow with lichen: the kind of slopes one finds along the coast in many parts of the world, at home in the north too, familiar, dependable and clean. Below them the beach, an even, white border to the south and north, as far as the eye could reach. Beyond it the sea, beyond that the universe: clouds, sun, moon, stars. And if one had not learnt in childhood that the earth was round, one could hardly have avoided discovering it here. For the horizon was drawn in a protracted bow.

The day had acquired colour and taste. It was a day for idling, for roaming about. For brief moments, minutes at a time, she would be able to join it in her own way, through the mesh of the net she had woven herself into. All that was old and put behind her stirred itself, not dead, in spite of the years.

'I must help Marthe. *Bonjour*, Pierre. We shall eat at the usual times.'

She walked towards the house, against the wind, straight into its warm, scented embrace. The worn little path was firm and elastic, pleasant to the feet. Hoary plantain grew straight up out of it, and myriads of tiny clover leaves which could not grow taller or flower as long as human feet used it for their daily business, but grew there just the same, compact and lush. In a while the boy could take off his jersey. It was going to be as fine as anyone could wish.

She heard Pierre humming again, and paused. The same old opera, or whatever it was: 'Da, da, da, da, dadada—'

Deep down in her mind, far back in time, lay the same melody, cheerful, graceful, simple as if composed by a child, now awakening note by note.

'What are you humming, Pierre?'

'Humming? I don't know. Something I knew as a child I expect. Was I humming?'

But Alberta suddenly knew what it was: Mama in her shawl sitting at the piano between two lighted candles on the other side of the dark sitting room. A thick volume of old opera scores, yellow with age, which had been new when grandfather was young and which would not lean upright on the music stand, but slid down into a curve. It had to be given a push now and again. Mama gave it a push when she had a free hand, and played on: 'The White Lady. . .'

A glimpse of something so far back that it seemed to belong to another person's life, something she had heard or read. A quick series of reactions followed: I must have taken the wrong turning, when did I go wrong, where did I go wrong? I have come to the wrong place. And the strange, meaningless sensation that she had really known Pierre, this strange man in a strange country, always. Like a fleeting view seen through a rift in the clouds it all flashed past her and was gone. Pierre himself chased it away: 'Go in and write? Damned if I do!'

He puffed out his chest and looked round as if the sea and the slopes belonged to him, hummed another bar and fell silent.

Paper, pencil, the beret, I shall have to look after the children alone, he'll go at least as far as the Pointe du Raz, thought Alberta, unpleasantly practical again.

'Go in and write! Listen, Alberta.'

'Would you like to take something with you to eat, Pierre? I can find something even though Jeanne isn't at home. We have a cold chop, I can boil some eggs—'

Pierre shook his head, and Alberta immediately felt anxious in case perhaps there was something he wanted her to do, type a fair copy, proof-read, now that Jeanne was away. Alberta was not generous in such matters; she had more than enough on her own account.

'I'll take the children to the beach,' Pierre said.

'You?'

'Yes.' He looked at his wrist-watch. 'You have a good three hours until lunch, and a couple more afterwards, if you want them. I can warm the soup. There's no magic about that.'

'Cold pancakes and soft-boiled eggs,' interrupted Marthe instantly from a window below. '*Maman* said so.'

'The police again.' Pierre sighed. He looked at Alberta, clearly waiting for her to understand something on her own. When she simply stood there like an interrogation mark he came nearer and said quietly, emphasizing his words: 'You must *concentrate* on your material, use every opportunity to work with it. It's the only way. If you don't manage to add something, at least you can erase, tidy it up, create clarity.'

His hands were on their way out of their pockets again, as if he needed them to clarify what he was saying. Then he stuffed them down still further. 'Come along Tot, come along Marthe, fetch your things, we're going to the beach.'

'No, Pierre!'

Solicitude for this aspect of her well-being made Alberta uneasy and perplexed. She automatically searched in her mind for excuses behind which to hide and on the spur of the moment found plenty. 'The washing came yesterday. I promised Jeanne I would sort it and dampen it. We're doing the ironing tomorrow, Josephine is coming. Then there's the food and the children, and the rooms have to be tidied. On the beach I must try to do some sewing; Tot won't have any clothes to wear soon. And you have so much to do yourself—'

A look of boyish disappointment came over Pierre's face.

'I have!' He took a couple of steps away from her again, as if tired of this fruitless conversation with a dullard and wishing to emphasize that he would prefer to drop it. Alberta

492

scarcely had time to regret that she had involved him at all when he was back again.

'Even if Tot hasn't a thing to wear, what does it matter out here?'

'More than you realise.'

'Hm. And Jeanne, she—'

'She already does more than her share because she's so capable. Liesel and I—'

'Liesel and you! Listen, Alberta, you can't afford to be so fair and correct. You must—'

'Learn from Sivert,' said Pierre suddenly in a different tone of voice. 'There's much to be learnt from Sivert. He's all of a piece right through, he's imperturbable. Sivert does not let any opportunity slip through his fingers. And he'll reach his goal. You can be certain of that.'

'Yes, there are quite a few things to be learnt from Sivert.' Alberta could hear the coldness in her voice. She broke off. Marthe was standing there as if shot up out of the ground, her eyes like a little detective's. '*Maman* said that—'

'Have you put everything away?'

'Yes, I have put everything away.'

'Then off we go, children.' Pierre was already on his way down, walking slowly, his hands thrust down into his pockets, pulling his trousers askew.

He looked back. And there it was again, the glimpse of the man behind the mask, of someone she felt she knew, who wished her well.

'If it has really got to the point when you *have* to cook and sew, then cook and sew. In that case there's nothing to be done.'

He waved. He smiled. Not at her, but to her.

Automatically she waved back, looking as she did so from the one child's face to the other. Both were standing full of that unfathomable quality that children put up against all that is new and disquieting. Without a word they fetched their things from under the stairs: buckets and spades, and the old pudding mould over which they often quarrelled, and which Marthe carried tightly under her arm.

A notion struck Alberta that Pierre intended to play a game that would in the long run become too involved. 'Tot must take off his jersey!' she called, and felt as if she were letting all life's chores slip out of her hands. She heard the children start asking questions both at once about this and that, because children are so easily distracted by something new, as long as it is amusing.

Jeanne, she thought. Jeanne! We're doing nothing wrong. And yet it almost seems as if we're deceiving you.

For a while she wandered in and out of the empty house, up and down the stairs. Times without number she had longed to be there by herself, thinking that if she were granted that, however briefly—. Now she was by herself and merely felt irresolute and abandoned.

The house stood alone, naked and unadorned, without even a tree nearby, and turned its face to the sea to such an extent that it did not have so much as a small peep-hole or back door on the other side. Alberta liked it, with its white, rough-cast walls and its unpainted floors that smelt newly planed. It was a real house with two storeys and an attic, built to be lived in and for no other purpose. Since having a child she had noticed in herself a liking for stability, for dwellings giving protection against wind and weather and keeping in the warmth, instead of ones with skylights and other picturesque advantages.

She opened the large cupboard in the living-room and contemplated the washing lying in heaps inside, children's clothes and adults' all in confusion. A bathing suit belonging to the boy stuck out from the pile. Alberta remembered the rent in it and shut the cupboard.

She continued to wander about, tidying up, looking at Marthe's arrangement for trapping the flies. It was quite clever, Marthe would be practical. She went upstairs, made her bed and the boy's, fastened the shutters everywhere as Jeanne had prescribed. In Jeanne's and Pierre's room and in Marthe's little closet order reigned; the beds were made, the washing water thrown away, everything carefully hung up and laid aside. On Pierre's writing table stood Jeanne's photograph, stained and yellowed; one could see that it had been wet. It was the one he had kept in his breast pocket throughout the war.

On Jeanne's bedside table there was a snapshot of herself and Pierre arm in arm, so small it could convey no impression of the original Pierre to a stranger. Two slender, dark-haired persons were standing together, grimacing at the sun, Jeanne in one of the hazardous skirts of 1913, so narrow at the ankles that a normal stride was out of the question. The picture was not new to Alberta. Jeanne had brought it downstairs on one occasion to show them how ridiculous the skirt was. She had said: 'I have other pictures of course, but I've put them away. It would be unkind to have them out, don't you think?'

Marthe's big doll Mimi sat on its little chair looking straight in front of it with stiff, blue eyes.

Up in Liesel's room in the attic clothes were scattered about and the bed was only loosely covered over. Liesel always got up at the last minute. Alberta made the bed, threw the washing water out of the window so that it slapped on to the ground, put a pair of shoes neatly by the wall and hung up some clothes. Then she went down to her own room and sat on the bed.

The window was full of sky and sea, as long as you did not go right up to it. And all day long every corner of the house was filled with the thunder of the breakers, so that it seemed to sough and sing like a seashell. But sounds within the house echoed as if it were a drum, built as it was with only one layer of planking. Keeping one's intimacies to oneself is one of the luxuries of the rich.

Considering how her life had turned out, Alberta ought to have been overjoyed at being able to wander about like this in a house. But, as Sivert said, she was the kind who would never be satisfied; such people were a burden to themselves, and much to be pitied.

She listened to the sea for a while. Afterwards she found the folder with her papers in it, putting it on her little lop-sided table, that could not stand straight without a piece of paper under one of its legs, then took it down to the table in the living-room. It was round and the folder looked just as futile and out of place on the one as on the other.

She put a rug over her arm and took it out of doors.

A group of people in a home. They are held together by external laws and forced apart by internal ones. The tension between them is expressed in a number of small events, apparently without significance, in reality a screen for fate, who spins her mysterious threads behind it.

It often seemed to Alberta that she was wasting her time, tampering with something empty and meaningless. Why should she expose these persons' lives? Of what interest could it be to others? They were as grey as everyday. But she was bound to them, as one is bound to people with whom one has once associated. She might ask herself: Why did I want to get mixed up with them? It made no difference; she was just as involved.

It was as impossible to subtract from or add to them as it would have been to do so to her surroundings. They were themselves, conjured out of a multiplicity of old scribbles, just as others were conjured up and took shape in her mind, in bits and pieces, by means of thousands of small details, brief, unfinished utterances, apparently insignificant actions.

It had all come so far that it amounted to a pile in a folder. It had grown in slow stages and as far as possible in secrecy. But suddenly, when she had begun to believe that she had achieved a certain amount of order and coherence, new material had presented itself, at times in such quantities that she became sickened and felt she could not face it. It had come from the wrong direction and been the cause of much disturbance: innovations and renumbering of pages. The task threatened to be endless, and the old glint had returned to Sivert's eye a long time ago when he asked after it. Or he might say: 'Have you done any scribbling today?' And then she felt as if he had handled her roughly, and she did not know which she detested most, herself or Sivert, or the pile of papers.

Taking all of it under her arm she wandered down the slope, but not so far that Jean-Marie would not see her and call if he were to come with the fish. She felt no inclination towards working on her manuscript, it all seemed more than usually stupid and pointless, a story that was none of her business, that she really knew nothing about.

Where the opposite slope shelved like a little meadow, just right for lying on one's stomach looking out over the sea, just right too for propping up the folder, should the occasion arise, she stopped and arranged her rug.

The day unfurled itself, warm and beautiful. The tide was coming in fast. Slowly, inexorably the enormous bowl was filled. Shining tongues licked the sand, advancing with a hiss and retreating with a sigh, gaining an advantage each time, leaving behind them a floating border of lace that merged with the next tongue. The creation was accomplished. A higher level of universal order is created by the incoming tide.

Some way out she could see Pierre and the children. They looked like small, dark figures in a composition, Marthe rushing off like a puppy that has just been let out, squatting by the pools and then running again. Pierre was holding the boy's hand. Alberta knew that he must have taken Pierre's hand of his own accord, thrusting his thin little one into it and holding it tight.

There they were, all three of them, squatting round a pool. And although she was not fond of the beach because of the sandworms that sketched their curlicues everywhere so that it was difficult to know where to place one's feet, and positively disliked the revelation of marine life, she longed to be down there with them and felt lonely. The wind was blowing away from her, she could hear nothing, but the small figures were excited. She wished she had gone too. Such a pool is like a little aquarium of strange, green light and curious fauna and flora; a closed world, where the seaweed grows straight upwards and is a mysterious forest trafficked by tiny crabs and occasionally a big one, by shrimps, little fish, much that is even unidentifiable. Pretty stones and snail-shells glint at the bottom like jewellery.

Pierre was fond of children, at least in the sense that, when he wished, he could amuse them hugely. Neither he nor any other man possessed that endless patience, that faculty of being able to hang about with them hour after hour, of answering precisely and good-naturedly the countless questions they use to hold you fast. And those women who really do possess it are usually elderly or a little simple-minded.

She saw Marthe take off her shoes and socks, jump into a pool and paddle round in it, waving her arms. In a short while they all went northwards. Tinti-Anna's house hid them from her.

She looked at the folder with hostility.

What was she to do with this unexpected three hours of freedom? Freedom was something she felt embarrassed about and could not understand. Once she had had plenty of it. It had trickled away between her fingers while she loitered through life, sight-seeing, a member of an audience. When it eventually dawned on her that she had looked about her enough, that she glimpsed coherence, that she had something to say about life, then that same life had seized her by the scruff of the neck and had not yet loosed its grip. It seemed to wish to emphasize thoroughly that it was now too late. She was picking her way indirectly as in the old days at home.

And Pierre?

He tried to help her, now and again. Something indefinable, friendship perhaps, perhaps not even that, perhaps something a little more, existed at intervals between them. It might well have been pure imagination too, a trick played on her by her longing for warmth. It came and went, as such feelings do. It would certainly be forgotten one day. Already on the journey out . . .

A man changes in the aura of his wife. The way Pierre had sat, leaning his head against the wall of the compartment, his eyes closed, had seemed frighteningly strange. Even his old beret, worn crookedly, seemed to belong to someone else whose joys and sorrows, duties and responsibilities, were totally unknown to her. This new person, Jeanne, slept beside him as a matter of course, as if she were engaged in some task, that of sleeping in a sitting position in a train, a task she had taken upon herself and was carrying out irreproachably. There was nothing loose or inert in that well-constructed face, framed by hair as neat and smooth as it had been at their departure. When the grey, merciless dawn came, Jeanne still sat there, just as presentable, with Marthe's head in her lap, a picture of complete repose.

A *père de famille* on holiday. That was as it should be. It was no surprise to her. Far from it. She had felt it as violence, almost like pillage. But what should have been different?

Nothing, Alberta assured herself, and suspected despondently that everything would be, whether on account of Jeanne or somebody else. Time after time she had pushed back her own hair, heavy with smoke and smuts, which fell uncomfortably into stripes between her fingers. The friendship between Pierre and Sivert was not to suffer, however, that had already been clear at the station the previous evening.

But it had altered. It was not her imagination. It had altered considerably. She quickly taught herself to behave towards Pierre as one does towards an acquaintance. She was flexible.

Even during the preparations for their departure she had been given a salutary ducking into everyday reality. She had been kept busy running about, sewing, pestering Sivert for scores of things. When she saw Pierre again, a busy man about to set out with his wife and child, she felt as sorry for herself as if she were quite helpless. I can't stand ordinary kindness any more, she thought. It goes straight to my head. She shook hands with Jeanne and said, 'Madame'.

But she needed Pierre, needed his quiet understanding, his support when necessary, the fact that he sometimes took her part against Sivert and made Sivert give in. It had become good to have Pierre there, not least against Sivert, not least—

He had remained friendly, no-one could accuse him of anything else, polite and friendly, kind and obliging. All the same—

Today he, who was always the soul of patience, had hummed, turned angry, gone to the beach in working hours, as if the postman, his publisher and Jeanne had all ceased to exist. He had suddenly referred to Alberta's shapeless manuscript as if it were something to be taken into account. Was this good or bad? It was disturbing.

Sivert must have said something. Sivert was odd in that way. He thought nothing of what she did; nevertheless he had to talk about it. It was impossible to make out what Sivert's intentions were.

She too had been out on the slopes occasionally with pad and pencil, had had difficulty controlling her temper when the subsequent inner restlessness had inconveniently affected her. She had had one or two short stories published in magazines at home and even been paid for them, small sums, that had disappeared into the ever-gaping holes. This was the official side of the matter, impossible to hide, never taken seriously by the world at large. On the contrary, it had appeared unwarranted, the last thing a wife and mother ought to undertake. It would have been preferable, for instance, to wash everything oneself, make all one's own clothes, turn the collars of Sivert's shirts inside-out when they were frayed. Jeanne did that to Pierre's; it was a great saving.

Alberta's scribbling was a burden that had to be borne, because she was made that way, for the sake of peace, and to avoid making mountains out of molehills. Only Liesel and Pierre supported her openly. Neither of them could read a word she wrote.

Could she not afford to be fair? Behave like Sivert? Pierre was a man too, that was why he could talk as he did. He understood a good deal, but not everything. And yet something in her profoundly and boastfully agreed with his male talk.

If only she could pull herself together and gain possession of both her child and her work! As things were, Alberta felt she possessed neither. There was still more she did not possess, and when life offered her a moment like the present, her longing welled up, flooding over everything else and paralysing her, as it had always done.

Sweetness and bitterness were mingled. Sivert, Sivert, can't we try to manage together? We have Tot. Tot! I owe him so many moments I would not have missed. But I have to look to find them. I always remember the bad things first and most clearly. I admit it.

Concentrate on her material?

She leafed through the pages in the folder, struggled for a while with the wind for control of her straying papers, and put them away again. It was all dead, approximate, loosely formulated.

Pierre and the children had reappeared on the other side of Tinti-Anna's house and settled there. Pierre was leaning on his elbow in the white sand, his head bent as if reading. It was probably one of the pamphlets which he carried round in his pockets, which came from Paris, and which Jeanne disliked. Tot and Marthe were digging with their spades. It looked a peaceful little group, and Alberta longed more than ever to join them. She scowled at the folder, then lay on her back with her face turned away from the others and towards the wind, looking up at the sky. A procession of solid, white clouds were sailing slowly before the off-shore breeze, all kinds of country and summer scents and sporadic sounds of work from up in the village in their train. There was a wet, slapping sound from the washing place over at the stream. The world was full of people with their affairs well in hand who were achieving something. What she had was flimsy and tattered, without a beginning or an end.

There were moments when it was different. They came like thieves in the night, at the wrong times. Images, word sequences, that immediately seemed serviceable, floated up from the depths of her mind. An unexpected clarity of thought seemed flung at her. She had sometimes been alone with it in the evening, when the boy slept and Sivert was at the *Dôme*; it accompanied her to bed, got her up during the night as in the old days, to jot down sudden ideas, sentences, single words. Even her body felt it, and became strong and supple from the back of her neck down to her big toe. Sivert was woken by the light and grumbled. She would think: If only I could wake up like this in the morning, knowing that she would not. Yet she would sleep with a strange certainty that everything would be put right in the end, even what was most difficult, painful and heart-breaking.

The next morning she would be dull and heavy. The day with all its demands stood waiting at her bedside. The boy would whine from the moment he opened his eyes. Perhaps it would be one of the days when his face was white as chalk and he ate paper, and she could not take him out because it was pouring with rain. The time came when there was war on top of everything else. The boy was not yet a year old. The value of money dropped like a barometer reacting to an earthquake.

And she would see the intoxication of the night for what it was, a flight from reality. The day was the morning after, when she paid for her foolishness and in a daze washed the child's clothes, stirred saucepans, watched the boy to see that he did not get hold of paper, and took him out as soon as she could. More than anything else, she felt she must get some colour into that white little face. It was white when she left with him, and white when she came indoors again. Or blue with cold. It hurt her so much to see it that she grew bad-tempered.

If by chance she was able to sit down with her scraps of paper and fit them in where they belonged, or make them the foundation of a new little structure, this was only uphill, boring, hopeless work. What she put together grew grudgingly, infinitely slowly. Yet she knew that if she continued to pile one stone on top of another for a while, unwearyingly and whether she wanted to or not, through hope and doubt there would come a moment when it looked as if there was a solution to the problem, and from then on it would be easier. Like a puzzle, it took a long time before you saw how it was going to turn out. The scraps of paper grew into pages, then into piles, and were put away in the folder. To expand them further—it was laughable, as Sivert so often demonstrated. But this was the only way that she could see. To what? From what? Oh—she would be able to buy something, take Tot to the doctor when she thought this was necessary, give him this and give him that, a better place in which to live, better living conditions; she would be able to abandon her antiquated winter coat. She could think of things like that without feeling a traitor.

The larks sang on, invisible in the enormous space, the sound of the sea grew louder, the sun was baking hot. Alberta kicked her sandals off her bare feet, turned her clothes up in one place and down in another, surrendered herself piece by piece to the wind. It felt good, good enough to send her to sleep; it satisfied her old hunger for fresh air. She was overcome by inertia. She had thought she would experience the day through the mesh of the net. She had become one with it through a large hole.

Erase, was that what Pierre had said?

Suddenly she was through her inertia and beyond it. She turned over the leaves, struggled with the wind for the pages, knew where previously she had only suspected, made thick lines, corrected, added . . .

She leaned the folder against the slope as if it were a desk.

At two o'clock the sea lay white as milk in the sun.

But if one went right down to it the blue of the sky bobbed and dipped as pale shadows in the swell. The seaweed and stones showed through clearly a long way out. The horizon was a thin line of shading. Gulls hovered at an angle on splayed wings, sweeping the surface with their wing tips, snatching at something, screaming . . .

The enormous bowl was brimful, its contents lying edge to edge with the shining white sand, rocking gently against it. The flowers of the oyster plant and sea holly were reflections of sea and sky. Everything was clean, soot-free. The creation was accomplished.

They were taking off their clothes in Tinti-Anna's little boathouse, which adjoined her living-room. It smelt of tar, sun-baked wood and pigs in there. For the pig lived next door too, on the other side. You could hear it grubbing in its trough outside, grunting, pushing itself against the fence.

The boy was standing without a stitch on, slender and slight, stunted by several years of deprivation. But he was a little brown, however shallow it might be. And he was exhilarated by what the new day had brought, telling Alberta all about it while she dressed him in the little bathing trunks which she had brought to propitiate local propriety. Marthe had stamped on a crab and killed it and *Ton-ton* Pierre had been cross with her. But *Ton-ton* Pierre was kind. He had carried Marthe, he had carried Tot, found a big starfish for each of them, helped them to make sand-pies. They had made lots, but the sea came so quickly and spoilt them.

Alberta got him out into the sun, Marthe was already wading. Pierre was crawling a little way out. His head was almost beneath the water, his arms appeared alternately in an even, fast rhythm, in a movement that came from the shoulders. A damaged hand was no longer of importance, the spray hid it.

Alberta, who had actually put twenty to thirty words on paper and had also erased a good deal, was seized with such physical elation that she ran straight out to swim without so much as looking about her. Behind her she heard the children, used as they were to having her at their beck and call, Marthe shouting, Tot setting up an injured howl. He's naked, she thought. He's in the sun and the fresh air, he has everything I've hungered to give him until I felt it in my own body, he has what he most needs. Let him howl—for a little while at any rate.

She was intoxicated. The endless sea, white in the glare, green as glass when she looked down into it, with each stone, each swaying alga and tangle of seaweed clear at the bottom; the bell of the sky above her; her own healthy body, thin and muscular, so brown that it looked as if she had a little white bathing suit on when she was naked, the unexpected speed with which she shot through the water, everything contributed to it. Now the feeling of unbelievable possibilities was with her again, of an existence lying parallel to the one she led already, but on another level. It was close to her. But she felt she would have to leave her mind and body in order to inhabit it.

She lay on her back and kicked up a column of spray. Water splashed over and about her, the sunshine was broken up in it, her face and eyes were smarting with salt. The sensation it gave of power and delight was as strong as if her metamorphosis had already taken place.

An extra shower blinded her, she heard the splashing and snorting of a sea creature. Pierre was swimming past her towards the shore. When she could see once more, his legs seemed to be whirling behind him like propellers a good way off. He had said nothing as he went by. It made her uneasy, chilling her and reminding her of the old days at home, as if she had let herself be drawn into flippancy and suddenly come to her senses.

But shortly afterwards, when she reached the shore and emerged step by step from the salt sea into the sea of air, pulling down her wet, clinging suit, he said 'Bravo!' without a trace of irony. He and the children were sitting cross-legged in a row, Pierre brown and hard, his long muscles still shining and damp. He had buried his right hand in the sand as usual. At this time of day it was obvious that the bullets and bayonet thrusts that had disabled the man had struck a fine example of homo sapiens. The face that went with it must have been fine too.

'That bullet knew where it was going,' Eliel was used to declaiming, when the subject came up. He and Sivert had once tried to make sketches of Pierre. But Pierre had noticed, slung his beach robe round him and gone to sunbathe elsewhere. 'Idiots!' called Jeanne from the bottom of her heart, following him. 'Tactless creatures! He was in the war, this man, while you—!'

'Bravo!' Pierre repeated. 'One day you'll swim the Channel.'

'Don't make fun of me.'

'I'm not making fun of you. You've learnt quickly. When you began—'

'I'd never swum before. At home the sea was too cold, nobody thought of doing it. It did look hopeless at the beginning.'

She saw herself lying on her stomach in shallow water, while Liesel held her under the chin and Jeanne commanded, 'Up

with your legs! Up with your legs! Think of a frog. Up with
your legs!'

'Nothing is hopeless once Jeanne takes an interest in it. It
would be—.' Pierre's voice deepened. 'Poor Jeanne, if anyone
deserves to succeed—. Did you swim, Marthe?'

'I did, but Tot didn't,' Marthe informed them. Her eyes and
ears were alert to the conversation as she sat filtering sand
through her fingers and toes.

'Come along, Tot, let's go and swim. The sea's nice today.'

Pierre got up and stood waiting, broad-shouldered and
narrow-hipped, brown-skinned, slightly blue round the loins,
silhouetted against the sky and sea. Alberta felt a pang of
joy and despondency when the boy grasped Pierre's hand
tightly in his thin little one and went without resistance. She
always had to argue with him, persuading and reassuring. It
was difficult to get him into the water, mistrustful as he was
and unused to it all. When the question of how to deal with
him was mooted, not even Jeanne would advise firmness. 'If
it were Marthe,' she said, 'I'd just drop her in, and it would be
over and done with. But this little one—!' The two wrinkles
that did not suit her, would appear in her forehead. She
seemed to be thinking: I'm glad I don't have any responsibility
for *him*.

Now he was going with Pierre as if there were nothing the
matter. They splashed and strode about at the water's edge,
the boy laughing aloud. Now they were going in, the water was
up to the boy's knees, then under his hollow little breastbone,
now almost up to his neck. It was too much, he was going to
cry. But when Pierre put him on his stomach and supported
him in shallower water he tried eagerly and ineffectually to
swim. When he returned to the shore and Alberta wrapped
him in the bathrobe he was beside himself with pride and
happiness. 'Tot swam,' he said. 'Tot swam with *Ton-ton*
Pierre.'

'What a clever boy!' Alberta rubbed him in the cautious
manner that made Sivert so impatient. 'Take hold of him
properly,' he would say. 'He's not made of glass.'

It seemed to her that his little heart was beating faster than it should; she rubbed even more cautiously, changed his bathing trunks and took out the biscuits and chocolate that were part of the ritual. Marthe was there at once: 'We're to share the extra one. *Maman* said so.'

Alberta shared it out. 'We'll write to Father and tell him Tot swam,' she said.

'He didn't swim. Besides, my Papa was there. When my Papa is there it's easy.' Marthe put down what was in her hands and ran into the water a second time, firm and brown in her faded red bathing suit, ruthless and superior. She swam around near the edge of the water, splashing to draw attention to herself. She was a year older than Alberta's child, could read, write, do sums, was used to the water from former summers and made of sterner stuff. Probably the same as Jeanne was made of. It was strong material.

Tot burst into tears. He stamped his feet, threw away his biscuits and chocolate and bellowed, while Pierre hauled his child back to the beach and gave her a well-aimed slap on the bottom. His hand managed it very well. 'And that's for you. Nobody asked you for your opinion.'

'But it's true. He didn't swim.'

Howls from Tot.

'He didn't swim.'

'Be quiet.'

'He *didn't* swim.'

Marthe suddenly arched her back and put her hands behind her to protect herself; another slap was on its way. She stood up to it for a moment, then threw herself on her knees in the sand, as if the slap had sent her there, and looked up at Pierre inquiringly, used as she was to receiving chastisement from Jeanne. Then she made up her mind, threw things about and howled too.

Alberta and Pierre looked at each other like two people who have caused a fiasco together. Then Pierre's expression turned blank: 'Pick up your chocolate. And the biscuit. Put your clothes on. Stop howling, you've got nothing to howl about. Hurry up.'

He bent over the boy: 'You swam, Tot. *Ton-ton* Pierre

knows you swam. Next time you'll swim even better. Get his clothes on him, Alberta. We'd better go home.'

Pierre looked disheartened. He disappeared behind the large rock where he dressed and undressed. Alberta took the children, still crying, each in a different key, into the boathouse. The day was darkened with scolding and tears, as all days were, sooner or later. And yet the boy was not quite as outmatched by the robust little girl as he had been when they arrived, and there had been perpetual friction. He had been so unused to other children that she had felt raw herself.

'Walk in front, children,' commanded Pierre when the procession moved off. As clearly as if she heard or saw, Alberta felt how the two sniffling children were immediately changed from opponents into hostile conspirators with common interests and a common front. They continued to walk, each on his own side of the path, but with their thoughts and ears directed the same way.

'I can't stand her when she's spiteful,' Pierre said, when there was sufficient distance between them.

'She was only telling the truth. And Tot *is* too sensitive.' All the elation had gone out of her. She was still trembling from the blow that had hurt the boy. He had conquered his fear. It was no small thing. Then Marthe had come along and—

'Some truths are worse than lies. It's brutality, no less.'

'She's only a child, Pierre. Children are brutal.'

'I expect you're right.' Pierre's voice was so toneless that Alberta thought: It doesn't take much to depress you. Then she remembered how little it took to make her depressed. She fell silent. Besides, the children had slackened their pace. Marthe was pulling a piece of sea holly to pieces, walking more and more slowly. Alberta could see her listening under her sunbleached dark hair.

Nothing was said for a while. The children were dragging their feet. Marthe dragged her bathing wrap demonstratively behind her as well, as if trying to provoke more of Pierre's unaccustomed anger. It led nowhere. Tot's kneebones seemed painfully large in contrast to his thighs and calves as he walked. It is not true that love is blind; one sees twice as clearly.

Sensitive? More than that. Suddenly, without apparent reason, the boy could become bad-tempered and whining. Jeanne called it nervousness. Sivert said he was spoilt and took after his mother. For Alberta it was an exhaustion she shared. She could not bring herself to scold him. The boy seemed to find life itself difficult; he saw that this was how it had to be. His mind was composed of memories of city air, winter dampness, cold, disturbed sleep, itching bug bites, insufficient food: vague anxiety about everything and nothing.

Marthe had spent most of the war in Dijon, with Jeanne's parents. She had toddled on lawns under tall trees, had milk from their own cow, eggs from their own chickens, fruit from the garden, sat on the laps of kind old grandparents, played naked in the sun. Jeanne had a whole album full of pictures, in which the cow, the chickens and everything else were visible. Not once had Marthe been snatched up out of sleep and carried down to the cellar, not one day had they been short of butter, firewood or sugar for her, even though the whole of the old avenue up to the house had been sacrificed because the army had needed big logs. Jeanne had sat, thin, but beautiful, seemingly incandescent with patient waiting beside a large hearth with a blazing fire, knitting warm clothes for Marthe, for Pierre, for unknown soldiers. This too appeared in the photographs. Pierre was in some of them, home on leave and in uniform. But there was not one in which he did not turn his face partially or wholly away. He had received the ugly cut on his cheek almost as soon as he got out to the front.

'Hurry, Marthe. Run. There's the postman. Ask him if there's anything for us. Off you go.' Pierre's voice was full of relief; something was happening, something innocent, about which they could talk easily to each other.

Marthe ran. Tot began to walk faster.

'We'll put them to bed early, shall we?' Pierre said quietly.

'As early as we can,' Alberta too spoke quietly. Her thoughts went abruptly to Jeanne.

Up at the house Marthe called: 'A telegram for *Tante*

Alberta. She has to sign for it. *Les Modes* for *Maman,* letters for Papa. And the newspapers. And a telegram for—'
Alberta was already running up the slope.

*   *   *

'That's all, Pierre.' Half a chop, two fried eggs, some fried potatoes. If only Jeanne had been home. Or Liesel. 'You can't have had enough.'
Alberta gestured apologetically towards the simple still-life on the table. The lamplight on the cloth, the bowl of dahlias, the background of wide, darkening sky through the open windows, the gusts of mild air from outside flapping the curtains, would have been becoming to a luxurious meal. Their cigarette smoke rose in beautiful whorls and rings, the ceaseless noise of the breakers was like a heavy accompaniment to the larks and gulls. But on the table were two plates, two cups, a couple of small dishes and the bread basket, all of them empty.
'If only Jean-Marie had come with fish.'
'Good heavens, Alberta!' Pierre pushed away his cup and leaned his palms on the table, shutting his eyes as he did when he was trying to collect himself. The gap left by the amputated fingers straddled defencelessly, painful to see. 'When will you stop talking about food? Mending, washing, food, mending, washing, food, like a parrot. What was I trying to say?—now don't interrupt me—get it all out of your system as quickly as you can. You can cut it down and polish it, put in new material and make alterations later. Break into the action, get to the important part. You'll have to rewrite it plenty of times as it is before you find a tone that doesn't seem too grating to your ears. In the meantime things may occur to you that you had no idea were in the material. And it doesn't have to be sent to the publisher's tomorrow. For God's sake organise yourself so that it won't—'
Pierre stopped. His fingers curled, he clenched his teeth, baring them slightly, and went on talking, now fast, as if the seconds mattered, now slowly, with difficulty: 'Get it out of

you while you still see it fresh. Something may happen one day to make it all seem ridiculous, and you won't be able to face it any more. If there's anyone who has the right to come after you with a whip and say: 'Write this and that, thus and so, have it ready by such and such a time . . .'

He's talking to himself, not to me, thought Alberta. But he's talking. He hasn't gone down to the beach as he usually does in the evenings. He's forgotten his hand, forgotten the cut in his face, exposing them both to the lamplight. He looks like a symbol—no, two—of human beings' ill-treatment of each other and of their struggle to survive in spite of it. If Sivert had been sitting here he would have forgotten him too, until Sivert decided that that was enough and said something to put a stop to it. He would not have forgotten Jeanne. He would not have talked like this, but gone out, asking whether she would like to go with him.

Alberta had to make an effort to follow him. As soon as the conversation left ordinary matters she felt giddy, that same giddiness that had lain in wait for her all her life as soon as anyone broached subjects she tried to hide. Besides, Sivert's telegram lay open on the mantelpiece demanding attention. From both she sought refuge in trifles as if they were small rocks to which she could cling for safety.

'I can smell mussels, can you?'

'The tide's going out,' Pierre replied curtly. 'Now listen to me. I may not get the opportunity to tell you again.'

Alberta acknowledged the reprimand and felt her eyes grow larger. 'I am grateful, Pierre.'

'If only there were any other course for you to take. But I can't see anything else for it, you will go this way sooner or later in the belief that it will lead to control of your life and your child. Perhaps it will. You do want to control everything yourself, Alberta.'

'I want to, yes,' answered Alberta ruefully, a little defiant and derisive. A thought sequence passed rapidly and vaguely through her head: The moments when you want to and must do so are few, those when you want to and cannot are numberless. Victory goes to the latter.

'You more than want. When I saw you for the first time I had the impression of a person in disintegration. Now—'

Is it possible? thought Alberta. She saw herself as someone at the bottom of an abyss.

'You might need support. But one day Sivert will . . .'

Is it only Sivert you want to talk about? Only about Sivert? She was gripped by loneliness, Pierre and Jeanne would go off one day. She would be left with Sivert.

'He's completely absorbed in his own affairs. That is his strength.'

But now Pierre seemed to feel he had rowed out too far. He added quickly, 'You know how much I admire Sivert. He is my friend, he is an artist. I—we ought to have drunk his health this evening. I don't grudge him his success. Nor you. Now everything will be easier.'

Alberta sat twisting a teaspoon between her fingers. She thought: We were talking about me. Say more, say things that make me feel better. Sivert, Sivert all the time. He doesn't even see me. I have turned myself into a doormat for him, and it has led nowhere.

'You must assert yourself beside Sivert, Alberta, let him see that you, too—. I felt I wanted to say this to you.'

Pierre got to his feet, walked up and down, leant against the mantelpiece, the ornament of the room, and absently read the telegram again.

'You must come to terms with Sivert.'

Alberta again felt reprimanded. His words were surprisingly hurtful. She suddenly saw herself and Sivert in the years to come. It was endless. 'We haven't quarrelled.'

'No, no. But you must accept him as he is, be patient with him.'

'I did accept him as he was and I was patient, to the point where we almost lost our lives, Tot and I. Yes, Pierre! If fire broke out he would save his canvases first.'

'You must be patient and accept him as he is until you have achieved something, until you are equals. Then Sivert will see you differently, and everything will work out all right.'

'Then Sivert will hate me,' Alberta said giddily. She bit

her lip hard. One did not say such things. One only thought them in moments of depression. Gratitude for what Sivert had, in spite of everything, managed to give her and the boy lay hidden beneath much else, ready to flame up in and out of season. Often she was too tired to acknowledge it. Now it was there like a warm wave, released by her bitter words. Pierre was a friend, he felt and understood. But it was Sivert who worked and paid, Sivert who for years had brought with him a kind of life and excitement merely by coming home with a wet canvas in each hand, or a package of food, or money from the pawnbroker's. It was in Sivert's arms she ought to belong.

'I don't know what I'm saying,' she said.

Pierre did not reply. The murmur of the sea and the untiring refrain of the larks became intrusively distinct. How many could there be up there in the sky? How long were they going to keep it up? It was some time since sunset.

'Since you have to stick together,' said Pierre.

The word divorce had never crossed Alberta's mind, yet Pierre's words made her feel as if a door had slammed in her face.

'Yes, you're right, we have to stick together.' Her voice was hard. She went on twisting the teaspoon and thought: That's what he was getting at. Now he'll go.

But Pierre blew a smoke-ring and picked up the thread where he had dropped it. 'Don't let yourself be paralysed by the bad days, when nothing happens. Something is lying there, turning into something, something you don't know how to grasp. You feel a wastrel and a criminal. If you try to help, you catch hold of an arm or a leg and everything is at a dead-lock, like an embryo lying in the wrong position. Yet you must go on tugging and pulling. Life demands it, one must live.'

Jeanne demands it, thought Alberta. He didn't go. He still has something to say to me.

'Then you have to turn the whole thing round and try another approach. That one is wrong too. The day you feel yourself grasping the head, then delivery begins in earnest, the day—' Pierre paused, lighted another cigarette with the old one, continued: 'When evening comes you may have no more than ten serviceable lines. But ten lines that open up for the rest.'

He stood looking at her with the same expression. Then he laughed. 'It would be better for you if you were able to cook and sew. But you can't.'

Through her giddiness Alberta thought of the distressing fury she could feel when Sivert brought out his 'Have you done any scribbling today?' Here was the explanation. Sivert's tone was too similar to the one he used to the boy: 'Have you had a nice time today?' It was painful to write, it was not a game. She had to be far advanced with her material before it ceased to distress her with its shapelessness, its reek of raw matter, of stillbirth. Pierre was right to talk of embryos. It took a long time before these lumps from the depths of the mind turned into something she could bear to expose to the gaze of others. Here was Pierre, who had written several books of distinction, corroborating the truth of it.

'All in all it's a luxury for the rich,' Pierre said, still talking about writing. 'But at any rate see to it that you get something out of you while you're still capable of accepting what you produce, while you're still naive enough to do so. We can fear our own work finally, shun it, flee from it like the plague, find incredible excuses for avoiding it. Hurry up and get something down before you reach that stage. Earn money, earn money, buy yourself peace in good time, peace to be yourself. Here you are, wasting your time! Even the washing-up—'

'I haven't touched the washing-up.'

'Good.'

At the same moment a bed creaked upstairs in the echoing house. A child suddenly cried. Alberta and Pierre looked at each other guiltily. *'Voilà.* Is it yours or mine?'

'Mine, of course.' Alberta was already on her feet, hurrying out into the passage and up the stairs, which were in complete darkness. 'Have you any matches?' Pierre called after her, 'In case you need them?'

'Yes, thank you.'

Up in the bedroom the fading twilight fell in stripes through the shutters. Alberta pushed them open. The sky with one pale star and a piece of ink-black sea became visible. She could see to walk.

Over in the cot the cries had turned into screams, which became more angry after her arrival. She glimpsed a tangle of naked legs and sheets; the blanket was on the floor.

'What is it?' Her voice grated on her ears. She tidied the bed and rearranged the blanket.

'It's the sea. I don't want to hear the sea.'

'You must go to sleep, then you won't hear the sea.'

'It's the sea that stops me from going to sleep. I don't like being by the sea.'

'But in the daytime you love the sea. Then you like hearing it.'

'Not at night-time.'

'Now Mother's going to turn the pillow, and then you'll go to sleep.'

'Mother must sit with me.'

'Nonsense,' said Alberta. But the pillow was hot with fever, and the boy's body burned to the touch. Quickly, stealthily, she put her hand on his chest, under the nightshirt. It beat too violently inside there, she knew it did, and nobody would get her to change her mind. It distressed her almost to the point of loathing and disgust. It was too much; it was one of the things that gave her nausea, the feeling that she could not bear it because she was in any case quite helpless. It turned her own heart into a hard, hammering little lump.

'What were you feeling for?'

'Nothing. Now little boys must go to sleep.'

'Sing to me.'

'Sing to a big boy like you?'

'You said I was little just now.'

'Not so very little.'

'Sing about Colin, then I shan't hear the sea.'

'But it won't hurt you to hear the sea. It's nice to hear the sea.'

'The sea's not nice. The sea's wicked. Sing to me.'

The boy's small hand, sticky and hot, lay in Alberta's, gripping it tighter now and then as if to assure itself that it was holding her. Unwillingly, cross with herself for her unwillingness, thinly, a little out of tune, and as softly as possible, she sang. The melody hit on the wrong notes continually and distressed her with its inadequacy. Were those footsteps on the path outside? Pierre was probably walking up and down out there, smiling to himself at how badly she did everything.

'Fais dodo, Colin, mon petit frère,
Fais dodo, tu auras du lolo—'

'Sing louder!'

'Maman est en haut, qui fait du gâteau—'

'Louder!'

'Papa est en bas, qui fait du chocolat.
Fais dodo Colin, mon petit frère,
Fais dodo, tu auras du lolo.'

It was ridiculous from every point of view to be singing to a boy nearly six years old, ridiculous to sing as badly as she did, ridiculous too that little shift of emotion which generally accompanied the naive song. A song about childish poor man's comfort, of the happiness of a full stomach; two children, one bigger boy, one smaller, a cold, miserable room, a candle burning low in a candlestick. Nobody was making anything for them; outside the world was full of similar rooms. Soon all the candles would have burned out.

'I don't expect he cared for milk when he could have chocolate.'

'I don't expect he did. Now go to sleep.'

'Perhaps it was only something his big brother thought up to get Colin to sleep. I expect he only got milk really. But there's nothing nice in milk. They had as much milk as they wanted, didn't they?'

'I'm sure they did.' Alberta recalled with bitterness the days when they had by no means had as much milk as they wanted. It was a good thing the boy did not remember them.

It was at last quiet in the bed. The child's hand still clung to hers immovably. She turned her head and looked out.

516

The darkness of the late summer evening was falling fast. The last trace of red along the horizon had been erased, the larks were silent. Only the breakers continued their eternal motion, up with a hiss, back with a sigh as if for the whole world's grief and distress.

The lighthouse at Penmarc'h had been lit. She could not see it, but its beams swept the surface of the sea, soundlessly and as regular as a heartbeat. The offshore wind must have met an air current that threw it back again. It came in, filling the room with spicy air, and was gone again. Now and then it smelt of the ebb-tide.

Now she could hear Pierre's footsteps clearly on the path outside. There they were—now he stopped—and went on again, wandering without purpose, moved a little way away, again came closer. There was a puff from his cigarette. She was seized with fear in case he might disappear for good, and go off on one of his usual evening walks along the beach. Carefully she began to disengage her hand.

'You put me to bed too early.'

'What do you mean?'

'You and *Ton-ton* Pierre want to sit and talk to each other.'

'Grown-ups always sit and talk to each other when children are in bed.'

'This evening you will talk more, because *Tante* Jeanne is away. And *Tante* Liesel is away, Father is away, everybody is away. Then you will talk a lot. You will talk about things that the others must not hear.'

'Tot!' exclaimed Alberta in despair.

'Father wants me to be called Brede now.'

'Mother wants you to be called that too.'

'Why do you say Tot then?'

'We called you that when you were little.'

'Sing about Martin too.'

'No, now you're going to sleep.'

'I shall tell Father you put me to bed too early. You put Marthe to bed too early as well. I shall tell *Tante* Jeanne. Marthe was silly and fell asleep, because she's a girl.'

'You fell asleep too.'

'I was only pretending. I heard you talking. Sing about Martin.'

'Will you go to sleep if I do?'

The boy considered for a moment. 'Yes,' he said.

And Alberta was in for it again:

> *'Danse Martin, vieux camarade*
> *Pour amuser les petits et les grands . . .'*

This song generally made her feel emotional too. The eternal tragedy of man and beast lay behind it, the tramping along the high road, fatigue and hunger, courage in spite of everything. This evening she felt nothing. She watched her son tensely. He lay peacefully, his eyes closed.

The song was finished, she began to withdraw her hand.

'Did he have a ring in the bear's nose?' came instantly.

'Is this going to sleep?'

'Are all bears called Martin? Do they all have rings in their noses?'

'Not the ones who are wild and live in the forest.'

'How do people catch bears?'

'I'll tell you in the morning. Go to sleep.'

'I shan't if you go.'

'You're very naughty,' exploded Alberta. She leaned her head against the bedpost in utter dejection.

'Sing to me again, then I'll go to sleep. You put me to bed too early.'

And Alberta went on singing. About Marlborough, about the three little lambs, about the art of planting cabbages:

> *'Savez-vous planter les choux*
> *à la mode, à la mode,*
> *savez-vous planter les choux*
> *à la mode de chez nous?*
>
> *On y plante avec les doigts,*
> *à la mode, à la mode,*
> *on y plante avec les doigts*
> *à la mode de chez moi.'*

She felt like a second-rate hurdy-gurdy, going on and on. She could no longer hear the footsteps outside.

She wanted to go downstairs to Pierre.. This one evening. She was sitting with her child, wanting it. Pierre would have gone on talking. He had things to say to her, things he had kept hidden until now, and there had been no occasion to say them before. He had the occasion this evening. Miraculously all the others were away. The house was quiet and strange on account of it, solemn as if in anticipation. Only the boy was present, seeing to it that she did not talk to Pierre. She was not even allowed to do that, to talk to Pierre.

When she came downstairs the only sign of life came from the moths whirring round the lamp. Alberta carried the lamp out to the kitchen, cleared the table in the half-light, and carried the dishes out, clattering them unnecessarily and carelessly, and punishing herself by lighting the primus. It started smoking immediately and she felt savage with hatred for it. She pumped wildly, the smoke got worse and worse. On the floor by the water pump two black snails stretched their horns towards the light, moving their slimy bodies slowly and tenaciously. She found a twig and threw the snails out of the window, the one after the other, with an angry, accustomed, firm gesture. The kitchen had an earthen floor. In the evening it seemed to breed vermin and creeping things, especially round the water pump, which stood there looking as if it belonged to some village square.

The primus burned at last with a little flickering, ragged, evil-smelling flame, an insult to the fresh air from outside. She stood holding the palms of her hands against the sides of the kettle, just as she used to stand with the coffee kettle at home long ago, keeping a watch on the temperature. There always seemed to be a temperature to watch, and certain habits stay with one to the end of one's days. When she had stood like this for a little while the heat moved from her fore-arms right up into her shoulders, the old, painful, soothing sensation. It kept its value in the winter.

519

She did the washing-up, the whole day's crockery and sauce-pans. On the wall, where the towels hung, Jeanne had written in a large, clear hand: Glass, China, Kitchen utensils, Hands. Alberta used the glass one for the china and the kitchen one for her hands, hung them up again any-old-how and shrugged her shoulders at her own childishness. The moths came tumbling in, dashing themselves in confusion against her face, the smoke from the primus still hung, noxious and disgusting, between the walls. It seemed to her at this moment to be the air of life, a suffocating aura that enclosed every breath of fresh air and in which everything decisive took place.

Had it not been exactly the same, worse even, that afternoon last winter when she—when Pierre—?

He had visited them several times, Pierre Cloquet, *Prix Fémina* and *Croix de Guerre*, married and the father of a little girl slightly older than Tot, one of Sivert's many acquaintances from the *Dôme* and one of those who had been 'out there', all four years of it. They compelled a rather oppressive feeling of respect, one tended to feel uncertain and perplexed, more insignificant than usual in their taciturn company. This one had, in addition to everything else, a face like a mask and was a writer. Why had Sivert wanted to drag him home?

But the times were past when she and Sivert got on better alone. A third was usually welcome, as long as he fitted in, and she and Tot had a few clothes on. Gradually she came to like his strange expression, blank, apparently concentrated on something in the distance, and his low, monotonous voice. He suited their surroundings, he seemed to belong.

That afternoon nobody would have been welcome. With black fingers and hair on end, wearing one of Sivert's old painting smocks that she had inherited for household use, she stood struggling with the primus. It was smoking so badly that soot was falling all over the place. Tot was on the pot. He had a cold and she dared not take him across the yard in the November rain; the Spanish influenza was at its height, especially among children. And all of a sudden there was Pierre standing in the doorway with Sivert, who also had a cold and immediately demanded a clean handkerchief.

Alberta could not supply him with one.

'Why not?'

'But Sivert, you know very well why not.'

'Oh Lord!' Sivert struck his forehead. The laundry had not been paid for. 'Damnation. But a few handkerchiefs? Such small things. Is it necessary to—?'

'They have to be boiled,' answered Alberta curtly. 'It's difficult enough to boil everything else as it is.'

As she said it she happened to look Pierre straight in the eye. And his were no longer blank, they were those of a confidant, almost of an accomplice, not those of a judge, and not merely sympathetic. There was an all-forgiving irony in them, kindness. It had been a fleeting and unbelievable moment. A current of life went through her, years' forgotten warmth shifted. It made her think of someone raised from the dead who gets his first glimpse of the light again.

He and Sivert busied themselves with money, digging loose change out of their pockets and pooling the results, and left in haste to fetch the laundry and new cleaning equipment for the primus. Alberta had time to tidy herself and her surroundings while they were gone, and everything was so normal again that she must only have had one of her foolish moments. Sivert brought out his latest pictures, he and Pierre discussed politics and art, as usual. Pierre sat there as he normally did, looking at her absently now and then, talking about Jeanne and little Marthe, his permanent subject of conversation. Alberta finally managed to get a cup of tea on the table.

He had been alone in Paris at that time, attempting in various ways to start writing again, even to the extent of sending his wife and child away for a while. He had a half-finished manuscript which he had begun before the war, a continuation of the book for which he had been awarded the *Prix Fémina*. The publisher wanted it, as he had gone as far as he could, and further, during the war years. It was imperative that Pierre should deliver it. But he achieved nothing, according to Sivert; he fled from it, to cafés, to friends, to revolutionary meetings in Montmartre. Alberta never heard him mention either his work or himself. 'Poor devil,' Eliel used to say.

It was after that day that she had begun to feel there was support in Pierre, and started to count on him, to reach out to him in her thoughts every time there was something the matter. She was happy when he came, and desolate when he left. Somebody cared a little as to how she felt. She was no longer simply the eternal culprit, who deserved what she got, and serve her right.

Disintegration, had he said? A strong word. It struck home. He had used it without hesitation, without even searching for another. She herself had sometimes wondered what this inner and outer composure that she inhabited really was? Passivity or courage, self-renunciation or self-control? Disintegration?

Whatever the reason for her composure, her old restlessness had returned. She caught herself thinking about her appearance, looking in the mirror, a thing she had almost forgotten about. One evening when Sivert had been at the *Dôme* and the boy was asleep, she had taken out her papers: not the short stories she pieced together in an emergency, the others, the pile in the folder. A long time had passed since she had last looked at them. A cold defiance had loosened its grip on her.

Then came the journey here. And Jeanne. But Jeanne in Dijon and Jeanne here were two different things. And two different things the simple knowledge that Pierre had a wife, and spending the days in her company.

The boy, Alberta and Liesel—at times Sivert and Eliel— that would have been for better or worse, like everything else in life, but she would have been able to calculate more or less in advance how things would turn out. But Jeanne . . .

Alberta's heart sank at the thought of how empty it had become, how little there was that could be called her own, in the life that was hers. Without Jeanne no Pierre.

She had gone outside to sit on the bench in the dark. The dew was falling, but the earth beneath it was warm from the sun. The stars had come out, boring into the disc of the sea with thin swords that were broken by the swell, carried in fragments to the shore and lost in the faintly luminous border of froth along the low tide line. Even now that it was dark she could see clearly how emphatically the curve of the sky pressed down on the surface of the water; the eye could follow it all the way round. Two enormous sections had been fitted together with geometrical accuracy. Penmarc'h lighthouse signalled life, death, life, death, with unfailing precision. Everything conformed to the natural law, eternal, serene.

Pierre had gone. He had lost patience, she supposed, even though it was their only chance. And what did she expect of him? Assert yourself beside Sivert, come to terms with him, work on your material continually, peg away, keep going. A kind observer's wise reflections, the good, sensible advice of a friend. He had crossed the chasm he himself had created between them and given it to her, in order to bring her out of the lethargy into which she had relapsed, to rouse her.

She had managed to write a little today. Pierre had helped her to look after the children, feed them, put them to bed, relieving her in every possible way. And yet—

Was that all you were after? she thought, and was suddenly as embarrassed as if she had compromised herself without redress. For deep inside her there was an obstinate murmur: You were really after something else, really, really. You've been observing and watching and thinking. It can't only be out of interest in my wretched writing of which you're completely ignorant.

A figment of the imagination; ordinary friendliness, that had gone to her head. It had been too much for her. But tomorrow Jeanne would be here. In a few days Sivert would arrive. She would be sober then, if not before.

She had leaned over Tot at dinner-time, standing there with the telegram, and said, 'Father's coming home soon, and *Ton-ton* Eliel,' happily and enthusiastically, as such things ought to be said. But her heart had been anxious. It was not only to the good that Sivert was coming, not only to the good that he was coming with money. Plenty of money.

Tot had given one of his convulsive jumps for joy. They could not really be described as jumps either, for he did not leave the ground, merely moved his arms and legs energetically and in vain. 'Father's coming,' he shouted. It had made her wince like a false note.

Sivert—? Tot—?

The day Pierre came and told them that Jeanne had found a cheap house in Brittany for the summer, big enough for at least two families, Sivert had been all enthusiasm. So had she. The Spanish influenza was raging for the second time. Pierre would not advise them for or against it. He was not so sure that the sea would be good for the boy. 'You ought to ask a doctor.'

'The sea?' echoed Sivert. 'What could be better than the sea?'

Alberta agreed with him. Everything in her reached out towards this new possibility. All the same she thought they should ask the doctor. For many reasons.

'Nonsense,' said Sivert. 'These Frenchmen spoil their children. Have you ever heard of a child who couldn't stand the sea?' Alberta had not. Nor had Eliel. 'Damnation,' he said. 'If a person can't stand the sea, what will he stand? Nothing.' Liesel hesitated; she had certainly heard of it. Alphonsine was exceedingly hesitant. But Eliel and Sivert said in chorus: 'Frenchmen and womenfolk!'

A short while ago Tot's heart had hammered like that of a frightened little animal. Her own hardened and stuttered as soon as she thought about it.

She started. Pierre had come up so quietly in his sandshoes that she had not heard him. He felt the ground with his hand and said quietly, as if he did not want to wake the children, 'Don't sit there, the dew is falling. I hope you left the washing-up, Alberta?'

'I couldn't leave it for Jeanne and Liesel. Coming home to dirty dishes . . .' She got up obediently.

'But Josephine? What about Josephine?'

'There's enough for her to do as it is,' said Alberta in an experienced tone of voice. She thought of Jeanne's face and of what she would have said if she had found the kitchen sink full.

'I ought to have helped you.' In the dark she could see how Pierre made a fumbling gesture as if to take his damaged hand out of his pocket. He was haunted by the memory of the time when he had had the use of two hands and done what he liked with them. 'To be honest, I lost patience. Is the tyrant asleep now? You sat up there for more than an hour, a full hour by the clock and let yourself be bullied. I left.' She could see his shoulders move as if in apology.

But Alberta, who at once felt more cheerful and full of gratitude because he had come, managed to ask a difficult question in the same quiet tone of voice. 'Is it the heart that can't stand the sea, Pierre?' She could hear the uncertainty in her voice. Curious, how easy it is to talk beside the point in everything one says.

'It's well known that the sea doesn't suit everyone,' Pierre said evasively, and his cautious words seemed to open her veins. All her strength ebbed away. She had worried over this, hinted it to Sivert, aloud and in writing. He had replied and written, 'Nonsense', and much else besides. She had stopped worrying, or pretended to herself that she had. But what others see acquires terrifying reality, gives one confirmation.

'I grew up by the sea myself. It suited me as a child. Sivert too.'

'It needn't be anything serious. Tot may well grow up strong. But if I were you, Alberta—I'm telling you for the tenth time, find yourself a living. You're wasting your time like this, and it's not as if you're good at it, you're clumsy.' Pierre said the final sentence in his usual voice, as if wanting to break the low, intimate tone on purpose.

'I'm not as clumsy as all that.' Years of drudgery with tasks that she really could not master, and carried out as if she were all thumbs, had made Alberta sensitive on this point. She had at least taken up the struggle, with honesty and goodwill. She did not really demand appreciation for anything whatsoever besides these things. She replied with irritation, 'What do you know about it?'

'Quite a lot. More than you think.'

'Of course, you have Jeanne.'

'Yes, of course, I have Jeanne, I have Jeanne. That explains everything, doesn't it?'

Alberta said nothing. Now *Pierre* was irritated. They were difficult, these men from the war. He was usually the first to give Jeanne the credit on every occasion: 'Thanks to Jeanne. Jeanne's magnificent. Jeanne's splendid. She manages everything. I wouldn't get far without her.' How many times had Alberta heard it all? 'Marthe will be pretty, but she'll never be like Jeanne. All of them were after her at home. There was nobody who didn't know who Jeanne Fauvel was.'

Jeanne here and Jeanne there. Yet one must not imply that she belonged to Pierre. But Alberta knew very well that it was not the words, but the tone. She regretted them.

And she was punished. Pierre yawned. He explained that he had walked quite far while she was sitting upstairs, and was tired. They had better go to bed.

He preceded her to the house, stopped to let her enter first, fastened the door securely, asked politely whether she had matches, whether there was enough oil in her lamp, whether she had water upstairs, something to read. She must be sure to tell him . . . with such icy, correct kindness, that there was no escape. She could only take what she deserved and pretend not to notice.

And worst of all, when they had reached the landing and were about to go to their rooms, Pierre said, 'Perhaps I tend to interfere more than I should in my friends' affairs. Forgive me. Goodnight.'

'Goodnight,' answered Alberta, utterly discomfited.

'Non, ce n'est pas vers toi que je me tourne, mon enfant.

'Tout ce qui bat en moi de vrai et de meilleur, le Dieu, la part de l'âme, cela ne te concerne pas.

'La question palpitante, que je suis, mes actes, leurs dessein, tu es né pour les contredire, puisque tu dois les dépasser, et toi, que j'ai porté dans mon ventre neuf mois, tu ne seras jamais devant moi, devant mes yeux mouillés, contre les baisers de mes lèvres, qu'un étranger, qui part en emportant mon sang.'

Alberta put the book down and picked up another. Her eyes were smarting from reading too long in the poor light. She tried to find composure, failed, and went on opening book after book. They belonged to Liesel. Books written by women.

'*J'ai un tel besoin, si vous saviez, de bras autour de moi. J'ai besoin qu'on s'approche, qu'on me vienne en aide. Personne n'est venu.*'

She sat upright in bed. The night was painful and restless. Someone to share with! To share, if only in the wind chasing round the house in the dark and pausing to sigh among the four or five trees beside the brook in the little valley a short way off; in the waning moon that had risen and was erasing the flickers of light coming through the mist from the lighthouse. Someone to say things to . . .

She was roused by a disturbance in the house. When she was properly awake she could distinguish the hurried tapping of heels on the stairs, doors opening and shutting, voices.

Jeanne and Liesel were back. They had come in the middle of the night.

She heard Jeanne: 'That's the chocolate, here's the material for your shirts, that's for Marthe's nightdresses. Did you take your medicine? Did you have the chop? Of course not, they're asleep, nobody'll hear. Won't you have something to eat? I'm ravenous. Here are *your* parcels, Liesel. And everything has been all right here? We dined at the Hôtel de l'Epée. It was expensive, but there you are. It's only once. Did you manage to get what you wanted sent by the postman?'

She heard Pierre's voice now and again, mumbling and indistinct. He was talking as quietly as he could.

Through the mist the dawn was breaking.

* * *

Jeanne moved about the house, brisk and efficient. Up and down the stairs went her tapping heels. She always finished her share of the chores in good time. Afterwards she would sit

with her handwork, indoors or outside on the grass, according
to the weather.

With beautiful regular stitches she would sew some well-
made, absolutely correct garment for herself, for Marthe, or
for Pierre. At her side would be more work, cut out and
tacked. Soon she would embark on that too. She finished them
incredibly quickly.

Alberta usually sat there too with one of her extraordinary
pieces of sewing, supposedly a garment for the boy. Although
she cut them out according to the right measurements and
used a good pattern they always turned out oddly as did everything of that kind that she undertook. There was something
hopeless about it. She wanted to be able to do this at least, it
was necessary that she should. But life went on and on, and
nothing that she embarked on turned out as she had intended.
If Pierre came by he might look at her ironically, or with
irritation, or with slight amusement. It all depended on what
kind of a day it was.

Jeanne was not a silent soul; but neither was she particularly
informative. In her slightly too high-pitched voice she would
talk about ordinary subjects: Marthe, the difficulties of the
times, the necessity for housewives to find something to do as
well.

She had friends who had begun to take up weaving. Or they
sewed and embroidered and sold the results, tried painting on
parchment, or journalism. Their husbands had come home
from the war and had failed to get their jobs back, they were
disabled, blinded, crippled; or they had not come home at all.
Life was quite different from what it had been before, and
impossibly expensive.

She assured Alberta kindly that Tot was browner and more
lively. 'Oh yes, of course he is, Alberta. The country might
have suited him better?' Jeanne shrugged her shoulders.
'Possibly. Very likely.' If she had seen him at an earlier stage
than at the last moment at the station, she might perhaps have
advised her against it. But here he was and it was much better
for him than Paris. She asked Alberta's advice concerning
colours and thread, talked fashion, literature, cooking. Of

Pierre she said: 'If only he could pull himself together and get out a longer work. It's so important.'

On top of her workbasket there usually lay the most recent issue of *Les Modes de la Femme de France,* a publication about which Pierre teased her. He accused her of being a member of *The Honeycomb,* a supplement in which subscribers exchanged experiences and philosophical reflections, over pseudonyms; and of getting advice from 'Enigma', who read horoscopes at five francs apiece.

'Be quiet,' Jeanne said. 'I'm not so stupid. If I didn't take *Les Modes* Marthe and I couldn't look as we do on almost nothing.'

Jeanne had all the good qualities you could think of. She was useful, respectable and trustworthy. She meant well, nobody's intentions were better. Nevertheless to be with Jeanne was like ceasing to live.

She could arrive full of plans, energy and busyness, always with a thought for others; slender and beautiful, in gay, practical clothes, lovely to look at. It was just that there was never a moment's peace. What was quiet and essential in one withered and died.

'Don't forget your strengthening medicine, Pierre. Then you must lie down for a while. You'll work all the better for it. Marthe, you've scratched yourself; don't touch anything before I've put iodine on it. You ought to look in on Madame Poulain, Alberta, before she sells the rest of those sandshoes, she only had a couple of pairs left. If you're going, would you mind buying a reel of cotton for me? Has anyone seen the paper? There was something in it I wanted to read to you. It's so true, as he says, that man who writes that we must not imagine peace has come yet, it is only a new phase of the war. I don't think Tot ought to be in the sun for such a long time, Alberta. It's different for Marthe. Who's going to shell the peas? You or Liesel? I did them last time. Whoever does them must remove all the withered pieces from the pods and we'll boil them up for soup tomorrow.'

Jeanne, so good-humoured, so full of activity. What would have become of a great many things out here, without Jeanne?

Getting supplies was difficult, vegetables and groceries had to be fetched from Audierne, eight kilometres away. Thanks to Jeanne everything went amazingly far. But tasks one had happily forgotten, anxieties one had pushed aside in one's consciousness, apprehension for tomorrow usually followed in her train.

The clatter of a typewriter came from the open window above. If it stopped, Jeanne noticed at once. Her sewing dropped into her lap, and she sat with upraised head, in her forehead the two small wrinkles that did not become her, forgot what she was talking about, absent-mindedly quietened the children.

When a few minutes had passed and there was still no clatter, Jeanne got up and disappeared inside the house.

Alberta looked down towards the bricklayer's cabbage field. Blue-green as verdigris it dipped steeply into a depression. In the middle of the field stood Liesel's painting parasol, and beneath it was Liesel.

She, too, had a good ear for the typewriter. As soon as Jeanne had gone she put her things down and came plodding through the tall cabbages, which reached up to her thighs. She pushed them aside with her hands as she walked, plucking a couple of large, mottled caterpillars off her skirt on the way up.

'She plagues the life out of him, Albertchen. At least we don't do *that* to Sivert and Eliel.'

'We shouldn't get very far with it either.' Alberta raised her voice and spoke naturally, as one has a right to do when saying things anybody may hear. 'How can you stand those caterpillars! There's one on your shoulder. It's revolting. Now it's climbing on to your hair!'

Liesel picked off the caterpillar coolly and threw it over the stone wall. 'Plenty of things are revolting. Painting is revolting too. I was bored with it a long time ago. If it were not that I had to—'

She sat down and threw her arms round her knees. People usually disappeared in the course of time. They whirled round in Alberta's range of vision for a while and were gone; she could think of many. Liesel was still there, as gangling as a schoolgirl in the short dresses that were now the fashion, her handsome face drawn and thin, a little too freckled to be attractive, and with a suspicion of early furrows running from the sides of her nose down to her mouth. Her coil of plaits was not firm and shining as it used to be, but tended to hang askew and get untidy. It was beginning to be obvious that for Liesel the years were passing, grey and without lustre.

'You really must buy yourself that new brush, Liesel, with hair like yours. And now Eliel is coming back.'

'Hair?' said Liesel. 'Eliel?' she said. 'Look at my hands, Albertchen. Thin, loathsome winter hands, although I'm in the sun all day. Before, when I went to the sea, it made me prettier. But it's this eternal influenza. I'm going to cut my hair when I get back to Paris. Nobody has long hair any more. As for Eliel—does he care what my hair looks like?' And she whispered again, 'If I were Pierre, I'd speak my mind one day. He works from morning till night. She goes about it the wrong way. There ought to be limits.' Liesel coughed.

'You caught a cold on that trip during the night, Liesel.'

'Yes, I did,' Liesel said. 'But I saved the price of a room at the *Lion d'Or* and got two tubes of cobalt blue instead. And Jeanne obtained peace of mind. Everything was in order and respectable here. It's true that Pierre had been idle, the washing had not been touched, and you had put the children to bed in the middle of the day. But the worst had not happened.'

'Who can possibly know?' said Alberta with irritation.

'That sort of thing hangs in the air, Albertchen. You wouldn't be able to deceive Jeanne for as much as a day.'

'I won't listen to this nonsense, Liesel. Is it *you* who thinks up such rubbish?'

'Why else should she decide to come home as soon as the last train had left?' said Liesel undaunted. 'It came over her all of a sudden. We combed the town for a farmer who was going this way. We might have been sitting in a vice, there was so little room beside him. All the way from Quimper to Pont-Croix, and then we walked.'

'She was thinking of Marthe, naturally.'

'You don't believe that, Albertchen.'

'Talk out loud,' whispered Alberta. 'Otherwise they'll notice.'

'Of course they won't. But why are you sitting here? *She* can look after the children. *She* can prepare the meals. She sits here in any case, and she's made for that sort of thing. You should see about finishing whatever it is you're writing.'

'Sssh,' Alberta said, from that hidden dread of many things that she could not always explain to herself. 'I work now and again. It's just that one can't do it as a matter of course, Liesel.'

An exchange of words could be heard through the open window above. It was mostly Jeanne who was speaking, insistently, persuasively. Now and then she paused as if to give Pierre the opportunity to reply. He did so briefly and quietly.

'Talk out loud, as if nothing's the matter. Here she comes.'

Jeanne came, silent, with the two unattractive wrinkles in her forehead. She sat down and bent over her work as before. Her mouth was sad and tired.

The typewriter started again, a light, nimble clatter that made Alberta feel that if only she had a typewriter ... Jeanne's forehead smoothed out. She bit off a thread and said, 'It's so much better for his own sake ...'

'But he does work, Jeanne!'

'If you can call it work!' Jeanne drew more thread from the reel and narrowed her brown eyes short-sightedly as she re-threaded her needle. 'If you can call it work! He could write them all into a cocked hat if only he'd pull himself together. Short stories are all very well, and he must write them if we're to live. But if he doesn't get that novel out soon ...'

Stitch after stitch she sewed, regularly, beautifully. They all lay in the same direction, each one as small as the last. The movement of Jeanne's little finger each time she drew out the thread was perfection.

Her beauty would last. It lay in the perfect structure of the cranium, the unassailability of her teeth, the abundance of her hair, her even, golden complexion: in a healthiness that defied everything. In spite of wrinkles and furrows Jeanne's beauty would make an impression to the end, and continue to smoulder in the deep-set eyes far into old age. Jeanne with white hair would be a magnificent old lady, one of those one looks at with astonishment, who are slender and chic, vital and active until death.

From each earlobe there dangled a tiny pearl. They were beautiful against her skin and her dark hair. Pierre had put them on her the day he was given the *Prix Fémina*. Madness of course. But a man must be allowed a little madness now and again.

Sometimes the machine would stop again. Footsteps would come rattling down the stairs. Pierre would stride past them, his hands in his pockets and his beret demonstratively awry, as if it had been thrown on his head. He would look neither to right nor left.

In dismay Jeanne would mutter, 'Would you believe it!' with sudden tears in her eyes. Marthe would notice immediately and come to put her arms round her neck, kiss and caress her. *'Petit maman,* don't cry.'

'He must get some exercise, Jeanne,' Liesel might say.

Alberta would sit, uncertain whether to try to console Jeanne or not. On occasion Jeanne had looked up at her with a strange expression and said, 'It's the war; he came home so changed.' To this Alberta had nothing to say. The women had stormed the hospitals; Liesel had offered her services, had no qualifications and simply came home again. But she had offered. Alberta had merely existed, while darkness enclosed her and her small world. She had perceived it as darkness, not being able to cope with it in any other way. Through the washing and the wakeful nights she had watched it thickening endlessly. The years had passed, one after the other. She had felt as if she and the sickly child were on a rock out at sea, with the tide coming in and night falling. The Spanish influenza came. Children died like flies. But Sivert had not been threatened in life or limb, and this was undeniable.

Nor had Eliel. There had been a period when they wanted to go to war too, coming home with serious expressions to tell her about other Scandinavians who had enlisted. 'If we have to experience this, we want to be in it,' they said. 'It won't last long, and it won't be repeated in our lifetime.'

Alberta and Liesel went round for days on tenterhooks. Then it was rumoured that one of the Swedes from the *Dôme* was in hospital somewhere in the provinces, with one leg amputated and the other in danger, after only one day of this experience that would never be repeated. A Norwegian had lost his sight, a Dane was dead. Sivert and Eliel did not mention the matter again.

Since her trip to Quimper Jeanne had begun to harp on matters which she had only hinted at before. If the machine stopped she might say, turning down her mouth as if sucking in the corners hard: 'It was unanimous, they gave *him* the prize.'

Alberta and Liesel knew this. 'Yes,' they said.

'For his *first* really *big* work. *I* had never questioned his talent. When he gave up the law and wanted to do nothing but write, it was I who stood by him. He became involved in a literary côterie in Paris, one of these cliques, you know. My parents wanted me to break off the engagement.'

'Oh?' Liesel and Alberta exchanged glances. It was not like Jeanne to make such confidences. Yet there she sat, making them.

'Naturally. It's a gamble to be an author, isn't it? An insecure kind of life. Even his mother was against him. Not I. I believed in him. We had been engaged since we were children.' For a moment Jeanne was almost breathless. 'When the telegram came, saying that he had been given the prize— what a triumph! I had had a hard struggle, I can tell you. They wanted to marry me off to the son of a landed family at home. I come from the Dijon district. But I held out, of course. And after a victory like that they all gave in. We married, were happy for a couple of years. And then the war came.'

She paused, and closed her eyes for a second, gazing inwards at her heroically survived martyrdom. She had the right to do so. She had been heroic, victoriously fighting out the long, tenacious struggle with anxiety and hopelessness, which was what the war had meant to women. Alberta suddenly lost her thread, her hand trembled. She saw what it must have been like to have Pierre 'out there' those four long years. For some reason Jeanne's words pierced her like awls.

The machine started again. Jeanne fell silent, But immediately afterwards it stopped. She dropped her sewing. Marthe, who was making a pattern of pretty stones in the grass, being a little too demonstrative about it while clearly following the discussion, turned her head.

'Pierre!' called Jeanne.

'Jeanne!' exclaimed Liesel softly. 'Jeanne!' said Alberta.

Footsteps on the stairs, strides taking at least two steps at a time. Pierre went past them, his hands in his pockets, his beret askew. He was in great haste. Tot, who was sitting on the ground, looked up. Marthe scattered her stones and snail-shells and ran to Jeanne. But Jeanne pushed her away. 'Go and play!'

Then the words suddenly tripped over one another. 'His friends—didn't I get out of bed, even when they came came in the small hours, even when I was pregnant? Wasn't I just as good-tempered when they had raided my larder and turned everything upside down? As if I were not one of the côterie, I as well as the others! All I ever heard was: Kind Jeanne, marvellous Jeanne, just the kind of wife a writer should have. I'm not allowed to see what he writes any more either. I, who used to read every word before anyone else.'

She got up and ran into the house, Marthe following. Then Liesel nodded three times at Alberta, sucking in her cheeks as if she had had something confirmed. Originally it had been one of Eliel's affectations. Liesel had caught it from him.

'*No,* Liesel,' Alberta said involuntarily. 'Oh no, Liesel.'

She put her hand to her breast as if to defend herself.

'*Yes,*' said Liesel.

At lunchtime that day Pierre was exquisitely polite to Jeanne and Jeanne more than usually solicitous towards Pierre, but more subdued than usual. She did not bother to help clear the table, but went upstairs with him.

In a while the others heard her sobbing and Pierre talking quietly and soothingly.

Tonight, thought Alberta mechanically. Tonight...

The night came and was indeed one of those when she had to put her head under the blankets in order to avoid hearing Jeanne's intense, effusive whispers, her silence and contented sighs, the creaking of the bed in their room.

*   *   *

The path up to the village went through the bricklayer's farm-yard. Children swarmed in and out across the threshold, apparently dropped into the world as frequently as the laws of nature permit. Their mother was coming from the fields carrying a large basket of cabbages on her head for the cows. They were kept indoors at mid-day because of the sun and the flies. She herself resembled a large, slow-witted animal going about its business. Her pale, round eyes were quite empty, without conscious expression, and she was pregnant yet again. Her heavy belly swayed before her like a large drum; she moved in an even, patient jog-trot.

People said the bricklayer hit her on Saturday evenings, for then he was drunk; hit her and made her pregnant, if she was not so already and he was not dead drunk. He had not even been away at the war, as he was already lame. There had therefore been no intermission.

Some of the children had their father's fretful, crafty expression beneath red eyebrows, others their mother's listless, stupid one under white ones. Judging by this family, the laws of heredity were simple and clear.

'*Ann amser zo brao*, fine weather today,' said Liesel and Alberta, as was the custom. The day was indeed fine: an offshore breeze, a sea like milk, boats out on it, moving banks of cloud, warmth; the pleasant sounds of work in progress, of threshing and whetstones on the farms.

The woman did not reply. She did not seem to be aware that they were speaking to her as a human being. She jogged on in her clogs and disappeared into the barn, with a shoal of her offspring crowding after her like frightened animals. Their stockings were wrinkled, snot ran from their noses. One had his trousers unbuttoned; they slapped against his little black rump. The others pressed themselves against the wall and stood there with their fingers in their mouths, scowling at Alberta, Liesel and the children, as if they could be suspected of anything.

A sympathy akin to irritation, a desire to do something brutal, to seize this sluggish creature and shake her, came over Alberta: Hit back, kick, put up a fight, take your children and leave.

But it is difficult to leave with one child, let alone several. All the collective degradation women have to suffer tormented her every time she passed this farm.

She felt Tot's hand gripping hers more tightly, saw Marthe inspecting everything about her with the arrogant air of the well-brought up child, caught sight of the expression in Liesel's face against which she was helpless, and quickened her pace. 'We must hurry.'

'We're not to speak to those people,' Marthe said reprovingly, when they were out on the path once more. 'They are not *comme il faut. Maman* says they have lice, and that we must never play with them, because then we'll get them too. They are *malpropre,* dirty people.'

'Dirty people,' repeated Tot, who did not usually imitate Marthe.

'They are people you should be sorry for, poor people, who have learnt nothing and don't know any better.' Alberta raised her voice harshly and looked down into her son's face. The bricklayer could not have been as poor as all that, since he was the only bricklayer for miles around. She felt strongly that her explanation was unsatisfactory. The boy's eyes met her own for an instant, and then looked away as usual.

'It's their own fault if they're poor,' Marthe insisted. 'They should not be poor. Lazy people are poor.'

The boy repeated, 'Lazy people are poor, lazy people are poor.'

'I expect other people are too.' Alberta could hear the irritation in her voice.

But the boy went on repeating, 'Lazy people are poor, lazy people are poor.'

And she let the children have the last word, the convenient word that people prefer even in childhood. Involuntarily she looked across at Liesel, who was walking alone, her face old and pathetic. Shortly she said, dropping her voice: 'And someone like that can have children, Albertchen. Full of children. An idiot.'

We ought to have gone by the road after all, thought Alberta. Liesel's remark was quite natural. But behind it there lay a morbidly developed sensitivity for certain matters. It increased with the years and could occasionally bring Liesel quite out of balance. She had bouts of weeping, convulsive sobbing that would not stop. It was then that Eliel would shake his head and say, 'Women! They're all the same.'

'I can't bear to see it, Albertchen, the way those children are brought up. It makes me feel ill.'

'She's so wretched herself, Liesel. One can't expect anything else.'

'I don't mean that either, I mean—' Liesel stopped. Marthe was obviously listening. It was not the moment for going into the subject more deeply.

At Josephine's and Jean-Marie's house only Jean-Marie's mother was at home. Through the open door they could see her busily polishing the table while keeping an eye on the pig, which was loose outside, and the chickens. The wall of the house was bright with dahlias, the old-fashioned, round kind one had such a desire to hold as a child. Fuchsia and pelargonium crowded each other behind the window panes. They looked pretty in contrast to the white-washed little house with its border of grey stone and its light blue window frames. Alongside was the outhouse, the black and white flank of a cow visible in the doorway; behind it all the cabbage field, blue-green as verdigris. It was pleasant on the little farm; it was all as neat and tidy as one could wish. It smelt of the cowshed, pigs, the sea, flowers from the country, in a warm blend. There was even a tiny fig tree, slanting and distorted by the wind from the sea, the shadows of its glossy leaves flickering above the well. A curious feeling of being at home was unavoidable here; Alberta was always reminded of certain words: At home we live in a village, Mademoiselle. We have a cow and a pig, potatoes, cabbages, the sardine fishing . . . Today the sea is as white as milk in the sun . . .

'*Ann amser zo brao*, Tinti-Marianna.'

'*Zo brao ann amser.*' Tinti-Marianna put down the cloth, dried her hands and came out to the doorway with them hidden under her apron as decorum demanded. 'Came in time, Josephine? Hens plucked yesterday. Good!'

Tinti-Marianna spoke French as a Negro might. Freckles were scattered over her thin, brown face. Stripes of pale red could be seen in her grey hair through her head-dress of white tulle. Her round, blue eyes seemed spun into a net of wrinkles. 'The gentlemen are coming, the gentlemen are coming. Good! Tinti-Marianna pleased, the ladies pleased, the little gentleman pleased.' She nodded in the direction of Tot, who was vainly attempting to approach the pig. 'Jean-Marie at sea. Fine weather. Fish this evening. Good.'

'Good,' said Alberta and Liesel, nodding. 'Good, Tinti-Marianna.'

'Do you wish you were Josephine, Albertchen?' asked Liesel as calmly as if she were asking where Alberta was going. They were out on the path again.

'Don't be ridiculous.' Alberta laughed. After a pause she said, 'Not that I were Josephine, but perhaps that I resembled her. Although—I don't know, Liesel. One wants to be oneself, in spite of everything.'

'Hm,' Liesel said.

From the open country they turned into the narrow lane that led up between outhouses and dung-heaps to the centre of the village, where the main road passed through, and the church, the priest's house, the mayor's house and the inn were situated. The sun beat down on the little square, not a leaf moved in the elms along the churchyard wall, and the shadow beneath them was heavy and blue.

Fully grown trees were normally only to be found far inland. Here eight of them stood in a row, thanks to the houses which sheltered them on all sides. Each time Alberta saw them the effect was always one of overwhelming luxuriance. An old, never quite satisfied longing would seize her for precisely this kind of summer, for warm abundance, such as she had experienced on brief holidays in the inner fjords as a child. On the journey out, when in the morning the train had steamed among green hills alternating with rich deciduous forests, she had been on the point of calling out that here was the place to stop, here the moment of time they should seize. Here was the murmur of bees, quiet breezes through the foliage, wild strawberries that could be plucked without changing your position, perhaps someone who would come and say that it was late, and call them home to a meal out of doors, under the trees. Jeanne was sitting crocheting in silence, her face kind and beautiful. She had looked up and smiled at the children, who had settled down, each in someone's lap, their wide, shining eyes reflecting the green light from outside. The fatigue of the journey was dispersed by it. Alberta was reminded of the rowan tree above the shoemaker's roof; this was what it had symbolized year after year in another life. The park at Versailles belonged with it, and other parks, in the life that had followed.

'Quick, Alberta,' whispered Liesel.

Madame Poulain's door was open as usual. Alberta and Liesel tried to hurry past. For what was there to say to Madame Poulain? But the children walked slowly, dragging their feet. Before they had rounded the corner she was standing on the doorstep.

'*Mesdames*! One moment! And the little ones? Are they to go past my house?'

'Another day, Madame Poulain. Someone is coming by the train. We—'

'The gentlemen. I know. But only for a moment. I have had *news*.' Madame Poulain's eyes were full of tears, they were brimming over already.

'Oh!' said Alberta and Liesel. 'Oh, Madame Poulain!'

Marthe was already inside, and had taken up her position in front of the shelf of dolls. They were small and cheap, and stood in their cardboard boxes as if in open coffins, staring stiffly into thin air with stupid eyes. They were made of calico or the kind of material that comes apart at the touch of a raindrop, stiff with sizing. At home Marthe had Mimi. Mimi was as big as a baby, could shut her eyes, had thick ringlets of real hair, hats, frocks, coats, three changes of underwear. Jeanne had made all her clothes. She was put to bed at night and dressed in the morning, usually on command; the rest of the day she just sat. But in front of Madame Poulain's dolls Marthe was lost in contemplation, lifting the small dresses, carefully touching the ringlets which were not attached to their heads, but only to their hats, so that it was simple to establish that the dolls were bald.

Jeanne was in the habit of saying, 'Not one *sou* will I spend on those rags. You are not to buy a hoop for Tot, Alberta, I'd like to make that clear. Give him one to take to the Luxembourg Gardens in the autumn. He won't be able to roll it on these slopes; it's not healthy to run too much near the sea, it strains the heart. And Marthe will give me no peace.'

Madame Poulain was looking for something in a drawer. Now and again she brushed the corner of her eye with her finger. 'One of his friends has been here ...'

'Oh!' said Alberta and Liesel again. They would have liked to find words, but it was difficult.

'Yesterday, *mesdames*. He has been a prisoner ever since. He saw my boy fall, just managed to take what was in his breast pocket, then everything went black. He knew nothing more until he woke up and found himself a prisoner. A grenade, *mesdames*. He assures me—he says my boy was dead before—before—'

Madame Poulain changed the subject. 'Here is the photograph of me. This is my daughter-in-law. Just imagine, she has gone into Audierne today again to get a mourning veil! As if I haven't got good enough veils here in the shop. But of course it's the new doctor, I know that. He's young; he survived it unharmed. She is young too, of course, and pretty. And it's three years since my boy disappeared—'

Alberta and Liesel looked at the worn wallet Madame Poulain was holding as if it were alive, and at the two photographs she had taken from it: the young fiancée who had married him as soon as the order came to mobilize, because she insisted; Madame Poulain herself, a pleasant middle-aged woman without a trace of white in her hair and a cheerful expression on her kind, understanding face. Now her hair was as white as snow. Alberta hesitantly mumbled something to the effect that it was better to know for certain.

'For certain? Yes, I know I shall never prepare him for burial, never put a pillow under his head, never even know where he lies. And that it is no use hoping any more. Before I had hope, in spite of all the things they said. Now they tell me: It is only his body that is gone, Madame Poulain. Only? You know yourself, Madame, how much we love that body from the first moment we handle it. It is a part of us; if there is anything wrong with it, we too are ill, if it is happy—oh, you know how it is, Madame, you have a little boy yourself.'

Her words affected Alberta as only the truth can. Helplessly she looked at Madame Poulain, powerless to contradict her. She turned, looking this way and that inside the little shop. Sewing things and knick-knacks, cheap toys, cheap soap, cheap perfume, doubtful brands of hair-oil. She wished she could say something comforting, but found nothing beyond reaching out her hand to Madame Poulain across the counter. And she began negotiating the purchase of a reel of white cotton.

'Thank you, Madame. It helps me to talk to you, Madame. You are so understanding. The others say: His soul is in heaven. The parish priest was here yesterday and said so. How do we know? However much of a priest he is, he does not know more than we ordinary folk. We have to be chastened, he said. Why start the whole business, I said, when it's all such a failure and can't be improved? What sort of a God is that? And my daughter-in-law in Audierne today again! It is only we mothers who do not forget, Madame. He is growing, your little one. Mine was not so robust either when he was small, he was quite delicate. Yours will grow big and strong later on, like mine.'

'Do you think so?' asked Alberta eagerly, suddenly involved. 'Do you think so?'

'Of course. Wait until he is thirteen or fourteen. Mine had such bearing, Madame, a way of carrying his head, such shoulders. It all came at that age. You ask whether I shall go there? Yes, Madame. It will be my first journey and my last. I come from Audierne, so did my husband. We have never been the kind to move about. We had the boy, you see. Anything we managed to save went to him. He spent a summer in England for the sake of the language, and another in Germany; he had almost finished training to be an engineer. We did our best. And when you think that he might have been shot by his German friend! They wrote to each other often. Yes indeed, Madame. He was a fine boy too, like mine. I even have a photograph of him. I say again: what sort of a God are they talking about? I didn't start this shop until I was widowed; it took half an hour in the wagon with the furniture, and I never thought I'd make any more journeys. His friend described the place to me as well as he could, but everything is in such confusion there. People can't find their own farms any more. I shall have to lay a wreath on the ground. Or on any one of the crosses. If it is not my boy it will be some other mother's son. The cotton, Madame, here it is. And the little ones? What are the little ones to have today, my angels?'

Madame Poulain looked round and took, in spite of Alberta's protests, two rubber balls from the shelf. '*Spoil* them? They *ought* to be spoilt. They can never be spoilt enough. One day you are left regretting all the things you never did—yes indeed, Madame.'

When they were outside again, Liesel said, 'How you talk. Everybody thinks a thing like that is beyond me.'

'Oh, Liesel! Don't start on that now, please,' Alberta said under her breath.

'No, there's no necessity to start on it. Here they come,' replied Liesel curtly.

A little way off two men were walking towards them along

the road, the one tall, the other short and thick-set. They were carrying suitcases, and coats over their arms, and approached quickly, at a brisk pace. In silent agreement Alberta and Liesel sat down on the stone wall to wait. Tot pressed himself up against it. His little face was stranger and more unfathomable than ever. In the middle of the road Marthe jumped and skipped demonstratively with her new ball. They would have preferred not to have taken her with them, but Jeanne had said, 'The stove is smoking. And we have more than enough with the kitchen and laying the table, Josephine and I. If we're to have Marthe hanging about—'

Alberta's heart still thumped a little with excitement when she was about to meet Sivert again after they had been parted for a while, if only a few hours. And she could still sag with disappointment after their first exchange of words. She still felt this anticipation, more consciously, more impatiently insistent than before. Were they never to grope their way to something different, Sivert and she? Was this journey's end for them? It could not be possible.

Fond of him? Of course she was fond of him. Life had welded them together, they were two people close together in the infinity of that relationship. Something that must have been yearning for him ran, hidden like a rootstock, beneath all their dissension and ill-humour.

There he was. The suitcase he was carrying was brand new, that was the first thing she noticed. It shone with nickel at each corner. And what else was different? He was tanned and handsome, but he had been so before he left. He was in new clothes, from top to toe in new clothes, the visible confirmation that they were over the worst for the time being, perhaps for good. But there was something else too, something indefinable.

The clothes fitted him, the hat suited him. It suddenly made her deeply happy to see it, and brought him closer. Aspects of Sivert that she had struggled to perceive seemed to become real as a result. Affection welled up in her. Why not stand shoulder to shoulder, why disagree? We have a child together, now we shall have a following wind. Let us set sail like good friends. But deep down there lurked a familiar, hurtful thought: It's difficult enough when we're poor; it will be worse if— Rubbish.

'There's Father. Run to meet him, give him a hug.'

The boy gave one of the strange leaps that did not take him off the ground. Only now did he seem certain as to who was coming. Now he had reached Sivert, who put down the suitcase, took him by the arms and lifted him up. 'Let's have a look at you, boy! Brown as a berry, eh? Swimming like a fish?'

'Ouch!' the boy exclaimed. His arms were hurting.

'Hmm.' Sivert shook his head. 'Alberta's damned sentimentality again. Can't even stand being touched. We must play another tune now, there must be an end to spoiling and coddling.'

He patted his son on the head in a fatherly manner. 'We're a big boy now, called Brede. Brede Ness. I shall have to look after you a bit more, I can see. Now you shall go swimming in the sea with Father. Hello, Alberta, hello, Liesel, nice of you to come and meet us. And there's Marthe too. Hello, Marthe.'

'Tot *can* swim,' came breathlessly from Tot.

'That's good, boy, that's good.'

Sivert's conversation was friendly and just as it should be. There could be nothing the matter with her. Yet his eyes glittered, the old glitter that Alberta could not stand at one time, and kept having to forget afresh in order to make progress. It could disappear for long periods at a time. Now it was back, forcing itself up from the bottom, confident and watchful.

She must get away from it, past it. He must be different.

'Sivert!' She gave him both her hands. 'How splendid you look. And how handsome you are.'

She meant it. He looked handsome and well-dressed, he cut a fine figure. And this new quality about him . . .

'Hm, yes,' said Sivert. 'It was about time,' he said. 'I haven't spent much on myself the last few years. I thought it was my right for once.'

'Yes, of course.' Alberta was amazed at his tone and the words, even though what he said was quite correct. Sivert had not been reckless about clothes, or anything else; circumstances had forbidden it in any case, and nobody had accused him of it. He seemed to be waiting for accusations.

'*Hei paa dig*, Alberta, how are you?' It was Eliel, tall, slightly stooping, handsome as a peasant, with his too-white teeth in his strong, tanned face. 'We shall all have to deal a little more roughly with that boy, if we're to make a man of him. Well—what do you think of Sivert? What airs he's putting on, isn't he? Look at his clothes, look at his suitcase. Yes, I must say—Damned beautiful out here at any rate. Enough to make a man wish he were a painter.'

'Welcome back, Eliel.' Alberta gave him her right hand, leaning down to handle the suitcase with her left. She was struggling with a completely new feeling of uncertainty towards Sivert. What he had said about looking after the boy, and Eliel about dealing with him more roughly, made her heart beat anxiously, as if she glimpsed a conspiracy. The suitcase stood there solidly in the middle of it all. It was nice that he had had bought that, at any rate, nice that they could buy things.

'What a handsome suitcase.'

'It is quite handsome,' said Sivert. 'I thought I should have a decent one.'

'Yes, of course.' Pleasure in the development of Sivert's concern for his outward appearance mingled so strangely with Alberta's feelings. He seemed to be thinking about something else all the time.

They had sat down on the wall to rest, he and Eliel. They swung their legs with their hats pushed on to the backs on their heads. Eliel had had his success last year, and it could indeed alter a person. Now Sivert was sitting here and was altered as well, in that utterly unexpected way of his. There was something nonchalant about his newly clad person, something daredevil, which had not been a part of his personality before. He shoved his hat even further back and looked at the sea with an expression of boyish defiance which made her uneasy. He seemed to be meditating mischief. 'Damned beauti-ful,' he said. 'This has to be done big, if it's to be done at all, no niggling.'

I'm even impatient of his happiness, thought Alberta, full of contrition. She sat down beside him with the boy. 'Come along, Tot. Let's sit here with Father.' Sivert's gaze returned from the distance and he took the boy on his knee. Alberta asked him where his new canvases were, had he not brought any with him? They could not be in the suitcase? He had worked at such a rate when they first came out here that he had used up all his material by the time he left. He had been forced to borrow from Liesel. Somewhat carelessly Sivert replied that Castelucho could send what he needed—if he needed anything; he had not made up his mind yet. Sur-prised beyond words Alberta said nothing. Would he not be needing canvases? Sivert? Diligence itself?

There had been changes for Liesel too when Eliel's large group was sold, such great changes that it was incredible that she had agreed to them. On the other hand—it was not easy for Liesel. As the war years passed she had been sent less and less by the family in the photograph, and now they sent noth-ing. The war had taught one geography, if nothing else. There had used to be some mystery about Liesel's fatherland, as there is about the Balkan states, and nobody had really bothered to find out where she came from. Then the day came when everyone realized she was from Estonia. During the brief period of Bolshevik rule her family had fled in panic and were still living on sufferance with poor German relations, even though their country became independent later. Liesel struggled to make a living out of her painting, meanwhile pressing Eliel for every *sou* she could, cold-bloodedly, almost with *schadenfreude*. 'It's good for him to part with it,' she said.

Now she was sitting on the grass border below the wall, her arms slung round her drawn-up knees, her usual position out here, cross-examining him methodically: Yes, he had locked the door properly and given the key to the concierge; she had promised to water the flowers and look after the cat. No, he had done nothing about the mattress yet, he had had other things to think about. There was no hurry, surely, so why talk about it now? Yes, yes, there was a new pane in the attic window. *Cleaned* the place after him? No, he hadn't. Surely there would be time to do that when they got home?

He spoke as if it was a long time since he had given these things a thought. Liesel did not look at him, merely continued asking her monotonous questions, sticking out her lower lip after each reply. She was watching a pile of clouds moving slowly across the sky. Not a muscle moved in her face when Eliel suddenly leaned forward, put his arm round her shoulders and shook her a little. Could they not talk about something else? Even at the Versailles people were not discussing their troubles any more. Why be worse than they were?

With a spacious gesture, the confidence of a peasant, he drew Liesel's head closer. Alberta was reminded of the way one draws a horse's head to oneself, in a gesture of confident mastery. There was also something of the capricious colt in Liesel's sudden toss of the head in order to free herself.

From her position out on the road Marthe watched them from under her eyelids, running about with her ball with the sole purpose of hiding this fact.

Sivert pushed his hat on straight, took Tot's hand and seized the suitcase. 'Come along. A bathe before lunch, what do you say to that, Eliel? After all that train dust? Here's the whole Atlantic waiting for us.' He threw back his shoulders and took a deep breath, nonchalantly drew out a new gold watch, looked at it quickly and put it back into his waistcoat pocket. The effect was all the more surprising since it had no chain. As if by magic it appeared and then was gone. Did I actually see that? thought Alberta. But Tot exclaimed, 'Father has a new watch, Father has a new watch. Tot wants to see it.'

'You may see it when you say "I" and remember that your name is Brede. Brede Ness.' Sivert nodded down at the boy. 'Then you may look at the watch as much as you like. Then Father will teach you how to tell the time.'

Josephine waited at table, clumsy and attractive in her Bigouden costume, red-faced and eager to do everything correctly. Eliel and Sivert watched her. She was new to them, having returned from a visit to her parents since their departure.

'Damnably picturesque,' Sivert muttered.

'Sculptural too,' Eliel assured him. 'Such solidity, don't you think?'

When she poured out for them or offered them a dish they teased her: 'Ring on your finger? Husband or sweetheart? Is there hope for anyone else?'

'Jean-Marie's wife,' whispered Alberta informatively.

Josephine glowed, herculean and healthy, without urban scruples. 'Husband, *messieurs,* husband, come back to me safe and sound from the war. I can assure you he is not one to waste his nights.'

And when a moment of amazed silence followed this remark: 'I could very well do without it. It means nothing to me—but for him! You know what men are!' The age-old feminine refrain, which they believe raises their status and gives them superiority.

Fresh silence. Josephine looked perplexed. It was evidently no use. She gave up trying to make herself understood by these city folk and fell silent. With a somewhat strained expression Jeanne brought up the matter of the sale of Sivert's big composition. She also asked him how things were in Paris. 'Tell us, Sivert.'

And Sivert told her, ready and willing to be cross-questioned by her and by Pierre, who was in high spirits in his quiet way and listened attentively. At other times he could look so astonished when he was in company. It came over him sometimes, making Jeanne's eyes and hands uneasy. Now her gaze moved incessantly between him and Sivert, full of confidence, of excessive satisfaction. If he notices it, it will be too much for him, thought Alberta.

'Everything is as usual on Montparnasse,' reported Sivert. 'Except that the girls get more and more like the boys, all of them with their hair cut short.' He didn't mind. It suited them. Yes, the composition had been sold. He would have made money on it a couple of years ago, but one had to be satisfied with things as they were. It had gone to his home town. One of the city fathers, who had seen it on exhibition at home, had come on a trip to Paris and decided to be generous. Came to the studio one day and initiated the transaction. Yes, he had said he was coming. But there you see, one shouldn't really be out of Paris. However lovely it might be here Sivert had not thought of staying long this time either. Heaven knew what it would look like when it was hung. Objects of that size were not suitable for private collections; though it was said that many people had been able to build amazingly large and beautiful houses during the war.

'The neutrals,' said Jeanne. There was silence for a moment. Her voice had been colourless, yet running over with bitterness and contempt. Pierre resumed the conversation. 'It was exhibited a couple of years ago, wasn't it?'

'In the spring of 1917,' Sivert informed him. 'It found a buyer none too soon, I must say. I sent it home with a friend. If I had been at home myself—' Sivert shrugged his shoulders, used to accepting life's difficulties.

'*Eh bien*, Alberta?' It was Pierre. His sudden question made them all look at her. Then they looked away again, and Alberta smilingly drank with them, when they drank a toast to Sivert. But the wine lay like vinegar on her tongue. She remembered all too clearly the occasion when the composition had been sent off and what subsequently happened.

Strangely enough it had arrived in Norway safely. There were all sorts of reasons why it should not have done so: hundreds of complicated formalities, mines in the North Sea, submarines. Sivert had driven to the station with it as if seeing off a person. Rolled up, long and cylindrical, it stood up by his side in the cab. It meant well-being and a future; it meant everything. It was going home. At home pictures were selling like hot cakes.

The cab fare had been begged as a loan from three different sources. It had been that kind of a day.

For a long time they had heard nothing. Then news came. It had arrived, had been included at the last moment in an exhibition held jointly by some of his friends. Newspaper cuttings arrived. Sivert was praised. He was given one of the more generous stipends.

And he had wanted to go home, by himself, alone. At home artists were not only selling their work, they had commissions enough for themselves, their children and grandchildren. Art was being sold as never before. He could not consider taking Alberta and the boy with him, for many reasons. One was the difficult journey. She did not wish to undertake it either. But she had realised for the first time that she could not rely on Sivert. Not that she would allow him to leave her and the delicate child, with conditions as they were then. Besides, he might have been torpedoed.

She suggested as much. Sivert laughed and said 'Nonsense!' The outcome was that she used harsh words, repeating them over and over again, behaving as she had behaved only once before and had never imagined she would again. And Sivert did not go. But this was one of the things that stood between them.

'*Skaal*, Alberta! Didn't I say Sivert would come back a rich man?'

'*Skaal*!' Alberta suddenly drained her glass and held it out for more. Pierre smiled crookedly in admonition before pouring her the wine, doing so awkwardly with his left hand. She was usually cautious with wine, and this was cheap and treacherous, bought up in the village. The glass she had emptied had already gone to her head.

She nodded to him in confirmation. Yes, she would like some more. Then she put down the full glass untouched, suddenly quite sober. Through the murmur of the others' voices, through the quickly alternating mixture of French and Scandinavian which had come about in their conversations, she heard Sivert say quietly, almost defensively, 'Of course I've been working, working like the devil. You work all the better for a love affair, you know that. *Skaal*!'

'True enough. *Skaal*, brother.' Eliel drank deep, while Pierre and Jeanne smiled politely at the strange words they did not

551

understand, and went on talking about the Treaty of Versailles, what was being said in Paris and what they were saying abroad.

But what had Sivert said? It was very unlike him. He was not the kind of person whose feelings and thoughts you could guess at. On the contrary. He had presumably thought and felt much that she had never suspected in the course of the years. Some people gave themselves away continually. Sivert never did. It was new for him to mention feelings at all.

She looked across at Liesel. She was never sure how much Scandinavian, and Norwegian in particular, Liesel understood. She was sitting sucking in her cheeks, feeding Tot piece by piece with Jeanne's celebrated apple cake. She was not looking at anybody. Perhaps she had not heard.

'More apple cake? No, Marthe. We mustn't spoil your digestion. Can a child eat as much as it likes? Perhaps your Vikings can, Eliel, but here we have to look after our stomachs. Marthe's is as regular as clockwork. Why? Because I have given her healthy habits.' Jeanne wiped her offspring's mouth energetically. 'Are you really going to have more wine, Pierre?'

She looked imploringly at Pierre, who filled his glass and emptied it. 'It's sweet of you, Jeanne, but I don't think anyone has yet seen me drink more than was good for me.' His voice was absent-minded and monotonous, his expression blank. It was one of the moments when it looked as if Jeanne's occasional remarks might be true: 'He's not concerned about anything any more. He's not affected by anything. It wouldn't matter to him if we were dead.'

What was Pierre thinking about when he sat like that? Did he not think at all? He had not only injured his face out there, he had not only lost three fingers. According to what he had told Sivert once something had been shot out of his brain, he had an empty space in his grey matter. As he was sitting the emptiness would open out; he literally saw it and progress was blocked.

He was supposed to have said, 'Three fingers. Well, I can't

shoot any more. If only they had gone a little earlier and not at the very end perhaps I'd still have been fit for something.' This was Pierre's sickness, that he believed he was fit for nothing. But his machine clattered from morning till night, and Jeanne would not hear of any empty space. *'Une idée fixe,'* she said. 'Just get over it. The doctors say so too.'

Now she got up quickly from the table. 'I think everyone has finished. You help Josephine, Marthe. We'll have our coffee outside.' The wrinkles had appeared in her forehead. Her voice was high-pitched.

'I'm afraid the sea isn't altogether good for the boy, Sivert.'

Alberta was standing with her back to the window in their bedroom, watching Sivert unpack the new suitcase. New underwear, new socks, tie and bath-robe, a shaving set she had not seen before; books in yellow jackets, which he placed on his bedside table without more ado. He put a large, angular parcel, clearly meant for Tot, on one side. He handed another to Alberta; it was small, oblong and hard. She could tell that it was a box and felt a pang of remorse and emotion: That I could mention it at this moment. I could have waited. It's not pleasant for him. He has thought about me, he's giving me something I haven't had to ask for.

'Thank you, Sivert.' She fumbled with the narrow red ribbon, unable to open it in her haste. There were so many things she needed. She hoped Sivert had not been extravagant. She felt a sudden rush of joy at the thought that perhaps he had been precisely that.

'Not good for him? The sea? What rubbish. Nothing could be better.'

'He gets so easily out of breath, he sleeps less and less.' He's still afraid of it, was on the tip of her tongue, but she stopped herself in time. 'Have you a knife, Sivert?'

'He's as brown as a berry.' Sivert searched his pockets. 'He's never looked as healthy as he does now. You coddle him too much. But naturally a boy ought to be brought up by his father, or he'll be mismanaged. I see more and more how unevenly he's developing.'

'Pierre says—'

'Pierre! In the first place he's a weakling himself, in the second place he's a Frenchman. You must admit they're not as hardy as we are at home.'

'Jeanne says so too.' Alberta's throat constricted. She felt her impotence as if it were a physical defect.

'Jeanne and Pierre!' said Sivert.

'There's nothing wrong with their child.'

'No. But they do tend to coddle her. This business of her stomach. A healthy child can eat whatever it likes and whenever it likes.'

'The sea *isn't* good for Tot,' said Alberta vehemently.

'Now listen, Alberta, you *look* for excuses to make life difficult for me. It's always been the same. I've thought so plenty of times. Isn't the sea any good either? Here I am, doing my best; I provide you with this, that and the other, and it's never right. I believe you do it on purpose so as to give me no peace. I took it to be typical woman's nonsense, along with much else, but—'

'You have come to the conclusion that it's not so typical after all.' Alberta was suddenly enraged. Her anger and resentment flamed up into her forehead. She spoke quietly but her voice was like ice.

'Yes, I have come to that conclusion. One does draw one's conclusions. Let me tell you something. Other people don't share your attitude towards me. Some people feel quite differently.'

'They haven't had a child by you,' answered Alberta. 'To be your friend, Sivert, can be bad enough. But to have a child by you is God's retribution.'

She did not know herself where she found the words. They came tumbling out, spiteful and over-solemn, in this same cold, quiet tone of voice. She did not recognise it; she had not possessed it before.

Sivert had found the knife that had gone astray among the things on the bed. He put it down roughly beside her on the window-sill. 'God's retribution,' he repeated with emphasis. He too spoke quietly, with icy deliberation. 'I shall not forget that,' he said. The words struck her like daggers, piercing surfaces in her mind that were sensitive and fearful; surfaces that gave her pain long afterwards if touched. Slowly she left Sivert and the unopened little packet. She bled with remorse and sorrow for herself and for him, for the fact that they scarcely met before they brought out the worst in each other. Their child was no bond uniting them, he was a symbol of dissension. And yet she had to believe that both of them meant well.

Downstairs Josephine was talking to Jean-Marie, a cheerful, loud-voiced exchange in the local dialect, impossible to understand beyond the brief introductory phrases about the weather that were essential to good manners. The children were with them. It was impossible to slip past unobserved. Alberta ordered her expression as best she could.

Jean-Marie had put the basket of fish down on the steps. In amongst the seaweed a few plaice slapped their tails languidly, a heap of sardines glittered like silver in the sun. He, Josephine and the children were standing in a ring round the catch looking at it; but it was impossible to tell whether that was what he and Josephine were discussing.

Jean-Marie was wearing his handsome reddish-brown sailor's tunic, loosely cut and open at the chest. It was made of the same stuff as the sails of his boat and suited, far better than one might have expected, his light chestnut hair, pale blue eyes and countless freckles that no amount of sunburn could hide. He was no charmer, but at least he had changed since the days when he had plodded round in his shirt sleeves and unbuttoned waistcoat, armed with a feather duster, in a fourth class Paris hotel, and was only called Jean. A basket of fish on his head suited him better than a bucket in his hand, or the occasional chamber pot. A person's background contributes something too. Sea and sky are more flattering than dark, unaired staircases. He and Josephine had a robust, natural matter-of-factness about them which almost made them a handsome couple. He swept his blue cap off his head and said, '*Ann amser zo brao.*'

'*Zo brao ann amser.*' Alberta hoped they would let her pass.

Then she saw that she could not behave so strangely. She stopped and looked at the fish. 'Splendid, Jean-Marie. Kill it, Josephine. Don't let it lie there like that.'

Jean-Marie had not displayed the slightest astonishment at seeing Alberta turn up with a boy almost six years of age, nor at the information that the shortest of 'the gentlemen' was the father. He had explained at once that he for his part had married when he was home on leave during the war, and that he was quite satisfied with the result. Josephine lived up to his idea of a good wife in every respect, and he expressed no regrets for the lost fancy of his youth. 'The shortest one?' he had said. '*Bien*. One must have someone.'

Now he was looking at Alberta with some surprise as he praised the fish and emphasized their qualities. 'We caught mackerel too. But I said: The ladies are expecting their men. Then there's nothing like a good meal. Look at this.' He weighed a large plaice in his hand, turned the corpse-pale stomach upwards and slapped its tail reprovingly. 'Steamed, with a good *hollandaise,* or plenty of parsley in the butter. Here, Josephine.'

Josephine took it all into the kitchen. The harsh sound of a knife cutting into the live fish, the helpless slapping of cold, wet muscles reached them outside. Sivert came down at the same time, and the children turned their excited faces towards him and the parcel he was carrying. He put it down, struck his hand with his fist, lifted the boy so high in the air that he gasped from fun and fright, then did the same to Marthe, who screamed with delight. Then he shook Jean-Marie's hand jovially, told him to put on his cap, and embarked on a conversation about the fishing, the weather, the old days in Paris, and the war. There was no lack of topics, and Sivert was clearly not one to allow his conduct to be disturbed by an unpleasant exchange of words. He looked cheerful and elated, even trying to draw Alberta into the conversation. 'To change the subject, when is it high tide today? We had to walk almost a kilometre before lunch, Eliel and I, to have a swim.'

He turned secretive about the contents of the boy's parcel. 'What do you think is inside? Try to guess. No, you must open it yourself. Use your fingers.' Trembling, clumsy with excitement, the boy started untying the string.

Unlike Pierre, Jean-Marie did not mind talking about life in the trenches. He did so without bloodthirstiness, almost with conviviality. Once he had been buried in a crater by a grenade and was dragged out half dead; a couple of times he had been wounded. As far as one could see it had left him with no external or internal scars.

'The German soldiers?' Jean-Marie shrugged his shoulders. 'Poor devils like ourselves, Monsieur. They probably wanted to go home to their wives and their work just as we did. If only we could have talked to each other, come to an agreement to send the Kaiser and Poincaré out to fight instead; there would have been some point in that. We threw boxes of sardines across to them, and packets of cigarettes. If there happened to be fresh water nearby we arranged times for going and fetching it. When the officers weren't looking we signalled all kinds of messages to each other. Once they lighted small Christmas trees on their side of the wire. It was beautiful. We had fun too. You have to find something to do. One day we carried a top hat along our trench. They thought the President was visiting us and shot at the hat. That gave us a good laugh. Afterwards we lifted it up so that they could see the pole and the bullet holes. I expect they laughed too. Did we *shoot* at *them* later?' Jean-Marie shrugged his shoulders. 'What the devil were we to do, Monsieur? If there was an attack it was in earnest.'

But even Jean-Marie would not comment on the use of bayonets. 'Filthy,' he said curtly.

'Well, Alberta? Going out for a walk?' Sivert glanced at Alberta, who was still standing there for the sake of appearances. His eyes seemed never to have glittered more than at that moment.

'Yes,' said Alberta. She turned and went. Sivert's cold, threatening words suddenly seemed unimportant beside his carefree behaviour now. That too was unlike him. It was something new that he had brought with him, something more dangerous, more cunning than the obstinate manner in which he bore a grudge. For a second she thought: I must pull myself together and pretend; I mustn't let them stand here and see—

But she could not manage it. With her mind at a standstill she walked blindly down the path. She heard the boy say, 'Where's Mother going?' heard him rustling the stiff paper, and Sivert's reply, 'I expect she'll be back.'

When had she begun to be afraid of Sivert? Perhaps she had always been afraid, and simply forgotten about it in between? Now she was lying there, so afraid that her heart stood still for sudden, painful moments at a time. He was asleep at her side, breathing evenly and calmly. Over in the cot it had been quiet for a long time too, as if Tot was less restless when both of them were there. He had been scared out of his wits when Sivert had taken him into the water that afternoon, his strange little face distorted, not daring to make a sound. But afterwards he had danced his curious little war dance, and stood stiff with the convulsive effort to put a brave face on it while his father rubbed him energetically with the towel. For Sivert to look after him physically was also new. Previously he had contented himself with shaking his head at Alberta's decrees.

She raised herself on her elbow and looked out at the room. The pale glimmer, like moonlight, that fell in stripes through the shutters flickered and was gone, flickered and was gone, as the Penmarc'h lighthouse revolved its beam. It was some time since the rocking and creaking of the bed in the attic had ceased. Alberta had heard it and thought: How can she? How can she in this house, where you can hear every sound, if for no other reason. But I'm the only one who knows how much can be heard, for I'm the quietest of them all.

The last time Sivert was here she had curled herself up into a defensive ball, raised a wall of silence, told him lies, because of the echoing house and the boy in the same room. The child kept them apart; it was no longer possible to forget that he was there and might be lying awake. She would do the same thing now, if necessary. So far there were no signs that it would be.

Someone was snoring upstairs. It was Eliel. The only other sound was Alberta's hammering heart against the background of Sivert's breathing and that of the sea. The tide was coming in. It would be high water in the small hours.

She could still hear Josephine's well-meaning *'Bonne nuit messieurs, bonne nuit mesdames, au plaisir.'* The last plate had been dried and the last snail thrown out. Josephine had curtsied and pulled the door to behind her, as if shutting them solemnly in, three couples in all. The slightly disconcerted faces, Eliel's ready laughter that elicited no response and died away at once, the awkward evening that followed—Alberta wished she could erase it all from her memory.

When she had started to take Tot up to bed, Sivert had interfered: 'I'll do it.' It might have been attentiveness on his part, unexpected relief from her chores. She knew it was something else, something vague and undefined.

Later on—they had been in bed for a while, and Sivert had just put out the light after looking through his yellow books, cutting the pages here and there and yawning—she had managed to say: 'I spoke too harshly today, Sivert. I'm sorry. I didn't mean it.'

Reluctance to say this, mingled with panic, compulsion and fear, forced the words to her lips. She had meant what she said.

'Yes, you have a sharp tongue,' said Sivert lightly. His tone let it be clearly understood that her apology was of no importance. And he turned over on to his side. In a moment he was asleep.

Over on the window sill she could just glimpse the packet. It lay there, small, oblong and merciless. Neither she nor Sivert had referred to it. Tot had not referred to it either when she had said good night to him. An unopened packet was not one of the things a child could normally tolerate. He must have been told.

The stairs creaked. Cautious footsteps were coming down. They passed the door and continued downwards, stealthily, nimbly, pausing now and then. Alberta would not have heard them had she not been awake. It was Liesel, for Eliel was still snoring. She must be barefoot, she was so quiet.

There was the front door opening, now it was closed, for a moment there was no sound, then the footsteps crept across the gravel in front of the house and were silent again as they reached the path. And now Liesel had her sandals on. She had gone out. She was not going to a certain place.

Suddenly Alberta was struggling with her bathrobe in the darkness, trying to find the sleeves, groping under the bed for her own sandals, fumbling and clumsy in her fear of waking the others. A tremendous feeling of anxiety came over her, relief too. She was not all alone in the depths of the night; and now there was something for her to do. What could be better for a soul in need?

The moon, in its last quarter, hung low and crooked just above the horizon, like a badly slung, ill-treated light. The air was kind and soothing to the eyes. Evenly and without pause the huge sweep of the lighthouse beams swept the surface of the sea and the sloping land. In the illumination of one of them Liesel came into view and disappeared again. She was sitting on the grass hugging her knees, not very far away. Alberta's tension left her. It was replaced by fatigue. What had she feared?

At the next swing of the beam she saw that Liesel was swaying backwards and forwards. Her face was tilted upwards, her eyes closed, her lips pressed tightly together as if she were in pain. Alberta hesitated, halfway across to her.

'Is that you, Albertchen? Are you out too?'

Liesel's quiet voice was larded with something else, bitter, resigned scorn.

'I heard you go downstairs. I was awake. What's the matter, Liesel?'

'The matter? The matter? There you stand asking what's the matter, you, who cannot rest either.'

'There could be many reasons.'

'Could there be many reasons? No, you know very well there's only one reason, one single reason. Come along, let's walk, let's walk fast!' Liesel got to her feet and ran forward, her bath robe flapping behind her black in the darkness, tripped and almost fell.

'We can't see the path, Liesel. The lighthouse only makes it more confusing. I'll fetch something to sit on.'

'Sit!' exclaimed Liesel contemptuously. 'With the restlessness I have in my body! I could fly on the sea.'

But when Alberta came out of doors again with a couple of coats she had found hanging in the hall and the tablecloth from the sitting-room, Liesel agreed to sit down. 'Eliel's raincoat,' she ascertained, spreading it out on the ground. 'My old coat,' wrapping herself in the second garment. 'What have you got there? It feels like the tablecloth? Why didn't you take—?'

'I didn't want to take Jeanne's rug,' said Alberta brusquely. 'It's lying on the armchair, I know.'

Liesel helped her to wrap herself up in the tablecloth. They crept together on the coat and said nothing for a while. Of course Alberta knew what was the matter; she had known it all along.

She looked over at the house. There it stood, unreal, faintly luminous in the light of the crooked sickle that was the moon. The door looked severe and solemn. Inside the boy and Sivert, Jeanne and Pierre, Eliel, Marthe, were asleep. Who were they all? Did they really exist? Were they more alive than the doll Mimi who shut her eyes as soon as she was put down? It was as if she sat looking back at a past existence, a door closed for ever. Only at the thought of Tot did Alberta feel a faint emotion, as if she had been away for years: guilt, pity, longing, sadness, something indefinable. But each time the illumination from the lighthouse swept across the house it became threatening, intrusive, almost gloating: Don't delude yourself. I shall keep everything that is mine.

Liesel gave a big sigh of relief. 'I'm glad you came, Albertchen, it's a good thing somebody came.' The sentence had a familiar and painful ring, reminding Alberta of another difficult moment.

'I'm glad I heard you, Liesel. It was good for me to get out of doors too.'

'There, you see, we *must* get out at night now and again, and we're not the only ones! Albertchen!' Liesel gripped Alberta's arm. 'Now, at this moment, the world is full of women who can't rest, who are up and about while a man lies snoring. There are so many of us. In Paris I sometimes pace up and down the passage outside like a madwoman. Sometimes I think I *am* mad.'

'Now Liesel!'

'I *hate* men.' Liesel hid her face in her hands and coughed.

Alberta did not contradict her. Not at this moment of candour and at this time of day. Her view was neither strange nor incomprehensible; it was the kind of feeling that came and went.

'Is that how it is again? he says, when all I want is to put my arms round his neck. Is that how it is again?'

Alberta could not stop herself thinking: Then why on earth *put* your arms round Eliel's neck? More than once she had felt like asking why Liesel did not look for someone else. She was still young, good-looking, when she occasionally went to the trouble of smartening herself up, still pursued as soon as she appeared in public. Her relationship with Eliel was somewhat of a mystery. They had no child to bind them together. They both strained at the yoke, Liesel in words: 'He's not worth bothering about; he's a miserable egoist'; and Eliel, as far as one could judge, in deeds. All the same, there must have been something between them, old, strange feelings that neither of them would admit to possessing any longer. Eliel, for instance, could simply have gone home during the war. He had not done so.

But even in the dark and at a time beyond reality Alberta could not bring herself to ask. Did she herself know why she did and did not do things? Should Liesel know any better? Life was not simple and lucid, it was full of contradictions. Liesel accompanied Eliel like a cowed but still rebellious animal, suffering when he chased other women, kicking out when he condescended to show her affection, grumblingly, almost greedily accepting her daily bread from his hands. Where was the tender, self-forgetful Liesel who had said, '*Ach*, family life wouldn't suit him, Albertchen. Artists have to be bachelors, especially sculptors.' She and Eliel were not legally married. Yet all the compulsion and pressure, wrangling and animosity that it can bring with it were there just the same.

'I'm unjust too. It's my own fault that I'm not normal.' Liesel took her hands away from her face, and her voice was icily calm.

'Of course you're normal!'

'No, I'm not. I've been damaged.'

'What nonsense! You must forget all that. You—'

'Forget? Did you say *forget*? When I've been—put outside.' She spoke in the same cold voice, calmly and monotonously, even though she seemed to be spitting out her words. 'Unable to give or receive happiness, dead as a stone internally. They shattered me, they destroyed the nerves. Oh, Albertchen — all the ugly things boys say to you when you're growing up, the crudest things that we didn't even understand — the day comes when you do understand, and it's all true.'

As if on cue the beam from the lighthouse swept over Liesel's face. The grimace with which she spoke appeared like a weird still from a film and was gone again. 'It's not strange for a man to get tired of you and want someone else. We must be reasonable, mustn't we? But if only I had a child Eliel could do as he liked. Then I'd be all right again, I know I would. All that has gone wrong would be wiped out. Imagine that there should be a penalty for what I did! It's enough of a penalty in itself, but no one who really knows dare say so, for fear of being sent to prison.'

Alberta said nothing; a gasp escaped her, too slight to be heard. She remembered how she had sat with Liesel feeling that she had escaped some disfigurement, a blemish on her body; remembered that her aversion for doing the same thing had been mainly concern for her body, an instinctive fear of harming it, a terror of being maimed and defiled.

But how would Liesel manage, alone with a child? She ought to know what she was talking about, too; she who had been Alberta's help and refuge in all kinds of difficult situations, prepared to go to any lengths for Tot, though often at her wits' end to know what to do.

'Eliel's child, Liesel? Would you really want that? When you are not so very fond of him any more? A child is a tie. And there are other men. Are you so sure you—?'

There came the question. Of its own accord? It's time had come.

'I'm not sure of anything,' answered Liesel sharply. 'That's just the trouble. What can one be sure of in life? I refuse to —you know very well what I mean.

'Shamming!' The cold scorn in Liesel's voice defined the limit of the feasible. 'Shamming. If you do that you must feel affection, love, as they call it. I shammed for a long time. In the end I shouted at him, I became spiteful, foul-mouthed, hysterical, according to him. Besides, there is no-one else for someone like me. I'm the kind who will put up with anything from the one person it happened to be. We are *faithful*, Albertchen, on top of everything else. To be faithful when you are happy is easy enough, it comes naturally. We're the kind who are faithful in spite of everything, without knowing why, like a dog. Genuine fidelity, in other words. Wait and you'll see—' Liesel raised her hand to check Alberta, who had opened her mouth to protest. 'But at least I could have a child. Some people are still able to—'

And suddenly, without transition, Liesel sobbed: 'He might have been nearly seven years old. When I'm old and still childless perhaps, I shall be saying twenty-five, twenty-six. If I had another child I would believe he had come back to me.'

Alberta sat in confusion and distress, alternating between sympathy and a desire to contradict her. She could find nothing to say. 'He,' Liesel had said. So it had been a boy? Like Tot? This fact gave it a fearful clarity, bringing it close, terribly close. Fidelity, on the other hand—what had that to do with it?

'A little Eliel? That might not be much fun.' The words dropped out unexpectedly. Alberta listened to the jocular undertone in her voice with disquiet. This was no joking matter. It had clipped Liesel's wings, hindered her growth.

But getting her to laugh was a well-tried means of diverting her attention. Alberta turned to it instinctively from many years' habit. In spite of everything Liesel's laughter was not so far below the surface as one might often think. There it was already, bubbling beneath her sobs. 'It might not be much fun, but I'd lick him into shape, don't worry.'

Her face appeared in the light of the beam, in close-up, the corners of her mouth quivering between tears and a smile, the teardrops hanging from her eyelashes and her hair falling in disorder over her forehead. 'If only success didn't make them put on such airs, these men of ours. That's what happens. Just like boys. Sivert's already in full bloom, that's obvious. Yes, let's just laugh at them, Albertchen.'

'They ought to know we laugh at them, they take themselves so seriously,' she said shortly afterwards, with a wicked glee, a hidden rancour that Alberta recognised. Then Liesel dried her face and her voice was calm and resolute. 'Eliel would never stop me from doing what I thought right where a child was concerned. He could just try.'

'It's a matter of money, Liesel.' Alberta suddenly felt insignificant. Liesel was strong in her way, if only in her stiff-necked clinging to Eliel. More than once it had seemed like cowardice, like an incomprehensible lack of pride. With a tight expression round the beautiful mouth that was no longer as red as it used to be, but had acquired a tendency to look a little blue, she remained in the clammy air of his studio, whatever happened. It almost looked as though he gained amusement from seeing how much she would put up with. She seemed to put up with everything. Until suddenly one day she was again good enough for Eliel, who was a confoundedly good sculptor, but not much of a man. Alberta had seen many like him on Montparnasse as the years went by. 'Our men are unfaithful too,' Alphonsine had said once. 'I'm not saying they aren't. But not in such a primitive way as yours from the North. Forgive me for saying so. But then—' Alphonsine laughed—'Unfaithful? They are *merely* primitive. They don't go any further than that.'

'Money, yes indeed.' Liesel sounded tired and defeated. 'Money.' She sighed. Alberta at once felt the pressure of the trap she was caught in herself and had always dreaded; the struggle with things which were simply too much for her. She did not have them in her grasp, nor in her head. We know too little about how we ought to live, and we exist as haphazardly as savages, having children and unable to take it in. Once we have them we are bound in chains stronger than iron. Fidelity, said Liesel. Surely the word was too grand, even if one called it canine fidelity.

The crust of moon, now minute and wrapped in mist, was about to disappear behind the inky blue surface of the sea. Raw vapour rose as if extracted from the ground, making the stars indistinct. There was a change in the weather, a suspicion of damp in the air.

'I suppose we ought,' said Liesel. Slowly they walked up the slope. Suddenly Liesel's head was on Alberta's shoulder. It bored in between shoulder and throat, looking for a place there, like a child. 'Tenderness, Albertchen. Tenderness! That's what we need more than anything. It keeps us alive. Men's tenderness, children's tenderness. Work is all very well, it's as necessary as food and drink; I wish I had some proper work to do. But it's not *enough*. Don't tell me it's enough. We need so much tenderness, far more than the men. How else should we dare to commit ourselves to all that's so difficult? That's how nature has arranged things to get her own way. As long as we're given tenderness we can put up with anything. But that's what these fools will never understand.' Liesel rolled her head from side to side, butting with it.

'No, they don't understand,' Alberta said, feeling that she knew it all even better than Liesel.

'Fall in love with many of them?' Liesel raised her head and tossed back her heavy plait. 'We could do that too, if only it were not so depressing. But it is depressing. So we hang around and are good to come back to when the others are tired of them.'

She loves Eliel all the same, thought Alberta without surprise. In herself longing for Sivert, fellow-feeling and mother love lay side by side with fear and animosity. In love with many of them? Her thoughts went to Pierre, and then suddenly to Tot: perhaps he had kicked off the blanket?

They reached the door. Tacitly they took off their sandals. Of course Liesel dropped one of hers on the staircase; it fell down a couple of steps, making a disproportionate amount of noise in the sleeping house. But no-one was disturbed; everything was silent and continued to be so.

'I talk about nothing but myself, but it was good of you to come, Albertchen, good to talk,' Liesel whispered guiltily on the landing, smoothing the palms of her hands down her body, as if smoothing something away from her.

'Good night,' whispered Alberta.

'Good night.' Liesel did something she had done only twice before, in a moment of desperation in an attic, and when Tot had come into the world. She kissed Alberta.

Inside the bedroom there was warmth from the two sleepers, from their breathing; warmth and fresh air, thanks to the windows which were always kept open. In the flash through the mist from the lighthouse Alberta groped over to the boy's bed to feel whether he was properly covered, then groped to her own. A small remnant of warmth left under the blanket welcomed her and enclosed her. Sivert's breathing was as regular as clockwork.

A yearning for everything to be right and inevitable between them was insistent in her mind. Her disquiet had vanished. Liesel had talked of tenderness. Alberta would get the better of herself, open the box, thank Sivert, make good the wrong she had done as far as it was in her power. She lay watching the dawn erase the alternation of light and darkness, noticed that the lighthouse must have been extinguished.

But after she had been lying like this for a long time she suddenly raised herself on one elbow and said aloud: 'That's right, sleep, you great oaf.'

Of which Sivert remained totally oblivious.

*   *   *

Cold, driving rain shut them in for three days. As fine as smoke it filled the air, laying a damp film over everything, indoors and out. Tot's teeth chattered when he came up after his bathe; Sivert saw to it that he was not allowed to escape.

Alberta struggled with the primus and got warm milk into the boy as quickly as she could. 'Stuff and nonsense,' Sivert said, accepting a cup with alacrity, rubbing his hands together. 'Foul weather, but it's splendid I must say. Nothing like the sea.'

He had installed himself at the small upright table in the bedroom, and drew there, supporting his sketch book between it and his knees; he wrote letters there too. The present had been a fountain pen. 'I thought it might be useful for when you did your scribbling,' he had said when Alberta thanked him.

'Of course it will, Sivert, it's a lovely present.'

For the time being he borrowed it himself for his correspondence, while the boy played on the floor for hours with the aeroplane he had been given. That did not worry Sivert. He was wonderfully patient, and in this respect far better suited to looking after children than Alberta. Sivert always managed in some way or another; hindrances or disturbances did not exist for him, and he never had a moment's boredom.

Alberta was in the sitting-room with Jeanne, sewing. Even when they were silent for long periods at a time she seemed to be unable to think. Time merely passed. She had felt for a long time that Sivert's mere presence extinguished her true existence. Jeanne's presence did not improve matters.

Marthe was tramping up and down the stairs. She had built some kind of many-storeyed house out there with stones and shells left by the tide. Jeanne had forbidden it and told her to play in the sitting-room with Mimi, but Pierre had said, 'Let her do it. It amuses her. It doesn't make any difference to me, I assure you.'

A little further off the typewriter clattered in fits and starts with oppressive silences in between. If they lasted Jeanne's sewing would sink into her lap as usual, and she sat with wrinkled forehead, about to lay it aside. As if it suspected this, the typewriter would spring to life again. Among the other sounds Alberta could tell when Pierre tore out the paper and rustled a new sheet as he put it in.

'He has become so morbidly self-critical,' Jeanne worried. 'He has a mania for throwing away. Pages the others would have given years of their lives to have written go into the waste-paper basket, I know it. If only I could save some of it. But he's always too quick for me and burns it. If that smoking stove is used for nothing else . . .'

Then she relaxed again, and started talking about the things women usually discuss amongst themselves. Having Marthe had been a difficult business. When one was narrowly built——yes, Alberta was not so broad either, but it had been a question of Jeanne's life, hers and the child's. Thank God she had been at home with her parents, and had had her mother at her bedside day and night.

Unpleasant memories floated up in Alberta's mind. Incoherent and dissatisfying as dreams they lay in wait in her consciousness ready to surface at the slightest opportunity. There was something the matter with them.

The worst had been the cold. When everything that could be hung had been hung round the stove, a corner screened off where the warmth could pause for a little on its way out of the room, she had achieved a temperature of eleven degrees centigrade . . .

A little child lying asleep, radiating peace. But someone else lying awake . . .

Every time the child had fallen asleep, warm and satisfied, holding one of her fingers tightly in his tiny hand, she had felt a new, mysterious understanding of hidden matters. Time stood still, all demands were silenced.

But when he screamed endlessly, an injured, angry, protesting scream, Alberta felt united with all bad-tempered, bitter women who had had more than enough of it. Children and mothers have rights; it began to dawn on her to what extent they were ignored and neglected.

To Liesel, who came regularly to help her in whatever way she could, she said, 'I should have done as you did.' But deep down she did not mean it. When the child fell ill and Sivert had refused to go for the doctor, when she realised that he thought it would be just as well if the whole business were brought to an end, she had been provoked to malice. Foot by foot she had driven him out of the door with words as merciless as those she had used when he had wanted to return home. It was the first time she had attacked him; it had been an unfamiliar and terrifying experience. And the first time she had seen him as he used to be, someone she really disliked. This feeling came and went. He had fetched the doctor. The danger passed, the days began to go by, no one can stand living in perpetual enmity. Better times came. But nothing hidden is ever really forgotten.

'You had Tot in hospital, didn't you?' Jeanne's voice was kind and sympathetic. 'It's not supposed to be so bad, according to what they say.'

'No, it's not so bad,' said Alberta, and meant it. Her emotion when they laid the child beside her for the first time stirred again in her mind, a sympathy that on the instant had filled her eyes with tears. There existed nothing more helpless or more dependent on human good-will. She had never taken an interest in babies. Suddenly she was holding one in her arms, one that was hers, so tiny, so strange, yet so familiar, so inevitable.

Her first coherent reflection had been: Now I am truly vulnerable. Now I can be hurt as never before.

With it came distrust. No child was more open to injury, none more threatened in life and limb. From the first moment all the world's wickedness was lying in wait: insensitive hands that picked him up too roughly, footsteps and voices that might frighten him. As soon as the child was brought to her, dressed and ready, she saw that the correct concern was lacking. They treated his vacillating little head so recklessly; they did not always put a hand beneath to support it. Neither did anyone seem the slightest bit interested in what all the painful little grimaces might mean, as if it was sufficient for a child to be born, changed and fed. She promised herself that if only they escaped without accident things would be different. We, she thought, as if she had been thinking it for years.

Sivert came and went, sat by her bed, brought news from the world outside, and looked at the boy with an expression which Alberta considered critical and out of place. And she was left alone again with the new, alarming thought that she was the one who was shackled for life by this ostensibly light, yet indissoluble bond.

When she came home she soon realised that she and the child had really been well off where they were.

'Of course it's not the same as having one's mother there.'

'No, of course not.' Alberta was filled with wonderment. Mama? Mama in that contingency? Impossible, unthinkable. None of all this would have happened if Mama had been alive. Alberta would probably have stayed at home to this day like a second Otilie Meyer, only more ugly, less kind, stubborn in her spinsterhood. She did know as a rule what she did *not* want. She would never have fallen into the trap there; it had been too obvious, too grossly constructed. An oddity, ageing early, a 'discard' as Eliel put it? Slightly deranged?

Her affection for Sivert, latent and shackled as it was, suddenly flared up. Whether to Sivert or another, her surrender had been neither a miracle nor a horrifying experience. Something utterly complete had taken place, releasing new warmth, enabling nature to blossom. It had been a step further, away from bondage, towards full knowledge of life. They tell lies and talk nonsense about this as about so much else. One day one experiences it oneself and it assumes the right proportions. Alberta's distant memory of a night with another was wrapped in unreal mist. Life's tangible realities were gradually erasing it. It was Sivert with whom she had lived after all, Sivert by whom she had had a child.

'What are you thinking about?' said Jeanne. 'You look so pensive.'

'Oh, nothing,' answered Alberta, caught off her guard, because she really had been thinking for a moment. 'Nothing, Jeanne. And you?'

'Oh, me!' said Jeanne gloomily.

'If only it would stop raining.'

'If only it would.'

They fell silent. Tot's aeroplane was still whirring across the floor upstairs, Marthe tramping on the staircase, the typewriter clattering. The panes were running with wet.

Amongst the pictures shifting ceaselessly in our hearts, the film we watch at intervals, Alberta suddenly saw herself whirl round in confusion, holding an impossibly small glass in her hand. 'Faîtes pipi,' said a voice. 'Where, where?' she stammered helplessly. 'There!' came the impatient reply. 'Try, make haste.' She was pushed into a narrow room with white tiled walls, a high ceiling like a shaft, it was a shaft, it was the bottom of the world. A moment later she handed over the full beaker. One masters astonishing situations when forced, discovering oneself to be incredibly resourceful ...

She was sitting up to her neck in water in a bath tub, forsaken by God and man. They had closed the door and gone away, as if she were quite capable of looking after herself. Suppose they forgot her? Suppose the pain came back before she was safe in bed? With sinking heart she stared at the door.

There they were! She breathed again.

But it was only a hand which snatched her clothes from the chair on which they were lying, placed some kind of white linen robe there instead, and closed the door again. She called. Nobody answered. She was a prisoner, with no chance of flight.

What was happening was inevitable. Outside night lay over the city; the profound, late hours of the night, when cars are infrequent, lonely wanderers suspect. Far, far away, in another world, lived people she knew who were close to her: Liesel, Alphonsine, Sivert, Eliel — shades, left behind in an earlier life, incapable of helping her. Nor had they any suspicion of how bitterly forsaken she was in this machine composed of curt, white-clad persons and shining tiled walls, which had her in its clutches and would not release her again until she was transformed, one become two, or until —

She was not afraid, but uneasy, as if there were some danger of the air giving out . . .

What was that?

It was a typewriter that paused and stopped. Jeanne lowered her sewing, the machine did not stir. Alberta, always ready to feel anxiety over matters about which she could do nothing, sat an the edge of her chair, an old habit of hers, as if Pierre was about to get into trouble, and it was partly her fault. It suddenly seemed as though she and Jeanne had been the custodians of this typewriter for an eternity.

'The short story,' said Jeanne. 'It *must* go off today, the postman will be here in three quarters of an hour. And these famous articles about this, that and the other that he's begun to write. We shall never get back to the book, I don't suppose. He promised me—'

'Yes, but Jeanne—'

Jeanne did not answer. She put down her sewing, got up, went upstairs. Nothing could be done for Pierre. There were her heels tapping across the floor of his room.

Ill at ease, Alberta sewed large, unsightly stitches, so unsightly that she started without hesitation to unpick them, a rare event. If only the everlasting rain would stop. It forced them all so close together that it was suffocating. That was the scraping of a chair. And what was that? Oh, Tot's aeroplane. Wasn't the typewriter going to start up again? No—Pierre was coming down!

His footsteps came tumbling down the stairs together with rattling, rolling stones. Alberta heard Marthe exclaim, 'He's tramping on my drawing room! That's my dining-room! The bedroom's one big mess! *Maman*!'

Pierre stood in the doorway. His blank expression searched the room : 'Is my beret here?'

'Are you going out, Pierre?'

'Yes, Madame, with your permission or without it. You are sewing, Madame? An admirable pursuit given that you can master it to perfection.' Pierre wandered round her in search of the beret, paused by the fireplace, raised the pile of newspapers lying on the mantelshelf, rustled the pages, suddenly laughed his curt, sad laughter: 'Magnificent. Capital, Just listen: "Bettina has entered the Beehive. Dear Bees, I hope many of you will welcome her; she loves you. She belongs to the rose-red clan, loves dancing, pretty clothes, art and sports, loves laughing, singing and running—"'

Jeanne entered the room. Her face frozen, she went across to take the magazine from him, but Pierre lifted it up high so that she could not reach it, and relentlessly read on: '" Blue Butterfly, if you wish I can provide you with details concerning Rouard, the baritone, if you will send me your home address and a photograph." Ha ha, thank God the war spared Rouard, the baritone! As long as he's alive, there's hope.'

And Pierre seized the beret which had in fact been lying under the newspapers, threw it on his head and rushed out. They heard him snatch something from a peg in the hall, saw him heave his raincoat over his shoulders as he strode down the slope, turn into a shadow in the drizzle and disappear.

Jeanne sank down on to a chair and for a moment she looked so tired that for once Alberta felt she was the one to be sorry for. Marthe was there at once with her arm round her mother's neck and her 'Petit Maman.' Jeanne pushed her away: 'Go and play.'

'He's spoilt it all, my dining-room and my drawing-room too. My drawing-room was chic. Papa is wicked.'

'If that was all he spoilt!' Jeanne stared stiffly in front of her and repeated, 'wicked', as if the word had only just acquired meaning for her.

Then she pulled herself together. 'He's not wicked, he's ill. Build it up again, Marthe. You have all the stones still, you must remember how they went.'

'My dining-room,' whimpered Marthe, 'When I think of my dining-room.'

'Off you go,' said Jeanne angrily. 'I will not listen to one word more.' Marthe disappeared.

'I shall become wicked too, I suppose.' Jeanne sobbed a dry little sob, hastily dried a single tear. 'That's how I got him back. Like *that*! He used to be so considerate, so good. He always listened to what I said, asked my opinion on everything. Nothing could have been more foreign to him than spite and sarcasm. He was hard-working, he was—'

'But he still is, Jeanne.' Alberta could no longer refrain from attempting to plead Pierre's case. She wanted to say. You only make things worse, but stopped herself in time. 'But he is hard-working,' she repeated.

Then Jeanne looked her coldly in the eye and said. 'What do you know about it? Nothing. But where Pierre is concerned. You and Pierre!' Her voice was on the instant so barbed that Alberta involuntarily rose to her feet.

'Sit down. It's quite safe to sit down. I'm not the revolver type, I don't carry a dagger. If you think I'm so scared of you—'

'I think nothing.' Alberta listened to her low voice, ice-cold above a violent inner tumult. 'Nothing, Jeanne.'

But Jeanne brushed her hand across her face as if brushing away the remnants of intoxication, of an aberration. 'We shall all go mad soon. You must forgive me, Alberta, Everything plays on my nerves so. It's this rain too. I—I beg your pardon.'

'It's of no account, Jeanne, no account at all,' said Alberta, as Jeanne went quickly past her on her way out of the room.

She sat down again. Her heart hammered and thumped. She jerked the thimble off her finger and let it disappear into the muddle in her work-basket, as if to divest herself of something, to make herself lighter, more mobile. She felt herself ringed by evil, dangerous forces. If only she could do as Pierre had done! Put on her coat and go. Never come back. Drown herself rather than stay here a day longer.

There was a whirring across the floor above. Someone in a sou'wester tramped past the window. It was Jean-Marie with fish for dinner. In that case it was time for Tot's snack, for the honey that Alberta got inside him by trickery in his milk on these raw, damp days, without either him or Sivert noticing it. It took a great deal of honey to make it taste.

She went out to the primus with the feeling she had had on so many other occasions in life, a feeling of acting under compulsion, of being a pawn in a game that was being moved in accordance with certain rules, whether she wished it or no.

Jean-Marie, his wet oilskins glistening, was standing at the kitchen dresser, cleaning mackerel. With a deft movement of his hand he removed all the guts at once, rinsed the fish under the pump and put it in a dish that was standing ready. *'Voilà, voilà!* Now all you have to do is put them in the pan. Josephine said you had better boil them since the stove is smoking and she's not coming today. *Ien eo ann amser,* it's cold today,' he said, looking at Alberta to see if she understood, and laughing.

'Yes, it is cold. Thank you, Jean-Marie.'

His expression changed to one of wonderment. He looked at her a little more closely, bent over the fish again, wrapped the insides up in newspaper and prepared to leave with it. At the door he paused for a moment with his hand on the latch. Then out it came.

'I don't think he understands what he is about, this husband of yours. A contented wife doesn't look like that. If Josephine were to go about with a face like yours—*ma foi,* I'd say to myself, you are a blockhead, my friend.' And Jean-Marie went out of the door, shaking his head. Alberta was left speechless.

Eliel came down from the attic and threw himself into one of the basket chairs. 'Disgusting weather! If I'd known what it was going to be like I'd have stayed in Montparnasse. You come here to sun yourself and enjoy it and then it turns out like this. Liesel? She's in bed, says she has a slight fever. This damned weather again. I suppose. Apropos the weather— has Pierre gone out? Almost two hours ago? Quite right too, damn it. But what about Jeanne? And the little girl? It's so unusually quiet indoors. You can only hear the boy. Clever little girl, Marthe, I must say, swims like a good 'un. You've been too soft with the boy, Alberta, you must put a stop to it.'

'And you must see about marrying Liesel,' answered Alberta angrily, amazed at her own sally. 'Don't force her to force you.' But she was thinking: Why am I interfering? It must be the oppressive atmosphere that's making me so foolish. Now I suppose he'll ask what I mean by it.

But Eliel said, 'All right, and when are you and Sivert going to get married?' His voice was remarkably gentle. He sat looking at the floor.

'The boy will grow up—' said Alberta. The uneasiness she always felt when she thought about the future gripped her. She did not like looking ahead.

Eliel looked up. He was drawing in his cheeks as if amused at a child's naiveté. It was a habit of his, the one he had passed on to Liesel.

And Alberta suddenly felt even more uneasy. If there was only one way of putting a difficult situation to rights, and if this too had to be surmounted, and if the result did not prove to be tenable—what then?

Eliel got to his feet. 'Aren't we going to eat today?' he asked, looking at the clock. 'Isn't it time to—?'

As he spoke Jeanne's heels could be heard on the stairs. They tapped into the kitchen and were silenced by the earth floor out there. Tacitly Alberta followed her and began peeling potatoes, while Jeanne lighted the primus. Marthe too lent a hand; 'Yes, *Maman*. I will, *Maman*.' Nobody said a word beyond what was necessary for the preparation of the food. Alberta knew that for some reason Jeanne was greatly worried about Pierre.

They had held back dinner for a long time. Sivert and Eliel were getting ready to go out into the early, overcast twilight to search, when Pierre suddenly appeared in the doorway.

Alberta could not remember having seen him in such high spirits before. He was elated, loudly teasing Jeanne who, agitated by the long wait, hung round his neck without scruple, groping for him. She seemed to be feeling to see if he was in fact alive, but it was perhaps just to verify how wet he was. She laid her head against him over and over again, repeating that he was wet through.

'There, there, there,' Pierre said. 'I am alive, *voyons*, I shan't melt because of a little rain. Have you been waiting? I do beg your pardon.'

He held her close, patted her hair, hugged Marthe. It was clear that the hours of walking had done him good in every way. He and Jeanne disappeared upstairs, Jeanne eagerly insisting that he must change.

And, just like a man, Pierre ate as if he had not seen food for a long time, clearly relishing being back home again, calling for wine and getting it without any objections being raised. He, Eliel and Sivert discussed long walks that they would take, the three of them alone, 'without women and children', as soon as the weather permitted. In any case, a change would not be long in coming. Pierre could feel it in the air, see it in the movement of the clouds, had talked to a fisherman he happened to meet. Those people knew what they were talking about. In these parts bad weather lasted for three, six or nine days. This was a three-day bout. It would clear during the night.

Pierre was so exhilarated that he forgot his hand. He rubbed them both together several times.

'*Oui mon ami, oui mon ami,*' said Jeanne, amenable to anything, filling his glass herself, making no mention of his work. Eliel and Sivert exchanged whispered remarks now and again: 'He did that very well. That's the way to treat them. About time she learnt a lesson.'

Liesel sat drawing in her cheeks in Eliel's fashion. She did not say much.

That evening Alberta was on her way down to fetch a book. On the stairs she met Jeanne coming up. Jeanne was carrying a lighted candle and a jug of hot water; a suggestion of vapour betrayed that she had just been using the primus.

With her hair falling forward on to her shoulders in two plaits and in a charming nightdress of crepe de Chine and lace she looked more beautiful than ever. The candle flame was reflected in her black eyes as they looked calmly into Alberta's.

A young wife on her way to her husband, perfectly within her rights.

Only when she had gone did it strike Alberta that neither

of them had uttered a word this time either. They had only
looked at each other.

*　　*　　*

'This Freud, Liesel, do *you* understand him?'

Alberta was out of her depth. Names buzzed in the air.
There was Freud and there was Einstein. She noticed them in
the newspapers, noticed that books were being published about
them and by them, and that was all. Since Eliel's and Sivert's
arrival she had had an uncomfortable impression that Freud
was behind everything they said and did; he seemed to be
ubiquitous. He inspired fear, if only because Sivert and Eliel
had in some way managed to appropriate him as an authority
on their side. One evening they discussed him with Pierre.
Pierre said: 'He has discovered new territory. To go further
and treat this territory as if it were mapped, a region in which
we can travel without more ado—*parbleu*! It can be dangerous to establish mysteries. Besides, in this as in so much else,
it was the poets who understood about it first, and always have
since time immemorial. It was their field. If science comes
along now and steals it—very well!' Pierre seemed to be
saying: Let them steal it, and the trouble and risk as well.
Then we'd be rid of it.

Jeanne looked up anxiously, wrinkling her forehead. 'Is that
the man with the dreams? The man who only sees nastiness
in everything? Nobody has the right to dream any more. If
you think it's respectable to dream that a chimney is being
swept, you are mistaken. It's highly improper. Some of my
friends accept it all as if it were Holy Writ. It's terrible to run
into them nowadays. But it's the fashion. It was the same with
Bergson before the war. Pierre, you don't really mean that
writers will ever become superfluous?'

'They became superfluous a long time ago,' said Pierre
sullenly, and suddenly retreated into himself as only he knew
how.

Alberta said nothing. She was cautious in such matters, not
least in Sivert's presence.

579

'Freud? They dug him out of Dr Freytag's crate,' Liesel informed her. 'Do you remember when they dug out Nietzsche?'

Alberta remembered it very well. 'When you go to Woman do not forget your whip.' She and Liesel had heard the quotation to excess.

'I wish we were rid of the whole crate,' Liesel said. 'Those books aren't any good to Sivert and Eliel. They ought to have been handed over to the police, but Eliel refused.'

The books had been left with Eliel when the mobilisation order had come. Dr Freytag had just completed his qualifying examinations. His French citizenship was in order and he was to start practising in the autumn. 'Austrian, but French in heart and soul,' he used to say when he introduced himself. As a doctor he was sent straight into the field. Since then nothing had been heard or seen of him. One rumour on Montparnasse had it that he was discovered to be a German spy and shot, another that he had simply disappeared like so many others. The years went by. Eliel had begun to look on the crate as his own property long ago.

When Alberta had asked Sivert recently to tell her something about Freud, he had said, 'That's not so easy on the spur of the moment. He throws new light on the mind, completely new light. It's of great value, especially for an educator.'

Alberta had walked away. Sivert's tone of voice had said more plainly than words: It is enough for me to know about it. His reference to his task as an educator made her start, his nonchalance wounded her in an unaccustomed way; as if Sivert had demeaned himself without the slightest necessity for it.

She was sitting on the grass with her sewing. Sometimes she sewed with such violence that it seemed like flight. The stitches succeeded one another rapidly and awkwardly. Two ugly little trousers were ready, and she was mending the old ones. But once in Paris Sivert could stump up. She and the boy were going to have decent clothes, at least for the street. Surreptitiously she tried to catch a glimpse of what was in

Jeanne's workbasket. Alberta thought: *That* dress, *that* coat; not so bad, not too expensive either. Something in that style might suit me. She felt an insistent longing to be beautiful while she was still young, a longing to see Tot in nice clothes.

Jeanne had not cancelled her fashion magazine, although she had threatened to do so the day after the scene with Pierre. 'I'd better give it up, if it irritates him so much. But just now, when I have to make clothes for Marthe and myself for the autumn—no, it's out of the question. He is so changed. I shall have to stop leaving my things about on the mantelshelf.'

Jeanne did not sit quietly any more. She would suddenly rush into the house or over to the village, taking the children with her. She went by the road to avoid the bricklayer's house, and assured Alberta that it was nice to have Tot with them. Both she and Pierre were very amicable, perhaps even more amicable than before. It sometimes struck Alberta as incredible that she should have said things to him that one does not say to anybody, that it was he whom she had asked for advice, from whom she had sought support: this stranger with his efficient, beautiful wife, his model child, his blank expression.

Between him and Jeanne was the same knowledge of each other as between herself and Sivert, as between all couples; and the same intimacy when the occasion arose. Alberta bit off her thread and clenched her teeth, promising herself to be more reserved another time.

If she were left alone for a while, Liesel would come up from her painting in the cabbage field. No great alterations were made to it, only that sometimes Liesel had figures in the foreground, sometimes none. Alberta said, 'Don't you think you'd better start on something else, Liesel, instead of standing there among those disgusting caterpillars?'

'I've put a lot of work into it,' Liesel replied. 'It binds you. And it's the kind of thing that might sell. White clouds and the sea, a boat, simple and easy to understand. The clouds are the best; I shan't touch them. It very probably would be better to stop, but I can't. I'm not like that. I'm on the wrong tack with my painting in any case, Albertchen. Once I was just getting hold of something, and even got a picture into the Autumn Exhibition, do you remember? Then I lost the thread.' Liesel shrugged her sloping shoulders resignedly.

It was one of the days when she preferred simply to sit. Inert and pale, with dark rings under her eyes, she would settle next to Alberta and whisper: 'Not this time either, not this time either. If there's no change soon, I don't know what I'll do. I'll go away from it all, go on the streets—'

'Nonsense, Liesel. One doesn't go on the streets.'

'And not I,' said Liesel, with that ring of bitterness that so easily came into her voice. 'Especially not I, Albertchen. But I'm on the prostitute's side. Either they're unnecessary, and if so they're a disgrace to us all; or they are necessary, and in that case they should be given ordinary respect like other members of society.' Liesel spoke as if challenging the world. She jutted out her lower lip with a contemptuous, hard expression, that ill accorded with the rest of her personality.

Alberta glanced at her sideways. Liesel was getting more and more into the habit of making unexpected remarks at unexpected moments. 'You ought to rest today, Liesel. And what made you think about prostitutes?'

'I often think about prostitutes. I think about a lot of things. Life is unjust. One sees it more clearly every day.'

Unjust? The word immediately sent Alberta back to the time when Tot was small. The summers had passed, nauseating and heavy. However they struggled through them, the feeling that injustice was being done towards herself and the child increased. The winter had its claims. With the spring there came a fierce obsession, the desire to see the boy playing in sunshine in a meadow, to cease being perpetually anxious, perpetually nervous. It was a drag to go to the Luxembourg Gardens: dusty streets all the way there, dusty streets all the way home again. And what good did it do him? Sitting low down as he did in his little push-chair, close to all the dirt whirled upwards by people's feet, she might just as well have dragged him behind her along the cobbles. Usually they ended up under the trees on the Avenue du Maine, among other mothers with tired faces and small, pale-faced children. When she occasionally took the boy to a park, he was seized with a kind of dumb wildness, and could scarcely be kept away from the lawns. It had been just the same when they came here. He had lain full length on the grass, clawing on to the ground, refusing to get up again, giving Marthe the opportunity to exult spitefully, 'He hasn't seen grass before, he hasn't seen grass before.'

'If I didn't have to try to earn money, and if I were not so stupid and useless, and if the war had not come and made everything so difficult—I'd have liked to be the kind of person who tries to put it all right. You know, suffragettes and that kind of thing. It sounds dreadful, but . . .'

They were far from all that, Liesel and Alberta; their hands were full with their own small affairs. And Liesel spoke as if in apology. After all, one gave up being a woman in the accepted sense, attractive to men, charming, if one went in for something like that; one became as it were sexless. Merely to think about it was to break with so much.

Instead Liesel mounted her hobby-horse, the one she rode perpetually. 'Some of them want to abolish the penalty. I've read about it. I suppose they think that would be the end of the matter. But it would only be one more convenience for the men and a penalty for us in any case, since it's penalty enough in itself. They can't ever have been through anything themselves; I suppose they're old maids. I'm sure they mean well, but—

'They can't have had children, at any rate,' Liesel said, jutting out her lower lip. She turned a pale, freckled face with large eyes towards Alberta, a fanatical face. 'Can you understand how it is that now, when masses of people have been shot and they're crying out for children everywhere, they don't *help* women with this problem and look after the children if necessary? Can you understand it?'

'No, Liesel.'

'The world is so awry, it will never be put right again. I agree with Madame Poulain, why start the whole business if it's to be burdened with so many drawbacks? It shouldn't be allowed. It's nothing to laugh about, Albertchen. But why are you sitting here? Take yourself off, now, while Jeanne and the children are away; go down among the rocks and stay there till dinner-time. What was it Pierre said the other day— that one has duties towards one's characters? I must say that if I were a writer . . .'

You're as good a writer as any of us, thought Alberta. You once rewrote Eliel until he was unrecognisable, at any rate. She said: 'I'm not a writer. But you're almost a painter; all you've got to do is pull yourself together. Rest today and find a new motif.'

'I'm nothing,' said Liesel wearily.

The fine weather had returned. Heavy with calm the sea lay in the sun, milk-white, with small rocking blue shadows here and there and a thick blue streak for horizon. A slight mistiness in the air gave warning that the summer was coming to an end.

The men were carrying out their plans for long walks. They walked to the Pointe du Raz, to Penmarc'h and Douarnenez, coming home at sunset, stuffing themselves with food while they recounted their adventures, promising generously to go into Audierne the next day for more provisions.

Alberta could not help feeling let down and badly treated on these occasions. They might have taken me, she thought; I've been able to keep up since childhood, and I'm not the sort who never stops talking. As if she were the only one to suffer! How Jeanne's anxieties had increased, for instance. 'It's all right, I'm sure it does him good,' she sighed. 'But it would have been even better for him to have finished his work. It doesn't matter to the rest of you. But the book, the book, when I think of the book! If it were ready, he could do what he liked,' she added, frowning.

But Alberta admitted to herself: I miss Pierre. He takes no notice of me any more, and yet it's empty and aching without him. He's the one who makes life worth living here.

Their trips down to the beach were not the same as before either. Jeanne's considerate activity was more irritating than ever. And Tot, who could go stiff with fear when Sivert was looking after him and made no discernible progress where daring was concerned, was perverse and obstinate with Alberta.

'Everything has become so horrid, Liesel.'

Liesel admitted that it could be more pleasant. It was a pity about Jeanne, but she had the worst of it. She probably regretted it in her fashion, she was more friendly these days.

'Yes. That only makes it worse.'

'She's not happy,' Liesel said, 'the way she takes things.'

'She doesn't have to be unhappy because of me.' Alberta noticed the slight hesitation in her voice. 'He's so incredibly kind and patient most of the time. If he were not fond of her— He doesn't even look at me.' She stopped. Now she had certainly revealed something, to Liesel and to herself. She sewed feverishly.

'He daren't look at you,' stated Liesel calmly. 'Not any longer. And is he fond of her? She may have cause, even if he is fond of her. Besides, is that a necessary reason? She's the one who plagues him, that's sufficient. Since the day we went to Quimper she hasn't been able to hide it. It broke out then. I can't understand why you didn't notice it long ago.'

'I did and I didn't. What was I to notice? We did nothing wrong, we never have, never exchanged a word that—'

'That's not necessary either. I noticed it a long time ago, I noticed it on the train journey.'

'Now you're exaggerating, Liesel.'

Alberta blew hot and cold. Liesel alternately fanned her unrest and choked it. A not entirely foreign idea played in her mind: He has a child, I have a child. So it's impossible, even if—even if— She killed it in the usual way: Fond of Jeanne. Deep down very fond of Jeanne. If it came to the point, if something were to happen, the end of the world for instance, he would choose to be with her and Marthe at the last, as I would want to be with Tot and Sivert. In love with Pierre in *that* way? Love another woman's husband like *that*? Of course not. It's just that I've made a mistake with Sivert. Why can't you be different, Sivert? So that I could find peace with you? So that I wouldn't have to stop myself from almost searching for somewhere else to go? My own fault, that everything is not as it should be? Yes—but not mine alone. Ours. And nobody's.

Her thoughts centred on Sivert, on all that was new about him, on his passivity, night and day. She had lied to him the last time he came. She would do the same again, put on an act perhaps, stop bathing. Some things were unthinkable, as matters now stood. But the inmost possibility of everything coming right between them lay in their embraces at night.

If Sivert made no approach he must have a reason for it, a new reason. Supposing someone else stood between them already, what then? Then there would be herself and Tot. Would she be in despair? No—as long as it would be possible to put the rest of her life in order. They would have to marry for the boy's sake, and then divorce again. The idea made her feel a little giddy. But that Sivert should have another, that he was not alone? Good, so far as she could see, good.

Suddenly she dropped her sewing. In astonishment she followed her line of reasoning. Her life, which had been a narrow little patch, broadened out. She saw that it was spacious beyond the enclosure, so frighteningly spacious that it took her breath away. But it was open and free on all sides for those who had courage and vigour, something to journey with. Everything was possible, as long as one dared and was strong.

'What are you thinking about now?' asked Liesel.

'I don't know. There's so much to think about nowadays. I'm becoming nervy, I scarcely get any sleep.'

'Go and *write*. That's what you ought to do. Write badly, if you have to, but earn some money.'

'What do you think is the matter with Sivert, Liesel? There's something.'

'He *has* earned money. It always goes to their heads.'

'There's something else too.'

'Something or other always comes with it,' said Liesel wisely. 'If I were you, I'd put my energies into turning my writing to account. Every line you've put together has been printed. But as long as you go on producing short pieces and paying Sivert's paint bills with the fees—'

'That's not true, Liesel.'

'No, I know you've bought shoes for Tot and paid for shoe repairs and the instalments at the grocer's, and that there was no other money in the house, and that you had to.'

'I had to. You would have done the same in my place. It's only fair for both parties to—'

'If I were in your place and had a child, I wouldn't sit sewing. I'd earn money and leave it to others to sew. Oh, Albertchen, if I were you—with a little boy who needed me.' Liesel tilted her head backwards and shut her eyes as if to look into a dream world in peace. 'You are foolish, foolish, even more foolish than I.'

Alberta hung her head. Now they had come to a point which she could not quite explain to herself. Someone who has not even contributed one complete, undivided feeling to the household has incurred great liabilities, very great ones. Sivert had picked her up when she had gone under.

'I'm afraid,' she burst out. 'That's why I sit here pretending.'

'Afraid of what?'

And now Alberta failed to understand how her reply could cross her lips. 'I'm afraid of Sivert.'

Liesel did not answer immediately. After a while she said: 'One more reason.'

One of the young wives from the farms came by with her little child. It had just started to walk and was at the stage when it refused to do anything else. If she took it up on her arm it kicked to be put down again. Foot by foot they plodded along. Her bent back looked so patient, as if it had grown this way once and for all. It was the third child she had taught to walk, her fourth year of marriage. She looked up and smiled, not wearily but humbly. It struck Alberta how stooping most women's work was. Man stretches: he rows, or reaches out for stones or planks. He is often bent beneath burdens, but woman bends over almost all her tasks, except when she hangs up washing. Perhaps that is why she likes doing it; then she too stretches, giving pleasure to her body. She spends years bent over small children . . .

'Listen, Liesel, I think I'll go down for a while all the same. With my papers.'

'At last a little common sense,' said Liesel. 'But get away before Jeanne comes back, or it'll come to nothing.'

With her folder under her arm Alberta walked quickly downhill in the direction of the cliffs. Like a mountain landscape on a scale for children they broke into the white stretch of beach a little to the north of Tinti-Anna's house. Panic seized her, an irritating eagerness to begin. Writing was something for people who could do nothing else. Some of them earned a living by writing, not just the genuine writers, others too. They produced nothing of importance, but they lived by it, it seemed. The thought that she might be left alone with the boy was far from new; before he came into the world it had lain in wait and had since reappeared at intervals like an attack of pain, a cramp in the region of her heart.

Towards the end of her term she had thought she would try seriously. An unexpected calm had come over her when she moved in with Sivert. She had sent strange letters home, fabricating their contents in order to divert the attention of the world from what was happening. She had taken devious routes more than ever before; the autumn had come and with it people from whom she had every reason to hide. She had been calm all the same. With Sivert they had a roof over their heads, the child and she. That was the most important thing, although the roof was not very satisfactory and needed replacing as soon as possible. She had intended to earn her living and help to provide for their needs. The worst would be over when the baby was born. In her imagination she saw herself writing successfully. Nothing was lacking. And Sivert *could* leave her. Such things did happen.

He had probably thought along the same lines. He had said once: 'The two of you have my pictures, you know.' Alberta replied: 'Don't talk like that, Sivert.' But before an artist's work turns into money and clothes and food he may have been in his grave for a century or more. It was impossible to forget this.

The worst had been far from over. It had not merely been a matter of learning about the needs of the infant's body, recognising and feeling them as if they were her own. It had been a matter of satisfying them in the face of the impossible, of struggling to do so night and day. Bad times came, so bad that her mind shrank from remembering them; it flinched as the boy had done when they bathed him in front of the stove. His tiny shoulders had contracted with cold, his mouth became square with pathetic, helpless crying, his eyes older, experienced, upbraiding. Alberta caught herself wishing foolishly that she could fluff out her feathers like a hen, that she resembled an animal: furry and warm, they never failed their young. Every woman, including Alberta, had the right to memories other than these.

Sivert had been unable to get anything painted and gradually became thoroughly tired of the whole business; it was unavoidable. His mouth tense, more reticent as the days went by, he helped with the shopping, the meals, even the washing, doing it efficiently, as he did everything. But he had no rest at night, and the line full of napkins intruded into the motif wherever they hung it. 'I thought I was a painter,' he muttered one day, 'not a washerwoman or a maid.'

Alberta herself was more wretched than she could have imagined anyone could feel. When they finally fetched a doctor to the boy she had her own bill of health written up at the same time. She was anaemic and her milk was too thin. She had to eat such and such, rest, avoid this and that, try to go away with the child for a change of air.

'Yes,' she said, looking into the wise eyes of the elderly man, knowing that they saw through her and everything in the studio, knowing that the days would pass just as before. Shortly afterwards war broke out. Everything they ought to have had disappeared little by little: butter, sugar, money, coal.

The second winter—no, she would not think about it. She

had sometimes said when she prattled to the boy: 'Tough, that's what we are.'

She came down among the cliffs, found a place where there was a natural bench in the warm granite wall, seated herself comfortably, turned the pages of her manuscript. Duties towards imagined characters? In that case they ought to be different from the ones with whom she had involved herself, a capricious, easily offended company, who never said or did anything when she sought them out, but attacked her at night, beside the primus, at the child's bedside, and were gone again before she had time to turn round; who tried to arrest her attention when the living, who had every right, had already done so, and who expressed themselves vaguely, in banal phrases and without profundity.

Concentrate on her material? Alberta's material was fluctuating and billowing: a cloud formation illuminated now from this side, now from that, and which then disintegrated and disappeared; a mirage, that vanished and was all of a sudden there again; a whirling nebula containing glimpses of voices, accents, faces, gestures, landscapes, streets, interiors, all of it appallingly like everyday life. If a thread lay hidden in it somewhere, it was well hidden.

Ten lines that open up for the rest, Pierre had said. Alberta's misfortune was that almost any line could do that. She could approach her theme from one direction, or from another, or from yet a third. Then she had countless lines, paper piling up, full of words: ill-behaved words that would not sound right together, would not be subservient, but had a frightful tendency to appear over and over again in proximity, to steal from each other. Words like 'suddenly', for instance, the most intrusive of them all. They resembled precious stones in that they were independent of their setting.

Sivert had colours and broad brushes, he could work backwards and forwards over the canvas, hinting here, emphasizing there. Without getting in his own way he could create a lucid frame within which to work. Alberta lost one glimpse for each that she was given, grasping at dots instead of outlines. Out of two hours' day-dreaming perhaps one or two sentences would be released. Haphazard external impressions interfered, confused her, broke off the thread. She wished she were deaf and blind, wished she lay ill in bed, shut off from the outside world so that she could concentrate. The result was that she fled from it all.

Except in the strange, rare moments, when it seemed to her that this imperfect thing with which she had no patience—there *was* something to it after all. It was not yet in print. It was still possible to handle it, to approach it more closely, encircle another piece of fog.

Alberta stopped turning the pages. What business had she here? She was playing truant from the things she was capable of doing, although with difficulty and badly, for something uncertain and elusive. She sat twisting her fountain pen and looking at the sea. The tide was coming in. With long, lazy tongues the water licked at the land, creeping up behind and beneath the seaweed that grew round the smooth, slanting rocks, lifting it, rocking it, letting it float and dip, releasing it again, seizing it more greedily the next time. A wisp of cloud sailed across the sun; the enormous surface of milk and silk was changed at once into molten metal; the sand to the south and north dazzled the eye excruciatingly, as if the light were thrown down on to it by a shade; the screaming of the gulls took on a deeper tone. The wisp sailed on, the world lay there again, dissolved in heat haze, the sun was burning hot. A day for idling, for wandering; for living relaxed, without thought, without worry; a day from which to return renewed.

Alberta leaned back against the granite wall and closed her eyes; she kicked off her sandals and let the folder slide off her lap. She heard a thud and a suspicious rustle of paper. Out of pure cussedness she did not look down, but continued to sit stretching her toes in the light, burning layer of sand that the wind took with it everywhere as soon as it blew. She thought: If a puff of wind comes and takes something with it out to sea, there's no harm done. A moment of dejection, the kind that drains away all one's strength, had come over her. Shortly she felt burning tears trickle from under her closed lids, down her cheeks and into the low neckline of her dress.

She gave way to them and found relief. She looked up for a second, but nobody was there, she could weep freely. She gave way completely and sobbed without so much as drying a tear. I must stop going out alone, she thought. I shall have to stay near the house minding my own business. Soon it will be time to bathe. I must go home, look after Tot, it's my duty. Liesel can do it instead of me, and she does it better, but she shouldn't waste her time. I shall let myself drift on just the same in the current I have thrown myself into. The only person who can clear up the mess I have made of my life is myself, and I haven't the strength, the resources, the courage.

She could hear the sound of the sea more clearly when she shut her eyes. It was good to sit still, to listen to it, giving rein to her tears and her misery. Many years ago she had sat like this, listening to the teeming sound of the sea as the tide came in, while her tears flowed and a great, soothing emptiness melted away the rebellion in her. Her longing for life, her disappointment in it, the sea was suited to both. She had ended up composing poetry that time. Poetry!

If only it were really good for Tot to be here, she would stay willingly. They could live together in this white-washed house, she and he; perhaps she might even pull herself together and write—Alberta's train of thought did an about turn and she guided it elsewhere. Her longings would have plenty of time at their disposal, all kinds of longings. Once impossible, always impossible.

She remembered first hearing the sea on the journey out. They had changed trains for the second time, and suddenly found themselves out in the open. It seemed to Alberta that she had not been out in the open like this since she lived at home, in the north. The station had not been roofed in. There were a few tiny coaches, and a locomotive of amazingly simple construction which stood spewing out black smoke against the wide sky.

Dragging suitcases and travelling clothes, dulled after sitting up all night, she dazedly picked her way amongst sleepers and rails, gaining a confused impression of her surroundings, which were new and yet profoundly familiar. Sivert was carrying the luggage too. Liesel was looking after the boy. He hung back and stumbled over the rails, overtired and cross. Liesel helped him up patiently, laden herself with her easel and bag of paint brushes. Eliel was not properly awake yet; he flew into a rage over a dog, which for unfathomable reasons decided to bark at him and him alone. 'Devil of a cur. I'll damn well give you something to remember.' Eliel kicked out at the animal into thin air; the dog was already far away. He stumbled over one of the rails too, which made him even angrier. Jeanne walked, correct and beautiful, beside Pierre, who was also struggling with his burdens. She had Marthe by the hand.

It was then that something reached Alberta. It filled the air, it was everywhere, lying behind and about all other sounds. She could not quite make out what it was.

The little train smelt of stale tobacco and bowled along with them as if running along the ground. She sat, so tired that she was quite bewildered. But once when the train stood still the air was filled with a roaring, an enormous, monotonous song on two notes. It rose and fell, came and went like a breath from somewhere in space, taking her back years in time. Involuntarily she got to her feet.

'It's not the first time you've heard the sea, surely?' said Pierre.

'The first time for many years.'

From now on she listened at every station. The roar increased in dimension, closed round her, limitless and secure, an embrace. It was then that the expectation, the faith that here beneath the enormous dome of the sky almost everything would come right had stirred in her strongly; in spite of Jeanne, in spite of the fact that Pierre was different. And here we are, all of us miserable, sobbed Alberta to herself.

Pierre, for instance.

'He's ill,' said Sivert one evening after a walk to Penmarc'h with Pierre and Eliel, when they had evidently talked together intimately. 'No doubt about it. He says he's no longer interested in his characters. That's not the talk of a healthy person. He says there are days when he feels dead. Nothing stirs in his brain. But he has a wife and a child, he's up to his ears in debt. He wishes he had never come back. Besides, he knows very well that he's not as he should be. He says he can see it in his handwriting.

'No, he's finished. If he were not, it would surely be just as natural for him to write as it is for me to paint. He has come to the point where nothing can be expressed any more, nothing can be said. He stands outside himself, he says, watching himself, unable to take himself seriously any more. So you see, Alberta . . .'

Sivert's report, thought Alberta. But he interprets things too literally. In part that's what must make him dangerous . . .

'He's too old for competition, he says. Old? He's still in his thirties, thirty-seven or eight. If you start feeling like that at his time of life there must be something wrong.'

Sivert walked about, undressing and making his comments. He had come to the conclusion that on many matters Jeanne had plenty of excuse. To be sure she was a family nuisance and an infliction, but it was not easy for her. If Sivert was not entirely mistaken, it was she who had arranged all the advance payments—

'Alberta! Has it come to that?'

Alberta started as if stung. It was Pierre, in the flesh, blocking out the sun. She had difficulty distinguishing his face, from the way he was standing and blinded as she was by her tears. Yet she knew it was the real Pierre standing there looking at her right through that strange mask of his. He had slung his jacket across one shoulder, his hands were in his trouser pockets. He made a movement as if to withdraw them, but drove them down again.

'Oh, it's you?' she said stupidly. He was in fact standing there. As an initial measure she laid the palms of her hands against her swollen, blotched face, looked at him again through her fingers, and then with bent head began to put her disarranged person to rights, pulling her dress straight, grubbing for her sandals and putting them on. As best she could she dried her eyes, wiped her nose, smoothed her hair. It was one thing for him to appear, another the moment he had chosen.

Pierre was busy picking up sheets of paper and putting them in a pile. He displayed great precision, studying the page numbers carefully, finding his way with their help. They had been struck out frequently and new numbers put in their place. Alberta felt exposed, body and soul. Everything embarrassed her, from her ugly handwriting, countless crossings out and dreadful scribbled numbers to her own condition. If only she were not looking like this. She was no backfish any longer, and crying did not become her. Jeanne, on the other hand—. It was a good thing Pierre was incapable of understanding her scribble.

When Jeanne cried there was something pearling about it; as crying it was perfect. Round and bright the tears rolled down her cheeks and hung in her long eyelashes, without spilling over into a devastating flood.

Pierre stood holding the pile of papers under his right arm, took out a handkerchief and dried his forehead with his left hand, stuffed the handkerchief down again and swept his beret off his head. 'Supposing a gust of wind had come along instead of me.'

'It wouldn't have mattered, Pierre.'

'All right. Not today. I can see that. But perhaps tomorrow.' He put the papers into the folder and tied the ribbon. '*Voilà*. Saved for posterity for the time being. But I might not come along another time. Is there any room for me?'

Alberta had put herself more or less to rights; she sat dabbing at her wretched face. She smiled her thanks, knowing that it was a foolish smile.

'Here—' Pierre took out cigarettes, put one in her mouth and lit them both. 'It always helps a little. Well—here we are, Alberta.'

'Here we are.' Alberta had to laugh at her own foolishness. 'I thought you were at La Pointe.'

But Pierre explained that they had not walked more than half-way there. Eliel had had a blister for the last couple of days, and now it had worsened, so that he had been forced to go to the chemist at Audierne and have it dressed. Afterwards he and Sivert had sat eating pancakes at Mère Catherine's, although their lunch packets had been more than sufficient and the tour had not materialized. They would probably arrive soon, though Eliel's foot was bad. Pierre had walked back along the beach. It was longer, but cooler.

'And there you have a tidy manuscript.' He nodded in the direction of the folder, which was lying on a small shelf in the cliff looking ridiculous. 'I wish I had as much.'

'Don't laugh at me. I don't suppose there's anything there that can be used.'

'It's raw material, at any rate. And if you've got the raw material out of you—' Pierre shrugged his shoulders. 'Just squeeze out what you know, even though it may come out untidily and sound false. You always know something, and one thing leads to another. Afterwards you can put it in order, over and over again as if each day were the last and the accountant was to come tomorrow. What are you doing when it comes down to it but juggling with your experiences, building with them, but differently from life? Remember, you can do this only so long as you can take yourself and your life seriously. If you can't do that any more—I expect I've said this before, but you're the kind of person one has to din things into. I don't suppose it's really any use talking to you at all. But I'm glad I ran into you today.'

'Are you?'

'I was rude to you the other day, rude and churlish. Not to you alone; I've apologised to others as well. I behaved badly. But—send a man to hell and then demand of him that he shall sit pottering with the same things as before—' The words burst out of him, he threw his cigarette butt into the sea. 'To come home having saved your skin isn't everything. And the Lord preserve us, I'm told I'm ill, I'm given medicine, I must learn to pull myself together. Damn me if I'm not just as healthy as anyone else. I'm healthier, because I'm no longer blind. I can see so clearly that it makes my eyes smart. Shall we go, Alberta?'

'I suppose we must.'

'I mean go away from it all. You would have nothing against it either. But you daren't. You'll never get away.'

Alberta glanced at him sideways. There he sat, fortuitously inclining towards her again. But he was talking about himself, and that was new. And his concluding words lacerated her to such an extent that she wondered for a moment whether he had said them in order to observe their effect, to study her. He had leaned his head against the cliff and shut his eyes, but that proved nothing, he had ears. She forgot about it just as quickly as it had occurred to her. His face was almost as it must have been before it was cut to pieces and distorted: a calm, strong face, a good one too. A person who could afford goodness, who did not need to look fierce in order to look manly. Boundless fatigue had, like death, wiped out all superficialities and brought out the essentials.

'You think I'm mad.' Pierre opened his eyes, looked at her, smiled crookedly; his expression was blank. 'Now you think I'm mad. But many madmen have been more right than the righteous.'

'I think you're unhappy.'

'Listen, get rid of this mountain of paper before it suffocates you. You must steal a march on yourself. So that you don't find yourself one day standing like a cow in its stall expected to furnish a certain quantity of—literature.'

The word had a bitter ring in Pierre's mouth. 'Literature. They think it has something to do with a mission, don't they? If you're fortunate you'll go down to your grave on that assumption, without having noticed that people grasp nothing beyond what they themselves have experienced. If it was any use telling them anything in print the world would be a different place. They have been told quite often. All the same—if only I were given a little breathing space to take a look at myself and my ideas, I suppose I'd try sending them a few more packets of truth. When you've been out there, it doesn't look quite the same as before. *Enfin*—let me tell you one thing, if you're going to enter the miserable business, then keep at it so that the devil himself can't catch up with you. So that you can defray the expenses of a few years in hell, if the worst happens, without straightaway falling into another one.'

'Pierre—'

But Pierre changed his tone. 'Jeanne was splendid. She always has been splendid. Without her—! Simply coming home to a wife and child for us out there was — — that somebody should be sitting waiting for you, without letting you down! If anyone is worth sacrifice—'

Not to have let you down was the least she could do, thought Alberta, horrified. She remembered the crowds of soldiers leaving the railway station. *Les poilus,* overgrown with hair and dirt, caged birds and other strange objects hanging about them, cats and puppies on their arms, animals that had sought refuge in the trenches and attached themselves to the men who were now bringing them to safety. She remembered their eyes: disorientated, full of wonder, eyes such as one might imagine the dead to have, if they really do wake up again in the beyond, or men coming up from a mine.

Pierre had not been like that, she knew. He was not the kind to permit his misery to come to the surface; he had not been an ordinary infantryman either. He would most certainly have made himself presentable so far as he could, and adopted his mask.

She remembered the severely wounded on stretchers. All traffic along the pavement in front of the station had been stopped. White bandages from head to foot, deathly pale faces, bloodless membranes for eyelids. These men had been strong and healthy, among the strongest, the healthiest.

Not to have let you down was the least she could do, she thought again.

But Pierre went on talking about it. 'She wanted to make use of her small dowry all the time. I tell you, Jeanne—'

He picked up a handful of pebbles and began throwing them into the water as if aiming at the invisible cigarette stub. 'But when a man is at war and may be killed at any moment—! She has her parents, it's true. They're good people, and we borrowed from them. But you can't go on like that for years. I wrote to the publisher, I promised anything, a continuation of the best-seller, even a war book. A war book! I! He took the risk. Now I'm trapped, a more or less honourable man.' Quite a large stone flew far out, incredibly far considering that it was thrown with the left hand.

'Supposing you wrote something else?' said Alberta cautiously.

'The book *sold*,' Pierre said. 'People want to hear more about the characters. If there's anything I really hate—. Besides, they're dead. Fictitious persons can die too. Jeanne said once, 'Surely you can let the war come and change them?' Clever of Jeanne, wasn't it? But when they're already dead? When I can neither see nor hear them any more?'

'You'll soon come through it. You work so much, after all.'

'It may look like it.' Pierre suddenly spoke in the tone of voice that meant he wanted to shut himself in. Alberta took care not to look at him. She sat watching the rocking seaweed. The sea released it no longer, but kept it perpetually on the move. In a little while it would have disappeared. In a little while they would have to go home.

'It didn't work out here quite as we had expected, eh, Alberta?'

'Nothing ever does, surely?'

'There's something in that. I work? One flimsy short story after the other, soup on sausage sticks. There are days when I can't see clearly, can't react properly; but away it must go, it's been promised, the postman will be here any minute. It's not work, it's prostitution, one might as well be a whore in a brothel. Here you are, go upstairs with this one and that one. It's humiliating, you haven't the time to make even the smallest claim on yourself. Sometimes at night—'

'At night?'

'I get up occasionally, and scribble in a notebook. It relieves me for a while—I've laid an egg. I don't know yet what it will lead to. Not to where the creditors imagine, I can predict that much. I manage to get off one or two brief articles of the kind Jeanne dislikes. She's afraid of—poor Jeanne. Every day I say to myself, you have *her*, your child, food on the table, what do you lack? Write and be glad you're alive, that you have arms and legs, that you're not a helpless cripple—are you crying again? Now listen, Alberta—'

'I cry so easily. It's only my nerves.'

'You have good reason,' said Pierre curtly. 'It's just that I'm not used to seeing you, and—I don't like it. And here I sit complaining when I ought to be trying to help you. That's what happens when one makes one's apologies. Now listen, *ma petite Alberte*—'

'If you say *ma petite Alberte* you'll make it ten times worse.' Alberta hastily withdrew the hand Pierre had taken. She forced a laugh through her tears, though by this time she was really crying, and it was smothered by her sodden handkerchief.

Then Pierre's hand was on her shoulder, shaking and patting it encouragingly, at once reminding her overwhelmingly of Jacob. Now it was round the other shoulder, drawing her slightly—

'Mother!' said somebody above their heads.

The next moment Tot was holding her tightly round the neck, looking at Pierre as if he were thinking: This is my business, not yours.

'Is that you? Where have *you* come from?'

Everything was unreal and strange. Tot was not an affectionate child. It was a long time since he had responded to a caress, let alone given one of his own accord. It was in fact a long time since anyone had caressed her. A child's arm round her neck, a hand shaking her shoulder, it was too much, too good to be true. Sivert's caresses were not in the same category. Simultaneously she felt as if she had arrived at an open, exposed place in life, where a disquieting wind blew and from which she could see the numerous paths that crossed it in all directions. She dried her tears and clung to Tot, the fixed point in her existence.

'I've come from over there,' pointed Tot. 'We're there and we're going to bathe. *Tante* Liesel said you were here.'

'Have you been here long?'

'A little while.'

'And you said nothing?' Alberta looked in bewilderment

from her son to Pierre. He was sitting studying the boy.

'I said something now.'

'Yes, now.'

Tot stood there, still holding her by the neck, and said for the first time, as far as she could remember, 'I' about himself. 'Come along then, we'll go and bathe. Come along, Tot.' Pierre got to his feet.

'I shall hold Mother's hand,' Tot said, refusing to let Alberta go.

At Tinti-Anna's Marthe was splashing about at the edge of the water in her bathing suit. She informed them that Jeanne and Liesel were inside the boathouse. They had Alberta's things with them, and chocolate and biscuits. Everything was back to the accustomed routine.

Alberta sat down for a moment in the warm sand, knowing that she did so in the hope of having the child's arm round her neck again. It came too. She laid her cheek against it and felt warmed by it through and through. The ice is cracking in me, she thought. I must have been frostbound.

And then she sat naked and bereft, cold to the marrow. Someone had jerked Tot's arm away from her neck. She turned round and looked up into the glitter in Sivert's eyes. 'We can't have that kind of thing,' he said. 'It's not proper.'

'Are you mad, Sivert? Are you out of your mind?'

Alberta was enraged. She looked from Sivert to the boy who was standing there, the expression on his face stranger than ever. 'Are you mad?' she repeated.

'On the contrary. I know very well what I'm about. I've learnt a good deal recently, about the upbringing of children amongst other things, and particularly that of boys. Matters that there's probably no point in discussing.'

Eliel, who was limping about on one foot with the toe of the other bound up, drew in his cheeks. It made Alberta even angrier.

'Oh, hold your tongue, Sivert. Have you been reading something again that you haven't the capacity to understand?' The malicious words scorched her tongue. She was about to stretch out her hand to the child, but changed her mind. It must not develop into an open quarrel. She met Pierre's blank expression, and knew that if she were to find support anywhere it would be from him. He had seen, understood, he would speak to Sivert. She clenched her teeth. Now there would probably be much to resist. Now things were beginning to look serious.

Jeanne and Liesel came out of the boathouse, Jeanne lovely, slender, attractively tanned in her dark blue bathing suit, Liesel suspiciously thin and round-shouldered in rust-red, sweetly feminine and a little ungainly. She sat down in the sand and said she would only sun herself.

'Are you back already?' Jeanne exclaimed, looking about her in surprise.

'Sivert and I got a lift with a farmer from Audierne.' Eliel held out his foot. 'We came by ambulance.'

'And Pierre?'

'I came by the beach. You haven't asked Eliel what he's done to his foot?'

'No. I don't suppose it's so very serious. But I'd like to ask what's going on here. You all look so strange?'

'Only natural events, Jeanne. Quite natural. We are as we normally are.' Pierre opened his left hand as if letting a bird fly.

PART TWO

. . . two green horses, two green dogs, green as copper . . .

Alberta was looking at them from the side. Strongly illuminated from above they stood out in relief against a wall of green leaves, which were lying in shadow and appeared blue.

They resembled casts.

But when she patted the dog nearest her they all turned their heads and regarded her with gentle, beautiful animals' eyes.

She was sitting on a bench asleep. Their departure hour was seven. She awoke. It was twelve, the horses and dogs were gone, it was too late. Anna Sletnesset sat there; she laid her hand sympathetically on Alberta's. But it was too late and the road in front was thick with dust as if carpeted with felt. It was straight and endless, she knew it stretched out for ever, stretched out beyond what she could see.

The thought of it oppressed her, it took her breath away. Dust settled over her face. She tried to brush it off, her hand was full of something greasy and stiff, and she realised that she was struggling with the dirty window of the compartment. It must have blown open. There was the throbbing rhythm of the wheels, there Eliel's snoring, there Liesel's dry little cough, scarcely audible above the din of the train. Had she dropped off for a long time or only for a moment?

She wiped her face and bent anxiously over Tot, who was lying with his head in her lap. He was sleeping quietly. What a good thing.

A glimmer of light filtered in, outshone the small lamp in the ceiling, revealed faces. Slowly they came into view, coarsened or hollowed, each according to its cast, by the night on the train. All of them were sitting as before, apparently jolted right down inside their clothes. When she had looked in other directions for a while, she could no longer avoid looking at Pierre. In the grudging light she felt rather than saw that his eyes never left her.

In embarrassment she raised the blind.

The dawn was greying. A narrow brook flowed solitary and intricate among the meadows, carrying the weak light of the sky through the dark landscape, then disappeared at the edge of a wood in the distance. A bird flew up out of the bushes at the side of the track; its piping could be heard for an instant. A landscape without distinction which one passes on a journey and immediately forgets; and wonders where it came from when one day it re-appears in the memory, more distinct than any of those looked at more carefully. Meadow, wood, air and water: these life-giving four.

Cautiously, so as not to wake the boy, she stretched up to the draught from the half-open window, and eagerly breathed the air from outside. It tasted of dew and grass, tasted of all she needed most bitterly and had once weaned herself from believing in. She closed her eyes.

When they had travelled out, and she had encountered the same air for the first time after the endless night in the train, she had felt her features soften, as if an astringent mask had fallen away. A dream had plagued her during recent years, recurring time after time. They were being immured, Tot and she; she could hear the clatter of the trowels, feel the air thicken—until all of a sudden she heard nothing, screamed, thrashed about and woke Sivert.

Now the boy was going to fill his lungs day and night with air as fresh and strong as this, even fresher, even stronger. It would fill his blood with oxygen, assume solidity in his muscles, glow in his skin, his eyes, his lips, at last, at last. A few more hours, and it would begin to force its way into the slender body, transform it, perform its miracle. The bad dream would lose its sting. And she too—

She dropped the blind and looked down at the child's face

in her lap. It seemed paler and thinner than ever in the grudging light and somehow twice as dirty as Marthe's. His black hair lay flat and lifeless about his forehead, one of his legs had fallen from the seat and hung down in full view of the adults, pathetically thin in the calf. Bothered by the sight Alberta leaned forward, brought it carefully into place again and drew the blanket over it.

Marthe was bursting with health as she slept under the railway soot. Her mouth pouted as waywardly as ever, ripe as a fruit. If she awoke, Jeanne only had to whisper to her a little and give her a pat or a smack, whichever was necessary. And Marthe would sigh and go back to sleep.

Alberta had hungered to see her own child like this, greedy for food and sleep, hungered for it for the sixth year. Getting him out into the sunshine and fresh air on a beach had been like carrying him to a new birth; at last he would be born after the full period of time, noisy, naughty, like other children.

But the things one longs for seldom happen. Other things happen instead.

Again she met Pierre's eyes; she could see them clearly now. There came the same sudden brilliance in the air about her, the light-hearted, sweet delirium, that she had felt repeatedly of late. It was as if gravity disappeared, she no longer denied it to herself. Then Jeanne's glance crossed hers. Calmly, without shrinking, Alberta parried it. She could look Jeanne straight in the eye, Sivert too. She had deceived neither of them.

Jeanne was no longer asleep. Perhaps she had not slept at all. Again and again Alberta had felt her eyes on her. Slowly the grey light chiselled her form, showing that Jeanne had altered since the previous time they had sat together in the train. She continually changed her position, and there was an expression round her pretty mouth as if she were clenching her teeth spasmodically. Alberta had words ready on her tongue: Don't take me seriously on top of everything else. What I get has nothing to do with you, and what you have nobody can take from you. It was unnecessary to add it all up; you could have spared us that with safety. What could I have done to you? No-one could be less dangerous. In a few hours I shall be out of sight.

One does not say things like that. They throb through one's brain with the rhythm of the wheels and get no further.

Jeanne started up and looked about her. 'Pierre, you're not asleep. You haven't slept at all.'

'Yes, of course I have.' Pierre too started up as if dragged out of deep slumber. He rearranged the blanket over Marthe, who was lying between them, and they sat as before, leaning their heads against the wall, their throats outstretched, unsteady and uncomfortable.

'You're not asleep. I can see you're not. I've seen it for some time. You must change places with me, or you'll be fit for nothing tomorrow.' Jeanne's voice was sharp and high-pitched.

'Today, you mean. Don't wake Marthe. I'm quite all right.'

But Jeanne was already on her feet, making the child sit up, disturbing the whole compartment. 'Rather than know you're sitting like this. Take my corner. No one needs it as much as you.'

Marthe began to cry, Liesel stood up, prepared for anything, and shook Eliel. Jeanne gestured impatiently and deprecatingly. Pierre said: 'Certainly not.' Eliel looked about him uncomprehendingly, pushed himself more comfortably into his corner and snored on. Liesel shook him once more. That was his voice, high-pitched and aggrieved, rough with sleep: 'What? Snoring? Me? Of course not.' And he resumed his snoring.

But Jeanne had her way. She took Marthe, whimpering, on to her lap again and gave her a smack, both with a violence that did not disturb Marthe in the slightest . 'You are naughty, *Maman,*' she said, turned over to make herself more comfortable, and went to sleep.

It was yesterday evening's dispute that had flared up. Pierre had argued that the women should each have a corner, but then gave in to the pressure of opinion and took the fourth himself. But during the night he and Eliel had changed places. Jeanne could not get over it, not over that either.

'You who have been to the war,' she said, firing her last shot. It was directed at Pierre, but levelled at Eliel.

Alberta looked across at Liesel. She was sitting with her back partly turned towards her and her face in towards the wall. She had folded her arms tightly about her and drawn up her shoulders. In spite of the heat inside the compartment she looked as if she were frozen.

Happily out of it all, Sivert was sleeping quietly behind the overcoat he had hung up. One of Sivert's gifts was that of staying out of things on certain occasions, a talent which sometimes drove Alberta to rash, ill-considered action. Had she not once gone over to him in public and pulled his chair away when she thought he ought to get up and he had made no move to do so?

The train stopped with a jerk. Eliel yawned, shook himself a little, and drew the blind back from the window in the door. It framed a section of a station building and people going past. Neither the house nor the people were typical of Brittany any more. Outside it was a lovely day. Liesel leaned forward, looked out, coughed her little cough. Her stooping shoulders, her long, supple neck, her head with its coil of plaits thoroughly askew after sitting up all night, were silhouetted for a moment against the lighter background.

Alberta felt a deep pang of longing for the sky and the sea, for fresh air. But the boy began to whimper.

'Do think of the children.' Jeanne was holding up a section of blanket protectively in front of her daughter's eyes.

'*Pardon.*' Eliel dropped the blind. The compartment again became dim.

'Children fall asleep again quickly,' said Pierre.

'Can you guarantee that? He is nervous, this little one. And it's quite enough to have one of them crying, don't you think?'

In distress, Alberta leaned over her child. Dulled and distant from sudden, limitless exhaustion she attempted to quieten him. He continued to fret for a long time as if in physical pain. It was fortunate Sivert was still asleep. *He* slept like a log.

Automatically Alberta looked for Pierre's gaze and found it. It was in position, it was waiting for her. For a second they looked at each other.

The hours passed. They were approaching the city. Once when the train stopped a crowd of people with bright morning faces joined it. With light luggage in their hands they ran alongside the row of carriages, off to the capital on a brief visit. It became crowded. The children had to sit on the grown-ups' knees and went on nodding there. The blinds were right up, the faces of the adults exposed mercilessly to the daylight. They wore the disorientated expression that comes of a night awake; a stamp of disolution, of guilt and homelessness. Thus do criminals look at each other, with evasive eyes, brief, twisted smiles, when they have given up and been caught. Eliel looked as if he had woken up after a spree, with his coarse, thick features. Pierre's scar was ugly in the darkening stubble on his face, two naked lips meeting at the wrong place. Alberta noticed it and thought: If there were any question of coming close to it, coming close to it now . . .

She had known for a long time that it would feel perfectly natural. With alarm she realized how quiveringly close she was to giving herself to him. It lay just below the surface, in spite of Tot, in spite of Sivert, in spite of everything. If she were free, if she had control of her life, of her child; if Pierre were free, with no child, she would have no doubts at all.

When did it come? How did it come? When did it start to grow? It only seems as if such things happen suddenly. One day it was there, in the atmosphere, obvious to everyone.

Was it when she had realised that Pierre had talked to Sivert about the episode at the beach, and perhaps about other things? And Sivert had come upstairs and sat down, looking at her with the glitter in his eyes.

'What are you looking at, Sivert?'

'At you.'

'Is there something the matter with me?'

'That depends on one's attitude.'

Was it when, driven after a while by the uneasiness and

embarrassment of sitting there with Sivert, she had gone down-stairs to the sitting-room and received a shock? For Pierre was there, and she had not known. Immovable as a statue he had stood leaning against the mantelshelf and simply looked at her, he too. They had both stood looking at each other. Alberta did not move, said nothing. The feeling that if she made a remark or a movement something fatal would happen, nailed her fast, paralysed her tongue. She smiled momentarily out of sheer bewilderment. Pierre did not smile back. She came away giddy, leaving the room with bowed head and hammering heart, as if she had been scolded. She went out. When she came home she walked straight upstairs as if dream-ing and looked at herself in the mirror. Why? Was it to find out whether she already bore some visible evidence or not?

Sivert? It had happened that Sivert had tossed his head, behaved with authority and a proprietary expression when anyone took an interest in her, however fleeting. This simple mechanism had functioned through the years without breaking down; only the occasions had become fewer and fewer. She had never given him any grounds for it.

He had no grounds now either, not according to his way of thinking. And it would be wrong to say that he was taking it seriously. He took it sarcastically and rather maliciously. This time they were equals. Alberta knew very well that he went to meet the postman up in the village, and that he re-ceived letters with an unfamiliar handwriting on the envelope. She ought not to have been afraid of him any more. But she was, so much so that her heart sometimes stopped short; and she scarcely dared exchange normal conversation with Pierre in the hearing of them all. She had become adept at avoiding meeting him alone.

Once when they met on the stairs he had said, 'Alberta.'

'Yes, Pierre,' was all that she replied. She listened to her voice, its busy tone incredibly easy and light. She had hurried past without pausing. Talking to him might open a door to her strength, the little she had, so that it would drain away like blood from a severed artery, leaving her helpless. And what should she say, for her part? Now I have arrived. I took a long, stupid path, but I found the way here at last. I am grown-up and I know what life is and what I am doing, and that I want to be here. Here I can unfurl into a person.

She must not say it. She had entangled herself to such an extent that she had cut off any retreat. He too, as far as she could see.

Time and again she had said to herself: If he were not so tired of everything, if Jeanne did not nag him as she does, if we had not met just at this time, he would not even have noticed me. If everything were as it should be between me and Sivert I would be invulnerable. We're in the grip of circumstances; they're playing with us, duping us. And if only Jeanne had not become suspicious and Sivert full of malice, then—then—

It was no use. The same dark desire was in her still. If she followed it she would go away with Pierre. For good, for evil, for anything whatsoever with Pierre. At any moment and travelling light.

She gritted her teeth. She must not give it rein. Everything passes, life wipes out its own traces. One day this feeling would have left her as blossom and foliage leave the tree. She would do without it. A plant dies without sustenance. She looked up, met Pierre's eyes, allowed her own to rest there briefly, moved her glance slowly away, while the pain the thought had given her died, as acute pain does. They had the present, a bloodless shadow of a present. Today, in a couple of hours, each of them would be going in his own direction. Afterwards it was impossible to predict anything.

It had begun to pour with rain. It drummed on the roof and drove against the window panes. A couple of the other passengers were talking to each other. Sivert and Eliel were bending forward, elbows on knees, enjoying themselves. Isolated words reached Alberta: 'Yes, so help me . . . my opinion too . . . would be no alternative. Listen to me, old chap.'

They were dazed no longer. There was that cheerful nonchalance about them that had been so striking on their arrival in Brittany. Sivert sat slapping his hand repeatedly with his new gloves, another unfamiliar gesture. It was as if the proximity of the city was going to their heads. But when had anything gone to Sivert's head before?

When he glanced over at Pierre he had the same slightly malicious expression as when he looked at Alberta. It did not appear in his features, it lay beneath much else in his eyes and wedged itself up from the bottom in grey glimpses. The next second his thoughts were elsewhere. He gave himself an extra slap with the gloves and looked resolute. Pierre presumably noticed nothing. He seemed to have forgotten Sivert's existence.

The suburbs appeared. Small, ugly villas, fine old houses behind walls, new banal gardens and old ones full of shadows and mystery, ivy in cascades, glistening with rain. This headlong journey back to streets and noise struck Alberta as sheer madness. They ought to have stayed out there, found some means of putting up with each other. Tot's heart had beat unevenly, but was it any better for him to be anaemic? It was not late autumn yet; the evenings were mild. Far out the sea glittered with moonshine; close to the land the moon itself rocked in the swell. Like an enormous balcony jutting out towards the universe the ocean lay there day and night. At high tide it surged stronger than ever, offering itself to the equinoctial gales. They would come.

Sivert had got the idea that Alberta ought to write. Before, when she had referred to the subject, he had not answered: an unequivocal manner of expressing his opinion.

'I'll look after Brede,' he had begun to say, 'if you want to scribble.

'Well, you have a pen,' he added.

'Aren't you going to paint?' asked Alberta to gain time and decide what attitude to adopt; perhaps also to show that she was not blind.

Surely she could see that he was not painting? He was doing some sketching, but Castelucho had not sent either canvases or paints. He occasionally took out the sketches he had made earlier that summer, whistled, and put them back with their faces to the wall. Everything pointed to Sivert's early return to

Paris. It was remarkable how light-heartedly he and Eliel regarded the journey in and out, twice each way during the course of the summer, as if there were no question of money or inflation.

'Penny wise, pound foolish,' he had said once, when the matter was raised. 'Working capital,' he said. 'If you have it, you must take risks. That's one lesson I've learnt.'

The day the storm came Sivert had been lying out on the slope near Jeanne. 'I have something to read, so I'll stay here until it's time to bathe. You go if you want.'

He took from his pockets the exhibition catalogues, art brochures and other pamphlets that he always carried about with him. Among them there inadvertently came letters which he quickly stuffed back again. He offered to look after both children if Jeanne had anything else to do.

'Oh, I!' said Jeanne. 'I have no talent. I'm just a simple housewife. You go, Alberta, as your husband suggests.' She looked up and sniffed the breeze, which was heavy with sea-weed and salt. 'I shouldn't be surprised if we had a storm before nightfall.'

Alberta left them. It all seemed odd and disquieting. For obscure reasons she did not like the fact that Sivert and Jeanne together watched her go. It had nothing to do with jealousy; it was an inexplicable uneasiness of another kind.

From the window above the typewriter clattered like some warning ally, or so it seemed to her. The atmosphere was stifling and her head was heavy. She did no work to speak of. She sat in her accustomed place, leafed through her manuscript, struck out here and there, moved pages from one chapter over to another and back again, while her thoughts revolved round very different matters, vacillating like a swing between insane possibilities and cramping heart-sickness.

She must have sat there for a long time. When she looked up a rust-red stripe lay along the horizon, and everything else was the colour of lead, sea as well as sky. The silence, the boundless metal surface without a ripple, the screech of a solitary gull that seemed to be the last one in flight from the earth, struck Alberta with sudden anxiety. She went home quickly, as if pursued. On the stone steps outside the kitchen door Josephine's clogs stood as usual; but their appearance was not as usual. In the nauseating light that grew paler minute by minute there was something significant and sinister about them. All summer Alberta had seen clogs standing in front of the doors of the houses. All it meant was that one could not cross the floor in them; they clattered noisily and spoiled the wood. Josephine glided round the house in her stockinged feet, nimbly and noiselessly, up and down stairs. Her clogs were attractive out of doors.

Now they revealed their true essence all of a sudden and appeared to be a warning, fulfilling a mission. They stood pointing towards the house. They said: In, not out again.

One attaches no importance to such impressions; they occur fleetingly and one passes on. Afterwards, when something terrible has taken place, they surface again.

An hour later the storm was upon them: a tremendous storm, that tore down slates and fences, altered the beach completely, threw mountains of seaweed up on land and brought with it a downpour that washed away roads and paths in the course of a few hours. It isolated them from each other. Only infrequently and at close quarters could they hear each others' voices and footsteps. They heard the rattle of the shutters, the heavy gusts of wind that were hurled against the house, then heard it give at the joints, sodden and buffeted. From the upstairs windows they watched the sea coming towards the land in row upon row of moving mountains, grey as rock, to be shattered against the beach. The spray hung at a great height beneath the lowering, turbulent sky; foam floated in the air, a rookery of white rags. They slapped against the panes or fluttered past, rising and falling on the storm, as far as the village and beyond.

It lasted for six days. Josephine had to spend the first night on the chaise-longue in the sitting-room, as it was impossible to open the outer door. In the morning Jean-Marie came to fetch her, bringing butter and four plucked chickens tied to his back. Arm in arm, he and Josephine crept over the crest of the slope and disappeared. For six days they were shut in,

except for one afternoon when it abated a little, and Sivert and
Eliel went out to fetch supplies, bent double, navigating before the gusts like ships at sea.

Liesel's influenza worsened. Usually nobody took it seriously; it was one of the things to which they had all become
accustomed. When they had said: 'You ought to go to a
doctor, Liesel, and get something for that cough,' they had
done what they could. She stayed in bed while the storm
lasted, eating nothing, her eyes glittering with fever, her hands
clammy and hot. Even Eliel said, 'That cold's a nuisance. It
can't go on like this.'

On the morning of the fifth day Sivert decided to return to
town as soon as possible. He began taking out his belongings
and packing them in the shining new suitcase. It was then
that Alberta was seized by one of her attacks and announced
suddenly: 'I want clothes and things too, nice clothes, nice
things.'

'Of course,' Sivert said, and sounded as if caught unawares.
'But after all, you can't have them out here.'

'I want to go to Paris and buy myself some decent clothes,'
said Alberta, sinking lower in her own estimation with every
remark.

'Well,' said Sivert slowly—he was standing at the table rearranging his belongings repeatedly, as if composing a still-
life—'Well, you can come with me if you like. There's no
longer any epidemic, so as far as that's concerned . . .'

It had sounded like a threat. Uneasiness crept over her, but
she shook it off. As a preliminary measure she started to look
over Tot's and her stockings. All summer they had both of
them gone without. She could not remember what was usable
and what was not. Perhaps she could throw away the worst
pairs and escape darning them.

Jeanne was upstairs with Pierre; she was there for a long
time. The storm reigned, nothing could be heard. But later
on, when she and Alberta were preparing lunch together in
the kitchen, Pierre came down and wandered in and out singing to a tune of his own:

'Je souhaite dans ma maison
une femme ayant sa raison
un chat passant parmi les livres . . .' [1]

He did not continue, but returned to the first line: *'Je souhaite dans ma maison une femme ayant sa raison.'* In spite of the weather each word could be heard clearly, so loudly did he sing. His expression was hard, his mouth twisted out the words. He remained briefly in the sitting-room and then went upstairs again.

Jeanne's hands trembled as she chopped up parsley at the kitchen table. She put the knife down, went across and lifted the lid of the pan of potatoes. When she came back again her hands were calm. Without altering her expression she chopped the rest. But the atmosphere in the house had become almost impossible to breathe.

The explosion came later, as they were eating. She got to her feet, pushed her chair back violently, and gripped the edge of the table so that her knuckles whitened. Her words tumbled out pell-mell. She referred to her expectations during her engagement and throughout the war, her struggle and her anxiety. 'Shall we talk about Mondement?' shouted Jeanne. 'About Soissons and Chemin des Dames and La Fère? I know a bit about those places. I was not present, and yet I was there. Or shall we talk about 'House X'? I know that book by heart. I can repeat whole pages of it, word by word. You wait for years. One day you find yourself sitting there with a child, waiting. There is no horror one does not experience. But what are you in the end? Are you so much as a comrade? No. A housekeeper, a nursemaid, a—a—a—'

'Be quiet,' said Pierre. 'Be quiet now, Jeanne.' He went over, put his left hand over her mouth and his right, his wretched, fingerless stump, which he hid so carefully, round her shoulders. He did that for Jeanne. He said: 'Come along, we'll go upstairs. You're saying things you don't really mean.' His voice was low and tender.

[1] Guillaume Apollinaire

But Jeanne shouted: 'That Alberta! What's she sitting staring at, that Alberta! With eyes like that!' And burst into tears. Pierre began to force her to go upstairs. Then Jeanne threw herself on his neck exclaiming, 'I don't know what I'm saying, I don't know what I'm saying, I don't know what's the matter with me. Forgive me!' Then they left. Her sobs and Pierre's low voice could be heard for a moment from the staircase between two gusts of wind.

Nobody said anything for a long while. The door out to the kitchen had been ajar the whole time, Josephine, who had come back again during a lull, was out there, and Jeanne had shouted so loudly that even a hurricane could not have drowned her. The scandal was complete. The thought hammered in Alberta: She was adding up the bonds, the ones that cannot be broken, the ones that sooner or later would draw him back again if he were to leave her. You cannot free yourself from them.

Pierre came downstairs afterwards and tried to explain it away. He did not say much, and he blamed himself: 'My fault, my fault entirely. Here I am letting my nerves run away with me, without thinking of Jeanne's. The soldiers weren't the only ones whose nerves were disordered by the war years; the civilians' were too, the women's above all. Even Jeanne, who is so brave—she's not more than human. All she wants is what's best for me.'

He paced up and down for a bit. Then he said: 'We've decided to leave. Our stay here has become meaningless, we're getting nothing out of it. Marthe is missing school to no purpose. But there's nothing to stop the rest of you from staying. The house is paid for for the next three weeks, and . . .' He stood staring at Alberta as if in distraction, with wide, tired eyes. He supported himself against the mantelshelf.

'I had thought of leaving in any case,' said Sivert. 'I think Eliel has too. But perhaps Liesel and Alberta would like to stay.'

Alberta stared into Pierre's staring eyes and said no. She was thinking that that slightly tender conscience, which comes of not loving wholly and unconditionally was something they had in common, he and she.

'Not much longer now, a quarter of an hour, the ticket collector says.' Sivert, who had gone out into the corridor, came back to report. He began rearranging the suitcases so that it would be easier to pick them up, brushed his clothes, made a new crease in his hat, and sat down ready. Jeanne started to busy herself. Undaunted by crossness and opposition she rubbed engine soot off Marthe's face with cotton wool and eau de Cologne. 'We are on a train, *mon enfant,* we are not at home.' Marthe stopped complaining. She repeated emphatically: 'We are on a train, we are not at home,' pouting and docile under the ordeal, while Jeanne rubbed and rubbed until she shone.

Alberta was reminded bitterly of the bottle of eau de Cologne she had wanted to buy at the last moment in Audierne, and had not done so because Sivert had thought that was carrying virtue a little too far. It had been the same on the journey out. In the morning Jeanne had unpacked various attractively and practically arranged toilet articles and provisions and prepared to refresh her family. She handed Pierre ready mixed mouth wash in a bottle and nodded in the direction of the place to which he should go, as if he were incapable of finding the way on his own. She offered Alberta eau de Cologne, and Alberta washed her son's face and put him in a rage. It was obvious to everyone that the process was quite new to him and that he was thoroughly opposed to it. He stood there in his unsuccessful dungarees with his hostile little face, exposed to the tender mercies of Jeanne's secure, motherly eye. Sivert did not improve matters by saying, 'Aren't you going to shake hands with the little girl?' The boy squirmed and simply said 'No'. Marthe looked at Sivert with the calm disdain children display towards adults. Jeanne said, 'Don't bother him.'

'Alberta!'

It was Jeanne. She had turned and was handing her the bottle and the packet of cotton wool, now as then. 'You can't possibly use the water in the W.C.; take these.'

Something in her eyes made Alberta put extra warmth into her voice as she replied, 'Thank you, Jeanne.' She was not Jeanne's adversary, and had no intention of being so. It would be good if that were clear.

Sivert intervened. 'I'll do it. Come here, boy.'

Alberta relinquished the articles, went outside and stood at the window in the corridor. They would soon be there. Factories and working class districts slid past, glimpses of wet asphalt, slum children playing, people stopping to look at the train. The white-washed house on the green slope suddenly stood in front of her more clearly than those she was looking at. White clouds, piled up like eiderdowns, were sailing above it, the clogs were standing at the kitchen door, dwarf clover grew along the little path. The live lobster, which, to Alberta's horror, Jean-Marie had taken out of his tunic and handed her as a parting gift, extended its black claws slowly and with hesitation. She dared not touch it, Josephine had had to intervene. The pot was brought, the most frightful execution took place, the bright red lobster was brought triumphantly in to supper and greeted with ovations from the men. She heard the sound of the sea, heard Madame Poulain's parting words: I've been thinking. I've come to the conclusion that the creation is far from complete. It is wrong to tell us it is, and that God found that everything was good. If He exists, He must be in despair over how incomplete it all is, especially mankind; for we have many talents but not enough sense to make use of them. I am only a simple woman, Madame, I cannot instruct anyone. But this is my belief.

'What are you thinking about, Alberta? That we shall soon be there?'

She started. Pierre was standing beside her, looking at her.

'Yes, something of the sort.'

'It always ends with an arrival. Was that our purpose in leaving? It is written somewhere: *Le vrai voyageur part pour partir.*'

'Is it?' said Alberta giddily. As if the words had removed covering layers in her mind she realised how much she loved

travel for it's own sake: the thump of the wheels, the changing, curving lines of the landscape, the furrow that seems to
make a circular movement around you, arriving at strange
places where everything is fresh and new as it only can be
when you have never been there before and will not be staying
long.

She smiled, not daring to look at him. Immediately afterwards she did so in astonishment, for Pierre said, 'No, it's not
the dome of the Pantheon. But what can it be? In weather
like this you can't distinguish the one from the other.'

At once words began tumbling hurriedly out of her own
mouth; she was not sure what they were, only that they were
unexpected, stupid, and far too numerous: 'No, it's not the
Pantheon. It's, let me see, it's — — no, it can't be the Pantheon, I'm sure of that.'

She went on repeating it, breathlessly and at random.
Jeanne had put her head in between them, her black eyes
looking from her to Pierre and back again. 'Fancy being able
to say so with such certainty, Alberta. You must know Paris
very well. Even for us it's difficult when it's overcast. We're
provincials, but all the same . . . How unfortunate that it
should be raining. Not a cab to be had, I don't suppose. Sivert
and Eliel have promised to rush on ahead and do what they
can. Have you the tickets ready, Pierre? Can you be quick
about getting a porter? Don't let everyone else go in front of
you, even if they are old ladies. You're much too unselfish
about such things. Think of tomorrow. You have to call on
Monsieur Chollet at nine o'clock. You must be rested and in
good spirits, to give him the impression that—After all, young
writers spring up out of the ground like mushrooms these
days, and some of them have talent. You must go to bed at
once, have a bath and go to bed, eat your supper there and
have a good night's rest.'

'Don't worry, Jeanne. A lot of money has been placed on
me. If it's to bring in any profit the best thing is to put in more
while I'm still alive. No one knows how long someone like
myself can keep it up. Now's the time to put me in a position
to produce.'

Pierre's voice was quiet and cold. Alberta stood embarrassed at being a party to their conversation, irritated that she had let herself be drawn into a foolish piece of play-acting which had been nothing but a fiasco. What had been the point of it? What had they to hide, she and Pierre? Jeanne was still talking in a high-pitched, nervous voice. 'Why do you always have to harp on that? It's unjust of you. They have been most obliging. They could simply take your manuscript, force you to hand it in. They're running a business, not a — a —'

She paused. When she had said 'take your manuscript' Pierre had laughed, that curt, almost silent laughter of his. It always made her unsure of herself. He stood looking at her, his eyes blank. More words came pouring out, low and faltering: 'If you're given another respite—a chance to get this piece finished—you can apply for the stipends, you can—as soon as you've produced something new.'

'Why not beg on the doorsteps?' Pierre neither raised nor lowered his voice. He looked at Jeanne a second longer, turned, gave Marthe his left hand and went towards the exit. Jeanne closed her eyes and slowly shrugged her beautiful, tailor-made shoulders. A jerk that made them all stagger passed through the train. It stood still.

Now there was nothing for it but to descend and get away from the mob. In front of the station the violent and unaccustomed combination of drumming rain and the noise of the street engulfed them bewilderingly. At great danger to life and limb, their coat collars turned up and shaking the rain off themselves, Sivert and Eliel ran hither and thither in the road after taxi-cabs, were stopped and sent back by the police and ran again. Marthe was carrying Mimi, wherever Mimi had come from. Jeanne buttoned Pierre's raincoat up to his neck and told him he must not move; all he had to do was stay quietly and shelter. Pierre acquiesced, was kind to Jeanne again, patting her on the cheek and smiling crookedly and absently as he watched the traffic with disorientated eyes. A reflection of old tenderness and of the soldier's wonderment at life behind the front was visible for a moment in his face, making Alberta feel an intrusive and somewhat ridiculous figure. A new, devastating thought slid into her mind: They have furniture and a home, he and Jeanne, a small world of their own, a shell they have built round themselves. It does not consist merely of chairs and tables, of objects that can be seen and touched. For better or worse it lives, it is a living web, it exists or goes under with the people who inhabit it. It was in the Rue Notre Dame des Champs, near the Rue de Rennes. Sivert had been there, but never Alberta. She held Tot's hand more tightly.

Sivert and Eliel had found cabs. Jeanne, Pierre and Marthe took the one. In a daze, Alberta felt them take her hand in turn, heard herself saying *au revoir* and how pleasant the holiday had been, first to the one, then to the other.

'I shall be terribly busy to begin with,' explained Jeanne. 'Must get Marthe off to school, make clothes for her, help her with her homework. She has missed almost a month. Then there's everything to be got ready for the winter. But later, in one, two, three weeks—I suppose you take Tot to the Luxembourg Gardens now and again, Alberta?'

'Yes, of course, Jeanne.'

'Then we'll see each other there if not before. I always go near the big fountain.'

'So do we,' answered Alberta mechanically. She watched the car drive away and mingle with the countless others moving down the street. Not even Marthe's little hand waving from the back window distinguished it from the rest any longer. Numbly she allowed herself to be packed into the other cab. She had a profound certainty that nothing of what had just happened could really be possible; that all the things they were saying and doing were not really as they seemed.

They sat squashed together, luggage everywhere, outside and inside the vehicle. They did not say much, only yawned now and again. Tot stared out, his intensely blue eyes wide from fatigue in his blackened little face that no washing had improved. Past them rushed rows of houses, people, traffic, all of which had the peculiar property of being exactly as they had left them. Rain dripped from umbrellas, from gutters and awnings; from chestnut trees which, confused by city life, were flowering for the second time with small, scattered, pathetic flowers; from plane trees, their bark peeling in flaps, and from trees like the ones belonging to a Noah's Ark, round at the top and unnaturally dark. The air coming through the open window smelt of hosed streets, a unique mixture of vapours impregnated with water.

Only Sivert seemed to be entirely at ease, rested and cheerful. He was still slapping his hand with his gloves. After a while Alberta felt as if she were being whipped; she cringed, waiting for the next stroke. He was as brown as tanned leather and contrasted almost shamefully with the pale people on the pavements. Every year he and Eliel acquired the same solid, even patina. It made them look younger and handsome as peasants. Their eyes and teeth glittered competitively. This time the sea air had deepened the beautiful basic colour by several shades. The china blue of Sivert's pupils contrasted so surprisingly with his skin and his black hair that it was unpleasant.

At the Parc de Montsouris they put down Liesel and Eliel. Liesel took leave of Alberta with a limp, hot hand. 'When I think that Eliel left it all in one big mess. You're lucky, Albertchen, to be going to a comparatively tidy home.'

'Comparatively?' said Sivert. 'And I even scrubbed the attic stairs.'

'Yes, Sivert's the man with his papers in order.' Eliel giggled. 'Besides, Liesel can move to a hotel. There's nothing to stop her, it would be better in every way.' He commandeered his final piece of luggage and kicked the door shut. '*Hei paa Er*. We'll see each other at the Dôme, Sivert? As usual? *Maa saa godt.*'

He put his things down and waved. Liesel waved too, a couple of small gestures. The last Alberta saw of her she was standing upright, her arms hanging down at her sides and a dull, bewildered expression on her face.

At a good speed and with plenty of room they drove on to the Rue Vercingétorix. Sivert was humming in quiet snatches. When in obedience to his instructions the cab turned into the courtyard, rounded the little shrubbery in the middle and stopped at the door of the studio, Sivert swung into *forte* and finished on a strong, long-drawn out note. Yet again Alberta's heart was constricted by inexplicable fear: fear of his strength, of his repose, of aspects of his character that she would never really fathom. Yet again she felt her absolute dependence on him as highly dangerous; it came and went, alternating with very different feelings, with old devotion, almost sympathy.

While he settled up with the driver she looked up at the walls of the houses round about. They looked as if they were about to collapse on top of her, so high were they. She had not remembered that the air was *so* heavy. She ought to have stayed at the seaside with the boy. Unconsciously she squeezed his hand so hard that he cried 'Ouch!' and drew it away. What were these potted plants that were standing in the way round her legs? The flowers had stalks that were far too long, as if they had been stretching towards the light. Behind her she heard the concierge: 'Here I am with the keys, Madame, and the most recent letters. *Mon Dieu,* how sunburnt you are! And Tot! Tot! Do I see any difference? A great difference, Madame, a great difference. He is not plump, he never will be, he is tired after the journey, *voilà.* A whole night on the train, *n'est-ce pas?* But wait until tomorrow when you take him out on to the street. Then you will see children who have not been to the sea. I shall say nothing about Monsieur. He is magnificent. Monsieur is always magnificent, with or without sea air. Is everything as it was when you left? I hope so, Madame, I hope so. I can answer for the flowers at any rate. They have not lacked water. Today they are outside, as you see. Nothing does them so much good as a shower of rain. We have had such a heatwave. The summer is sultry in Paris. We have not one single case of the Spanish sickness left in this *quartier,* thank God. I was at the chemist's only yesterday . . .'

Madame Morin bent down, helpfully moved fuchsias and pelargonias so that the entrance was free, rattled her bunch of keys and opened the door.

'Thank you,' said Alberta, suddenly recognizing her own

plants, whose existence she had forgotten. 'I can see they have been well looked after. They've grown.'

On the threshold she paused. Through a haze of fatigue she recognized the interior again too. Was that how it looked? And how unused it smelt. Quickly she went to and fro in the large, rather dilapidated room, opening windows to let in the air. It was tidy, everything was in its right place, the floor was clean. Sivert was not the man to leave a thorough mess like Eliel. In that respect she had much to be thankful for. She vainly attempted to feel something more for this, their home, Tot's home.

She heard Sivert's relieved, 'Well, that's that,' when the cab had gone, and the boy's footsteps sounded across to the corner where his toys were. She looked down at the letters in her hand. The one was a *pneumatique* for Sivert; the other had Australian stamps all over it and was from Jacob.

Jacob? She could forget him for long stretches at a time, until all of a sudden he would remind her of his existence in one way or another and heighten her feeling of having deserted her own destiny. When did she take the wrong turning? Where did she take it? The only persons she recognised at all times as part of her life and knew she was close to, were Jacob and Tot: this odd little stranger she longed for and did not know how to win.

'Magnificent?' repeated Sivert with irritation, putting the last suitcase down on the floor and wiping his forehead. 'Magnificent? What does she mean by that? A pretty irrelevant expression, it seems to me. Is the good Madame Morin beginning to be impertinent?'

He put the *pneumatique* that Alberta handed him quickly in his pocket, as if he already knew who it was from and what it contained. In passing he asked about Alberta's letter.

'It's from Jacob.'

'Fancy that.'

But Alberta suddenly realised what was strange about the room. Two brand new cushions lay on the divan in the corner, on top of the ones she herself had stitched together at great pains and with limited materials. She stood looking at them

624

for a second. They were attractive, and made the place brighter. She recalled occasions when she had had a desire for many well-matched cushions. A wild notion prodded her, but did not seem to accord with anything else. She said nothing, put her letter aside, and began to unpack what they needed for their immediate use.

* * *

Although the days had long since turned into weeks, looking upwards still gave her the same feeling. The houses seemed to be leaning over her threateningly. They bordered closely on the remains of the low old studio buildings, their enormous brick walls rising upwards, the lower half covered with ivy, the upper with advertisements for Byrrh, Dubonnet, Pneus Michelin in giant letters, Man-size bottles paraded up there together with the inescapable apparition made out of car tyres and a cigar, that had once frightened Tot so much.

Out in the street, beyond the gate and the low house belonging to the concierge, storey was piled upon storey: identical windows, all of them open, washing on lines, bird cages and window boxes, a rectangle of the ubiquitous flowered wallpaper visible on the inner wall of the narrow rooms; women going to and fro, leaning out, carrying children on their arms, sewing something, polishing something; high up a balcony running along the length of the façade, above that attics under the steep roof; and when she tilted her head back as far as it would go, the sky, a grudgingly measured, crookedly and badly cut sample, in so far as one could see that the material existed at all.

Behind much else in her consciousness Alberta had, since her return, been reluctant to admit that she had lived here for years with her child and that she would continue to live here for an uncertain length of time. Tot was breathing in the same air as in previous years: the heavy city brew of exhaust and food smells, exhaust and scent, exhaust and tired vapours, exhaust and dust. It hung in the streets unaltered from year to year. If it was scattered by a shower of rain, a few hours of fresh night breeze from the country, it oozed back just as quickly, tenacious and satiated, from the houses, the cars, the people. Once, a long time ago, she had inhaled it like a stimulant. It was one, but, like most stimulants, it was a slow poison too.

When she had finished tidying up in the morning she went to the milk shop and the vegetable and fruit barrows. Tot went with her and helped her to carry the things, unapproachable, undaunted by the cries that greeted him on his way. 'How he has grown.' 'He's brown.' 'Yes indeed, and more robust.' 'All the same I'd give him cod-liver oil in the winter, if he were mine, cod-liver oil from Norway.' '*Oh là là,* the damned war, not a child who isn't marked by it, except for those of the rich, they always manage of course, all they have to do is leave in good time.' 'Come here, Tot, and say good-day and you shall have some grapes. They're not bad for him, Madame, on the contrary.' 'He has a serious air, that little boy, it makes quite an impression on one just to see him.'

Every comment was well-meaning, every one cut Alberta to the quick. 'Thank you,' she would say. 'Thank you Mesdames. Shake hands nicely, Tot.' She nodded and smiled to the neighbourhood children, who stopped in their play to watch the boy. He had had a couple of friends among them when he was small; they had come into the courtyard to play. It had always resulted in tears and been brought to an end by each new epidemic. There was no trace of them any more, and Madame Morin said: 'Boys of his age in here, no Madame. Toddlers are a different matter. He would learn bad habits, and I would get into difficulties with the tenants. They're working folk, they need quiet. You can imagine yourself how it would be if there were shouting and screaming here, fighting and throwing of stones. Now he is pleasant and well brought-up, approved of by everyone. My cousin from Saint-Denis comes to spend a day with me every autumn. I'll ask her to bring her boy with her, he's nearly six years of age too.'

Too well brought-up, thought Alberta, impotent and guilty. And so am I. I ought to fight for this, struggle and not give in. He needs friends again, kind ones, not too rough, not too

626

pliant either. I dare not let him run loose on the streets. A good thing that idea has not occurred to Sivert. A good thing he . . .

For Sivert, on the contrary, said: 'The boy will probably find someone to play with. I daresay a solution will be found.' He seemed to be saying, 'Don't interfere. I have my plans.' Paralysed in the face of the mystery of Sivert's plans, which were perhaps completely out of her range of vision in any case, Alberta could not bring herself to ask further questions.

She would sit beside the shrubbery in the middle of the courtyard, sewing, shelling broad beans, or doing some other task, while the boy pottered about, in and out of the open studio door. She could see straight into the corner which did duty as a sitting-room: two divans at right-angles, book-shelves on the wall above them and a table in front, draperies and cushions, two new ones in Hungarian embroidery amongst them, looking bright and luxurious; at the end of one of the divans Tot's corner with his rocking horse, bought after a struggle, the chair and table that Sivert had made some time ago, the box with old objects that the boy himself had col-lected and put away. Out of doors strong, baking sunshine lay like a flaming puddle between the houses for a brief while, then began to move, creeping upwards along a brick gable, sliding over at an angle to the next and the next, higher and higher as the day progressed. Indoors the air had something clammy and mildewed about it that Alberta never managed to dispel. Every time the boy disappeared through the door she was on the point of calling him back, but stopped herself so as not to nag.

Minute by minute she had to force herself to sit there at all. Longings passed through her in unnerving confusion: the long-ing to be a peaceful woman, looking after her husband and children competently without yearning for anything else, watching them prosper and grow about her, receiving diffident, rough caresses for reward, pats like blows, embraces en-dangering life and limb; the longing to be back in possession of the old, modest freedom that had once been hers, to use it properly and sensibly, making room in it for Tot, for the future, for interests beyond the immediate, for knowledge;

the longing simply to get to her feet, take the boy by the hand, and go. Where? Out into the city. Down into the Rue Notre Dame des Champs to where it joined the Rue de Rennes. What business had she there? Whatever happened she would not reveal anything, confess anything, she would grit her teeth above her secret. Nevertheless she wandered about down there in her thoughts, imagining sudden meetings on corners, words casually spoken that made life good and candid.

She brought herself home again. There was a scent of box from the low hedge surrounding the shrubbery, which consisted of three aspidistras and a skinny fan palm, grouped in pots round a deformed acacia. She tore off a leaf now and again, crushed it between her fingers and inhaled the astringent perfume, which became so strong in the sun and reminded her of Versailles. Smoke blew down from nearby chimneys, black nauseating coal smoke; and the woolly, pale wood smoke, that had hung thick in the kitchen as soon as they lighted the impossible stove, making her eyes smart, smelling of burning undergrowth and Lapp camps, came back to her, one of the things in life she had not appreciated sufficiently at the time. She remembered the smell of hay and flowers, seaweed and salt, pleasant working sounds, drifting clouds, Jean-Marie plodding over the hill with a basket of fish on his head the second day and turning out to be the Jean of long ago. She had not been surprised, nor had he. For much had happened, and life was no longer surprising except perhaps where Sivert was concerned. Jean-Marie had told her about his wife, a splendid wife in every respect, away for the moment because of illness at home. She would be ready to come and help them later if they needed anybody—

'Tot!'

The boy looked up from what he was doing.

'The mirror is pretty now.'

'It's the sun,' he said briefly and continued with his play.

It was the sun. And it was just as well he no longer ran indoors every time a window, swinging on its hinges in the house at the other side of the street, threw reflections into the far end of the studio, into Sivert's big mirror. Emeralds and rubies caught fire along its edge. When the boy was small he had been seized with that mute wildness: each time it happened he had stood on tiptoe trying to catch the splendour with his hands; then refused to go out again, and sat down, his face radiant, waiting for it to happen again. 'It's pretty,' he would say to himself. 'Tot thinks it's pretty.'

There was no need to regret it. It was good for him to be out of doors, good that he was growing bigger and more reasonable. But values always slipped between her fingers before she had time to come to her senses and realise that she possessed them. She must have lost the ability to grasp the fleeting moment during the endless years of the war. And yet every second became precious, acquiring value of its own as soon as she thought back to the first night when the bombers could no longer be expected, to the deep, unaccustomed peace of the morning after with its atmosphere of resurrection and new life, of limitless possibilities.

'Why don't you come and help me for a while, Tot? Here, take some beans and we'll see who can shell them the fastest.'

'You shell them the fastest, and you like doing it. I don't.'

'Are you sure I like doing it?'

'It's what mothers do.'

'That's true,' said Alberta. The boy suddenly seemed to resemble Sivert in a way that was almost horrible: Sivert's ability to dash cold water over one's enthusiasm and extinguish it effectively and at once. It was not right that a child should be so like an adult. The thought worried her, as if she had been unjustly severe towards Tot. She put the things down to take him in her arms, but did not do so. One can be reserved in one's love for a child, just as in other relationships. Since the episode on the beach he had withdrawn into himself again, twisting mutely away from her, refusing to agree to her suggestions but doing so when they came from Sivert. She could have put up with a great deal if only he had been different.

She caught herself down in the Rue Notre Dame des Champs again. Pierre had found a solution satisfactory to all parties. What solution? What indeed? But something had to happen. Her longing was so great that surely no-one could

long so much without something happening. She must be
liberated, or else die.

The men from the studios round about passed by now and
again. 'What a good little boy he is, Madame. You don't
often see such a quiet child. He looks a thoughtful little soul.'
And they patted him on the head.

The models came, squatted down and tried to talk to him.
'What a sweet little boy. Oh, what blue eyes you've got, I've
never seen anything like it, blue as the sky.' And they turned
to Alberta. 'I'm crazy about children, utterly crazy. You're
fortunate, Madame: a husband, a beautiful child, peace and
quiet. As for us—He's a bit thin, but very sweet,' they concluded, and hurried on.

Madame Morin came. She was a large, masculine person,
feared by her neighbours, brusquely friendly towards Alberta.
The fact that Alberta had settled here, had a child and stayed,
in contrast to the rest of the women-folk who frequented the
studios; and that she looked after the boy instead of simply
putting him outside to play, had given her standing. Madame
Morin addressed her as Madame Ness, although an occasional
letter would arrive for Mademoiselle. She even held her up as
an example: 'If only everyone behaved like Madame Ness.
She's *comme il faut,* a good mother.' Oh indeed, thought
Alberta.

Now she had spent the summer in the country. This made
her highly respectable, an ornament of the whole courtyard,
a person Madame Morin took pleasure in conversing with.
'You're right to take advantage of the sun, Madame, right to
keep Tot out of doors as much as possible. Now that he has
become stronger you must keep him that way. Not all mothers
look after their children like you. But then we do have a little
bit of green here, it is a great advantage. I don't draw a bucket
of water that doesn't end up out here: water for scrubbing
the floors, for washing the dishes, both of them are excellent
for vegetation, I assure you. The summer is so dry in Paris.
Enfin, one does one's best. And Monsieur is still working
out of doors? He is industrious, I grant him that.'

'Yes,' said Alberta. She thought she detected a slight under-tone in Madame Morin's voice, as if she had really wanted to say something else. Had she not made some remark the day she came in and noticed the two new sofa cushions? If Alberta had had a confused notion that, in spite of everything, perhaps they had been meant as a surprise for her, this had been thoroughly dispelled.

'Nice to see that Monsieur thinks of Madame,' commented Madame Morin.

'I was expecting guests,' Sivert said, as off-handedly as only he knew how. 'So I bought them. I thought a little colour would be an improvement.'

'Well, well, Monsieur wanted everything to look its best in Madame's absence. An interior is judged according to the woman who lives in it. That's how a husband reasons. It's charming, it's touching.'

'My word, how she does poke her nose into things,' said Sivert angrily in Norwegian, rattling canvases against the wall and pretending he was no longer following the conversation.

'We shall have to put her in her place soon, to stop her getting too meddlesome,' he said when she had gone. Alberta trembled for a couple of days in case he should attempt such a thing. But nothing happened, and she breathed more easily. Madame Morin could not be put in her place; she occupied the place she already had with justification. When the shortage of fuel, butter, sugar, milk and proper flour had been at its worst, and Sivert had come home empty-handed from the queues, she had saved the situation more than once. 'A child must not lack for anything. We adults can manage,' she would say, putting small paper bags and packets on the table, or placing a bucket of coal inside the door. Perhaps she did stand with arms akimbo expressing her humble opinion about one thing or another, since she had looked in anyway. But Tot got soup, warm milk, porridge, warmth from the stove. It would be impossible to dislodge Madame Morin.

The attention excited by the cushions was irritating to all concerned. Alberta felt she was being pitied for her simplicity, it made her want to shout: 'They're there with my full approval; I like them.' It made her think uneasily: Supposing it's serious between Sivert and this other woman—then, then—

At once she saw Jeanne, heard her saying, 'Sit down. It's quite safe to sit down. I'm not the revolver type, I don't carry a dagger. If you think I'm so frightened of you . . .' She saw Marthe, sound, healthy and secure, and guided her thoughts elsewhere.

Liesel whistled when she saw the cushions. She said: 'He's starting to buy things. We recognize that symptom, thank you.'

Sivert was out of doors, painting. Sometimes he came home to lunch, sometimes not. There was no need to wonder whether he had company on these expeditions; there was much to betray the fact. The *pneumatiques* he stuck in his pocket, whistling, betrayed it. On the canvases he brought home Alberta saw Paris again, a city pale with moist air, a city of light coloured stone, autumn colours and sunshine against a heavy, pastel blue sky. Was Sivert's latest work good or bad? Something of Cubist geometry and ascetic colour appeared here and there in his flamboyant palette; the effect was as if a stranger had shared in the picture. He himself was pleased. 'At last I'm beginning to find my own style,' he said.

He was, and always would be, surprising. Did he not take Alberta and the boy unasked to Galeries Lafayette one day? Tot was given plenty of new clothes, Alberta a dress, coat and hat. When she went over to look at the price tickets and let them fall again because they seemed to her fantastically high, Sivert had said: 'Try it on. You can try it on, after all. It's expensive, but never mind.' she had come home with things she had not even dreamed of possessing.

'It's too big an outlay, Sivert. I'll take the bus down and change it.'

'If you're pleased with it you're to keep it,' Sivert said. 'Then at least you'll have something.'

He said nothing to the effect that now he would not have to listen to nagging about clothes for a while. On this occasion Sivert was generous throughout, merely slapping himself on the hand with his gloves before putting them down. 'I'm glad you found something you liked,' he said, when Alberta finally thanked him and hung the clothes neatly behind the curtain in the attic. She wished it could have been possible to say a little more, but it did not seem to be.

It was a long time since she had owned clothes she liked wearing, clothes that suited her and suited each other. When she went to the Luxembourg Gardens in the afternoon with Tot she looked like a comparatively carefree woman, with all her affairs in order. Tot was a well-dressed little boy with a vanishing layer of sunburn on his strange small face, with thin calves and large knees sticking out of small nautical trousers, a checked ball under his arm and a hoop. Mothers of a different category from the ones on the Avenue du Maine, handsome women with beautiful embroidery, often in mourning, talked to him and to Alberta, graciously inviting him to play with their children. Occasionally he would agree to throw his ball. When it was discovered that he was Norwegian, the ladies would ask, leaning forward with anxious faces: 'Norway is a friend of France, isn't she?' Alberta assured them that she was. She smiled with them at the children and held her sewing as naturally as possible.

A gnawing feeling that time was passing and something quite different ought to be happening possessed her day and night. It was an old acquaintance, the kind one never manages to shake off. She often looked round her involuntarily, and sometimes felt a pang at the sight of a back, a way of walking, a contour. Ha, ha, Alberta, you've gone round staring at shadows before, she thought. Even Jeanne was nowhere to be seen, although Alberta consistently stayed in the part of the Gardens where she had said she was to be found.

On the way home they walked along streets abandoned by the sun which resembled dark chasms between the houses. The air was thick with petrol vapour and food smells. Tot dragged his feet and whined, as if the shadow and the waning day oppressed him. But in spite of it all Alberta could feel herself moving in the light, weightless fashion of those in love.

When she opened the studio door stale air struck her. Not

until the cold weather came would there be any kind of ventilation through the few panes that it was possible to open. She left the door wide open, and the long evening began to pass.

Sivert came home briefly for dinner, though often he would not appear even then. 'I must be off again,' he would say, 'But if you want to go out, just go. Tot's old enough now. It's time he learned to be alone in the evening occasionally.' Sivert looked at her sideways; she felt as if he were studying her.

'I shouldn't dream of it.'

'You're indulging the boy.'

'I'm only thinking of the possibility of fire.'

'There won't be a fire.'

But Alberta pictured Tot alone in the big studio, where the darkness unfolded itself out of the corners like black mist, remembered how he would sometimes wake up, frightened and restless, and said no more.

It was when he was finally asleep that her longing became unbearable. She wandered up and down the courtyard, through the branches of the acacia sketched in the gravel by the nearest street lamp, watching the play of living shadows in the lighted windows on the opposite side of the street, a theatre of silhouettes in friendly, unfriendly, indifferent, sometimes affectionate inter-action: good performances, taken individually, under uncertain and temperamental direction. Until, little by little, the shutters were closed everywhere and the performance was over. This happened early in the evening. The actors were working folk.

She sat down with a book in the corner that was the sitting-room. Sivert had bought a considerable number of new books. Under different circumstances she would have devoured them, lived through them, perhaps been changed by them. Sivert was no fool. He could unexpectedly rise to a higher level very successfully, bringing home literature that made her wonder how he had found it at all. It was one of the characteristics that had always brought out her former affection and her regret for what ought to have been and never was. Now she put the book down without knowing what she had read. It did not occur to her to write. She went outside again and wandered up and down. It was quiet in the narrow streets, dark in the studios. Nobody lived in them besides Sivert and Alberta. Dark at Madame Morin's. From the Avenue du Maine came the jangling of tram bells, the senseless, angry hooting of motor cars. Alberta's footsteps crunched unnaturally loudly, as if somebody were walking at her side or immediately behind her.

She had experienced loneliness, the will to live, blind desire, the play of blood and nerves in walking and breathing, affection, gratitude, a sense of duty, understanding, but never before this unconditional longing for another, as if she herself were only a half, lost and astray. Against this feeling she could now weigh and measure the life she shared with Sivert. It had withered rapidly, losing the first buds early. The boy had monopolized her, there had been no way of avoiding it, and one receives according to what one gives, in this as in much else.

Sivert first became passive, later indifferent. He had once been fond enough of her to pursue her, but he probably had not imagined things turning out as they did. She herself had been satisfied, she supposed, until the needs of the child had destroyed the framework. Things could look like this when the horizon had widened and one had progressed round them.

Beneath all her pondering, for and against, there was hope. Pierre would find a solution, make a move in one direction or another, turn up again at the very least. Tomorrow she would know. The post would come, a telegram would come. Now, in a little while, it would come. Telegrams were delivered even at night.

Nothing came. The uneventful moments linked themselves to each other, endlessly, pitilessly, as they had done so many times before. She was worried by suspicions that the man expects the woman to act in such a situation: to take the responsibility, even the initiative. She would not be saddled with that, not even for Pierre. Jeanne had won him back, and this was the most suitable, the most fortunate, the only reasonable solution. Won him back? She had never really lost him, he had only been tired. And here was Alberta taking it all seriously, longing with every drop of blood in her body to such an extent that she felt it in her face, her breast, her lap; peering into the past and the future and believing herself to be in the grip of the power that governs the world and upsets fate. Ridiculous.

But when she awoke in the early hours, her head heavy, half unconscious with veronal, her pillow was wet with tears. She sat up in bed, stretching out her arms in the clammy, airless darkness, as if other hands were ready to grasp hers, to draw her with them, if only she could find them.

Sivert slept, his breathing regular as clockwork.

She heard *about* Pierre, in snatches and inadequately.

Liesel came, pale, somewhat out of breath but, according to herself, stronger and more energetic than before. She inspected Alberta's new clothes, feeling the material. 'Nice. Suspiciously nice. A silent apology, or else an advertisement for his generosity. Difficult to tell yet. It's that Swedish artist. Sivert and Eliel are equally mad about her, but Sivert has priority; you know how men are. They sit at the Dôme with her, paying for one drink after the other. She's the type who can take plenty—doesn't get drunk on half a glass of wine like us. It's called priority, isn't it, Albertchen?'

'I expect so, Liesel. So it's the Swedish artist? You see, I know nothing about it. What's she like otherwise?'

'Not Sivert's type, I shouldn't have thought. Expensive to run, fox furs and lots of rings. They say she has money. And she sings. Men have a weakness for that type. She's in the habit of bursting into song when they're sitting with her at Leduc's so that everyone turns their heads to look. If somebody comes and plays outside she joins in with soprano and alto and God knows what. Apparently she's studied singing. And we're not like that, Albertchen. I have some of it from Eliel and some of it from Alphonsine, whom I met the other day. She asked after you. She's married her mechanic now, and lives in Vanves, in a villa with chickens. When she's in town she eats at the usual places. We're to go out to see her one day. She has got quite fat. Marushka is back on Montparnasse. She still seems to manage, heaven knows how.'

Marushka was somewhat of a mystery. She got nothing from Russia any more. On the other hand two relations had landed themselves on her, two destitute refugees who had arrived in Paris after an adventurous journey through Sweden, Norway and England. Marushka kept them, painted, was as chic and well-dressed as before, but did not look well. 'Either she's burning the candle at both ends or else she's been as stupid as I was. No-one can tell me there's nothing the matter,' said Liesel.

The little medical student from Canada that Alberta knew, the one who had been expecting a baby by Foresti the painter, was up and about again, thin as a ghost in her white smock. In bed for nine days. Liesel had visited her at the hospital where she worked. The child was being fostered at Vincennes. She was worried about it because she could not afford to pay very much. She had said: 'If I have to go on the streets, then there's nothing else for it.' But all she said about Foresti was: 'Such a fine person, in his art, in every way, if only he didn't drink.' 'They always say that about their revolting men,' said Liesel. 'Of course she never hears from him. Potter is supposed to be back.'

Potter? thought Alberta, in distraction. Wasn't Liesel beginning to remind her a little of Potter, expressing herself in the same brusque, hard fashion, only not quite so cynically? Perhaps once upon a time Potter too had been young, gentle and charming?

Jeanne was beside herself because Pierre was always going off to meetings on Montmartre. He seemed to have become a thorough Bolshevik. His book was not finished yet.

At last. Alberta felt her heart flutter. At last we're getting to what is important. She devoured the words, pretending only moderate interest.

'Oh, Liesel? How are Pierre and Jeanne anyway? Who is she afraid is going to steal him from her now?'

'You,' answered Liesel dryly.

'I?' Alberta laughed a false, ringing laugh and was suddenly weightless, full of sweet dizziness. 'Surely she's given up by this time. I'm stuck here. I don't even see him.'

637

'That's no guarantee. Eliel says Jeanne wants to take him home to Dijon again. If you don't do something, Albertchen, she'll get her way.'

'Now, Liesel.'

'I'm going to speak my mind,' Liesel announced. 'I'm not keeping my mouth shut any longer. I'm tired of it, so why not speak frankly. It's a pity you and Sivert have a child and Pierre and Jean too. It takes money to arrange such matters, and that makes it difficult for people like ourselves.'

'How you do talk, Liesel!'

'Yes, yes,' said Liesel in a tired voice. 'Yes, yes.' As if she was saying: The world must go its own way without me.

She did not stay long. A new restlessness had seized her, an uneasy busyness. She was off to Colarossi's to sketch or else home to cook the dinner. Alberta watched her go, thinking that she had become alarmingly thin inside her clothes at the back. She thought: Liesel must pull herself together and go to a doctor. I ought to tell her in such a way that she understands it's imperative. And she forgot her for her own affairs again. If she had fought to keep a little calmness and presence of mind, it was dispelled now. Everything dangerous was again let loose. She tossed between two parallel lives and was pummelled weak and senseless. Her daily existence could not be the right one.

She took out the letter from Jacob. It was easy to find in her handbag. Through the brief contents she attempted again and again to see him as he must look now. But the picture he had sent her once, standing on the deck of a ship, got in her way. It had erased the memory of him as he was when he had left home. She remembered broad shoulders in a new seaman's tunic, remembered his lifting his sea-chest now with the right, now with the left hand, and that he had whistled and talked to Papa as one grown man to another. But his face was missing. And nothing was left of the schoolboy, or of the many anxieties of their years together as children, besides a pair of red fists sticking out of outgrown sleeves.

Now Jacob had sheep, not many by Australian standards, but he hoped for more. During the war he had threatened to enlist. Then he had had no sheep, but merely sheared them for others and was sometimes out of work. He no longer said, 'I'll stay for one more year'; he said, 'for several years'. He told her about the sheep, about the house he had built himself with another fellow, about how they looked after themselves, what the war had meant for people like him. And as a post-script: 'If that man not marry you or you want to marry him, come over here with the boy. If I get married, you and he can live here all the same. I'm all right, not a rich man, but you would not go without. I'll go and send money for the ticket if you want. That big boy of yours, I often think of him. Give him a good kiss from his uncle. Keep cheerful dear, take good care of yourself.'

Jacob's Norwegian became less Norwegian and more English with every year that passed. He had not found land in Norway, but sheep in quite another part of the world.

'Do you remember you have an uncle, Tot?'

'I have an aunt too.'

'An aunt, a grandpapa and a grandmama in Norway. And an uncle in Australia.'

'Australia, where's that?' The boy did not look up from the piece of wood into which he was hammering nails. She could hear that he was asking out of politeness, a child's politeness, that can be far more chilling than an adult's.

'It's far away on the other side of the world. It takes several months to get there by boat. Uncle Jacob has sheep, lots of sheep.'

'Does he?' said the boy, just like Sivert. Shortly afterwards he asked: 'Is a grandpapa only Father's father?'

'No, Mother's too.'

'But you have no father?'

'He's dead.'

'Dead? What's that?'

'It's—it's—it's falling asleep forever.'

'Can't anybody wake you up?'

'No.'

'I see.' The boy hammered away at his piece of wood and fell silent.

When he was a few weeks old Alberta had written about him to Jacob, telling him the truth without wrapping it up in explanations: I have had a child, Jacob, a little boy. Jacob had replied: That's all right, Alberta. If you need me, let me know. A cheque for five pounds was enclosed in the letter.

At home in Norway they knew about it too. She knew they knew about it, though she did not know who had passed on the information. For a time she had ransacked her brain, trying to present the matter in a way which would break the news while keeping them at a lifelong distance. But she had never sent the letter, and she soon became indifferent to what they thought of her up there on the other side of the war. They were no longer able to send travellers to descend on her. Events had proved even stronger than Aunt. She no longer heard from anyone in Norway.

Marry? She and Sivert? They must, for the sake of the boy. Everything would be better if they did. Sivert must be of the same opinion. It must happen before the boy started school; there would be expense and inconvenience. Would it be dissolved afterwards . . . ?

'Come here, Tot, let's read our ABC.'

'No,' Tot said and went on hammering.

And Alberta, who wanted to prepare him on this point, to give him some literary superiority, and really had managed to get him to learn a few of the letters, bent her head over her sewing again. She ought to exert her authority in a good many matters. The reason for not doing so must have been her paralysing uncertainty about Sivert.

She ought to work at something lucrative. It became more pressing with each passing day. In thought she scrutinized her inefficiency thoroughly, found nothing but her writing and turned from it despondently. Never had it seemed more ridiculous, more distant, more impossible than now.

She applied herself to household tasks, mending and darning far beyond what was profitable and reasonable, cooking in new and more thorough ways, even baking in an upturned cake box on the miserable primus. Then she would have periods of doing nothing as if addicted to a vice for which she despised herself.

Occasionally she was seized with savagery. This was her life, it really was *her* life, these uniform days that passed, one after the other. It was no longer something that occurred; it was a drain she could less and less afford.

Then she would catch sight of the boy's head as he bent over something, and thought: I shall never leave *you*. As if somebody had proposed that she should.

One day she was able to tell Sivert that Pierre had been there. She felt as if she were telling him that a spirit had manifested itself. It had been brief and unexpected as a vision. She was sitting outside the door. Suddenly Pierre was standing just inside the gate, then coming towards her round the shrubbery. She had no time to be surprised, no time to blush or turn pale. Mechanically she stroked Tot's hair; he had immediately come to her and clung to her as he seldom did. Pierre had stood looking at him the short while he was there, they both looked at him. Pierre asked her how she was. Very well, thank you, and he? From her confused brain she produced a conjecture about his departure to Dijon. Pierre shrugged his shoulders, he was not sure. A couple of times she noticed him glance, wearily and ironically, at her sewing, and it gave her confidence. All the same, the atmosphere quickly became raher oppressive. 'Sivert isn't at home,' Alberta informed him. 'Well, never mind.' Pierre patted Tot on the head, said something about just wanting to look in, since he had been in that district, and left. He left! Only then did Alberta realise that he had altered; or he had let the mask fall for good, one of the two. At the gate he turned and called out a greeting from Jeanne and Marthe, as if remembering something urgent at the last moment. Then he was gone. Alberta was still bewildered, restless in her arms and hands, as if something had been torn away from her by force. Instinctively she hastened to tell Sivert about the visit, to minimize its importance and steal a march on Tot. 'Fancy, Pierre looked in.'

'Did he?' Sivert replied. 'That fellow? What's he fooling about with nowadays?'

'Fooling?' Alberta instantly regretted taking up the challenge. Sivert's eyes met hers briefly, and a mixture of triumph, inquisitiveness, satisfaction was in them. Satisfaction?

'Yes, fooling. Surely it ought to be possible to slap together that everlasting book in a hurry, when he has spent so much time on it; an experienced fellow like that. But he's lazy, that's the trouble. He's not the only person to have gone to the war. A man ought to be able to pull himself together and make a new start.'

'You yourself have sometimes said he was ill.'

'Depends what you mean by ill. There are people who hide behind the notion that they're ill, run away from life into illness,' stated Sivert categorically. 'But of course, in this old-fashioned country they just pander to such cases. It'll take centuries before they catch up.'

'Catch up with what?'

'Oh, various matters.'

'What an authority you've become.'

'I keep up to date; I've studied one thing and another during the past few years.'

'Dr Freytag's box?'

'Amongst other things, yes. To change the subject, I may bring a visitor here one of these days. A Swedish girl who paints, a very pleasant acquaintance. You might perhaps wear your new dress. And I suppose we ought to offer her something to eat?'

Alberta paused on the way from the primus to the table. She almost dropped the dish with the ham and lentils. She was about to protest. She was not unfriendly, but the situation was a false one. She had a desire to call out, 'It's no good this way, we must tackle it differently.'

'Very well,' she replied. 'When will you be coming?'

'I thought Thursday, at about half past four. See that Tot looks decent, won't you? He could wear his new clothes too, perhaps? I meet her at the Dôme. We're going to look at some of my pictures.'

'Will it be the first time she's been here?' asked Alberta as indifferently as she could.

'Ye-e-es, no as a matter of fact she has been up before. I value her opinion highly. A wonderfully talented person. A strange person. She originally studied singing. Then she became obsessed with the idea that she wanted to paint. But there, she has other obsessions too.'

'Oh?'

'A strange person, as I said. For a woman, at any rate. Remarkable. I've never met anyone like her. No coffee for me, thank you. So if you're not having any—'

'I *am* having some,' said Alberta, pumping her enemy the primus so hard that it smoked.

'Well, well. How is it you can never learn to deal with that poor primus?' Sivert took over, and succeeded, in this as in everything else. Then he began to inspect his pictures, displaying some of them along the wall, and putting others away. As if quite by chance he went across and rearranged the sofa cushions, trying out different effects. Silly Sivert, thought Alberta, with sudden affection.

When the gate moved on its hinges her heart began to hammer. She heard footsteps and voices, pulled herself together and went to the door. Sivert and a tall stranger with so much fur round her shoulders that she resembled a returning trapper, were just rounding the shrubbery. She felt their eyes on her. She thought mechanically: No worse!

'Come in,' she said. 'I'm so glad you could come.'

'Yes, I'm so glad too, to be meeting Sivert's wife. We've talked about it so often. But some things never seem to come about here in Paris. There is such an enormous amount to get through. Fru Ness knows how it is. But what a pleasant place to live in, how attractive those plants are. This is the way to live, not in an ordinary, banal hotel.'

A powerful hand took Alberta's. And Alberta felt as if it was quite normal that they should touch each other, as if it was inevitable. She pressed the hand hastily and preceded them indoors. She heard Sivert say: 'Yes, it is pleasant, don't you

643

agree? Isn't that what I told you, my dear, this is how you ought to live.' The rapid, accustomed 'my dear' at once seemed to her more decisive than an open embrace. With trembling hands she rearranged the tea table.

She had bought a tart and some nice little cakes, made delicate ham sandwiches, brought out the best cups, flowers and fruit. But the stranger would eat nothing, she never ate between meals. She could scarcely be persuaded to take a cup of tea without sugar, with a cigarette which she herself took out. She smiled indulgently at the things Alberta offered her, as if at a children's party. 'It'll soon be aperitif time,' she said. 'You should have remembered, Sivert, that I never take tea and that sort of thing. Such a pity Fru Ness has gone to all that trouble.' Abstractedly she looked at the boy, who was watching her shyly, threw away her half-smoked cigarette and immediately lighted a fresh one. 'What a sweet little boy you have.'

Sivert struck himself on the forehead. 'What an idiot I am! I'll run round the corner for a bottle of Dubonnet. Or would you prefer Byrrh? Italian vermouth? Amer-Picon?'

'What I'd really like at this moment, Sivert,' said their guest slowly, staring at him, 'is an ice-cold absinthe. And that you cannot get me.'

'Nobody else can either. It's been illegal since the beginning of the war.'

'What of it? If we were to give up what is illegal, what fun should we have? I drink absinthe every day. In that way I at least avoid that kind of complex. You look shocked? My dear, you can always find someone who can get hold of it. But hurry up and show me your pictures. We're going back to town again soon, aren't we?'

Sivert threw out his hands, powerless where absinthe was concerned. They both left the useless tea-table and began to inspect Sivert's pictures, which he lined up along the wall. Alberta listened to the stranger as she expressed her opinions, and had to admit that she did so clearly and wisely, without hesitation or deviousness. She listened to Sivert's respectful, almost grateful, 'Do you think so? I suppose I've seen it myself, but—. Too anecdotal? Not constructive enough? Merely sketches, preparatory work? I understand it from your point of view. But don't you think that—? Well, I'm glad you think so. Thank you.'

This is how they suit each other, thought Alberta involuntarily, as if she were marrying off a young, inexperienced Sivert. At the same time she could not help feeling exceedingly embarrassed on his behalf, if only for the fact that he was so small by comparison with her.

She was tall and well-built, with restless grey eyes which contrasted oddly with the childish bow of her upper lip. Her profile was clear-cut and strong, she was beautiful. But her complexion was sallow, her hair lank and dull. She looked as if she had lived through a good deal.

She was smartly dressed. Alberta had seen the same type of clothes at Lafayette and had an idea of the price; they were the kind whose price tags one did not even bother to read. She had taken off her fur; it lay in a heap on the chair she had left, teeming with tails and paws. And Alberta felt even more sorry for Sivert. He was so innocent where women's clothes were concerned. They all seemed to him to cost far more than they ought, and that was that. Suddenly she seemed to hear Potter: 'Men don't think with their brains, dear, they think with something further down.' No—Potter had said the heart. She did not deny men brains. It was Alberta's black soul that did that.

'Taking her home—oh, isn't that a dirty trick? She's hard up for a man, he wants to clean his body, that's all.' The way Potter had talked on many occasions. Alberta felt as if she had her sitting here on the divan, whispering the hard, brusque sentences in her ear. Again she rearranged the tea-table, to give herself something to do and to get away from the nastiness of her thoughts. What right had she to remember them? She wished Potter had never expressed an opinion on anything.

Alberta felt humiliated by the whole situation, by her own state of mind, by the new dress she had put on, the table she had taken such pains over. If Sivert and this woman wanted to live together, why not come to the point without mincing matters? The situation was difficult enough as it was. But men seemed to have a mania for inviting their paramours home. Alberta pictured Liesel pouring out coffee for well-built, well-dressed Swedish girls who talked terribly loudly, had use for Eliel for a time, and took him. Or acted that way. Eliel also acted that way. He seemed purposely to heap Liesel with indignities.

Alberta went outside, leading Tot by the hand. Fortunately he went with a good grace without adding another defeat to the number. Madame Morin was standing in the courtyard, inspecting the shrubbery. They embarked on an animated conversation. Alberta did not have to listen to the vivacious exclamations from indoors every time Sivert turned a new canvas round. She talked at random about this and that, about the weather. Suddenly, the sound of singing came from the studio. A deep, rather rough, but true voice moved up and down in operatic recitative and then dropped into speech. Madame Morin leaned over: 'That's the one. Now she's singing. She was here when you were away too. Not to my taste. Women like her cause nothing but trouble. Be on your guard. You know what men are—No, this year the box hedge is not as it ought to be. I've watered it, I've pruned it, but what can you expect? It was scorching all July and August.'

Sivert and his companion had come to the doorway. He looked at Alberta, who went towards them with a toss of the head, saying effusively, 'Must you go already? How kind of you to come. It was a pleasure. Sivert has talked about you so often. Do come again very soon now that you know the way.'

Again she had the powerful hand in hers. Red fox furs and restless grey eyes flickered in front of her. 'Charmed to meet Fru Ness, charmed to meet your sweet little boy. It's very pleasant here, I think, so peaceful and pretty. Well, now I'm afraid I must rush off, Sivert.'

'I'm coming, I'm coming,' Sivert slapped his hand with his gloves. 'Good-bye Tot, good-bye Alberta. I shan't be late.' His eyes seemed to be apologizing for the situation.

She was left behind with the silent little boy. When the gate banged shut he said: 'That was not a nice auntie.'

646

'Oh yes, Tot, of course, a very nice auntie.' Alberta turned and looked into the sitting-room corner. Each little detail had cost her willpower or persuasion, fumbling and bother with needle and thread, maintenance, cleaning, resignation. Something had inspired her, something she had wanted to create in here. It had never turned out as she wanted. Now the new cushions led their own threatening life on the divan, and the ashtrays were overflowing with half-smoked cigarettes with a strange aroma.

A feeling of intense loneliness and helplessness seized her; and of pity for Sivert.

When he came home she had been in bed for a long time, pretending to read. As he got into bed he said : 'That reminds me, Jeanne wished to be remembered to you.'

'Jeanne?' Alberta propped herself up on her elbow and shut the book.

'Ran into her on the way down. She's leaving for Dijon tomorrow with Marthe. They're letting the apartment for the winter. She would have come up, but has had so much to do. Hoped to come to Paris just before Christmas, and would look in on you then.'

'Oh?'

Alberta failed to say more. Jeanne was leaving, Marthe was leaving, the apartment was being let. But what about Pierre? Had they ceased to take him into account? He was not dead, nor had he disappeared. He lived and breathed a few *quartiers* away. Her head swam. Then she noticed Sivert's sidelong glance, quick, cunning, his eyebrows slightly raised. 'I suppose Pierre is leaving too. In a few days. It's the best thing for him. He wished to be remembered to you too, by the way. Just caught a glimpse of him.'

'Thank you. So they're leaving?' It was possible to say such things coldly and quietly.

'Yes, they're leaving. Things are getting worse instead of better with Pierre here in Paris. He doesn't even write any more, not even short stories. His publisher is said to have lost patience completely. He said, "Not one more sou until I have

647

the manuscript on my desk." It's tactics to put pressure on poor old Pierre. But Jeanne has to be responsible for the rent and the taxes, food and clothes and insurance. They say Pierre is scarcely ever at home; he's taking part in readings and that sort of thing.'

'Readings?'

'Yes. There are some people, actors and intellectuals, who have decided to put on plays together, art for the masses and so on, all of it free. Jeanne's quite right when she says he can't feed a wife and child on that. According to Eliel, they've been in a fantastic state. He was up there the other day. Jeanne and Marthe hadn't any food even. Now she's delivered an ultimatum and is going home. If he doesn't come to some arrangement with the publisher and finish that everlasting novel of his he'll never see her or Marthe again. Not surprising either.'

'If only he could write in peace—. There are other things he wants to do.'

'It's no damned good sitting down and saying there are other things he wants to do. You have to finish one thing at a time before you start on anything else. Look at most of the people who have been to the war. They take up the threads where they left off and are happy to do so. I'm beginning to think that Pierre is pretty spineless. I used to be sorry for him, but now that I've seen at close quarters how confoundedly difficult it is for Jeanne—. It's no fun to have to go home because her husband can't keep her.'

'It won't be much fun for Pierre either.' Alberta spoke bitterly, angry with herself because she could not defend him any better. Pierre's weakness was only on the surface. In reality he was stronger than any of them, braver, richer in goodness. But how could that be proved?

'Then he'll have to behave like a man, so help me,' Sivert said. 'I must say he's not much of one.'

'He has the *Croix de Guerre*,' replied Alberta in her impotence.

'Ye-es—maybe it's easier to earn that than to face everyday life.' Sivert turned off his lamp.

Alberta turned off her lamp too. Almost immediately she turned it on again, grasping for her book as if for a lifebelt. Grumbling, Sivert turned over on to his other side. A moment later he was asleep.

* * *

'It's me, Albertchen.'

'Come in Liesel. Quietly. Tot's asleep for once. Fetch a chair, we can sit outside. It's mild this evening. Nice of you to come.'

Liesel stood unexpectedly in the doorway, faintly illuminated by the lamp that Alberta had turned on in the corner by the divan. She was so out of breath that Alberta was frightened and said, 'But Liesel! Have you been walking too fast again? You know you shouldn't. Sit down. I'll make some tea. I'm so glad you've come. I'm all on my own—'

'Albertchen, put on your new clothes, your dress, coat, hat, hurry.' Liesel sat down holding her throat as if to release her exhausted breathing.

'But my dear Liesel, I never go out in the evening, you know that. Tot—'

'I'll stay with Tot. Get your things and go.'

'Go? Where should I go?'

'Down to the corner of the Avenue du Maine, Albertchen. Outside the café. Pierre is waiting for you.'

'Pierre? At the corner? Hasn't Pierre left?' asked Alberta foolishly.

'He's there, he's waiting for you. Don't ask me to explain so much; I've got a stitch, I've walked too quickly, as you say.' Liesel put her hand between her shoulder blades and coughed.

'Can't he come here?' asked Alberta severely to cover herself.

Liesel nodded in the direction of the attic, where Tot was asleep. 'He probably wants to talk to you alone. Besides, he wants to take you out. Get yourself ready and go.'

Alberta had already brought down her clothes and was in

the process of changing, powdering her face haphazardly in the inadequate light. She had not thought for an instant of refusing to go, but she begged for persuasion as one begs for stupefying drugs. While doing so she attempted to gather her strength, the little she had, searching it out from the corners of her mind and putting it where it would be sorely needed, in her voice, her cadences, her expression. 'What an extraordinary idea. At this time of day.'

'Do you think so? There must be something the matter.'

'The matter? With Jeanne? Or with Marthe?'

'I don't think so. Nor do you. Now hurry. I met him outside the Dôme.'

'I don't want Jeanne to be able to make any more accusations,' began Alberta. She had buttoned several of the tiny buttons on her dress wrongly and had to do up the long row all over again. 'Jeanne takes everything in one way.'

'Jeanne is in Dijon.'

'But Sivert is here.'

'Sivert is at Montmartre this evening with the Swede and Eliel. Don't get home too late, that's all. Don't bother about the buttons, Albertchen, it looks all right as it is. Do you think he'll notice? We could put our clothes on back to front without their noticing. Now go.'

'I am going. Where did I put my gloves? And my handbag? Thank you, Liesel.'

'Is Mama going out?' came a wide-awake voice from the attic.

'It's all right, Tot. *Tante* Liesel is here.'

'Where's Mama going?'

'Out for a little while.'

'Out where?'

'Out for a walk. I stay at home all the time,' called Alberta despairingly. Liesel pushed her out of the door and shut it behind her. She heard the child's voice once more, but could not distinguish the words, and felt torn in two, as she ran across the courtyard and through the shadow of the acacia.

In a strange, high voice she called 'Cordon' to the unsuspecting Madame Morin and was out in the Rue Vercingétorix.

At this time of day it was as strange to her as being on a stage.

Pierre was not standing at the corner. He was a little way beyond the lamp, and so close that it made her start. The man with his right hand plunged down into his pocket so that his raincoat was pulled askew was neither a vision nor an optical illusion. He was walking towards her, passing through the circle of light. His scar was thrown into sharp relief for an instant, as if to emphasize that it was he and no other, the man marked by the war, who could never again become the man he used to be. He took Alberta's hand quickly, squeezed it hard, and kept it, thereby adding to the impression that something unusual was happening. Her whole body was trembling. To hide it, she pulled at her hand and met the darkness in which his eyes lay as bravely as she could. 'Very well, thank you Pierre, and you?'

'I have not asked how you are, Alberta.'

'Haven't you? I thought I heard—' Alberta attempted a laugh. It rang forced and lonely.

'Will you dine with me?'

'Dine? It's after nine o'clock, nearly ten—'

'Well, call it supper if you like. But don't start making objections. I know it's nearly ten. An unheard-of time for someone like you, I know that too. But we never meet. I miss you. Spend this evening with me, Alberta, keep me company for a while.' Pierre spoke impatiently and rapidly. The last words came with a rush, breathlessly, as if he had been running. He led her quickly in the direction of a cab standing at the pavement a short distance away; it seemed to be waiting for them as if they were its masters. The chauffeur leaned out, saw them, started up without waiting for orders, obviously knowing where he was to go. They jolted off so violently over the uneven cobbles that Alberta hit her head on the roof and her hat came awry, making her even more confused. Then they swung out on to the Avenue du Maine, gliding easily and quickly over the asphalt. 'Ah!' Pierre said, as if things were taking the right course. He leaned back, still talking, but more calmly, in a conversational tone. Brokenly and in fragments, like an echo, the sentences reached Alberta through her own inner tumult:

'— — busy during the day — — Sivert's new côterie—not my type—suits him and Eliel even less—ought to stick to their art, they understand that — — this Swedish woman—don't like her—a bundle of nerves — — Paris is deluged again with loafers from all over the place — —'

'She paints, Pierre.'

'Of course, it's part of the equipment. *Enfin*—I may well be the one who is impossible—keep out of all that, Alberta.'

'I am out of everything.'

'Hm,' said the echo. 'What about your work?' it said. 'And Tot?'

'Oh heavens, my work! Tot is sleeping better, thank you.'

'Listen,' Pierre moved closer, and began talking so fast he scarcely paused for breath. 'Write a novel "full of action". Have you noticed the bands round the new, uncut books this autumn? "Full of action" is written on every single one of them. Not those of the advance guard—they're digging down in the subconscious, they remind me of people in the old days who came home from expeditions to unknown lands without being able to prove they had been there—those don't have much sale—no, the picked troops, the ones whose editions run into high figures. They're crying out for action, external action, that gets the characters moving so that they run round each other in circles and make scenes. Fires, houses falling down, not business houses, that's passé now, simply houses, avalanches, accidents, wild beasts. All of them are useful. Daring, memorable scenes. The main and the secondary characters must pair off once or twice, so that we know all about it and are present when it takes place; that's what they turn the pages to look for first, the publishers and the purchasers, for the same reasons.'

'This summer, Pierre—'

'This summer I expect I said a good many impractical things. Wise sayings I had stopped paying any attention to myself. This advice is better, remember it and earn money. Raise the temperature of your manuscript to boiling point, add a fire or two, don't take it too seriously, the majority of people read superficially. See to it that it's three hundred pages long. Not any less, then the book will be too thin, and they want something for their money. Not any more, then it will be too expensive. There are limits to what they will pay for that sort of thing. It's just a matter of being industrious, you must never lose sight of that. Yes, Alberta, I'm talking out of sheer impotence.' Pierre leaned back in his corner and fell silent, as if the stream of talk had been cut off with a scissors.

Tired, thought Alberta. Harassed, distressed, one of his bad days.

Without any idea of where they were she looked out at autumn yellow trees in the magic light of the arc lamps, at people walking in and out of the shadows of the leaves as if between the wings of a theatre, at cars, buses, trams, feet moving, leaves falling, all of it against a backcloth of milky night mist. It was like travelling backwards in life, to places she had loved once and which could no longer command her attention. She recognized the large red gladioli round the fountain at the Rue Soufflot, glimpsed the railings of the Luxembourg Gardens behind them, lost the thread. Dark, narrow streets, a growing feeling that something decisive had happened. A thought occurred to her, it was on the tip of her tongue, but she kept silence. She was about to ask after Jeanne, but did not. As if she had done so, Pierre said, 'Jeanne is in Dijon. I suppose you know?'

'I heard she was leaving. How is she?'

'Splendid. She's with her parents. It's the best thing for her.'

'Yes, in a way—'

'In every way. Here we are.'

Alberta got out. The street was quiet, crooked, poorly lit, old. In front of her was one of the usual small restaurants: a few tables between laurels in tubs on the narrow pavement, an awning, coloured electric lights along the edge of the awning, an open door, open windows revealing an empty room where three or four men in eager conversation were putting their heads together over the remains of a meal. A waiter stood listening to them idly. Out of doors the walls were half in darkness. Pierre's hand guided her to a table where there was a view of the laurel trees and the cobblestones in the road.

An unexpected feeling of irresponsibility suddenly took charge of her, soothing anxiety, lifting gravity. 'Where are we, Pierre?'

'Oh, at a small, simple place. The waiter is a friend of mine from the trenches. I've been eating here recently, the food's good. If you'd prefer to go to d'Harcourt it's just round the corner, a couple of blocks away.'

'Of course not!'

'Good. *Good,* Alberta. Read this to me, will you? Let's have a proper meal.' Pierre pushed across the little wooden frame with the menu written in faded blue pencil and leaned his forehead on his clenched left hand. After a while he put his hand on her arm, patting it each time she came to something suitable. She heard herself speaking quietly and evenly, as if she had been reading the menu to him for years.

'We shan't get any of this, Pierre, it's too late.'

'Then we'll have something else. Are you to decide what we shall be allowed to have?'

'Of course not!'

He patted her arm a couple of times more, removed his hand and called for the *garçon,* turning his face towards the window as he did so. The light fell directly on him. Alberta was shocked. She could not help thinking of death: a man torn out of a trance who had seen death. Impulsively she put her hand on his. He took it, kept it, smiled, called once more. She heard the tramping of a wooden leg.

'*Mon vieux!*'

'*Mon vieux!*'

They slapped each other on the shoulder. Pierre was still holding her hand. Everything was magically right, safe and good. It could not last. But it was happening now. It was wrong, but they were in it together. Without really seeing him she nodded to the man with the wooden leg as if he were an old acquaintance. His brief, appraising glance fell naturally into the picture. Their table received special attention; a clean cloth was put on it, a dusty wine bottle and flowers brought out. All the sympathy that every couple, legally united or not, finds in Paris, lapped round herself and Pierre. She listened to the discussion about what they could and could not have,

rather as a queen might be imagined to listen to her subjects'
proposals: benevolently, somewhat absent-mindedly, raised
above the matter, but ready to acknowledge their good-will.
The wooden leg tramped in and out. The voices at the table
indoors rose and fell. Another couple arrived and sat down
between the laurel trees; their faces seemed out of focus, they
were deaf and blind to all else but each other. The shadow
took them under its protection. Props all of it, good props, true
to nature, as if on a stage.

'Pierre, is something the matter?'

'On the contrary, on the contrary.'

'The book's finished!' exclaimed Alberta. The unfortunate
thought that had occurred to her just now assumed words on
its own, and flew out of her mouth before she could stop it.
For a brief moment it seemed to explain so much: Pierre's
long absence, his fatigue and weariness, his hunger at an unaccustomed hour of the day, the fact that he took a cab. She
was at once given reason to regret her rash remark. He released
her hand, drummed on the table, put on his mask and his distant voice, laughed his painful, brusque laugh. 'Correctly put.
The book's finished. *Finished*. You always hit the nail on the
head. Listen Alberta, I thought you were one of those people
who understand things without having it hammered into them
verbally. I am mistaken. Time after time I am mistaken. It's
just that I haven't seen you for so long.'

'It was stupid of me, Pierre.'

'It was stupid of me too. I ought not to have carried you
off like this, since I cannot manage to be different. *Pardon*
Alberta. You look pretty in that coat and hat. It's nice to see
you in clothes that suit you.' Pierre gave Alberta's hat a little
push, so that it sat more crookedly. '*Voilà*. That's how it
should be worn. You haven't even got sufficient sense to put
your hat on right. Never have I seen a person get in her own
way to such an extent.'

'Am I to be scolded for that too? I know how it should be
worn. But here you come in the pitch dark, at night, and drag
me out. We only have the one lamp; you saw yourself how

far that reaches. I have to carry it with me all over the studio. I had to hurry. The car jolted—'

'I scold you from habit. I always feel like scolding you. Heaven help us, you were sitting out there with your damned sewing the other day. I almost took it away from you and tore it up. You look ridiculous with it. Comic. Deplorable. You can't sew. I can sew better. And yet you sit there as if bound and gagged with thread. You are in Paris, and not of it. You live as if you're in the back of beyond. Everything passes you by. You hear nothing, you see nothing, you take part in nothing. You remind me of the bricklayer's wife; yes, Alberta, the bricklayer's wife in Brittany. You are no idiot—'

'Nice of you to say so.'

'Listen.' Pierre fumbled for words, then spoke rapidly again. 'There's something I'd like to show you some time. I've thought it out. Today's Tuesday. Come with me to Montmartre when we've finished eating. Not to the foreigners' Montmartre, the Rat Mort and the Moulin Rouge. To some friends of mine. You'll see new people, hear music too, all sorts of things. I think you'd like it. Please don't mention Tot or Sivert. Liesel is with Tot. It's all arranged. I'll take her home afterwards.'

'I'm not saying a word.'

'But it's on the tip of your tongue. I know you. Tot, Sivert, washing, sewing, Tot, Sivert, washing, sewing. One could set it to music.'

'What do you want me to do, then?' exclaimed Alberta, laughing aloud for joy because she was being scolded in the old, proper way, because they were both talking at once, because Pierre was looking at her as he had done in Brittany, and on the train, because his hand was on hers; because he had said she was pretty. A message that she must get a grip on herself passed through her brain. For the image of him had been taken from her, she had been freed of it and made too light. Visible and tangible, fully materialized, he sat there, resembling and not resembling the memory she had kept of him. His mouth was mobile; it was defiant and sad and patient, sometimes smiling. Something behind the mask that no cuts and scars had defeated, came out in flashes, blinding her, so that she had to look away. His scar was worse than she had remembered. There were dark flecks, that she had not noticed, in his grey-brown eyes; they were visible whenever he turned towards the window.

'Yes, what are you to do?' Pierre paused. 'What are we to do? One of us is looked after too much, and the other too little. What are you laughing at now?'

'At ourselves. We're so peculiar,' Alberta said, and knew that this was not keeping a grip on herself.

'It's good to see you laugh. Laugh more. It suits you.'

But Alberta was serious again. She must watch herself. Currents from reality had reached her. She was back in the studio, where perhaps the boy was asking for her and could not sleep, where perhaps Sivert had come home. She also heard a voice from the morning of time, distant and oracular: 'Laugh my girl, you look attractive when you laugh.' Mrs. Buck, Beda's mother. She had always made Alberta retreat into her shell, if she had dared to come out of it for a moment.

'I mustn't be late, Pierre.'

'I know you mustn't,' said Pierre, in a cadence that blocked any approach to him, releasing her hand. There she sat. It is woman's lot when she has had a child to act as a damper on man's happiness, a brake on his initiative. The one who can at all times throw off her ties and be ready for his every whim is a lantern unto his feet and a light unto his paths; not she with the sewing, beside the cradle and the cooking pots.

The wooden leg came tramping back with soup tureen, bread, plates, all of it skilfully balanced along one arm, up to the elbow. He looked searchingly from the one to the other, and then began to talk at random, as if engaged to do so. 'We ought to have gone to Berlin. That's what I've just told those fellows in there. Yes, *mon vieux* Cloquet, yes. The Boch signed the Versailles Treaty. Good. We know what that means. Signatures? Paper, *mon vieux*, paper. When it suits them they call it paper openly. No, we ought to have gone to Berlin. Or at any rate as far as the Ruhr.'

'Hold your tongue, Michaud. You talk like an old maid.

You're always so warlike—you have nothing to sacrifice. One would think you had been there. Give me more soup and hold your tongue. You can't see farther than your nose.'

Michaud shrugged his shoulders and ladled out the soup. 'Here's your soup. It's one of your bad days, I can see that. Nothing to bother about, Madame. Fine fellow, Cloquet, as I should know. Carried me in his arms like a child to the rear, when I lay there with my foot just about cut off. Under enemy fire, Madame. But he has not seen his village wiped off the face of the earth as if it had never existed. He does not have his old parents sitting on sugar crates in a house made of corrugated iron. Fine fellow, Cloquet, but he has his bad days, and he doesn't really understand all that sort of thing. One just has to pretend not to notice. Is the soup good, Madame? Sufficiently seasoned? I added a little lemon when I warmed it up, just a *soupçon*. I'm afraid it was perhaps a trifle green. The proprietor has gone to the cinema with his wife.'

'Now listen, Michaud—'

Alberta noticed Pierre's spoon lying abandoned in his plate and felt his impatience quiver in her own nerves. At the same time she saw a vision: gun smoke, whining bullets, one soldier carrying another, the scar in his face, the crooked jaw. Life's hard journey, man's toil and danger. Michaud, the average type with the ordinary face, who had come as a boy from his village, a little stunted by his early uprooting, a little narrow-chested, was no longer a nobody from out there, one of the many anonymous men with wooden legs. He was a part of Pierre's background, a necessary part that it was good to know about. She looked up at him and said, 'Delicious soup, thank you, really delicious.'

'More bread, Michaud. We're hungry. Come up one evening to the Rue Gabrielle and air your thoughts a bit. I've told you so before. Be off. Now then, Alberta, why aren't you eating?'

'But I am eating.'

'You're waving your spoon about like a child who has not learnt table manners. There, you spilt some too. *Enfin*, you're laughing. Good.'

'And you carried him, Pierre? Under enemy fire?'

'Nonsense. There wasn't a shot. They were retreating. Besides, the stretcher-bearers were coming. And he was unconscious, he knew nothing about it. He gets on my nerves with his chatter. Once he starts—'

'I feel sorry for him.'

'He's a good boy! One of the innocent pawns in the enormous game. He attached himself to me like a dog out there, God knows why. Puts many of us to shame; he manages in a way, as long as he's allowed to talk. I expect things would be better for a good many of us if we stood up and talked. We're always quarrelling, he and I. If we never stop looking backwards we shall never move from the spot. I should have kept away from here this evening, we ought to have gone somewhere else. But it's difficult to keep away from war comrades. We seek each other out as sheep seek out the flock. I found this place by accident one day as I was going past. He's kind, takes everything in good part.'

'It was the right place to go.' Alberta recklessly emptied her glass as if it contained water.

'Oh?' Pierre stared at her. 'What's that you're bringing, Michaud? Roast veal?'

'You *asked* for it, Cloquet. It's cold, but here is mayonnaise. There's the bread.'

'I *asked* for it? All right. Now look after that couple over there. They've forgotten what they came for.'

Pierre was over his ill humour. He ate and talked as if it were a long time since he had indulged in either. 'When you've shared the same trench you go on doing it, you don't float up again. You fight for years in groups and crowds, and then all of a sudden you have to sit alone at a desk and concentrate on things of the mind. It's no good, Alberta, it's no use trying. You have to go on fighting. People can't be put back like clocks. You have to find your place in the ranks. The damnable thing is that if you want to give a good account of yourself, you must first of all be self-supporting. That's why I tell you: write thus and so, earn money. I tell myself the same thing. Not to mention everything Jeanne says.' Pierre's voice became monotonous, his expression blank. 'Poor Jeanne.'

Alberta picked at the veal, got nothing down, gulped her wine carelessly instead, found nothing to say, but felt her eyes widening. Her thoughts touched on the unfortunate novel, and Pierre said suddenly, 'The novel has form too. You set people in motion who use three hundred pages to express what one normally could explain to the world in twenty. Belles lettres, as it's called. It takes a great deal of time and energy to produce it in such a way that people don't notice they're swallowing pills. If they do, it's called tendentious and it's not asked after any more, nobody reads it. If you've seen reality from the wrong side, seen how much drudgery the world is still in need of, you no longer have the patience necessary for such extraneous work. You have to attack directly. I don't know what will become of me, Alberta. I've written a few short articles; I suppose I must write in spite of everything. I'm not fit for anything else.' Pierre smiled crookedly. 'I even got a fee today.'

'Did you?' Alberta turned her head away. For the wine she had drunk so thoughtlessly suddenly inundated her brain, placing everything strangely at a distance. Pierre's voice seemed to be packed in wadding. Her own was independent of herself and had to be kept under strict control. Let Pierre talk. He needs to. He can't mention these things to Jeanne.

From an immense distance she heard him saying '. . . good to be with you, Alberta. You're quiet. You talk with your eyes, not your mouth. All these words destroy me. Why are you looking away? Are you tired? Would you prefer to go home?'

Alberta shook her head, smiled, guarded her tongue, looked away again. She felt secure, as if wrapped up and protected. Pierre wished her well. It was good that somebody did. Faces that once had sought hers gathered in the air, looking at her. They had not simply wanted to own her and take her to bed with them and have her to cook their food. One had scolded her because she did nothing, another was scolding because she did too much. Once one of them had scolded because she had said nothing, though goodness knew why; she had not quite understood and was afraid of misunderstanding. At any rate, it seemed that one should stick to the people who scolded. One of them had died. Her sorrow afterwards now seemed like an illness that she had survived. The pain had been terrible, she knew, but she could no longer remember how it had felt. And Sivert? Of course, she had been alone, that was how it was. The fate of many. Liesel's too, although she had managed to deck it up well. What Liesel had said was true: we want to love the person it happens to be. Alberta had decked it up a bit at times herself. Subjection was not always caused by love . . . mysterious things in life . . .

'. . . besides I'm a man,' said Pierre's voice. 'We men are always faithless to something. Only women are capable of being faithful. When I was supposed to be studying law I wrote novels, and now when I'm supposed to be writing novels—'

'But Pierre.' Alberta summoned up her strength. It was no longer easy to speak.

'Now don't say, but you do write. Don't say it ever again. Do you know what I did today? Now, a short while ago? I've put an end to my sewing, Alberta. I had some sewing too, it was called a manuscript. It exists no longer. Burnt up. Gone I was struggling with a pile of papers and now I've mastered them.' He gripped both her hands, gathering them into his single one.

Now we're both drunk, thought Alberta. Very drunk. Poor Pierre, he hasn't eaten properly today, that's what it is. I must hold his forehead, then he'll feel better. She freed a hand, reached his face, he caught it, pressed it against his cheek, his deep-set eyes were large and close, his mouth trembling. 'You think it was a novel, far advanced? The part I had written before was an attempt at least, a collection of persons who had begun to behave, in the innocent way people did behave at that time. As for the rest—a cock-and-bull story, pages full of disconnected type, *empty* pages. They filled out the pile well enough. It looked as if there really was something lying on the desk. I had it to hide behind. I locked it away in my suitcase when I went out and took the key with me. I shammed illness

661

too; at least I didn't contradict them when they said I was ill. I'm not ill. I'm different. For a long time I hoped it would not be for ever, and that they were right when they said everything would improve when I had published my work. I let myself be put to sit at the desk; I sat there, I waited, I tried. One wants to, you see; one tries to settle down again. Jeanne had done so much for me, and now she believed this book meant the whole world. I should have spoken out at once— I should have said, I am not the man you think I am any more. Besides, none of us are the same, Jeanne's not the same either. The Jeanne I was in love with as a boy was not like this. The war has changed her too. It has been hell, Alberta. If only I had completed my studies or could master a proper trade.'

Pierre removed his hand, laid it flat on the table, and contemplated it. 'There are plenty of people who have to manage with one hand now,' he said.

'So unlike Sivert's,' Alberta heard her voice say in the distance. She studied his hand too, and had to make an effort to do so, frowning. She was suddenly so tired that she could scarcely hold her head up. Nevertheless everything Pierre had said was stored away clearly in her mind for later use. In a while her fatigue would overwhelm her. While she was still capable of it she must tell Pierre that she had understood, and then she would go to sleep. As loudly as she could in order to make it clear, making an effort before each word as if clearing hurdles, she said: 'I understand everything, Pierre. Everything. You could not bear the manuscript any longer, there are other things you want to do. Something to do with social— questions. It's difficult to understand, heaps of things one has to know and read.' She unexpectedly caught sight of a word which seemed to her to be deficient, but unavoidable. 'Statistics,' she said, and repeated it a couple of times. 'Statistics.'

'But Alberta?' An amazed, amused, rather touched expression had come into the face in front of her. That was what happened sometimes, men did get strange expressions, it didn't matter, it would pass. Alberta nodded seriously to the strange face. Her own sank lower and lower towards the table. Then suddenly an arm was holding it, her hat was taken off, and she was leaning on Pierre's shoulder. 'Never mind about statistics. You're drunk, *ma petite*. And I never noticed. I ought to have been looking after you. What are you bringing, Michaud? *Ananas au Kirsch*? Take it away! Give us mineral water and strong coffee. As quickly as you can, Madame is not well. Off with you.'

Alberta felt somebody stroking her head. Michaud was laughing. She was standing a short way away, laughing too. From even further off there came the voices of a man and a woman: 'Is Madame unwell, Monsieur? There is a chemist on the corner. May we help you to take her there?' 'Thank you Madame, thank you, Monsieur, it's nothing, a little fatigue, it will pass,' said Pierre from somewhere up in the air. He was holding a glass to her mouth, cold water trickled down her throat, she sank down into fog and slowly emerged from it again as if getting her head above water, and felt normal. Now Pierre was holding a cup of coffee to her mouth. 'Here you are, good and strong. It helps. You don't feel ill? No? Only drunk a bit too much? *Ma pauvre petite*. It's no good taking you out. That's right, another sip—and another! Better? Hm?'

'I'm not used to going out, Pierre. It's years since—'

'All my fault. I talk and talk and never give you a thought.' Pierre's voice was hoarse and thick with emotion. He was holding her uncomfortably, using his undamaged hand for the cup and leaning over her with it. For a moment his face was close, very close, the scar, the crooked jaw, the mobile mouth, sad now, the searching eyes, the saucers of shadow beneath the cheekbones and temples. She felt his breath, a good, healthy scent like the fields and woods in spring. Then she turned her head slightly and was free, sat upright, emptied the cup and held it out for more. 'I'm sorry. I can stand so little. It comes all of a sudden but passes quickly too. I heard everything you said, Pierre, even with my head full of wine.'

'Now I expect you want to go home?'

'What's the time? We mustn't forget about Liesel.'

'Liesel, yes. I don't like the look of Liesel these days. She seems poorly. But when we're out together for once— It's just gone half past ten.'

'I suppose you'll be leaving soon, too?' Alberta managed an even tone of voice, innocent and without overtones. Then she remembered what Jeanne had threatened, and was covered with confusion.

'Leave?' repeated Pierre dryly. 'No. The bill please, Michaud.' He rummaged in his pocket. Like most men he carried his money loose, and had to take out pamphlets and brochures before he could find it. She took out her compact, righted her hat and smoothed her hair. They seemed to be the actions of an established couple; it felt both good and bad, filling her with sweetness and giving her support. It was emphasized by Michaud's farewell: *'Au plaisir, Madame.* Now you know the way—.'

The night air lay cool against her face, sobering her completely. She and Pierre walked along together as if they had done so always, rapidly, lightly, with matching strides. The joy of walking with someone whose rhythm was the same as her own increased. She thought of Tot, and Liesel; they seemed to be standing in supplication far away. She turned her back on them. I'm staying with Pierre for a little while— just once.

'It's devilish at home in the empty apartment, Alberta. I go there as late as I can. I don't care for cafés any more either. Thank you for staying with me.' He put his arm under hers, they walked even more comfortably. He hailed a passing cab. Paris, as it is late at night, began to pass by. Pierre talked as if he had forgotten all his anxieties: '—a few soldiers from the front who stick together. They've begun to collect other comrades, play for them, read to them—a way of passing the time together to start with, a continuation of what we did out there when we had the chance. We read something or other. Now we have music as well, lectures. All of a sudden it's developed into full soirées. Soon we shan't have room for everyone. Those who have come once or twice bring others with them: wives, sweethearts, friends, people who haven't the money or the opportunity for expensive entertainment. It's at

Larbaud's. He and Suzanne are marvellous, they let us meet in their studio twice a week. We sit on top of each other, there's so little room. We've had an enquiry from trade union headquarters—whether we'd care to affiliate with them. They have big evening meetings with artistic programmes, a huge orchestra, turns by first class artistes, all free of course. There's a great deal of interest being taken in these things in artistic circles just now. We don't think we have enough to offer yet, we're not used to appearing on a stage. Though not only minor artistes and amateurs appear at our place. If we're lucky we may hear unexpectedly good turns this evening. We shan't stay long. Just so that you can get an impression.'

Pierre was talking as if he was at last being given the chance to do so. He sat leaning forward crookedly. Light from outside fell on his face momentarily. He looked as if he were telling her about customs and habits in a land he had visited, far away. That was good, since he was not paying so much attention to Alberta, who sat well back in the corner, weak after her intoxication, dull and a little ashamed, above all unresisting. She had lost her strength; it had ebbed away from her, away from her voice and her face. Each time the light shone on her she felt defenceless, at the mercy of anything.

'. . . To stick together,' said Pierre. 'Share with each other. That was what we learned out there besides killing. They ought to be thankful if we manage to drop the latter habit, and if anyone fails to do so, nobody should be surprised. Your career, they say to me. Your name, they say. Your living. You have no time, they say. Once I had time to sit all night long discussing literary problems, and nobody said a word. My living? They don't pay much at my publisher's now, it's true. They can't. New little periodicals championing new things can never pay. But you can't feed a wife and child by sitting like a broody hen on an old novel that never progresses playing with dead dolls, struggling with old, worn-out forms that you can no longer fill, searching for conclusions to things one wrote years ago in another world. *Enfin*—I've thrown out the ballast. I'm a villain and a scoundrel. But at least I can begin to look round for new truths, new ways of describing them. And then there's this wind from the east that's begun to blow. How far it will blow me I don't know. Poor Jeanne, she already sees me as a bomb-thrower and an executioner, or put up against a wall and shot. I've become malicious and have several horrid bogeymen to frighten her with: Marx and Lenin, Monatte and Monmousson. She puts her hands over her ears and flees. She has fled all the way to Dijon. Will you be afraid too, Alberta?'

'I know too little to be afraid, Pierre,' said Alberta, and it was true. She felt her eyes were large; it was her way of listening. The world widened. There it was beyond the fence, with possibilities, tasks, demands on her and on everyone mature enough to meet them. Pierre sat simplifying it for her, adjusting down to her level, perhaps a little lower than absolutely necessary. But that was her own fault. She always gave the impression of being more ignorant than she really was. As they passed the next lamp she saw that Pierre was no longer absent. Now he was looking at her.

'If I had any money I'd take up my studies again. That could give me an honest living. A lawyer can be useful. But I have no money.'

'No, money—' said Alberta, feeling her armour grow out again, her strength return. If all other barriers were to fall, this one would remain: money. She might just as well prune her emotions accordingly.

Tobacco smoke met them, hanging like mist under the glass panes in the roof, billowing above a tightly packed assembly sitting with their backs to them in rows. A deep, distinct female voice was clearing a way from the bottom of the room, reaching its goal effortlessly above all the heads, word by word. They came clearly through the quietness and the thick air. Not one of them was lost, not one jarred or struck a wrong note. They were supported by the masterly movement on which they rose and fell, gentle and penetrating. In free verse they discussed what could have made a fifteen year-old into the boy he was, lively, generous, cheerful, industrious, with

rich artistic and literary talent. Not the poverty and courage
of his childhood alone, but the people who had gone before
him: men who came home from work in the evening and perhaps felt a pathos they could not explain when the smoke
from the chimney rose up thin and light against the golden
sky; women who worked hard, wearing their hands red in cold
water, and had no time for anything more; a little girl perhaps,
who, stiff from holding a younger child on her lap, sat on the
pavement in a dark street somewhere dreaming of green lawns,
birds, roses, running water. All of it so that, later in time, this
boy might write poetry.

> *... Qui sait quel trésor, comme un fruit unique*
> *Mûrit depuis toujours en tout enfant qui passe?'*

The voice changed, and became full of bitterness:

> *'Qu'importe ce trésor o mon ami*
> *Aux trafiquants du monde!*
> *Ils nous ont pris, toi, moi, nous tous,*
> *Hommes parqués, matériel humain,*
> *Comme on prendrait la menue—paille*
> *Pour nourrir un feu,*
> *Prodiguant les poignées après les poignées ...*

There was a disturbance amongst those sitting nearest to
them; room was made for Alberta and Pierre. Several people
leaned forward and nodded to him, a couple of them shook
him by the hand. Then they turned towards the platform again,
towards the voice and the small figure up there in a blouse
and skirt, the omniscient face, no longer young, the thin hands,
the simply arranged hair.

'Who is she, Pierre?'

'Madame L. of the Théâtre Français. She is reading Vildrac,
one of the few who has the ability to express something of
what went on out there. It's about a friend who fell.'

Alberta looked about her. Seldom had she seen a more in-
congruous audience, never one more attentive. There was
something hungry about the bent backs, the upraised chins.
She recognised eyes that she had seen outside the stations

667

during the war, looking at things they scarcely dared believe. The majority were men, many of them in working clothes, pullovers with patched elbows, frayed collars without ties, here and there an empty sleeve, here and there faces more damaged than Pierre's. But a few were in their Sunday best. An elderly woman and a couple of young girls were dressed up to the nines. Squeezed in among the rest sat unimpeachable ladies and gentlemen in simple, irreproachable clothes. The voice, which for a moment had been interrupted by applause, caught her attention again.

> Jean Ruet aussi est mort;
> Il avait vingt-quatre ans;
> C'était un gars de Saint-Ay
> Dans les vignes sur la Loire.

> Jean Ruet a été tue!
> Qui donc aurait pu croire
> que celui-là mourrait?

Jean Ruet's brief fate was presented in verses so blunt, so apparently artless, that the effect was that of a straightforward, accurate report. Jean Ruet had been young, light-hearted, a good comrade, a clever worker; a kind brother, who, himself a dancer, had taught his little sister to dance; a cheerful fellow who took the girls by the waist and kissed them down among the vines.

> Il était si vivant que c'était plaisir
> De le regarder vivre!

> Hélas! J'ai vu ses traits
> S'amincir et se fondre
> Pendant qui'l répétait
> L'adresse de sa mère.

> Beaucoup d'autres aussi
> En France, en Angleterre,
> En Prusse et en Bavière,
> En Flandre et en Russie.

> Beaucoup d'autres Jean Ruet
> Qui chantaient sur la terre

En y plantant la vigne
Le houblon et le blé
Sans penser aux casernes.

There was a moment's silence. Then the applause broke like a storm. Alberta looked at Pierre. He nodded, his eyes blank.

Someone pushed a grand piano forward across the floor. A thin man with a great deal of hair sat down and played with long, supple fingers. And melodies began to trickle into Alberta, a tinkling procession of clear drops. She had not listened to music for a long time. It was like a call from another life. It was good and bitterly painful. She had a sob in her throat. Then she suddenly realised how desperate this music was, how full of anguish and bitterness. It made her feel like the inopportune witness to an outburst of emotion. A voice in the treble was in *extremis,* it insulted, scorned, wounded. Another followed, pleading, anxious, deprived, it too *in extremis.* At her side Pierre suddenly whispered, 'I've written to the publisher. He'll get the letter tomorrow. I've told him briefly—'

Words and music advanced together towards a threat, an imminent catastrophe. 'Yes,' said Alberta, not daring to look at him. Her heart was hammering. Someone must intervene—something tragic would occur!

And it was over. The pianist was sitting wiping his forehead. There was clapping and cries of bravo, he rose and bowed. 'What was it, Pierre? I didn't recognise it.'

'Something by Scriabin. An *étude.*'

But Alberta thought: *Etude*? It ought to be called Shriek, Shriek.

'Have you noticed the audience? They're rather out of the ordinary.'

Yes, they were. Many of these men in dungarees and patched pullovers were sitting with sheet music in their hands, writing notes in the margin, pointing out bars to each other, whispering together. Those without music moved closer and leaned over the others' shoulders. The man at the piano began

669

to play 'The Moonlight Sonata'. The first movement filled the room with heavy calm.

'Look at them,' whispered Pierre. 'Sometimes they bring the whole score with them, though goodness knows where they get them from. We have a string quartet here. They've probably finished already. Have you ever seen people listening like this?'

'No,' Alberta said. She felt lazy and backward, a person who had let everything in life pass her by.

The man at the piano rose. In a flash an eager little fellow with sheets of paper in his hand and one sleeve hanging empty was up on the platform and speaking at a tearing pace in a high-pitched voice: 'The average reader is superficial by nature, thoughtless and lazy. He soon puts down the most talented writing if it demands the slightest effort on his part . . .'

'What sort of a character is this?' 'Where did you find him? What does he want?' 'Get him down. This sounds dangerous.' 'But it's the truth!' Pierre got to his feet. 'Let's go, Alberta, it's late, and this may go on for a long time.' He pushed his way out, making gestures of recognition to right and left, leaning down to listen to whispered explanations: 'He must be allowed to continue, *mon vieux,* he has prepared it so carefully. It's about reading. What can you expect? He has reading on the brain. It's Yence, you remember Yence. He can't keep his mouth shut. He's a good fellow, and no fool. When are we going to hear you, Cloquet?'

'When I have something to say. No, not this evening. I was only looking in—Oh, Suzanne!'

A small, simply dressed person with short, smooth hair and eyes enlarged by spectacles was standing in front of them. 'Must you go, Pierre? Is this the Norwegian friend you told me about? How kind of you to come, Madame. I hope we shall see you here again. We meet again on Friday. Maurice will be sorry not to have seen you, Pierre, but I can't get hold of him now, he's sitting so close to the front. Yence? Somebody Maurice found, one of the ones from out there, as you can see. He must be allowed to have his say. It's his contribution.

He's so fond of speaking, and it does him good. *Au revoir,*
Madame, I mean it.'

'Suzanne Larbaud,' explained Pierre. 'First prize at the Con-
servatory. She's incredible, two children, a home, pupils, plays
in the quartet, plays in the Colonne orchestra, helps Larbaud
with these soirées. If he opened a menagerie Suzanne would
find a way of helping him and find room for it. She's that sort.
But he appreciates her too, they're happy.'

'She's attractive,' Alberta said. Her head was whirling; she
felt paralysed by impressions and unaccustomed fatigue.

'Hey, taxi!'

A cab again, as if they were millionaires. Pierre's face without the mask, leaning forward in the light from an arc lamp
to look at her. 'Sleepy? Not sorry you came? No? You know
all this is still trifling, just a small step, the nearest at hand for
people like myself. A way of keeping up with your comrades.
We will not be divided again into different social classes. You
know, Alberta, when men have shared all kinds of misery, as
we have . . .'

'I should like to come with you again, many times, if I
could, Pierre.'

'What about your concierge?' asked Pierre. 'Is she reliable?
Liesel ought to go to bed earlier. She ought to have been doing
so long ago.'

'Madame Morin goes to bed with the chickens. You don't
think there's anything the matter with Liesel, surely?'

'There might be. She is getting thinner. And Eliel—. They
live in their own world, he and Sivert. Gifted artists. Beyond
that they're not dependable.'

Paris rushed past. A glimpse of the hectic flood of light on
the boulevards, the deserted streets again, narrow and dark,
the Seine reflecting the lights. Pierre was talking about Jeanne.
'She can't stand all this. She wants me back in the circus again,
chasing acquaintances and prizes with my tongue out. If you
knew how many literary prizes we have in this country,
Alberta. It's terrible. A fearful method of rewarding work.
That artists and writers should allow themselves to compete!
Those who don't are always wrong, Jeanne says.'

Jeanne! thought Alberta. The book burnt. Jeanne left for good? No, it couldn't be true. It must be more complicated than that.

The corner of the Avenue du Maine. The car suddenly stopping. Pierre helping her out, holding her hand, thanking her for coming, still holding it. Something to the effect that if Liesel did not come within such and such a time, he would take it that she had gone home. 'Be careful in the dark when you cross the courtyard, Alberta.'

'Take something to make you sleep tonight, Pierre. Don't lie thinking about you know what.'

The sound of the bell. Alberta's voice calling 'Madame Ness'. The gate opening and slamming again. The horn of a car far away.

Nothing had happened; much had happened. Alberta's feet felt as heavy as if she had been on a route march. The gravel crunched unnaturally loudly.

Before she reached the door she saw that Sivert was home. His shadow fell for a moment on the curtain across the big window, rose to its full height, and disappeared again. Only the top of his head formed a slight curve along the window sill. He was probably sitting reading. Odd that he had not gone to bed. Her heart thudded as she walked towards the door.

'Good evening, Sivert.'

'Good evening. Well? So you've been out for an airing?'

'As you see.'

She took off her outdoor things and hung them up, then went up to the attic to see to Tot. Her heart continued to thud.

'Liesel sat here?' Sivert's tone was that of a kind cross-examiner and put Alberta immediately on her guard. Was not this the way notorious criminals were led to confess?

'Yes, she did. She was kind enough to do so.'

'It's rather late to be out,' remarked Sivert in the same tone.

'It did get late. I was with Pierre.'

'Oh, were you?'

'He hasn't left yet.'

'I can well imagine it. Our good Pierre is not a man of action. Poor Jeanne. The mere fact that she can't get him to meet the kind of people he should, people who could be of importance to him—'

'I know all about that, Sivert.' Alberta prepared herself for bed, coming and going in and out of the shadow in the large room, glad of its protection. She thought: If only you would leave me in peace; I don't attack you. Sivert was reading again.

Then he raised his head from the book. 'Did Liesel say nothing?'

Alberta paused in the middle of the room. Sivert's tone was no longer kind. Now he really was interrogating her; his eyes pierced her through the shadow. 'I'm asking you, did she say nothing?'

'Nothing in particular.'

Sivert slammed the book shut, putting it down so roughly on the table that Alberta involuntarily said, 'Hush, Tot!'

'Worse things can happen to Tot than being woken up.' Sivert was on his feet and was walking up and down. He stood still. 'Women! There's nothing more irresponsible than a woman of that type.'

'What are you talking about now, Sivert?' Alberta's rage was mounting. Sivert's attitude was unbearable. She looked him straight in the eye and did not look away.

'I'm saying that the next time you go out waltzing with Pierre or whoever it may be, I wish to be excused from having Liesel to sit with my boy. It would be infinitely preferable to have nobody. Liesel's lungs are diseased. If the possibility had occurred to me that—'

'The possibility was not so remote,' Alberta heard herself say. She sat down in a chair feeling her fatigue and impotence creeping over her like a flood which she could no longer stave off. It was rising, it would seize her, it was useless to struggle. What had Sivert said? And what had she meant to say herself? It had been something else.

She heard Sivert from an immense distance. His voice

673

reached her again. 'At last Eliel got her to a doctor the other day. The X-ray came yesterday, there's no doubt about it. And then she comes here and sits with the boy as if there were nothing the matter. Without saying a word. I thought she was at least adult. Eliel, poor fellow—'

'I suppose you pity him most?' Alberta at last found her voice. She held her head, trying to think clearly. It couldn't be true? Not like that? Liesel ill? Really ill? But we've survived everything, she and I. We may feel unwell, but we get over it.

'I do pity Eliel most. If he had not felt responsible, if he had not had so much *sense of honour* . . . This has been going on for years, and I must say he hasn't had much of a life with Liesel. Then it turns out that—God knows what he may not have caught too. She sweats at night until she's wringing wet. He has to get up, help her to change. That was what made him suspect something was wrong. He's a healthy person himself, not used to illness—'

'Stop, Sivert. You are not to talk about it like this. Not like this.' Alberta confronted Sivert and told him so to his face. She spoke so calmly that she scarcely believed it of herself. At really bad moments it was possible to behave like that. 'Now stop talking about it for tonight.'

Sivert answered by immediately turning the lamp right down. In the cold vapour that hung in the air she heard him undressing quickly and without fuss.

She fumbled her way across to the kitchen shelf, found matches, took out two sleeping powders and emptied them into a glass of water. Her heart was cold as a stone, closed and tight. Only in her brain was there flickering movement still: melodies, verses, the after-swell of words, music and wine, vibrations it was not accustomed to and could not shake off. She lighted her way up the stairs, and lay down in the high iron bedstead beside Sivert, while the heavy darkness of the veronal already began filtering upwards from the darkness within her, expunged her and became one with the night.

But in the mysterious no man's land between dark and dark she felt for a moment an arm about her neck, warm breath against her face; a man's voice, slightly hoarse as if talking to a child, asked, 'Better now? Hmm?'

* * *

It was a quiet, late autumn, mild, with pale sunshine. The flower beds in the Luxembourg Gardens were filled with the wild, hectic splendour that gives warning of frost at night: dahlias, enormous gladioli, defiant and strong with leaves like swords, Michaelmas daisies, golden rod. In amongst the yellow foliage the black outlines of the trees became daily more distinct; the summer's shade beneath them dissolved into airy, blue lattice-work. The sky above and the atmosphere about it all were disquietingly light and soft, as if the scene were painted in pastels and could be blown away. Tomorrow morning the iron hand of winter might have been there, and wrung the world dry and withered, or storm and rain might have ravaged it. Each day might be the last.

Alberta and Liesel were sitting together on a bench just as in the old days, without Tot; an unbelievable situation which even repeated itself, and had in fact done so several times. 'All to the good, as long as we can meet here,' Liesel commented. 'I know Sivert won't let me inside the door. Eliel said so.'

'He can't have meant it, Liesel,' said Alberta in embarrassment. 'Eliel must have misunderstood him.'

'He didn't misunderstand him. They pretend I'm gravely ill, both of them. They're scared to death of me. As if it were something serious. The X-ray? You can find anything on an X-ray. They say they're not at all easy to read. And when I actually feel stronger than before, more energetic . . .'

'But you must follow the doctor's orders now, Liesel.'

'I follow them as far as possible. I take medicine and strengthening things. I ought to rest, go out in the fresh air, eat well, be lazy, all the things doctors always suggest in all cases. I *am* out in the fresh air. I can't *lie* in the studio passage for hours on end. It smells of the w.c. and the sun only comes there for a short while. Besides, the whole house would notice.

I've set up a new still-life too, a big one. I must finish it before Eliel starts on something monumental again. He threatens to.'

'What does Eliel *say*?'

'Eliel? He wants me to go home. Where should I go?' Liesel looked up at Alberta. A hectic little red rose flamed in each cheek as she did so. 'You can imagine for yourself, Albertchen . . .'

Alberta could. To go home was impossible. The family in the cabinet-sized photograph were in Germany. Liesel would not fit in with them. *'Sie sind alle furchtbar gut, aber . . .'* She refused to go there. 'Not after all we have gone through on account of that nation, Albertchen. I am sufficiently French, sufficiently Russian. Besides, I can't throw myself on my family. It's difficult enough for them without me.'

'What about the country then, Liesel?' Alberta asked hesitantly.

'Don't mention the word sanatorium. It gives me hysterics. Those places are terrible, worse than prisons for people like us who can't pay.'

'But for a while—only until you were better. I'm sure the doctor suggested it.'

'Yes, yes of course. Hush. I told him I lived in open surroundings, with sun, fresh air and green trees. He wanted to come and see me. We shan't open the door if he does, I shall see to that. Why should I go and catch something *here*?' Liesel touched her shoulder blade. 'It's never happened to us before. We've never *caught* anything, just like that. But if only Eliel hadn't begun nagging and I hadn't gone to the doctor, it would have passed by itself. We wouldn't have known about it. If you want to be made really miserable, go to a doctor, my father always said. He didn't die of any illness, he died after a fall from a horse. At home we were never ill. We slept on a balcony in summer, we children. We heard the trees soughing when the wind blew, we could watch the stars. A big balcony, just like a room. I shall never sleep like that again.'

Liesel tilted her head back and looked up at the sky. 'Eliel doesn't sleep in the attic any more. He stays downstairs.'

'It would be better for you to sleep there. The air's fresher.'

'He's arranged it like that. Men always make the arrangements. They talk so much about complexes, he and Sivert.
One must not have complexes. It's beginning to dawn on me
that often it's simply synonymous with ordinary consideration
for others. Besides, it's *his* studio. St Sulpice is striking twelve,
Albertchen. You must go in ten minutes.'

'Yes, yes,' said Alberta, pretending there was time enough.

Her whole being longed for the moment when she could get
up from the bench and go towards her goal, towards the
moment round which all the hours of the day revolved, leading her to it and away from it. The boy was in Meudon with
Sivert and the Swedish woman. Sivert had suddenly remarked
one day: 'You complain that he never gets any country air
and that you never get anything written. I'll take him with me.
Then he'll *get* country air and you'll *get* something written.'

'I'm not complaining about anything.'

'It amounts to the same thing. It's always in the air. It will
be good for him to come with me for many reasons.'

Country air was good for Tot, nobody could dispute that.
With the old, familiar feeling of letting everything slip out of
her hands Alberta got him ready every morning, hiding things
for him in Sivert's lunch packet and painting equipment:
extra stockings to change into if necessary, a jersey, the
checked rubber ball, biscuits and chocolate for the afternoon,
a bottle of milk, apples. Day after day most of it came home
unused, and Tot said, 'Father thinks it's silly to take all that
with us. Father laughs about it.'

'Does he?' replied Alberta, feeling that her obstinate nature
was not entirely dead and destroyed. 'Well, you're taking it
with you.'

'Auntie laughs about it.'

'Then she must laugh.'

But when Alberta sat on the edge of his bed in the evening,
and Sivert was at the Dôme, she would ask him deceitful and
humiliating questions. 'Tell me, is Auntie nice?'

'Father's nice,' said the boy, going on to tell her about things
he had seen and heard in the course of the day, on the train
and elsewhere. 'What did you do then?' 'I sat in the grass and

677

watched them painting.' One evening he said: 'Auntie painted me with the ball.'

Alberta leaned forward, just managing to brush his cheek with her mouth. 'Good night,' he said, turning his face to the wall. Her kiss met the empty air. Torn apart by warring emotions she went downstairs and dried her tears in the corner of the divan. The next morning, aching, she watched him disappear through the gate. Then she hurried to tidy up and rushed to the Luxembourg Gardens as if she had wings: to sit on a bench with Liesel; to eat with Pierre at Michaud's. We are two people and more than two: there were moments when she felt her mind to be an ill-lit battlefield, on which a struggle was raging back and forth. There were many people fighting there. One might well ask where what we call ourselves really begins and ends.

'Time to go,' Liesel said laconically.

'Come with us for once, Liesel.'

'I didn't know you were a hypocrite, Albertchen. Besides, the weather may change any day now. Even I can't arrange that for you. Sivert can't take Tot with him when the autumn rains begin, however much he wants to disgust you. For he intends to drive you out. That's how men do it. So that in desperation we take the first step, just as they lure us into carelessness when they want to catch us. That's how they free themselves of responsibility. They're terribly cunning. I believe he's miscalculated with this woman of his, but it's of no consequence. To take Tot with him on his expeditions—a dirty trick, as Potter says.'

Of no consequence? thought Alberta. No, whatever it may be, it's not of no consequence. We are bound to a wheel, he and Pierre and I. It's whirling us round. The way we stand in relation to each other when it stops one day is certainly of consequence.

With a little farewell cough Liesel departed. And it was just as painful to see her go as it had been one morning a few years ago, when she had banged on Alberta's door in the middle of the night because she could not bear to be alone, and had crept under her eiderdown, lying there like a frightened little animal, tossing and turning and groaning. Eliel and Sivert were at the Bal des Quat'z Arts. They had let it be understood that they did not intend to deny themselves anything, if the opportunity chanced to offer itself.

'Lie still, Liesel. You're so restless.'

'I can't sleep.'

'Nonsense. Try.'

'Do you believe, Albertchen—do you believe he would simply . . .'

'No, I can't believe it, Liesel.' Alberta trusted Sivert. She thought it most improbable that a person who shared the good and bad things of life with another should fail her so easily in important matters.

'But if—I'm saying, if—'

'I wouldn't put up with it.'

'No, you wouldn't, would you? But then we'd have to—then it would be . . .' And Liesel wept.

In the morning she had gone home, shattered by sleeplessness, her courage barely reinforced with a cup of coffee. Sivert had not come home. She had suffered bewilderingly and indescribably, such as one only suffers for short periods in one's life; afterwards it is different. She seemed to be transfigured by anxiety and pain. In her rather aggrieved manner she continued to be only fond of Eliel, who had made it clear long ago that he attached no importance to it.

Twice Alberta turned round to watch Liesel, but Liesel did not turn. She disappeared down one of the avenues, her back thin and her shoulders sloping.

And Alberta's feet acquired wings. It was a good stretch from the Rue Vercingétorix down to Michaud's. She covered the distance twice a day, unaware of her feet until she was on the way home.

At the first turning in the little street she would see Pierre's head in the right place between the laurel trees, bent over some reading matter. She might also catch sight of a white napkin gesturing among the tables, disappearing through the door: Michaud.

Then Pierre seemed to feel she was coming; or he became

impatient. He would raise his head. And the new expression, an old one really that had reappeared, would spread across his damaged face, blotting out the traces of war. He would stuff the pamphlets in his pocket. 'Five minutes late. Women, women. Not a thought for Michaud's omelette.' And then: 'I never dare to believe you will come, Alberta, that you will come every day. I have to see you before I can believe it.'

And Alberta's defences, if she had any, would melt away. His arms were about her shoulders, his kiss on her mouth, for all the world and Michaud to see, sealing the fact that this was how it was. She was at journey's end.

The little restaurant buzzed with activity at this time of day. Students with their sweethearts, shop people from the *quartier*, the couple who had been there the first evening, and were habitués by now. The woman nodded protectively, in complicity and complete understanding: We are inside, you and I, we know about life and happiness. Michaud thumped about with only time for a greeting and for taking their order. He just managed to say, 'Ah, there you are, Madame! *Tant mieux*. I began to be afraid somebody might want your place.'

And the moment had arrived when Alberta had taken off her gloves, arranged them with her handbag on the table, righted her hair and her hat, and powdered her nose. She and Pierre sat for a while gazing into each other's eyes, silent and smiling: like other couples, like all couples when they meet.

When they spoke, they did not discuss the impossible. 'Well, everything all right?'

'All right.'

'Still free to come?'

'As long as it lasts. As long as we have this weather, I suppose.'

'Well, it doesn't harm Tot to be out of doors.'

'I don't like this woman, Pierre.'

'Nor do I. A bundle of nerves, hungry for life as they say. Although they seem to limit life to certain particular aspects. I sat listening to her once at the Dôme. She tampers with herself and her mental processes according to the latest recipe. It's the newest vice. It will bring at least as many people out of balance as the church's tampering with souls, but in the opposite way. The triumphs of knowledge are one thing; all these dilettantes who immediately take advantage of them are a different matter. If only they kept to themselves, but they practise vivisection around them too. Personal problems? In nine out of ten cases the person who has found his place in society has solved them. I don't wish anyone back in the trenches, but I wish some of them could be plunged into a slum district. She's supposed to be talented. Very possible. She's not Sivert's type, at any rate, and their taking the boy with them—

'It has one advantage,' Pierre brought his eyes back from the distance; they looked directly at Alberta, full of kindness, irony, tenderness. They studied her and continued to do so. The air around her began to tremble with light. 'You really do squint.'

'I'm afraid so.'

'Afraid so? No, it's amusing, it suits you. I've often wondered what it was about your expression. Now I know. Alberta squints. But only enough to make one feel uncertain about it.'

'Here comes Michaud.'

'Let him come. Besides, I'm sitting as stiff as a ramrod. Do you know what I've been doing today, Madame? I've been sitting here working. All morning. There's always something on one's mind, as long as one casts about a bit and breathes deeply and sweeps away old rubbish. Courage suddenly returns.' Pierre brought a few folded sheets of paper half way out of his breast pocket, then thrust them back again. *Voilà.* Your move, Madame. I shall expect to see you with some pages too. You're not an experienced gambler, however, it shows in many ways. Put the things down and be off with you, Michaud!'

'If you think I have time for gossip, *mon vieux*—! You'll have the chicken after the omelette, won't you? I can recommend it.'

'Chicken? Are you mad?' Alberta picked up the wooden-framed menu and glanced over it. 'Stewed veal for two, and nothing else. We aren't millionaires.'

'Very well, Madame.' Michaud winked craftily. "The chicken.'

'I haven't a sou, as usual, Pierre. I don't like this. I can't let you spend so much money.'

'Don't you know how over-confident you become when you have a few lines on paper? There's no limit to what you permit yourself.'

'I know that. But I know too that—' Alberta hesitated. What did she know really? She received confirmation of some of her suspicions when they talked, that was all. 'I know nothing really. I haven't tried it out. Are you really writing something new?'

'It feels like it. We'll see. It will be—will be—well, we'll talk about it one of these days. If we're given more of this weather I shall sit here tomorrow. I feel so damned unhappy in the apartment. The people who are going to have it aren't moving in until the first.'

'No,' said Alberta. Her heart turned over, paused, then began pounding again slowly. Now they were near to all the things it was useless to talk about, which would only make them depressed and silent. She tussled with the wing of her chicken and avoided looking at him. And she was right, he said nothing for a while. When he spoke once more it seemed to be with difficulty.

'See to finishing that manuscript of yours, Alberta. It looked to me as if it was at the point when something ought to be happening. Let it expand to three hundred pages or burn it, so that new blood can flow into you. Mental thrombosis—that can kill you too. I don't know how these things are in your country. Here you can make money out of novels, at any rate to start with, but if you don't follow up with successes, you have to live on charity. But who knows? A few produce happily once a year. Then even scribbling can keep you alive.'

Now they had come to the point where Pierre used to say: You must come to terms with Sivert, assert yourself against Sivert. He said it no longer. He said. 'Sivert's making some strange moves these days. Do you never think of making any counter moves?'

'Think of it? I have none to make.' Alberta's heart was pounding again. 'I can't produce once a year, either. I feel it in my bones.'

'You're no gambler, as I said. But perhaps it's not easy to gamble against Sivert.

'Eliel and Sivert!' said Pierre abruptly. For the first time Alberta detected a trace of contempt in his voice. He had referred to Eliel and Sivert frequently in the course of time, referred to them in a tolerant and quite friendly tone, admiringly too, as long as he judged them by their art. 'But then, I'm no more than a bungler myself,' he concluded. His mouth was defiant, his expression blank.

Michaud served them their coffee. Most of the people at the nearby tables had gone, the happy couple had gone, Michaud was no longer busy. He struck Pierre on the shoulder. 'Out of humour, *mon vieux?*'

'On the contrary.'

'He has his moods, Madame. He has it from out there. It's over, *mon vieux*. We knocked them out. It's not right to present such a face to Madame. It's beautiful weather. You've worked well all morning—'

'If you don't hold your tongue, Michaud, and take yourself off—'

'I am taking myself off. I know you. Don't attach any importance to it, Madame. He's like that. It doesn't mean anything.'

'Pierre snarled after him. Then he said, 'Poor devil. He means well.'

'Yes, he means well,' said Alberta. She remembered that she might be looking at the laurel trees and the cobblestones, listening to the thump of Michaud's wooden leg, getting her coffee put in front of her by his thin, worn hands—red from rinsing glasses and sticking out of sleeves that were too short— for the last time. Was there not a change in the weather, a new quality in the air? Or was it simply a cloud obscuring the sun, a shadow in the mind? She searched for words, for something to say that would chase it all away and remove the sting of Pierre's bitter remark, of the blow he had so unreasonably given himself. Then he hauled a letter out of his pocket. It was from Marthe.

He unfolded it and quoted a few lines. Marthe was at a new school, a difficult transition. On the other hand she was not the kind to let herself be bullied. 'Do you think I lack affection for my child, Alberta?'

The abrupt question confused Alberta. 'But of course not.'

'She belongs so very much to her mother. I've been away so much, it shows. I miss Marthe.'

'It's only natural. You—you notice it when a child turns away from you,' said Alberta bitterly.

'Yes, there's that too. I've been annoyed with Sivert more than once, and I've told him so. You know that.'

'It's no use as long as he has these ideas.' It occurred to Alberta that ideas were weapons that Sivert had forged for himself. Behind them stood Sivert himself, obstinate, strong, difficult to understand; one day he might well seize entirely different ones. Suddenly she shuddered, got to her feet, busied herself over leaving the restaurant. The sun had left the street, which now resembled a shaft. The afternoon approached, long and tenacious. She had to go home, make purchases, prepare the dinner, see to something she had left unfinished. They would come home, he and the boy. The painful feeling of dissolution, uncertainty, false situation, would hang in the air making a dangerous undertaking of every step and every word. Her own feeling of having broken faith, of the lack of firmness and purpose in her life, would be waiting to receive her. The momentary horror at the fact that she and Sivert no longer shared their lives, the curious pity she had for him, similar to the pity one feels for people asleep, lying there at one's mercy, she would be spared none of it. Nor the vague fear. Nor the hurt in the fact that the boy lived at home suspecting nothing, that he turned away from her when she sat on the edge of his bed.

'Are you going already?'

'I feel restless, Pierre.'

'Hm. Hi, Michaud.' Pierre rummaged in his pockets for money, found none, blushed a flaming red, which quickly subsided while his expression turned blank. 'Never mind about that, *mon vieux*. I know all about it. *Ça s'arrange.*' Michaud wiped the cloth with his napkin and shook it out. 'You both have credit here.'

'I honestly forgot, *mon vieux*.'

'Your head is full of other things. One cannot remember everything.'

Alberta fought down an impulse to go up to Pierre, put her arms round him, say something. Instead she pressed Michaud's hand so hard that he looked at her in astonishment. 'But you'll be here tomorrow won't you, Madame?'

'If the weather's fine.'

'The weather? We have excellent tables indoors too. A corner, all to yourselves. If it rains I shall keep it for you.'

'Thank you, Michaud, thank you.'

She heard the thump of his wooden leg a couple of times as they left, and suddenly disliked the sound. It had something final about it, the sound of a club striking. At the corner she paused, turned her face upwards towards Pierre, closed her eyes and waited.

'Here, already? *Mon petit enfant!*'

'Kiss me, Pierre.'

He did so. At the brisk pace Alberta loved, the perfect rhythm that filled her body with joy, they walked through the small streets and the Rue de Tournon, into the Luxembourg Gardens, up into the remote, deserted path towards the Observatory, which was theirs.

'Alberta, you can tell me nothing that I don't already know and understand.'

'Nor you me.'

'All this is so wretched, so petty and stupid. I can't even offer to take you out to a meal without—. My small pension goes straight to Dijon.'

'Don't talk about it.'

'But you'll come tomorrow? We have Michaud, after all.'

'I hope I can, Pierre.'

'The concierge?'

'I daren't.'

'She looks trustworthy.'

'It's not that.'

'If something's the matter—Would Liesel—?'

'Liesel does what she can, she always has.'

'Yes, poor Liesel. I shall never forget that she let me know you were alone nowadays. You have to take the initiative, Alberta, the way things are.'

'We've had a wonderful time together, Pierre.'

'Had?'

'Kiss me, Pierre.'

Today was the first time she had asked him to kiss her, the first time she let it happen without turning her head away again at once as if she had burned herself. Kiss, and the world can collapse, all your strength melt away. Longing becomes more agonizing than ever, everything within you that recognises neither reason nor the law seizes power. Kisses are not playthings; Alberta had never understood how anyone could regard them as such. She was afraid of them, cautious as if dealing with fire. Now they were over her like a storm. She was lost in each of them and woke from each like a new person in a new world. Then something penetrated her consciousness, an ice-cold stream from reality. 'I'm mad, Pierre, we're both mad—standing here in the middle of the path—it's late.'

She was already on her way from him, her feet were moving, the distance was increasing.

He accompanied her for a few paces, still holding tightly to one finger. 'Tomorrow, Alberta? I shall not be able to bear it if you stay away.'

'As long as I'm able to, my love.'

Now her finger was free too. His quiet, concentrated face, the eyes alight, continued to accompany her as she ran uphill.

When she got home the key was in the door. She could see it from the courtyard gate. Her heart beat heavily and painfully.

Sivert was sitting at the table. The small box in which he kept money and papers was open in front of him. 'Well, so you've been out?'

'As you see.' And this time Alberta could very well have pretended that she had only been shopping, for she was carrying her purchases, but she said, 'Pierre wishes to be remembered to you. Did you come home again?'

'Had to turn back, I'd forgotten something. We're going out later. I'm expecting a carpenter.'

'A carpenter?' Alberta did not pay much attention. Something to do with frames, she supposed. She walked about, putting her things down, and went across to Tot, who was sitting on the rocking-horse in his outdoor clothes.

'So Pierre is still here? Is he still harping on those theories of his, the obliteration of the individual and so on? I mean his bolshevism.'

'I've heard nothing about the obliteration of the individual. I shouldn't have thought he would be any more obliterated by being given his share in the good things of life than he was after getting tap water and street lighting. I should have thought it would lead to new freedom, greater freedom.'

Alberta was unused to expressing opinions about such matters and listened to herself in amazement. Where had she found such words? If Sivert had not been sitting there, if he were not the person he was, probably she would never even have thought them. He developed them, as pictures are developed on plates. The plate might well have remained undeveloped.

'Pierre's theories. You're as teachable as a parrot.'

Alberta considered for a moment and was certain that she had never heard Pierre say this. Had he already led her into his way of thinking, so that she continued of her own volition? Or was it because they had both been to the bottom in different circumstances, and seen things from below? Sivert had been to the bottom too.

He was rummaging in the box, lifting out papers and putting them down. 'That's odd, I had a hundred francs in notes here yesterday. Now they've gone.'

'But that's dreadful.' Alberta sat down, thoroughly shocked. A hundred francs was a lot of money, even at the present rate of exchange. 'You must have put them somewhere else, Sivert. They can't have disappeared.'

'They have. They were in here.'

'Have you looked in—?' Alberta paused, racking her brains. There were not many places in which to look. 'Are you sure you took them out of the bank, Sivert?'

'Tot, run across to Madame Morin and ask for the hammer. She borrowed it. I may need it when the carpenter comes.'

Alberta noticed Sivert's clenched fist lying on the table beside the box. Her old anxiety gripped her strongly and without reason. There was something about his voice too. She was flooded with homesickness for Pierre, for kindness and silent understanding.

'Have you looked in your best clothes? The inside pocket?'

'Alberta.' He was standing in front of her. 'You might just as well admit it.'

Alberta stood up, as if Sivert were a wall she had noticed at the very last moment. Her thoughts whirled like lightning in her head: Be careful, don't misunderstand him. And then: You did not misunderstand.

The blood rushed to her head, then drained away. Mechanically she went over to find support in the real wall. Sivert followed her. He followed her!

'Tell me the truth, Alberta. I can see it in your face.'

'Do you realise what you're saying?' The words seemed inadequate, pale, empty, without weight. She could find no others.

'Yes, yes, yes. For your own sake let's get this over before the boy comes back. For your own sake.' Sivert spoke quietly and quickly; his eyes, much too blue, never left her face. Alberta shrank away along the wall. Even her lips felt cold and she had difficulty in speaking. Now she and Sivert were so far down that they would never be able to come up again.

'Answer me, at least. I'm saying that as long as you admit—'

'Admit what?'

'Good heavens, I know women have their little weaknesses. Liesel, for instance. I don't attach so much importance to it, in fact. But I must know where I stand. I can't allow myself to be—. You must see that yourself. What have you done with the money? Is there any of it left?'

'I haven't taken your money, Sivert,' said Alberta, suddenly quite calm and resolute, to this utter stranger who was standing in front of her. 'You're mistaken. You must look again, think again.'

'I have looked and I have thought. I don't ask such questions without reason. Well, here's the boy with the hammer. Here's the carpenter too, at the gate.'

'Carpenter?'

'He's coming to look at the divans.'

Anything wrong with the divans? thought Alberta in bewilderment, on the periphery of her consciousness. She watched the carpenter from further down the street taking off his peaked cap: *'Bonjour messieu-dames'*; watched Tot, immersed in what was going on, circling round him and Sivert; watched Sivert clear away cushions and cover and turn the divan upside down: 'I want one exactly the same as this.'

Alberta had sat down again. She noticed she was sitting with her hat in her hand, and put it down mechanically on to the floor. As if from a blow on the head, she felt immense fatigue and a lack of coherence. There were empty holes in her thoughts, gaps from which she returned as if from the hereafter. In one of them she heard Sivert saying, 'If your terms are reasonable I'll take two. But in that case it must be solid work, strong legs that will stand a long journey, for instance. And first-class springs. I could have gone to the Bon Marché, after all. When can you let me have your estimate?'

A journey? What had Sivert said about Liesel? He had talked about her as well, hadn't he? His money? Two new divans? *Two*? Tot—what am I to do about Tot? Until something has been arranged? Tears began to trickle down Alberta's face. To hide them she went up into the attic and sat down on one of the beds. Her thoughts had frozen into a couple of phrases and failed to free themselves: Nothing is arranged, nothing prepared, nothing is arranged, nothing prepared . . .

Again she heard Sivert: 'A fortnight? Not before? Well,

well, as long as I can be sure of them. Leaving at once? No, in a few months' time. But I may need the divans before then. Hell and damnation—wait a moment!'

There he was coming upstairs, standing in the doorway in his shirt-sleeves and with a foot-rule in his hand. 'Are you there? I just want to make a couple of measurements up here. If you wouldn't mind moving for a minute? Thank you.' Sivert studied the ruler and made notes in his notebook, calmly and impassively.

'Are they to stand here?' asked Alberta dully.

'Here, yes.' Sivert was on his downstairs already. 'Yes, the measurements are all right. There's enough room. You can start on them as soon as you can.'

'Very good.' She heard the carpenter leaving. They discussed measurements and materials all the way to the door. The carpenter said, 'Madame,' into thin air to the invisible Alberta. 'Monsieur,' she called back, with the feeling that her voice did not carry at all. Their footsteps crunched on the gravel outside. They were still talking.

Sivert came back with the boy, who was asking questions eagerly. They clattered crockery downstairs, and Sivert lighted the primus. Alberta got up, weak at the knees, went downstairs like a sleepwalker, crossed the room and picked up her hat.

'We're just making some tea to take with the sandwiches,' explained Sivert. 'It's late, we shan't go far. Probably to the fortifications to do some sketching.'

A little later they wandered off together across the courtyard. Alberta stood back from the door, watching them go. Tot strode along on his thin legs, conscientiously carrying the bag of brushes. In the palm of the hand she was pressing against her cheek she still held the softness and the warmth of his body and his face. She had hugged him before he left as if snatching him to her, and squeezed him close, holding his head against hers for an instant. She seemed to hold vulnerability, innocence and simplicity itself in her hands. She released him, or he twisted away from her. She watched the narrow back, the thin nape of the neck, the dent in it, moving away—

She had to hold on to the frame of the door to stop herself running after him. She thrust her clenched fist between her teeth so as not to scream.

'There, you see, Albertchen. He wanted to disgust you to the point of driving you out. What did I tell you? You've put up with a good deal, but you couldn't put up with this. How could you? Not somebody like yourself. Of course he hasn't lost a sou.'

'He must have done, though I can't think how it happened.'

'Have you written to Pierre?'

'I've sent a *pneumatique*.'

'He won't get it until late this evening, in the middle of the night perhaps. He's scarcely ever at home. What did you write to Sivert?'

'Oh, only a few words. "You have won, I can't stand it any longer." It's worse where Tot is concerned. Just imagine not being able to say good night to him this evening. We must come to some arrangement. I can't bring him here. Do you think Sivert has left him alone, Liesel?'

Alberta looked round her in bewilderment at the depressing little hotel room, where a single candle flickered in its holder and cast shadows up the walls.

'Sivert has got what he wanted, *voilà*. He's quite capable of leaving Tot.'

'Then I must go home at once.'

'Stay here until we've talked to somebody else. I've sent a message to Alphonsine. I sent it when I read your letter. She always has good advice, but she can't get here until tomorrow morning. Nor can Pierre. Sivert won't leave the boy the first evening, not the first. Put on your coat and we'll go out. We'll have a meal and then go to a cinema.'

'A cinema? That's the last place *you* ought to go to Liesel.'

'The air is awful in the small ones, I agree, but the price is reasonable. I go to the cinema nearly every evening. Two hours of oblivion.'

'You're worse than a child.'

'The last cigarette, Albertchen, the one they give the condemned prisoner. I don't expect he'd want to do without it.'

'What a way to talk. It's up to you to get well again.'

'I'm joking, I am well, the whole thing's a lot of nonsense. Sivert ought to be horse-whipped, he uses such cheap weapons. I suppose he thinks you haven't kotowed to him enough.'

'Not enough? Have I done anything else? What could I do? We have a child. You have no idea, Liesel, what it means to have a child by the wrong man. But it's my own fault. Do you think he'll leave him? Our little boy?'

'I have a very good idea. No, he won't leave him. And we must come to some agreement before you go home, come to some decision as to what you're to say. You can't stay here tonight; you'll go out of your mind.' Liesel looked about her. 'No electric light even. We lived more elegantly in the old days. What did you want to come to this hotel for?'

'I don't know. I stayed the night here once a long time ago. I had fled from a *pension* and didn't want to go where anybody might recognise me . . . You want a child by Eliel—'

'Not any more.'

'Liesel!' Alberta raised herself on her elbow and reached out her hand in remorse. Liesel took it. 'Put on your coat and come with me.'

'I haven't the money, nor have you.' Alberta thought anxiously of the miserable sum she had hurriedly obtained at the pawnbroker's for her old pieces of jewellery. They had become fewer over the years and their value had not increased with inflation, strangely enough. 'Fetch something from the nearest dairy, and we'll eat here. I believe some of the chestnut men have appeared on the corners.' She looked round for her handbag.

'I help myself to money every day from Eliel's trouser pocket. He doesn't keep count, and doesn't notice if I only take a little at a time. Don't mention chestnuts, please.'

Alberta was sitting upright, staring at Liesel.

'We can't go without,' said Liesel in passionate self-defence. 'Not without anything at all. We clean up around them if nothing else, cook and darn socks and pose if necessary. We must have something in exchange. I've finished with begging, I take it. They go round with money loose in their pockets, they sit for hours at the Dôme every evening, they deny themselves nothing where they and their women friends are concerned. I do it when Eliel has gone you know where; he goes there in his bath-robe. Yes, you can stare, Albertchen. Let me tell you something. Once you've begun to degrade yourself, once you've done it really thoroughly—.' Liesel lost her breath and coughed. 'You make me talk too much.'

'My dear Liesel, I haven't said a word.'

'But you're staring at me. You can stare. If I were certain you weren't afraid of me I'd offer to stay with you tonight. There's infection everywhere; it's one's resistance that's important. Tot—'

'You're to sleep in your own bed, not in discomfort here with me. The sheets are damp too. I remember that from last time. Feel them. I have veronal with me. Now I'm coming.'

Alberta had at last found her voice. Sivert's mysterious remarks about Liesel had been glaringly and unexpectedly illuminated. She had been dazzled and confused for a moment.

'You ought to be careful. Eliel might get suspicious, he might exaggerate its importance.' She picked up her coat, which she had instinctively spread over the doubtful blanket before lying down, tidied herself up, and put an arm round Liesel's sloping shoulders. 'How I should manage without you, I don't know. Do be careful.'

'I *am* careful. If Eliel knows anything—,' Liesel frowned, '—then he knows too that I put the money back as soon as I can. The concierge at Colarossi's has the landscape I painted this summer for sale. We'll go to Baty's. There'll be nobody we know and the food is decent. It has to be if I'm to get anything down.'

'Stop thinking, Albertchen. Eat. Would you like something to drink?'

'No, thank you.' Dully Alberta looked about her at the

crowded restaurant. The air was thick with steam and tobacco smoke; conversation was half drowned in the hubbub of voices and the clash of crockery. Baty's must have become fashionable. It was not quiet as they had expected, but jammed with people. Alberta had wanted to leave, but Liesel had pushed her into a seat just inside the door.

Nobody they knew. But types, of the kind they had become used to seeing through the years: Mediterraneans, elderly spinsters, very young models, chic in their touching way, naïve newcomers from Scandinavia, all expectation, Americans, Americans, Americans. A new cast in an old play, that could simply be called Montparnasse, all of it presented as if through water or misty glass, heard as if through a wall. Watching, one can forget one's pain, then feel it again, like a toothache. A little thought whirred mechanically on its own somewhere inside Alberta's head: They have no children—they have no children—

Suddenly she noticed a deprecating, apologetic expression in Liesel's eyes, and then felt a slap on the shoulder. 'Alberta! Where *have* you been all this time? Here in Paris? *Comment?* And we never meet? How stupid! I must sit down. Is it true you have a child, a little boy? Are you still living alone, or—? You don't look very happy? But these things come and go, that's life. *Enfin*—you have a child. They say it brings happiness. I have an aunt and an uncle on my shoulders—the Revolution—got out of the country without a sou—Aunt's jewellery, but nothing else. My work suffers. But I've had something at the Indépendants nearly every year. One must try to keep afloat, *n'est ce pas?* Do you think I have changed much, Alberta?'

'No, of course not,' answered Alberta, bewildered by Marushka's nervous torrent of words. She looked distractedly into her ravaged, powdered little face, that was incessantly nodding and smiling to people round about.

'Duty, family, *oh là là,* I know all about that now. Though they are darlings, I'm fond of them. *Enfin*—to be frank with you, I have a friend, not young exactly, over sixty, but kind.

Without him I couldn't manage. I have my good days now and again, go to the Riviera, he's rheumatic. We both enjoy gambling. I always lose, but there you are. That's the place to be; there you can take a holiday from your life. You know, the sun and all that. During the war I worked in a hospital, looking after the wounded—I trained as a nurse once upon a time as a young girl, I know all about it. You came across women who were quite incompetent, who had got in through some connection and only got in the way. They were the despair of the doctors. Women always find a way of flirting—'

'I'll go and pay,' said Liesel, getting up.

Marushka put a hand on Alberta's arm. 'Just imagine your having a child. It's courageous of you, but it pays. I was unlucky too, I don't know how it happened. One is careless sometimes. *Enfin*—I found myself in that condition and had to do the same as Liesel. I took it in time, but still. Filthy business, you're never the same afterwards. But there, it's happened since then too. When you have a run of bad luck . . . That's life, one mustn't take it too seriously. Won't you come up one day? You must see my paintings. Where do you live? You must show me your boy. Potter's back. Short skirts don't suit her. But you don't look happy?'

'No, I'm not happy, Marushka.'

'*Pauvre petite*.' Marushka squeezed Alberta's hand, suddenly and surprisingly resembling her old self. 'Listen—is it money? I can see that it's money. I haven't any at the moment, but one day soon—Rue Vavin 35 *bis*. *Courage. Au revoir*. You can rely on me.'

'Thank you, Marushka.'

Outside Alberta collapsed into nervous sobbing, her head against Liesel's shoulder. All the way up to the Rue St Jacques she wept, asking jerkily, 'Do you think Sivert is at the Dôme— Tot alone? We must go and see, go and see. Do you think Sivert is at the Dôme—Tot alone?'

But she passively allowed Liesel to guide her, accompany her upstairs, take off her dress and shoes; swallowed obediently the two powders, lay down docile and shivering on her outspread coat with her dress over her—met two lips in the no

695

man's land between dark and dark—they were there, they were waiting for her—and fell asleep at last.

. . . Madame Morin was to be divorced. Alberta helped her with her arrangements, full of understanding for her and for Monsieur Morin, who was dead, it was true, but walked in and out all the same.

The corner grocer was there. He looked different, but it was he. Alberta and he were conversing. Then she noticed appalled that she was saying *tu* to him. He looked at her, calm, serious, sure of himself. And suddenly she felt between them that terrible complicity that can exist between a man and a woman, the physical and mental understanding that defies all reason, all laws. She felt guilty, and at the same time guiltless and in the right . . .

But the child in her arms was struggling and kicking, its mouth sought her breast, it sucked, released it, its downy head sank to one side, its eyes dulled with repleteness and sleep, she was filled with a great peace and gentleness . . .

Then one of Marushka's Hungarians from long ago said: '*Machen Sie bitte den Mund ganz dreieckig—lassen Sie sich doch ein Ei geben.*' Alberta looked down at her salad, she had no money for eggs, and hunger possessed her like a nightmare. In desperation she fled with the child in her arms, but her feet would not move. They would not move, and Sivert wanted another woman—

'Don't cry, Albertchen, don't cry.'

Liesel was bending over her, stroking her forehead. 'You were having a bad dream. You had better wake up. Have some coffee. Alphonsine is here too.'

Alberta looked up. It was day, grey, ordinary day. Bewildered and exhausted she saw Alphonsine standing dangling her lorgnette between two fingers, and for a moment could not distinguish dream from reality. It was all one. Obediently she drank from the cup Liesel held to her mouth and listened to them talking. 'Will you go to the chemist's then?'

'Yes, I'll go.'

A door slammed. Liesel had gone. Alberta returned to reality, to the cruel and difficult condition that is life. Alphonsine had sat down on the edge of the bed. 'Here, wash your face, it makes you feel fresher. I'll hold the bowl. Now we must use our time while we are alone. It's ten minutes to the nearest chemist, and she'll probably have to wait a while. Talk about friendship! She's been sitting here all night. She looks like a ghost. So you've left home, *ma pauvre petite*?'

Alphonsine had put on her lorgnette. It was her habit in decisive moments. She was wearing her big skunk collar, which made her look bourgeois, and had indeed become fatter as Liesel once had said. But her face still kept its firmness and determination. The red hair, painted mouth and green eyes still contrasted violently with her powder-white skin. Her teeth were just as strong. As if in parenthesis she took the tube of veronal from the bedside table and studied the label. 'Too strong. Knocks you senseless. Bromide, valerian, *tisane* are all right. Not this.'

'I need to be knocked senseless, Alphonsine.' Alberta was already longing for the heavy, imageless sleep she knew she had slept before the dream began, for new, profound darkness.

'We must find out what's to be done. So you've left home.'

'He insulted me,' said Alberta evasively. 'I had to get away for a bit, I couldn't stand the sight of him any more, his voice, his—his footsteps. I—I couldn't go upstairs and lie down beside him as if there was nothing the matter.'

Alphonsine looked at her omnisciently. 'You ought to have gone to bed downstairs for the time being. Well . . ! Can you remember my saying once, "Not that one"?'

'I remember.'

'I told Liesel the same. How many times has she come to me complaining, "He's in love again, somebody from his own country is here again. He's ardently in love." I've had to laugh. Herr Eliel ardent? Herr Sivert ardent? They're good artists, that's what they're ardent about. They're ardent about anything that serves their art, *tant pis* for the rest of us. In my opinion Liesel is withering away for lack of ardour, besides lack of fresh air. Men can live in a sculptor's studio, but we

can't for long. Now her lungs are diseased. *Enfin*—so you've
left him.'

'Yes—for the time being.'

'Ma pauvre petite, what do you mean by the time being?
That man is capable of using it against you. He has already
wounded your feelings.'

'He thought I had taken money,' Alberta said, her lips stiff.
Merely saying it was humiliating.

'Le salaud! Didn't I tell you he was up to something? I've
never liked his eyes. Not honest eyes, in my opinion. You
have a child, a little boy. How old is he now—five, six?'

'He'll soon be six.' Alberta suddenly remembered that it
would soon be Tot's birthday. The thought plunged her into
an abyss of despair.

'Six? Time flies. I've seen him once or twice of course. I
lived at Morlaix for a long time, as you know. My friend lay
there wounded. We're married now and live at Vanves, Rue
Murillo. You must come and see us one day. Now you must
go home as quickly as you can, cost what it will. I don't know
the law. But children's officers and people like them never see
further than the end of their noses, I know that. One hears
enough. There's something called abandonment of the marital
dwelling. That's serious. And if there's another woman . . .'

'There is another woman.'

Alberta was sitting bolt upright in bed. Her head was heavy
as lead and she felt giddy, but one thought cut through, sharp
as a knife. She flailed with her arms to get the coat off and Alphonsine out of the way. 'I couldn't bring him here. The boy,
I mean. I had to think first.'

She was out on the floor, shivering, unable to find her way
into the dress that Alphonsine was pulling over her head, then
straightened and buttoned up. 'Fighting over children, I've
seen a little of that. Here, wash your face a bit more. Have
you a pocket comb? Let me help you. These small hotels—
they're a disgrace. Look at the soap dish. I can scrape the dirt
off it with my nail.'

'Had to have something cheap.' Alberta was looking stiffly
at the door. 'Somebody may be coming.'

'Liesel ought to be back soon.'

'No, somebody else. I've sent a *pneumatique* to someone.'

'Doesn't this person know where you live?'

'Yes, of course.'

'*Eh bien,* anyone who really wants to get hold of you is sure to find you. Here's Liesel. Look, *eau de Mélisse,* a good spoonful. It will calm you.'

Alberta swallowed it. She would have swallowed anything without a notion of what it was. She stared at Liesel, who did indeed look like a ghost and whose eyes were filled with guilt and fear as if a crime had been committed.

'I'm going home, Liesel. If Pierre comes—if Pierre comes, Liesel, say I had to go home. I didn't dare to wait any longer. Greet him for me, Liesel.'

Liesel nodded, clearly prepared to wait for Pierre as long as it might be necessary. It occurred to none of them that they could leave a written message. 'Imagine our not realising,' said Liesel. 'That I could have been so thoughtless, Albert-chen. But we'll never be the sort to understand this kind of thing.'

As she spoke there was a knock at the door. 'We'll wait downstairs.' Liesel drew Alphonsine with her. 'Come in,' called Alberta. Involuntarily she breathed deeply, hastily righted her hat and supported herself against the table. Help and consolation were on the way, protection too. An embrace, a kiss, a few kind words are great things. She expected no more than that.

The door was not locked. It opened slowly. Jeanne stood on the threshold. 'It is I,' she said, nodding absently at Liesel and Alphonsine as they went out.

There is nothing to be done about some things in life. It was Jeanne and nobody else. 'Sit down,' said Alberta tonelessly, feeling her features sag, their tension dissolve. She moved one of the doubtful-looking chairs. Jeanne looked at it, opened her handbag and took out a handkerchief.

'Here's a newspaper.'

'Thank you. These small hotels are dreadful. Well, here I am. Listen, Alberta, I was so nervous out there this summer.

So many things made me nervous. We must talk in peace and quiet.'

'Is it necessary?'

'I have the impression that it is necessary.'

'How did you know I was here?'

'Because I have read your letter. I arrived in Paris this morning, I travelled overnight. This was under the door.' Jeanne opened her handbag again and put Alberta's *pneumatique* on the table. 'Pierre has not been home since yesterday. His bed had not been touched. *Where* he has been—.' Jeanne shrugged her shoulders.

Silence. Anger and mortification struggled in Alberta to such an extent that at first she failed to express them. She opened and shut her mouth a couple of times without making a sound.

'And obviously you don't know either.' Jeanne made a gesture in the direction of the message.

'Are you so sure? People do meet. But of course he's been with friends. He finds it difficult to stand it at home.' At last Alberta had found a tone in which to talk : dry, sober, serviceable. If only she could keep it up.

Jeanne made no reply. She sat looking straight in front of her with an expression of utter fatigue. It made Alberta sorry for a moment. The feeling passed when Jeanne spoke. 'I am candid, Alberta. I go straight to the point, so that people know where they are with me. Let me tell you at once that I understand you. As a woman I understand you. You and Sivert are not happy together. Why, I don't know. I find Sivert very attractive, a good artist, a sensible person. I should have thought that it was you who were too—too complicated, too—*enfin,* it does not work. Sivert has begun to take an interest in somebody else—'

'Thank you, Jeanne, but I'm sure we shall cope with that ourselves, Sivert and I.'

'Good. Then let us consider Pierre. He finds it difficult to settle down after all he has gone through. If there is anyone in the world who understands his difficulties, it is I.'

'*Pardon,* Jeanne.' Alberta could not repress a smile and a new ring in her voice. She knew the smile was spiteful and venomous, an ugly smile to which she should not have stooped. It sat on her face like an unworthy, disfiguring mark. 'Please make haste,' she added. 'I am in a hurry.'

Jeanne was unaffected. She continued where she left off. 'No one knows better than I what is the matter with him. Do you think I like being demanding? Don't you think I too would like to ape his views, to be a companion to him in that way? I am doing my utmost to get him on an even keel again, to bring him back to where he belongs, among the top young writers. I try everything, even to the point of leaving him and telling him it's all over if he doesn't follow me and finish his book. I know what that book might be. I know the beginning let alone the part that preceded it. He did not follow me; he stayed here. He doesn't even write to me. It is your fault. And what does he see in you? You are not beautiful. Intelligent—?' Jeanne paused for a moment as if to consider the matter. 'You are probably intelligent. But in any case you are *understanding*. If there's anything men can't resist, it's that. The person who can appear at the right moment and be understanding—'

'Something in Alberta had struggled to the surface, cold and merciless. 'The book has been burned,' she said, in the same tone of voice as if she were saying, 'It's raining.'

'What?'

'I said the book has been burned. It no longer exists.'

Silence. For a second Jeanne looked as if she had been struck, but it passed quickly. 'When did he do that?' Searchingly, but without enmity, she looked at Alberta.

'The other day.'

'How do you know?'

'He told me so himself. He was relieved. It meant liberation. It stood in his way. It was dead, Jeanne, he could not put life into it again.'

'*Mon pauvre Pierre,*' said Jeanne, and all Alberta's cold wrath dissolved. She took out her handkerchief. Tears, no longer rounded or perfect, trickled down her face. Now Jeanne was ravaged by weeping.

Silence.

'Listen, Alberta, I was allowed to do what I wanted, don't you see? To marry the man I loved? He was well received by my family. While he was at the war they helped us, right up to the day when Pierre would no longer permit it. They lost practically everything. My father had put his money into a sugar refinery. In this country the whole of the sugar industry is in the north. You know how the enemy advanced. Everything was razed to the ground, the machinery destroyed. The shares are not worth much at the moment. He has his little country property, vegetables, fruit, milk. He had to cut down the big trees in the avenue and sell them—'

'I've heard about all that, Jeanne.'

'*Enfin*—they did their utmost. Am I to go to them now and say, "Pierre will not keep me, he cannot keep me. You will have to take me back again. Here is the child I had by him."? Besides—' Jeanne moved the chair next to her roughly— 'Besides, after a few months, a year to be generous, he would probably want to come back to us again. A marriage is a marriage, the links are too numerous, too strong, you must not imagine—'

Jeanne paused, biting her lips. 'I cannot give Pierre his freedom for your sake. Because he cannot free himself, however much he may wish it. We have a child together.'

'My dear Jeanne.' Alberta's anger had gone. She was merely tired. And if it had been necessary to make her give way, she had already done so. Had she even gone so far as to think about all this? No, she had avoided it as if they were obstacles she dared not face. They *were* obstacles.

Jeanne continued: 'I'd like to see the two of you in a couple of years, you missing your child and he his. Or perhaps you've thought of letting Pierre support Tot too? I don't know how you have thought it out. Pierre and I had a civil marriage. I deferred to his wishes. These things make no difference to me. It would not be impossible for him to free himself, if he really wished. But I should have to insist on support, to begin with at any rate. And he—in his present state, to support two children and two wives—! I look at it from the practical point of view. One of us must. I shall not mention my feelings for him.' Jeanne sobbed a dry little sob and came no further.

'All he needs in his present state is peace. Peace and quiet.' Alberta had a desperate feeling that it was imperative to say what was important, no more. To put an end to it. To get away. A little spite might do Jeanne good; it would do no harm.

'He has these new ideas on the brain. It's not so surprising for someone who has been through the war. But it's a misfortune for him. Who are these people he meets? Oh, good people, I'm sure, I'm no snob. But they're waiters, tailors and shoemenders, a few literati who have never succeeded on their own account. And before? The centre of an intelligent circle, invited all over the place. Yes, you can smile, I don't suppose you have any idea what it means to be the object of attention in a city like Paris, what chances it opens up. Well—you don't understand that sort of thing. But perhaps you do understand what it means to break up a home. The home may have its drawbacks, one may wish it were otherwise. But it belongs to the child, it protects the child. One has no right to—'

'It's quite true, Jeanne. And I had no intention—'

'Perhaps you think, she has lost him all the same. That's not so certain. Just you get out of the way and then we'll see. You're a mother yourself. You must be capable of imagining what it would mean to be left alone with a child. You ought—'

Alberta raised her hand deprecatingly. 'What do you want me to do, Jeanne?'

Jeanne pointed at the blue letter. 'Tear that up. Write another. Tell him that you—are not going to meet him again—for the time being at any rate. Keep away, in other words.'

'I haven't been running after him.'

'No, you don't follow him in the street. But there are many ways of doing it. You go with him to these meetings, you listen to him, encourage him, dine with him. I know all about it. You're doing the very opposite of what he needs. If this were to continue it would lead to misfortune for all of us. It it not far off.'

'Very well, Jeanne.'

'Here's a *pneumatique*. Here's a fountain pen.'

'Thank you.'

Alberta wrote. She wrote in a dream. The words appeared of their own volition, springing out of the paper. 'I have thought things over. We shall not meet again.' She paused for a moment, pulled herself together, and added, 'Pierre' in disproportionately large letters, which wavered in all directions. The signature, 'Alberta', on the other hand, was quite neatly written. Then she folded the letter, stuck it down, wrote the address, gave it to Jeanne and felt her spine sag.

'Thank you, Alberta. This is the best thing for us all. After a time, I'm sure that you yourself . . . Let me give you a piece of advice, stick to Sivert. He's a good man, the father of your child.'

'Is he really?'

'Don't let's part enemies. We're not enemies. We've met at an unfortunate time. If it had not been for this damned war and for all that we've been through—'

'No, of course not. None of this would have happened.'

'That's just what I think. *Au revoir*, Alberta.'

'*Adieu*, Jeanne.'

The door closed behind her. Alberta remained seated for a second, then threw herself across the bed, wept the burning, dry weeping she had experienced before, no more than a grimace. It passed rapidly. The moment to give in to it had not yet come. Quickly she collected her things and went downstairs. Liesel and Alphonsine were waiting in the dark little vestibule. They did not say much, nor did Alberta. Together they took a tram. It was raining outside, windy and autumnal.

Outside the studio she hesitated for a while, looking in through the windows which went down to head level. Sivert and the boy were sitting at the table playing Halma. They moved the pieces with concentration. For an instant Tot glanced over at the window, but turned back again at once.

Alberta opened the door.

'Here's Mother,' said the boy as calmly as if she had left five minutes ago, lifting his head from the game.

'Yes, here she is, I do declare.' Sivert's voice was quite normal too, as if nothing had happened. And perhaps it had not. God knew.

'Is everything all right, Sivert?'

'As you see.'

Alberta had taken off her outdoor clothes. She stood behind the boy with her hands about his face, lifted it towards her, scrutinized it, bent down and hugged him to her. She thought: If I have to live in hell . . . Hack off a heel and cut a toe, the shoe will fit.

In a fit of feverish gaiety she sat down at the table, knocked down the pieces and began placing them upright again. 'Now you shall play with Mother. I'll get something to eat in a minute, Sivert. Look, I'm going to move this one, Tot.'

Her face was burning and she felt unwell and tousled as if she had spent a night sitting up in the train.

The boy was asleep. Sivert had not gone to the Dôme. He was wandering up and down outside with his coat collar turned up against the chill of the evening. It was drizzling and still windy. But the moment had come when matters had to be discussed.

If one gives way to fatigue, it becomes endless. It was no use giving way to it now. Alberta put on her coat and went outside as well. It was too cold to sit. She joined Sivert and they walked up and down. It was some time before Sivert spoke. Each time the light from the lamp on the pavement outside fell on him she glimpsed his face. As so often before it was impossible to draw any conclusion from it.

'It seems there are quite a few things you are unable to put up with, Alberta.'

'It's not so easy. Do you still believe I've taken your money?'

'No, it's not easy,' answered Sivert, obviously knowing a

great deal about the subject. 'But a person ought to be able to defend himself. I thought you had more pride, I must say.'

'Than what?'

'Than to come back, once you had left. As far as the money's concerned, I don't know what to believe. At any rate it's a highly singular story. I could have shown you the door today. As long as the boy was there I didn't wish to do so.'

'You do so now, then?'

'We needn't use words like that.'

'What words have you thought of using?'

Sivert did not reply immediately. They went on walking. It was dark in the studios, a faint light showed through Madame Morin's blinds. Sivert stopped, and glanced at Alberta quickly. The lamplight caught the glitter in his eyes. 'What would you say, Alberta, if I told you that I was in love with someone else?'

Alberta gave a start. These were decisive words, affecting the fate of all three of them. She felt her strange pity for Sivert for an instant. At the same time his silhouette seemed to change as he stood there: look at his shoulders, his legs, the line of his chin, his hat! Is that how he looks? Just as when she had first known him.

'You don't have to tell me that, Sivert.'

'No, no. But what have you to say?'

'I say that we must settle matters accordingly.' Alberta felt as if she were walking on quaking ground. It was impossible to tell if it would hold when she took the next step. How on earth were they to settle matters?

'Yes,' said Sivert. 'That's what I think too. It's fortunate that we're not legally married. Now we shall avoid a great deal of bother. You don't want to know who it is?'

The thought stirred coldly in Alberta: It's none of my business. She said: 'Need I ask about something I know already?'

'I've been meeting a good many people recently.'

'Then perhaps I am mistaken.'

'I don't know if you are. But it's the Swedish painter, in fact.' And Sivert embarked on an account of which Alberta did not understand the half, such a swarm of old and new anxieties were creating havoc in her mind. Nevertheless, she quickly understood, as if with senses other than her hearing, that this had to come about and that it was to a great extent her own fault.

'Yes, yes, Sivert. It may well be so, Sivert.'

He gave a brief lecture on woman as mother and mistress; she was either the one or the other, seldom both. Then there were those who were neither the one nor the other.

Exhaustion drifted through her brain as black patches. Her anxieties reappeared now and again, and thoughts for which she failed to find words immediately: something to the effect that we are not divided into categories, we would like nothing better than to be both. But it takes strength and the right conditions. Not even a plant will develop all its qualities in any kind of soil. It was useless to explain this to Sivert now.

Then he said something that left her wide awake. 'You said, I love you, first.'

'Did I? It must have been at some moment—? It must have been in your arms?' Alberta searched her memory confusedly. When had she said these amazing words? And had it been so wrong? Had he not just accused her of—?

'You did. And it's a mistake. It's the man who should say that sort of thing first.'

Suddenly Alberta did not know whether to laugh or cry. 'You—you ninny!' she exclaimed in despair. It was a word Sivert had taught her. At home they said booby.

'Another expression I shall not forget,' announced Sivert. 'I shall remember that word, you may rest assured.'

But Alberta repeated the word and made matters worse by saying nincompoop. And she left him to prepare herself for the night with clenched teeth. When Sivert came in a little while later she was already in bed, knowing that she had not improved her position in any way. There would be much to negotiate.

Sivert's breathing was as regular as clockwork. Alberta could not sleep. One can be so tired that no powder will help, not even two. Delivered, delivered, delivered, delivered, said her heart, punching out the seconds. Tot tossed restlessly in his sleep as if life itself was too burdensome for him.

The first to say I love you? Yes, there had been times when she had believed Sivert to be different from the man he was. The misleading moment of engulfment. It must have been then.

Sivert did not say such things. 'Hh, Hh,' said Sivert, keeping his words under control—unless he had finally brought himself to say them now. Alberta smiled maliciously at the thought. He would be incapable of it.

She remembered that she had become effusive at times. Perhaps someone who had kept silent for much of her life does so easily. It must be true that it was dangerous to keep silent, as Frederick Lossius had said one summer at home. It did not do to be effusive. It irritated people. They would have none of it. Not Sivert.

There had also been moments when his name had paused on her lips and refused to be spoken, because she really ought to have been saying another name. God knows which of all the names in the world? And moments when she had had the feeling that she had approached something strong and good-natured in the belief that it was not dangerous. Then either its paws or its jaws had engulfed her, and there she was, trapped.

He was right. One came to men like Sivert of one's own accord, once one had laid a hand on the back of his neck. They were charged with the patient waiting of generations for what finally comes of its own accord. They keep to the letter, and have done so for thousands of years.

What had she felt for him? Gratitude because he had broken into her loneliness? Yes, mainly that. Sympathy? Sivert had been alone too. The lunatic feeling of ownership for what one finds it difficult to do without? The feeling the animal has for its master? A brief period of infrequent moments, a hectic blaze of body and mind, a wave of passion which had more to do with the two strong arms round her in the darkness, the mysterious proximity of another living being, than Sivert himself.

And yet—as her antipathy had thawed there had come a blind faith, an unconditional surrender in those strong arms. When she had struggled incompetently to produce meals, clumsily and arduously patched and darned, sewn her unsuccessful creations, fought with dust and fleas, it had been for Tot's sake and out of fear; but also out of tenderness. In order finally to experience a little tenderness.

Anything that she had got out of it had really come from her own hungering blood, her indomitable determination to experience happiness.

Why had they stayed together? In the first place because they had to. There had been no other way out, though Sivert seemed to have found one now. In the second place out of the urge to create continuity, to complete what has been begun; out of egoism, fear of loneliness, a desire to share one's life with whoever it turns out to be. If he does not answer to one's original ideas, one makes a fantasy picture and glues it on to the outside. It will serve for a while.

Supposing the war had not come? It was useless to contemplate. Who can tell how things would have turned out if everything had been different?

Alberta sat bolt upright in bed. One thing had struck her with fearful clarity: Sivert had not abandoned her when she was pregnant. He had not acquired anything so burdensome as a bad conscience. He had plodded on with his burden. But one must not demand more than patience in such cases, it seemed. Sivert had been patient. Sivert had done his duty. The fault was hers, for not having found herself a livelihood. There was the hitch, there the stumbling-block. She was the debtor. She lay down exhausted and dared not think further in any direction.

The following evening Sivert prepared to go to the Dôme. Alberta threw on her coat and went with him outside. 'There's one thing we must discuss, Sivert, the sooner the better.'

'Well, what is it?'

And Alberta got it out, the most difficult, the most burning of all questions. 'Have you thought about us?'

'About you?'

'Yes, Tot and me? What arrangements are we to make?'

'Of course I have.'

'Yes, and—?'

'I shall have to take the boy.'

'You?'

'Yes, I. I can support him. You ought to be quite glad to be free, so that you can finally devote yourself to what you want to do. Besides, after what has happened— You simply left. If you had any rights, you lost them then.

'You're not really a mother in that sense of the word,' continued Sivert, when Alberta failed to respond.

'You and she?' she said at last, quietly, as if to clarify the matter. 'Have you gone mad, Sivert?' she got out finally, very loudly.

'Mad? No, I'm certainly not mad.'

'I believe you must be.'

'You believe, you believe. I've given up trying to make you see reason, Alberta. During the first years I thought— But that's not the question now. The question is solely the welfare of the boy. He'll have a wise person for stepmother.'

'Stepmother?'

'Stepmother. Can you find another word for it? A wise person, who will know how to bring him up, how to make a man of him. What do you give him? Spoiling and nonsense. Have you ever been *fond* of him, when it comes to the point? You've constantly had something to find fault with. All that talk about mother love is a bit of a fable, I suppose. A stranger may often be just as suitable. You will be given the opportunity to see him, in so far as it's possible. I don't intend to leave you without support. We shall be reasonably comfortable. But of course I don't know what you will decide to do ...'

All Alberta could feel was a desire to hit Sivert, hit him in the face. At the same time she knew that if there was one thing she must not resort to, it was this. And she knew why she had been afraid of Sivert. This was why. They were standing at the decisive point in their lives. Something had been spinning in secret. Now it was a completed, dangerous web with threads stretching forwards and backwards in time; it was impossible to see the beginning or the end of it. She went across to the wall, to support herself against it.

Fond of her child? She was knotted with anxiety for him; with distress because he was as he was and not different; with anguish in advance on his behalf; with longing for him.

'We must be reasonable,' Sivert said. 'We must think of the boy first. I'm thinking of you as well. You must admit that with your attitude to life this will be the best solution. There's nothing to quarrel about. I have my work, I can support him, not you, not at the moment, at any rate. Legally my right to him is clear. Well, I must go now.' Sivert took out his watch and looked at it in the light from the lamp. 'Besides, did you want a child?'

'I'd have been an idiot to want one, placed as we were. Did you want a child?'

'No. A man doesn't want children as a woman does. But I did my duty towards him. I've supported him for almost six years—'

'Be quiet, Sivert, with your support.'

'There we go again. It's impossible to talk to you. I repeat, I have done my utmost, always my utmost, I have done all that a man *can* do. As for you, were you even capable of dealing with the situation when he came into the world? Most women manage that. But didn't I have to work like a maid? I lost eight pounds. I have never referred to it, but I did. I won't mention my work. Besides, I've provided myself with a book on the law, I know what I'm talking about.'

Alberta stared at him, petrified. Then she heard herself speaking, quietly, coldly, maliciously. 'I don't know how many pounds I lost. I didn't go and weigh myself. But—' And she went over and hit Sivert in the face. Now she had done it. Foolish or not, it was unavoidable.

Sivert flinched slightly. Then his face came into the lamplight, strangely thin at the tip of his nose. His mouth was a line, his eyes seemed nailed in his head by two contracted pupils in porcelain blue irises. The mask dissolved into cold laughter.

Alberta froze. This was Sivert's rage. And his rage was as assured as everything else about him, stubborn, persistent, unlikely to diminish when first awakened. 'We've thought of going home,' he said abruptly and matter-of-factly. 'In the early spring. We may go to Sweden for a couple of years. Now you know where you stand.'

He turned on his heel and left. The gate slammed behind him.

Had she wanted a child? No, she had been afraid, she had not wanted it to happen. Gusts of fear had passed through her when she realised she was pregnant, the fear of being tied, the fear that she might not survive. She knew she would never be able to take it lightly. And besides—take it lightly, in her position? The child would not have survived.

Only one fear had been greater, that of destroying her body, her healthy body which, unharmed, had borne cold and other deprivations and seen her through many situations. Pride and instinct asserted themselves violently. It was not for nothing that she had seen Liesel lying humiliated and destroyed, weeping and bitter.

What had happened? She had been searching for herself. Then the child was suddenly there, and everything in her had fought against it. Could the boy somehow have known, in his mother's womb? But he had smiled at her when he was old enough, and held her tightly in the evening before he went to sleep. With increased longing she remembered how, when he was a little older, he had woken up to be put on the pot. He had thrown his arms round her neck wanting to sleep there, a gesture of ownership as clear as noonday; a gesture too of unscrupulous confidence that had made her feel confident herself. She had arrived at something important in life, and she had arrived there unawares, as we so often do.

There had come a time when she had been opposed, stubbornly and silently. She had not understood what was happening; it had merely been in the air, disquieting and unpleasant. Now she understood. Now she understood a great deal, with stinging, ice-cold clarity. Is there anything a man is incapable

ALONE

of doing? He can take the child out of the womb, physically
and psychologically, born or unborn. His is the power.

She had had her way once. Since then it had been understood that beyond this she could not reasonably make any
claims.

On the other hand Sivert had bought this and bought that;
he had not gained much joy from it all. She wept under the
blanket for Sivert and herself. When her thoughts came to
Tot she had to stop herself screaming. They went in circles.
Somewhere outside the circle, in another orbit, so distant that
he could no longer be seen clearly, was Pierre. He was like
a dead man, someone whose existence is uncertain, whom one
can only miss. She found herself clinging to her pillow, thrusting her head down into it as if it were alive, and capable of
giving her protection and warmth.

Some days passed, unpleasant, unreal days, torturing passages between harbours of heavy, artificial sleep. It rained and
blew. Tot stayed indoors, Sivert was home some of the time
too. Alberta felt as if she were at a railway station. The train
would be leaving soon; it was no use embarking on anything.
Sivert spoke to her in an ordinary tone of voice about ordinary
things and as little as possible, as if at a departure, when all
the good-byes have been said and an awkward void has to be
filled.

If she took the boy out they only wandered about the
streets. Feverishly she talked to him, feverishly she found
things to do when they were at home, taking out games in a
display of gaiety which she felt she owed him: clumsy instalments on a sum of joy which she had not kept up to date, had
been piling up, and could never be paid off. He watched her
in astonishment. Sivert's irony hung in the air, but he did not
interfere. Every time he came home her heart stood still. If
something were to happen she would offer physical resistance,
cling to Tot, scream, call to Madame Morin for help, hide in
her apartment with the boy. They would have to knock down
the door and kill her before they could take the child. She
looked at the thin little figure, the strange little face, the dent

in the back of his neck, and knew that nothing was of the slightest importance compared with giving him up. Somewhere on the periphery of her consciousness she had vague notions of looking for help, of going to the authorities and putting her case before them. A mountain of money and paper rose up at the very thought, overwhelming her. The idea of going to strangers with all this was also overwhelming.

If she could have known for certain when she would be alone she would have sent a cry for help to Alphonsine. Soon it would be the boy's birthday ...

One afternoon, when Sivert had said he was going to sketching class and returned home half an hour later, Alberta's heart stopped dead. When he sent Tot across to Madame Morin it pounded in fear. She felt her legs disappear from beneath her. Then she suddenly felt a savage, furious strength, a desperation. She waited.

Sivert paced the floor, paused, resumed his pacing. Alberta held her breath. As if in a trance she repeated to herself: Keep calm, keep calm. As soon as the first words are spoken you will be stronger. Keep calm. She gripped the table, under the leaf.

'The devil take me if women aren't completely lacking in pride,' said Sivert.

'I suppose it varies?' Alberta could hear the hesitation in her voice. What was he getting at?

'I'm damned if it does.'

Silence.

'She's a mystery,' stated Sivert.

'Really? A mystery?'

'A complete mystery. Here we've—here I've—here I finally come and suggest that we get everything settled, so that we can make our arrangements. A man ought to be able to insist on that. She looks at me and she says, "But my dear Sivert, we've had a wonderful time together, we've been such good friends. It's been really beautiful occasionally, you know I think that. I've been very happy during the time we've spent together, but to go on for ever—!" Sivert threw his hands out in a wide gesture. 'Now it's one of the others, of course, that's what it is. *Women!*' He said the word as if conjuring up the devil himself.

And he made to leave, seizing his hat.

'Are you going out?' Alberta fought against an overwhelming exhaustion that made each word an effort.

'I must go and cancel the divans. What else can I do?' Only Sivert could have said such a thing so simply and straightforwardly. He was already out of the door.

Alberta looked about her. It was all more than familiar, yet she seemed to be seeing it for the first time. Look, there's the stove, an unparalleled luxury once upon a time. There it stood, unchanged in its outward appearance, a little rusty here and there. She must get hold of some blacklead, they would have to start the heating again soon.

She bent forward over the table; she whispered, 'If only everything were different.'

The boy entered in his quiet way. Sivert came back. 'What about your leaving, then, Sivert?' She wondered why she said it. Out of malice, perhaps.

'I shan't change my plans. I shall go home in the spring. With Tot. You must do as you please.'

* * *

It was the end of April, mild and still. The twilight was falling, dark with rain. Moist, blue-grey cloud hung in broad, loose layers above the hills, which looked as if they were merely a continuation of the sky. In front of the hills were bare, violet-brown trees, broken here and there by dark firs; in the foreground ploughed land and withered meadows just starting to green, ruts, lanes, one or two houses, stone walls.

It was a mild landscape, without contrasts. A broken-down barn fell in with it as if it had grown up out of the soil. The air was bland, tasting of vegetation, steaming earth and burning undergrowth. Smoke rose up, collected horizontally, lay floating on the breeze or dissolved into formless masses that displaced all outlines. Bonfires, tended by children, were bright in the dusk. There was quiet birdsong from the hedges and the undergrowth alongside the road. The murmur of hidden streams could be heard continually.

Since leaving the town they had followed the same road, edged with stone markers. It went slowly uphill towards the wood. Alberta was sitting up in front with the grey-bearded man who was Sivert's father. He did not look at her, but asked questions and gave answers to the air about him. With some difficulty and strain they exchanged remarks about the journey and the weather. At the back of the cart with the suitcases, the crate of paintings and the rocking horse, sat Sivert with Tot on his knee. Tot was asleep.

Sivert was doing most of the talking. 'Well, would you believe it,' he exclaimed. 'If the Evensens haven't built a glass veranda! And what's that at the side of the house? Surely it's not—?'

'I expect that's the garage,' said old Ness soberly. He shook the reins out of habit. The fallow horse quickened its pace for a moment and then resumed its jog-trot.

'Oh, so he's bought himself a car as well? Whaling certainly pays.'

'He's worth eighty thousand kroner now.'

'Is that so? Is that really so? Well, well. And what's that we can see above the trees? The new chapel? But it looks as if it's finished?'

'It is, more or less. The women have collected most of the money. Now they want an organ. And then the altar hangings. That's what they're busy doing now, Mother and Otilie, getting in money for that too.'

Sivert could well imagine it. Yes indeed, it was to the credit of the women of the village. But what about the altar-piece? Had they got that? Sivert thought an altar-piece was surely the most pressing task.

'Ho, ho, ho, ho,' cackled the old man. 'Yes, I'm sure you think so, master painter that you are. You can ask them, apply through the proper channels, as they say. I can't give you better advice.'

Well, Sivert did not consider the matter to be entirely out of the question. An attractive altar-piece, some well-chosen motif. There was no need to choose the Resurrection, it had become too ordinary, so had the Crucifixion. But the Annunciation, for instance? Or Mary's visit to Elizabeth? The price would have to be fixed remember that it was all in a good cause.

Female models, hammered Alberta's brain. Female models.

She felt dazed and light-headed after the nights in third class carriages and another on deck between Sassnitz and Trelleborg. Sivert had insisted on travelling via Berlin. He had inspected it indefatigably for several hours, right up to the last minute, while Alberta, crushed by exhaustion, lay on a hotel bed with Tot beside her, occasionally glancing up at a red flowered wallpaper and the Kaiser and his Empress framed to their knees, undisturbed by defeat and revolution.

A little sad and heart-sick she sat watching with astonishment the cold northern landscape which takes so long to unfurl into spring coming to meet her, surround her, disappear behind her. This was Norway. An unfamiliar Norway, yet at the same time surprisingly familiar, as if she had seen it long ago or in a dream. The small, round, yellow horse with its black mane and crupper askew, the apron which old Ness had so carefully buckled round her, the air, the colours, the stone markers, it was homelike and it was foreign, different from the glimpse she had once had of the south coast at Grimstad. Nevertheless it was like driving back into early childhood, experiencing afresh something old and forgotten to which she had been disloyal. As recently as in the railway compartment that afternoon she had felt as if she were only passing through, and sat full of sad recognition. Now, in the open cart out under the sky, she felt defenceless, forced to answer for herself, someone who had really forfeited her right to be here and yet came and insisted on it.

She should have belonged to this country. She did not do so. All the time she was here she would carry with her the smart in her breast, a kind of painful tenderness she could not take into consideration, could not bother about. She was doomed to long to get away again. That was her nature. That was the nature of life.

'Do you feel cold, Alberta?'

'No, of course not.' Alberta drew her coat up round her throat, realising as she did so that she was freezing. But it had been kind of Sivert to ask.

It was almost dark. They were driving alongside a fir hedge, naked and plucked at the bottom, overgrown and far too thick at the top. Alberta could not help thinking that one would have to search for anything more depressing than such a hedge, and that it had better not be here. Suddenly they swung in through an opening. 'Well, here we are,' said Sivert. Alberta remembered that the place was called Granli after the firs, and shivered more than ever.

From an old photograph in Sivert's pocket book she recognised the white house with its veranda and gables and the contours of the two women who were coming down the steps to meet them. The kerchief of the one and the apron of the other gleamed white through the dusk.

Day by day it slowly became greener round the black circles in which the fruit trees stood. Day and night there was the smell of burning undergrowth, that smell which had caught up with her year after year and was the same everywhere, on walks in the mountains at home up north, on the outskirts of Paris, in the garden of a farm down by the fjord. Once it had been a joyous sign of spring, intoxicating, liberating; now it had acquired a tinge of admonition and reckoning, surprising her in the wrong places and in the wrong circumstances, filling her mind with irritating unrest: How far have you come since last year? What business have you here? It was carried up from the garden, where Alberta and Otilie constantly had a small fire going; or it came drifting from somewhere else.

When twilight fell, tartly cool, bordering on frost, other fires showed bright in other gardens and out in the fields. Tranquil blue columns of smoke rose from them. Two lines of verse freed themselves from the chaos of memory and pursued Alberta with the persistence of music: 'The land stood dressed in bud, fragrance flowed from the leaf, Abel's thank-offering rose to the sky.' The transparent Norwegian spring with its strong scent of growth and burning was in them, as blood is in the body. Who wrote them? Björnson.

One morning it was raining, a silent, mysterious rain, full of promise, that had begun in the night and continued hour after hour. The earth greened intensely and magically fast, so fast one could watch it, round the beds in the garden; a garden which was far too cut up by its narrow, curving paths, where no one ever seemed to set foot except when they had to be levelled once a year. Meaty and red, naked and immodest, the rhubarb suddenly shot up out of the dark soil. The gooseberry bushes bristled with a pale mist of countless minute buds along the branches. When the weather cleared towards evening a chuffing sound came up from the invisible fjord, and old Ness took the pipe out of the corner of his mouth and nodded wisely. 'The first motor boat this year. Wonder if it's Evensens'?'

Alberta was exhausted and bewildered by spring. It was the second she had experienced within a short period of time. It had been over where they had come from. There it had been summer.

'I hope you're going to call me Mother.'

The clear, pale eyes were deep-set in the old woman's thin face under the kerchief, which kept slipping backwards and had to be retied. Cheerful and frank, but searching too, they looked at Alberta. 'It would be a pity if you didn't call me Mother.'

She put her hand on Alberta's and dropped her voice. 'What do you feel about sharing Otilie's room? She's kind, Otilie, not a scrap of badness in her. But she is *odd*, you know. She is *odd*. I wanted you to have the room to yourselves, you and Sivert and the boy. Then the rest of us could have slept downstairs. But no, she would have none of it. She's not married, that's the trouble. She doesn't understand. She can't understand. And perhaps it won't be for so very long, so we let her arrange it as she wanted. So that there should be no *bad feeling*. She thinks it's grand to have you up there in her room, you see.'

The dry, rough hand, so worn with age and work that the veins lay above it unprotected like roots on a forest path, shyly patted Alberta's, then suddenly withdrew, afraid of having dared to go too far. 'The time will soon pass, you'll see. If Sivert gets this bequest he's applied for I suppose you'll all be off again. And that's right and proper. Married folk must be on their own, not hanging about the old folk. I still understand that, old as I am. But you did us a kindness to come home while Father and I were still alive; and it would please us to see you happy the little while we have you.'

'Of course we're happy,' managed Alberta. She also managed the strange, very difficult word, 'Mother', and found the hand that had withdrawn. She smiled. 'I'm glad you asked me here and that I've come to know you,' she brought out. But that was all. Her lips closed tight.

She would have given much to be able to be truly honest in such moments, to be the simple, reliable person whom everyone finds straightforward; a person who, from the moment she had joined forces with him and to the end of her days, was securely and inevitably fond of Sivert.

'You come to me, if there's anything wrong,' said Sivert's mother softly, giving Alberta a little nudge. 'Come to me. And you know it would please Father if you were to *call* him Father.'

Alberta promised. And that obstacle was out of the way. But there were many more. God knew how it would go with them?

They were sitting on the kitchen steps, Old Fru Ness and Alberta. It had come about that they sat there together now and again, almost surreptitiously, even though they were visible from all directions. They did so when Otilie had gone down to the store, or down to the quay, or to town, and Alberta had avoided going with her.

If there were time, Fru Ness would bring out something to eat: jam and biscuits, glasses of cream that had been put aside for Alberta and Tot. The sun was warm at midday, shining directly down on them. Sivert's mother talked about her life, her marriage. From the time when, as an eighteen-yearold serving maid in the town, she had met Sivert's father, she had lived through everything in the unshaken certainty that he, who had first of all gone to sea as a carpenter for many years and then put all his savings into the farm, was the person whom she should accompany and to whom she should accommodate herself in matters large and small.

Over by the steps of the wooden storehouse, where the grindstone stood, Tot was busy. He had established himself, with the box full of objects he had collected, in a safe spot under the stairs. From there it was only a few steps across to the stable where the rocking horse stood in its stall beside Blakken, as was only right and proper. There he waited for the exciting moment when something had to be sharpened and the stone began to turn. He had begun to come over to them of his own accord when he saw there was something to be gained by it; he no longer had to be fetched and forced or persuaded to come. Sometimes he would stand watching Fru Ness and Alberta with his profoundly blue eyes; sometimes he would look round at all these new things and say to himself, in French: 'It's Norway.'

'Yes, it's Norway.' Alberta spoke only Norwegian now, and the boy understood it or should have been able to. But he seemed to be half-heartedly protesting against it all by keeping to the foreign language. 'We shall be friends,' said old Fru Ness. 'We shall be good friends, as soon as he settles down. I must say I think he's thin, Alberta, though he has put on weight. I was frightened the first evening, he looked so poorly compared to what we're used to here. But I expect he was thoroughly tired after the journey, as you said. I'm wondering what we shall do with him when school begins in the autumn. If you're here then, of course.'

'We must put his name down,' Alberta said.

'You must talk to Sivert. He will have to decide. If you're leaving again soon, then—'

'But he must go to school, wherever we are. He must start—'

ALBERTA

'You talk to Sivert. He knows best how it should be.'

'Yes,' answered Alberta tamely, but without rebellion. There was something disarming about Sivert's mother. She preached the doctrine according to which she lived, no more and no less.

Alberta was sharing Otilie's room. They were up in the north gable, in a large room with two brown-painted beds, a wash-stand, Otilie's chest of drawers with a mirror above it, and a table in front of the window. The air, which never felt the sun, hung full of a sweet, enclosed smell impossible to disperse. It was supposed to be a temporary arrangement. Part of the house was being rebuilt with an eye to summer visitors, and the south gable was uninhabitable for this reason. Sivert was sleeping on the sofa in the sitting-room and had put up a camp bed down there for Tot. Out of doors the brittle spring continued, slightly more advanced, but still tinkling with last night's ice.

The very first evening Alberta had felt suffocated. There are many kinds of nakedness: Otilie's was the unhealthy kind, un-aired and distasteful, never completely unclothed. When she took off her dress and stood there in her old-fashioned corset, with ugly, bare arms which were too thick at the top and wrinkled at the elbows, and assumed a different expression from her usual one, she seemed to Alberta to be an outrage against all modesty, something impure from which she would have liked to turn away, but which she was forced to look at; let alone when Otilie washed herself in the morning, with her clothes turned down to her waist.

Her washstand was crowded with half empty medicine bottles, old pots of ointment, and vaseline. There was a greasi-ness and dustiness about them that permeated the air. That un-pleasant smell one often associates with elderly, rather fat women, accompanied Otilie and all her belongings. If Alberta was forced to undress or dress in her presence, she did so with cunning. She slipped quickly in and out of her clothes as if attempting to vanish. The simple, natural action of splashing water over herself, upright and unclothed, was impermissible up here in this room; it had to be filched briefly and in bits and pieces. Gritting her teeth, Alberta defended her body so that Otilie should not get a glimpse of it.

The Bible lay on the table beneath the window. It had the funereal trappings of the Lutheran Bible Society, a coal black cover, with a cross on it, its mere appearance evoking images of graves, crumbling bones, the corner of the churchyard at home where withered flowers lay rotting in a heap. When old Ness brought out his downstairs in the sitting-room and leafed through it with coarse, careful fingers to find a text, the impact was quite different. But when Otilie sat by the window, which was hermetically sealed against the evening twilight, in grey felt slippers, a shawl over her bedjacket, muttering as she read, turning the pages and sighing over text after text, Alberta crept under the eiderdown so as not to die of mental and physical nausea.

She told herself that Otilie could not help it, that life had made her as she was, that she ought to be sorry for her, and that their stay here would not last for ever. Once again, here was one of those tracts in life that had to be traversed holding one's breath and shutting one's eyes. Time after time she had run into them and coped with them by going at half-speed, sometimes switching to another track and steaming away along that. The days might encircle her like a vice. Then the only thing to do was to keep calm, not lose her head and make everything worse by ill-considered action. Tot slept with Sivert downstairs and was dressed and undressed by him. Tot got air through an open window. That was a big thing, the most important of all.

'Hew down the tree, and cut off his branches . . . nevertheless leave the stump of his roots in the earth, even with a band of iron and brass, in the tender grass of the field; and let it be wet with the dew of heaven, and let his portion be with the beasts in the grass of the earth . . . and let seven times pass over him. They shall drive thee from men, and thy dwelling shall be with the beasts of the field, and they shall make thee to eat grass as oxen, and they shall wet thee with the dew of heaven, and seven times shall pass over thee, till thou know that the most High ruleth in the kingdom of men, and giveth it to whomsoever he will.

'And whereas they commanded to leave the stump of the tree roots; thy kingdom shall be sure unto thee, after that thou shalt have known that the heavens do rule.

'Let not mercy and truth forsake thee: bind them about thy neck; write them upon the table of thine heart.

'Our Father, Which art in heaven . . .'

Alberta's thoughts were suddenly released from the mumbling, monotonous voice, and were again on their own somewhere, half overcome by sleep: Thy kingdom shall be sure unto thee, after that thou shalt have known that the heavens do rule . . . Let not mercy and truth forsake thee: bind them about thy neck; write them upon the table of thine heart . . .

This was what men had had to impose on one another. There was nothing inevitable about life. Thy kingdom shall be sure unto thee, after that thou shalt have known that . . . thy kingdom shall be sure unto thee . . .

Outside an enormous soughing passed through the wood. The wind was rising, fresh and free. Seven times have passed over me, she thought. And seven times seven . . .

An old man with a white beard and spectacles, dressed in a grey habit, staff in hand. He put down his staff and spectacles. Kindly and calmly, but with decision, he took a pen and writing materials from Alberta and put them to one side on a desk. 'There, there,' he said, in a voice like a schoolmaster's.

'Who are you?' asked Alberta dispiritedly.

'I am Time,' answered the man. He picked up his staff and spectacles, and left slowly, unhurriedly . . .

A fearful emptiness spread in and around her. It had all gone, the desk with the things on it, the old man. She was alone in the universe, dispossessed of a good of which she had no understanding.

It was irrevocable. It could not be put right again.

* * *

'Some people use unbleached material for kitchen curtains,' said Otilie. 'It's not a bad idea.'

Unbleached? Yes, unbleached—Alberta's thoughts took a daring turn and lighted on the word domestic. God knows why? Probably her inner defences were functioning. She said it in desperation. But it happened to be right. Otilie nudged her playfully in the ribs. 'Domestic, yes indeed. You're not so wide of the mark when it comes to the point. Be a dear and run down to the store for me. It's good for you, you're the one who's married and a housewife.'

Every now and again Otilie made it plain that she did not take Alberta's married status very seriously. It was plain from her questions: 'Do you make much jam in the autumn? I suppose there's plenty of berries and fruit down there? Do you send out *all* the washing, Sivert's shirts too? But my dear, don't you even wash *them* yourself? It must be an expense for him?' She looked suspicious when Alberta offered brief, hesitant explanations. The question as to how far she and Sivert really were married hung in the air. A marriage performed by a French mayor was clearly more than questionable to Otilie.

Alberta went over to the store, uneasy and unused to it all. Housewives from the nearby farms stood with their baskets in front of the counter, studying the shelves with calm, clear eyes, knowing precisely what they wanted and did not want. The verger's wife and the doctor's wife might be there, poking expertly at the meat, turning over the various pieces, connoisseurs. They remembered last year's prices for porridge oats and sugar, and would remark, 'Fancy, it's going up again, two øre the kilo, it's all money after all,' considering whether they should buy any at all under such circumstances.

Alberta always forgot to ask what anything cost. It never occurred to her to ask for cardamom by weight because it was more expensive in small packets. Her blind eyes failed to notice that the price per kilo was very different when sold this way. 'But mercy me!' exclaimed Otilie when Alberta came home with a neat little packet. 'Work out what it would come to if you had bought more. Are we to *give* that money to Larsen? No fear!'

And although Otilie was just about to start baking, in an enormous apron, and had flour lying in heaps on the pastry

725

board, she took off the apron and went to change the cardamom. Clearly Alberta had not been the right person to send.
Perhaps spices and so on cost nothing where she came from,
in spite of the war. Here they had learned to save during the
years when they had eaten whale fat, remember that.

Alberta had to admit that Otilie was right, she was no catch
for Sivert. If you undertake to do something you should do
it properly, as competently as you can. If you go in for house-
keeping you should know how to do it. She looked back with
contrition on an endless series of ill-considered purchases.
When had she last given a thought to the price per kilo? Her
system had been the opposite: What can I buy for the money
I have today?

Occasionally the housewives would talk to her as she stood
among them, waiting at the counter. They talked about the
spring and the summer. It was a busy time for those who had
their own homes. No sooner were the spring cleaning over
and the summer clothes ready than it was time for making
jam and juice, salting beans, canning for those who had the
equipment. Some people wrapped hay round the glass jars,
that worked too. How did they do things in France? What
was that? So much fruit and vegetables all the year round
that it was unnecessary? Well, fancy that! They looked at her
in disbelief: That *must* be pleasant! As if they were saying:
Imagine roast pigeon flying into your mouth. Obviously it was
not quite proper that life should be so easy.

It hurt Alberta as if they were prodding her. She would
never be purposeful and conscientious as they were. Should she
therefore have gone through life alone, without love, without
children, without—? Something was wrong somewhere.

She genuinely tried to be of use, offering her services and
taking pains. There was nearly always something wrong with
the result. In the course of the years she had worked out
private little methods which decidedly did not meet with ap-
probation. 'Do you do it like that? Mercy me! Is that French?
There are some funny people down there, I must say.' 'It's my
way,' said Alberta, so as not to compromise the Republic. If

anything succeeded she felt strangely proud and relieved in her degradation, as if she had obtained credentials.

In all this Sivert left her completely alone. Nor could she have expected anything else, she was there on sufferance. Not that he took the side of the others exactly. Sivert was on his own side, that of himself and his painting; he manoeuvred forwards between various obstacles and came out of it with profit. Now here, now there in the terrain Sivert's painting parasol would appear. He might come home with his easel and box on his back, a damp canvas in each hand: violet ploughed land, a patchwork of green fields, a heavy spring sky above, perhaps a rainbow. He had become completely non-cubist again. He would stand by the kitchen steps scraping the thick lumps of the heavy, newly ploughed soil off his shoes, thirsty for coffee, hungrily enthusiastic about Otilie's wheaten cake and doughnuts. With his mouth full he would turn round the canvases, which he had put down facing the wall outside, rub his hands together, continue eating and drinking. Or perhaps he would put on his best clothes, walk the seven kilometres to town, where he had numerous irons in the fire, call on Consul This and Doctor That, full of optimism about selling his pictures. Or he would disappear up into the attic, where he had made himself a studio with overhead illumination from a skylight, and sketch, draw and paint.

Between whiles he would put on his oldest clothes and help old Ness with the rebuilding. They hammered, planed, sawed and measured. Sivert knew how to handle everything; he was not impractical as a result of being an artist. He could even cut panes of glass and fit them into the window frames. Only the doors and the brasswork had to be ordered from town; he and his father coped with the rest. Old Ness had been a carpenter before turning to farming, so he was naturally a handyman. Sivert must have inherited it. When Alberta came and rather awkwardly kept them company for a while in the pleasant scent of sawdust and fresh wood, and stayed making conversation so as not to feel a complete outsider, expressing her surprise at how clever Sivert was, he smiled indulgently: 'I've helped Father since I was a youngster.'

'Sivert's very useful to me,' Old Ness said. 'He wasn't much more than a lad when he began helping in all sorts of ways. He was handy on land and handy in a boat. Now I hear he's handy at his painting too. I have to rely on what I hear. The likes of me don't understand that sort of thing. Doesn't surprise me. Sivert has always been clever with his hands.'

'Hm,' Sivert replied .'My hands?'

'Yes, your hands. That's what you do it with, I know that. Of course you have to use your brains as well, as with everything else in this world. I couldn't even saw through this piece of planking without using my brains.'

'You're quite right, Father.'

'You're chaffing me,' snickered the old man, thoroughly pleased with Sivert, whatever he might do. 'But I do know a bit about it. There's more speculation to painting Mary and Elizabeth than to sawing across this piece of planking, I grant you that. Far more. But both of them need brains and deliberation. Look out! Might have expected it—hit your hand that time.'

'You make me think about so much else. Ouch!' Sivert sucked his damaged finger, shook it and laughed. 'All right, Tot, now you shall come with me to see the grindstone.'

He took the serious little boy by the hand. Alberta followed them, embarrassed, at a loose end. Once she had hooked herself on to Sivert; now he was monopolising that part of her which was the boy, drawing her after them, to the grindstone too. She took her eternal sewing with her everywhere, even though Otilie had revealed its shortcomings mercilessly. She had simply taken it away from Alberta one day, held it up for everyone to see, and said, 'Mercy me! What on earth's this? Don't they use sewing machines in France either? This is the oddest way of facing a garment I've ever seen. Whatever you say, you must come from a backward country. Imagine doing that by hand! Now run upstairs and fetch my machine. It's threaded with black cotton so it'll be just right.'

'It's my own way of doing it.' Alberta snatched the garment back again. 'I've sewn a great deal by hand. Sometimes I had the long seams machine sewn.'

'You don't say! Perhaps you don't *know* how to use a sewing-machine?'

'No, I don't know how to use a sewing-machine.'

'But, goodness me, you must learn. I'll teach you when I have a spare moment. I've never seen anything so crazy.'

'Let Alberta do things the way she's used to,' mediated old Fru Ness. 'It will be all right, I know. The boy looks very smart, *I* think.'

'That may be so. But we're not living in the nineteenth century. I shall have to run it up for her myself, if the worst comes to the worst.'

In spite of it all Alberta still slunk round with her sewing, her soul numb and dead, in the wake of Sivert and Tot. She felt as if she were back at the beginning, as if life had brought her home again to the place she had come from, in all her uselessness. Only the outer circumstances were different. Incredibly she was married and had a child. And she had relatives in Kristiania who did not even know she was here.

Aunt and Lydia, how would they take it all? They would be grateful to Sivert for marrying Alberta. They would have as little to do with him as possible, but insist: 'The best thing that could happen. I'm sure he's a good fellow.' They would be lady-like and distantly gracious when they met him, were he the devil himself. They would present him with ashtrays and ties; and sigh with relief when he and Alberta left. They were not going to meet him, as long as it was up to her. This relationship was not one to be displayed. Emergency measures seldom are.

Day and night she could feel her heart beating, always more strongly at night. Her sleep was no longer loose and ragged; she lay tossing in the stuffy atmosphere. Torturing restlessness jerked her limbs, her heart tried to hammer its way out. If she finally did fall asleep, it was only to struggle vainly and in desperation with mysterious vague objects. One night she was climbing up a ladder to an attic. It was narrow and in disrepair, grey with spiders' webs, in some places quite shaggy. She had to bend double to pass under beams. Occasionally she struck her head against them and hurt herself. Twice she called out, loudly and complainingly.

A short distance in front of her went the person who was showing her the way, a young, girlish figure she only glimpsed before she disappeared round the curve of the stairs. When Alberta called the second time, an answer came from above: You have arrived.

Stumbling, she reached a wall. In a corner there was a black hole, just big enough for her arm to pass through. She put it in, groped in the empty air inside, understood nothing, called again, heard her own voice in a cracked howl.

Then an answer came from the other side of the wall: You must break through.

I can't!

You must break through. The voice died away like the wind dropping. Silence fell.

She was gripped with boundless fear and uncertainty: her grey, narrow surroundings, the impossibility of going forward, the impossibility of going back. She screamed aloud—

'Alberta!'

Otilie was standing over her, Sivert was in the doorway.

'This is terrible, Alberta,' he said. 'We'll all end up in the madhouse if you go on like this. What's the matter with you? Are you ill?'

'I was dreaming.' Alberta felt as if she had been torn up by the roots, and that they were hanging naked in the air. If only Otilie had not been there. But there she stood in her slippers, wearing a skirt under her bed-jacket and the big, grey check shawl round her shoulders, looking down at Alberta, shaking her head. 'There is only One Who can help here, Our Saviour Jesus Christ. For nervous distress is distress of the soul, after all. None will make me believe otherwise.'

'Yes, yes, yes.' Sivert spoke impatiently and brusquely, nodding at the other bed. 'Go and lie down, Otilie, will you? I'll sit here for a while.'

He crossed the floor and sat on the edge of Alberta's bed. He had put on his trousers and vest over his nightshirt, his chin was unshaven, and he very much resembled a shoe-mender. 'Are you ill, Alberta? Do you feel any pain anywhere?' He took her hand. 'Then what is it? This is the second time you've screamed like this in the middle of the night. What's the matter with you?'

'Nothing. Nothing, Sivert.' Alberta turned her face to the wall.

'You must realise it's disturbing for the rest of us.'

Alberta stubbornly contemplated the wall. After a while she said, 'I shan't sleep any more tonight. Just go to bed, both of you.'

'Go to bed!' exclaimed Otilie. 'Easier said than done!'

'Go outside for a moment, will you, Otilie, so that Alberta and I can talk?'

The door opened and closed.

'I agreed to bring you home,' began Sivert, 'because I realised that the boy was of great concern to you.'

Silence. Alberta could not utter a word.

'I have said nothing to anyone here that was not to your advantage. It's entirely up to you if everything is to seem all right between us. I think I have been as considerate as possible, done my duty, behaved—'

'Like a man of honour,' suddenly came from Alberta, quite involuntarily. She had not the slightest intention of being spiteful.

'Put it like that if you wish. I suppose it's your way of being witty. I recognise it. However, you are staying here, with your child. It should in a way be pleasant for you. You can have nothing to criticise Father and Mother for. Otilie has her peculiarities—'

'I've—become fond of your father and mother, Sivert.'

'That's good. We do our best. This is no mansion—'

'Sivert!'

'All right. But you must do your best too. Pull yourself together. Or you'll have to go somewhere else. Tot is happy. I was beginning to think that you too . . . It's healthy here and—'

'It's true, Tot's happy.' Again Alberta glimpsed the ray of

731

hope that put everything else in shadow. Sometimes she was blind to it. 'I will pull myself together, Sivert—go for long walks, to help me to sleep. Things will be better. I'll—I'll do my utmost.'

'If only the room in the south gable were in order, you could perhaps—do your scribbling there. If it would help. But it will be some time before—'

'Go to bed now, Sivert. This shan't happen again, I promise you.' Alberta turned back to the wall, heard Sivert sigh and go, Otilie come in, cough and get into bed. They exchanged a couple of phrases in the doorway, but Alberta could not make out what they said.

Longing which she had learned to suppress because she had to, because there had been no other solution, was suddenly alive in her, as if she had been plundered at that very moment. She murmured her incantation: 'Tot's happy, Tot's happy,' trying to concentrate her thoughts on it.

'Break through.' The words from her dream came to her, linking themselves with the others, threading themselves between them: 'Break through, Tot's happy, break through, Tot's happy . . .'

Alberta felt her eyes widen. She raised her head slightly from the pillow.

*   *   *

The road which wound past the farm between two stone walls took one further into Norway.

After ten minutes' walk the structure of the landscape changed and became all uphill and down, the fields on each side billowing and advancing, a sea of curving lines in violent movement towards each other, the foreground of round, rich forms in green and violet in full uproar. Down in the hollows were old barns, fences, aspen trunks the colour of plane-trees, firs, young birches white as chalk marks. Furthest away and eternally blue were the hills. But the houses people lived in lay always on the crest of a wave.

Perhaps as in the old pictures God's finger would one day

appear out of the thin layer of cloud, pointing down at a ploughed field. Here and there a band of boys might come into sight, in bright blue shirts and dark red jerseys, colours which would clash horribly anywhere else. Here, with budding alder bushes for background and a purple haze farther off they acquired a mysterious depth and richness, melted down and became priceless as inlaid stones. An extraordinary country, thought Alberta, struck. Is it surprising that every other person here is an artist?

She met children on the road. 'G'morning,' they said, even if it was afternoon or evening. They looked at her frankly, without shyness, their eyes clear under sun-bleached hair. They looked amazingly secure and sure of themselves, talking loudly together in the strange, rather rough melody which is the Norwegian language.

At the top of a steep slope the wood began. A path, brown with pine needles, curved away between the tree trunks. Blue hepatica grew in bouquets amongst the dead leaves. Rolled up like brown hair in curling rags the ferns stood in groups, still with a long way to go. On the south side of the pine trees the ants had been building: enormous old heaps and small new ones, ceaseless traffic. It is concentrated where Norway's stone skeleton lies bare.

One day the ferns had raised their heads and stood with tall, swaying necks, making her think of sea-horses that stand upright in the water. There were catkins on the birch tree. The aspen had them too, and the tree was so splendid that one might imagine oneself at the Mediterranean. It was purple and chenille, with a smooth strong trunk, southern in colouring; Alberta could find no other words to describe it. It was a miracle standing against the blue sky.

She walked this way every day and sat on a tree stump, letting the sun sift down on her through the branches, noticing what had happened since yesterday, reading a little, busying herself with the manuscript she had smuggled out under her coat. It was uncomfortable balancing it on her knees. Piles of straying pages would constantly slide away from her and have to be collected again. But when had anything been comfortable? She thought of the past winter and admitted that quiet, woodland air, mild warmth, security for the boy, were in fact comforts of the first order. If it were a Sunday morning and the wind was in the right direction she could hear the chapel bell, hoarse and mocking. Tot went with the others to church. He submitted for the sake of the ride, so that he could hold the reins going uphill, when Blakken was walking. Godless Alberta was nowhere to be found when the cart was ready to leave.

The manuscript lay in its folder, dead, roughly drafted and loosely written. She had to breathe life into it, or at least pretend she was doing so; or die herself, slowly perhaps, but surely. There was *one* way out, *one* possibility, and four points on which it depended: get it finished, write out a fair copy, not allow herself to be halted by doubt, keep her head high as long as possible if there should turn out to be no other solution.

Her thoughts continually stole away and had to be caught again. Time and again they sought sanctuary in the letters from Liesel that had come from Königsberg.

Liesel had been forced to leave Paris; it had been that or the hospital. There had been two of them to persuade her, a young, energetic doctor, and Eliel. One windy day in March Alberta had accompanied her to the station with one of her sisters, who had come to fetch her. The sister was not at all like Liesel; she was short, fair-haired, plump, primly and unattractively dressed, and wore steel-rimmed spectacles. She spoke only Russian and German and looked at everything about her with suspicious eyes. Liesel had moved to a hotel, and lay weeping and coughing on the bed in a comfortless room, pretending that she had always lived in this way. She had refused to go to the Hôtel des Indes.

Eliel had come up to say good-bye. He refused to come to the station for fear of compromising Liesel, thus emphasizing his delicacy of feeling. He had brought a little statuette with him. It had been standing on the bedside table when Alberta came up for the last time, and tears had come to Liesel's eyes when she looked at it. Otherwise she had been surprisingly calm. Not a tear, very few words. But when the train began to move and she was forced to let go of Alberta's hand they had both cried openly.

The tram on the way home had been halted by a modest funeral, a slow little procession of black-clothed people on foot behind the simplest kind of hearse. Among them was a woman in a long veil, supported by other women. Behind them, on top of the coffin, was a wreath: its broad ribbons flapped, were borne outwards by the wind, floated on the breeze for a moment and fell again. Alberta was just able to read: *A mon mari*. In spite of the words she was left with the painful feeling that she had been watching Liesel's funeral.

But Liesel wrote: 'I shall recover. I am still in bed, but the fever is dropping, I can knit, sew and write letters. Everyone is kind to me. Nobody has commented on the fact that I didn't become a painter. As long as you stop wanting things for yourself, I suppose you can live anywhere, Albertchen. It's bourgeois and terribly anti-French here. I shall not be able to say a word when I have to go to coffee parties later on. I shall not attempt to describe how they dress. It was a good thing you went home; otherwise you would have caught some illness or other too. The artistic, poverty-stricken life isn't much fun in the long run. The men can do it, but not us. After all, you always wished Tot could live in the country.'

In one of her letters she said: 'If I believed that powers who might help could hear me I'd call to them to make me get well more quickly. I need to so that I can start earning. I've thought of starting as a dressmaker when I get up. Do you remember, I used to sew quite neatly? It's no use painting here, and I no longer have any talent. I had once, but it has disappeared. I don't believe anyone is listening, Albertchen. Sometimes I imagine how it would be if an atom in my body began calling to me from its point of view, and how impossible it would be for me to do anything for the atom personally, even if I heard it. Do you think me stupid? You see, they talk to me so much about God. It's so difficult when they give this personal name to something so completely unknown. It's a kind of capsule into which they put it and then expect you to swallow it whole. I've heard from Eliel a couple of times. It's nice of him, but he seems like a stranger. He was really very patient with me all those years, and I really loved him right to the end, although I was often malicious. But now it's all so far away. He says Pierre is back in Paris. He has left Jeanne for good and is living with a Russian woman, a communist, somewhere on the Boul' Mich'. You will hear about this through Sivert in any case. Pierre is supposed to be trying to start a newspaper, but has no money.'

At this place in Liesel's letter Alberta felt the same painful stab each time. Nevertheless she re-read it. Pierre's calm face with the light in his eyes, as she had seen it the last time, became overwhelmingly distinct. She knew that he had gone to Dijon with Jeanne. They said that Jeanne had taken Marthe by the hand and fetched him from Michaud's. He spent his time there, and nobody knew where he lived.

Deep in her mind Alberta kept a secret certainty: Whatever may happen, it doesn't matter. Something *must* happen; life never stands still. We shall not meet again, but if we were to do so everything would be just as it was that day and the rest merely in parentheses. His kisses were branded on her mouth indelibly. Down at Granli her knowledge of it retreated; it avoided Otilie's room as all winter it had avoided the studio and Sivert's presence. Up here in the wood it turned into physical certainty again, mind and body unfurled in burning desire . . .

She bent over her manuscript.

'For heaven's sake, are you writing in the middle of the wood?'

Alberta started, and looked up into a kind, wrinkled face tied up in a kerchief. It looked at her, laughing. She had to laugh back. 'Yes, it is rather absurd, isn't it?'

'Yes, I should think it must be? Not that I know anything about it. And on a tree-stump into the bargain? Have the summer visitors started coming already? They don't usually come before the schools finish.'

'I'm not a visitor exactly. I live at a farm called Granli—I—'

'At Granli? I know all about Granli. I'm a member of the

women's association for that district. The meetings we have there are worth going to. Otilie *can* bake. But for heaven's sake, you're not—you're not Sivert's wife, from Paris?'

Yes, Alberta was.

'Well I never! And here you are, sitting in the wood.'

'It's peaceful and pleasant here.'

'It is peaceful. Yes. I know others who are just the same. My summer visitors, for instance—the husband is always off in the wood. He's an author, he is, writes books and for the newspapers. He gets his ideas in the wood. Then he writes it out up in his room. Are you an author too?'

'No. There are so many kinds of writing.'

'I expect there are. I live over there. Was on my way up from the store when I saw you sitting here. Would you like to come and have a look at it, since you're so near? It's an old farm, over two hundred years old, and run down in some ways, but people say the house is attractive, and the store-house. The road has disappeared since they made the new rural road twenty years ago. It's often difficult for us when the snow comes in winter, and our horse hasn't ever been outside our land; he just draws the plough and the hay and the muck. And he brings in firewood for us. He's like a child, he's so spoilt. Animals get like that. We're a bit out of the way, we can't get the electric light, though that would make things easier. But you know how it is, when your family has lived for many generations.—But what does Otilie have to say about it? About your sitting up here?'

Her final question decided the matter. Alberta collected her papers and got to her feet. She looked into the many kind laughter wrinkles and laughed herself. 'I don't know what she has to say about it.'

'She is *peculiar*, you know.'

'Perhaps she is a little.'

'She's not married, that's what it is. She ought to have had a man like the rest of us. Then she wouldn't have become so *domineering*. Not that we don't need to be domineering sometimes. The menfolk—but you're still young.'

To this Alberta prudently said nothing.

The path broadened into an overgrown road. Shortly afterwards the wood opened out, grass slopes and ploughed land came into view. The farm lay on a ridge: a smoke-coloured log house in a good position, a tumbledown outhouse, leaning and crooked, with an open barn door like a gaping mouth at one end and manure coming out of an opening like an outlet at the other. It resembled other outhouses, but this one was old and done-for. But the buildings stood in the open. The wood had drawn well back from them. An enormous tree stood at one corner close to the wall. When they came nearer, Alberta saw that it was a chestnut tree; the buds were already fat and shining on the branches. A cat got up from a flight of steps, stretched itself, came over and rubbed itself against their legs, purring loudly.

'Well, fancy meeting Sivert's wife! And I go that way so seldom. We have no help on the farm, we plod along ourselves. My husband's up in the woods today. If I'd known I was going to have a visitor I'd have made time to bake some waffles. But you shall have coffee. Well I never, Sivert's wife! He's made a name for himself. Now, you just sit down—

'But the Lord save us, you have a boy too, don't you? Yes, didn't I hear something about it? And you've brought him with you from France? I don't suppose he can speak Norwegian, can he? That must be strange.'

She rattled the rings of the oven that was standing in the fireplace.

Alberta looked round. The walls were built of logs so thick that nothing could hang straight on them, just as in Kjeldsen the smith's house at home in the north. Through the open door she could look across a wide hallway into another large room. A broad flight of stairs with a banister led upwards. 'You have plenty of room,' she remarked mechanically.

'Yes, plenty of room. If there's one thing we do have, it's room. In the summer we take in visitors, as I told you. They have to take us as they find us, a long way from the road and short of water plenty of times. But it's so *peaceful*, they say, so *quiet*. They're the kind of people who like that. But they're not coming until August. He can't take a holiday from the newspaper before then. You shall see their rooms.'

They drank their coffee. The woman studied Alberta over the edge of her cup with intelligent, deep-set eyes. Her wrinkles occasionally contracted, craftily and sympathetically. 'Are you happy to be back home in Norway?'

'Oh, I don't know.'

'You couldn't find kinder people than Ness and his wife.'

'No, you couldn't,' said Alberta honestly.

'So it's Otilie, is it?'

'Yes, it's Otilie.'

'She likes to be the one who makes the decisions. It's often difficult for the old folk, I know that. They say Otilie fell in love with our old vicar. That's what they say. But he came a widower and he left a widower. Would you like to see upstairs? Then you must have a look at the animals. I have such splendid cows too. Balder is up in the woods today with my husband. Balder's our horse. And I have fifty chickens.'

They went to the outhouse and looked at the animals. The cowshed was in good condition inside with panelling everywhere. Alberta politely patted the rump of a cow. Then they went upstairs: a spacious landing, high thresholds over which they had to step carefully, blue-painted log walls everywhere, old, greenish window panes, two big living rooms, one on each side of the landing. In one of them the sun poured in on to a large table standing between the windows. The branches of the chestnut tree swept towards one of the windows on a light current of air. There was simple furniture, an old-fashioned bench-sofa, a four-poster bed bulging with eiderdowns beneath a white bed-cover. Some dried wreaths above the sofa gave out a strong, sweet scent. The farmer's wife went across and let in air. 'I hang these wreaths up in the autumn against the moths. It's almost too much of a good thing.'

But Alberta had, without thinking, put her folder down on the table. There it lay as if it had come home. She almost felt at home herself. The moment had something dreamlike about it.

'Is this room left empty?'

'Yes, of course it's empty. Nobody will come here before August.'

'I—I wonder if I might be allowed to sit here for a while during the daytime? I'll pay for it.' It occurred to Alberta that perhaps she might produce short pieces in between and earn some ready money. Now she was gambling high.

'Pay for it? I'll have no payment, not at this time of year.'

'It's—I'd like to keep it to myself—for the present.'

'Come as often as you like, then you won't have to sit in the wood. You shall have the key, then you can go in and out as you like. If I'm away one day, the key to the outer door will be under a stone on the steps. I'll show it to you.'

'You will be doing me a great service.'

'Why not, when it's standing empty? It'll be nice to have you. People must have *peace* for work of that sort, I know that much. Otilie shan't get to hear of it. The men needn't poke their noses into everything either. It isn't always to the good when they do. My name's Lina Haugen. Haugen's the name of the farm.'

'Mine's Alberta Ness. Thank you, Lina.'

Lina laughed with all her wrinkles again, in reality still young, only dried and weather-beaten, as country people are. 'We can fox people too, can't we?'

When Alberta went home she left the folder behind.

She walked down the hill towards Granli. Between the tree-tops she could see the farmyard. Old Ness was pulling Blakken after him. Tot was sitting on the horse's back. He leaned forward and patted it on the neck. As Alberta turned in through the hedge she heard him saying, 'Yes, Blakken, yes, nice Blakken. Gee up, Blakken, gee up.' His voice resembled those of the children she met on the road. The strange, rather rough little melody had become his. His legs pummelled Blakken's sides like drumsticks. The horse was quite unaffected. Ness walked sedately, so did Blakken; neither of them threatened danger to the child on horseback. And the child knew it, and was fearless, safe and secure. When Alberta came over to them and the procession halted, she leaned her cheek against the firm, warm neck of the horse, as if it were Blakken she had to thank for the fact that Tot was turning into a different boy, day by day.

'That rocking horse has had it's day,' whinnied old Ness. 'And of course Blakken's getting on now. He has plenty of sense.'

*   *   *

It was almost mid-summer.

It seemed to Alberta that she had never seen such a wealth of leaves and flowers before. The meadow was full of sorrel, heartsease, lady's mantle, herb bennet. Between the rocks behind the storehouse grew limewort in broad purple patches, speedwell, germander bluer than Tot's eyes, cinquefoil and lady's slipper. Above them all rocked the myriad corollas of the wild chervil.

In the wood the pines and firs had bright new shoots. The pines carried theirs vertically, the firs let them hang down in draperies and furbelows.

A black horse was cropping the grass on the bridge to a barn. Behind the horse, the red barn, and the thousands upon thousands of wild chervil heads showing through the grass, it was blue, like deep water. You thought it was water. Then it turned out to be a hill. It was like nothing else, could not be anywhere else in the whole world: Norway.

Alberta saw it all, took it in with her mind, looked at it with astonishment. All the same it did not penetrate. For the first time in her life nature was a frame and a background, not the boasting and demanding thing that makes itself one with you, almost painfully.

She had bound herself to her manuscript like a knot. She felt as if she were in a heated house, in which one exit had been left to her. It was beautiful outside, of course, but . . .

A painful tingling night and day; practically no sleep, a tattered veil that descended on her momentarily, headache, heartache; a strange little boy, who had to be reached from

741

a new angle, along uncertain, untried paths. Keep me away from our child, Sivert, be the one who has the power. Perhaps I shall claim my place before you expect it, by taking a round-about way. Got you, Sivert!

In the garden peonies stood along the wall of the house. Small, hard, opinionated heads on overgrown stalks stuck up above one another and suddenly burst one day into a luxury of silken petals. The mock orange blossom bush by the summer house was covered with buds, making one think of young brides, of everything untouched. They opened, and the intense fragrance contrasted strongly with the bud that bore it; with Otilie too. Alberta picked small twigs in secret, took them aside and inhaled their scent like a forbidden, slightly dangerous stimulant.

Birds called and answered each other in the wood so passionately that the one had scarcely begun to pipe before the other joined in. Soon after midnight the dawn was reflected in the windows of the neighbouring farm. There was a sound of accordion playing, no one knew where from. One felt there were couples wandering along the paths all night.

If Alberta did manage to fall asleep, she woke again at the first birdsong. Or perhaps Otilie had turned over in bed. Otilie's bed creaked loudly.

Her body felt palsied with fatigue. But her brain teemed. Image succeeded image. Words came to her, inevitable, irres-istable, the only right ones. But if she sat up in bed and reached for the paper and pencil she had hidden under her pillow, the spell was broken. A short while would elapse. Then she would grope her way towards heavy, clumsy sentences, the one piled on top of the other, grating on the ear. And she was afraid that Otilie might wake and notice what she was doing. It did not improve matters.

The result was small pieces of paper, new piles of small pieces of paper which were carried up to Haugen and were the cause of radical changes. It was impossible to ignore them.

Decisive things happened at daybreak. It is then that the birds lay their eggs, birth and death are given release. Then,

too, the brain is ready to arrange and put together, to precipi-
tate words with content and significance, part of a sequence.
They seemed to Alberta to float up from the mysterious life-
stream itself, which, dark and secretive, reaches down into the
depths of the mind. They were brewed of bitterness and sweetness. But to reach for them was often like reaching for soap
bubbles. When she opened her hand there was nothing there.

At last the time would come when Alberta dared to open
one of the windows. Half fainting she got out of bed and did
so. It was the evening and night air Otilie was so desperately
afraid of; she was less discouraging towards the morning air
and sunshine. Alberta lay feeling how the atmosphere in the
room slowly became seasoned with the element human beings
principally live on and so sorely need.

She must have dozed off again. The next thing she would be
aware of was Otilie demonstratively shutting the window because she wanted to dress, her splashing in the washbowl, the
emphatic manner in which she put down her mug, a manner
full of disapproval.

Not that Alberta's excursions went unnoticed.

'You certainly do go for long walks,' said Otilie. And one
day she said: 'It's all very well for those who have the *time*.'

'Alberta needs them for the sake of her sleep, Otilie. And
she's on holiday here with us in a way. She's sleeping better
now.' Fru Ness nodded at Alberta behind Otilie's back. Her
eyes said: You just get away. I'll see to the rest.

Alberta slunk out. She could hear Otilie saying, 'Sleep? I
don't know that she sleeps so much better. She's still restless.
I repeat, nervous distress is distress of the soul. People who
don't even go to church on Sunday ... '

Sometimes Alberta did not get away. For the sake of peace
she had to stay at home and help. Otilie had real talent for
starting some enterprise just as Alberta had thought, quite
reasonably, that the coast was clear for a while. Cleaning
chores that nobody had dreamed of doing were her speciality.
Then her cheeks turned red, her false teeth slipped awry, and
her shoes squeaked more loudly than usual. Then no one

dared argue with Otilie. Fru Ness shook her head in despair behind her back. In the midst of carrying buckets and polishing windows Alberta would be seized with savage, furious longing for the lonely, desultory life of idleness she had once led. Then she simply thought of flight.

Perhaps she would not get up to Lina with her new pieces of paper until the next day. A few of them brought clarity, others nausea and fear, all of them bother and rewriting. She would be seized with hatred of this old manuscript, and a desire to destroy it. Life passes, we alter, we change position in relation to things, seeing them from different points of view. Here lay a pile of paper which it was impossible to revise, there was no time. Alberta was a minute pack animal in front of an enormous load which should have been pulled away a long time ago. The whip lashed, August approached. If the load had not been moved by then it never would be. She saw the future as a hopeless struggle which already made her tired and old. Many manuscripts like this would be required, preferably one a year. Then even scribbling might keep her alive. She felt doomed to the galleys. She wished she could take up dress-making like Liesel. That was work you knew how to do once you had mastered it.

'A luxury for the rich,' Pierre had said once. 'Three hundred pages,' he had said too. As far as Alberta could make out she had many more than that, although she hoped it would shrink in print. Half in delirium she struck out and cut down, took sections out and put them back in again. Sometimes she had the feeling that she was knitting the product, or making a patchwork quilt. Words were added to words and had no more meaning than stitches and rags. Together they would perhaps turn into something one day, but wall after wall of doubt had to be broken down, doubt that this irrelevant story could possibly interest anyone. Alberta knew it all of old. For the first time she was struggling with it under the whip. Sick with anxiety she paced up and down the floor. Her brain stood still.

Then a small incident might occur. Through the open window there would come a sound from the farmyard, calling, footsteps. Lina had let out the cows on to the grassy slope;

they would not be allowed into the meadow until after the hay-making was over. Now she was calling from the steps: 'Keep your head to yourself, Beauty! Will you keep your head to yourself!'

Beauty would not keep her head to herself. Undisturbed she cropped at the fresh clover under the barbed wire fence until Lina approached her with uplifted stick. Then she turned and moved away, certain that she would not be seriously chastised.

But Alberta was thinking: What a language! What a concise and descriptive and direct language, full of clarity, clothing thought compactly. My language. And she seemed to feel a flick of the whip. Illumination fell on the many pages. The wheels she had set in motion took purchase in her. Reality ebbed away, she had passed into timelessness. She would hurry back to Granli much too late for something or other and strangely insensitive to this deplorable fact.

One day the meadow was nodding with moon daisies. A warm wind passed through the grass, combing it with its fingers. Everything curtsied after it, now here, now there. 'We haven't had such a fine summer since Sivert sold his big picture,' said Fru Ness.

After sunset the clouds sailed gilt-edged under the light sky. All was abundance, warmth, fragrance and peace.

One day Sivert and his father simply cut down the miracle of flowers in the meadow with their scythes. But in the evenings there was the smell of new-mown hay. Tot went out and rolled in it, shouting aloud for joy.

*　　*　　*

The summer was so far advanced that the green had deepened in colour and become monotonous. The willow herb stood in tall, strong clumps. The evenings started earlier, and already had a hint of autumn in them. When it was quite dark an illumination hung above the woods to the south, showing where the town lay.

In the afternoon Sivert sometimes said, 'Will you come to town with me, Alberta?' Sometimes she did so: from old habit, because it was good to walk in company with someone, a change to see different surroundings; perhaps too because it would attract attention at Granli if she did not go.

They did not talk much, and only about neutral topics. Alberta had the feeling of being with a man she knew slightly, no more. Sadness that it was so would flood warmly into her as she watched him disappear into a house with paintings under his arm, landscapes and compositions created by his placid mind and strong, practical hands. He had returned to his former style of painting. The wealth of colouring that had been Sivert's strength and distinguishing characteristic had flowed again. She was glad to see it as one is always glad to see things functioning normally.

She wandered about the narrow streets round the market place while she waited for him, or sat on a bench in the park. If he had collected a fee they would go to a café, and the time would pass pleasantly, as it does at a chance meeting of acquaintances. It sometimes struck Alberta as quite incredible that they should ever have slept together, and that they should be the father and mother of a child. Occasionally Sivert would push money towards her across the table. 'I suppose you need some to throw around too.' 'Thank you, Sivert, I have all I need.' 'You must tell me then, if there is anything.' Sivert would put the money back in his pocket. 'Yes, thank you.'

One day when they were sitting like this, he said, 'I've decided to stay here for the winter. I have orders for a couple of portraits.'

'Have you, Sivert?'

'One of them is of a whaling captain, at least he's gone ashore now. Those people have money. A real character, should be amusing to paint. It's possible that I may be asked to paint the daughter as well. Beautiful girl. Fine-looking. Unusually pleasant too.'

'Oh?'

'I may get the commission for this altar-piece too. It doesn't look entirely out of the question. I shall go to see the vicar one day. It would probably be best to put down Brede for the local school. He can begin there at any rate. It would be too far for him to go to town for the time being. Tot's coming on well.'

'Yes, he is. I'm so happy about it, Sivert.'

'I always knew he'd grow into a fine boy. You looked at the black side all the time. Perhaps mothers are like that.'

'Perhaps so.'

There was no longer any friction between them, only a strange emptiness, a rather distant sympathy; just as when people make brief contact and think: That could have been pleasant, but it can't be arranged. She could sit looking at him as if he were a stranger. A sailor perhaps? Yes. Not the jolly kind with a sweetheart in every port; the tenacious kind, who rows out to fish and drags nets, looks after lobster pots, does his job, in fact. With amazement she remembered how she had alternated in her feelings for him. Many would have called it sensuousness; on the contrary, it had been spiritual, a need to solve the riddle that was he.

When it came down to it it had not been complicated. The solution lay so close at hand that this was perhaps one of the reasons why it had taken her such a long time to find it. Sivert was so completely himself in all circumstances, without any notion that he ought perhaps to behave differently, that such and such would look better. He was not the kind to hide the fact that he was aware of advantages; he was aware of them and said nothing. It was merely that he had a keen eye for business, an instinct as natural as that of a wild animal. 'Yes,' he always said, when Alberta insisted that he had been reasoning again in such and such a way. 'Yes, of course.' And if she were to say to him, 'You wanted to drive me out, Sivert. Liesel was right. I believe you made up all that about the money,' he might well answer, 'Well, yes. What else could I have done to get rid of you just then?'

And the daughter of the whaling captain? Was there anything in the offing as far as she was concerned? If so she must be prepared, so that she could take up the fight over the child on more equal terms. Alberta felt a wild panic, her heart pitched unevenly in her breast. She felt sorry for Sivert too, he was gullible in such matters; he might be disappointed again. Then she thought: Sivert is a wall; I shall demoralize myself in the long run if I go on striking my head against it. I mustn't feel sorry for him. I have enough with my own affairs.

'Won't you buy some little thing for Brede, since we're in town for once? He'd be so pleased.'

'Very well,' said Sivert. 'If there's anything you think he'd like—that isn't too expensive.'

They found something or other. They came home. The boy came running to meet them, full of adventures, full of expectancy. He was handed the little parcel and was obviously and noisily enraptured. He jumped into the air. He had become strong and secure. He rushed about showing everybody what he had been given: in and out of doors, to the kitchen, the stable, the storehouse, the woodshed, eager and at home. Children from the neighbouring farms looked in and asked whether Brede was coming out. Brede answered them in the local dialect, cheekily and loudly. He no longer bothered about his French, although Alberta and Sivert both tried to keep up the language with him.

Alberta felt a bitter happiness at seeing it all. Her laughter at the tricks he played verged on tears; she had to swallow hard on the occasions when he threw his arms round her in new frankness, more friendly towards everyone except Otilie. She sat watching him when he was wide-eyed with concentration on what was going on round him. She thought: Perhaps he will remember this for the rest of his life. A little piece of this moment, the taste of this or that, the smell of it will stay with him down the years: a smile perhaps, the ring of a voice.

He hung about Fru Ness's skirts, calling her Grannie. He followed Sivert and Sivert's father, carrying tools, helping to harness the horse and make hay, sharing actively in the life of the farm. It was evident that this child, who could not thrive in city air or by the open sea, did so in the country a couple of kilometres away from a fjord. But if Otilie tried to take him on her lap and show him the child Jesus in her illustrated Bible he twisted away from her. When he was alone with

Alberta he would say, 'Aunt Otilie isn't pretty. Aunt Otilie has ugly teeth.'

'Aunt Otilie is kind,' attempted Alberta.

'No.'

'Otilie hasn't a way with children,' said Fru Ness. 'She means well, but she simply *hasn't* a way with children. Not married, has none herself, that's what it is.'

But Otilie would say, 'Suffer the little children to come unto me. Of such is the Kingdom of Heaven. Who will lead this child to Jesus? Not those whose duty it ought to be, it seems. If he is to come to Him, it looks as if it will have to be through others.'

One evening when the family had gathered on the steps she said, 'I was just thinking. How did you have Brede baptised? After all, they're Catholics down there, as far as I know.'

'Yes, they're Catholics.' Sivert barely glanced up from the local paper, which he read from end to end every evening.

'I suppose you had to go to the consulate, then? Or the legation? Or perhaps there's a Scandinavian church down there? For it seems to me that such a sacred ceremony would not be very dignified in an office. And who were the godparents?'

'We've wondered about that, I must say.' Old Ness took his pipe out of his mouth. 'Wondered who the godparents were. Here at home those who aren't present can have their names entered just the same. I don't know how things are there. We didn't want to write and ask either. But now that Otilie's brought it up . . .'

Alberta looked across at Sivert. Sivert was reading the paper.

'Brede isn't baptised,' she said. 'He was registered at the mayor's office.'

There was an astounded silence. 'Surely you can't mean—?' began Otilie. Sivert folded up the paper. 'It ought to have been done, of course. Naturally we thought about it, but there was so much else to think about. Then the war came.'

'But gracious me, you're not going to let the boy go *unbaptised*?'

'No, no, Otilie, we'll see about it.'
'It would be nice if it were done, I must say,' said old Ness.
'Yes father, yes father.'
Alberta said nothing. She and Sivert had never discussed it, and that was the truth of the matter. For a moment she pictured the boy being led up the aisle, the centre of attention, put on display. Then she thought: As long as I see that it's done quietly, they can do as they like. He's grown strong and boisterous here, grown as I hungered to see him. Everything else is unimportant.

Up at Lina's things went their uneven way. August approached. Lina was already remarking that one of these days she would have to clean the room properly, take out the furniture and bedding, scrub the floors and clean the windows.
Alberta was in a fever. She went to bed and got up in the morning with a burdensome feeling of guilt. In spite of all her work the manuscript was still loose and ragged in many places, vague, insufficiently thought out.
When one day Lina said, 'There's no help for it, you must let me in on Friday at the latest,' panic took her breath away. 'Of course I must,' she replied.
'If they weren't using both rooms—'
'But they do.'
'You can sit here as much as you like during the winter. We have plenty of firewood from our own trees. There's always a lot of snow but I expect you can ski? There'll be plenty happening down at Granli before the autumn. I hear Fru Ness is having the women's association for the first meeting this year, and that will be soon. But you take your time until Friday.'
It was Wednesday. Alberta was half unconscious with anxiety. Without quite knowing what she was about she erased and added. Sentences grated in her ears, flat, empty of content. She caught herself in contradictions and lapses of memory. Fictional characters can die, Pierre had said. It seemed as if Alberta's had never had a spark of life. Hollow exhaustion,

the result of revolt against the pressure, threatened time and again to make her impotent. Previously she had sometimes felt that the material evened itself out on its own, when she had laid stone upon stone long enough. The feeling abandoned her when she was in a serious hurry. She could only see an unmanageable chaos, and feel it was too late to do anything about it.

Out in the fields Balder was drawing the plough, turning again and again on a stretch of earth full of heartsease. Behind him came Lina's short, silent husband. Balder pulled when he wished and stopped when he wished. He swished his tail, dragged the reins well forward and made himself comfortable for a while, cropping a few handfuls of grass, setting off again of his own accord after a suitable interval had elapsed. Balder did the work, Balder decided on the tempo, Balder's heart did not beat unevenly. Alberta, who had come beyond exhaustion to a kind of madness when her fountain pen ran away with her, shut her eyes when she raised her head in order to avoid seeing this perfect equilibrium between what had to be done and what the animal thought he could manage.

On Thursday, in a trance, she wrote some final words which sounded sentimental, knowing she would find no others and that no further alterations were possible. She would have to venture it. It was the only card she had to play: a problematic card. She gathered her things together and said good-bye to Lina, who dried her hands on her apron. 'Thank you for everything, Lina. You've been such a help to me.'

'Nothing to thank me for,' said Lina. 'It's been nice having you here. I understand enough to see you're a kind of author too, it's just that you don't want anybody to interfere. *I* shan't breathe a word. My husband never asks about anything.' Lina nodded in the direction of the ploughland. 'He's a bit peculiar too, you know. Well, I'll be coming down one of these days, to the meeting.'

'That will be nice, Lina.'

Before Alberta entered Granli with the folder under her arm she stood for a while watching from the road. Otilie was sittin on the steps, shelling peas. At last she got to her feet and went across to the storehouse.

You can get through a good deal. Even if your mind is raw with anxiety, you finally get through a meeting of forty-five women, presided over by Otilie. If you were being sent to the scaffold tomorrow, you would get through it.

Alberta knew enough about the ways of the world to realise that it was no use embarking on a literary career at the beginning of August. Nobody was at home, everyone on holiday, including the mysterious powers she was about to accost. In a fortnight perhaps . . . three weeks . . .

The moment for sinister schemes was not ripe in other ways either; scarcely was the folder safe in her suitcase before discussion about the meeting began at Granli.

'*We* must have it this time, Mother.'

'It's not our *turn*, Otilie.'

'The doctor's wife is expecting at any time. *She* can't have it. The Evensens have summer guests. Then it's our turn. It's impossible to say no. It's not done.'

Fru Ness righted her kerchief and sighed, not without reason. They could scarcely get away with less than two hundred and fifty *smørbrød,* Otilie had explained that at the start. It was doubtful whether even that would be enough. They had to allow for the fact that almost everyone would come now that it was between the busy seasons. Then there would have to be small cakes and at *least* five big pastries. They ought to have doughnuts too, but those would have to be baked the same day if they were going to be good. That meant such a bother and fuss with all the cutting of bread for the *smørbrød* as well. After a few days of discussion Otilie gave up the doughnuts to Fru Ness's and Alberta's great relief. She did not stop talking about them, however. Although she said it herself, doughnuts were one of the things she really did know how to make.

Alberta felt a kind of armour growing round her. Old ~motions from the times when parties had been given at home ~re renewed in her. 'You'll wear your best, won't you?'

Otilie reminded her. 'And make the boy look nice.' Alberta hastily lengthened Brede's sailor's suit which had become too short.

And the house filled with women. Along all the walls and in all the rooms downstairs they sat, in black dresses with a touch of white at the throat, gold brooches, their hands folded in their laps until their embroidery was brought out as if on command. At the table in the middle were the leaders of society: the vicar's wife, the teacher's and precentor's wives, the wife of the store-keeper, a few whalers' wives. Alberta retreated again and again to Lina and a couple of farmers' wives along the wall, as she had retreated to the potted palm in another life, only to be brought out again. 'Be a little sociable,' whispered Otilie, red spots in her cheeks. 'Tell them what it's like abroad, since you've been there.' Altogether Alberta felt she was the object of considerable curiosity on the part of the centre table, as if she had been engaged for the purpose of entertaining them. Lina nudged her understandingly in the ribs each time she was fetched away. Brede was hauled to right and left and told to bow.

The vicar arrived, went the rounds shaking hands, stood in a doorway, said a few words and prayed a prayer. His wife read about work in the mission field. Old Ness was present in his Sunday best, his beard newly clipped, but Sivert basely stayed away.

The coffee arrived. Alberta, red as a lobster, ran here and there with cream and sugar, cups and saucers. Life repeated itself in an astonishing way. Conversation at the centre table became lively. It concerned prohibition, boot-legging, home distilling, poor relief. Smuggled liquor was being landed at the most incredible places; it was found hidden in the woods and in the homes of completely innocent people who suffered all kinds of unpleasantness. The world's wickedness was endless. The doctor was being called out to people who had drunk the poison and lay at the point of death, having lost their hearing and their sight. Home distilleries were being discovered al' over the parish. When the factory ships of the whaling fle there. I was thinking—of staying there for the time being.'

'Not to your relations? You'll have to stay in town then?' Old Fru Ness stared at her in perplexity. 'I wonder whether Sivert can manage that,' she added thoughtfully. 'Whether he'll feel he can just now.'

'I shall see to it myself. I mean, I must have money for my ticket. I had thought—'

Alberta paused. This was like throwing herself into the sea. But she had thrown herself into the sea several times before in her life. 'I had thought of asking you to lend me ten kroner.'

Sivert's mother said nothing. Alberta talked on, as one does when a difficult pause must be filled. 'I often think of how it would be if one day I were to be left alone with Brede. I must start doing something, I must find a living. Some people live by writing books. I've written a few trifles and got money for them. Now I'd like to try something a little bigger.'

Old Fru Ness was still silent. She stopped walking; her expression was blank, difficult to interpret. Alberta looked at her standing against the yellow-green evening sky, thin and workworn, a person who had lived by honest striving for others, without a thought of any reward other than their happiness and progress.

'A novel, you mean?' she finally asked gropingly. 'What they call a novel? I heard you were busy with something of the sort. I didn't like to ask since you hadn't said anything. But it must take rather a long time? But there, I don't know anything about it. Still, it must be very uncertain?' she said, in a more determined tone. 'Wouldn't dressmaking or something like that be better?'

'I can't sew. I can't learn to either. I'm all thumbs. And the novel is more or less finished. I must get it typed, I must do that first of all—'

'You could learn to sew as well as anybody else,' said old Fru Ness, a little sternly this time. 'It's funny what you can do if you really *want* to. But you're not like us, I understand that I don't mean to scold, I mean that's how it is. And if you have faith in this you must have your ten kroner.'

'Thank you.' Alberta took her veined hands. 'You shall have it back. Soon perhaps.'

But Fru Ness looked at her cunningly. 'So that's what you've been doing up in the wood?'

'Yes, that's what I've been doing.'

'Hmm. Well, Otilie had better not hear about it beforehand, there'd be such a fuss and palaver. I can't quite fathom what we're to do. Have you talked to Sivert?'

'No.'

'You must talk to him. Explain it as best you can.'

'I came to you in order to avoid that. I'd like to manage alone.'

'Hm.'

There was an embarrassed pause. The burden of all the circumstances of life became so heavy for a moment that it took Alberta's breath away.

'I wish I could make out,' said Fru Ness finally, 'I wish I could make out how things are between the two of you. Sometimes I have the idea that there's nothing between you, nothing at all. I've often regretted that Otilie got her way over sharing her room with you. It can't be right when it's like this. If it were not that she's so peculiar—it's not nice to have to say it, but—it's almost as if she *grudged*—grudged you—She's not married herself. It's a misfortune for a person.'

'We understand that,' answered Alberta, in embarrassment.

'Yes, Sivert says the same. And it's as well for the sake of peace. But it's wrong, quite wrong. If I believed you were thinking of staying so long, it would never have been like this. Now Sivert has found so much work here. I shall talk to Otilie.'

'Don't do that,' said Alberta without thinking. 'There'll be bad feeling,' she added, to rescue what was beyond hope.

'I'm sorry for my boy, I am.' Fru Ness was stern now, really stern. 'Indeed I am. What kind of a marriage is this? Has he a wife or hasn't he?'

'He has no wife.'

'That's what I thought, Alberta. Just what I thought. What did you want with each other, then?'

'It's not so easy to explain. We believed—' Alberta threw

out her hands helplessly, thoroughly miserable. She had to go through with it.

'Perhaps you'll not be coming back to us?'

'I shall come to see Brede. I am his mother, after all.' In sudden self-assertion she raised her head and looked at Fru Ness.

'*I* think you should stay, and come to an agreement with Sivert. I expect all you need do is give way a little. Goodwill gets one far. That would be the right thing to do, Alberta.'

Silence. Then Alberta said. 'Will you promise to keep Brede here to start with? So that he won't have to change schools and—perhaps have a stepmother.'

'Stepmother?' Fru Ness gave a start. 'Is there any question of a stepmother as well? I've never heard anything to equal it.'

Alberta could control herself no longer. She wept openly. 'I suppose Sivert will want to marry again. It's only natural. And the boy is not to have a stepmother. Keep him here, you and Father—until . . .'

'That's for Sivert to decide.'

'You will decide too, I'm sure.'

'All this is dreadful, just dreadful.'

'We mustn't make it worse than it is. You're a mother yourself.'

'And so you're going out to work, Alberta? For I can imagine it's hard to write too. Are you leaving us tomorrow?'

'Don't talk like that, it only makes me cry.'

Alberta really was crying. After a while she felt the knotted hand on her back. 'Don't take it so hard. As long as we're granted our health. Are you sure you'll get this novel of yours published, though? It's so very uncertain, after all.'

Alberta dried her tears. 'I expect it will work out all right,' she said mechanically, a sentence she had learnt at home. It was useful when things looked most problematic. 'I shall try to get something to do on the side. On a newspaper or something like that.'

. . . Full of people. A small, crowded restaurant with tables outside and laurel trees in green tubs.

'Do you sell it to take out as well?'

'Of course. Here you are, here's the menu.'

'Food . . . I knew French once, now I've forgotten it . . . but it's to be for six persons, cheap and good. It's really cheating to be buying it here. I ought to have prepared it myself. It should have been on the table by now, they're sitting waiting.'

'Roast veal? Cold roast veal? Yes, everyone likes that. Dead, boring, pale-coloured food, sliced corpses, but everyone likes it. For six persons, thank you. Is this the way out?'

I must hurry home and apologise. I shall arrange matters better another time . . .

A door slammed. Alberta sat up. It was Otilie going downstairs. She had decided it was high time Alberta woke up.

She had been asleep, although she had lain awake half the night. She had to collect her limbs and her thoughts piecemeal. It was not a new sensation. But it was new for her to be standing in the middle of the floor as if facing something she had not noticed until it was right in front of her. It was new for her to go across and look at herself in the mirror, examining her face as she had not done for a long time.

What was that? A grey tuft, hidden under the rest of her hair, above her temples. When she swept it back, all at once, it appeared. Look at that, she was greying early like Mama, and like her would probably do so in the manner of nervous people, with sudden white tufts here and there, not evenly and finely distributed like people who are placid. But Mama's hair had been quite fair. It had hidden the grey until she was far advanced in years.

That thin line running downwards from her nose? That too followed a course she recognised, even though it had not come far yet. There was something fateful about it. The rather angular way of walking that she had noticed lately was her own. She had lost her light, easy step, or put it aside on purpose perhaps.

She dressed, packed her smallest suitcase, took out her manuscript and leafed through it for a while. Much of it had been written in panic, and looked like someone else's work. All of it could have been shaped better, expressed better. But each word had come floating up singly from the unknown depths, where the truth hides itself and then rises again, in different guise, unrecognisable as a dream, but irrefutable. That was what she had to support her, to use in her defence, should fate one day demand a reckoning: a new reckoning.

She hid the suitcase under the bed. She would catch a train in the early evening. Immediately after supper would be the easiest time to leave unnoticed. Then Sivert would be reading, old Ness would be reading too. Otilie was going out. Brede —no, she would not be able to wait until he was in bed.

The day passed. She could not have lived through a worse one.

She had smuggled the suitcase downstairs into the garden, under a bush. She came out on to the steps. They were all sitting there, except Otilie. Fru Ness had the boy on her knee. She was telling him a story and he was listening wide-eyed. Alberta came down, paused at the foot of the steps, and found nothing to say.

'Going for a walk?' asked Sivert.

'Yes. Good night, Brede.'

'Good night,' answered Brede briefly. 'Go on, Grannie.'

Alberta stood for a moment irresolute. Then she felt her eyes welling over and ran out of the yard. She heard Sivert say, 'She's in a hurry.'

She had to run, so as not to look back. She thought: If it had been any good talking, Sivert, we'd have done so. For a long while she saw Fru Ness's eyes: they had looked right into her own across the boy's head. They had been neither severe nor mild: they had resembled those of fate, or of the blind.

She controlled herself and walked more calmly; she must not attract attention. The evening was similar to the one on which she had arrived. The air was already cool, with the first acrid taste of autumn. They were burning branches in the gardens. It was the kind of evening in early autumn that resembles an evening in spring.

She met people. They were standing in groups outside their

houses or talking to each other over the fences. There were mothers and children, husbands and wives, acquaintances. The peace of evening was on them. They stood at ease, finished with the day, waiting calmly for the night. At least, it seemed so. A few nodded to Alberta. Nobody asked where she was going.

She walked along, certain of only one thing. She had finished groping in a fog for warmth and security. The mist had risen now, there was clear visibility and it was cold. No arms round her any more, not even those of a child: naked life, as far ahead as she could see, struggle and an impartial view. She would go under or become so bitterly strong that nothing could hurt her any more. She felt something of the power of the complete solitary. Then she remembered Brede and knew that she could never be quite so invulnerable after all.

A young mother with a child on her arm took one of its small hands in hers and waved it at Alberta. 'Wave to the lady.'

Alberta nodded and smiled, waving back. The memory of the soft, tender warmth, the easy weight of a child a few months' old remained like deprivation in her arms. She pictured Tot, when, changed and dry, he lay kicking in his clean napkin. Small as he was, he too could be seized with delight, kicking with socks on his tiny feet, and laughing when Alberta caught them.

At the Evensens' the mare had a foal. It followed its mother closely. She was placid, the foal was placid. Everything was as it should be, and no one remarked on it. Alberta clenched her teeth. I'm actually beginning to grow up, she thought.

At moments she felt quite faint. For this might go completely wrong. She would offer her manuscript, ask for an advance, get it copied, look for work on a newspaper. Supposing nobody accepted it? Would she retrace her steps? Would she be capable of doing so if necessary? It must not be necessary. In the worst case she would have to try anything. To stay with Sivert on sufferance led nowhere, not even into the heart of her child. She would have to approach him from another direction: first as the strange visitor, half forgotten, bringing small presents and sweets; later, if fate was kind, as an equal guardian—as his mother.

Did she have any desires? To go out into the world? To find anyone in particular? One does not desire the impossible. The person who has once taken life in the wrong way must finally accept life as it is.

The truth, Pierre had said once. To tell a little of the truth.